Praise for *Mr. Darcy Takes a Wife*

"Wild, bawdy, and utterly enjoyable sequel.... Austenites who enjoy the many continuations of her novels will find much to love about this wild ride of a sequel."
—*Booklist*

"While there have been other *Pride and Prejudice* sequels, this one, with its rich character development, has been the most enjoyable."
—*Library Journal*

"A breezy, satisfying romance."
—*Chicago Tribune*

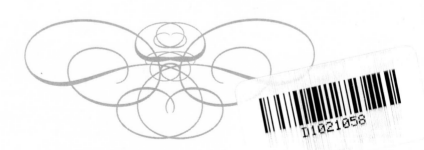

Also by LINDA BERDOLL

Darcy & Elizabeth: Nights and Days at Pemberley

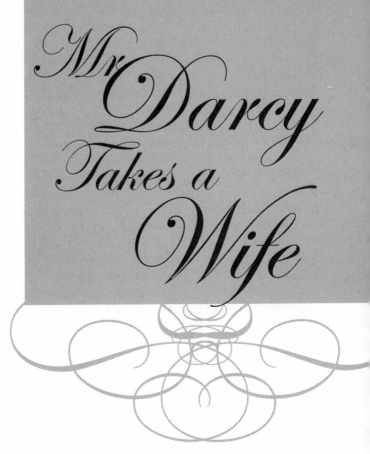

Mr Darcy Takes a Wife

Pride and Prejudice
Continues

LINDA BERDOLL

SOURCEBOOKS LANDMARK™
AN IMPRINT OF SOURCEBOOKS, INC.®
NAPERVILLE, ILLINOIS

Published by Sourcebooks, Inc.
P.O. Box 4410, Naperville, Illinois 60567-4410
(630) 961-3900
FAX: (630) 961-2168
www.sourcebooks.com

The characters and events portrayed in this book are fictitious or are used fictitiously. Any similarity to real persons, living or dead, is purely coincidental and not intended by the author.

Library of Congress Cataloging-in-Publication Data

Berdoll, Linda.
 Mr. Darcy takes a wife : Pride and prejudice continues / by Linda Berdoll.
   p. cm.
 ISBN 1-4022-0273-3 (alk. paper)
 1. Darcy, Fitzwilliam (Fictitious character)— Fiction. 2. Bennet, Elizabeth (Fictitious character)—Fiction. 3. Married people—Fiction. 4. England—Fiction. I. Austen, Jane, 1775-1817. Pride and prejudice. II. Title.
 PS3552.E6945M7 2004
 813'.54--dc22

                         2003027655

Printed and bound in the United States of America
BG   20   19   18   17   16

For Phil

preface

The renowned (if occasionally peevish) lady of letters, Charlotte Brontë, once carped of fellow authoress Jane Austen's work, "…she ruffles her reader by nothing vehement, disturbs him by nothing profound: the Passions are perfectly unknown to her…what throbs fast and full, though hidden, what the blood rushes through, what is the unseen seat of Life and the sentient target of death—*this* Miss Austen ignores."

It is forever lost what Jane Austen might have made of *Jane Eyre*, hence we shan't dally with such a conjecture. And however we are moved to defend Miss Austen's unparalleled literary gift, we cannot totally disregard Miss Brontë's observation, for it was quite on the money. Jane Austen wrote of what she knew. Miss Austen never married, it appears her own life passed with only the barest hint of romance. Hence, one must presume she went to her great reward *virgo intactus*.

As befitting a maiden's sensibilities, her novels all end with the wedding ceremony. What throbs fast and full, what the blood rushes through, is denied her unforgettable characters and, therefore, us. Dash it all!

We endeavour to right this wrong by compleating at least one of her stories, beginning whence hers leaves off. Our lovers have wed. But the throbbing that we first encounter is not the cry of a passionate heart. Another part of her anatomy is grieving Elizabeth Bennet Darcy.

Part One

As plush a coach as it was, recent rains tried even its heavy springs. Hence, the road to Derbyshire was betimes a bit jarring. Mr. Darcy, with all gentlemanly solicitousness, offered the new Mrs. Darcy a pillow upon which to sit to cushion the ride.

It was a plump tasselled affair, not at all discreet. His making an issue of her sore nether-end was a mortification in and of itself. But, as Elizabeth harboured the conviction that she had adopted a peculiar gait as a result of her most recent (by reason of matrimony) pursuits, her much abused dignity forbade her to accept such a blatant admission of conjugal congress. Thus, the cushion was refused.

Dignity notwithstanding, the unrelenting jiggle of the carriage demanded by the puddles bade her eye that same pillow wistfully as its soft comfort lay wasted upon the empty seat opposite them. As she clung to the handgrip, she knew it was indefensibly foolish not to admit to her husband that he was justified in suspecting that she needed it. But at that moment, not making a concession to him was a matter of principle.

Suffering both from the road and from knowing herself unreasonably miffed, she submitted to the silent chastisement that she must learn to accept the perversely quixotic turns of her new husband.

As each and every muddy mile they travelled diminished the distance betwixt Elizabeth and the awesome duty that awaited her as mistress of such a vast estate as Pemberley, she became ever more uneasy. It was not that she had only then fully comprehended what awaited her, for she had. At least as comprehensibly as it was possible.

Hitherto, there had been the excitement of the wedding, and moreover, the anticipation of connubial pleasures with Mr. Darcy that buffered her from the daunting *devoir* that lay ahead. In soothing her newly appreciated trepidation, her husband was of no help whatsoever. Indeed, they had no more than stepped from their matrimonial bedchamber before he had reclaimed his recently relinquished mask of reticence. And with it, that maddening hauteur. One peculiar only to him.

It was only subsequent to their engagement that he had ceased addressing her as "Miss Bennet" in lieu of her Christian name. Delightful as that transfiguration was, her previous understanding in regards to her name was usurped in the throes of passion. For in the considerable heat generated the previous evening, he had repeatedly murmured "Lizzy" in her ear.

To her dismay, their re-emergence into company bade the Master of Pemberley serve compunction by abandoning that much-appreciated endearment. This disappointment would have been less egregious had he not insisted upon addressing her as "Mrs. Darcy" not only to the help, but privately as well. Her alteration from Lizzy to

Mrs. Darcy had been vexatiously abrupt. Therefore, Mrs. Darcy was profoundly aggrieved and sat in petulant silence much of their trip.

This lack of conversation he did nothing to mitigate.

Indeed, it was a repetition of the ride from their wedding to their London honeymoon nest the day before. She had convinced herself hitherto that his quiet could be attributed to nerves (owing to the compleat lack of reserve that night). Presently, she had not a clue.

Upon thinking of that lack of reserve and the resultant kindness done upon her person, it bade her not to think so meanly upon her husband, silent or no. If he had truly been disquieted in apprehension of their wedding-night, might not his present reticence come from unease? It occurred to her that the more firmly he seemed in his own charge, the greater was his perceived threat to it. Hence, his wall of defence. At one time, she might have been amused to think herself such a disconcertion to the arrogant Mr. Darcy. But no more.

Impetuously, she took his hand. In no manner did she want him to believe her a peril to his well-being.

The carriage, evidently unhindered by the weightiness of her ruminations, endeavoured on. Hence, she wrested her attention from them and peered out the window as they ambled down the fashionable avenues of Mayfair. There, even so fine a carriage as theirs excited few heads to turn and watch as they passed.

But once upon the road north, a legion of staring eyes could be detected through the obfuscatory yellow fog that clung persistently to the streets. Unaccustomed as she was to being the occupant of such an elegant coach, Elizabeth was a little off-put to be the object of such general scrutiny. Mr. Darcy, however, as was his habit, practised an impervious gaze just at the horizon, reflecting neither distaste nor notice of the gawking.

They broke their journey for a spare midday meal at a plain but tidy inn. This rest occasioned the innkeeper and his wife into whimpering subservience, thus enlightening Elizabeth to the extreme deference she must weather as Mr. Darcy's wife.

The brevity of their stop was in all probability ultimately a good thing, blessedly truncating as it did the publican couple's display. The next fit of veneration from a person of lesser birth than the Darcys (i.e., just about everyone) would not be so unexpected. Elizabeth promised herself that she would practise Darcy's patrician inscrutability and elude the urge to tell those servile persons they had undoubtedly mistaken her for someone else.

Whilst still partaking of their meal, Darcy apologised unnecessarily upon the austere winter dressing of his county.

He said, "I am happy, Elizabeth, that you have seen Derbyshire in the summer. I fear the gloom of winter does not show it at its best."

Such was his formality, she could not help but respond in kind, dipping her head and smiling as if she was responding to a stranger at a dinner party.

Small consolation, but at the very least he was calling her "Elizabeth" once more.

Whereupon she endeavoured in her thoughts to retrace their steps that forenoon, wondering what, if anything at all, she could have done to cause his emotional retreat from her.

For had they not parted from each other's arms reluctantly and in all good humour?

The single unseemliness bechanced in her dressing room. He was compleatly unaware of it. And as this impropriety was of an extremely personal nature, it was absolutely unobserved.

Her bath had been drawn before she appeared. When she saw it there, hot and inviting, she was struck by an odd caprice. With little contemplation, she took the bar of soap and dropped it in the tub, allowing it to sink to the bottom and melt. Thereupon, she wrapped herself in a towel and let the steam curl her hair into an untidy frowse. In time, a waiting woman appeared to help her dress and curl her hair into a reasonably fashionable design. Elizabeth allowed the maid to believe her bath had been compleated. All this subterfuge was to a single end. She did not want to wash her husband from her body.

It was not premeditated. The decision was not made until she looked into the clear, hot water. She did not want to be daintied. She wanted to be able to smell his aroma emanating from her own body. If it was common to want to do such a thing, so be it. She deliberated the possible unbecomingness of her conduct no further.

The second half of their journey proved vastly more rewarding than the first.

Once the impenetrable noise and slush of London had been shed, the wintry countryside for which he apologised was quite inviting. And, their re-entry into the coach allowed her to claim the pillow she had earlier refused. She attempted to place it under herself with as little notice as possible. But once the coach door had been slammed shut, Darcy made a point of helping her to situate it. As to why she was utterly mortified at his chivalry, she could only guess. For was it not his doing that she needed the pillow in the first place?

It may have been that unspoken thought that passed betwixt them when they exchanged an exceedingly explicit gaze, but it was broken as the horses lurched forward.

The team strove on. And sitting shoulder to shoulder with her new husband in the bright, very public daylight, she was visited with an unshakeable, if indecorous, recollection. As much as she endeavoured (and mightily she did endeavour), Elizabeth could not displace the image from her mind of her husband's body. Naked as God made him. And aroused.

With all her being, she wished she had some cold water to flick upon her face, for she could feel the rush of heat building from her bosom. Her flush was so pronounced, she hypothesised that the bumping of the carriage was making her ill.

"Yes, I am feeling ill. 'Tis not my husband's nearness. 'Tis not the thought of him naked and flesh proud. I am feeling ill. It must have been the blood-pudding."

Silently, she fretted that the relentless throbbing in her chest might cause her permanent affliction. She did so not want to be a sickly wife. But in her heart, she knew herself not truly ill. Would she want so very much to leap into his arms had she been afflicted? As she lay her head back against the seat, quite unknowingly, she emitted a deep sigh. Regrettably, she thereby gifted herself further disconcertion by reason of his hand alighting upon her knee.

Uneasily, he queried, "Pray, are you unwell?"

It occurred to her to tell him that if he kept his hand upon her knee, he was in imminent danger of learning just how well she was, but she quashed the notion.

"I am quite well, I thank you," she said.

That assurance evidently did not persuade him of the felicity of her health, for his hand began a small, reassuring caress. This manipulation was unsuccessfully ignored by Elizabeth. For as he gazed impassively out the window at the passing countryside, the seemingly independent action of his hand expanded to an outright stroking of the inside of her thigh.

Soundly, she clamped her hand down atop his, certain that if she did not stop him, her eyes might actually roll back in her head. This constraining grasp was largely ignored. His fingertips continued their caress. In time, the rocking of the carriage and his rhythmic stroke influenced her own hand to relinquish its grip. Lulled into a nearly trance-like state, she almost gave a start when he spoke.

"Indubitably, it will take a period of adjustment to become accustomed to each other's all and sundry personal habits."

"Yes."

She steeled herself for a reproach upon any of her more prevalent personal shortcomings. As punctilious as she knew he could be, she was determined to weather any criticism with forbearance.

"My own routine is thoroughly entrenched."

She nodded in acceptance of this irrefutable likelihood.

"Yet, I have an admission."

"Have you?"

"This morning, I could not bring myself to bathe. I could not bear to wash your scent from me, Lizzy."

It had been a heady two months' engagement. Indeed, with two promised daughters in close company with their betrotheds, one might have expected Mrs. Bennet to have been beside herself with vigilance of chastity. But she was not. The exceedingly advantageous marriages were set. The only insult that she imagined could now befall them was for either of the intended bridegrooms to drop dead before the wedding.

Hence, when both couples had sought the outdoors and, therefore, separate paths for some time alone, her primary concern was that neither of the gentlemen in question caught cold.

Notwithstanding their mother's peculiar inattention to virginal honour, Jane and Elizabeth Bennet endeavoured to comport themselves during their periods of betrothal with a politesse so precise as to demand society overlook their sister Lydia's decidedly divergent road to matrimony. Entering into this delicate balance of love and propriety, however, obtruded the very weighty matter of immoderately aroused libido.

The entire quandary might have been circumvented had Elizabeth not allowed (welcomed, invited, summoned) a kiss from Mr. Darcy. For a union that had not been christened by greater affection than the holding of a gloved hand, that was a moment of considerable excitation.

First, one must understand that the distance between Mr. Bingley's estate of Netherfield and the Bennets' house of Longbourn was traversed with the regularity and certainty of the sunrise in the short months of the Bennet sisters' engagements. Upon fine days, Mr. Darcy and Mr. Bingley travelled the three miles upon horseback; upon foul they came by coach. Upon fair days, Bingley and Jane, followed by Elizabeth and Darcy at a discreet distance, walked out to stroll.

It was upon one of those perambulations that this kissing business was initiated.

And, thereupon, temporarily terminated. For Miss Bennet's and Mr. Darcy's tender moment came coincident to an extended rainstorm. Hence, all subsequent visits with Elizabeth's intended were relegated to Longbourn House and the company of assorted sisters, parents, and servants. Mrs. Bennet might turn a blind eye to affection betwixt them, but it was quite unlikely that all would. This was a considerable vexation, in that after that first kiss, Elizabeth thought of little except the anticipation of the next.

That interim was appropriated by a second hazard. The first, being housebound by reason of inclement weather, was quite beyond anyone's control. The second, no less so. For when she received the letter from Elizabeth advising her of the impending marriages, Lydia Bennet Wickham did not offer her nuptial congratulations by post. She came herself. Lydia had written to her mother to expect her, but such was her haste, she arrived only hours behind her missive.

Regrettably, the Wickhams' marital bliss had lasted little longer than it took the rector to pronounce them husband and wife. Howbeit, in the excitement of parading about as Mrs. Wickham, Lydia did not detect this for several months. Indeed, understanding the youngest Bennet sister's nature (shallow, fickle, and dim), it would not be unreasonable to assume that had the Wickhams remained in London, the abundance of shops there might have kept her insensible of it for years.

But in the gloom of Newcastle, household felicity was not abundant. And, not introspective by nature, Lydia was unable to enjoy the single thing Newcastle did offer in abundance (besides coal), that of quiet (if sooty) solitude.

Reading bored her, sewing was a chore, and walks were, to Lydia, only a means to cover the ground between where she was and where she wanted to be. Activity lay by way of engagement balls and wedding breakfasts. Citing her extreme affection for her sisters (dubious) and homesickness for Longbourn (unquestionable), she applied to her husband to return home.

Lydia two hundred miles away? Happy thought for Wickham. ("Yes, dearest Lydia, you must be with your sisters, but I am not certain my heart will bear your absence. Do not tarry longer than you must and then hurry home to me!")

Lydia thought she might well tarry as long as possible. For while being ensconced in north England may initially have been regarded as an adventure, its allure waned more precipitously than did her husband's. The shops were sparse, her friends were even fewer. Those she had soon wearied of hearing how she, the youngest of five sisters, had usurped the title of ranking daughter by becoming the first wed. Her own consideration of that coup paled when she read the letter telling of the engagements of both Jane and Elizabeth, for she had only bested them by six months.

And even in the infinitesimal area of her intellect that Lydia reserved for contemplation, it occurred to her that the proposals Elizabeth and Jane had secured eclipsed hers considerably. Although she knew Wickham more handsome by half than either Mr. Bingley or Mr. Darcy, and certainly more charming (well, Mr. Bingley was amicable, but Mr. Darcy was absolutely dour), the few months of her marriage made her understand one great profundity: Beauty and allurement were not the only attributes of importance when selecting a husband. Money was paramount to both.

But Lydia's consideration was specific to legal tender, not title or position. Some amongst the gentry would suffer any indignity to maintain, or obtain, position. That alone meant nothing to Lydia. Even she knew title and money were not necessarily synonymous in the vast country estates. Some baronial and ducal homes were in debt up to their leaking roofs. One of her few good qualities was that she was not a social snob. She loved money, true. But her adoration was birthed by the misfortune of her being a spendthrift. Her purse was always in need of replenishing. She desired the exactitude of money, not the encumbrance of wealth.

Hence, a man of position and wealth who could actually produce currency was, to Lydia, truly a prize. Mr. Bingley and Mr. Darcy (who both had those two exceedingly advantageous attributes in abundance and were happily in the additional circumstance of available cash) were to Lydia as much a matrimonial trophy as had their heads been mounted upon the wall.

It came to pass that providence had seen to it that Lydia's dowry of fifty pounds per annum and Wickham's paltry army pay did not compleatly embrace Lydia's wants nor Wickham's gambling debts. In the light of that injustice (and as it had long been her position that charity did, indeed, begin at home), Lydia saw no reason why all the Bennet sisters' good fortune should not be communal. Upholding a second strongly clutched belief that the end always justifies the means, Lydia realised it might be necessary to subdue her sisters' possible reluctance to share in their future husbands' plethora of funds. Thus, she strove to become, not only their dear youngest sister, but their confidant and teacher as well.

For, if the loss of her brief status of First Daughter was imminent by reason of new marriages, she still clung to the single feat she held over her *virgo intactus* sisters. She alone knew what would befall Jane and Elizabeth upon their wedding night. She alone was in a position to *explain it all* to them.

Their mother would not. Mrs. Bennet's only advice to Lydia had been (this was not prior to their actual carnal union, but she advised it all the same), "Bear up, Lydia, and be brave. Suffer as you must and make certain your husband knows it."

Copulation as recreation would have bumfuzzled Mrs. Bennet, for although her mother thought of Lydia as the daughter most truly after her own heart, she did not share Lydia's concupiscence. (Lydia knew that their mother had to have consummated relations with their father, but was it not for the undeniable existence of herself and four sisters, she would have argued that possibility to the death.) Lydia sought amorous congress just as studiously as her mother avoided it.

And whatever were Wickham's drawbacks as a provider, he was a prolific and masterful lover. As it happened, Lydia knew this as fact because he told her so emphatically and often. There were, however, not as many opportunities for Lydia to admire her husband's self-professed masculine achievements by the sixth month of her marriage. Had the appellation of wife not elated Lydia so, she might have noted that Mrs. Lydia Wickham's nether-regions were not sacrificed to Venus by Major George Wickham one-tenth as often as when she was Miss Lydia Bennet.

That was regrettable, but had to be forgiven. For even Lydia knew that Major Wickham was so fatigued by his exceedingly weighty and tedious assigned duty of telling the sergeant major what to do that, come evening, he could scarcely pull off his own boots. Exhausted or not, Lydia had some success at cajoling him into accommodating her, but she soon learnt there are only so many bodily orifices to penetrate and without the enthusiasm of her poor, weary husband, her gratification was limited.

Longbourn would be a merry distraction from drab Tyne and Wear. And, as Lydia gradually discovered as the miles grew between her coach and Wickham, distance does invariably soften one's matrimonial travails. So by the time Lydia reached Hertfordshire, the memory of her husband's libido had been resurrected to premarital prominence. Hence, she was quite anxious to share with Jane and Elizabeth the fortune that was soon to befall them (even if it had to ensue with lesser lovers than her Wickham).

With as much ado, bedlam, and brouhaha as she could incite, Lydia arrived by hackney coach into her mother's outstretched arms. She kissed the air in her father's direction, then bypassed Elizabeth, Jane, Kitty, and Mary altogether to offer her heartfelt (and prodigious) congratulations to her future brothers-in-law.

Lydia arrived at four in the afternoon. By five they had supped, and fifteen minutes after six o'clock the men retired to Mr. Bennet's library to enjoy a decanter of port. The Miss Bennets and their mother anticipated conversation with Mrs. Wickham in the west parlour. She, however, had urgent business to attend to with Elizabeth and Jane. With whispered entreaty, she herded them into the first available bedroom. Once there, Jane sat upon the side of the bed in apprehension. Elizabeth chose to stand with arms folded, her posture reflecting a compleat understanding that all this urgency was undoubtedly in preparation for the disclosure of another of Lydia's schemes.

Her premonition was not unrewarded. For Lydia closed the door and, without taking her hand from the knob, turned. Thereupon, she issued a tremendous, if melodramatic, sigh. She went to both sisters, took one hand of each in hers and clasped them to her bosom.

"Oh, to be a naïve young girl again!" Lydia, the wise matron of sixteen, gushed directly to the twenty-two-year-old Jane. "You know nothing of men and their carnal cravings, do you, my dear, sweet, innocent sister?"

Jane, of course, did not. But all three knew if Lydia wanted to disconcert someone with graphic delineation, Jane would be the victim of choice.

Watching the manipulative Lydia homing in upon Jane as if singling out a lamb for slaughter did not sit well with Elizabeth. Lydia, however, was so enthralled to be in a position of authority that she did not see Elizabeth glaring at her. Jane's wide-eyed, wary look invited Lydia to expand.

"There are things you must know, Jane, Lizzy."

She looked over at Elizabeth, whose countenance bore the distinct expression of one who knew herself far more ignorant than she would have liked. It also beheld a pronounced distaste for being enlightened by a younger sister, particularly Lydia, the unparalleled Queen of Theatrics.

As if reading her mind, Lydia said, "If you believe our mother will advise you, Lizzy, do not be so foolhardy."

She then repeated what Mrs. Bennet had told her about the wedding bed, punctuating it with a merry laugh. Noting a compleat lack of sisterly camaraderie upon the subject of their mother's marital shortcomings, she hastily prattled on.

"Indubitably, you believe Mr. Bingley and Mr. Darcy are compleat gentlemen. Surely, it is thus that they strive to be. But they are men and beneath their chivalrous manners lurk barely tethered desires of the flesh!"

More than one Sunday the vicar had warned of carnal pleasure, hence it was understandable for at least Jane to be alarmed. However, if Jane was held in fright, Elizabeth was not. Her disdain for Lydia's pompousness was compromised somewhat by curiosity. Intelligence available to young ladies upon this subject was intentionally meagre. Decorum and society demanded benightedness.

Yet Elizabeth managed to respond mildly, "How kind of you, Lydia, to have come all this distance to warn us of carnal cravings of the unwed."

Not compleatly oblivious to the mockery from the headiness of her singular position of matrimony, Lydia replied, "Of course not, Lizzy. But you would do well to listen to my admonishments lest you be taken unawares by Mr. Darcy's conjugal embrace."

"Pray?"

Elizabeth's reluctant interest at hand, Lydia returned to the sanctuary of Jane's more genuine one and came directly to the point.

"When you give yourself for the first time, you must be prepared. For, are you not, when your lover takes you the pain will be unbearable."

Believing Lydia's superior practise in this had to be accepted, Jane's eyes widened even more (physical pain, for anyone, was the very thing which Jane held in greatest repugnance).

"Lydia," Jane said, "do you think it best to talk so unguardedly? Is this not private?"

"Yes," Lydia agreed, undaunted. "I am speaking to you both privately, am I not?"

Of course, the only way Lydia knew to speak was without caution (privacy was hardly a hindrance upon her, either). Hence, Lydia continued unrestrained.

"It will be glorious beyond words, but you may cry out to God to take your life!"

"Lydia, really…"

"'Tis true, Lizzy!"

Lydia turned to Elizabeth, lifting her chin defensively, "You know nothing of this…one must assume."

No, she did not. It was a quandary, for she was very keen to hear the details that were kept so scrupulously from the ears of maidens. However, she did not want to lend encouragement to Lydia (whom she knew needed little) nor to have Jane terrorised by hyperbole. That was clearly Lydia's impending effect, if not intent. For Lydia returned her attention to her eldest sister, whose face had lost all colour.

"Your husband's manly instrument will swell big and red and hard and angry and enormous…"

Here Lydia struggled for adjectives, and having accidentally lapsed into repetition, strove on, "And when he first puts it up your nonny-nonny it will be with such force as to render you prostrate with ecstasy and pain."

She lowered her voice in a highly conspiratorial whisper, and said, "Once he thrusts into you, he will again and again and *again!*"

Lydia had to take a swallow. In fortune, for with each successive "again," Jane's eyes widened and she leaned farther away from Lydia, and by the third "again," was almost prone upon the bed.

Lydia concluded with a deep sigh, "It is a sweaty prospect. And his spendings are sticky. And his larydoodle does go limp with great dispatch after he has had his way with you."

Lydia had frowned at the thought of these drawbacks, but perked up, remembering, "But, if he can just stay with it, he will bring you such rapture that you will sing about it for days!"

Jane and Elizabeth were silent.

Thus Lydia, supposing it was of a stunned nature due to her oratory, added, "Of course, that is the lover that Wickham is. You, sisters, may not be so fortunate as I. For my husband is endowed with an organ of far grander proportions than other men."

Lydia leaned forward conspiratorially again, "And this is what is most pleasing to his lover."

Elizabeth narrowed her eyes and asked Lydia how she found validation of this information.

"Why, Wickham told me," she replied without a hint of question.

Elizabeth was not in a position to know whether George Wickham's apparatus was, indeed, superior to any other man's. But, to her, the very fact that vapouring cock-a-hoop boasted of something automatically called its veracity into question.

Looking at the scepticism written upon Elizabeth's face, Lydia hurried to assure her, "You cannot imagine anything so frightening as the sight of Wickham's excited member!"

"I am sure I do not want to imagine Mr. Wickham's excited anything."

"You will see a great deal far sooner than you might anticipate, Lizzy, if you are not cautious with your affection before you wed."

Lydia held up her fingernails and inspected them diligently as she said, "For a man's ardour does not await the wedding vows."

Of this, Lydia knew well and Elizabeth only raised her eyebrow in reminder.

Lydia saw the look and snapped, "Do not eye me so severely, Lizzy! If Mr. Darcy is half the man as Wickham, his flag will fly quite readily at the smallest provocation, I assure you."

"You do not mean, Lydia," Jane interjected, "that a gentleman is quite without his own will in such a situation?"

"I mean," retorted Lydia, "that if you allow Mr. Bingley to kiss you too ardently, he will be aroused to such lust his loins will ache and his engorged lance will burst from his nether garments to ravish you! Wickham's waggled at me more than once!"

"Lydia!"

Lydia replied self-righteously, "I have no say in the nature of men. I am merely the bearer of the information. If you do not choose to believe what is a verifiable truth, 'tis your folly, not mine," and, with the timing of a true thespian, she then rose and quitted the room.

Jane sat upon the bed in a befuddled stupor. Elizabeth knew her dear sister's sensibilities had been abused far beyond immediate reclamation. Was she not so curious, her own might have found insult, too. But this time, the usual annoyance Lydia incited in Elizabeth was compounded by being at the mercy of her own ignorance.

Even with no brothers to have enlightened them, Elizabeth was marginally informed upon nature's intent. She had seen boys, of course, at least boy babies. Hence, she held some notion of the rather flagrant configuration of the male of the species. She was uncertain why she held Darcy's…person in such interest, but until Lydia had importuned them, she had not taken the time to study the matter.

Elizabeth endeavoured to think of something soothing to say to Jane. But with her own mouth agape as it was, Jane was rising to leave before she could. Jane patted her hair distractedly and murmured about something that needed her attention. However, she stopped at the door, her hand upon the knob, and stood a moment, deep in thought.

Thereupon, she turned and bid Elizabeth, "Pray, Lizzy, there is something I do not understand."

"Yes, Jane?"

"If it is so very painful to his wife for…a husband to…do his duty, why would she want him to be large?"

A perfectly good question.

George Wickham was not a happy major.

"*Spirits*" the sign had read.

In all the good humour of one who has yet to know himself disappointed, Wickham had run his glove reassuringly across the shine of the brass buttons that lined his uniform jacket, tossed his red cape back across one shoulder just so, and made his entrance into the anticipated merriment.

But he took no more than a step or two inside the door that had borne the designation of a drinking establishment. For upon his intrusion the patrons stopped all discourse, abandoned their ale, and glared in baleful silence at the fancy soldier in his pretty uniform who had just barged into their refuge.

If the sight they beheld was distasteful, Wickham was even more affronted.

Indistinguishable from the gloom of the room only by reason of the startling whites of their eyes, twenty-odd black smudged eyeballs stared at him. The two score of orbs had widened, then narrowed just menacingly enough to tell Wickham he best take his leave post-haste. That was most probably the only common ground he thought he might find in accordance with this plebeian pack of humanity. He very nearly fled.

Once at a safe distance he spat, *"Bassimeçu,"* over his shoulder, his arrogance reinstated with the assurance that no man in that odious excuse for a tavern would understand the insult.

He picked up his step all the same.

Although his scepticism had been on high alert, he had been assured by those who vehemently sought his egress from London that Newcastle was an ambitious but pretty coastal port surrounded by grouse moors.

Wickham, who loved nothing better than to insinuate himself into good society, had not thought much of such a bucolic milieu. He should have held out for better. Bath, perhaps. However, establishing distance betwixt himself and Darcy had been uppermost at that particular moment (hasty leave-taking and the resultant insulation of miles was the single constant in his life). Hence, the felicity of an assignment in the north-easternmost reach of England rendered itself ever more probable. Reality saw that Newcastle was, indeed, small, and had a port, but there was nothing pretty about the place. It appeared industrious, but hardly fashionable.

He and Lydia were not a ten-foot out of their hack coach before Wickham realised a dual insult upon his person. The high lustre of his boots was already besoiled with soot and there was not a bootblack in sight to polish them.

His boots' hasty begriming bade him look about to see whence it came. There was no single culprit, for he saw nothing but cinereous stone buildings, slate streets, dingy windows, drab people, and a sky thick with smoke. It looked as if, quite literally, a film of coal grit filled every crevice and dusted every face in the town.

"Like shipping coal to Newcastle," Wickham repeated miserably to himself as he spat upon his wife's lace-trimmed, cambric hanky and dabbed at the toes of his jackboots.

This first impression of the town not at all promising, Wickham had looked to the moors. And again he had been disappointed. If there were any hunting retreats of the wealthy about, by the time the Wickhams had arrived in mid-December, they were long abandoned. Were they not, clearly from the seedy look of Newcastle, people of station hied directly to the hinterlands and fro, compleatly bypassing town. An altogether reprehensible situation.

Further injury awaited. For even more than hobnobbing with those elusive people of property, Wickham favoured gambling with them. Hidden behind his façade of well-mannered sociability stood a man who, after all respectable persons had gone to bed, liked to prowl the night for similarly-minded men flush with funds. Wickham liked his cards lucky, his whiskey smooth, and his women loose. There were a number of taverns, but as Wickham had soon determined, they were tended by grubby men with thick forearms instead of lusty barmaids (who might enjoy a little debauchery in a back room). And nary a den of iniquity amongst them.

Was the denial of winsome wenches not test enough, Wickham discovered the clientele of these establishments far worse than the proprietorship. It would be a struggle to name the most offensive to him amongst them: the filthy coal-haulers who did not bother to slap the dust from their clothes, the dock workers foetid with briny water, or the infernal sheep men, fresh with coin from marketing the aging lambs that weaning missed. Was a decision demanded, Wickham probably would have given the nod to those unholy shepherds, who stunk of the Cheviot flocks they brought down from the frost-browned hills and drove through the streets, thus demanding good people leap for a doorway lest they be engulfed in dust and trampled by hundreds of tiny little cloven hooves.

Wickham despised farm animals.

If he thought his ignoble introduction to the nightlife of Newcastle to be his ebb, sadly, he discovered more diversional setbacks were yet to be encountered. For the paucity of barmaids bade ill-chance of feminine company in general. If the shop-keepers had daughters, they kept them hidden, which probably proved them prudent men in a town overrun with nothing but shipbuilders and coal men. And the army. The caution of those fathers was ill-luck to Wickham, for in light of the meagre competition, a fine crimson officer's uniform would be quite an enticement to seduction. The only remaining avenue of beguilement was within the spousal ranks of his few fellow officers. But as Wickham was one of the few (and the only one below colonel) to have a wife, even a little innocent adultery was unlikely.

Indeed, things looked very grim that winter for Wickham, reduced as he was to taking womanly company and a game of chance with his superior officer's wife (who was of Methodist persuasion, despised music, played nothing but Whist, and, to Wickham's perpetual misfortune, adored his company). Thus, his evenings of sociability were spent in pointless deliberation of whether to avoid Colonel Sutcliffe's insufferable wife or his own.

No happy outcome there. Had it not been so finger-numbingly frigid, Wickham would have simply mutinied for the garden and a smoke. For Lydia's only merit had been as a temporary romantic conquest. Not particularly pretty, as a maiden she did have a somewhat fetching forwardness that promised she did not hold much prudence of affection. Under the stern fortress of matrimony, however, her desirability to her husband had waned disastrously. She had become the proverbial millstone about his increasingly constricted neck.

It was ever so cold in Newcastle, even for northern England in the winter. The chill was exacerbated upon Wickham's realisation that the single reason he had married Lydia Bennet was to solve his most immediate bother, that of an embarrassing shortfall of funds and an unruly mob of unhappy, impatient creditors. Because of Wickham's tonsorial fetish and relentless wagering, that "bother" reinvented itself four times a year, hence it was creeping upon him again with a vengeance, even in Newcastle.

Indebtedness had never been much of a barrier to Wickham's peace of mind so long as he could find one more shopkeeper to dupe into allowing him to purchase on account (although tailors, as a rule, were a mistrustful bunch). But such obligations had landed him in his present ignobly garrisoned regiment.

As it happened, by the time of his and Lydia's extended tryst in London, he had left a trail of outstanding bills that was extensive even for him. Moneylenders had him teetering upon the threshold of a sponge house and more than one had a shilling laid down for his arrest, hence debtors' prison was not a mere threat. Desperation had begun to make a nasty crease betwixt his usually unfurrowed brows.

Was that not vexation enough, to be confronted in London by an obviously indignant Darcy whilst in lascivious company with the unwed, underage Lydia would have been quite unnerving to any man who valued his *bursa virilia*. But as a man of considerable practise with confrontation, be it broker or cuckolded husband, Wickham had hastily deduced from the absence of sword and seconds that Darcy was not there to demand satisfaction for some injury. Indeed, Darcy did not intend Wickham mortal harm just then; for what Darcy wanted of him, he needed him very much alive. From an impetus unapparent to Wickham, Darcy had gone to great trouble to find their little Soho lovenest to (of all things!) demand that Wickham redeem Lydia's virtue through marriage.

At the time, it had been an utter mystery as to why Darcy sought them out when in the past he had but turned up his nose at Wickham's numerous amorous indiscretions (except for that unfortunate miscalculation with Georgiana). Then, however, Wickham had not taken time to question. Thrown into a position of negotiation, dickering over specifics took all his concentration. Wickham's finely honed sense of personal aggrandisement immediately ascertained that, for whatever reason, Darcy would do whatever was necessary to see that the marriage took place.

Darcy pledged himself to Wickham's creditors in exchange for a wedding and the promise of settling in a northern regiment with the Regulars. Wickham had jumped at the opportunity (incarceration being a nasty alternative). The puzzle surrounding such an intervention had not truly bedevilled Wickham, however, until he had settled with Lydia at the new post. From the ill-house of vanquishment, Wickham was certain some malevolence had been done to him by Darcy's hand. But it was nothing at all so covert, the Wickhams soon learnt. For not a month after landing in Newcastle, Lydia received the letter telling of her sister Elizabeth's engagement to Darcy. It was almost as much an astonishment to her as to her husband.

"I cannot believe her good fortune, Wickham, for he is easily the richest man in England and I know she despised him not six months ago. What could have changed her mind so decidedly?"

The question was asked more to herself than Wickham, so after barely an instance of reflection, she opined, "I can tell you why. A man of that rank need only offer his affection and Lizzy, for all her airs, cannot call herself above any other woman in wasting no time in accepting."

She snorted a short laugh and looked to her husband, who had glanced at her when he heard her announcement, but upon seeing her look in his direction he hastily returned his attention to his papers. That his wife's conversation only seldom required response was one of the few advantages her husband still found in her company. He watched out of the corner of his eye as she turned back to her letter and allowed himself a sigh of relief.

Wickham could always call upon himself to foster an outward mien of ingratiating, if somewhat smug, charm. But Lydia's reminder of Darcy's wealth tried even his countenance. That ominous, superciliary crevice deepened upon hearing that the very lovely Elizabeth Bennet was to marry his nemesis. Wickham's invidious nature allowed jealousy to rear its ugly head, momentarily allowing the reason he had slighted her to slip his mind. But, in the vacuum that was his soul, the wherefore of not pursuing such a comely young woman soon wafted back to him.

It was the sparseness of her dowry. What a lark! Darcy had chosen a bride that he, Wickham, had found unworthy. Gleefully, Wickham played with that notion. That conceit, however, did not last much longer than it took to think it. Almost instantly, he was brought to wonder just what particular charm Darcy had discovered in Elizabeth Bennet that he himself had overlooked. Of course dowry meant but little to a man of Darcy's wealth, but then conversely, position and rank meant all.

Why had Darcy, who could have his pick of any woman in England, chosen a wife with such questionable connexions? Wickham's puzzlement over Darcy's intervention with Lydia was displaced by his pondering of such an unusual match. It was only a temporary amusement to Wickham to think that the great Darcy's wife held the same low connexions as his own. If he smiled, it was fleeting. As much as Wickham hated to admit it, he had married a wife with the same fifty pounds a year as her sister. And he certainly had not the resources to elevate their station as had Darcy. That was not a rewarding rumination. He strove to think of something else.

But he could not.

Perhaps Wickham was not the cleverest of men. However, when it came to plottings, his mind knew the region well. Rarely was he out-manoeuvred. It was only a few minutes before he bore the full brunt of just how thoroughly Darcy had outwitted him. Quite unbeknownst to Wickham, he had held in his hand the key to the Darcy fortune. Georgiana Darcy's thirty thousand a year was paltry compared to the sum Wickham could have blackmailed Darcy for in exchange for saving the Bennet family name from ruin. As unlikely as it was for Darcy to marry beneath him, he most assuredly would not double the insult of position by connecting himself with a family disgraced. Realising he had held such a trump card over Darcy and not cashed in upon it was of significant vexation. In bargaining, knowledge is everything. If Wickham had held any notion of Darcy's intentions for Elizabeth, he could have discovered, monetarily, just how very dearly Darcy wanted to marry her. In the acute vision of hindsight, no figure seemed too outrageous when it came to Darcy getting what he wanted.

Not only had he botched the bargaining opportunity of a lifetime, he was marooned in Newcastle. Moreover, he was married to a young woman whose attention, which he had once supposed lent itself in enquiry no more profound than the prettiness of her newest bonnet, had somehow birthed an uncanny knack for sniffing out his every infidelity. Lydia's brittle temperament was accompanied by a compleat lack of trust in her husband's faithfulness.

And dogged she was. Wickham could not fathom how any one woman could be so simultaneously obtuse yet clever.

Looking again to his wife, he then just as hastily looked away, not wanting to invite her conversation. She was licking the last residue of chocolate from her fingertips with no less noise than a cow sucking its foot from the mud. He prayed that her indecorous desire for bonbons was the source of her ever-increasing girth and she was not with child, for a wailing infant would be the last straw upon his ill-temper.

Narrowing his eyes in reinvigorated concentration, Wickham thought of his situation again. There was only one promising possibility upon his horizon.

Within the letter announcing the impending nuptials betwixt Darcy and Elizabeth was imbedded the merest beginnings of a scheme. Undoubtedly with the Darcy marriage, the true story of his banishment from Pemberley would be known, thus that avenue of misdirected sympathy had withered. But perhaps another benefit would take its place. For now that he and Darcy would be brothers-in-law, perhaps he would be readmitted to Pemberley, his unsuccessful and unfortunate (only by reason of its lack of success) seduction of Georgiana put in the past. For Pemberley was vast, reflecting the extent of the Darcy wealth. Might Darcy's wife have sympathy for her sister and her sister's husband? It was a notion worth pursuing.

As a man with no occupation of the heart, Wickham could uncover no answer to the perplexing question as to why Darcy chose to marry a simple country lass with poor connexions and no fortune. But then Wickham was often troubled by Darcy's motives. They seemed not to have reason, at least not one familiar to Wickham, for he believed Darcy was no better than any other man, he merely had better means of obtaining what he wanted. And, for whatever reason, Darcy wanted to marry Elizabeth Bennet.

Exiled from London and all good society, an insipid cow for a wife, Wickham was in high dudgeon.

Damn that Darcy!

Money held all the nobility to be had, Wickham knew. And why it was all Darcy's was a question that would dog him relentlessly.

Preceded by Lydia (who seemed particularly satisfied with herself), Elizabeth returned that night to her sisters and mother in the parlour. It took a little longer for Jane to appear. Moreover, she had no sooner settled herself into a chair than the gentlemen rejoined them, quite unwitting of the temper of the room.

For when Bingley took his usual seat next to Jane, she bore the exact expression one would have conjured a chicken to possess hearing a fox circling the hen-house.

Poor bewildered Bingley attempted conversation with her, but Jane was so spooked, she could hardly respond to her baffled fiancé. Had she thought she could whisper it without losing her countenance to mirth, Elizabeth would have liked to reassure Jane. For she was certain that, regardless of what Lydia told them, Bingley's privates were unlikely (especially in company in the parlour) to burst from his inexpressibles as if an enraged squirrel.

Besides, Elizabeth was having her own difficulties of disconcertion.

She may have found some amusement in Jane's unease, however, she did not at all in her own. Notwithstanding how roundly overwrought she knew Lydia's description of sexual congress must be, the very explicit picture she had detailed seized Elizabeth's mind quite unreasonably. And this was not to abate, for Darcy claimed a seat upon the sofa next to her, undoubtedly bringing his easily agitated male instrument with him.

Everyone else seemed quite unruffled.

Mary poured tea, offering some to Mr. Darcy. He rose and walked to the tea table. Thereupon, with cup in hand, he took an interminable stroll the length of the room back to his seat next to Elizabeth. Elizabeth studiously inspected her shoes until he sat down again, quite determined that her gaze would not alight upon that explicit bulge in the fork of his unhintables (of which one was not even to speak, let alone stare at). Until that moment, it had never occurred to her to decry the unforgiving, leg-hugging fashion of gentlemen's breeches. It was now impossible for her to think of anything but Mr. Darcy's tights and what they contained.

Once he was again seated, Elizabeth thought it safe enough to allow herself to lift her eyes from the floor and did manage conversation without once looking at his lap. Jane, however, still had not regained her powers of speech and the situation was not helped by Lydia, who found it necessary to traipse about the room offering sweet biscuits to Bingley and Darcy.

Elizabeth's apprehension over Mrs. George Wickham's visit was considerable. For Darcy became uneasy with the mere mention of Wickham's name. Being forced into company with his wife would clearly be abhorrent. And Lydia's nature did not cooperate in protecting Darcy's sensibilities. For along with her display of the tray of sweet cakes was a generous presentation of her bosom, one she did not withdraw even after a firm refusal, coaxing each gentleman to reconsider a treat. This forwarding of Lydia's appurtenances was exceedingly embarrassing to everyone who witnessed it, but did have the advantage of irritating Elizabeth's mind away from Darcy's manhood.

Hence, the evening passed with no less unease, but at least it was yielded from Lydia's disorder, not her own. Upon his leave-taking, Darcy stole a moment in the vestibule to bestow a kiss upon Elizabeth. All her preparation for the moment was for naught. For this time when they kissed, he drew her tightly against him. Through the wool of his jacket, the satin of his waistcoat, and the gauze of his shirt, she could not truly feel his body, however the impression of it was enough to weaken her knees. And when she retired for the night, that impression did not waft away.

Their period of engagement might have passed thusly, chaste but for fervent kisses exchanged in foyers and amongst secluded oaks, had Elizabeth not committed an indiscretion of considerable vehemence.

She was certain, however, the fault of her lapse was not entirely hers.

For had Darcy not kissed her with such exceeding warmth that evening, she would not have begun to ponder his lips as she had (in defence of pondering any other part of his person). And had she not pondered his lips so insistently, when he pressed her back against a convenient oak and kissed her that next day, she would not have taken his lower lip betwixt her own and so decidedly bitten it.

The particular etiquette of reducing one's beloved to masticatory morsel had never once been addressed to her so far as Elizabeth could recollect. Hence, instinctively she covered her face, aghast with mortification. Certain that such an unbridled act would have, at the very least, affrighted him to flee, she was therefore astonished that he had not. Not only had he not taken flight, he drew her hands from her face and kissed her again. This kiss was neither chaste, nor warm. It was a long, deep, white-hot kiss of passion and howbeit Elizabeth had never been kissed thusly, she recognised it even without the attributing adjectives.

That kiss was replaced by another, then another until one was indistinguishable from the last. This pleasuring was accompanied by an embrace so firm their bodies were rendered quite indistinguishable from each other as well. (It was impressive how much writhing could be managed with so little room betwixt them, so secure was their clinch.) Her lungs were just beginning to tell her that she must take a gasp of air, when he quite abruptly quit the kiss. It took her a moment to realise that he had.

He turned away. His shoulders heaved, keeping the same deep rhythm as her own. She put her hand across her eyes and closed them. After a moment (perhaps when oxygen returning to her brain allowed conscious thought), she understood he was right. As much as she did not want him to rise from her, she knew he must. There could be no other generous end to their hunger for each other than compleat union.

Accepting the rightness of his decision (not an outright endorsement, more a concession), her single most pressing concern was not a matter of compunction, but that what had transpired was not evaded. She could wrestle with self-censure in private; she needed to talk with him about her…his…their…. Indeed, that was the problem. What was this? It felt uncommonly like naked lust.

Adjusting her bonnet, Elizabeth said to his back, "I had no idea such feelings could be so frightfully fierce."

He dropped his chin to his chest momentarily, then turned about to her. He bore an expression quite unlike any she had ever seen upon him. If one described it as truly pitiful, Elizabeth would have argued. For it did not elicit pity from her, but surely sympathy. She wanted to embrace him, soothe him, cosset him like a child and assure him everything would be just fine. This pathos was quite unapparent to him.

"Yes, I am afraid my conduct is quite unforgivable."

Quite unapparent to him as well was her complicity. Should she disabuse him of the notion that she was a victim of his appetency rather than a willing accomplice?

"Perhaps our conduct has been too unrestrained, but hardly unforgivable. You are too harsh upon us."

Upon her use of the collective, he looked at her directly. In a determined little fit of coquetry, she turned her head slightly akilter and smiled fully. Which amused him, for it was clear her entreaty was a presumptuous tease. Yet, he stood his ground. His hands reached out for her, but they only cupped her face, his thumbs tracing the curve of her cheeks.

"Your father would have good reason to run me through."

"And lock his daughter in the attic for good measure," she countered, both knowing the unlikelihood of either occurrence.

But their remarks announced a return to better humour. Hence, they turned toward the security of Longbourn House, a habitat that would quash any disinclination toward propriety. Her virtue was not compromised in deed, Elizabeth knew, but it was besmutted considerably by her own intentions.

It was difficult to concede any issue to Lydia, but Elizabeth knew she would have to reassess her heretofore unwavering stance against Lydia's imprudent, unmarried cohabitation with Wickham in London. She yet believed it impossible of herself to expose her family to the same degradation and ruin as had Lydia. It was now, however, much easier for Elizabeth to understand the very violence of the compulsion to do it.

Elizabeth did not grant Darcy clemency that day. There was no culpability with which to hold him, for she was not affronted. They were promised. Lessers with such an understanding would have been hockling merrily in the hayloft as soon as the match was made. Those weddings often only occurred when a baby was too high in the belly to be denied. Granted, they were not lessers and merry bouts were out of the question. However, she would gladly have granted her intended full immunity would he kiss her just the way he had again, now that she no longer feared that she would abandon caution and indiscriminately bite his lip once more.

She knew she would not. This happenstance occurred not by virtue of her inciting indiscretion and his counter remaining out of topic for them. She would not because, when he drew her so firmly to him, however entertained her attention was by his lips, her thoughts had wandered from them. With absolutely no cognisant endorsement from her, they travelled thitherward to that unfathomable part of his body that she felt pressed so hard against her leg.

As surely and as certainly as the sunrise, Bingley rode to Longbourn the next day, but he rode alone. Only a letter accompanied him, tucked neatly into his vest. It bore Elizabeth's name in Darcy's unmistakably precise script.

5

At the age of eight and twenty years, Fitzwilliam Darcy had neither professed love nor fallen victim to it. It was simply not in his nature to entertain frivolity. Stealing kisses or bandying for some damsel's affection was insipid. As it happened, prior to his acquaintance with Elizabeth, he had never once pursued a courtship. Hence, neither sweet nothings nor the whispering of them were within even marginal propinquity of his sensibilities.

His affairs had been cursory and to the point. That point being carnal gratification, not romance.

A compliment may have been paid upon a woman's beauty whilst in her embrace, but even those were more observational than adulatory. He simply had no tongue for flattery. Truth be known, he had not the wherewithal for expressing amorous feelings at all, so foreign were such inclinations to him. Whereas love had captured him quite decisively, reticence to revelation was not an easy transformation—not even when addressing the object of his new and exceedingly vigorous regard. Truly, he wanted to shower Elizabeth with every manner of tribute. Had he been able, he would have celebrated her every virtue, extolled her beauty, blessed her goodness, kissed her toes and the ground upon which they trod.

However sincere the aspiration, he simply had not the means to explain the shades of his love. To feel such fierce emotions and yet be unable to profess them adequately was ghastly. It occurred to him that he should plumb Netherfield's library (the books were not Bingley's, they came with the lease). His poetic inclinations favoured Pope, but he believed Blake might offer some inspiration.

That is, if he could keep his wits about him long enough to concentrate upon reading. For howbeit his voice was unable to pay her tribute, his body was announcing his desire for her in a most ungentlemanly manner.

When, in the throes of that increasingly amorous kiss, she bit his lip, it incited him to an exercise of his passion the extent of which he had not thought possible. Hitherto, such a loss of self-restraint would have been inconceivable. To have to turn away just to keep his arousal from being revealed was an outright mortification. He had stood, his back to her, desperately seeking to redirect his thoughts. The weather, scripture, anything but Elizabeth standing behind him lush and desirable (and undoubtedly mortally affronted).

It was miraculous that she had seemed neither angry nor insulted. As it happened, she bore no greater pique than a raised eyebrow and a rather peculiar expression. But the encounter had rendered him so out of sorts, he had taken his leave almost immediately. Upon thoughtful recollection, he understood that howbeit her bite heated his blood, it was her passionate response that fanned his flame. And that aroused no little compunctious self-examination.

For her demeanour and her circumstance claimed Elizabeth an innocent. She was chaste and it was his duty to protect her honour, not take privileges. But the volatile combination of their love, her innocence, and his lust was inciting his once sternly controlled mettle to unprecedented heights.

This would not do. It was insupportable to take such a liberty no matter how cussed the temptation. He was a gentleman, she a lady, their courtship could be affectionate but absolutely circumspect. His passion would be tethered, regardless of the provocation of her eyes, at least until their wedding. Certainly he could wait that long to kiss her throat. Smell her scent. Caress her body. His better judgement, clearly, was not only beclouded, it was very nearly trampled by desire.

It had not always been thus. There was a time, a very long time ago, when things were quite simple.

By the time he was nearly fifteen, little beleaguered Darcy. Already reaching a goodly portion of the height he would eventually realise, his bearing reflected that advantage. He was a hand-span taller than Wickham, who was more than a year older, thus inspiriting considerable ill-will from that young knave. Wickham's disposition fancied slight at every turn and took umbrage no less from God above than mortal man. Contrarily, Darcy's cousin, Geoffrey Fitzwilliam, was older still but had not the height of either. Yet if his ego suffered it was unapparent.

Wickham's, however, flailed about quite unreasonably. Though his own height would eventually almost equal Darcy's, Wickham was then most displeased, their rivalries intense. Wickham was quick, even anticipatory, but Darcy's height advantage was solicitously enhanced by superior strength, thus feats of agility were not a close contest. That the outcome was hardly a factor did not render the competitions any less wicked.

In time, Fitzwilliam accepted his limitations and (discretion being the better part of valour) abandoned both Darcy and Wickham to their races, clashes, and bouts for the arena that equalised all men: the back of a horse. In Fitzwilliam's stead, Wickham and Darcy strove onward, the latter in the happy circumstance of a natural winner. In defence of his continually abused ego, Wickham eventually (if petulantly) announced he was too old for boyish games. Lacking Fitzwilliam's good sense to stomach the inevitable, the height affront nettled Wickham's conceit of himself considerably.

Wickham had considerable ego to fester. Upon the death of his father, Mr. Darcy's steward, the elder Mr. Darcy became Wickham's benefactor. The adolescent Wickham had come to live on the upper floors in Pemberley. Having all the benefit and none of the attendant responsibility of station, Wickham's self-regard was distended beyond all proportion. Whilst engaging in bootlicking the elder Mr. Darcy, he deliberately fostered the impression that his position was entailed higher than it was to servants and villagers alike. Some were taken in by his swagger, others were not. Young Darcy was not, but neither did he understand that beneath Wickham's unctuous bearing festered substantial treachery.

The single advantage Wickham held over Darcy was by reason of age. He regaled Darcy with tales of scullery, chamber, and serving maids at Pemberley from whom he had been able to obtain favours biblical in nature. Already a practised cynic when it came to what tales Wickham told, Darcy's newly aroused libido, nonetheless, instructed him to listen more keenly than independent reasoning would have thought prudent.

Even as persevering a Lothario as was Wickham, there was further gall at Darcy's unwitting hand to be endured.

Young Master Darcy's burgeoning masculinity graced his countenance with unusual fondness, bestowing a handsomeness that perhaps did not exceed Wickham's, but certainly rivalled it. Hence, unbeknownst to him, Wickham's tide-pool of romantic opportunity was being eroded by defection. (Hampering Wickham too was a complexion that had a tendency to inflame under stress. The more his skin pustulated, the greater his vexation. Altogether a nasty turn of luck.) Because Wickham spent so very much of his time admiring his costume and feathering his bangs, he was blind to the understanding that one unaware of his own beauty always exacts more interest than he who preens. And whilst Wickham picked at his skin and patted his hair, Darcy looked in a mirror only to make certain he had no unsightly food stuck betwixt his teeth.

The stage was set for a battle as old as time.

For a time, the various intended prey of Wickham's foul designs admired Darcy's lack of self-regard from a discreet distance. However, one Abigail Christie, chambermaid, soon put herself into the young master's path. A year less than twenty, she possessed fine skin, a retroussé profile and pretty auburn hair. If her countenance suggested innocence, however, it was deceiving. A weakness for male attention had compromised her virtue more times than the vicar wagged his finger. Upon occasion she lifted her skirts to Wickham, but even she knew he had little to offer beyond his over-promoted position (and she immediately recognised his own sceptre of love was not half so inflated as his opinion of it). Still, a bum-tickle with the son of a steward was a considerable step up from a bit of hay beneath the under-gardener.

As a veteran of amorous rites, she considered herself quite the doyenne upon the appraisal of male pudenda. When she heard house gossip that Master Darcy's *virilia* was exceedingly well favoured by nature, her interest was…piqued.

It was difficult for Darcy not to have taken notice of Abigail over her half-year's employment. Wickham belaboured the various attributes of any of the female servants remotely close to child-bearing years (that being over twelve and under fifty; Wickham was nothing if not democratic in his lechery). Darcy's curt opinion, however, initially saw Abigail a bit too snub-nosed and thick-waisted. He began to reassess his position after experiencing a few unusually close brushes with her body.

That these encounters with her invariably happened in an otherwise spacious environment was quite myopically overlooked.

'Tis noted that it was more by her own design than caprice of fate that she found many chores in the bedchamber of young Mr. Darcy, frequently dawdling about her tasks in order to linger near. To an objective viewer of these doings, it would not have been a surprise when Abigail deposited herself in his room one quiet mid-afternoon. Darcy, however, was taken quite unawares when he bechanced her there and his expression betrayed this. With dispatch, his surprise was usurped and converted forthwith into excited apprehension. Clearly, she had not come into his room merely to change the bedding.

Again, she walked near him and stood idly twirling a copper ringlet that had escaped her cap. Shifting nervously from one foot to the other, he reddened, then frowned in a vain attempt to appear unruffled. His colour certainly did not abate when she, with an audacity he had yet to experience, asked if he had ever touched a woman. At that, he dropped his eyes to the floor, not wanting to admit he had not. That reaction, of course, announced the very thing he hoped to hide. When she took his hand and placed it upon her bosom, the size of her waist was little impediment to her desirability.

Abigail's inexpert genesis of this seduction would have warned a more experienced lover that, however practised she was in the basics of amour, she lacked finesse. The youthful Darcy was oblivious to such nuances, however, and her clumsy seeking of his manhood easily provoked its attention. That garnered, Abigail simply laid back upon the bed and drew up her dress (this being a wordless and universal sign of invitation). And, as a lad of considerable vigour and no little heat, he needed neither encouragement nor instruction (yea, some instincts are, indeed, stronger than others). He mounted her, spent (far too quickly he was certain), and, undeniably ignorant of the protocol under such circumstances, rolled away.

She rose, smoothed down her dress, adjusted her cap, and kissed him full upon the mouth.

"Will Aye find you here to-morrow?"

He nodded emphatically. She did, then, and for several days thence, Darcy not tardy once.

This embarkation into the rites of amour was not only inspiriting, but quite illuminating. Betimes, even off-putting. Upon the culmination of his second coupling with his newly designated paramour, said lover rather vocally reached achievement. Wickham had, in his many oratories, explained to Darcy there was a great deal of thrashing about whilst undergoing this act. However, Abigail's crescendo was of a magnitude to persuade him she had seizured in some manner. Hence, he was quite horrified he might have to explain her demise. To his considerable gratitude, her recovery was prompt. That his uppermost concern was not her possible death, but the scandal it would invite, should have warned him he was not actually in the throes of deep, abiding love.

Nonetheless, with their next assignation, she asked him if he loved her. He said, yes, he believed he did. (As this declaration was proffered post-insertion, pre-emission, one supposes the true depth of his adolescent affection must be taken with a grain of salt. His loins ached, and if he believed it was for her alone, Abigail was not one to argue the point.)

Nary a word of any of this did Darcy tell Wickham, but he thought of little else. And though Darcy was himself discreet, Abigail was not. Word spread post-haste (with more philanthropy than precision) of the young master's virility. From the objectivity of time, had Darcy been privy later to those whispered comments, he would undoubtedly have allowed that virility in that specific instance was possibly confused with youthful enthusiasm.

Beyond her undying, virginal devotion, the one thing Abigail had not offered to Darcy was that she had been sharing her favours with Wickham. But, once eliciting a profession of love from young Darcy, Abigail refused to lay with Wickham. He was not amused, even a little. Wickham called her several names that were not complimentary. She spat out some rather harsh character complaints herself.

"Muck slattern!"

"Deknackered dung heap!"

Trading unpleasantries with Abigail did nothing to appease Wickham's insulted ego. To be spurned for the younger, wealthier Darcy was gristle he refused to swallow. With the air of a true Samaritan (and no little haste), he went directly to Darcy's father and told him of the exact nature of his son's latest avocation.

Darcy ranked his father's good opinion far higher than any other, and when called to answer for such carnal indiscretion, he was mortified to his very bones.

In his first formal discussion of manly honour and integrity, Mr. Darcy told his son that his position was one of such import that he must never be ruled by anything other than the highest of motives and the worthiest of principles (trysting with servant girls, obviously, was neither). He told him he must never exploit his circumstance nor use it selfishly (trysting with servant girls was both). It was not revealed, nor did he ask, how his father learnt of his improprieties. Darcy never suspected George Wickham, for his conscience could not be entirely convinced divine judgement had not exposed him.

If there was any divine intervention, it was visited at that time only upon Wickham. For there was a hasty realignment of the female servants at Pemberley. Wickham was extremely vexed to see that all the newly-assigned chambermaids were great with girth and age (averaging ten stone in weight and two score ten in years). In his humiliation, Darcy noticed neither this nor that Abigail disappeared from Pemberley compleatly.

This episode unquestionably altered Darcy's life, introducing a lifelong pattern of stern self-control. As he grew older, his natural reserve became a buffer, leading some to believe he felt himself above their company. If his manner came to be led in pride and conceit, it was borne of a perpetual stream of obsequious deference from men and women alike. In adulthood, he was known as a man of clever intellect and superior understanding. His manners were impeccable, if somewhat haughty.

Darcy was not vain, but he was proud, expecting perfection of himself, and would not brook less from anyone else.

His reserve was already firmly in place when he and Wickham left for Cambridge. But once there, he found concealed in his belongings a piece of paper bearing a London street address written in his father's hand. He came to learn Harcourt was a house of good Mayfair address, known to most men of means. It was a place they could discreetly pass company with a woman possessed of both beauty and refinement. This lady required no commitment beyond a few hours of one's time. A major rite of passage would have been for his father to escort him to such a place for his introduction to manhood. As that horse was already out of the barn, so to speak, his father chose to guide his son thusly.

With the single lecture his father had given him still ringing in his ears, Darcy had every good intention of taking his studies quite seriously and he set the address aside. Even with the caterwauling Wickham underfoot in constant search of his next conquest, Darcy strove to seek the moral high ground. So often did he rebuff Wickham, who constantly prevailed upon him to join in his rounds of drinking and wenching, Wickham took to calling him the "Archbishop."

The sobriquets with which Wickham gifted him mattered little to Darcy, for in actuality, his libido was not necessarily inconsolable. He was merely less vocal about the women with whom he joined in physical congress. And, upon occasion, congress he did. But each of these rendezvous was, to his mind at least, unsatisfactory. If he disparaged Wickham's bent for vulgar establishments and round-heeled women, Darcy could not say with utmost conviction his road was an improvement. For each instance of intimacy he consummated gifted him, not with satisfaction, but with new restricting axioms with which to lead his life.

There had been a rather titillating, if unexpected, experience when he was just eighteen with the infamous (he belatedly learnt) Twisnodde twins in their coach one night. But he had been so consumed with guilt for such debauchery, he was visited for months with the terror that he had left either or both of them with child. (For due to circumstance of drink, he could never absolutely swear whether he had had them both, or one or the other twice.) He vowed (first axiom) he would be most cautious within whose garden he spilled his seed; and (second axiom) never, ever drink more than one glass of wine per evening.

As he grew older, he occasioned affairs with women of station and allowed himself a passing interlude with a noted actress. He found her a disappointment and (third axiom) kept to his own social level thereafter. His understanding of honour demanded he never take a virgin, nor lie with a woman married or promised (four and five). Ultimately, though, he began to recognise an all too familiar expression upon the countenances of those with whom he intended intrigue. Just before carnal egress commenced, an expression of excited apprehension appeared. That, of course, announced that word of the generosity of his lovemaking (and that with which God endowed him, upon its behalf) had preceded him. He abhorred transgression of his privacy, and, in time, this abhorrence overtook any pleasure he might have had with his liaisons. His sixth axiom was instated: He would avail himself of no women of his social circle.

Of course, eliminating virgins, wives, the affianced, the forward, ladies of lesser rank, and those in his social circle from the reservoir of possible feminine gratification left little alternative. Finding no favour in self-gratification, he saw the irony that the two strongest needs he held—that of passion and that of privacy—were so perversely conflicting.

It would have been customary for a man of his position to take a mistress, but he did not seek a woman to dress his arm. His warm constitution sought only release, not company. Believing it a profound failing not to keep one's physical needs under the same good regulation as one's emotions, he strove to harness them both.

After a period of abstention marked by a profoundly ill-temper and a great deal of fencing, he decided, as a matter of expediency (seventh and final axiom), he would visit a lady at Harcourt. There he could chamber with diligence and privacy, safe in the knowledge that commerce exacted no threat of entanglement.

Once the urgency of that no-small need was taken care of, he could concentrate all his attention upon stern regulation of the rest of his sensibilities. That austerity was necessitated by the staggering onslaught of ladies in want of young Mr. Darcy for a husband. Eligibility, of course, demands little from its inhabitant. And, from his latent perspective, Darcy saw there were no wiles too unworthy, no scheme of cunning too disreputable. Each hopeful seductress saw the usual feminine arts and allurements met with devout stoicism. In this climate, it could be understood that Darcy held, if not conceit, at least a certainty of success when a woman's affection came into question.

When he went with Bingley to Meryton, the flagrant occupation of Elizabeth's mother in obtaining matches for her five daughters with men of wealth influenced Darcy to believe Mrs. Bennet to be exceedingly ill-bred. (Every mother's duty was this objective, but to be too overt was unseemly.) However, his appreciation for Elizabeth's fine eyes soon came perilously close to nullifying disregard for her family. That would not do. A man of his station could never consider marrying injudiciously, even though his good friend Bingley was tempted by Jane Bennet. Darcy hied to London and went, with considerable haste, to Harcourt to remind himself of his seventh axiom. However, the very entanglement he had hoped to avoid was already well underway. At Harcourt he consummated carnal union, but found little release and no pleasure.

The following April when he had chanced upon Elizabeth visiting her cousin next to his aunt's house, Rosings Park, he realised he could no longer deny his love.

Her flat refusal of his proposal of marriage flabbergasted him. Personal prudence had seen that he had never been refused by a woman for anything, ever. Angered and mortified, it was of no comfort to him to know that she realised his vanity. Clearly it had led him to believe her in serious want of his application of marriage.

With impetuosity hitherto unknown to him, he repaired to London, resolving never again to think of Miss Bennet. But when last he visited Harcourt, he sat in sullenness, enveloped in a black desultory cloud. The woman before him was not Elizabeth Bennet and he simply would not have her. He left angry, but at no one but himself.

It was not a feeling to which he was accustomed.

There had never been any doubt in his mind about his world or his place in it. Until he met Miss Bennet, his mind was in the same staid, structural order as his life. The fault of his disorder lay entirely at her feet. Therefore, with perverse pig-headedness, he vowed if he could not have Elizabeth, he would bear celibacy. All axioms were excised.

Fortunately for his constitution, Elizabeth relented, lest he might have actually burst. Although no one else, not even his beloved, knew it, Darcy had reached a state of utter capitulation to her. As a man of considerable personal courage, there was a single thing that he looked upon with unmitigated fear. That was the moment when she would learn of his unconditional surrender. He hoped she would be kind.

Viscountess Eugenia Clisson was revered as the most beautiful woman of St. Etienne. Her daughter Juliette was cast in her image. By reason of that resemblance, one might have expected her father to look upon Juliette with increased favour after his beloved wife's death, not, in his grief, refuse to look upon her at all. But he would not.

Viscount Clisson spent his days at his wife's grave. His evenings were spent commiserating his loss with his mistress and a carafe of rather good Bordeaux. He spoke little to his sons (who were used to dismissal) and ignored Juliette (who was not). This unhappy alteration in Juliette's situation might ultimately have been resolved had not her father's inattention to political upheaval kept him from currying favour with whatever entity was in power in France at the time. He, perchance, could be forgiven for not keeping closer watch, for even those under more rapt attention found it a dodgy business. Rebellion and chaos ruled. Even so, the Viscount could only weep for his wife, gulp his wine, and make love with his face, finding in all three a much better occupation of mind and body than government. He eventually saw his error in judgement, but by then, it was too late.

In the last shuddering breath of the eighteenth century, French dynasties were abolished, power inverted. Royalty was alternately in and out of favour. Unfortunately, it was out of favour when Viscountess Clisson died, allowing unguarded insurgency to usurp the Viscount's property. His vineyards were burned, cattle slaughtered, and property confiscated. Six soldiers of the revolution, their wives, nine children, four chickens, and a laundress stood without contrition upon his portico as Clisson vacated his villa to them. He weathered this affront with little more than a sniff of his aristocratic nose (happy enough not to lose his head along with his house), but his evacuation was only as far as his own goatherd's shanty. There he ensconced his mistress in one of the two rooms. The goatherd, his wife, and seven children appropriated the two-sided windbreak used to house milking does, oblivious to the odour and the goats' inconsolable bleating at the intrusion.

Hence, except for a matter of decor, Viscount Clisson continued to mourn just as he had (albeit the alteration of scenery required a little more wine). And as they were all over fifteen, *enfants d' Clisson* were left to fend for themselves in the single adjoining room. That it was a bit crowded was the kindest thing that could be said for the accommodations, hence, the children of *pere Clisson* looked for better elsewhere. Her brothers took officerships in the French army. Juliette took out a powder puff, dusted her exceedingly lovely bosom, and boarded a coach for Paris.

There, word had it that poverty abided more easily than in most of the great cities of Europe. Still, the newly impoverished Juliette realised quite with dispatch that being poor lay not amongst her proclivities. Having the refinement of the privileged, her mother's beauty, and not a whit of her father's insouciance, it took her no more than a se'nnight before she found introduction to a Marquis of the most meritorious ilk (that of longing for feminine company). He was not handsome of face nor figure, but was endowed with considerable riches and had more charm than his wealth would have demanded of him.

Juliette's decision to align herself with the Marquis was an excellent notion in that he required nothing more of her than to grace his arm at the theatre every other night (his wife accompanied him alternately) and allow him into her bed three times a week. He bestowed gowns, jewels, and a generous allowance upon her. And, as providence inspired the Marquis to embrace an affection for wine which rendered him asleep mid-coitus more often than not, quinine pessaries and a little luck assured motherhood did not jeopardise her employment.

However, another encumbrance did.

It soon fell apparent that the happiness of Juliette's situation was to be exceeded only by its brevity. For her middle-aged lover was arrested for crimes against the revolution whilst asleep in her bed, hence they were both whisked forthwith to the La Force Prison. As she had been in his company, Juliette was found guilty of the Marquis' offence as well (she never determined exactly what this was, presuming it his flagrancy of wealth and Bourbon blood, both of which he held in copious quantities).

Even with so severe a transgression before the court within the *Palais de Justice*, until her sentencing Juliette's greatest vexation was what indignities prison would inflict upon her complexion. The tribunal in charge of their fate, however, saw her penalty differently. And, as misfortune would have it, shorn of her glorious tresses, she stood in the tumbrel directly behind the impugned Marquis as it wended its way to the guillotine (that, unequivocally, being a far more heinous end than bad skin). Although they were not the only ill-fated in the cart, Juliette and the Marquis were first relegated from thence by reason of station (amongst those remaining were three Carmelite nuns and a man who had feisted in court). Thus, Juliette was standing at the foot of the scaffold pondering her own impending doom, when a basic quirk in the law of physics was exhibited.

For the Marquis' affection for drink was exceeded only by his affinity for food, this brace of indiscriminate habits rendering his an exceedingly corpulent neck. Upon its release, the guillotine blade fell soundly (acceleration, velocity, and force). But when it encountered the Marquis' apoplectic neck (mass) the blade merely wedged itself, denying the doomed man immediate decollation. The Lord High Executioner gaped at the sight in disbelief and then looked to his deputy in bewilderment. In all their beheadings, this had happened not once.

It is suggested that the Lord High Executioner's post was an exceptionally demanding employment. Yet, it was not compleatly without its reward of applause. That was not what he heard then. The crowd had ceased its cheering and begun to jeer. Ominously.

Juliette had never given her lover's throat much thought, hidden as it was beneath his many chins. But at that moment, it would seem, the significance of the Marquis' endomorphic anatomy only escaped the notice of the three Carmelite nuns, who still stood in the tumbrel awaiting their own execution by singing a very pretty (and appropriately mournful) dirge. For it was foremost in the minds of everyone else. The driver of their cart, the gaseous juror, the bloodthirsty crowd of onlookers, the *gendarme* who held a vigilant gun upon the felonious nuns, the Lord High Executioner, the Deputy Lord High Executioner, and, presumably, the Marquis himself.

The Lord High Executioner ceased his bewilderment and immediately ordered the Deputy Lord High Executioner to finish the job lest the crowd turn upon them. The Deputy Lord High Executioner saw no choice but to relinquish the dignity of ritual and climbed atop the wood moulding that held the blade in an attempt to force the contraption to do its job. Unfortunately, his efforts were to no avail and incited the increasing disdain of the crowd. In the face of that ever-escalating malevolence, the deputy had the excellent notion to jump up and down upon the top of the blade and only from thence was success at last found.

Such was the Lord High Executioner's immense relief, he was felled by a swoon and dropped to the floor of the scaffold across the Marquis' newly decapitated corpse. The Deputy Lord High Executioner, however, did not faint, for the show was not over and no theatre wings held a more anxious performer. For the Lord High Executioner in a faint left his role quite empty and his deputy saw his first opportunity to escape his own thankless job. For the severing of a head could only be compleatly appreciated upon its display.

The Deputy Lord High Executioner retrieved the Marquis' sundered cranium from the basket where it had landed and held it aloft to the ovation of the crowd. Alas, the Deputy Lord High Executioner was not used to bowing nor to royal pate adornment, hence when he dipped his chin and pointed his toe, lifting the Marquis' head high, its weight separated it from its adorning wig. The Deputy Lord High Executioner flung away the empty peruke and was sent upon a run after the head, for it rolled about for an absurdly long time before coming to a stop, its features fixed with a look of appalled (and extended) incredulity.

A torrential guffaw imbued the crowd and whilst that merriment ensued, the Deputy Lord High Executioner managed to recapture the head and hold it up long enough to reckon protocol satisfied. Thereupon he seized the opportunity to declare the day's festivities over, lest the loss of his own head provide a needed encore. (Reasonably, the Lord High Executioner himself would have escaped this affront, for he was still at the mercy of oblivion and it would provide the crowd no entertainment at all to witness the beheading of a man insensible of the insult.) The Deputy Lord High Executioner hastily vacated the scaffold and tugged his employer from atop the truncated remains of the dead Marquis. The Deputy Lord High Executioner was taller, but the Lord High Executioner was heavier (having, by reason of his gloriously ignoble occupation, similar predilections as the Marquis), hence, the Deputy Lord High Executioner had to grab the Lord High Executioner by his boots in order to drag him down the steps of the scaffold. The Lord High Executioner's head hit each of the ten steps, one by one, rendering him even more benumbed.

The *gendarme* who stood holding the gun upon the malefactors still in the cart was much occupied by his duty, hence could not help load the Lord High Executioner onto the tumbrel. Thus, the Deputy Lord High Executioner ordered those same felons to assist. Throughout these horrifying proceedings, the nuns had stood mutely in the cart, their mouths agape (due less to shock than the fact that they had stopped singing mid-note). But their oath of duty bade them render aid. The intestinally indecorous man, however, was still in a snit over his bodily functions condemning him and refused to help. With only four in service, it was an ungainly procedure to hoist the Lord High Executioner onto the cart and had the disadvantage of landing the back of his head in the middle of a generous pile of manure still clinging to the floor of the tumbrel (by reason of its recent service as a dung cart).

Of course, the Lord High Executioner was not immediately aware of this, hence, it was not of immediate concern to his deputy. What was of immediate concern was that they take their leave whilst the crowd that had swarmed to the Marquis' torso was still busy ridding him of his fashionable attire (his tasselled shoes had already disappeared).

The Lord High Executioner's deputy encouraged the driver of the cart to make haste. This sallying encouragement was, indeed, needed, although the driver should have known it imperative to make away. But the man hesitated. For his duality of position demanded that he drive the prisoners to the guillotine and return with their headless bodies, whereby he would be paid to bury them. The Marquis' body (along with remuneration) still lay atop the scaffold. The Deputy Lord High Executioner immediately saw the driver's dilemma (for he, too, was a man of wages). Upon his pointing out that if the mob overtook them, there would be little need of money, off the little waggon went, its two wheels groaning and squeaking. Progress was, however, a little slow.

Juliette had watched this entire event unfold, quite entranced. She did, however, have the presence of mind to jump into the retreating cart. The leap was impressive for one who seldom leapt, but because her hands were still tied behind her back, the landing was not nearly so pretty as the jump.

Yet no less fortunate, for she landed face down atop the face up, but still senseless, Lord High Executioner. Although she was of slight frame, the percussion of her landing roused him to consciousness, and providence claimed fortune in that the crevice of her unpowdered, but still lovely, bosom wedged upon his nose.

Because the Lord High Executioner's swoon had lent him amnesia of the recent unfortunate incident, he was compleatly beguiled by the fragrance (and bounteousness) of Juliette Clisson's *décolletage* as the cart rattled away.

Although what came to pass was not entered into historical reference, it was still part of it. For, although the Carmelite nuns and feisting man did not, Juliette escaped the guillotine. And if in time it were suggested to her that a lady should be admired for her mind and not her physical charms, she would not argue. Nevertheless, she knew her wit did not save her that day. Perhaps her mind told her to run after the cart, but it did not land upon the Lord High Executioner's face. Nor was it her mind the Lord High Executioner kissed that night before he fell into glorious wine-induced sleep mid-coitus.

Dinner at Netherfield in the company of Jane, Bingley, and his sisters was turning out more poorly than Elizabeth could ever have imagined. In Darcy's absence, she had not wanted to come, but Caroline Bingley had insisted she accompany Jane.

"It will do you good, poor dear."

If being the recipient of Miss Bingley's frequent "poor dears" was not Elizabeth's least favourite thing at the moment, it was amongst the bottom three, bested only by being tied up in a sack with rats, or being wife to her cousin, Mr. Collins, in that order. Comportment at Bingley's house a week after the news of Darcy's unceremonious decampment had turned absolutely funereal. Surprisingly, the same could not be said at Longbourn. Upon having been informed of Darcy's leave-taking by Jane, Mrs. Bennet looked upon the matter with unlikely wisdom.

"Not to fear, Jane. Mr. Darcy dare not break the engagement less than a fortnight before the wedding. The marriage is secure."

Yes, the marriage was secure. Elizabeth knew that as well as her mother. The marriage would take place regardless. Regardless of what? That was what worried Elizabeth. Eleven days before their wedding, Darcy had left Hertfordshire without warning. Not knowing what could have precipitated such a ghastly impetuosity upon the part of so deliberate a man was extremely vexing to Elizabeth, and his letter (actually no more than a note) had shed little light:

Dearest Elizabeth,

I regret I must away upon business. I shall return in time for final arrangements for the wedding.

Yours,

F. Darcy

When Bingley had handed Darcy's missive to her that day, he smiled. But it was an odd little smile, one accompanied by a slight twitch in his left cheek, as if it was less determined to present a happy face than its owner. Obviously, he was at least minimally aware of the note's contents and his unease did nothing to appease Elizabeth's. Taking the letter with more angst than she would have liked to expose, Elizabeth excused herself from Jane and Bingley intending to retire to the privacy of her bedroom to read the letter. But such was its brevity, she had it read halfway up the stairs. Standing upon the landing, she refolded it. Then she opened it and reread it. She refolded it.

His note was economic at best. Compared to the verbosity of his letter responding to her refusal of his marriage proposal, it was not merely terse. It was very nearly rude. Could he not at least have used the word "love" once? "Yours," he had signed it. She signed her letters to her aunt and uncle with more affection. Her only comfort was that he had not written that he wished her "health and happiness." An invective such as that would truly have been an outrage.

Daring not to press Bingley for details, Elizabeth spent that evening listening to the contrived gaiety of his and Jane's conversation and gave her sewing much more attention than it had ever known of her. And whilst she embroidered, she thought again about why Darcy could have left with such haste, with not a word to her.

Certainly not because he thought he could express himself better by hand. It was unlikely a less flowery correspondent could be found in all of England.

Uninfluenced by Jane and Bingley's pretence that all was well in the realm of romance, Elizabeth sat in silent misery. In her meditation, speculation was unavoidable.

Had her unguarded response to his kisses cost her his regard? Until then, she had held only the vaguest notion of contrition for her behaviour. The provocative abandon she had felt only the day before had degenerated into a black cloud of humiliation that threatened to follow her into perpetuity.

"Yours," indeed.

After Bingley took his leave, Jane came to Elizabeth.

"Perhaps you don't wish to speak of it, Lizzy, but I must tell you that Charles is just as perplexed at Mr. Darcy's away as are we all. He spoke not a word of it. It is said he took his leave before first light."

"Truly, Jane, I am vexed that he would leave so. But there are often unforeseen circumstances at such a vast estate as Pemberley that might well have necessitated his immediate attention."

That answer sounded as contrived as it was and Elizabeth attempted to mitigate it with a smile, determined not to appear inordinately fretful. But she fretted. And the cost to her nerves and ego were considerable under the guise of "sisterly" solicitation from Bingley's sisters, Caroline Bingley and Mrs. Hurst.

Hence, their dinner that night at Netherfield was insufferable, seated as she was betwixt Caroline ("You poor, poor, dear Eliza") Bingley, and the bibulous Mr. Hurst, who had no conversation beyond a disparaging comment upon each dish just consumed and a preference for the one upcoming. Elizabeth had no opinion upon any of the ten courses of the meal, for she choked down only enough food to keep Caroline from remarking upon her lack of appetite.

Looking down her narrow nose, past her exceedingly long chin, Caroline clucked again and again to Elizabeth (who knew not if it was meant as a comfort or a threat), "To think, Jane will soon be our sister," pausing dramatically before adding ominously, "as shall you, Miss Eliza."

Sister to Caroline Bingley. Happy thought, indeed.

Having been thwarted in a rather overt and lengthy play for Darcy's affection, Caroline Bingley was not even marginally successful at appearing happy at their engagement. She professed absolute euphoria at the match. If she had displayed even a little coolness of manner, a certain reserve in her voice when she spoke to her, Elizabeth might have felt some sympathy for her disappointment. But as it was, the more fervently did Miss Bingley vow her everlasting devotion to her new "sister" the more firmly she announced herself an unctuous hypocrite.

At the head of the table, Jane to his right, Bingley and his betrothed were conspicuously in their own world. Howbeit their besmitten countenances only emphasised her singular status at the table, Elizabeth was grateful Jane was unwitting of Caroline's thinly veiled insults about the Bennet family's circumstances.

"What a sweet country frock, Miss Eliza! You must be frightfully happy to know soon you shall afford fashionable ones!"

Elizabeth was bereft. Four days until their wedding and she was still without even a word from Darcy. Trapped with the Bingley sisters behind an obscenely becandled épergne subjugating clearly half of the table whilst watching Jane and Charles look lovingly into each other's eyes, Elizabeth felt a great deal of self-pity.

Hence, the clap of thunder that rattled the windows was most unwelcome. The accompanying rain meant she and Jane would be overnight guests as well. Breakfast on the morrow must be partaken in the same unhappy manner as dinner. Briefly considering feigning illness, Elizabeth emptied her wineglass and set it down rather soundly, thus inducing a stare from Mr. Hurst and its hurried refilling from the footman. She was tempted to upend the glass again, this consideration taking her attention just long enough for the evening's entertainment to be decided upon as cards. Given the manner in which fortune had trespassed upon her most recently, she fancied her partner would be Caroline Bingley and silently groused to herself.

Another clatter of thunder culminated with the crash of the front door loud enough to dislodge the portico, and the party synchronously jolted in their chairs. The wind that rushed in blew out many candles from the vestibule to the dining-room, sending the servants bustling to resecure the light. But before they could, another horrific rattle of thunder erupted, this one punctuated by a show of lightning that revealed a spectre at the door of the dining-room. Louisa Hurst shrieked.

But Elizabeth did not. Still, she was startled. For the convulsion of flickering light revealed the very face she saw every time she closed her eyes.

"Darcy!" Bingley declared.

That proclamation was met with a gradual re-lighting of the candles, which unveiled the condition in which Mr. Darcy had entered the house—soaking wet. He handed his hat to a servant, who then yanked and heaved mightily whilst endeavouring to relieve him of his saturated greatcoat.

Bingley bounded from his seat, hand outstretched to Darcy, "I say, Darcy, come sit by the fire or you shall catch your death!"

(Mrs. Bennet would have been very alarmed. Were three days enough time to take pneumonia and die?)

Apparently the drenching Darcy took had come only from an impetuous, umbrel-laless dash from his coach to the house and he convinced Bingley he had not been so foolish as to make the trip upon horseback. After waving off Bingley's concern, Darcy looked through the dim light at each dinner guest. When his eyes lit upon Elizabeth, they rested their search. Elizabeth saw that they had, as did everyone seated at the table, for all eyes followed the same course as did his. To say she was disconcerted would be understating it by half. His appearance was so sudden, she had not time to decide what to say, much less how to feel, particularly since the room seemed quite anxious to register it. So, her cheeks did what they did best. They coloured.

Excusing himself for dry clothes, Darcy quitted the room almost within a minute of his introduction. There might have been cause for Elizabeth to wonder if he had really been there had not she continued to be scrutinised by her company. (Mr. Hurst held his oft-replenished wineglass halfway to his mouth for clearly a quarter-minute, which was evidently a record abstention for him.)

There was enough time to compleat the meal and retire to the comfort of the draw-ing room before they were joined by a now-dry Darcy. He bowed and spoke to every-one there before he came to Elizabeth. All Elizabeth wanted was to have a private conversation with him, but it appeared he was in no great haste to have one with her. For he merely took her hand, barely brushing his lips across it as he sat down next to her, immediately initiating a conversation with Bingley.

The evening was spent in that perverse manner. Darcy sat next to Elizabeth, very nearly touching her, but had hardly a comment to her beyond the storm. Darcy and Bingley nearly had their foreheads touching, so confidential was their conversation. Elizabeth only learnt through determined eavesdropping that Darcy's wet arrival had come about by reason of a stop at Longbourn.

Darcy told Bingley (and more than one Bingley sister who was eavesdropping as well), "There I discovered the Miss Bennets were dining at Netherfield. I feared their carriage might be caught in this storm, thus I strove on."

It appeared to Elizabeth that Mr. Darcy had gone to a great deal of bother and grief to find her so he could ignore her. Yet, when agreement was made to retire and Miss Bin-gley called for a servant to show the Miss Bennets to their bedchambers, Darcy caught Elizabeth's hand, allowing the others to quit the room and leave it to them. At last.

Howbeit she fought it dearly, Elizabeth felt herself trembling. The defence she had fashioned to ward off the worry, vexation, and humiliation over his departure had just collapsed. Relief that he had returned and anger over the manner in which he had taken leave were threatening to make her cry. She did not trust herself to speak. It was he who needed to explain himself, not she to inquire.

But he offered no explanation. He offered a gift. Elizabeth eyed the small silk-wrapped present in his hand meanly. Did he fancy he could treat her so thoughtlessly and buy her forgiveness with a trinket? She eyed the silk again. Even an expensive trinket? If she was, indeed, to become Mrs. Darcy, this must be addressed.

Her hesitancy to take the package from his hand induced Darcy to draw the end of the bow himself, thus revealing within the silk a sapphire the size of his thumbnail. It was surrounded by three rows of diamonds and swimming in a sea of pearls. It was only when he held it up that Elizabeth saw it was a necklace, the sapphire and diamonds its clasp. She saw, too, that if he thought a gift would buy her happiness, he did not fancy such felicity purchased cheaply.

"My father gave these to me as he lay ill the month before he died. He told me my mother had wanted me to present them to my wife. They belonged to her."

Thereupon, he placed them about the neck of a thoroughly chastened Elizabeth.

"My costume, I fear, does not do such a treasure justice," Elizabeth finally managed to say. "Miss Bingley is anxious to help me improve my wardrobe…something in brocade, I think she suggested…"

In her discomfiture, it was not what she wanted to say. She looked up at Darcy and said what she did want to say.

"I thank you."

"Lesser beauties, of course, might need brocades and other such finery. But upon you, Elizabeth, it would be redundant."

She fingered the pearls gently. He placed his fingers even more gently atop hers.

The tip of his forefinger located the largest pearl as it nestled in the indention at the bottom of her throat and rolled it lightly against her skin.

"You made a special trip to Pemberley for this? Could you not have sent someone and not have disappeared for so long? Sir, do not think me ungrateful, for I am not. But it has been an agony…"

Her trembling voice announced the strain of the previous week and Elizabeth was afraid the emotion of the moment would make her weep.

"Yes," he said, then, "No…I did not…" he stopped again.

It was apparent any further explanation for his leave-taking would not be easily offered. Abnegating to that self-evident truth, he abandoned any accounting for his departure and turned Elizabeth about to look at herself in the mirror upon the wall behind them.

"So very lovely," he said quietly, but as he spoke, he was looking at her countenance reflected in the looking-glass, not the pearls.

Her gaze returned his there in the mirror. And through that surrogacy, a communion more intimate than had hitherto been encountered took place. And within the length of that gaze, he encircled her in his embrace, his arms beneath hers. He kissed her neck just beneath her ear. And as he did, she watched his expression alter from shared intimacy to private anguish. Was it his dead mother's pearls about her neck? There was no opportunity to query, either in the mirror or directly, for he took her formally by the hand and led her out of the drawing room and to the stairs.

Once there, they were overtaken by Miss Bingley come in search of Miss Eliza to show her to her room. In place of a goodnight kiss and profession of love, Elizabeth was led away by her cunning, chattering hostess. Hence, she could only take a fleeting glance over her shoulder at Darcy, hands hanging uselessly at his sides.

Troubled, Elizabeth sat in the middle of the plump mattress in her rather fine room at Netherfield and considered seeking Jane for a talk. But the house was asleep and she was not certain to which room Jane had retired. It would be imprudent to sneak about the halls knocking randomly upon doors in her dressing-gown. A light rap upon her own door stole her attention from pondering propriety. She brightened. Perhaps Jane had found her. Then darkened. Perhaps Miss Bingley wanted to inquire as to the suitability of her accommodations. By the time she padded across the room, she had steeled herself for the cloying sweetness of Caroline's solicitations.

Therefore, the expression she bore when she opened the door to Darcy was not a particularly inviting one.

So dramatic a change did her countenance make, it was quite obvious his appearance was not anticipated. Her alteration of expression did not influence his, thus revealing he expected her astonishment. Automatically, she put her hand to her now vacant neck. Had he come to retrieve his mother's necklace?

Without hesitation, she took a step back with the door, in mute acquiescence to his admittance. In any other circumstance, she would not have acted so rashly, supposing the probability he came to wish her goodnight. But he was in his shirtsleeves and his face still bore stifled traces of the wretchedness she had seen in the mirror; hence, her reaction had been instinctive.

He stepped into the room. She closed the door, exceedingly aware that the single layer of muslin cascading from her trembling shoulders was beginning a shimmy over which she had no control. She endeavoured to halt it by leaning back against the door. One must suppose that he took note of her gown as well. For once in the room, he stood very still and took a lengthy study of her person, from her loose hair to her bare toes (which curled under the inspection).

Unexpectedly, he turned and walked away from her into the middle of the room. He reached out and rested his hand upon the top of the post at the end of her bed, and, looking more into the air than at her he spoke.

"I fear I must apologise for taking leave so suddenly and without explanation…"

At this, he glanced at his own hand reposed atop her bedpost and, rather self-consciously, removed it and placed it upon his hip. Elizabeth gave a slight nod, but did not speak.

He continued. "I could have sent my man for the necklace, it is true. But I chose not. I had to take leave…from you, us…lest I…forget myself. Compleatly."

With an unlikely blend of contrition and indignation, she said, "I supposed you had made your escape from the shameless libertine you have ascertained your intended to be."

At this, he looked at her in sudden realisation that she thought that he had gone, not in defence of her honour, but by reason of her comportment.

"It is myself I do not trust, Elizabeth, not you."

It took a few moments for the magnitude of his confession to settle upon her mind.

But, it ultimately did. Evidently, his passion was more indocile than her own. Both relieved and amused, she asked, "You came to me in the night to tell me you do not trust yourself alone in my company?"

As she said this, she walked toward him, feeling a little giddy at his expression of confoundment. Furrowing his brow slightly, he deliberated upon that for a moment.

"It appears, indeed, I have."

By then, she had reached him and taken his hand. The coldness of hers allowed him to change the subject from dissection of the reason why he stood in her room at that hour to the mundaneness of the chilliness of it. He busied himself demanding she find her slippers, robe herself, come stand by the fire, none of which she was able to do, for he drew the duvet from the bed and wrapped it about her shoulders.

All this fussing did not persuade Elizabeth of his self-appointed stewardship of her health. But the solicitude was not unwelcome. She climbed upon the end of the bed, tucking her bare feet beneath her. Upon her knees, his chest was just the right height for her to nestle her head there.

"You are right, Mr. Darcy. It would not do to stand up with a bride with a red, sniffling nose."

Smiling, he stroked her hair and whispered, "I left here to protect you from the fever in my blood, Elizabeth."

He lifted her chin.

"Only to return here to find you steps from me all night long."

It was unlikely that Elizabeth had cuddled against him guilelessly, for they still had not kissed. It is just as unlikely that she did not understand that his sense of honour would not allow him to take the initiative of seduction with an innocent, even if she was his wife-to-be. Hence, she assumed the reins of her own chastity, threw off the quilt and kissed him upon the mouth.

That might have startled him, it might not have. Regardless, the gesture was understood compleatly and was hardly spurned. And from her knees upon the edge of the bed, the stratagem of bodies and lips was at an optimum. Still, each anchored the other with a firm grasp of hair and kissed repeatedly, each one deeper than the last.

When he had explored her body that day against the oak, there was the considerable hindrance of corset and petticoats. Hence, even though his search was diligent and had not been without reward, it remained ultimately futile. Her night-gown, however, offered no such impediment; any pleasure he received when he slid his hands across the fabric was exceeded only by her own. All of which demanded their wrestling about escalate into a feverish near-frenzy.

The only obstacle of costume was his, for, although he had doffed his coat before he sought her room, his waistcoat and tie were still in place. The tie was no true impediment to sate her desire for his body, but his waistcoat was. Had his hands not been so diligently employed, he might have ridded himself of it. But since they were, Elizabeth's took upon that task, barely executing the violation of his buttons before their bodies toppled back onto the bed.

In all the candour and impertinence of truly united desire, he climbed atop her, his hands searching for the hem of her night-dress. That found, thus were her calves, knees, and backs of her thighs. And each was stroked to quivering, unadulterated surrender.

Now, into this fray, arrived a little argued presumption. When very nearly embarked *in flagrante delicto*, it is postulated that the female of the species' attention is less, shall we say, monopolised. And in this specific instance, that truism was validated. For Elizabeth was the one who heard the knock upon her door and Jane's voice.

"Lizzy? Lizzy? I cannot sleep. May we talk?"

Elizabeth stiffened, then lay still. Her quitting the embrace alerted him to outside intrusion. It was testimony to his determination to have her full participation whilst he luxuriated in her embrace that bade him cease his quest to possess her as well.

Jane repeated insistently, "Lizzy!"

They looked at each other, chests heaving. "If I do not answer, she will believe me ill and awaken the house," Elizabeth whispered.

He dropped his head to her shoulder in frustrated acknowledgement, then advised her, "I will not hide under the bed, Elizabeth."

"I would not marry a man who would," she answered matter-of-factly. He kissed her for that, very nearly rekindling their passion.

Then he rolled away, sat up and said quietly, "Can you give me a moment to…collect myself?"

The reason he needed that restoration had been fully apparent, and Elizabeth, having no knowledge of such matters, wondered how long it would take for him to become…presentable. Even with Jane rapping at the door once more, she granted him whatever time he needed to…settle his ardour.

Elizabeth called out, "Coming, Jane."

She rose slowly, followed by Darcy whose arousal had subsided, but who was fumbling with the buttons on his waistcoat. When they reached the door, neither had compleatly collected themselves, but they were intact. Elizabeth opened the door boldly. Jane looked apprehensively at Elizabeth, then her gaze over-swept her sister's shoulder and stopped. Her eyes widened at the startling sight of Mr. Darcy, who loomed quite large behind Elizabeth in the doorway. He bowed to Jane curtly, revealing a head of thoroughly mussed hair, and spoke quite formally.

"Good evening."

Thereupon, with as much dignity as one could muster in such a situation, he walked out of the room and down the hall.

Jane watched him as he took his leave, then tilted her head just a little to catch every last glimpse of him as he rounded the corner to his own room (possibly to make certain she truly witnessed what she thought she had). Then, still in the doorway, she looked at her sister's equally dishevelled tresses.

"I feared you and Mr. Darcy had quarrelled." She again looked down the hall, now vacant of Mr. Darcy's passage, "But I dare say any disagreements betwixt you have been mended?"

Indeed.

Nary a word had passed betwixt Elizabeth and Jane regarding the blatant impropriety of Elizabeth entertaining Mr. Darcy in her bedchamber (and in her nightdress). This was not by way of censure, but because Jane and Elizabeth's sisterly bond was unusually strong. Jane endeavoured to find goodness in all God's creations and she loved Elizabeth unconditionally. Hence, no matter what her eyes told her, she did not for a moment believe anything untoward had occurred that night.

This benevolence allowed Elizabeth a reprieve from explaining that if it did not, it was not for want of trying.

The day Mrs. Bennet married off her two eldest daughters in extremely advantageous matches was cold and bright. As the two couples stood in the vestibule (Jane aglow with purity and Elizabeth wearing quasi-vestal white) Mr. Bingley's eyes were almost as fulgent as the winter sun, but Mr. Darcy was quite solemn.

This august occasion was well-nigh put into a pother by reason of another relative. For the obsequious, obtuse (and far too ubiquitous) Mr. Collins waited as long as he dared for the request. It being not forthcoming, he then hied from his vicarage in Kent to apply for the exceedingly illustrious duty of presiding over the wedding of Mr. Darcy to his cousin, Elizabeth Bennet. So very anxious was he to officiate, Elizabeth thought it fortunate that it was she who happened upon him first, lest his fawning embrace have to be pried from about the illustrious Mr. Darcy's knees.

For, as he was wont to announce upon the heels of his introduction, Mr. Collins came under the personal condescension of Darcy's aunt, the Mistress of Rosings Park, Lady Catherine de Bourgh (a distinction he embraced a bit too acutely). His own self-satisfaction with the felicity of his situation was exceeded only by his compleat ignorance of public regard. This happy alliance of oblivion and conceit made Mr. Collins an unusually contented man.

There was, however, a single cloud upon the perpetually sunny sky of his disposition. Indeed, it was a forbidding one. For Lady Catherine's extreme displeasure over her nephew's engagement to Miss Bennet rather than to her daughter, the bilious Lady Anne, was vocal and virulent. And for a sycophant of Mr. Collins's well-rehearsed sensibilities, it was a fiendish dilemma. But, ultimately, with whom he should ally himself was not a really difficult decision: Rosings Park was closer, but Mr. Darcy richer. Hence, just days before the wedding he stood before Elizabeth, his handkerchief mopping his perpetually bedewed upper lip.

"Dearest Cousin Elizabeth, perhaps you feared it too much to ask of me, thus I take it upon myself to offer my services at your wedding."

Human folly had always been a great source of amusement for Mr. Bennet and, as her father's daughter, Elizabeth as well. As the most ridiculous of men, Mr. Collins should have incited considerable merriment. However, Mr. Collins had expectations. Upon Mr. Bennet's death, by reason of the unforgivable sin of begetting five daughters, Longbourn was to be entailed to his sister's son, the said same vicar from Kent. The magnitude of this particular injury was compounded by Mr. Collins's once entertaining the notion of uniting Longbourn with the Bennets by marrying Elizabeth.

Disabusing the tenacious little vicar of that idea was no easy endeavour. Her eventual success was but a miserly triumph, for she only managed to deflect him upon her good friend Charlotte Lucas. (Charlotte may well have been plain, twenty-seven and not of romantic sensibility, but Elizabeth believed even those desperate straits were not enough for her to sacrifice herself upon the altar of insipidity.)

Hence, it was with little compunction that Elizabeth disencumbered her toadying cousin of the considerable vagary that he would read them their vows.

"I thank you, Mr. Collins. You are very good to offer. But we did not wish to impose upon you, as a member of the family, any other duty than that of honoured guest. Bishop Peel shall perform the ceremony."

Thus Mr. Collins could boast (and did regularly, as he was always in need of a new boast) that he was passed over only for a clergyman who sat in the House of Lords.

A festooned high-flyer took them from the church to a commotion-filled wedding breakfast at Netherfield. Mr. and Mrs. Darcy bade their farewells that forenoon.

The Bingleys were to honeymoon there in the bosom of his family, the Darcys to travel first to London, then make an early start for Pemberley the next day. That was as one would have foretold. Mr. Bingley wanted to share his happiness; Mr. Darcy sought to enjoy his in privacy. Hence, for the trip to town the sporty open carriage was exchanged for a closed Landau, brandishing two postilions, two footmen, six horses, and a fully laden boot.

It was early evening when the resplendent coach arrived at the Darcy London townhouse. The newlyweds' egress from it was appropriately consequential, but for a courtship so rife with unrequited passion, it had been a strangely torpid trip.

Forasmuch as their simmering desire had seethed into a teeming boil at Netherfield, one should anticipate that once the union had been blessed by God, there would have been at least a minimal exchange of affection. That occurrence would have been quite unobjectionable to Mrs. Darcy.

That amorous juncture did not occasion.

Howbeit Mr. Darcy held her hand tightly and even kissed it several times, her glove was not removed. What little conversation occurred betwixt them originated from her. So barren of passionate inclinations was their journey, she concluded (a little petulantly) that marriage evidently stifled both her allurement and his abandon. Little time did she have to nurse injury, for they were whisked to a lavish supper.

Pemberley was certainly a stately home, but its grounds and gardens were not

formal. The townhouse was swimming in recherché glory. Much in want of appreciating the distinction of the meal, Elizabeth had not the means.

Once again, her appetite had vanished. The only consolation for her disquiet was
that Darcy was afflicted as much as she. They sat in reserved acceptance of the soup
and fish, but partook little. By the time the second entrée made its appearance, he
waved the rest away. Had there been other guests that would have been scandalous. As
it was, she issued a silent prayer of thanks. They rose from the table, her hand upon
his forearm, and from thence, he forsook her to the stewardship of a maid.

Her heart beating resoundingly in her ears, Elizabeth followed the plump lady-
maid to her dressing room like a dutiful schoolgirl. There she found the night-dress
she had meticulously embroidered carefully arranged. Upon it lay a silver-encrusted
comb, brush, and hand-mirror. As it was unknown to her, she premised it another
wedding gift from Darcy. It bore no note. Without invitation, the maid plucked her
hairpins out and set about putting the brush to good use. Elizabeth watched the
doings in the looking-glass and dearly wished she could talk to Jane.

For all her self-possession, she suddenly felt a strange longing. In the cavernous
house, her body and soul entrusted to a man whose nature she had not a notion of
unravelling, she missed her home. Or at least Jane.

The leap from fiancée to bride seemed a little too precipitous just then. Was that
not test enough, a decision fraught with possible mortification begged to be made.

Should she get into their bed and await him, or should she give him time to precede
her? When she peeked through the door, she saw there was no resolution to be reached.

Howbeit she opened the massive door only a crack, the glare behind released a
shaft of light rendering it impossible for her to behold what lay within the dim candle glow of the bedchamber. When she opened it a bit wider, a form was revealed
stopped mid-motion next to the bed. At first, Elizabeth could not discern who it was
and, in her embarrassment, very nearly leapt back behind the door.

Only sheer will (admittedly fortified by a finely honed inclination to curiosity)
induced her to take a second look. Propitious fortune allowed her to descry whom the
crepuscular light yielded.

It was her husband.

In his hand, he held a silver bowl, the floral scent wafting from thence announcing
the rose petals it contained. When her eyes adjusted to the darkness, she beheld an odd
expression upon his face, one she did not recollect of him. His gaze undefined made
her uneasy and she shifted from one foot to the other, uncertain should she flee back
to her dressing room or close the door behind her.

Abruptly, he set the bowl upon the table and hastily began to tuck in the tail of his
shirt. For she then saw, howbeit he was dressed, it was not properly. His feet were bare
and he appeared to be wearing only his shirt and trousers. His being *en déshabillé*
should have assured her he was tie-less as well, but that conclusion was not the one
that was drawn. For that was what she noticed above anything else. Neither his bare
feet, nor his prevailing shirttail, but that his collar button was undone, thus exposing
his neck. His neck being under such diligent study, it gave her a start when he strode

to her. Hence, he was upon her before she could do more than gasp.

With a swoop, he lifted her and carried her to the bed. But she did not truly remember him lifting her, nor any scenery upon the excursion. She was brought to her senses by the overwhelming redolence of roses that engulfed her body and thereupon by his mouth when it covered hers. Whatever reticence had been in his charge was surrendered to her with a ferocity quite unparalleled in her exceedingly explored imagination. Only then did she perceive his wetness, but she did not question what discaution of his bath bade him rise and come to their bed before her.

She was only sensible that his shirt and small-clothes clung to him, hindering her hands from sliding across his body. Evidently, this was an irritant to him as well. For he rose from her and begat a fierce struggle to divest himself of them.

Because she had felt of his body in full cry, and therefore appreciated the ampleness of his...credentials, Elizabeth had harboured a certainty she would not be taken unawares when she saw them. Yet, she could not help but stare (by reason of its tumescence, his torch of love just so happened to be trained directly upon her and it was difficult to disregard). When she finally wrested her eyes from thence, she raised one eyebrow slightly as if to question the viability of what nature insisted was, indeed, possible. In that he sought refuge from her gaze beneath the counter-pane with considerable dispatch, she concluded that her dumbfounded expression was less subtle than she hoped.

Her attention to passion, however, was reclaimed from the distraction of the size of his instrument for it forthwith. For he commenced to industriously explore beneath her gown.

As those caresses became increasingly urgent, she understood an escalation of affection was called for.

Having viewed just what would be inserted into her person to effect the eagerly anticipated act of copulation, it occurred to Elizabeth (in the very small part of her consciousness not compleatly swamped by desire) that there might be some heretofore undisclosed manoeuvre for her to accommodate such a commodious organ.

In light of how very commendably he was executing everything else, she surmised he would know that as well.

She bid, "What am I to do?"

Gentle, guiding strokes influenced her to allow him betwixt her thighs (an objective she found quite tolerable), this *demarché* culminating in the discovery of her womanly portal. Due to his exceedingly admirable ministrations, therewith, her womanly portal was quite anxious to be traversed. She moaned. However, he did not rush to possess her. The firm but gliding caresses she had enjoyed ceased.

"Elizabeth, you are so very small. I cannot bear to hurt you."

Relative size of aperture and appendage were hardly lost upon her. Pain, at that moment, did not seem quite so insurmountable to her.

She whispered, "You must."

Undoubtedly he knew he must. Undoubtedly, he knew he would. Even for a man with no experience piercing a maidenhead, innate wisdom, one must suppose, would tell him to do it slowly, gently. Ultimate desire, however, often obliterates discretion.

Unrehearsed as she was in coupling, when his body became quite taut as he initiated ingress, she conjectured it took a great deal of concentration upon his part to emit his seed. Therefore, it was quite unexpected when his restraint finally collapsed. He grasped her hips and thrust into her, hard. With repetition.

Most anxious not to cry out in pain, she very nearly did. Fortuitously, she was rescued from it by an assiduous search of her throat by his tongue. Needlessly, he murmured words of love and regret against her ear. For after the initial concussion of their encounter, the injury to her person was overridden. Indeed, her blood was stirred in a most unseemly manner, prompting her to run her teeth down his exceedingly admirable neck. This, regrettably, incited from him another newly invigorated impaling assault convincing her she was not quite as benumbed as she had begun to believe. But she bit her lips into silence and clung to him as he reached some sort of tumultuous crescendo, whereupon he gasped, shuddered, and moaned simultaneously.

In the quiet that followed, little was heard but the deep heavy breaths of expended exertion. He rolled from her. When he did so, she looked over to him and witnessed the back of his hand sweeping to a rest across his eyes. His chest was still heaving from the mingling of their bloods and he had already retreated from her.

So this was the act of love.

She felt as if she had just fallen off the roof of a barn and he had not extended his hand to help her to her feet. Lying there, desolate and resentful, she was uncertain whether to turn her back to him in a sulk, or simply smite him with a pillow.

In fortune, she had not the time to exact either recourse when he reached for her and drew her tightly to him.

He buried his face against her neck and stroked the small of her back, saying, "Forgive me, Lizzy. Forgive me."

Even in the winter night's chill, perspiration crept down his neck, and his damp hair now curled into sweaty ringlets. Instinctively, she wiped his forehead with the hem of her gown (which had lodged conveniently beneath her armpits), silently granting it best to withhold judgement until better informed of just what had come to pass. But forgiveness should not be an issue. Pain was the price to be paid of becoming a wife. She knew that. He must as well.

"Am I to consider myself now taken?"

He smiled hesitantly, then stroked her face, "Yes, Lizzy, you are now taken. And you are mine."

Within the confines of courtship, she had been "Elizabeth" to him, her name spoken with precise eloquence. But when their intimacy rendered her unto him "Lizzy," he lowered his voice huskily, the "z" sound tingling her toes. Peculiar how that small alteration allowed her to dismiss the entire issue of his post-coital disengagement. She announced to him that which he undoubtedly already knew.

"You have hair upon your chest."

It was there, but still sparse, promising the years would thicken it. She let her fingers inspect the thatch, allowing her to appreciate his bare chest clandestinely. His intrigue, however, did not lay with hers in his chest hair.

"Pray, can you bear it, Lizzy? I fear I must have you again."

Her admittedly limited education upon matters of amour had not included consecutive acts, hence this query was received by her as something of an astonishment.

"You can do it again?"

A pride of some consequence pressing against her thigh announced, indeed, he could. Had not Lydia insisted "it" became flaccid upon effecting achievement? Elizabeth chastised herself silently for listening to anything Lydia told her, then turned her attention to the matter at hand.

Concurrently trying to contain a smile and speak sternly, she said, "I will gladly suffer your love once again upon one condition."

Already of a mind he would acquiesce to any proviso, he had commenced to kiss her neck, but said, "Pray, ask anything of me."

"I found the velvet of your tongue quite unobjectionable."

He allowed that condition was agreeable. And this pact initiated a night of serial coitus, each successively more privileged than the previous, her gown soon cast aside altogether. Her nether region was still sore, but she would not admit to it, for his repeated lubrications did relieve the chafing.

The corner of the sheet he used to gently wipe the excess revealed, however, the blood her body had let, reminding him of the very thing she sought not to reveal. He laced his fingers through her hair and soothed her with repeated adulations of her beauty. Still, he was apparently confounded by the briefness of her womanhood.

To her increasing unease, amongst his purlings of love, he repeated, "You are so small."

Tom Reed was slightly akilter as he quitted the tavern. Hence, when he hit the door hard with the flat of his hand, it took its revenge upon his nose before he could clear it. In retaliation, he hit it hard again and this time when it was flung open, it stayed flung. Reed looked at it in smug satisfaction for a moment before he turned his gaze out onto the street.

One of his most trustworthy mates assured him that if he hung right past the knacker's shed, he could find a cockfight. He had done his best to entice Jack Lewis to join him. But Lewis would not budge.

"Ain't got time fer such, Tom. Aye gots to wait 'ere fer them gem'men. Make good money wi' 'em."

Pock-marked and snub-faced, Lewis was a bit fleshy for society's newest darling pastime of fisticuffs. Reed snorted at the presumption.

"Whot's fightin' if yer got rules, Jack? Brother of the Ring! What flummery! Yer'll git yer bowsprit smashed!"

"Aye've got me plans, Tom. Aye be no fool."

"Yea? Well, Aye'druther be a fartcatcher than a ninnyhammer w' beat conk."

Lewis only cackled and Reed betook himself out the door. In his inebriation (yea, even sober), Reed was not entirely certain of right from left and he reeled in the wrong direction.

Brimming were the streets of St. Giles Parish that night. Reed bumped into several people. Fortunately, they were in no closer claim of their wits than he and, by unspoken agreement, simply righted themselves without offence. As a man suffering from the convergence of an ursine bearing and caprine appetite, Reed routinely thumped anyone so presumptuous as not to clear his path. However, that evening his unsteadiness was fuelled by gin. That always left him in better temper than ale.

The happy crowd was about, as was Reed, by reason of a hanging outside Newgate Prison that afternoon. (Sentimental celebration of blood lust always included a fair amount of drink.) A number of folk claimed the multitude that day was as large as the one that witnessed the Haggerty/Holloway double noose in '07. Reed disputed that. Whereas nearly thirty people were crushed to death in the melee at that illustrious execution, not a soul did he spy trampled in today's mayhem. Undeniably, the entire spectacle was a disappointment. Only a pickpocket and sheep thief were hanged. 'Twas hardly bloody worth the bother.

Dual disappointment for Reed was that both were men. He had heard that the legendary Maggie "Snags" was to swing. Miss Snags (affectionately named thus by reason of her teeth, which she filed sharper than a shiv) had a propensity to use them somewhat gleefully upon those who crossed her. She was but a malmsey-nosed dishclout, but it would have been diverting to watch some petticoats dance about.

Hence, the single consolation of amusement was that the pickpocket was a portly man, his weight causing his decapitation. Reed cheered along with the crowd.

A speculation visited Reed briefly as to whether he might have access to either of the bodies once they had been thrown upon the tumbrel. He dismissed the idea by reason of there being too many constables about. Pity, for it was an undisputed truth that nothing had more power of luck than the right hand of a hanged man.

Here in front of him twirled two such amulets. The men guarding the bodies watched Reed as conscientiously as Reed eyed the corpses, thus convincing him they had already made monetary arrangement for adoption of the hands. In his disappointment, Reed looked up from the scuffling, cursing mob to the higher climbs of the inns surrounding the square. In those windows, he could discern the faces of the rich who watched the spectacle in unbesmirched self-righteousness from their rented seats.

He looked up, but did not tarry with his gaze, for if the moneyed class did not want to admit to more than a casual interest in such a lowborn exhibition, he knew them safer of their purses. Even Reed kept a close eye out for pickpockets; an assembly such as this was a fountain of fortune for the light-fingered. His own private little joke, he pretended a lack of vigilance in the hopes of luring an unsuspecting thief, happy for the opportunity to pound anyone. Either he looked too unprosperous or much too barbarous (possibly a combination of both), for no one bit. A few fights had broken out and Reed could not even break through the barrier of bodies to join the brawl.

That night upon Dyot Street, he gazed upon the throng of people and recollected why they were there. The execution was a reminder of his recent incarceration and was he of any sort of introspective persuasion, he might have understood his unusually intemperate turn. The gin turned a little sour in his stomach as he contemplated Newgate and vowed never to be taken there again. He was not so deep in thought as not to hear the coarse whistle of a young boy, who spieled, "What d'ye want, gem'men? D'ye like the dogs? We got 'em 'ere, gemmen. We got 'em 'ere."

Reed bethought the notion of entering the shabby wooden building. Betimes he was partial to watching terriers take on rats. A particularly ruthless bitch brought him a gold coin once. But he did not keep it long. As it happened, that had led to his imprisonment. Had he not wagered and lost it, if that joker had not angered him by winning it, he would not have had to throttle him. Was it his fault the bloke bled out? He did not throttle him all that hard, even kept his knife put away, he did. But the bloody constables took a sorry look at it. Blamed him. Took him in, locked him up. Had he not had the gumption to garrotte that guard, he would be picking oakum or on the Newgate treadmill still. Or, perhaps, would have fed the crowd more sport with one more noose filled.

Hence, no, he did not favour wagering upon the dogs.

But his misdirection did find sight of a familiar barmaid heading out for home. Frumpy and cheap, she had been his major source of quim since his "parole." He came up behind her, slapped her backside, and slung his arm over her shoulder.

"Abby me luv, where yer off to?"

"'ome."

"Yer need company, donna yer?"

"Yer spent all the company me needs, Tom Reed. Yer pockets are at low tide, are they not?"

"Not so flat as that."

At that somewhat wavering reassurance, Abigail Christie acquiesced to his company. When they arrived at her rooms a little ritual was enacted. She motioned to her boy to away and he disappeared behind a curtain with an armful of dirty babies. With great economy of movement, she found a bottle in a cupboard, and set it unceremoniously upon the table. She produced two handleless cups, clunked them down and poured the drinks without looking.

"Yer lay yer whiskey down better'n yer do yer men," Reed laughed.

Abigail appeared either uncomprehending of, or unamused by the joke. They emptied a few, thereupon Reed followed her to bed.

Reed had more or less taken up residence in the shabby lodgings, but he was never moved to ask about the father of her children. He surmised her husband was at sea. Fair enough. So long as she would let him in her bed for the price of a pint, he was in want of knowing nothing more.

By the time the sun made its appearance upon the narrow streets the next morning, it was nearly noon. The yellowed newsprint over the window kept out most of the light but none of the cold, and Reed awoke disgruntled and particular to his bearish inclinations. Scowling and scratching himself without looking about, he reached for his breeches left dangling upon the bedpost. He shook them out to put them on, then stopped before he had put a foot down one leg. He shook them again. He reached down and impatiently searched for the purse that had been pinned to his trousers, but to no avail. They were quite empty.

"Woman!" he bellowed.

If his menace was compromised by a costume consisting of ragged homespun and gaskins, he was quite unaware of it. He began to barrel about the room for someone, anyone, upon whom to vent his displeasure. No one came into sight but the same boy he had seen the night before.

"Yer there! Boy! Where's yer mother?"

The boy feigned ignorance, angering Reed further. Grabbing him by the neck of his shirt, he shook the gangly youth.

"Where's yer mother?"

"Donno, sir!" the boy answered.

Reed jangled the boy until he was certain he could hear his teeth rattle. Before the lad stopped vibrating, Reed struck him backhanded. A ribbon of blood trickled from one nostril, but the boy neither yelped nor cried.

At the commotion, Abigail intervened, attempting to calm Reed.

"Leave the boy!" Abigail called out angrily, thought better of it and said calmly, "Leave the boy."

Reed's interrogation was then aided with his fist full of her hair. Hence, its brevity.

"Was gonna buy us some tea and buns fer breakfast s'all," she explained sourly.

"Aye donno want no tea and buns and Aye ain't payin' fer none fer yer brats."

This, clearly, was of no extraordinary surprise. Abigail tugged a dress on over her chemise and gave up her sad attempt at coaxing a coiffure by dejectedly pulling the rags she used in place of curl-papers from her hair. Only about half had withstood Reed's fit of pique.

"Collector'll be 'round for the rent, too," she added.

As Reed's reaction to that bit of news was no more than a bit of hacking and snorting, relieving his nasal passages of the remnants of his hangover, Abigail announced an alternative plan.

"Yer don't help with payin' for the lodgin's, we're leavin'."

"'ud's naggers if Aye give a damn."

Contrary to his profession of lack of interest in her domicile arrangements, Reed glared at her and began to pick his teeth with a fierce-looking dagger. Initially, his undisguised threat was unseen, for Abigail was trying to arrange her stockings to hide the holes, a diligent but ultimately unsuccessful endeavour. He kept picking until she finally saw the blade. The intimidation incited Abigail to chatter on nervously.

"We'll head for Derbyshire, a goodly distance but Aye got kin there. Aye worked at Pemberley when Aye was the merest chit of a girl. Richer than God, them people are."

"You were never a chit of a gerl, Abby," leered Reed.

Unexpectedly, his tone altered. He lay back across the dishevelled bed and ruminated.

"Pemberley? Me brother boasts him a place on that coach. Said they weren't all that rich. Stays behind the house here in London." He lay there silently a moment and then bid Abigail, "Yer say it's a fine place, eh? Very rich?"

"The finest. The richest," she assured him. "Didn't yer brother tell you?"

No, his brother did not tell him. Not surprisingly either, Reed thought, knowing his brother had little gumption and no enterprise. Suddenly, better humour favoured him with a near-smile. This odd alteration of his features struck mother and son identically. They both recoiled.

He stood with a distant look upon his face, then slapped her behind again and said, "Thanks to yer, Abby."

Abigail had no idea what he was thanking her for, but she spoke not a word of question. Few people in the bowels of London questioned fate when it smiled. And providence looked quite happily upon Abigail if she escaped either a beating or a dip of Reed's wick. She did not watch as he walked out the door and up the street whistling absently.

"There goes a no-good muck of a man, John."

Without further comment, both began a furious compilation of meagre possessions to stuff into a dilapidated holdall.

Reed took advantage of the cold weather by stealing a ride clinging to the footboard of a closed carriage. He dropped to the ground as it rounded the corner of Haymarket and Monmouth, strolled up the street whistling until he spied a red brick mansion, and presented himself at his brother's quarters in back. When told he had a visitor, Frank Reed came directly, but seemed less than pleased when he recognised his guest. They had not seen each other but once since Tom's flight from justice as Tom had hit Frank up for half a crown. Knowing his brother as he did, Frank did not suppose it was a loan.

At Frank's dour countenance, Tom slapped him upon the shoulders, assuring him he had not come for more money. He wanted more than mere cash. Tom wanted Frank to open the bank.

He set about his plan post-haste by pressing Frank to promote him for the position of footman, that situation to become available forthwith. Tom took out his ever-present knife and commenced to pare his nails with it in front of the coachman who rode next to Frank. The intimidated man loved his life more dearly than gainful employment, took the hint, and fled.

Contrary to his brother, Frank had been a dependable and complaisant employee, hence, when he gave assurances of his brother's character to the rather prissy houseman, it was accepted as true as any other tale told in London. The houseman saw that the brothers held the greatest want of footmen, that of the same tall height and good leg. Additionally, Tom fit the newly vacated jacket. Could there possibly be anything else wanting? As easy as that.

Reed fancied the runty houseman's eyes spent a little more time than necessary looking him up and down than professional appraisal would have demanded. The position attained, he swaggered away, complaining over his shoulder to his brother who plodded sullenly behind.

"That nimminy-pimminy looks like that at me again, he'll be-a eatin' his danglers for dinner."

Frank Reed cringed at what he considered more than loose talk. Reed noticed his head hanging despondently as he walked.

"Ah, Frankie, me boy," he reassured him, "they're a waste on 'im anyways."

Yes, he could do it several times more than once, and with no little vigour. Light was barely filtering into the room, but Elizabeth was awake and contemplating that new understanding.

One might reason, considering the sumptuousness of the accommodations, her first observations when she awoke in the Darcys' palatial townhouse would have been of the furnishings (opulent), the wall coverings (lavish), the paintings (extraordinary), or the appointments (exquisite). But, by virtue that opposite her in the silk-sheeted bed reposed the handsome figure of Mr. Darcy, it would be understood if no competition existed.

Gaze she did upon her new husband, but from across the distance of a pillow. It was a test to keep from cuddling herself against him. His respiration was deep and peaceful. She dared not trespass on his sleep, for she knew surely he must be quite bedone by his endeavours. And as his thoroughly enthusiastic compatriot in amorous congress, Elizabeth supposed she should be weary as well. But as he was the verb of this act of love and she, the direct object, his flagging strength could be excused.

So robust (and extensive) had been their lovemaking, she had neither the time nor the inclination to analyse it at its coronation. Now fully explored and unconditionally admired, there seemed little left to ponder. What had been kept scrupulously arcane from her unwed sensibilities only the day before was a secret no more. Yesterday a maiden, today a wife.

With another look at her husband still somnolent, a deep sigh escaped her. Then, with covers clutched protectively against her own naked bosom, she carefully lifted the edge of the sheet.

She sighed once more. For there before her was the glory of her husband's body, revealed as such by the increasing daylight. The glimpse she had caught the night before had been astounding. But the light had been dim and she had not had time to savour it beyond taking profound notice of what was most incongruously obvious. Now that sleep finally cooled his pride, she could fully appreciate the breadth of his shoulders and the long, muscular leanness of his body. Her gaze, however, soon returned to his netherlands, for she was happy to have the opportunity to inspect them in covert leisure.

As she looked upon him, she pondered the only mysteries remaining. Firstly was the puzzlement of just where her own body found room to accommodate his member (for the answer to this, she would eventually make an awkward inspection of her person), and secondly (and even more curious), was the enigma of his true self.

His unpredictable and expeditious fluctuation from apparent immovable solemnity to volatile passion had left her shaking her head with wonder. Without a word, he had abandoned her for Pemberley a week before their wedding, then very nearly leapt upon her at Netherfield. Nary a word of love all the way to London, then he bestowed upon her a night of fervoured amour atop a bed of rose petals he had scattered there himself. She felt dizzy at the contemplation. But only fleetingly.

He stirred. Thereupon, he opened his eyes. This, before she had the presence of mind to drop the sheet beneath which she was peering blatantly at his naked body.

"Lizzy?" he said sleepily.

Either in lack of taking notice or of caring, she knew not which, he made no indication he was aware that she was eyeing his privates. She was happy for him to overlook such shamelessness and nestled impenitently against him. As he kissed her betwixt the shoulders, to her dismay she realised that her body was seeping again. Her cup, evidently, runneth over.

Her dignity was not yet mended from him so unceremoniously wiping his comings from betwixt her legs. The affront to her person (not to mention the abuse of a fine silk sheet) would have been addressed rather curtly had she not reasoned with such dispatch that his ardour was far too compromised for reproof. In fortune, for the repetition of conjugal acts and his subsequent edulcoration persuaded her that, in truth, it was not a grievance, but a courtesy. This enlightenment provided her understanding that if the first stains upon the bedclothes had been coloured by her blood, the besoiled sheets and untidiness of the entire venture generally fell to his secretions, not hers.

They were his, and her insides could discern the shuddering moment he cast them. That memory alone allowed her not to be affronted at the mess. Howbeit his fevered lovemaking had not yet yielded Elizabeth a sublimity comparable to his, she had not felt slighted. When she felt him pulsate into her, his *ne plus ultra* was hers. A slightly strangled sough escaped the back of her throat at the thought.

He brushed her hair back from her neck and nuzzled her there. His chin was scratchy. She laughed and put her hand upon his jaw, rubbing it. Odd, she thought, to see the fastidious Mr. Darcy with tousled hair and the shadow of a beard. Odd but not unwelcome. Dishevelment favoured him.

Suddenly, it occurred to her that it was probable she did not look quite as fetching as did he. Belatedly, she realised her time might have been better employed making herself presentable to her bridegroom than ogling his body.

Fully awake, he was eyeing her with silent intensity. Hence, ever more fervently, she wished that she had at least seen to her hair and located her gown. She believed she felt it by her toes beneath the covers, but dared not dive under the quilt after it just then. Pulling the bedclothes beneath her chin, she felt for it desperately with her foot. For her own nakedness had not embarrassed her in the darkness. The harsh light of morn and the unfamiliar, formal splendour of her surroundings coupled to invite severe misgivings of decorum. Even had he not stared at her so keenly.

But this close scrutiny, clearly, was not in censure, for he bid, "Pray, do you give me leave to look upon you?"

A formal request to examine her aspect. The politeness of which made her feel even guiltier about her own covert inspection of him. Intent as she was upon self-condemnation, she did not realise that he did not wait for her to acquiesce before he drew the covers from her.

Upon her unexpected baring to morning daylight and under his open gaze, she crimsoned. It was quite probable her entire being coloured. And that which could not blush, contracted. Owing to the fact that the two puckered components of her figure were that upon which he bestowed his attention, he took direct notice. However, he mistook the nature of their conversion.

"This room is far too cold."

He drew her close, bundling her in the covers. And then, before she could protest, he reached for and yanked an elabourate, tasselled pull-cord.

Before its tassel quit dancing about, two bellows-laden maids appeared to restore the fire. Their arrival precipitated Elizabeth's burrowing deep within the bedclothes. Her sensibilities demanded it. For to have servants wholly unknown to her witness her abed, compleatly stark-naked and with a man, was unconditionally mortifying. Even if the gentleman in her bed was her husband.

After much trampling about and the sound of the door closing, she whispered, "Pray, have they taken leave?"

He adopted a stage whisper to reply, "Yes, they have gone."

She peered out from beneath the counterpane and witnessed the manner in which he had greeted his servitors.

Covered only to the waist, her husband was propped upon his pillow, casually resting his head back against his steepled fingers. It would be obvious to anyone who might have dared to look that Mr. Darcy was quite without his nightshift, thus announcing Mrs. Darcy most likely in the same state of undress as she cowered beneath the covers.

Aghast that he would tease her in such a manner in front of the help, she exclaimed, "What cheek!"

"Pray, whatever do you mean, Mrs. Darcy?"

"You have left no ambiguity as to the nature of our…association!"

"I believe, Mrs. Darcy, they understood the nature of our 'association' before they entered the room."

There was a pause. A resentful pause. But, ultimately she could not fault his reasoning. Everyone who was married knew what they were doing. Fleetingly, it crossed her mind that she now knew what every married person was doing (or at the very least had done) as well. Faces flashed through her mind. When one set of them was Mr. Collins and Charlotte, she decided she would ponder that universal truth another time. The imperceptible grimace her ruminations bestowed upon her she shrugged away, for her husband rejoined her deep within the folds of covers.

"I planned poorly, Lizzy. We must arise if we are to reach Pemberley before dark."

Clearly, an admission of a misjudgement came with some cost to his dignity.

Hence, she nodded a little hesitantly, hoping he understood her affirmation was of understanding the need for haste, not that she agreed he had erred.

The stop at London had been an ideal compromise of time. It had been his plan to arrive at Pemberley the day after their wedding by mid-afternoon. Then, she would see it at its best. But his finely detailed agenda did not incorporate langourous loungings and supine delights. All his scheming went for naught. They would have to away soon. It was a hurry neither wanted.

Inevitably, thoughts strayed from their imminent travel, for he rediscovered her bashful bosom right where he last saw it, his lips endeavouring to beckon them from their shyness by means of affection.

Lying back, she revelled in the pleasure he bestowed.

"Must we?" she asked.

Utterly lost in the bounty of her body, he had forgotten what he had just said not moments before. He rose from her, unsuccessfully masking an expression of extreme injury.

"No, we do not," he said. "I am a beast to be at you so much. Forgive me."

Very nearly laughing at such a colossal misapprehension, she said, "I meant 'Must we leave?' I could stay here with you like this forever."

It was discovered then, that a man of sufficiently warm blood could, even under the disadvantaged impairment of four previous accommodations, re-achieve a *penis in erectus* of considerable magnitude. In light of foregoing acceptance and resultant pleasure, the owner of this temporary priapism sought to explore just how abundantly his wife's newly liberated *pudendum femininus* could receive it. Although she was willing (even eager), her nether-regions cried out. She kept her wailing womanhood silent until, in the final throes of release, he thrust even more fiercely, quite insensible that her ultimate confines had been reached. His moan at this apex was quite overwhelmed by hers.

Immediately, he drew her head to his chest, repeating, "This will not do. This will not do."

Wretched was she. Not only for her suffering body, but that she had been certain the vexatious pain problem had been rectified by her deflowerment. It had not. And she was not strong enough to bear it, thereby exposing her body's inadequacy to him.

"This will not do," he had said.

Clearly, he was as appalled as was she by her body's connubial inhospitality. Indubitably, he would demand the marriage be negated. It was a perfectly good reason. She could not perform her wifely duties, therefore she was unfit as a bride. The church would concur. He would be given an uncontested annulment. She would enter a nunnery in shame. There, she would pine away for him for the rest of her life. Her tombstone would read, "Her body was willing, but not fit." He would marry again. To a lady whose body was as generous as the Meryton well. A woman who would bear him ten children, all sons. He would never think of her again. Oh, wretchedness.

Before she had found reason or even anger at fate, which would have been a truer reaction for her nature, she bitterly (and with a great deal of self-pity) announced her obvious shortcoming.

"I am stunted," she proclaimed.

Still in heaving contrition atop her, he raised himself upon both elbows and inquired, "You are what?"

"I cannot accommodate you. I am obviously stunted."

Still raised upon his elbows, breathing heavily, but blinking at her remark in non-comprehension, he could only repeat, "You are 'stunted'?"

"Yes."

Impatient that he did not follow her reasoning, she explained to her exceedingly satisfied husband thusly, "My body obviously cannot meet your needs. I thought it was only at first, but you see now, it is not. I am stunted and cannot perform satisfactorily as your wife."

"Lizzy, that is absurd!"

"'Tis not absurd! You yourself said, 'This will not do.' Indeed, last night, you said again and again that I was too small."

"I said you were small, meaning..." he searched for an explanation.

"Paltry," she answered for him.

"No. I meant, small—diminutive—*petite*. Lush and tight."

At that unprecedented explicitness, he well-nigh blushed.

Then, hastily, he continued, "It was a compliment, Lizzy, not a complaint. As for my saying 'it will not do,' I only meant it would not do for me to continue to hurt you. That is my failing, not yours. I must rein myself in, for you are not too small, I am..." He flailed about for a delicate way to put it. "...rather large."

"Oh."

This was an interesting turn of events. The entire conundrum was the fault of *his* body, not hers.

She bid, "Do you mean too large?"

"I mean to say, you are small, but not too small."

"You mean to say, you are not large, but too large?"

"I am not all that large..." he made a frustrated little half-snort, obviously unhappy at the direction the conversation was taking, but that did not deter her curiosity.

"How large are you?"

"As you see."

"Well, you must understand, sir, my frame of reference is somewhat limited. Would you not grant I have no true way to compare it?"

He almost smiled then reclaimed it, not wanting to encourage further discussion of the meritoriousness of his member. But he was tardy by half, leaving Elizabeth feeling saucy enough to inflict a tease.

"Are you large enough to incite gossip? Are you large enough to be put upon display in Piccadilly?"

By then thoroughly defensive, he said, "I said I was large, not a freak of nature."

"I am just trying to get some idea of what sort of largeness we are dealing with here..."

"I should have just said I was not small."

"There is a very wide gap in definition betwixt 'too large' and 'not small.'"

"It will have to simply remain so, for I refuse to discuss it further."

He shook his head slightly, then said, "I truly believed I would be whispering endearments in your ear at this moment, not discussing *logistiques*."

"But, the dilemma has not been solved…"

"I promise you, Lizzy, it shall be solved," he said. "With very diligent practise."

They eyed each other with uncommon concentration. Had he held the unlikely notion that she was not of a mind to re-enact connubial rites, the quivering little *frisson* she elicited when he kissed the inside of her thigh would have removed all doubt.

One would travel miles upon the property owned by the vast estate of Pemberley before reaching the house itself. There was no true guidepost to announce whence it began, save for the road as it changed to gravel. This road snaked through the holdings with all due obeisance to the landscape, skirting hedged fields in the brown dormancy of winter.

The season saw few people about, only a harrower or two yet at their tasks. Although a smattering of flocks could be seen from the road, they were not well watched. Lambing had commenced. That was a nocturnal obligation, hence what few shepherds looked over them were kept awake midday only by the yapping of their dogs. This semi-somnambulism predestined that no one was much about to take notice as the coach travelled up the way, shades drawn in defence of eyes that were not upon it.

Employment inside this coach was perhaps as assiduous as the land outside lay fallow, for as it neared the great house of Pemberley, Mr. Darcy was in mid-instruction of Mrs. Darcy upon the merits of equestrian exercise. No bell tolled at the lodge gate; it had already been opened in expectation of the newlyweds' coach.

Thus, its occupants were unaware of their own imminent arrival. Hence, when the carriage drew to a stop, there was an uncomfortable pause before the door opened. Had anyone counted, one hundred and sixty-eight people assembled upon the curved drive of the house in reverent anticipation of meeting their new mistress, thus reasoning the vacant countryside. A slight murmur began to arise from the throng when they heard scuffling sounds and what might have been an embarrassed giggle from within the coach, but they silenced when Mr. and Mrs. Darcy emerged.

Mr. Darcy stepped out first, his bearing noble and appropriately proud. With no more than a glance from the master, the footman stepped back, allowing her husband to hand Mrs. Darcy down, her cheeks blazing. As she took her first step upon Pemberley soil as its mistress, an ovation erupted.

Nervously tightening the chin ribbon of her bonnet, she, for the briefest moment, looked heavenward. (She had been cavorting quite lasciviously in the coach upon their lands with their heir and namesake, hence, this may have been a silent prayer that no lightening bolt would strike her down at the behest of Darcy's forebears. One can only conjecture.)

Mr. Darcy, however, appeared to have no such qualms and took her arm.

Clinging dearly to him, Elizabeth looked at the twenty steps she must conquer to reach the door to the house. She took a deep breath and was certain she waddled like a duck with every one she took, impeaching the very propriety of her position and betraying what she had just been a party to in the coach. If she believed there was a lack of stateliness to her carriage, her husband thought better, proudly introducing each of the house servants to her by name. Three little girls were urged forward, presenting freshly scrubbed faces rosier than the flowers they shyly held forth.

The family awaited at the top of the steps. Miss Georgiana Darcy's eyes were bright with excitement, her hands nervously wringing a handkerchief. Next to her, Elizabeth espied the congenial face of Colonel Fitzwilliam. To his left stood one who could only be Fitzwilliam's older brother James, now the Earl of Matlock since their father's death. The brothers favoured each other considerably, the elder a slightly stouter version of his younger brother. Inside and out of the draft stood frail Lady Matlock, wobbly upon a cane and steadied by James' wife Eugenia. (The willful old woman announced she was determined to greet her nephew's wife standing.)

Those introductions compleat, more servants appeared. Elizabeth had thought everyone upon Pemberley must have stood outside upon the lawn, but it was not so. Her previous visit to the place had told her servitors abounded, but although a guest to the great house found great hospitality, it was nothing to the solicitations she now received as Mrs. Darcy.

It seemed there was a separate maid to tend to each of her ten fingertips. Her cape, each glove, and her bonnet were each plucked by a separate attendant. Her coach-wear was removed with such dispatch, had her eyes been closed, she would not have known anyone was there. It was a ritual to which her husband seemed quite accustomed, for a separate contingent of servants relieved him of his hat, gloves, walking stick, and overcoat as smoothly and precisely as had it been a well-rehearsed ballet.

Pleading weariness from the trip, they took their leave directly. As they ascended the staircase rather grandly, Elizabeth looked back over her shoulder in renewed admiration of the tasteful elegance of décor. It was not dressed with useless finery, but with furniture and paintings accumulated by the family for not just generations, but centuries. Her trepidation upon assuming the considerable responsibility and obligation of her position very nearly made her quake. Therefore, as she took the stairs, she endeavoured to call upon enough gumption to ward off such relentless intimidation.

Suddenly, the punctiliousness of the entire homecoming was irredeemably ruptured by a raucous scrambling of feet and claws punctuated by loud yelping whines and originating from huge, hairy beasts that scrambled headlong down the corridor in their direction. So intent were the enormous Irish wolfhounds on greeting their long-absent master, they had no qualms about going around, over, or possibly through his new bride to reach him.

Darcy simultaneously reached out to rescue Elizabeth (who had spun a revolution and a half) from tumbling back down the stairs and commanded the dogs, "Behave!"

Dizzied as she was, it took a moment to determine that it was not she, but the dogs that had incited his rebuke. When she recalled the moment, she would be ever grateful that she did not actually break her neck within the first quarter-hour of their arrival.

He held her close, but continued to scold the dogs, perhaps venting his fright for her upon them. She, however, pleaded their cause.

"Oh Darcy, they are simply happy to see you!"

With profuse apologies, the dogs' handler rushed up to retrieve their leashes. Mr. Darcy waved him away with a small aristocratic wave of his hand. It was one that Elizabeth was beginning to recognise as astutely as did the servants. With the dogs upon their heels, he showed Elizabeth into what was to be their bedchamber. Yet in a pother, both dogs proceeded upon a wild circle of the room, each provoking the other as if exacting a hunt of some undisclosed quarry. One dog (it was difficult to determine which) bounded across the silk counterpane, requiring Darcy to demand "Heel!" to still them. Evidently of the persuasion that it was best to desist before they were ejected, they dropped at his feet, tails whapping the floor.

Elizabeth knelt to pet them. (It was a treat, for her mother never allowed dogs inside Longbourn.) Once they were still, she could determine that one was grey, the other brindle. They kept their heads low, but their tongues sneaked out to lick her hand.

"What are their names?"

Somewhat abashedly, he answered, "Troilus and Cressida."

"Truly?"

"Yes. 'Tis true. My father sent them to me as pups my second year at Cambridge. I was seriously interested in literature and suffered the resultant melancholia. Homesick for Pemberley, I suppose. My father sent them to cheer me."

"You named them for such a tragedy? I cannot imagine you the victim of dolour," she teased.

Quite seriously, he said, "Then you have no idea what torture you once inflicted upon me."

Obviously still mortified by the experience, he hastened to change the subject by doffing his jacket and vest and commencing to wrestle with his cravat. The imminent exposure of his neck reminded her of the connubial bliss consummated in the privacy of his coach. Her blush was more from the pleasure of that indiscretion than that it was, indeed, an indiscretion.

She said, "I fancy you know your credibility as a gentleman has been severely challenged."

"Pray, how so?"

"Be not so innocent of countenance. I was not the initiate of what occurred in the carriage."

"What occurred, Lizzy?"

Not for a moment did she believe he knew not of what she spoke. It amused her that he wanted to hear her say it.

"The yielding of favours."

Stifling a laugh, he let her euphemism pass. "Cannot a man be at once a gentleman and husband too?"

"Indeed. But upon a public road?"

"'Twas a private road for the last ten miles," he assured her. "A private carriage upon a private road."

With that, he playfully picked her up and tossed her upon the bed and added, "Such as this is a private room, this a private bed."

The dogs plopped down upon the rug as decidedly as did their master upon the bed, but the dogs sat looking good-humouredly askance for what would next come to pass. What next came to pass was his hand sliding up her leg above her stocking and a caressing of her thigh. And that made it impossible for her remember that she was going to tell him about the day she first visited Pemberley and saw his portrait. Had she not been so pleasantly and thoroughly diverted, she would have told him she thought that was when she first fell in love with him. It was from his portrait.

Indeed, that previous spring when Elizabeth Bennet had done the unthinkable by refusing Mr. Darcy's proposal of marriage, it was a surprise there was not an audible and collective gasp from his ancestors.

For, not only had she, the daughter of a modest country gentleman, refused the hand of one of the richest men in England, she refused him emphatically and with little civility. If his vanity was injured, at that time she cared little. There was considerable conceit to wound. Indeed, his vainglory was the basis for her entire refusal. And because of his egregious faults, it was likely she would have spent her life in self-satisfied spinsterhood had not she taken a fortuitous summer tour of the north-country with her Aunt and Uncle Gardiner. There, she had bechanced upon the said same haughty Mr. Darcy once again. At one time thought irredeemably proud and disagreeable, his demeanour at this meeting was vastly improved. His love had not wavered; hers blossomed.

It had been a chance encounter. Now she had returned as Elizabeth Bennet Darcy, Mistress of Pemberley by reason of a chance encounter. If his precedents smiled down upon their union, Elizabeth had yet to see them.

As anxious as the Master of Pemberley was upon christening the marital bed with the Mistress of Pemberley, little intimacy could be initiated (or rather culminated). For the house was in an excited uproar, trunks hauled thither, the servants bustling about. All this commotion excited the dogs and they barked at every opportunity.

At the first knock upon their door, Elizabeth leapt self-consciously to her feet. It was her fervent wish that the servants not see her upon her back with their master so precipitous of their arrival. Darcy's reputation within the house had been cemented over a period of almost three decades. It was imperative to Elizabeth that licentious conduct not censure hers forthwith of her introduction.

She stood in resolute piety as the servants went about their chores. Darcy still lay languidly upon the bed. His tie was undone, his neck all but naked. Hence, Elizabeth's own libido corrupted her good intentions. She weathered such blatant seduction, however, and dutifully looked away, then busied herself with a turn about the room. In her intense need not to look at her husband's throat, she scrupulously admired the room's adornments, but was drawn to a miniature atop one chest. It looked very much like her.

"Darcy," she asked, "Pray, whose likeness is this?"

"'Tis you."

Confused, she said, "But I have not sat for a likeness."

"Indeed, you have not. It was done from my memory six months ago."

"But we were not even engaged six months ago."

"No," he said quietly.

The intensity of his gaze just then discomfited her. Her hands, quite of their own volition, set to straightening and smoothing her frock. Perhaps it was the unconscious need for reassurance that she was not standing before him naked, for she suddenly felt compleatly exposed. It was an odd sensation, not truly unwelcome, just unsettling.

A maid returned to the room announcing that Elizabeth's bath was drawn. Upon this occasion, she did bathe, the dust from their trip quite evident. Was that not an impetus, she would have bathed regardless. For she was now quite certain her body's respite from her husband's scent would be fleeting.

They were not yet engaged when Darcy happened upon that studio in Pall Mall. The throes of unrequited and all-consuming love had driven him to invent business upon which to attend just to keep insanity at bay. He had only been passing by when he found himself outside the house where Gainsborough once worked. The old painter was long-dead and Darcy had no notion of who, if anyone, still laboured within. It was an impulse to find his way 'round back and enter through a low door. The entire episode was quite rash.

A lone painter was at work. As he sat crouched in concentration at a small table delicately applying paint to a tiny piece of ivory, Darcy was able to poke about the place unnoticed. While the studio itself bore no particular distinction, a large assemblage of oils leaned against the wall at one end. Most were badly done discards. A few showed promise, but apparently were abandoned. Among those, one in particular caught his eye. Indeed, so struck was he that he very nearly gasped.

It was not signed, but as he owned several works of the artist, Darcy was quite certain that it was done by Gainsborough himself. However, it was one quite unlike that painter's usual aristocratic portraits and bucolic landscapes.

It was of a wood-nymph. A beautiful nymph, immodestly draped, sitting by a lake. It was not the brushwork that took his notice, but that the nymph bore such a startling resemblance to the form in which Miss Elizabeth Bennet visited his dreams each night. So striking was the resemblance to his unbridled vision, for a moment he could not breathe.

He did not favour the allegorical; indeed, he despised romanticism in art. Was his heart not quite so wounded, undoubtedly he would not have been taken with the desire to purchase it on the spot.

Better judgement prevailed.

However, if propriety did not allow him to hang a six-foot canvas of Elizabeth's naked twin upon the wall of the Pemberley library, he would do the second-best thing. He strode over to the artist, who only then realized a personage of import had graced his studio and rose in obeisance. With fifty sovereigns, the portrait of the nymph before him, and explicit instructions from the gentleman, the artist achieved a cunning likeness, but one of abbreviated pose and tiny in size. The painter thought the gentleman quite pleased.

When Darcy returned to retrieve the compleated miniature, he purchased that great canvas also bearing likeness to his beloved, for he could not bear another to look upon what he dreamed of each night. However, he took it not to Pemberley. He had it encased in a wooden crate and transported to the farthest reaches of his London home. There it sat, yet untouched this half-year later.

But as he now had enjoyed the quite singular pleasure of his wife's true form revealed to him, he knew he would have that wood-nymph returned to Pall Mall. At one time he had thought it quite impossible, but he now understood how truly inadequate the vision cast by his mind's eye had been.

As dinner hour approached, Mr. and Mrs. Darcy descended the stairs much in the same grand manner as they had taken them hours before. They conversed with their company before the meal was called, Darcy's closest relatives' opinion of his new wife obviously not polluted by his aunt, Lady Catherine. Colonel Fitzwilliam had once announced to Elizabeth he thought his aunt a bore, not in so many words, but he said it all the same. He paid respect to his aunt for she was his aunt, just as Darcy had done. Politic and kind, Fitzwilliam was thought of as a dashing-good fellow. Indeed, other than those of a gentleman, he appeared totally without airs.

Fitzwilliam's older brother was not as convivial, perhaps stricken with the importance of his lately acquired title. Lady Eugenia was less merry than anyone at the table, but in very conscientious attention every time her mother-in-law coughed. One might suppose this dedication fell to her extreme affection. Closer study would reveal it less filial regard than eager anticipation. The sooner the old woman lay toes up, the sooner she would be not only the wife of an earl, but also the Lady of the manor.

It was obvious that Georgiana readily relinquished her position at the head of the Pemberley table to Elizabeth. At this moment, that it relieved Georgiana of her burden was the single inducement that Elizabeth saw in her own ascension to mistress. For Georgiana was timid. Counterpoint to her brother in every way but reserve, she was blonde and ethereal as Darcy was dark and intimidating.

At the dinner table, Miss Darcy was content to be a listener, but in the drawing room, Elizabeth took every opportunity to coax her into conversation. However, Fitzwilliam repeatedly compromised her success. That gentleman was hasty to reclaim the easy friendship they had begun to form when they first met at Rosings Park. He talked to Elizabeth to the point of monopoly. Darcy played his part in this re-enactment of the previous April's circumstance as well by glowering at Fitzwilliam and Elizabeth the entire time they conversed. So conspicuous was his disapproval, Elizabeth was quite uneasy. She made more progress bidding Georgiana to talk than her brother, and the awkward evening played out with excruciating forbearance on the part of Mr. Darcy's new wife.

When their guests left for Whitemore and Georgiana retired, the newlyweds took the staircase rather grandly again (perhaps the only way to take such an august set of steps). The Master of Pemberley held his lady's fingers out and away at shoulder level (the majesty of their assent ever so slightly compromised by Troilus and Cressida scrambling in their wake). Elizabeth only took her husband's arm when they reached the top of the stairs. His grip upon her was firm, steering her away from the corridor door toward her dressing room and to the one that led to their bed.

With the closing of the door, he put his arms about her. Then, for a long moment, he rested his cheek atop her head.

"It is good to have you home with me," he said.

Still disquieted by his being so out of humour downstairs, she responded, "If this is so, why do you look so ill upon me in company? You stare as if I offend you in some manner. You have always done thus. 'Tis no wonder I once thought you disliked me."

"I hold myself to the strongest reproof if my countenance persuaded you of other than my love. For if I gaze intently upon you, it is most certainly not from dislike. Quite the opposite."

That said, he kissed her neck. Several times. This, whilst he began an undulating search for the pins in her hair. With quiet deliberation, he dropped them one by one to the floor.

"May I undress you?" he bid.

"I feel," she said, "as though you just did."

Quite unbeknownst to Elizabeth, a niggling annoyance was turning into a serious vexation for Darcy. Other than having her, he thought of little else.

As a man of considerable self-control, he had perfected *coitus reservatus* to his own particular art form, orchestrating each of his assignations with self-assured precision. With the single woman he cared most to please, his loins refused to await her pleasure. He was unable to muster more restraint than a pubescent schoolboy. And that thought was most abhorrent. It would not do.

By reason of extreme duress (lengthy abstention and obstacle of hymen), he could excuse himself for effusing uncontrollably into her the first time. But not the next, nor the next (nor the next several). The lush confines of her body usurped his wits compleatly. His will was totally lost to her. In retrospect, he reckoned that it had been thus for some time—just not with such graphic delineation.

If his evening's silence disquieted Elizabeth, that was unfortunate, but it was not without merit. He had found little amusement whatsoever in Fitzwilliam sporting with his husbandly parsimony by monopolising Elizabeth's conversation. Undoubtedly, his cousin knew he was one of the few men to whom he would allow such a liberty. Though he had stood in mute disapproval allowing Fitzwilliam his little joke, his taciturnity reflected intimate contemplation and a resultant steadfast resolve. For her first night in Pemberley, he would bring Mrs. Darcy to the same rapture she bestowed upon her husband. Anything less was indefensible.

His plan would not await her toilette. It must commence immediately. Undoubtedly, anticipation would seize all discretion.

Hence, the shedding of each layer of clothing betwixt their bodies was done expeditiously. Whilst this disrobing was performed with extraordinary mutual admiration by Mr. and Mrs. Darcy, it was not they alone who benefited. Though not for the same design, Troilus and Cressida did as well. After their garments dropped to the floor in a heap, Cressida scratched them into a compact pile and curled upon them, resting her nose upon her paws. Troilus, however, had no more than situated himself before the last piece of their wardrobe was cast aside, landing upon the dog's head and disconcerting him not one whit. He merely unearthed himself and added to their makeshift bed. There, lying in feigned repose, he and Cressida awaited the soft sounds of sleeping. It was only then that they would sneak upon the end of the bed to take their rest.

The dogs, however, were to be disappointed for some time. The master's bed-mate kept him awake. Conversely, their master kept his bed-mate awake as well.

Undeniably, Darcy was quite fond of his dogs (else they would not have access to his bedchamber). But their interests were not his just then. He held to his simple ambition. Ultimately, patience and Herculean self-control obtained success. Substantial success.

Her arousal burgeoned and thereupon ruptured into an intense convulsion of pleasure that was accentuated by a deep moan that began at the back of her throat and then wafted across the room.

A misfortune, for at this unidentified sound, both Troilus and Cressida commenced to howl. Mr. and Mrs. Darcy were so profoundly enthralled within their own pursuit, the dogs' yowling did not become apparent with any haste. When the dogs' accompaniment finally overrode their senses, Elizabeth released the grip she had upon her husband's hair. And (not entirely certain what she just experienced), covered her face in mortification.

"Please," she implored her husband, still breathing heavily. "Pray, tell me that noise did not all come from me."

At this enquiry, the steady rise and fall of Darcy's own shoulders evolved into the jiggling of laughter. After a few moments of collection, Elizabeth rolled over upon her stomach at the edge of the bed, and both gazed at the culprits. Each put out a hand and the dogs, aware they were the exactors of some untoward event, walked hesitantly over for a pat of reassurance. Thus obtained, Troilus thought it was an invitation to join his master and jumped upon the bed.

At this, Darcy said, "I believe some rules of conduct will have to be established."

He rose and dragged both Troilus and Cressida by their collars across the room (both in claw-scraping reluctance), then unceremoniously shoved them out the door. Elizabeth was not so certain that was the proper remedy.

"Oh Darcy," she fretted. "They will never forgive me for usurping their place."

He only smiled in answer to her compassion, but she came to learn he was acting in the best interests of all concerned. For had the dogs not been put out, all of Pemberley would have been kept awake most of the night.

12

M̲r. Darcy's engagement and wedding had kept him away a full quarter-year from Pemberley. Although it was midwinter and fieldwork was at a minimum, he told himself it was imperative to ride out and see to things. It was not, of course. The only true obligation of an owner of such a vast estate was not to lose the place gambling.

Darcy knew well that not only were there a hundred men to do his bidding, but his overseer, Mr. Rhymes, was exceedingly reliable. Still, if it was not obligatory for him to tend to things personally, it was essential for his own spiritual well-being. It was a restoration of his soul, if you will. He chose not to be idle and useless. Far too many people depended upon Pemberley for their livelihood, and if their fate rested upon him ultimately, it would be he who took on the responsibility.

Knowing the master would be out forthwith, for he was accustomed to the master's conscientious habits, a groom had Blackjack saddled early. Yet it was mid-morning when Mr. Darcy bestrode his horse and trod out the gate of the manor house, Troilus and Cressida trailing Blackjack's hooves.

Punctual by nature, Darcy demanded promptness from others and was unhappy for such a late start, knowing Rhymes had been cooling his heels for several hours. As Darcy rode along, he forsook his less than wholehearted sojourn into self-recrimination for his behindhand appearance. In its stead, he basked in a bit of vainglory. This because the wherefore of his own tardiness had yet to escape his mind's occupation. Indeed, Elizabeth's scent still wafted through his nostrils. He smiled as he thought of her in the bed that he left not an hour past.

It was a considerable relief finally to have checked his appetency long enough to gratify her passion. Under any other circumstances to be smug over such a miserly triumph would be quite ridiculous. In light of the fact it was lovely Elizabeth who held the reins of his galloping libido, he absolved himself of all censure.

In a lifetime of scrupulous attention to duty, he had never used his wealth in flagrant self-indulgence. However, he knew well that in a hired coach upon a public road, he would never have even entertained the notion of relishing his wife so thoroughly. Thinking upon that occasion, it struck him how very fortunate he was. For, if he did not hesitate to take Elizabeth into conjugal embrace in his carriage, one would suppose so new a wife might be taken aback, if not outright scandalised. It appeared the meeting of the minds he and Elizabeth had enjoyed as betrothed now blossomed into an ardent convergence of respective concupiscence.

Although their nuptial night had been incalculably rewarding, it bestowed upon him a serious caution.

At one time, he had been a veritable Sphinx when it came to professing admiration of a woman's physical charms before, during, or after physical congress. It had been his position that it went without saying he found whatever lover he bechanced to be with desirable, else he would not have been there in the first place. That presumption upon occasion caused no little consternation, but it was an idiosyncrasy from which he refused to waver. It was trial enough to have his person open for inspection; he flatly refused to be quoted.

Marital rites with Elizabeth, however, were a different matter. The level of restraint with which he had engaged her to him led him to express his appreciation of her unparalleled pulchritude with reckless abandon. He had ceded her his love unconditionally, hence he had little compunction about telling her that. However, unless he intended to divulge his past dalliances to her as well, he realised he was going to have to censor his tongue at least in the comparative. Her lips may have been the softest he had kissed, her skin the silkiest he had stroked, and her body the most voluptuous he had ever beheld, but he dared not say it.

The misunderstanding he invited when rapturing about Elizabeth's snug womanhood was a provident warning. She could very well have entertained the enquiry as to how he came to harbour an opinion about feminine apertures at all. It would take some discipline to tell her what he longed to share without exposing what he did not.

Not only had he need of expurgating his pillow talk, he feared that if he did not dampen his ardour for her in some manner, she was likely to flee the marriage to have any peace at all. Indeed, his legs felt a little shaky as he swung onto his horse just then, for he had not gone longer than six hours without possessing her since their wedding.

Surely, time and familiarity would soothe his blood; but as for then, every time they consecrated capital union, it only intensified his desire for her. He needed only picture her face in his mind, think of her soft breath against his ear (or, heaven help him, think of her sweet, pink, tufted demesnes) to be overcome with the need to take her once again. Thinking of her receiving him thusly, it was all he could do not to turn his horse about and find her (for he discovered with dispatch that riding his horse in a state of arousal was distressingly uncomfortable).

He was startled from these most intimate of thoughts by his overseer Charles Rhymes' greeting.

"Good day sir, Aye hope Mrs. Darcy is well."

Unnerved by hearing Elizabeth's name spoken aloud concurrent with such a deeply provocative contemplation of her as he was in, he cleared his throat.

Then, quite mildly, he said, "Yes, she is quite well."

Gathering his wits, Mr. Darcy hastily changed the subject from Mr. Darcy's connubial bliss, to Mr. Darcy's sheep.

"How does the lambing fare?"

"Only middlin'," Rhymes answered. "The ewes are droppin' 'em fine, but the swains can't seem to keep up with them. We need a good hunt."

That was Rhymes' subtle way of reminding Darcy of the length of his away. Darcy said they would have to remedy that, but did not say when. Hunts were weekly at neighbouring Pennyswope. Lady Millhouse would have had them daily would there be enough fox. As it was, their constant pursuit caused those upon her property to veer onto Pemberley. Of course this did not stop the chase, but the farther away the foxes ran, the less the likelihood of them being found. Thus, it yielded a plenitude of vermin upon Pemberley and the resultant havoc to the lambing.

One of the first matters of business that forenoon was to ride to the village of Kympton. As tradition dictated, Darcy had given instruction for the inn to provide food and spirits the day of his and Elizabeth's arrival for anyone who chose to share in the celebration of his marriage. Everyone in the county not infirm or immobile had answered the invitation.

When he and Rhymes arrived at the Fox and Hogget, the stench of stale beer still in the cups and disgorged upon the floor was overpowering. Darcy noticed there were still a few overindulgers lying about, one atop a table, and two (proving the euphemism) being literally beneath it.

Rhymes grumbled, "The sun's still gone over the yardarm for those sots."

It was half-past noon, but there were few signs of restoring the establishment after what appeared to be quite a fine time the night before. The pub-keeper's wife and a barmaid were making little progress in rousting the remaining victims of barley fever. The publican, a penurious man with the apt appellation of Phinehas Turnpenny, sat with two other hoary-eyed men, all three drinking their midday meal at the far end of the single large room.

When Darcy entered, those men who were conscious hastily rose. Turnpenny nervously wiped his mouth with the back of his hand as he eyed Mr. Darcy's approach. It was exceedingly unusual for a member of the Darcy family to come into town, and entering his establishment was unprecedented. It was understood the importance of the occasion would be the only reason Mr. Darcy would present himself to make remuneration.

Mr. Rhymes held the purse for Mr. Darcy and at his instruction gave Turnpenny two extra sovereigns for his trouble. The missus wasted no time in wresting the gold pieces from her husband, dropping them down her considerable cleavage.

Dispersal accomplished, Darcy made to quit the inn, but as he and Rhymes took their leave, the fellow felled by drink reposing atop the table coincidentally found God and sobriety.

Suddenly sitting bolt upright, he announced both by choking out a "Gads me life!"

Quite familiar with the workings of the intestines of men drawn to drink, Mrs. Turnpenny waved the broom whose handle had prodded him conscious, and hollered.

"Shoot that cat outside!"

In the face of certain mean retribution under the hand of a woman who knew how to exact it, the man struggled to his feet and staggered for the door. In no mind or time to excuse himself, he jostled Darcy and Rhymes aside to heave upon the threshold. This was to their advantage, for neither wanted to leave with the over-imbiber retching upon their heels.

The hacking, yorking, and gagging were interminable and blocked the doorway. In their wait, and not wanting to inflict his sensibility with watching the retching man heave Jonah in addition to the insult of listening to him, Darcy looked first at the ceiling and then to the floor. Thereupon, he began an unforebearing tap of his boot. He could not help but notice that the innkeeper and his compatriots-in-ale moved nervously about during this hiatus. One man stared at the wall behind Darcy before the innkeeper jabbed him decidedly with his elbow, eliciting a harsh "uh" from the man who then looked down at the floor.

It was not in Darcy's nature to find curiosity upon the instruction of another. But when the intemperate retcher refound stupefaction from the uncomfortable (and rather ludicrous) position that resulted from only his toes, knees, and forehead resting upon the floor, he still blocked the door. Turnpenny sidled over to the inebriant, put his foot soundly against the man's hinder-region, and shoved him, somersaulting, out the door. This gave Darcy opportunity to look to the wall behind him in search of what unnerved the men.

Initially, he saw nothing unusual and turned to go out the door behind Rhymes. The corner of his eye caught sight of a stanchion. Hanging from thence was a silk sheet. It was queer to see such a fine piece of fabric in such an ignominious establishment.

Rhymes took a broad stride across the foul puddle left by the now prostrate man and stepped out the door. However, Darcy stopped to take a closer look at the puzzlement. He paused but fleetingly. Then he strode out across the threshold, his long legs not having to take the great leap as did Rhymes' to evade the muck.

Had someone been in position to scrutinise Mr. Darcy's countenance as he quit the inn, they would not have suspected anything at all was amiss. His expression never wavered. It betrayed nothing but stern placidity. This was a considerable feat in that he had recognised not only the initial upon the bedcloth, but its unique paraph in one corner. It was his.

Undoubtedly, it was pilfered from his nuptial bed, for it was bespattered and bedewed with the denouement of numerous carnal infusions. He was roundly sickened to realise that the sheet he had used to wipe Elizabeth's virgin blood from her had then hung in inglorious lewdness inside a vile alehouse.

Having their most intimate moment violated roused him to such a loathing fury, he was almost provoked to do the unthinkable. But he knew that if he went back inside and retrieved the bed-linen, then beat the men senseless, it might soothe his immediate wrath, but would only inflate the business into legend and lore. It was best to take a dignified leave.

Stricken as he was with righteous indignation, he knew full well why it was displayed thusly. It was a coarse but unmistakable testimony of Elizabeth's virginity and his virility. It provided the common folk of the county reassurance of the enduring prosperity and continuity of Pemberley. The towns and the surrounding populations depended upon that very constancy. Understanding that, however, did not render it less objectionable.

However, as mortified as Elizabeth had been for the servants to come into their spousal bedchamber, he was grateful that she was insulated from the possibility of hearing about her newly impugned modesty. How his bedcloth from London had arrived so expeditiously of the arrival of their persons to Derbyshire, however, was an issue he chose not to confront at that moment.

Weathering such an indignity upon Elizabeth's behalf stole all the pleasure of his afternoon excursion. He drew himself onto the saddle. But before Rhymes did the same, Darcy gathered his considerable hauteur and held up his hand, palm forward.

"There is an offensive object hanging from the wall of that inn. Take it and watch until it has been burned to ashes."

Rhymes was accustomed to receiving succinct orders from Mr. Darcy. Still, this oblique demand was unusual. But, although he might have looked at Darcy a little queerly, he did not question him. Darcy observed the look upon the man's face and knew Rhymes not too dull to fathom when he saw the bedcloth what it was and why it was to be burned.

As he turned his horse for home, he endeavoured not to envision the tattered remnants of their privacy being waved about in drunken revelry.

With only an inkling of what weight her husband willingly took upon his shoulders, Elizabeth had lain that morning amidst the covers admiring their broadness as he sat availing himself of the chamber pot. That he could relieve himself from the comfort of the bed rather than perched precariously upon the pot, she thought (as one of five sisters) was somewhat fascinating. Configuration, it occurred to her, accommodated gentlemen far more conveniently than it did ladies.

Configuration was dearly upon her mind, thus she mused about it as she gazed across the wide, bare expanse of his back. The sight bade her sigh.

Yet, the shamelessness of disporting in such a deliciously wicked manner in the carriage the day past she had not compleatly forsworn. It had taken but one single look from her husband (in her defence, it was but one—but that one was profoundly provocative) to entice her to toss up her petticoats, crawl astraddle his lap and ride him like St. George. Had she any pretence to modesty left, his demonstration upon the subtle distinction betwixt a canter and a gallop dashed it to oblivion.

Not only had she impaled herself upon his virile member like a particularly lewd strumpet in the coach, the said same instrument had spent the previous night besieging her with ecstasy so unconditionally, she had been compelled to mimic a wailing banshee. The means was apparent, but the method of just how her husband exacted that beatitude upon her person still lay undetermined. She questioned it not, simply happy to be spared mortification for such unseemly comportment due to her husband's enthusiastic complicity. Deducing just how he could be at once so dourly correct and libidinously conducted was challenge enough.

As for herself, she fancied she had entered irrevocably the realm of wanton hussydom. Of all of her mother's many admonishments of decorum, the most vehement had been for a lady to remember to keep her knees pressed firmly together at all times. Clearly, it had been at least thirty-six hours since Elizabeth remembered her knees to have had more than a nodding acquaintanceship with each other. Nevertheless, she was not truly penitent.

However she might have liked to revel in recollection, she tarried no longer in her bed once it was absent of her husband. The day would begin her instruction of her new position. The first order of business after breakfast was for the Mistress of Pemberley to ascertain how to find the rooms upon the ground floor of the huge house without a map.

At breakfast, Darcy had partaken of his meal with a gusto not usually seen of him. His zeal she attributed to being at home again, it not occurring to her that he was famished from physical depletion. Still, such an unusual display of enthusiasm was contagious and Elizabeth followed him out, ostensibly to bid him good-bye from the courtyard. In truth, she welcomed any opportunity to see him ride off astride his horse. Silly crotchet, she told herself. But watch she did until he rode out of sight.

When nothing was left of his figure but the memory, she reluctantly turned back to the house.

One would expect a hall that size to have a house steward, and butler, if not more. Evidently, no one other than Mrs. Reynolds was in charge. At her ready was a red leather folio, in it well-worn sheaths of vellum detailing the staggering number of duties that fell to Pemberley's mistress. The handwriting was fair and flowing, apparently that of a cultured lady. Elizabeth was disposed to believe it had been written by Darcy's mother.

Handed the book, she sank to a chair quite involuntarily, stunned by the sheer number of responsibilities now in her charge. Even having held such previous trepidation over what she was commissioned to undertake, she still was overwhelmed. Hence, it was with great deliberation and resolve that she looked upon the lists, unaware that Mrs. Reynolds noted this purposefulness with approval. It was then that Georgiana appeared, timing her entrance subsequent to Elizabeth's receiving her duties.

"I must confess, Elizabeth, you see now the additional reason I was so frightfully happy for my brother to marry you. I can now sit and play my music all day without ill-conscience."

Georgiana then blushed at her own forthrightness. This surprising unity of candidness and jest from timid Georgiana came almost as close to flabbergasting Elizabeth as had her newly acquired domestic obligations, albeit with Georgiana more a marvel than a shock.

After a rudimentary tour of the house, Elizabeth persuaded her new sister-in-law to play for her upon the pianoforte as she meticulously perused her lists. Darcy came upon this harmonious scene mid-song not three hours after he had left.

He awaited the song's completion, then announced himself thusly, "I have taken the precaution, my good wife, of locking all the doors, lest you be so daunted by the weight of your obligations that you plan to flee."

"You cannot rid yourself of me all that easily, Husband."

Georgiana looked somewhat aghast at this playful exchange. However, Elizabeth and Darcy were unwitting of it, for he was busy explaining to his wife a convoluted version of why he had aborted the circumnavigation of his land.

So little did he like the weaving of tales, he abruptly altered the subject, "Pray, shall we picnic?"

So bright and pleasant the day for the season, Elizabeth needed no meditation to think it a grand idea and tactfully bade Georgiana to join them. Georgiana, in tactful reciprocity, declined.

On the presumption of Elizabeth's agreement to the outing (his own wishes still considered a divine right) Darcy had designed to have a fully laden basket at the ready. Yet, when he simply took up the basket in one hand and, with no more than a wave of his hand and a deferring step back, allowed her to precede him out the door, her countenance betrayed no little amazement.

She turned about and looked over her shoulder, "We are a party of two alone?"

Even at Longbourn an outdoor excursion with a meal would have been complemented by every servant Mrs. Bennet could muster to provide all the attendant pomp one could garner from so lowly an undertaking. Mr. and Mrs. Darcy appeared to be unescorted even by the dogs (for exhausted from their jaunt, Troilus and Cressida lay curled up asleep upon the sofa). Darcy assured her they were, indeed, to go unattended (for, to his mind, what other reason was there to go?).

If she thought it curious, she remarked of it not. "I ask no other to be of our party. I only feared we should be trailed by a contingent of servants carrying candlesticks, linen, and silver."

"If you would find favour with a grander occasion, it can be arranged."

"I doubt that not at all. But, no, I would not favour something more grand."

Once beyond the deliberately averted eyes of servants, he caught her hand. As he did, she looked demurely away, but an expression of barely contained delight overspread her countenance.

As they struck out upon their walk, her conversation returned to the quite serious matter of her new and numerous responsibilities as Mistress of the House. It was a sad lament, indeed.

"How am I ever to learn all that I must? I am not entirely certain I can find my way from our bedchamber to the morning-parlour without you to guide me."

"Be happy you have not married a duke, for at least you will not have to entertain foreign sovereigns," he laughed.

"A consolation," she laughed, for so it was (even though he had not absolutely excluded sovereigns domestic). "But I might have favoured marrying Duke Darcy. It has a pretty ring to it, does it not?"

"I would be known as duke of something, perhaps Pemberley, and you would call me Pemberley instead of Darcy," he reminded her.

"Pemberley, oh, Pemberley!" she effected a breathy scenario, then shook her head. "No, that does not excite my esteem. I believe I favour Darcy."

After a quarter-hour stroll past the pleasure grounds, through oaks and Spanish chestnut trees, they reached the appointed picnic spot that Darcy had, with all due deliberation, preselected. It was in a wood bosky enough for seclusion, but spare enough for the sun to warm. He spread the blanket, doffed his jacket, and tugged at his cravat as if readying for a feast (the nature of which she dared not conjecture). Rather, she took out the still-warm partridges, tore the bread, and pared the fruit. Whilst she laboured thusly, she hummed, endeavouring to be unmindful of the likelihood that she would never serve him from her own hand again.

It was a leisurely sup. Eventually his head found a comfortable nestle in her lap and she found occupation drawing lazy, tickling circles with a bit of grass upon his brow. Perhaps it was not their true design, but intimacy as tantalizing as this did invite affection to take its course.

Suddenly into this scene of pastoral serenity appeared a scruffy-looking man. He bore an ominously large gun, one whose menace to them was becalmed only by the sight of two scent-hounds thrashing about his heels.

For a man whose attention was seriously compromised, Mr. Darcy was to his feet with the utmost rapidity. In that instant, he put himself betwixt the man and Elizabeth (who had to be content with her view of the proceedings from between her tall husband's knees).

The poor man recognised upon whom he had blundered, and he was terrified to be caught poaching so close to Pemberley Hall by the master himself.

Darcy's initial alarm was quieted forthwith of ascertaining that the gun the man carried, ancient and rusting, was a fowling piece, one for small game and probably used to feed his family. Still, he glared at him quite relentlessly.

The unfortunate hunter upon whom this severe gaze rested just as expeditiously made not one, but two reckonings. Firstly, considering the disarray of their garb, Mr. Darcy was having a quiet tryst with a woman who was most likely his new wife, and secondly, that Mr. Darcy had not come here to look for poachers.

He backed away in hasty, nodding genuflection.

As Darcy stood watching him leave, Elizabeth subtly tossed aside the paring-knife she had taken into her hand. Not for a moment did she think her husband either unwilling or unable to protect them both. Taking the knife to her side had been quite involuntary. Still, as their marriage was young, she thought it best to disguise from her husband that she did not scruple sacrificing her gentility in the face of danger.

As he found his seat, Mr. Darcy was a bit vexed. It was not lost on him what assumptions that hunter had made. He groused to himself that the incident would only give more fodder to the Kympton inn gossips.

Quite unaware of her own humbling, Elizabeth lay back in blissful, fetching ignorance. Her spirits aflutter still from the fright, she lay gazing up through the tree limbs and endeavoured to ease her heaving chest.

Her husband was well aware of her heaving bosom, but in far less hurry for her to reclaim her breath. Indeed, in that dappled copse, it was easy for him to forget there were transgressions against their privacy.

It was at least eight hours since he had had her last. An improvement, was it not?

The poacher had feared no mantraps set, for the Darcy family turned a blind eye on what game was pilfered from their property as long as the privilege was not abused. However, as this foiled poacher moved away from Mr. Darcy as hastily and quietly as he could, he came in great intrusion, eyes to chin, upon one of the house footmen. For the second time in less than five minutes the poor nimrod was confronted by two separate men of great height and little humour.

This encounter would not end so benignly as the first.

Howbeit Mr. Darcy had looked quite forbidding, the man before him then looked not unlike Beelzebub himself. Not an entirely inapt analogy, for the footman hit the hunter full in the chest with the flat of his hand, knocking him to the ground. This most likely oft-practised manoeuvre was one of economy for the thug, for he seized the gun from his victim's hand as he fell to ground in utter loss of breath and with no means of retaliation.

Standing over the man as he gasped for air, the foul thief said, "Run if ye know what's good for ye and donno' cry for yer weapon, be happy wi' yer life."

In no position not to heed that advice save lacking the means, the poacher lunged away upon all four limbs until he finally struggled to his feet. Once upright, he called to his dogs to follow. As the dogs' instinct for self-preservation was at least as keen as their owner's, both had already started after him. But as they passed their tormentor, he took a wild swing with the gun-butt, it glancing off the rump of the one who had the misfortune to trail the first. That poor pup then yelped loud enough to startle them both to join their owner's headlong race for safety.

The footman was none other than the nefarious Thomas Reed.

Others who rode upon the Pemberley coach might harbour enough officious sanguinity to find pleasure in frightening the bejeezus out of a harmless trespasser. Few, however, would receive the sadistic thrill Reed did. Regrettably, his predilection for cruelty was hardly sated by an encounter that was fruitless of bloodshed. Had he not been so intent upon other prey, Reed might have pursued the hapless hunter.

As it was, he just laughed and inspected the gun he had appropriated. Finding it a deplorable excuse of a weapon, Reed cursed the man for being so impoverished. He grumbled a few minutes, then remembered why he was in the wood in the first place: the fair Mrs. Darcy, that beauteous bounty of woman-flesh.

Tom Reed had never been in love. Until he first set eyes upon Elizabeth, Reed's definition of "in love" was to rut a woman and not have to pay her. Amorous flame, as Reed knew it, lasted only as long as his erection. Moreover, not shelling out a copper to mount a woman did not take into consideration the nicety of consent. Those Covent Garden jack-whores were far too treacherous to cadge (and the French pox was a constant threat), but he could usually find a piece of work like Abigail Christie, jaded (or drunk) enough not to put up much of a fight. Admittedly, Reed did not mind a good, amorous tussle. (His only scruple was to make certain that if he was to take sick with the foul disease, he did not pay good money to become infected.)

Reed raised his nose and took an uncannily feral whiff as if to sniff out the scent of quimsy. Thereupon, head low, he strove on against the underbrush. His quarry was not difficult to locate. Although they were laughing and talking in low tones, they lay in a small glade in perfect view if someone chose to pry.

If given the choice of peeping or participating, Reed would have chosen the latter. As this ruling was not in his hands, he snooped.

The particular delectation of this pursuit had only come to him as recently as his employment on the Darcy coach. More precisely, it overcame him on his ensuing journey to Netherfield in the soon-to-be nuptial coach. There were a fair number of unplucked damsels about that Longbourn house, but none so succulent of plump dairies as was the dark-haired Miss Bennet.

Reed spent the entire return trip to London daydreaming of that alabaster damsel's pretty, harrumping like a lord that he would not be the one to dock her.

Like many a man of mean understanding, Reed had always held the opinion that most rich men were not much more than eunuchs or else they foined their servants, with nothing left for their wives. As for the rich men's wives, why would anyone want to diddle such harping shrews? The new Mrs. Darcy, however, was an entirely different matter. He would happily have his way with her if Mr. Darcy chose not.

This was not an entirely outrageous notion. For tall and handsome as they often were, it was not unknown for footmen to gratify an occasional gentlewoman. Reed had heard such stories, and now knew himself a footman. But his considerable conceit had not allowed him to consider that he could not, even by the most generous opinion, be called handsome. Never one to give up a notion on the merit of absurdity, he harboured the exceedingly improbable hope that Mrs. Darcy might some day favour him with her attentions.

At least he harboured it until he had heard from the other servants in the London house of what bechanced at some length in the Darcy bedchamber. Well, perhaps that comely minx would tire of Mr. Darcy and him of her. Patience has its rewards. Reed would wait.

Await he did, silently, upon the grounds of Pemberley.

Fortune had veiled the wildlife from the poacher within the slight canopy of leaves still clinging to the trees. The slow dance of foliage, brought from their limbs by the light breeze, that shrouded Reed then, also obscured his view.

Reed strained to see that which was concealed to him. The obfuscated scene he could make out did not quench his thirst for scrutiny. However, the twigs beneath his feet were already dry enough to crackle. Reed knew his quarry was already aware of intrusion and he was afraid to venture closer. He simply sat in silence, implying to his imagination what his eyes could not reveal and found lascivious pleasure enough in what he heard.

Notwithstanding her methodical commitment to collecting dirty mugs in the far corner of the tavern, the unexpected ingress of two gentlemen stole Abigail's attention.

By virtue of the nature of its business, the place was dim. The only light was a blinding glare from the doorway behind them. Hence, other than ascertaining that neither was a *habitué* of their low establishment, immediate identification of the duo was not forthcoming. She continued to eye the pair long enough to eliminate constable and debt-collector from the possibilities. Her interest was piqued, however, by the deference shown them by Turnpenny and his companions.

Once they escaped the harsh back-light of the doorway, she could see the man who led the way was middle-aged, plump, and a bit rumpled. The other stood slightly aloof, unsuccessfully masking a look of extreme repugnance at the fetor emanating from his malodorous surroundings. The disdainful gentleman was younger than the first, tall, immaculately tailored, and of exceedingly handsome figure.

Indeed, maturity had strengthened his jaw and broadened his chest, but he had altered but little. Had she not recognised his countenance, Abigail would not have mistaken the hauteur.

She had known it was possible that Darcy would come personally to settle his bill. Yet, to see him actually standing so before her in the shabby tavern took her aback. She, however, was the only ruffled party.

Not unexpectedly, he looked neither right nor left. He kept his imperious gaze upon the business at hand. Had he glanced in her direction, instinct would have bid her turn away. If there was any chance that he remembered her at all, she wanted it to be as a pretty sylph of a girl, not the daggle-tailed slattern she had become.

Abigail had traded upon the prestige of her long past employment at Pemberley to obtain a situation with the Fox and Hogget (albeit she had abused a portion of that goodwill by boasting about her past connexion with that estate). As talk was prolific at any tavern, case and canard were tossed about indiscriminately. Hence, Abigail found ample audience for her oft-repeated rendering of her tenure in that grand house. Although she omitted her dalliance with Wickham (for he was regarded as a truckling toff), her intrigue with Master Darcy had prospered with numerous retellings from tryst to *affaire d'amour*.

Interest was keen, for until Abigail volunteered her recollections, there had been a veritable dearth of information about young Mr. Darcy's amours. His comportment, as far as anyone could fathom, was entirely circumspect. He was known as a kindly landlord, but no one thought him a hail-fellow-well-met sort of likeness of his father. Although there was a consensus that a man of his obvious vigour must have succumbed upon occasion, not a single soul could cite an instance of indiscretion.

As nothing sends female hearts aflutter and tongues a-wagging quite so readily as a handsome yet distant countenance, that bailiwick was a hotbed of speculation about young Mr. Darcy by the time he finally became engaged. Talk blazed furiously, expanding into an absolute maelstrom by the time he arrived in Derbyshire with his new wife. She was known to be quite pretty, in a fresh-faced wholesome kind of way, not at all the sophisticate that would have been expected to become the Mistress of Pemberley. In light of her family's questionable connexions and Lady Catherine de Bourgh's displeasure at the match, the cauldron of local gossip had very nearly burbled over by epiphany. For what else are country-folk to do in the idleness of winter but smoke pork, stoke a pipe, and chew upon the doings of the rich?

Betwixt the initiation of Mr. Darcy's engagement and the culmination of his wedding, Abigail arrived at Kympton sans husband, sans two of her children, and very pregnant. As was her plan, she had fled back to her home county from London abandoning the bantlings begat of an extended left-handed alliance with a seaman named Archibald Arbuthnot.

No mother discards her offspring without remorse. Nevertheless, that regret was somewhat mitigated due to the nature of the older girl.

Poor Sally Frances had been a bit of a beleaguerment, having the misfortune to bear a striking resemblance to her father (red face and large ears) and an inexplicably obstinate nature. Indeed, when expatriated from her mother's milk upon the appearance of another babe, the lass had stubbornly refused to speak. From age two years to four and a half, she was silent. Abigail was flummoxed at this bit of intractability. It was obvious to everyone but Sally Frances that although her mother had two teats, she had but one lap. Abigail held steadfastly to the position that a child had to learn sometime that there was a time to stand one's ground and a time to accept defeat.

Owing to her mother's unrelenting disapproval, Sally sucked her thumb and clung to her half-brother, John, who dandled her about whenever he thought his mother did not see him.

"Belay that! Yer turnin' that gerl into a pampered little cosset, boy. Leave 'er be!"

Abigail's compunction over having forsaken her daughters was not overly employed in that she had wiped their faces and left them upon the stoop of Archie's mother's house. Mrs. Arbuthnot had a tedious but steady mending business. She would not forsake her grandchildren. John, however, was Abigail's alone and would have been consigned to the workhouse. That would be a waste, for at thirteen, he was a strong and able boy. Was he to labour, Abigail did not want it to be for naught.

The entire contretemps of decampment came about by virtue of a nautical calamity that did not occur. For although Cape Horn was an unforgiving promontory, the ship that boasted Seaman Third Class Arbuthnot had rounded it without incident. Abigail learned the Galatea was due back upon the upcoming Friday. She and John shed London Wednesday morn.

Although Archie was a bit dim, Abigail did not doubt that even he would determine that a year at sea and a wife half-term with child did not add up to marital devotion. Retribution by strop would be swift. Such was his history.

John was nimble enough to stay out of Archie's reach before his liberated pants worked their way down about his knees, thus restricting his manoeuvrability. However, Abigail knew herself to be not so quick. The only possible positive of the situation was that Archie and her bed-mate of late, Tom Reed, might draw the iron to each other and both end up dead. That outcome, however, was indefensibly optimistic. Hence, she took what she believed was her only recourse—to flee.

Indeed, it was with a bitter laugh that she realised she was returning to Kympton in the precise condition in which she had left.

Unfortunately, few of her relations were about to appreciate the irony. She had hoped to find her sister, for she had married a farmer and had her own house. However, it had been five years since poor Fanny was taken by childbirth fever. (Truth be told, it was a minor comfort that none of her true family was about to see she had lost her struggle with a tendency to lowness.)

Still yet in the county was Abigail's impoverished ex-brother-in-law, but his present wife and their eight collective children did not look favourably upon taking in two penniless relatives. Abigail could not fault them, but still cursed her dearth of luck. Alas, fortune worked to her disadvantage at every turn.

Had she not once been a fetching little hoyden? Yet she had the dismal luck to find a situation in one of the few illustrious houses where servicing the male members of the household was not considered a part of one's duties. Indeed, she learnt that, although intrigues abounded, getting one's mutton at Pemberley was a furtive business. This scrupulous adherence to morality had been set by old Mr. Darcy and was enforced with relish by that cursed Mrs. Reynolds—that woman could ferret out a dust-ball beneath a bed without once looking.

That old hag chose to cast Abigail out with only three months wages and the admonition to be gone. Until then, Abigail's scheme had appeared infallible. For however jealously he guarded his son's virtue, Mr. Darcy was a kind man. A gentleman such as he would never have callously expelled a woman with child, particularly when he knew her to be coupling with his beloved son.

Why, was the matter explored diligently enough, it might have been concluded that young Darcy had compromised her. He was young master of the household. Is not the girl always the victim of vile intentions? Regardless of the circumstances, if she and the indefatigable young Darcy engaged in voluptuous combat, a swelling belly should have put her to pecuniary advantage.

The singular mystery of the entire flap had been just who had exposed her condition. Was it that vile Mrs. Reynolds? Or did Mr. Darcy uncover it himself? If any money were put down, Abigail's wager would have been put upon Wickham as the cad.

Damn that Wickham and his jaundiced nature. Upon her presumptuous dismissal, she had gone to that blackguard hoping that he would intercede on her behalf. It galled her yet that he had the considerable brass cheek to snort a laugh at her dilemma. He offered his assistance only if she would split the proceeds. At the time, she scoffed at his offer. A misjudgement, that. If she just could have bade her time at Pemberley, belly under her chin and pointing a finger at his son, surely old Mr. Darcy would have coughed up some sovereigns. Bloody luck.

These disappointments much on her mind, she kept Mr. Darcy in her eye whilst he took care of his business. All the while, she scrubbed diligently, throwing sudsy water across the wooden plank tables, prodding the drunks awake. As he stood upon the threshold, she drew quiet and dared a glance his way. It did not escape her notice that he quite clearly took measure of his nuptial bedcloth hanging to the left of the door.

There was little doubt he recognised it. Fervently, she prayed he would somehow come to know who had pilfered it. If he did, accident could only uncover it, for it would not come from her. Tom Reed was a bastardly snake, and although he did not deserve employment upon such a fine estate, she held her tongue, fearing his retaliation. Old scores would have to remain unsettled.

It was just the night before when that muckheap of a man had appeared at the door of the Fox and Hogget clutching the silk sheet in his fist. Abigail had very nearly leapt at the spectre. She had been happy to believe she had left that miscreant in London.

With adolescent bravado, young John had hastily dropped his swill bucket and rushed to his mother's side, shooting menacing looks at Reed. Wearily, she shooed the boy away. She had dealt with Reed and his ilk before. She would again.

Moreover, it was most likely that Reed was the blighter who knapped her. (A clear determination of the perpetrator of her condition took deep study and was compromised not only by immoderate consumption of drink, but by the sheer number of possibilities.) Whilst still in London, it had been briefly under consideration to announce to him that he was the father of her unborn. The only reason for that proclamation was the unlikely hope he would give her a few shillings or take her in when her husband inevitably threw her out. That the first was a barmy notion, and the second not an improvement of circumstances, kept Abigail from breathing a word of it to him.

She should not have had to say a thing.

One of the multitudes of unwritten precepts amongst their society was that if one cohabits with an impregnated female and there is no one else to blame, that man is the father of record. Reed, however, was of the opinion that pintling a woman in kindle is gratis, as a slice or two off a cut loaf was unlikely to be missed. Therefore, the grounds of discord had been laid for some time before Reed showed up in Derbyshire.

The word that free food and drink would be availed at the Kympton tavern in honour of the Darcys' wedding had emptied the countryside. It was not surprising there had been nary room for another person in the inn when Reed, dragging an ever-reluctant Frank behind him, pushed into the place. Immediately he relinquished his hold upon his brother and scattered patrons by climbing atop one of the trestle tables. Issuing a curse decrying a serious a lack of creativity, he demanded the floor.

"Shut the bloody 'ell up!"

Gradually, the din abated. With a flourish worthy of a St. James courtier, he unfurled the silk and, pointing to the blood and stains, pronounced gleefully, "It seems the new Lady of Pemberley got herself busted! No hedge-docked wench she!"

He, commencing to count the seminal splotches, added, "Looks like she got pricked more than was she peddlin' 'er arse on Drury Lane!"

Exacting a little burlesque, he enumerated them, and the crowd burst into raucous laughter. Then, as the tally mounted, more than a few cheers erupted. In a stage whisper, Abigail conjectured to the barmaid next to her that if there were fewer than ten splotches, at least Reed would not have to remove his boots to number them all. Fortunately for the patrons, they were not subjected to the abuse of the exposure of Reed's stinking feet, because the bedcloth's jubilant emancipation was exacted by the crowd, resulting in its travel about the room.

When the sheet passed to Abigail for admiration, she held it up and winked knowingly, "You can bet the Lady wakes up smilin'. I've never seen a man nature hung better."

Dolly Turnpenny snorted, "What would ye know 'bout such things, Abbie? He wasn't more than a pup when you worked in that house."

"Boy he may've been, but his pillicock weren't."

She held her hands up and apart in demonstration of his approximate length, the generosity of which displayed a moderately inflationary memory. The women present, however, were in no mood to quibble preciseness in the face of such a possibility and nodded appreciatively. This allocution alerted Reed to Abigail's presence for the first time. He walked over and slapped her possessively upon the buttocks before plopping down in a chair next to her.

Thereupon, he turned back to his cohorts and guffawed, "Well, Abbie should know. That whore's been laid on every flat rock from Derbyshire to Kent."

Exacting her own little revenge (and cautiously behind his back) Abigail pointed to Reed and held up her little finger, her thumb touching halfway up. A burst of bawdy laughter, however, caused Reed to catch her announcement of the limited length of his carnal stump. The invidious contortion that overspread his visage was not felicitous. Inwardly wincing, Abigail laughed it off but kept a close eye upon him the rest of the evening. Because so much drink passed over, under and through Reed, she began to hope he would disremember a little jest at his expense.

That was not to be. Not only did a man of Reed's brutality have an extensive memory for such affronts, he liked to let them fester. It would not be vented in a fit of anger. Reprisal would be exacted with savage and lengthy precision. When Reed did seek her out, the inn had emptied and Abigail was face down upon her bed not much in her senses. Providence for her, for had she the means to try to fend him off, it would have only prolonged the abuse.

Her boy made a feeble stand at her door, but Reed's brachmard made an indention in his gullet deep enough to persuade him to take leave.

"Abbie's expectin' me."

Whilst she snored loudly in the corner, Reed shoved the boy out of the room. Then, without bothering to remove his boots, let alone his pants, he heaved himself upon her. That was what awakened her: The scraping of his boots upon the bedstead. She did not query as to whom rutted upon her; the rancidity of his breath identified him.

"Reed," she croaked miserably.

She might have struggled then, but in previous servicings, she knew that grappling only incited his lust. Moreover, time was her ally. He had a propensity for failing in the furrow. Regrettably, he did not that night. Vengeance came with malevolence and was paid for with considerable abasement. For a man of little imagination, Reed managed to spend the better part of an hour without duplicating a single degradation. Eventually, he tired of his play and left. Thenceforth, Abigail was sober. Sober she did not want to be.

Her head had ached when she had arisen. She drew a wrapper about herself, but the bright light made her lurch about blindly. When she finally managed to peer out the door to see if Reed was about, she stirred only her son. He was sitting with his back to the door, his knees drawn up beneath his chin, but hopped to his feet when he felt it open. The odd mixture of anguish and anger upon his countenance did nothing to soothe her.

By mid-afternoon her temples pounded ferociously. Any stale ale she found in the bottom of the mugs, she emptied down her throat. She drank steadily and much on the sly, for old Turnpenny would dock her if he knew how much of his brew she was consuming. But she cared little. Once Darcy had gone and the mugs were drained, she saw no particular reason to stay. She abandoned her tray and staggered to her room. It was empty—empty and grim. Rifling through their sparse belongings, she found a half bottle of gin. That was her drink of choice and she had been hoarding it. She plopped down two glasses automatically, smiled mirthlessly at the silent taunt, and then filled them both.

On the heels of drink, she had been suffering from a loss of senses for some months. That should have been a misgiving for pouring another, but it was not. It was a cure for her ills. She sought that blessed blackness again, took a glass in each fist and upended them both with precision. Then she repeated her sacrament. Eventually, one dropped from her hand. Empty, it hit with a clunk, but did not break before it made a lengthy, uneven roll across the length of the floor.

The room was dark when John Christie returned from mucking out the tavern's stable. His mother's body had not stirred from her seat. Her cheek rested against the table, both hands dangled. He did not reach out to shake her. He did not even go over to her. He simply sat on the side of the bed until dawn, staring at her lifeless eyes.

It was a sad business for one's mother to die. Abigail Christie's son knew that, if for no other reason than that the little congregation standing about gawking as her body was taken away looked upon him with a great deal of pity. His countenance, however, harboured no emotion at all. It was not that he was undespairing of his mother's death; he simply refused to put on a display of bereavement just because there was an audience before him expecting it.

For all his mother's bad judgement, limited initiative, and poor taste in men, he had still loved her. She had taught him there was no percentage in sentiment. That pragmatism kept any fright about his situation at bay just as certainly as grief. He knew weeping served no purpose whatsoever. That was a wisdom he would have liked to impart to Mrs. Turnpenny and various barmaids, for they all stood about shedding crocodile tears with considerable relish. It was Mrs. Turnpenny, however, who had hugged him to her substantial bosom (a difficult manoeuvre in that he was taller than she) and clucked about his newly acquired misfortune repeatedly.

"Oh you poor, dear, motherless boy!"

Her heartbroken lamentations upon the loss of his dear departed mother were mitigated, however, by the understanding that before his dear departed mother's corpse had been carted from the room, Mrs. Turnpenny had already re-let it. The ale-wench intending to take the room did have the good taste to stand aside until the lodgings were vacated.

Nonetheless, she stood with her belongings at the ready once the deed was done. Moreover, it was done with much haste and little civility.

Knowing the burial was going to be on the parish and thus frippery-less, the undertaker went about his duties with a look of abused sufferance. He wrapped Abigail Christie's remains in a tattered counterpane. Yet, still unable to outright abandon the niceties of his profession, he tied the corners in neat, if ragged, little bows.

As he and Phinehas Turnpenny (who was just happy to rid the body from his establishment) hauled her out, one foot escaped the shroud and trailed along the floor. It was not a pretty foot. It was bunioned and callused and her big toe added insult by protruding from a tear in her stocking. The entire party was distressed to witness this indecorous strait, but only John stepped forward to rectify it. Indeed, for a young man who refused to cry, it was with considerable tenderness that he tucked his mother's toe back into her stocking and foot beneath the counterpane.

So it was that the passing bell still reverberated in John's ears as he walked along the road leaving Kympton. Already his mother's face had begun to fade for him. He suffered to reclaim it, for he truly did not want his only recollection of her to be that one bunioned toe.

He had set out expeditiously in spite of the lip-serviced condolences. Mrs. Turn-penny had let out their room, announcing a realignment of help. Truly, he did not fault the Turnpennys. They were a bit miserly with the broad-beans, but they had turned a blind eye to his sharing lodgings with his mother when rent paid was for but one. Although he had done what he could to earn his keep in the Turnpenny barn, he knew business at the inn was selling ale, not putting up orphans. He had not expected otherwise. He had learned the true definition of sympathy in the mean streets of London. The kindest gift his mother gave him was to teach him to see to himself.

She had once said, "Son, I can't watch out for yer, yer've got to make yer own way. Nobody looks out for nobody else in this world."

Undeniably.

Hence, self-reliance, not mother love, was her legacy. That is why he did not cry and that is why he would not allow himself to grieve. Moreover, convinced as he was of his own pragmatic nature, he did not allow himself the indulgence of thinking of his now motherless sisters in London. For a young man of such sense and practicality should have no affection for babies. Yet, he could in no way account for why he, a practising cynic, had carried Sally Frances about when she was far too big to be riding upon his hip. Or, why he had hummed to Baby Sue and hid them both whilst their mother plied her trade with sweaty men atop the creaking bed.

Or, why he missed their sweet faces even then. London was a fair distance. The thought that he might never see them again nagged at the pit of his stomach.

The economy of his situation had no room for such maudlin ruminations; hence, he shook it from his mind in order to ponder specifics. Where was he to go? At least his mother's poor sense of timing had improved enough to have her die in the country instead of town. He knew he would be but a half-day from the workhouse in London. An orphan he was, but certainly too big a bundle for a foundling home.

John had been born in London, somewhere betwixt Whitechapel and Wapping. He did not know the street or the house. His mother did not tarry long anywhere, usually taking leave one step ahead of the collector. Initially, she was a barmaid. Quite quickly, that career evolved into another. London taverns had back rooms. There, with a little initiative, a fresh-faced lass could earn a half-crown a night. Regrettably, the office of doxy had several disadvantages, the foremost of which was that one did not stay fresh-faced for long. Fees dwindled with the exact rapidity of one's looks.

Abigail was no exception. Eventually, she walked the streets.

John spent his days with his own manner of scavenging. In the mean rookeries of London, scavenging, more often than not, overlapped into outright thievery. John held no pride in his cunning, nor was he ashamed. The only shame he felt was that he was reduced to thieving to eat. (Caught red-handed with a couple of rabbit skins, he was sent to the House of Correction for a fortnight. It was cruel place, but he was fed twice a day, that more often than he got upon his own.) His secondary employment was actually an extension of his first. For when his mother managed to snare a man to join her in illicit commerce, John was instructed to await. At the height of carnality he was to surreptitiously investigate the visitor's divested purse and gaskins for any far-things left unspent upon beer or her. As the nicety of disrobing was not often observed and his mother was just as often as cupshotten as her intended paramour, it was a true find when money turned up.

This was not a happy existence. However, not having known a better one, John thought not meanly of it. As to why his mother decided to make a home for that bandy-legged seaman was a compleat mystery to him. When John bewailed the more caitiff strains of that man's nature (brutal, demented, and flatulent), Abigail had laughed that strange little mirthless laugh she had and embarked upon one of her lessons in survival.

She told her son he lacked objectivity ("Yer blind, boy!"). For the very reason she stayed with Archie was precisely because of his profession. The man provided a roof over their heads (even if it did shelter beatings, which were fierce and prolific). Gone so long at sea simply meant less time she would have to spend with him.

Though of no true religious faith, every time the man sailed, John still managed to compose a little prayer to recite, the gist of which was that Archie's ninety-gun dread-nought be blown clean out of the water. However, at least so far as Seaman Arbuthnot was concerned, the British navy was omnipotent. Archie always came back, regular as rain. Moreover, upon his return, he would find a cudgel or draw off that strop of a belt and commence a bastinado. John was agile and thus adept at eluding the clumsy Archie (for spirits stole his sea legs). Others in the household, however, were not as swift, and this led to an appalling conundrum for young John Christie.

John could forgive his mother for many things. For prostituting herself, for finding comfort in gin, even for neglecting his sisters. However, the single thing for which he could not find forgiveness was that of which she had the least charge. She continued to beget children of Archibald Arbuthnot. Those children demanded John weather demons that no child should have to endure. He had to decide which of his loved ones' heads he would try to protect from Archie's blows. If he tried to shield them all, no one would escape punishment.

When Abigail was with child once again, John had known without being told it was not fathered by Archie Arbuthnot. He understood that was an aggravation to the basic evil of the situation. For although Archie was a vicious cur of a man, he had one quality worthy of regard: he would away. Thomas Reed was a continual sore.

Hardly the first grass widow of a sailor, it was understood with certainty that when this particular sailor found out that he was so public a cuckold, the insult to his manhood would be consequential. The means to exact his revenge would be harsh, possibly fatal. There was but one answer. Because the past year of growth had bestowed him six inches in height (even though but a half stone in weight), John came to believe that if he had not age upon his side, he was man enough to defend his mother's life.

He knew that should he survive the fight to the death that he intended to engage in with Archie, the constables would be upon him in an instant. (Authorities were not much inclined to intervene in family discord unless that disharmony resulted in bodily harm to a taxpaying breadwinner.) John had been jailed once. Even if Archie's life weathered John's substantial rancour, two offences meant Newgate.

Hence, when Abigail abruptly decided to decamp London, she thought it was her own neck she was saving. She had no idea she was rescuing her son's also.

The truncated Family Christie departed for Derbyshire under the cloak of night and fear of pursuit. Upon neither their journey nor their arrival did John query Abigail about her expanding waistline or her decision to take leave of London. She had not expected otherwise. It had been her tease that his most identifiable trait was his compleat want of curiosity. Although he had not corrected her misconception, he knew it was less a trait than a lesson committed to memory.

John knew how his mother got in the family way and by whom. He had learnt far more about basic urges of mankind from a cot in the corner of her room than had he sat centre seat in a professorial lecture. John never questioned why Kympton was the town they chose to light upon, for his mother's drunken loquacity had revealed where he was sired.

The road was dusty, crust having been reclaimed from the recent rain. John decided whither he had to go. Once that was done, he made no hesitation. He had not heard his mother's boasts in the inn the previous night. Yet she had told him the man who lay with her at Pemberley was his father. Was he of station? Was he still there? John had not a clue. But his mother had been superstitious, and in want of any other bias or religious persuasion, he trusted in it, too. Perhaps the place of his conception might somehow offer him refuge.

For even John knew it was a rich man's world and he took the most direct route there. On he trod in the dust.

16

It was nothing more sinister than the evening chill that drove Darcy and Elizabeth from their picnic. As they placidly circled back to the house upon the path, they came upon Fitzwilliam astride a rather noble-looking bay.

When he espied them, he drew to a stop and forsook his ride short of the court-yard, thus aborting their stroll. Neither the encounter nor the sharing of their prom-enade was less than a delight. For, as Darcy was wont to boast, Fitzwilliam was not only an esteemed cousin, but also a chivalrous officer, courageous cavalryman, and *raconteur nonpareil.*

Elizabeth shared his opinion.

Once pleasantries were given due, Darcy and Fitzwilliam commenced a lengthy recapitulation of the weather and rural doings that had not been fully explored the evening previous. As this discourse meandered into areas arcane to her, Elizabeth walked over to admire Fitzwilliam's horse. He was a tall, athletic animal and stood idly twiddling his ears, apparently as bored with the conversation as was she.

Commiserating their duality of neglect, Elizabeth talked soothingly to him whilst stroking his nose. He nickered when her fingers found the soft skin betwixt his nos-trils. She cooed back at him. This equine affection stole her husband's attention.

Darcy called, "When would you like to have your riding lesson, Elizabeth?"

Eager for such an adventure, she blurted out, "On a horse?"

Otherwise engrossed as she had been, one could understand the innocent lack of vigilance in her reply. Indeed, her countenance betrayed unadulterated guilelessness. Only for a moment. But when the magnitude of her *faux pas* became apparent, her face first blanched, and then turned a remarkable shade of magenta.

With careful deliberateness, he said, "Yes, Elizabeth, upon a horse. We shall come around to-morrow."

She narrowed her eyes at him, for he had not answered her directly, delaying his reply quite mercilessly. Indeed, initially he had pursed his lips. That might have per-suaded an observer that he was much off-put by the extent of his wife's monstrous gaffe. It was evident to Elizabeth, however, that he was merely trying to keep from laughing. As unsparing as he was and so deeply did she colour, the revelation that his merriment was entirely at her expense was not lost upon her. She was not compleatly successful at concealing her displeasure.

In the midst of this little skirmish, she thought to steal a glance at Col. Fitzwilliam. He was paying a great deal of attention to the toes of his boots, possibly whistling.

With all due insouciance, Darcy offered his arm to his wife and the three took the path to the house. But they had taken no more than a few steps in that direction before Elizabeth bestowed a rather violent pinch of retribution upon her husband's arm just above the elbow. In a show of his usual impressive self-discipline, he did not start at this infliction. He did, however, rest his free hand upon hers, for it was still poised menacingly upon his arm (perhaps this was in affection, more likely it was in defence of another assault).

In a gallant change of topic, Fitzwilliam inquired of Elizabeth why it was she had never ridden before. She knew "riding" in the sense that Darcy and Fitzwilliam spoke of it did not mean simply sitting atop a horse from one place to another (and spoken in company, certainly had no carnal connotation). They meant "ride to hunt."

For foxhunting was a ritual in Derbyshire as much as a sport. Hence, she explained why, as a gentleman's daughter, she did not ride, and her admission supported both her honesty and sense of humour.

"Our father keeps no hunters, Colonel, only one saddle horse, Nellie. She is dispro-portionately fat. Jane and I once spent half a day just urging her into a trot. So wea-ried were we by this endeavour, we quite gave it up."

"Well," Fitzwilliam said as they sauntered on, "Darcy here has quite the best seat in the county. However, as an instructor, no doubt, he will be quite relentless. Pray, be prepared to weather countless hours under his stern instruction."

"Yes, Col. Fitzwilliam," she agreed solemnly, "I trust you are quite right about that."

Unschooled that gentleman friends are betimes inclined to bedevil each other in covert ways, Elizabeth believed that Fitzwilliam was unaware of his *double entendre*. Fitzwilliam's countenance, however, beheld the slightest trace of a smirk, whilst Darcy looked quite unamused. Intent as they were upon their silent sparring, neither noticed the mischievous smile that had overtaken her until after her remark.

Thereupon both eyed her curiously. Her intent had been only to exact a small revenge on behalf of her husband's tease. The ambiguity that reigned over her coun-tenance, however, persuaded her husband and her husband's cousin that neither knew just who was the victim of what.

Regrettably, Elizabeth was utterly insensible of her small victory. Yet, she did bene-fit. For her second evening at Pemberley was spent much more congenially than the first, in that Fitzwilliam prudently forsook toying with Darcy's temper. In benign innocence, Elizabeth sat about enjoying their company, entirely unwitting that she was the perpetrator of a faintly risqué sub-plot.

By morning, Elizabeth was quite inspirited by the prospect of her equine initiation and rifled desperately through her garderobe for some sort of reasonable riding-dress. When all she could find amongst her belongings was muslin, lace, and a corduroy spencer, she became increasingly frantic. That would not do. The proper habit was essential, thus catapulted clothing passed over her into an ever-increasing pile of dis-cards.

Timidly, a maid tapped her upon the shoulder. She gestured in the direction of a cheval mirror whence hung an unfamiliar garment. In her panic, Elizabeth had over-looked it. When she finally espied it, she put her hand to her heart in silent apprecia-tion. For there before her was a compleat riding costume.

The habit shirt and jabot were of exceptionally fine cambric, but it was the jacket and skirt that were most stunning. They were green, but not merely green. They were of a verdancy so deep it seemed to have leapt from the farthest reaches of the forest.

Hesitantly, Elizabeth walked to them and lovingly fingered the detail. The collar was velvet and *passimeterie* edged the cuffs and adorned the tail. A brocade waistcoat peeked from beneath the jacket. It mimicked masculinity, but delicate tatting at the seams gave it a definite feminine identity.

She shook her head in astonishment, knowing it was all her husband's doing. As she was helped into it, she wondered, then she fretted, how he was able to have had it fit her so very well with no actual fitting. The only answer that did not grieve her was the hope of beginner's luck. She did so not want to believe he had ever done such a thing for any other.

Then, praise be, it occurred to her that he had a sister.

Donning a voluminous velvet beret, she nodded it appreciatively at her reflection in the mirror. The pert feather curling about the side bobbed cooperatively. Satisfied, she about-faced and went in search of her benefactor. Her benefactor (perhaps discomfited by prodigious gratitude) was unable to fully appreciate the allurement of her chapeau (howbeit she was tossing her head about quite fetchingly), for he was preoccupied by the inadequacy of her shoes.

"Pray, do you not have proper boots?"

She squinched her nose and reminded him, "My equestrian experience thus far required no footwear."

As Mr. Darcy was unaccustomed to cheek, he was unprepared with a rejoinder and endeavoured to ignore the allusion by clearing his throat. Elizabeth was roundly satisfied with the subtle crimsoning of his aspect and allowed him to escort her toward the stables and away from the topic of their connubial tutelage.

Amongst the whitewashed stalls and scrubbed cobblestones stood the even-tempered chestnut horse he had chosen for her.

"This is Lady," he announced and with the merest flick of his head, he sent the groom scurrying away. Clearly, he chose to leg his wife onto the saddle himself.

Once she was aloft, his begrudging of the groom's assistance became apparent, forasmuch as situating her properly necessitated the sliding of his hand beneath her skirt. Thereupon, he clasped her calf and positioned her knee around the pommel of the side-saddle with just enough firmness to incite a most unseemly fluttering in her stomach. If his fingers tarried thither, it was but fleetingly, for his doings were under intense scrutiny from a contingent of servitors.

Once persuaded she was well-settled, he eschewed a leg up himself. Indeed, with a leap and a heave, he mounted his own horse. As Blackjack was an exceedingly tall animal, Elizabeth supposed his method was a bit of *braggadocio*, most probably for her benefit. Hence, she was twice impressed. First with her husband's strength, and secondly, that he wanted her to witness it.

They took to the downs with slow deliberation. Elizabeth (surreptitiously, she believed) tapped Lady with her crop, urging her forward. Darcy, however, was eyeing her most diligently; hence, it did not escape his notice.

"I see you have a natural seat for your horse, Lizzy."

"Do I?" she said, flushing with pride that her intrinsic horsemanship was so readily apparent.

"Yes," he said, "and as fearlessly as you ride you will learn with dispatch. Or, of course, be killed."

Thus, her little fit of egotism was not snuffed, merely dampened. But she had not the opportunity to fully explore her burgeoning saddle prowess that first day of instruction, for Darcy chose not to traverse farther than the immediate demesne. That alone took some time. Ever eager, Elizabeth wanted to inspect the chase, but he insisted not.

"To-morrow forenoon you will thank me. For your limbs will ache and your...keel will suffer cruelly."

"My what will suffer?"

"Your...keel, your...breech...your hinder-end!" he concluded graciously.

"Oh," she laughed, finally recognising a euphemism. "Could you not say 'rump' to your wife and be done with it?"

"No, I could not. Perchance I should have begun with '*derrière*.' As it happens, I have no practise speaking of such things in company. Moreover," he took a scholarly tone, "as a verb, Lizzy, the word 'rump' has a vulgar connotation."

At that bit of news, she looked at him queerly, but he did not offer further explanation. Rather, he aimed them toward the stables, Elizabeth yet grousing because of their shortened ride.

In front of the horse barn stood Mr. Rhymes. He was talking to a tall, gangly boy, all wrists and Adam's apple. Darcy dismounted and then helped ease down Elizabeth (who at this point was beginning to appreciate the easing) before turning his attention to his overseer. Upon seeing the master arrive, Rhymes exacted a genuflection that compelled the lad at his elbow to mimic it. Directly, Darcy asked what it was the boy wanted. Rhymes related that, just orphaned, the boy had been put out and was looking for work at their stables.

During their dialog, the boy stood nervously wringing the hat he had pulled from atop a mop of dark curls. He watched the two men talk from beneath wary, hooded eyes.

Hereupon, Elizabeth's pity was provoked, but to her chagrin, she heard Darcy curtly declare that there was no need of another groom.

In his most stentorian voice, he said, "I think this knave is not fully the sixteen years he claims."

Rhymes knew Mr. Darcy well enough to understand this as a warning to the boy not to lie, and waited patiently to be told what was to be done with him. Doubtlessly, he would be set to mucking out stalls, just as did all who came up looking for honest work. However, before such instructions could be issued, Elizabeth interrupted.

"But Darcy, how is it you quibble about how old he claims to be? Should it not matter only that he is able enough to do the work? His mother has just died..."

She silenced herself mid-sentence, for Mr. Rhymes turned to her with an expression that could only be described as aghast. Darcy's face betrayed no emotion at all. That absence announced a displeasure of some magnitude. So emphatic was it that, as Elizabeth opened her mouth to make another entreaty upon the boy's behalf, she shut it. She shut it so decidedly it was almost audible. It was possible Darcy spoke further with Rhymes, but if he did, Elizabeth did not hear it. The roaring in her ears was far too deafening. Mr. Darcy took Mrs. Darcy's elbow and walked her silently back to the house. Upon the portico, his icy silence was supplanted by a voice cold enough to exact a chill down her back.

"Do not ever reprove me in front of one of my people again, Elizabeth."

Thereupon, he turned and took his leave of her. She stood upon the threshold for a moment in foot-shuffling mortification before repairing to her dressing room.

Darcy reappeared at dinner, but only at the farthest end of the great table. Conversation was stilted and sparse. Elizabeth was anxious to affix herself in the privacy of their boudoir to hash out the matter, but when it was time to retire, Darcy abruptly excused himself and called for his horse.

If there was anything upon Pemberley that needed his attention more than she did at that time of night, Elizabeth could not think of it.

Understanding she had transgressed a very distinct line, she still believed semi-public emendation was hardly a capital offence. Had she not abused him miserably in company before? Until that day, he had found that charming of her. She realised, however, that within the flirtatious bantering of courtship, she had forgotten that his position and his consideration of his position were implacable. So deeply had she been entrenched in her role as his lover, she had confused it with that of wife. Repeatedly, and with vehemence, she lectured herself that the Mistress of Pemberley must never redress the Master of Pemberley in front of the help.

She would have announced her contrition had he been there to hear it.

She took the stairs alone and with no small measure of self-pity. It was thus that she lay abed, fighting back tears, uncertain whether they were born more of anger or hurt. For he had not chastised her, he had not even spoken to her of her heinous misdeed beyond the one statement. Upon the veritable inauguration of their marriage, he had simply dismissed her. Dismissal was an indignity far more egregious than any quarrel.

Her wifely umbrage notwithstanding, their bed without him was dismal comfort. And as the advancing hours were announced by innumerable rings of the chimes, it occurred to her that he might have returned and taken a separate bedroom.

Her parents did not share a bed. Many couples did not. There was an ominously austere bedchamber just beyond the wall. It was ideal for martyrdom. Was her own husband announcing to her that did she displease him, he would take to his own room as if a petulant child? Not a happy thought. So unpleasant was that thought, Elizabeth decided she would seek this room in which he sought refuge from her and smite him with her pillow (a candlestick was handy, but might well have been lethal; she did not want to bludgeon him, simply to obtain his attention).

Fortuitously, before she had opportunity to enact this reckoning, their door opened. She heard her husband's footsteps as they crossed the room and his weight upon the mattress. Though he had not forsaken their marriage bed, she was not compleatly mollified. Yet of a mind to whop him with the pillow, she reasoned: One should not allow ills to fester.

From the darkness, she heard him say, "The boy will be second groom to your horse."

Who was to groom her horse was not of the utmost importance to her at that moment.

"Pray, where have you been?" she asked. "I have been tormented some cruel accident had befallen you." (Now that he had returned, it was far easier to admit she had been truly distraught. Moreover, plaguing his conscience ever so slightly was only fair.)

"It took some time to find that boy."

"I apologise if I abused you in company," she announced. "In the future I will keep my own counsel upon matters so wholly unconnected to me."

"The boy will be second groom to your horse," he repeated, and offered no further comment about the incident. Elizabeth recognized that was a manner of apology as well.

Understanding his concessions were infrequent, Elizabeth still believed his had more merit than did hers. For she thought, perchance, the boy's circumstances may have reminded Darcy of the loss of his own mother. That poignancy, however, lay uninvestigated. She did offer that the lad's tall, dark, and solemn countenance bade her envision just how Darcy himself might have looked at that age.

"Pish-tosh," was his disdainful comment, "I looked nothing of the kind."

She did not further the subject, but that resemblance was reason enough for her to give the boy consequence despite her husband's scoff. And because there is no better reason to have a quarrel than to reconcile with an abundance of vigour and enthusiasm, they did. Midmost of this reconciliation Elizabeth received edification upon the infinitive "to rump."

However, first person singular had nothing whatsoever to do with it.

Enlightenments upon life at Pemberley in general and being a wife specifically came with all due regularity. These wisdoms rained down upon Elizabeth with such dispatch, she occasionally had to stop and take a breath to be able to function at all. In all this befuddlement, the descent of her monthly terms was not remotely a comfort.

Whilst at Longbourn she was governed by a dictum set down by Mrs. Bennet. To wit, all menstrually enfeebled females would be consigned to bed for the duration, whether they felt ill or not. The only time Elizabeth ever fibbed to her mother was upon the occasion of her menses, for she knew herself to be quite hardy. This deceit (and Jane did worry for Elizabeth's health) began in adolescence and extended until her marriage. For with so many, it was difficult for the easily flummoxed Mrs. Bennet to keep up with each daughter's monthly cycle. Elizabeth only veered from this pattern upon the instances of her sister Mary's reproach. Not because Elizabeth took Mary's counsel, but if she did not stay abed at least a little, the punctilious Mary would tattle to Mrs. Bennet.

Now that she was a woman and a wife, Elizabeth refused subterfuge. If she were not unwell, she would not stay in bed and say she was.

Inevitably, ten days after her wedding, her courses descended and that avowal was put to the test.

It was another instance whereupon she missed Jane most deeply. Their entire life had been lived with a common bedroom wall. They had confided every secret, exchanged every dream. When Jane found Darcy in Elizabeth's bedroom that night at Netherfield, Elizabeth worried for what Jane thought, but never for what she might tell. Their bond was that compleat. And Elizabeth would have dearly loved to have her counsel that morning, for she had no idea how to tell her husband of her womanly woes. Or if she should tell him. Or even if he knew of such things.

Instinctively, she dismissed the idea that he might not know of a woman's reproductive cycle, for it seemed her husband was much more knowledgeable about her body than she was herself. At least, minimally, the female form collectively. She could only pray it was erudite in origin. For his countenance had betrayed not the least bit of astonishment upon beholding her in nature's garb (although she believed she had detected lust). But then again, she had no timbered appendage that he was to receive betwixt his legs. For even having had the privilege of viewing several Greek statues, beholding Darcy as God made him (and burdened as he was with the evidence of God's admonition to go forth and multiply), her own astonishment had well-nigh caused her to gasp.

Indeed, he had the appendage and she had the menses. Elizabeth sighed. She would have to tell him.

Hence, when her husband took her in his arms that night, indubitably in anticipation of connubial union, the woman, his wife, Elizabeth Bennet Darcy said, "I am afraid I am…indisposed."

This, of course, was an outright dodge. Although she had not stooped to the detestable term "unwell," it was certainly not the forthright announcement she would have preferred to make. (However, in her defence, "Sorry my dear, we cannot make the beast with two backs for I am riding the red stallion," was not a part of her vernacular.)

But exposition was unnecessary. For when she spoke of her indisposition from deep beneath the covers, he immediately put a concerned back of his hand to her forehead. Looking into the bright eyes of one in the pink of health, he made an all-purpose comment.

"I see."

Embarrassed, she could not look at him.

"Perhaps I should take my sleep elsewhere," he said.

He then kissed her upon her unfevered brow and quietly left their bed, putting out the candles upon his way out of the room.

Well. There it was.

It was quite evident the only interest he had in her bed was the kindness she obliged him there. Was there no possibility of conjugal embrace, he chose to sleep alone. Moreover, wifely poorliness clearly demanded not only abstinence, but distance as well. She, however, did not want to sleep without him. If she could not at least stroke his ankle with her toes or hear that sound that came from his throat when he slept upon his back, she thought their bed would be too cold to bear. Forthwith and quite miserably, she realised that she would have ample opportunity to acquaint herself with the deprivation.

Tossing restlessly whilst fretting about the one-fourth of her life that she would have to sleep without her husband, she heard a soft scratching at the door. To her feet in an instant, she padded to the door, but opened it only a crack, not entirely certain she had heard a noise. True, she had, for there, candle in hand, stood Darcy.

"Lizzy," he said, uncommonly hesitant, "Would you mind…I wonder if I might just lie next to you for a time…"

With more unbridled enthusiasm than she thought a demure lady should expose, she flung back the door and wrapped her arms about his waist. This, of course, did influence him she was agreeable to his company. Either in affection or rescue, she knew not which, he lifted her chin and stroked it with his thumb.

Then, whispering against her hair, he admitted, "I fear I am no longer able to find sleep without you."

She stifled her jubilation until entrenched again beneath the covers. There, she nestled happily in his arms.

"I thought you did not want to lie with me because…you could not…I could not…"

"Yield favours?" he compleated her halting sentence.

Having embarrassed herself further, she nodded her head then looked away. He would not have that, and drew her close.

"When you advised me you were indisposed, I believed you wanted to be alone."

"No. Never. No. I was simply mortified to speak of such a thing." She turned away, "I am still mortified."

"Pray, be not. 'Tis a part of you. The womanly part of you."

He kissed her upon the lips rather tenderly, which almost diverted her from other enquiry.

"How is it you know of such things?"

Somewhat defensively, he said, "I am an educated man."

"Cambridge offers a class in 'Female Affliction'?"

Parrying, he quoted, "'As leaky as an unstanched wench.'"

Indignant, she rose upon one elbow, "As leaky as an unstaunched what!"

"Shakespeare, *The Tempest*."

"That I know!"

She, of course, did not, but she did not want him to think her benighted, "I was simply outraged at the reference."

"Are you truly outraged? For you are a wanton wench, Lizzy."

His lips took a little nibbling path up her neck, then kissed her beneath the ear. She allowed that he was an excellent debater.

Thereupon, she sighed, "I fear I shall not have opportunity to be any type of wench for the better part of a se'nnight."

"That long?"

She nodded ruefully.

"Well, there is more than one way to 'crack your whip.'"

She blinked at him, then bade, "Shakespeare?"

"No," he said, "Me."

The gentle art of pleasure was explored that night, Mrs. Darcy quite confounded that she was capable of tending Mr. Darcy's natural vigours so…unconditionally. It was only with the morn that their bloods were truly mingled. Then, he took hers upon his finger-tips, held them aloft and announced, "When this ceases to come we will have begat a baby."

That, of course, was not a revelation to either of them. But with his words, he took their entwined bodies a full revolution across the bed. Elizabeth was uncertain did her head swim from the twirl, or the prospect of their shared child.

Hannah Moorhouse was more than surprised, she was astonished, when her mistress at the Lambton Inn handed her a letter bidding her to come to Pemberley Hall. As it happened, one of her brothers worked there as an under-gardener and she knew the estate well. She had even been as near as the postern, but could in no way account for having received a formally addressed letter from that place. It was but a single piece of vellum affixed with a red wax seal, but it was delivered by a liveried courier. Howbeit she looked upon her letter and touched it lovingly, she took an interminably long time before she mustered the courage to open it.

Moreover, she wanted to bask in the pride of literacy. Her instruction had come by way of the vicar's wife, and because that lady's own education was spotty, Hannah's was very weak in sums above single digits. None of her multitude of brothers could so much as read. Having been rusticated from their schooling for an ugly incident involving a toad, they all had repaired to the fields to earn their keep. Because they teased her unmercifully, Hannah would have much appreciated the opportunity to read her letter from Pemberley aloud for her siblings.

After looking upon it for nearly a half-hour, she carefully opened it. It was an invitation (it was in language an invitation, but no one would have received it as less than a summons), which had arrived early in the forenoon requesting her presence by four. That gave her a mere seven hours to prepare for whatever the visit would mean.

Hannah's plump face reflected her figure and she was given to be an accepting, obliging sort of girl. She knew obesity required its inhabitant to be jolly, but she was a bit shy to be all that droll. Humble, but very capable and not inordinately ambitious, Hannah had lived her entire life in Derbyshire and had been exceedingly happy with her position at the Lambton Inn.

Accepting, obliging Hannah was perfectly content to wait until she arrived at Pemberley to uncover the mystery of her summons. She left at half-past two, hitching a ride with a peddler, and sat in patient wait at the scullery door until precisely four o'clock.

When she entered the back parlour, she espied Miss Elizabeth Bennet sitting at an elabourately stencilled escritoire waiting for her. Mrs. Reynolds introduced her as Mrs. Darcy. Hannah had no idea the new Mrs. Darcy was the same Miss Elizabeth Bennet who had visited with her Aunt and Uncle Gardiner at the Lambton Inn the summer before. She remembered them as kind people, but they had left abruptly under peculiar circumstances.

Howbeit that was odd, Hannah was not a busybody. Another might have held a great deal of curiosity, but Hannah did not. Miss Bennet had married Mr. Darcy. Period.

The elevation of her station to Mrs. Darcy did not appear to inflate Miss Bennet's ego unduly. Her manner was still quite kind. However, Hannah did hold some apprehension toward the housekeeper, Mrs. Reynolds. Having heard from her brother that she held the whip-hand above the staff, Hannah eyed the old woman warily. She endeavoured to restrain her considerable skittishness of the old woman, for it kept her full attention from Mrs. Darcy.

After Hannah had assured Mrs. Darcy that the weather, the roads, and her health were splendid, Mrs. Darcy came directly to the reason she had bid her come to Pemberley. Would Hannah be agreeable to undertaking a situation of lady-maid?

Lady-maid to Mrs. Darcy! At that thought, two bright red splotches coloured high upon Hannah's cheeks. She flushed with pride and pleasure. She had no notion of why Mrs. Darcy would ask a person such as herself to hold such an important position. Even Hannah knew that most great ladies insisted upon a French lady-maid. She had seen one from Whitemore following the Earl's wife with more disdain upon her face than the great lady wore herself.

An agreement was met. Hannah understood there would be a period of trial for them both. With an ingenuousness not usually found amongst ladies of station, Mrs. Darcy suggested that Hannah might not favour the position. Hannah could not imagine such a thing. She would gladly have scoured the scullery and emptied the chamber pots in such a great house.

Even if Mrs. Reynolds was the harridan she evidently was.

Curtly, the housekeeper bid her bring her things to the house the next day, giving notice at the inn obviously not an issue. Having worked there, Hannah knew a great deal about caring for the needs of others, but none so privileged as those at Pemberley. She thought perchance that was why Mrs. Reynolds was so brusque to her, for her duties would be complicated and ignorance a disadvantage. But eager to please, Hannah wrapped up what few personal items she could call her own and vowed to remember all she must. In a small wooden box containing other keepsakes (a lock of her mother's hair and some buttons), she placed the letter written to her from Pemberley and set off for her new life.

She beat the cock to the morn to arrive at Pemberley by half-past five and stood, with all her earthly belongings, upon the threshold. Promptly at nine, she was ushered upstairs. Mrs. Darcy told her that because she had not had her own lady-maid before (Mrs. Darcy whispered the confidence to Hannah that she had shared one maid among five sisters) they would simply make their own rules about many things. Hannah's few reservations about her own ability to please evaporated. Her lady was kind, the house was beautiful, and a bed-closet to herself was more than she might ever have dreamed.

Because it was midwinter, society dictated that Miss Georgiana, her companion, Mrs. Annesley, and her lady-maid, Anne, soon quit the house. Her return to London announced that Pemberley had returned to its pre-wedding routine. With the newlyweds in residence, however, that was not quite so. Without need to question anyone, Hannah noted that Mr. and Mrs. Darcy shared Mrs. Darcy's bed each night, although the bedroom adjoining it (referred to by tittering chambermaids as Mr. Darcy's bedroom) had its pristine linens changed with the same regularity as hers. Evidently, propriety and convention were respected, if not actually embraced.

Hannah quickly understood that Mrs. Reynolds held the triadic position of housekeeper, butler, and steward over the male and female help because Morton, the erstwhile butler, was of infirm mind.

Old Morton's situation was a bit sad, as no one had ever had the heart to tell him he was no longer in charge of either the house or his faculties. Hence, when he remembered to issue orders, they were accepted with a bow and then ignored. The single duty the senescent Morton could recall was the morning snuffing of candles, and he spent most of his time shuffling down the corridors, extinguisher in hand regardless of the hour. This was a bit of a bother, but it did offer an additional position in the house for another servant whose sole duty was to trail him at a distance and relight the wicks. (One evening he did accident into the Darcy boudoir whilst Mr. and Mrs. Darcy were in connubial embrace. It was believed he methodically put out their candles just as he did all others. But as he was as blind as he was senile and neither of the Darcys of a mind to share the level of his intrusion with anyone, it did not enter into the annals of Pemberley lore.)

With her ever-present keys dangling from a cord at her waist, Mrs. Reynolds concurrently familiarised both Mrs. Darcy and Hannah with the one hundred and two rooms and history of the house. To Hannah, the place was daunting and Mrs. Darcy was quite in agreement. Indeed, Hannah overheard Mrs. Darcy telling Mr. Darcy about that very thing.

"I fear I should be unable to find my way back to the ground floor without leaving a trail of bread crumbs to follow," she had declared.

Evidently, that lament induced Mr. Darcy to undertake her tutelage himself. It was upon some of these excursions that the intentions of their meanderings veered from instructional into the realm of outright playfulness. Even as a child, Mr. Darcy was never accused of being frolicsome; hence, this was a bit astounding. A first-hand account of such doings was offered by a particularly rotund charwoman. She told Hannah (in the utmost confidence) about a most disconcerting experience.

Evidently, whilst rounding the corner of what was presumed to be an unoccupied floor, she espied Mr. Darcy himself jiggling the doorknob of a small closet.

"Aye asked the gentleman if Aye could be of assistance and held out me keys," she explained. "He claimed no. He shook his head, he did. Said he had no need of no key but when Aye walked on, he kept a jigglin' the doorknob!"

Then she lowered her voice and advised that when she came back, "He was not there, so Aye guessed him gone. Found what he needed and gone. But, no. When Aye come upon that door, it bust open, it did!"

The woman took a generous gulp of air before continuing, thus allowing Hannah's eyes to widen in anticipation.

"And who comes out? Mrs. Darcy, she does! Aye turned, surprised ye know? She bumped right into me. Bounced back she did. Right back into Mr. Darcy who was comin' fast right behind her!"

"No…" Hannah said, unsuccessfully containing her amazement.

"In a fright Aye was…Mrs. Darcy bumpin' into me, Mr. Darcy right there. Aye was in a fright!"

Another chambermaid stopped to listen (in the utmost confidence). The charwoman stopped to update the newest member of her audience upon the events leading up to this diversion before continuing.

"They looked at me, then back at each other an' almos' laughed, they did. Then they 'scused themselves and hurry on," she lowered her voice and raised an eyebrow as two more servants joined the assemblage. "Mr. Darcy, Aye never seen him no way but proper. Never even his jacket crook't. Not in all my days here. But he was then, he was. As they's walkin' down the hall, he fixes his jacket like this," she pulled at invisible lapels. "But he took no notice that his shirt was hangin' down in back. Down to his knees it was! Ye could see it each time he tookin' a step!"

"Ohhh…" announced that all privy to this dissertation were suitably impressed with the significance of the disclosure.

Likewise, house prattle was how Hannah learnt of the staff's belief that every bed in every vacant bedroom under the roof of Pemberley was being methodically christened in some manner by Mr. and Mrs. Darcy's passion. Granted, it took a great deal of snooping to learn this, but the Pemberley staff was nothing if not diligent.

Then there was the matter of the dogs.

Every servant, too, knew what was commencing in the Darcy bedroom whilst the dogs lay whining outside the door. Yet, everyone passing by stepped over Troilus and Cressida without a glance. Neither did they raise an eyebrow at the soundly shut bedroom door.

Hannah was a maiden, but she had brothers. She was not unwitting of what went on betwixt men and women, married or not. However, there were noises that came from the Darcys' bedchamber in the daytime that ordinarily would not have been heard even at night. Some detonations unexpected to be heard at all. In light of the unseemly noises, rustled beds, and whining dogs, the servants of Pemberley allowed that, clearly, there was a great deal of affection betwixt Mr. Darcy and his wife.

Ribald noises notwithstanding, there was that queer matter of the missing pier glass. A rather large, gilded mirror had hung upon the wall in Mrs. Darcy's bedchamber. One morning, it was not there. In foot-tapping annoyance, Mrs. Reynolds asked Hannah if she knew what betide it. She asked it a little pointedly for Hannah's taste. Did she think Hannah had somehow pilfered it? A huge mirror like that? What would she have done, Hannah thought defensively, packed it out upon her back?

Every spare moment was spent in search of that pier glass and the mystery was in no way solved when Hannah bechanced it under the bed whilst gathering Mrs. Darcy's night-dress one morning (Mrs. Darcy's night-dress was often in odd places). Hannah immediately called Mrs. Reynolds to inform her just where the wayward mirror had been located and anticipated an explanation or at least a retrieval of the mirror. However, Mrs. Reynolds merely thanked Hannah politely and said nothing more.

Hannah bade, "D'ye want someone to hang it back?"

Mrs. Reynolds shook her head. Hannah's lips formed the beginning of a query but Mrs. Reynolds pursed her lips and waved her aside.

That was peculiar. The old woman had been so concerned about the missing mirror, then when it was found, she wanted it left under the bed. Hannah could see no sense in it.

But there was sense in it. Those less innocent of sensual pleasure would have understood. If the Darcys wanted the mirror underneath the bed, there it would remain.

The old housekeeper kept a careful ear for the transferral of lascivious gossip by scullery maids in the kitchen, a watchful eye upon the chambermaids upstairs, but had no notion at all what to do about the whining dogs.

18

In the country, any illustrious occasion was scheduled by the moon. When it was to be full could be determined by the calendar. A clear night sky to guide the guests' coaches to the Pemberley ball, however, fell to serendipity. Everything else was being done by the staff, just as ably as it had in the past. Preparations being so well taken care of and out of her hands, Elizabeth knew she had no more influence over the success or failure of the evening than she did the condition of the sky. And that left her both relieved and anxious. Polishing the silver would at least have bestowed her something to do besides fretting, for worry she did. Her presentation to Derbyshire society was quite the event and curiosity would be rampant.

However, Jane and Bingley had arrived that forenoon and their presence was a substantial comfort. That inviting the Bingleys necessitated invitation to his sisters as well was not.

Caroline Bingley and Louisa Hurst were in obvious raptures upon being houseguests of Pemberley. But having perfected it upon Jane, they continued to hide their obvious dislike of the lesser-born Bennet sisters behind a demeanour of fawning insincerity. Elizabeth would have much preferred outright animosity, but Jane's love for her husband, and those he loved in return, was unconditional. Jane's wishes ruled in this matter, for the sisters were, after all, her in-laws. Elizabeth could, however, find some pity for them, for she and Jane, quite unknowingly, had foiled them twice. Once, when Georgiana Darcy did not marry their brother, and secondly, when Caroline Bingley did not snare Darcy for herself.

Aunt and Uncle Gardiner were to travel to Pemberley from London for the festivities, but Mr. and Mrs. Bennet did not come immediately. They were away to Newcastle for Lydia's first laying-in (Mary Bennet refused to visit the morally bankrupt Wickhams). And unless Lydia's newborn was more punctual than was its mother, they would miss the ball. Of this, Elizabeth was prodigiously (if somewhat sheepishly) relieved. Her first foray into Derbyshire society would be less agonising without the fear of humiliation by her mother. Kitty and Maria Lucas, who favoured a grand ball at Pemberley more than visiting a whining Lydia in grimy Newcastle, were taking on Mrs. Bennet's role as resident mortifiers quite nicely.

Elizabeth knew she would have to take ultimate responsibility for that embarrassment. For it was she who suggested Kitty invite Maria Lucas to accompany her when Mary (who found even less pleasure in a ball than in visiting wicked relations) had not wanted to come. For every dance, frock, fan, and feather that Mary Bennet saw as decadent, Maria Lucas found equally agreeable. She and Kitty were of the same age and both loved society. All would have prospered quite happily had it not been a matter of ill-timing. For Kitty and Maria came thither from Hertfordshire upon the immediate heels of sharing a particularly histrionic novel.

This work of fiction (a distinction lost upon the two girls) portrayed a heroine who had the misfortune of constitution that bade her fall into a dramatic faint at the least provocation, and, of course, at the greatest romantic moment. At the grand estate of Pemberley and in preparation for a particularly impressive ball, Kitty and Maria saw the necessity of perfecting this act of swooning in the unlikely prospect that a romantic moment might fall at their awaiting feet. Such behaviour had been overlooked with patient indulgence when they merely fell in the privacy and unobtrusiveness of Kitty's bedroom. But the girls harboured the notion that one must refine one's techniques for greater benefit of an audience (for there was no other reason to swoon) in the drawing rooms at Pemberley. Moreover, neither was of a mind to be outdone, one's swoon inviting the other, the synchronousness of which was lost upon no one.

It had been her family's hope that out from under Lydia's influence, Kitty's disposition might flower more judiciously. Evidently, Lydia's relocation to Newcastle only vacated the office of silliest girl in England and Kitty was determined to capture it. (If she did, Elizabeth preferred her reputation be earned in Hertfordshire.)

Upon Kitty's falling faint into Mr. Bingley's hands (which he had hastily emptied of teacup and saucer), even Jane reached the limit of her considerable good nature. She and Elizabeth each commandeered a breathless soubrette and escorted them upstairs. Thereupon, Elizabeth issued an ultimatum: Either they cease this swooning nonsense or they would be locked in the cock-loft.

Jane, quite seriously, worried for their health.

"Maria, Kitty, you must cease this at once. Mrs. Hurst knows a young woman brought to galloping consumption through just such imprudent conduct who died within days!"

Upon that pronouncement, Elizabeth looked at Jane as if she was *non compos mentis,* yet said not a word. She was of the opinion that questionable medical truths betimes dampened incautious conduct.

"One fatal swoon cost her life," Jane admonished. "Beware of fainting fits, young ladies, they can prove destructive to your constitutions."

Quite caught up in the moment, Elizabeth intoned, "Run mad if you must, Kitty, but do not swoon."

Much impressed by their brush with death, their romantic swoons were abandoned for solemn (with an occasional hand to the back of the forehead for emphasis) introspection. However, lugubrious expression did not last long upon such young countenances and by the day of the ball, Maria and Kitty were again in high spirits. The only remaining terror was the one they inflicted upon their trunks in search of the perfect ball-gowns.

Elizabeth had no such dilemma. Hannah had taken the frock she was to wear that evening for a last minute pressing. The mantua-maker said the colour was bisque. It was not. It was yellow, lemon yellow.

Creating a dress of simplicity and elegance was no small undertaking. Indeed, its birth precipitated the exhausting of more resources than a military campaign against a foreign state. Two waggons ladened with bolts of fabric, three seamstresses, a cobbler, and the mantua-maker all beset her in a single afternoon. The bother was substantial, but of the results, Elizabeth was exultant.

Now the evening that bid her endure such torture was upon her. And as she waited in her dressing-gown, she was conspicuously idle. Loose ends invited fretting and she began to worry that Darcy might not approve of her gown. In a turn of unadulterated coquetry, she had not allowed him to see it, hoping a dramatic unveiling would somehow render him in awe. As the time approached, that likelihood seemed to wane precipitously. Perchance her dress was not merely simple, but blatantly unsophisticated. It would have been more far more prudent to gather his favourable opinion prior to the ball. If he were even a little less than happy with it there would be scant time to rummage up a replacement. Whilst stewing and second-guessing, Elizabeth heard the unmistakable sound of her husband's boots upon the stairs, undoubtedly returning from taking care of some last-minute details.

It had been he who insisted she languish about whilst everyone else in the house toiled. She promised herself that in the future she would insist on some busy-work, even if it were polishing the silver. Idle and fidgety, she put her ear to the door and heard Goodwin filling his master's copper bathtub.

Forthwith of Goodwin's leave-taking was a splash as Darcy got into the tub. All of which begged a prank.

Elizabeth, of course, had heard that idleness was the devil's workshop. But without pedantic Mary to remind her of it, such a notion did not come to mind. Hence, the ruse she impetuously hatched to exact upon her husband was deemed particularly amusing. With great care, she peeked inside his dressing-chamber. There in his tub he sat. Humming tunelessly, he had lathered his face. Blinded by soap and wholly unwitting of her presence, she endeavoured to steal in upon him, but the door creaked.

He leaned his head forward and said, "Water."

Barely stifling a laugh at his mistaking her for Goodwin, she bravely lifted the heavy brass pitcher over his head. Unaware of how very near he was to being conked senseless by her unsteady grasp of the urn, he sat placidly waiting. Whilst hiding behind his back, she managed to pour without mishap. Thereupon, she wantonly foraged his bath water for the soap.

Regrettably, it was located before her exploration became overtly lascivious and with all due vigour and no little relish, she rubbed it against a sponge to create a good lather. Then she set to work scrubbing the length of his spine. Up and down, back and forth she scrubbed, eventually advancing her ministrations over his shoulders and halfway down his stomach. Unmistakably startled, he grabbed the hand that held the invading sponge. She let out a giggle.

Seeing it was her hand he clutched, he looked relieved.

"I thought Goodwin had taken leave of his wits."

As her ploy was unconditionally successful, she was inclined to verify that he was not out of humour at her hands by bestowing an uncommonly passionate kiss. That would have been a most uneventful climax to an innocent lark but for his reprisal. For from her perch upon the lip of the tub, she was quite caught up in the fervour of their kiss and at the mercy of gravity. With the merest flick of his wrist, she half-toppled into the water. This unexpected dunking induced a small shriek in surprise.

That was but a momentary reaction, for the slathering warmth of the water and his nakedness persuaded her to join him. Hence, he drew her legs over the side, both wriggling in accommodation of all four limbs. This situating was still in progress when Goodwin flung back the door from the hallway with obvious alarm.

"Is all well, sir?"

Upon seeing Mrs. Darcy in drenched, if splayed, splendour atop her husband, he stopped short. She dropped her head, shut her eyes and, in petrified mortification, prayed vainly that she would somehow be unnoticed. Folly.

"A slight accident," Mr. Darcy said mildly. "Could you put out more toweling? It appears Mrs. Darcy will be needing it as well."

She clenched her eyes shut in defence of what she did so not want to hear. Goodwin did as he was told and hastily left.

"Fitzwilliam Darcy! What must he think? You have humiliated me beyond measure!"

"Humiliated you in what manner, madam? You are in my bath, I am not in yours."

"That is what I mean, I am in your bath," the colour in her cheeks was not disappearing.

"Yes," replied Darcy.

"He knows that I am in your bath," she repeated.

Perhaps taking pity upon her he ceased his tease, "Yes. 'Tis my bath and my wife and he will think nothing of it."

Elizabeth frowned hesitantly, uncertain this was true. But as it was unlikely that Darcy would have someone injudicious in such close employ she rethought the matter. Reluctantly accepting that her mortification was mostly of her own doing, she reclaimed the sponge and began to relather his body, a pursuit, unquestionably, he did not disfavour. Thereupon, they embarked upon an ever-increasing exploration of the possibilities of aqueous achievement. This investigation was vehement, hence, water sloshed, then spilt onto the floor. A misfortune, for when those possibilities were discovered to be limited, he endeavoured to pick her up and carry her dripping to their bed.

It was then that near-disaster struck.

For the decision to move from the cramped quarters of the tub was made post insertion of his virile member. Indisputably, stepping out of a bath is not in and of itself a particularly tricky manoeuvre. However, if one's wife has her limbs wrapped about one's waist and one is determined to continue carnal union, the additional obstacle of a slick floor presents a high probability of mishap.

Which occurred.

He landed upon his backside, but it was not his chief concern. He feared that the explicit nature of their embrace might have subjected Elizabeth to impalement and thus violent injury to her…self. The laughter she attempted to stifle persuaded him not. Thus, this particular amorous infusion was compleated upon the floor, the slipperiness of which rendered the act as one of exceedingly ambulatory passion. This trip was of considerable length and ceased only upon the occasion of Mr. Darcy effecting seminous emission whilst Mrs. Darcy's head was wedged in a corner.

As they lay there in a puddle of bath water, Elizabeth was grateful Goodwin had the sense to stay out (she truly did want to limit herself to one mortification per day). Eventually, the combination of their nakedness, the water, and the chill of the floor influenced them that their position of repose was untenable. Untangling their limbs, they heard activity downstairs responding to the gentle tinkle of the dressing bell. In reluctant haste, they left each other's company then to dress, reclaiming decorum for the benefit of society's evening.

Born in the servant quarters at Pemberley, Harold Goodwin could not remember when he was not in the Darcys' service. His mother was a sister to the housekeeper, his uncle, manservant to Mr. Darcy, the elder. As a child, he carried laundry and learnt the art of polishing a gentleman's boots. He was but fifteen when young Master Darcy was born. Even at so innocent an age, Goodwin understood the magnitude of joy the family held at the birth of their son and heir.

And a strapping, healthy baby he was. That was apparent to Goodwin as he looked over his mother's shoulder whilst she tended the baby in her new duties as his nurse. Mrs. Goodwin had a great deal of practise with babies, Harold being her seventh, and not her last, child. But the number of surviving offspring was not what was paramount to the Darcys in selecting who to care for their son. Practise was mandatory and easily identified. Loyalty and discretion were needed even more prodigiously, but not so easily found.

It was accepted that Pemberley was as fine a house as one could want as a place of employment. It would require a number of years and introduction to other houses, other families, before Goodwin would understand that the Darcys' good regard was as generous a compliment as could be paid.

Even before young Master Darcy was born, Goodwin had abandoned the laundry and shadowed his uncle's footsteps to learn the precise art of being a gentleman's gentleman. A more gracious master was unlikely to be found. Indeed, Mr. Darcy had been a bit of an anomaly for an aristocrat. Kind and circumspect, he was affable and accessible.

Howbeit Master Darcy had inherited his father's height and dark good looks, he was most certainly his mother's son in outlook and demeanour, being reserved and reticent. Mrs. Darcy was the better part of a decade older than her husband. A handsome woman, she was exceedingly wealthy in her own right. Bookish and quiet, she stood counterpoint to him in every way but wealth. Together their match had almost tripled the land that belonged to the house of Pemberley.

Mr. Darcy had been a dutiful husband, Mrs. Darcy a dutiful wife. They were both exceedingly dutiful and proud parents. Clearly, duty ruled their lives.

When Mrs. Darcy was taken by childbirth fever after Miss Georgiana's birth, young Darcy had stayed in his room for days, refusing to attend the funeral or admire his new sister. Subsequent of that tragedy, the elder Mr. Darcy committed the single error in judgement Goodwin ever recalled of him. He bid Goodwin's mother to be nurse to the new baby. Another woman wholly unknown to him took her place with the young master. Goodwin understood Mr. Darcy's utmost concern for his motherless daughter. Undoubtedly the man did not understand it a double loss for his son, losing both his mother and mother figure in one fell swoop.

Hence, Goodwin was probably more forgiving and less judgemental when upon occasion young Darcy fought him figuratively and literally. For by the time of Master Darcy's twelfth birthday, he had been complaining with uncommon vehemence that he was far too old to have a nurse. He demanded that the matter be rectified forthwith. And if it were not, he would suffer humiliation so debilitating he would be wounded cruelly from it for the rest of his life. In that he had commenced to locking the poor nurse out of his bath, Mr. Darcy the elder was persuaded to acquiesce that his towering son was to have a manservant of his own. It was Goodwin who was bid to tend the young master.

In their pride, Goodwin thought his own parents could not have been more pleased had he been raised to the deity. Indeed, Goodwin became perilously close to designating himself such by the distinction. It was not, however, always easy to see to the young master. As sartorial faultlessness was foremost amongst Goodwin's duties to his charge, Master Darcy's disinclination to bathe became an outright war. Not only did he resist his bath, he showed a decided lack of interest in all matters of grooming to which general rowdiness lent more disrepute. Regrettably, this lackadaisical dispassion for matters of hygiene was accompanied by a revulsion for good manners as well. When observing the exceedingly fastidious and courtly adult Darcy, it never failed to amuse Goodwin to recollect the young man who once had to be wrestled into a bathtub.

There were only a few years during which Master Darcy exhibited unrestrained behaviour. All fell midmost of his second decade of life. Goodwin had never been certain if his mother's death had lent him such brashness or if it was merely the jubilance of new-found pubescent virility. For as diligent as Goodwin was about all aspects of Master Darcy's personal habits, it did not escape his notice when the young master was introduced into carnal necessities by that titian-haired jezebel, Abigail Christie.

Where Goodwin's loyalty lay was never in question. Therefore, he never entertained the possibility of reporting Master Darcy's doings to his father. This, regardless of how disapproving Goodwin had been. And disapprove he did. For, however necessary it would be for Master Darcy to procreate on behalf of his family, Goodwin despised the notion that the young man practise with vulgar women. Conjugal acts of generation were one thing, getting one's ashes hauled by a maid was quite another. It would not do.

The single time that arch rogue Wickham's means suited Goodwin's ends was when he went to Mr. Darcy and prattled about the young master's indiscretions. A miraculous alteration overtook him literally overnight. Darcy had ceased his rebellion. Indeed, it appeared his disposition altered irrevocably. No longer was he the rambunctious boy. In his place stood a young man who was a lankier, if reserved, version of his father. The same kindness and generosity was exhibited with his servitors, but conversely he was just as staid, rigid, and unyielding as his father was amenable.

In his thirty-three years upon the earth, Goodwin had not ventured beyond Derbyshire, but he accompanied young Darcy to Cambridge. George Wickham went with them, as Mr. Darcy was committed to that young man's education. However unhappy Goodwin was over the matter was of no importance. For young Wickham had been living at Pemberley for several years under Mr. Darcy's condescension by reason of his affection for his steward, Wickham's father. In Goodwin's opinion (had he been asked), Geoffrey Fitzwilliam was a far more admirable companion than that truckling

lickspittle and incorrigible Lothario, Wickham. For in addition to his faults of character, he was exceedingly jealous of his benefactor's son.

Betimes, this envy took perverse turns. More than once Goodwin had, unbeknownst to Wickham (and Darcy too), thwarted him. Covertness was an absolute, for
Wickham was a young man who held grudges that were deep and mean. Whilst at
.Cambridge, it had been a little entertaining to watch the perfidious Wickham turn in
circles, uncertain with which rich classmate he should next curry favour.

Rarely was he successful; his reputation as a tuft-hunter usually preceded him. And
when it did not, Wickham could usually be counted upon to sink his own boat.

When Wickham was caught, not only with a young woman in his room, but with
the answers to his tripos exam, Master Darcy had come to the end of his much abused
tolerance of his roommate. Inclined to let him be "hoist by his own petard," young
Darcy was overruled by his father. Had not Mr. Darcy interceded, Wickham would
have been cast out of Cambridge a fortnight before his finals with a first in nothing
but whore-mongering. Though rescued, even Wickham knew when one was disgraced
and made himself scarce when they returned to Pemberley. Master Darcy wisely chose
to take the grand tour with Fitzwilliam.

It was soon after their return that Mr. Darcy took ill. Upon his death, however, George
Wickham was front and centre, hand extended, awaiting what he believed was his due.

Goodwin knew he was hardly the only person who thought ill of George Wickham.
His misadventures had become legend amongst the Pemberley help. As highly as he
held Mr. Darcy's memory, Goodwin could not fully understand why that very astute
man had allowed Wickham latitude others found begging. A deep affection and regard
for Wickham's father, coupled with that man's premature death was the only reason
that Goodwin could fathom. But, of course, Goodwin did not pretend to know of that
which he should not.

When the young master became the Master of Pemberley in actuality, little changed
within the house. Mr. Darcy had been so ill for so long, his son had taken over his
duties with little more than a ripple in the water. Sorrow over their dead master on the
part of the house staff was gradually usurped by dedication to the younger. Indeed,
young Darcy had earned their respect long before he asked for it. As Master Darcy had
matured, his social obligations increased exponentially. Hence, Goodwin's enlarged
commensurably. His world broadened to include any number of illustrious homes, up
to and including the royal palace. If he found himself impressed by his master's station, Goodwin reminded himself, it was, indeed, his master's station, not his own.

As a man in service, Goodwin never questioned. But much to his relief, if Mr. Darcy
did not choose a life of celibate introspection, he was at least discreet in his pursuits and
utterly circumspect in his liaisons. (Other gentleman's gentlemen told tales of debauchery and excess.) That he had not to deal with inebriation and dissolution was a blessing. Unlike some gentlemen, Mr. Darcy expected Goodwin to be neither his shill nor
pimp. He was never asked to carry messages nor deflect injudiciously flirtatious ladies.

As an unmarried man who would expect to remain unmarried, Goodwin was,
however, not unlearnt in matters romantic in nature. That his master was inclined to
be cautious of his own reputation regardless of the provocation, bid Goodwin understand the position he must himself undertake. Relating to Mr. Darcy, no female

enquiry was answered, no invitation acknowledged. What Mr. Darcy chose to honour fell to his own discrimination and volition. No one else would be involved. Mr. Darcy's subtle requests eventually taught Goodwin of his predilections. When to be available and when not was followed precisely. Mr. Darcy was a private man. His wishes were law. All things were stable and predictable.

That is, until the tumultuous year of Mr. Darcy's introduction to Miss Bennet.

A remedy oft proffered to relieve undue anxiety is that of physical exertion. Hence one should have expected Elizabeth Darcy to be post-coitally languid. She was not. Howbeit her body was well-spent, her mind refused to be soothed. For despite Hannah's incessant fussing, Elizabeth was most unhappy with the flowers adorning her coiffure.

Impatiently, she yanked them out, then reconsidered. Without the flowers, she feared she looked plain. With them, she was certain she resembled an overgrown wisteria bush. Even her yellow dress no longer pleased her eye. It not only looked unstudied, it appeared absolutely artless. She gazed unhappily in the mirror and made a half circle. At every turn, it appeared fate destined her for ignominious habiliment.

First impressions were immutable. She wanted Darcy to be proud to present her as his wife to Derbyshire. Yet her circumstance and station would be appraised by her appearance, and not with particular generosity. She longed to look more urbane.

"Do you suppose," she queried Hannah, "I should consider wearing a turban?"

Before Hannah could determine whether that was a jest or not, there came a rap upon the door, the firmness of which announced it was Mr. Darcy. The merest flick of his head sent Hannah upon a curtsying fizzle out of the room. Across the length of the room stood his wife, and thither his gaze rested.

From beneath the veil of her lashes, she turned her eyes to him, and then hastily cast them away. It might have appeared to him a modesty, but it was not. She simply could not bear to see disappointment reflected in his eyes. Hence, she failed to witness his appreciative flush.

"How ravishingly beautiful you look, Lizzy."

Surprised and disconcerted, a grand rubescence graced her cheeks. Her mind groped about for some comment, but she could only think to inquire of how well his posterior weathered their recent indecorous undertakings.

"Pray, did you bruise yourself when we fell?"

"Actually," he said, "I did not think to look."

With that recollection, they stared at each other a long moment. Her flush not only deepened, but also crept down her neck and nestled into her bosom.

"Husband," she said, "you are a devastatingly handsome man."

The only rejoinder he offered was an embarrassed cough. Thereupon, in apparent relief, he remembered why he had come and thrust forward the box he had been concealing behind his back.

"I should like for you to wear this tonight."

She looked up at him and then to the green velvet box, which was tied with an azure satin ribbon. So pretty were the colours, she gave an admiring coo when she looked upon it. That sound continued long after she noticed that the azure satin ribbon was tied in a crude bow, almost disreputable. It was, as it happened, quite odd looking, such a fine box with a ribbon so badly tied.

It came to her then that her husband had tied the ribbon himself. He, a man who always had ribbons tied for his use, tied a bow upon the box for her. She thought that sad little bow was as lovely a gift as she might ever receive. She would prize it always. Her fingertips touched it affectionately, thus it took her a moment to realise he was patiently waiting for her to untie it. She truly hated to disturb it and her reluctant fingers fumbled when she endeavoured to undo the knotted bow.

Retrieving it, he easily opened that which he had himself wrapped and, with a bit of a flourish, held it out to her again.

Lifting the lid, she peered into the box. An elabourate diamond-cascade of a choker glittered within, more exquisite than any necklace she could have ever imagined about anyone's throat (and that included Lady Catherine and probably the Queen). Momentarily speechless, she looked at it, then back to him.

A bit stupidly, she bid, "This is for me?"

"Yes, it is for you," he smiled. "May I have the pleasure of putting it upon you? …You do wish to wear it?"

That he might actually have thought she would not was enormously ingenuous, and she stifled a laugh at such a notion by turning about for him to fasten it. It was heavy and cold against her skin, but the sensation was rather pleasant and the diamonds sparkled brilliantly in the candlelight. He stood behind her as she looked at herself in the looking-glass. Thereupon a possibility occurred to her.

"Was this your mother's?" she asked.

"No," he said, then leaned down and whispered in her ear, "It is yours alone."

In timid appreciation, a flabbergasted smile crept across her face. In light of his reserve, such generosity was overwhelming. She understood forthwith, however, that it was only ostentation that he abhorred. For Mr. Darcy, extravagance was an impossibility.

Touched by the gesture, not the gift, she knew not how to say that without sounding coy. Turning to kiss him, she said as lightly as she could manage, "I am now free to commit any indecorum. My countenance, my gown, all will be forgot. No one will recall anything of me but this necklace."

He looked then upon her with such silent intensity, she began to believe her response was not emphatically grateful enough. She considered additional plaudits. Her consideration was not only interrupted, it was severed irreparably when he abruptly grasped her beneath the armpits and plopped her atop her dressing table.

"However impolitic it is to contradict one's wife, I must disagree, Lizzy."

Jarred by this unceremonious act, she was fleetingly stunned. It fell apparent immediately, however, that the reason he had perpetrated such a manoeuvre was to overcome her height disadvantage whilst he ran his hands up the back of her legs and kissed her neck. She was uncertain if it was the stroking of her thighs or the kissing, but for whatever reason her neck refused to hold up her head. Thus, it dropped uselessly to his chest. Had her voice not been strangled within the flaccidity of throat, she would have spoken. In the silence, he did instead.

"Lizzy."

He said it only once, but he said it huskily. That singular calling of her name disturbed the very depth of her being, and though she truly did not mean to moan, she did.

That announcement of her passion granted him every liberty. Hence, from that precarious perch she found herself at the mercy of a husband in full cry, the entire appetency of which he did not withhold. Further foreplay an irrelevance, he simply thrust into her with all the considerable insistence and dedication of a pile driver. She could do nothing but cling to his neck and pray he did not lose his grip upon her lest she be cast to the floor once again.

With a gasp, he convulsed into her. He stood pressed against her for a moment heaving breathlessly. Then, he hoarsely bade her do the unlikely.

"Pray, do not bathe. Do not cleanse yourself."

She nodded. He still held her close, his breath hot against her ear.

"Every time I look upon you tonight, I want not only to know my seed is in you," his lips grazed her hair as he whispered, "I want to know you feel it running down your legs."

He kissed her hard upon the mouth, withdrew, then took leave of the room.

Dazed, she slid to her feet and stood leaning against the table for some few minutes mutely looking at the door that had closed behind him. Hannah's return broke her trance and she hastily turned away.

Whilst Hannah busied herself, Elizabeth was able to lift her eyes and look at her dishevelled appearance in the mirror. She made a feeble attempt to repair her hair, but her arms were too heavy to hold aloft. Thus, she gave it up and just stood looking at her own reflection. It was apparent Hannah would have to repress her gown.

Calling to her to help unbutton it, she looked again into the mirror. Disguising the flush upon her cheeks would be a problem.

Not to mention what a sticky business dancing would be.

Georgiana had returned to Pemberley for the ball and stood in the entry with Darcy and Elizabeth to greet their guests. Elizabeth smiled and nodded happily when she first espied her powdered and bejeweled, for she wore a pretty, pink gown that complimented her complexion. Georgiana smiled demurely, clearly pleased at her sister-in-law's approval. But when Elizabeth glanced at the handsome necklace Georgiana wore, she was mortified to see her own transcended Miss Darcy's twofold.

Indeed, that must have been Darcy's intent, for he did nothing that was not well-considered. She understood that his gift was for her, but realised, too, it was meant to send a message to the society that greeted her: "This is my wife."

(She surmised the other gift he left her, the one she was now quite aware of beneath her newly pressed gown as it progressed down her legs, must have meant, "*You* are my wife.")

Her presumption of curiosity from Derbyshire's finest was not a miscalculation. She knew there had to be a great deal of gossip about her connexions, undoubtedly fuelled by Darcy's aunt, Lady Catherine de Bourg. That lady's chief occupation now seemed to be that of making it clear to all and sundry that she had not and would not contain her displeasure at the match.

Ignoring such rencontre, Darcy made the introductions to his wife, allowing Elizabeth to understand which families were friends to Pemberley and thus to them. The Lord and Lady Millhouse, the Ducketts, the Allenbys. Nodding to each, they were introduced not only by name, but also by estate. Pennyswope, Greygable, Keenlysyde Manor.

However, when the family Howgrave stood before them, Elizabeth thought it peculiar that Darcy introduced only the husband and wife and not the young man with them, for it was apparent he knew him. Nevertheless, Darcy held an air of decided disapproval (the one he had mastered so well, owing to a great deal of practise) and the family moved hastily on when no attempt at pleasantries was made. Elizabeth saw the young man look over his shoulder at them as they walked on. Knowing if she turned and asked about them immediately, she would announce herself a gossip, Elizabeth could not help but do just that.

"Who was that young man?"

Darcy did not say anything immediately, as if to weigh his words.

When he chose them, he said, "The young man is Mr. Howgrave's son by his late housekeeper."

"He married his housekeeper?"

No wonder Darcy's disapproval.

"No, he did not."

Her lips formed the word "oh," but she did not make the sound. Far too hastily, the next guests approached. The many questions Elizabeth would have liked to ask her husband about the odd circumstance of the Howgraves were set temporarily at rest for before them stood Mrs. Dalrymple and her nephew. The lady was of a certain age and had a forefront whose gravity defied her corset (her breasts were so pendulous, had they been prehensile they might well have been useful). The young man, a Horace Chombly, employed a manner of dress that paid compliment to rather undeniable foppery and did little to disguise that he suffered a decided curvature of the spine. Together, they presented quite a sight.

Mrs. Dalrymple announced herself, "A dear friend of Lady Catherine's."

Even so, Elizabeth would not have taken half such delight at making note of the quite unbelievably broad backside of the Dowager Dalrymple as she waddled away, had not the good lady taken out her monocle and with a slight (though audible) snort, so openly inspected Elizabeth's person.

"I hope her report to her good friend, your aunt, is appropriately wanting of my appeal," Elizabeth asided, "for her escort does not lend her any generosity of taste."

Very nearly sniggering, Darcy agreed, "The good lady, I fear, has a finer estate and more worthless relatives than anyone else who comes to mind."

As time and the reception line wore on, Elizabeth found a great deal of amusement in gauging the time a lady (and indeed, invariably it was a lady) was introduced to her before that lady's gaze dropped to the choker about her neck. Never having any particular interest in gems nor the bejeweled herself, she noticed some women more subtle than others at appraising it. But the sight apparently struck one poor woman senseless. With any number of faces straining to see why the reception line was at a standstill, this lady appeared to be taking a carat count of the diamonds in her hostess's necklace.

In want of hurrying her, Elizabeth charitably leaned forward slightly and tilted up her chin to present a better look. It was then that she observed a frown cross Darcy's face and feared he thought her too frank with the woman. But when the lady moved on, Darcy's distaste left as well. It occurred to Elizabeth that her husband wanted his society to make as good an impression upon his wife as she did upon it.

Hitherto, the most extravagant ball Elizabeth had attended had been at Bingley's estate, Netherfield. She had then, most incorrectly, thought nothing could surpass it for elegance. Pemberley unadorned was unbelievably impressive. Pemberley in want of a ball was indescribably sumptuous.

The foyer alone was as large as many ballrooms and festooned to the hilt. The grandeur of the floral arrangements and the beauty of the decorations were far beyond even her fertile imagination. A seventeen-piece orchestra's overture announced the first dance, and Darcy took Elizabeth's gloved hand and led her to the dance floor for the first quadrille. The spontaneous applause was quite unexpected by Elizabeth, but was no surprise to her husband.

Such gestures of respect were to be presumed. Of course, their guests would applaud the first dance by the master and new mistress of Pemberley. From the first time he asked her to dance (or rather the first time she accepted) she had been very aware of the homage paid to her as his partner. The air of deference then was absolutely palpable. Unnerved to be the focus of such singular attention, Elizabeth was happy not to be forced to display a dancing form that stretched her capabilities. For her husband was the dancer she remembered. Graceful, but far too reserved to be called particular.

As the evening aged, the deference did not wane. Thus, Elizabeth began to see more clearly than she had ever before why Darcy had held himself in so proud and disdainful a manner as he had, for he had known no other life than one of opulent deference. Master of Pemberley was far more magnificent than any other station she could have imagined.

The vastness of the crowd precluded any intimacy betwixt them beyond an inconspicuous holding of hands. That chance alone was enough to keep Elizabeth near to her husband, but that he ran his thumb across her knuckles whilst they did was added inducement. When she was not at his side, giddy as a schoolgirl, she searched the room for sight of him. For her reward was sweet. Inevitably, as he had before they married, he would be looking upon her as well.

One of the greatest delights the evening held for her was the pleasure of seeing her husband take her Aunt Gardiner's hand and lead her out onto the floor. Her aunt, for all her life, had admired Pemberley from afar, and to see such a deserving lady honoured in such a manner was a true delight.

In her right as hostess, Elizabeth danced twice with Bingley, although he was kept quite busy chasing down dance partners for both his sisters and Jane's like coursing hares. Darcy even stood up with Maria Lucas. That her husband bespoke a dance with one who was neither an in-law nor of his station demonstrated that, now safely married, he had not forsaken his new-found (if only by a few degrees) humility.

Indeed, he danced more than society at large had ever known of him. He stood up not only with Jane (not at all a punishment for him), but also Kitty (who was). Although Fitzwilliam bespoke a dance with Elizabeth, he honoured Kitty and Maria once each as well. If it was thought particularly kind of Darcy for favouring Kitty and Maria with a dance, of Fitzwilliam it was not. His propitious temperament instructed him to choose a partner not by rank, but to avail himself as a single man to those most slighted. It was upon the conclusion of their dance when Elizabeth remarked upon that to him.

"Colonel, for a man who has little volition in whom he marries, you could serve yourself better by selecting your dancing partner by fortune rather than need. I believe the reverse is good enough for lesser young men."

Elizabeth was unafraid her comment was overly frank, for Fitzwilliam had often addressed his misfortune of being a second son. She was not unwitting that his prospects were limited to how well he married. Thus, her observation was a compliment, not a criticism. In recognition of that, he bowed formally. As he did, Elizabeth admired both his grace and goodness. Fervently, she wished Kitty were older. Less flighty. Not so silly. Possessed of a fortune. Colonel Fitzwilliam would be a kind and agreeable husband.

Elizabeth's little matchmaking reverie was interrupted by espying Jane, hence she forsook Fitzwilliam's company. In the tumult of travel and preparations, Elizabeth had scarcely had time to exchange words with her aunt or Jane. However, no sooner did the new Mrs. Darcy and the new Mrs. Bingley converge than they were besieged by a bevy of veteran wives, who, weary of their own company, had awaited opportunity to take the novices in as members of their privileged tribe.

Their initiation was inaugurated by the time-honoured tradition of exchanging articles of mostly unfounded news. Although gossip in and of itself was not unknown to Elizabeth and Jane, they were taken aback by the level of intrigue they had become privy to by reason of their elevation to wifedom.

One lady, pursy either from dancing, her corpulence, or the lascivious nature of her information, told the newly devirginated sisters that her middle-aged houseman evidently held dual duty as husband to their cook and lover to the second floor chambermaid. Perhaps incredulousness crossed Elizabeth's countenance when this information was proffered, for the lady offered a hasty reassurance.

"There have been no children by either encounter."

Not actually having leapt to that enquiry, Elizabeth could find no other comment than, "I see."

Upon this declaration, Elizabeth looked at Jane. Her eyes, not surprisingly, had widened to a precipitous degree. (Their office of maiden so recently discarded, it was clear they would both have to practise a more inscrutable expression.)

Elizabeth's own jaw very nearly rested upon the floor when further discussion disclosed that a lady, unrepresented in the conversing group, had barely found enthusiasm to attend the ball, so dissipated was she by the birthing of her ninth offspring. The happenstance of her predicament was not without sympathetic voice.

"I should think she might consider locking the door to her bedroom."

"Yes, if she is to find any peace at all."

Immediate upon this postulation, it was offered (behind the back of a hand) that the oft-engaged woman's husband had also impregnated any number of their servants.

A chorus of "tsks, tsks" was accorded. (It seemed that particular house's chief evil was fecundity.)

"And she has no idea it was her husband who had handled the maids?" asked one woman.

"He told her it was the gardener! That poor man suffered cruelly from the wife's displeasure, for the lord would not allow the man let go."

"And lose the seducer of record? Never!"

Tittering all about.

Much to Elizabeth's bemused disappointment, this conversation was quieted, for "maidens" approached their group (and maiden ears must be protected at all costs). As Mrs. Hurst and the maidens, Georgiana Darcy and Caroline Bingley, joined them, talk immediately turned to the more universally benign topics of matches and matrimony.

Miss Bingley, in her unceasing promotion of herself, said she understood that a baronet attended that night. Titles always piqued Caroline's interest, but it was the information that the baronet was two years into widowerhood that propelled him from diversion into outright quarry. Indisputably, such a man was in want of a wife. Thus, Caroline bade him pointed out to her.

"I dare say you could not do better if dullness is the true proprietor of distinction," declared a firm voice from the edge of the group.

Lady Winifred Millhouse had stood inconspicuously amidst them until she broke her silence with that observation. Caroline looked as if she wanted to huff, but apparently thought better of it.

Candidly, Elizabeth soon determined, was the only way Lady Millhouse knew how to speak. Of Derbyshire society in general, and Pemberley friends more specifically, Elizabeth thought she would like the Millhouses. The lord was interested in little but riding to hunt. His lady, a sturdy woman of middle age whose demeanour said she did not suffer fools gladly, was similarly inclined. As Elizabeth found considerable amusement in her remark about the baronet, Lady Millhouse clearly approved of her. Ignoring Caroline's petulance, she addressed the only issue of any import to her by asking Elizabeth when they would next ride to hounds at Pemberley.

"I fancy my husband would be the one to answer that question," Elizabeth told her.

Lady Millhouse found this not only a reasonable response, but a perfectly good excuse to leave the little enclave of prattlers. She abruptly took hold of Elizabeth's hand and set out to find good Mr. Darcy and inquire. They ventured not far before spying him talking amongst a group of gentlemen. Elizabeth would never have dared walk the distance of the room to join them. But Lady Millhouse's grip upon her was tenacious and she had little choice but to follow in her wake as she parted the crowd.

Darcy did not seem confounded that Lady Millhouse suddenly appeared in the midst of the coterie of men, nor that his wife was in tow.

"Darcy," Lady Millhouse said, forgoing Elizabeth's arm for his, "you have not told your sweet wife here when we will next have a hunt at Pemberley? Shame upon you. We must remedy this situation at once."

"We will within the month. I will send my cards around directly, Lady Millhouse."

As he spoke, he bore an expression of amusement that astonished Elizabeth. Lady Millhouse obviously had a position of friendship with Darcy that did not require the level of obsequious decorum of others. Quite probably, the lady was unlikely to offer it. This liberty was certainly not due to her station. Elizabeth surmised it something more significant. Indeed, Lady Millhouse enthusiastically took the reins of the conversation in a pertinacious detailing of their most recent ride to covert. Darcy seemed amused at this as well. But as the story became increasingly lengthy and convoluted, Elizabeth let her attention wander to the doings of the other guests.

The son of Mr. Howgrave's housekeeper passed by. Surreptitiously, Elizabeth watched him cross the floor. Darcy, who she had thought was in rapt attention to Mrs. Millhouse's recitation glanced at, then affixed a rancorous glare upon young Howgrave as he stopped before Georgiana. He spoke to her but a moment, then moved away. Upon his retreat, Darcy apparently quitted him as well.

Forthwith of the overture to the next promenade, Howgrave returned to Georgiana, apparently having bespoken the next dance. Obviously, Darcy had not quite let the young man out of his eye. For by the time Howgrave returned to claim his dance, Darcy had stridden halfway across the floor toward them.

Lady Millhouse stopped mid-sentence at the distraction. She looked at Elizabeth quizzically. Then they both watched Darcy as he advanced upon the couple. He spoke to his sister, took her hand, and walked her onto the dance floor, leaving young Howgrave standing rather flatfooted. The cut was not unapparent to the guests nearest, and even from a distance, Elizabeth could see the young man's face redden. That the young man's history was known to Lady Millhouse was betrayed when she spoke, not of him, but of Darcy, for there was the drama.

"Because he has never forgiven himself any fault, he can forgive no one else's," she sighed.

The remark was bestowed with affectionate understanding from someone who knew Darcy well. That the observation rode with such accuracy upon him made it all the more unsettling for his wife to hear. She had little time to ponder it, for just then Lord Millhouse took her attention, perhaps at his wife's silent instruction, and asked Elizabeth to dance. Of this she was most grateful, happy to have reason to move about. The air had suddenly become a little stale where she stood.

After a rowdy gallop across the dance floor with the blustery Lord Millhouse, Elizabeth excused herself to catch her breath in a corner of the room. From her vantage she could gaze upon her husband, who had bade Jane to dance again. It was a pleasant inevitability to know Bingley would seek her out in polite return; still she endeavoured to hide herself. This, only partly because she chose not to dance, but foremost because she did not want to have to beg off from sweet-tempered Bingley. Her earlier unease forgotten, she wanted to savour the sight of her husband from afar.

It was obvious the ladies of Derbyshire thought likewise. For of the female gazes that followed him (and there were many), all did not merely betoken respectful admiration of rank. Indeed, a few looks were positively unchaste. Elizabeth did not fault their acumen, for they were more sensible than she had been. It was she who, upon first meeting him, had concluded that a man of such beauty and wealth must, of course, harbour some ill-trait of character. She laughed at her own prejudice. For now that he was her Darcy, she knew him to be quite perfect.

The theatrical whisper of one who wanted to be heard broke her solitude. A woman's voice rose from the other side of a fan leaf palm. Elizabeth peered between the leaves and spied two women, one whose years had abused the better part of four decades, the other younger and a bit squat.

"Why, 'tis so good to have our Mr. Darcy back in Derbyshire, for he has been sorely missed."

Elizabeth recognised neither of them. That they knew who she was, and where she was, was of little doubt.

"Yes, manhood has suffered in his absence. Sport is never so attractive without him in the county. He has such strength of leg, he can stay a-mount long after lesser men fade."

They tittered behind their fans. The younger doxy closed hers and tapped her friend with it upon the shoulder whilst applying further euphemistic grandiloquence.

"He has a most impressive blade and knows quite well how to wield it!"

Taken with their own wit, they tittered again not unlike two exceedingly rude magpies. Elizabeth's face burned with indignation. How to respond? The Mistress of Pemberley should not acknowledge such defamatory utterances, she reminded herself. She would sacrifice her spirit to propriety and suffer, as those two vilifying…trollops undoubtedly knew she must. This most considered and correct decision made, she immediately cast it aside. She did not walk away but took one step that brought her purposely under the women's immediate gazes, which, if they were not quite at a level of alarm, at least spoke high alert.

Elizabeth saw she had chosen correctly. Clearly, the women did not expect confrontation from a naïve country lass. As she looked at first one and then the other, she summarily determined they both had more hair than sense. And, obviously, they had more sense than integrity.

Hence, it bedevilled Elizabeth not one dash to quietly, but quite deliberately, say, "I could not help but overhear your kind words about Mr. Darcy. You shall, no doubt, agree I am most fortunate to have so magnificent a lover for a husband."

She smiled brilliantly, turned, and walked away. That the two women's countenances held at first confusion then confounded incredulity, was not known to her. But as she strode off, she pictured it, and found considerable pleasure in the imagining alone.

Not surprising of such a grand evening, it was quite late when the last of the guests had betaken themselves home, allowing Elizabeth and Darcy wearily to ascend the stairs. They entered their bedchamber together, finally alone, but still dressed from the evening. Falling in fatigue back across their bed, she listened as he told her how well the evening had gone and how many remarks were made to him upon the beauty of his wife's countenance and amiability of her nature.

"I would think it unlikely for any of your guests to offer that they found your new wife held much queerness of temper and little pretension to beauty," she reminded him.

"Of course not. But one would have to have a great understanding of, say, Mr. Collins's ability to flatter to invent such compliments."

She laughed. "Yes, your guests will say the music was superb, the decorations outstanding. The only criticism one shall offer is that nothing scandalous occurred. No one fell drunkenly into the punch bowl; no young man's face was slapped. For that is the only true way to gauge an evening's success." (That his wife spoke without caution to the two female guests might have met the criteria of scandalous, but Elizabeth discounted it by reason of an audience of only two.)

"You were charming and beautiful tonight, Lizzy. I would not have cared were you neither, but imagine what pride I hold that you were both."

Their dressing rooms were forgone for the immediacy of their bed. They simply dropped their clothes where they stood and climbed beneath the bedclothes. There had been an initial spoon, but when his lack of dedication was announced by a soft snore, Elizabeth did not have the heart to awaken him. She drew his arm about her and snuggled against his chest.

It occurred to her that it was the first time since they married that they had not ended their day with amorous union. They had, of course, already made love twice that evening before the ball (well, they had made love the first time; she was uncertain exactly how to label the second, it possibly just an anointment). It was unreasonably avaricious to want him again, especially if only in defence of her own disorder.

For, as much as she did not like to admit it to herself, she was unsettled when she remembered the two loose-lipped hildings who spoke so crudely. Although they had spoken as if they had first-person knowledge, Elizabeth could not imagine Darcy cavorting with such vulgar pieces of work. True, he was eight years her senior. It was possible (alright, even probable) that he had been with other women. She supposed as well that was one to cavort it would have to be in less than virtuous company.

But it was easier to accept that in Hertfordshire, where he was newly in society. Derbyshire was another matter entirely. As she considered that he had spent at least a dozen years in his county as an eligible young man, every female face under age fifty that she had greeted that night revisited her. Suddenly, they were not just amiable guests, they were all former lovers.

"He knows how to use his blade."

That was what the woman had said. Yes, Elizabeth thought, he does know how to use his blade.

Providentially, he drew her closer and said quite clearly, "I love you, Lizzy."

Even in his sleep he knew what she needed from him. At that particular moment, no carnal act could possibly have allowed her to fall into so peaceful a slumber.

Their having unfurled the drapes to admire the moonlight the past evening allowed the morning sun to awaken Mr. Darcy prematurely.

For a man basking in the glow of unprecedented self-approbation, he did not suffer the abuse of nature without indignation. However, this *lèse-majesté* was mitigated by a single slash of sunlight which cast a milky glow upon his wife's bare back. He propped himself up on one elbow and gazed upon her form at some length.

Hours spent in restful sleep had not undone his self-satisfaction with the sublime success of the ball nor his wife's part in that success. Both had been triumphs. It was clear that all of Derbyshire had fallen under the spell of his wife's considerable charm. Those who dared to fault him for selecting a bride of questionable connexions had been silenced unequivocally. With Elizabeth now his wife, the pride he harboured as the Darcy heir, the master of an illustrious estate, and his station in general had ripened into unadulterated omnipotence. It was a most ambrosial sensation. One he wanted to share.

Drawing his fingers lightly down her spine, he tempted her awake. She responded to this intrusion by the Master of Pemberley by intolerantly drawing the covers over her shoulders. Undaunted, he loosened the sheet and trailed his fingers down her back again. She turned over, blinking in the bright morning light, and espying him looking down at her, smiled sleepily. At the sight of her so fetchingly in the altogether, his morning pride flowered into outright arousal.

He had seen her, of course, but gained no true inspection. In the pristine morning light, it was not an inquisition of her configuration he sought (for he had, upon a few occasions long past, perused a womanly portal). He wanted to memorise his Elizabeth. When he closed his eyes, he wanted to be able to bring every pore of her skin to mind, let her scent invade his nostrils so no distance could ever take her truly from him.

She acquiesced to his investigation a bit self-consciously, dovetailing her knees in futile protection of her modesty. He stroked her thighs at length with the backs of his fingers, thus convincing them to relinquish their sentry. Eventually, she lay back, eyes closed, entrusting herself unto him.

This presented him with a struggling conscience. Although he had kissed her womanhood before, it was only fleetingly. He longed not only to fill his nostrils with her scent; he wanted to saturate his mouth with her taste. Thusly, he would bring her to an ecstasy she had hitherto not experienced. However, would such a lascivious letch scandalise her? In the afterglow of a truly magnificent societal victory, he believed the time to test those waters was at hand. He dove in—so to speak.

She might have been a bit startled, but she betokened no alarm. In time, however, a sound escaped her throat that was quite unmelodious. Had she not entwined her fingers so fiercely into his hair, he might have heard her moan. As it was, he did not. Nevertheless, when the arching of her back announced that she was upon the precipice of an ecstasy yet unexplored, his loins would not let her experience it alone. Hence, this union was enjoyed with such unconditional vigour, it may well have endangered the groundsels supporting the house.

Quite foredone by passion, they lay in a sweating heap, she still clutching his hair. Not a bother, for her tenacious hold was proof this success exceeded that of the ball by some measure. That satisfaction was exquisite.

Bedewed by the maelstrom she had just experienced, she lay back to give them both a chance to catch their breath. He reached out and brushed the sweaty curls back from her face, anxious to hear her words of wonder at the pleasure he had bestowed upon her. He was not to be disappointed, for when she turned and looked at him, it was in absolute veneration.

"Pray, what did you do?"

For her to be awe-struck was his intention. To incite her to question him was not. Allowing that it appeared, indeed, she did expect an explanation, he decided it best to take an academic route.

"There is a Latin name for it."

He winced ever so slightly as he spoke the words, knowing that alone would not satisfy her. She was one of the most confoundingly curious creatures he had ever known. This was one of her quirks of character he most treasured. Odd, he thought, that he liked to speak so little, yet loved a woman who bade him speak so much.

She put her forehead against his and stroked his face, smiling at the brevity of his elucidation.

"Do not speak to me of Latin," she bid playfully. "Where ever did you learn of such a proceeding? Certainly not at Cambridge."

Forthwith, her smile evaporated, but her gaze held his an uncomfortably long time. All the while, his mind searched for an answer that would be both true and painless. He, however, could not find one. He was keenly aware that his silence confessed more compromising skeletons in his romantic past than any act he could have related.

During his extended silence, her chin began a barely discernible quiver, perhaps to accompany the tears that had begun to well up in her eyes. Blessedly for him, she looked away.

She whispered, "Of course."

"Of course," she repeated more firmly. "I fancy my testimony should be added to the others who indubitably can attest to the perfection of your technique."

Thereupon, she sat up on the side of the bed, drawing the counterpane protectively to her bosom.

"Lizzy," he said, sitting up next to her. "Lizzy?"

Looking only at the path of sunlight that crossed the floor, she announced, "How foolish of me."

He thought it perhaps best not to ask, but could not help himself, "Foolish?"

She laughed a curt, mirthless laugh, "I have always believed you a worldly man and that you might have 'known' other women. Foolishly, I chose to believe it only a possibility—possible, of course, being much easier to bear than absolutely. Had I come to you in full acceptance of that as fact, I should have been much kinder to myself…"

Not wanting to hear more, he lay back upon the bed and considered, then rejected (only with utmost discipline) the notion of hiding his mortified face with a pillow. She found her gown and drew it on, tying the sash with quick, ill-tempered little motions. Then, she flipped her hair from beneath the collar and stalked out of the room. He did not for a moment think that she did not finish her thought because she believed he did not want to hear it. She did not because she could not bear to say it. Not only had he rendered the possible to her a certainty, he had demonstrated it. Explicitly.

He lay there for some time, pondering whereby he had transfigured from omniscient to dolt in such an expeditious fashion. When the route was fully determined, he pondered the matter still.

Foolish, she called herself. It was he, not she, who was foolish. The single thing he had told her of his past connexions was that he had never loved another. Perhaps that was because that was the only absolute to which he could avow. He had the considerable ingenuousness to believe that was he not to initiate her too hurriedly into the various rites of love, it would seem as if they had uncovered these acts together.

'Twas a folly, but he had come to believe that her unconditional trust had somehow allowed him a retrieval of his own innocence. He had never made love with the abandon they shared (in his wonderment, he had, upon a few occasions, come perilously close to declaring that to her). The passion he ignited in her and the new heights he found in his own, all too easily exposed him to this serious misstep of over-ambition. He had to admit conceit was his undoing.

In his zeal to satisfy her, he had convinced himself he was compleatly selfless. Of course, he was not. His pleasures had been of a duality. The lovemaking itself, of course, but perhaps most enjoyable were the looks and words of adoration she gave him each time they reached achievement. Those punctuated by her smile were of peculiar satisfaction. Precisely like the one she had just gifted him.

That is, the one she had gifted immediately preceding her realisation of just how limited in spontaneity his act had been. (It did not help his conscience that, if memory served, the last time he had done that to a woman, she had used almost the exact words as Elizabeth, but then it had not been a criticism.) Quite despairingly, he begged himself only to remember how Elizabeth had smiled at him, but that memory was now ever besmirched by the chapfallen expression that had replaced it. How could he have believed that she would always be insensible to his previous...connexions? Did he think it possible that she would never suspect? That she would never ask? Foolishly, he too had hoped for a possibility rather than the truth.

Sitting up, he decided then he would go to her and beg forgiveness. Hurriedly, he endeavoured to compose his speech of apology. This employment, however, was not profitable in that he could not specifically determine for what he should apologise.

Should he admit contrition that he had been with other women? He wished then that he had not. However, all such connexions were before they had been introduced, hence, it was not truly an offence against her. Should he apologise that he had not confessed it? He still believed such an admittance from a man who considers himself a gentleman was unconscionable. He could explain that he had succumbed to lust rather than love, but, however true, he was disposed to think that would be of no particular comfort to her. (Nor did he fancy she would favour knowing he had bowed upon the altar of Eros with indefensible frequency and with so many different women.) A recapitulation of his amorous exploits sounded, even to him, uncommonly more debauched than he knew them to have been.

His contrition and regret, however, were compleat in having caused her to suffer. Any carnal pleasure he had ever received he would gladly have relinquished not to witness the look of hurt upon her countenance. Indeed, just then the vision of himself in monk's robes was not unobjectionable.

He was truly penitent. He did not know how he would find the words of consolation, but he knew he must try. If her trust were lost, little else would matter.

Gathering himself from the bed, he walked to her dressing room door and knocked
soundly. Elizabeth did not answer it, Hannah did. An expression of astonishment overspread her face. It was only when the maid took her leave with no undue haste, that he
realised her surprise stemmed less from his appearing at his wife's dressing room door,
than his want of appearance. He was naked as a babe save the bedcloth wrapped about
his waist (grateful was he that he had the presence of mind to reach for that).

Elizabeth sat in her bathtub facing away from him. Undoubtedly she heard him
enter but did not turn, she simply continued scrubbing her arms. She did so with such
dutiful concentration, it suggested that she felt herself somehow befouled. His eyes
dropped briefly from the sight, for that was more painful than her refusal to acknowledge him there. He was induced by her inattention to perch upon the edge of a small
chest, whereupon, he gazed at her purposely oblivious back.

Steeling his resolve, but still not knowing what he would say until he said it, he
finally spoke, "Had I thought for a moment it would have benefited you, I should have
confessed my ignominious past and thrown myself at your feet for forgiveness. However, as any women I have known meant nothing to me, I thought they would mean
nothing to you. Wrongly, I now see."

He paused, looking for a sign that his words were reaching her.

Finding none whatsoever, he then strove on, "I might have lived differently had I
known one day I would find you. If you believe nothing else, please believe my life
only began when we met. Your censure is unendurable."

As he fell silent, she did not speak, but ceased her ablutions.

In a moment, she said, "I thought myself a fool, and fatuous I have been. However,
never so foolish as today. It was absurd of me to reproach you for my own ignorance."

"No. You should reproach me. I took love before. It was not until I met you that I
gave love."

The generous honesty of that statement moved her to turn to look at him. The sincerity of his expression was undermined by the incongruity of the bedcloth he had
tied about his middle. She rose, knee deep in water, bits of suds clinging to her body.

"Can you find forgiveness for me?" she asked.

A little line of froth collected upon the tip of one breast and sat there, momentarily suspended. Had his forgiveness ever been in question, those few foamy droplets
would have ensured it. Nevertheless, as his was the most grievous trespass, he did not
have to question himself for the crux of his absolution of her.

When he rose to go to her to assure her she was very much forgiven, he tossed a
trailing end of the sheet over his left shoulder.

"Hail, Caesar," she announced.

"Which one?"

"The most handsome."

Caesar's toga fell away with her single tug, whereupon he stepped into her bath water.
Teasingly, she said, "You are only repaying my intrusion into your bath, are you not?"

"I am not. I simply have never been in a lady's bath before. Yours looks inviting."

"I am the first?"

"You are the first."

Thereupon ensued any number of professions and demonstrations of Mr. Darcy's love of his wife, and Elizabeth enjoyed them all.

After careful deliberation, she was inclined to believe that it was much better to bask in the pleasure of his experience rather than question it. For his part, Darcy learnt that smugness was never a virtue.

What he believed to be a particularly harmonious denouement to a particularly sticky subject was not yet at hand. Fortune had not allowed her to forget the two simpering chattermags remarking upon his "blade" at the ball. Once the fact of Mr. Darcy's encounters was unkenneled, specifics seemed fair game to his wife. It took not a day before she made a frontal assault.

"Am I to be advised of whose charms you have known?"

"No."

"I know 'tis ungentlemanly to repeat such things, but certainly you can understand I choose not to sit next to a lady of your intimate acquaintance at a dinner party quite unenlightened. If I am to be thought a fool, I prefer my own confidence."

He knew well he was again entering *territoire dangereux*, for she had an uncanny ability to winnow information from him that he knew he did not wish to confide. Independent decision of what it best to reveal and what not to inevitably fell to naught.

"I would never invest in such a conspiracy against you," he assured her. "I would never allow you to find yourself in such a position."

As he said this, he took a mental inventory of the guest list of the ball to reassure himself he was speaking truthfully. Once absolutely certain of that, he sighed in silent relief and vowed to himself what he had promised Elizabeth. Because he had so naïvely expected this moment not to come, he had no plan. However, he recognised the foundation when he saw it. With all due diligence, he would make quite certain that no woman whom he had "known" would be invited to their home. (Not a problem in Derbyshire, but London might be a bit of a dilemma. Diversions abounded; he could account for his own guest lists, but not that of others.)

Thinking the matter at last closed, he shut his eyes as well. They stayed resolutely thus, however she inveigled him.

"I would not ask you to name names—that would be insupportable," she persisted. "Perhaps you could tell me how many."

"I could not do that," he announced rather snippily.

"That frightfully many?"

"That is not my meaning," he declared in exasperation. "I should have said, 'I choose not to say.'"

"Less than five?"

As this interrogation took place atop their bed, he rolled upon his stomach and, in vain hope it would impede her, finally did draw a pillow over his head. Alas.

"More than five, but less than ten?"

The pillow groaned.

She pulled up a corner and said under it, "I am full curious is all."

Her words elicited another groan from her encased husband. Quite abruptly, her manner changed from playful to astonished. Releasing the entreated pillow compleatly, she uttered the unspeakable thought that had just come to her.

"You had a mistress!"

In his pillowed cave, he was trying most determinedly not to listen, but he heard that. She laid back, her arms folded across her stomach in apparent readiness to accept this undeniable and painful truth. Detecting something even more amiss, he pulled the pillow from his head and looked to her. Again, she did not return his gaze.

Unhappily, he understood this must be addressed. He would rather say "more than five" than have her think he had kept a woman—and he most decidedly did not want to say "more than five."

"I did not have a mistress."

"You no longer have to shield me. I am not compleatly naïve. I know men have mistresses. What is the word? *Inamorata?* I understand they wear a great deal of rouge."

Repeating again, with uncommon firmness, "I did not have a mistress," he managed to encroach upon her self-martyrdom.

Elizabeth had already conjured a picture of the fancied mistress in her mind, flaxen-haired, rouged, and buxom. Her imagination had endowed this mistress with every disreputable quality one woman could possibly entertain; hence she was reluctant to abandon the idea. Nevertheless, she soon did, finding more happiness in it not being true than pleasure in assigning the nonexistent mistress poor habits.

Offering her logic for examination, she said, "You said you favoured no women of our acquaintance. What other conclusion could one draw?"

Knowing just how deep and wide the tide-pool of opportunity for carnal embrace was, he thought it best not to share that information with her just then. He chose his words with extreme caution.

"If you know men have mistresses, you must know too that there are houses where men go that harbour women with whom to...(he struggled for a non-active verb)...associate." (Not entirely inactive, but benign.)

She sat up.

He cringed.

"A house? You mean a brothel?" she asked.

"Of sorts."

Now, thoroughly fascinated, she exclaimed, "You visited a brothel?"

Her exclamation, however, he interpreted as contemptuous.

"What would you have had me do?" he responded sharply. "Deflower shop girls as did Wickham?"

At this, she retreated in confused surprise (thus sparing him the retorted detestable suggestion that he could have remained chaste until marriage). Upon understanding his interpretation of her remark, she hurried her reassurance.

"I did not speak to reprimand you, but in amazement. For I have heard of such places."

Although he had a sudden, horrifying vision of Elizabeth scurrying about a bawdy-house, asking all manner of questions about the goings-on there, he was chastened. He realised his outburst was not a result of her remark, but due to his long-held contrition for not keeping his baser needs under better regulation. He had exposed this flaw to the very person whose admiration he most desired. Upon this internal revelation, his countenance reflected repentance. Discerning this, she drew to him.

In eager confidentiality, she bade, "Were there harem girls?"

"Just where have you learnt of harem girls and brothels, pray tell?"

Avoiding his gaze, she made great work of picking imaginary lint from the bedcloth.

"My father had a book, actually two books, he thought well-hidden in his library. One had illustrations. I was but a girl of no more than four and ten when I discovered them."

"Illustrations too?" he smiled, thinking of her surreptitiously reading her father's risqué books.

Thereupon he admitted, "This place was not so exotic."

Not really wanting to think much more of Darcy mingling intimately with the English incarnation of harem girls, she teased him, "So you did not deflower any shop girls?"

"No, I did not. The only woman I have deflowered is you, Mrs. Darcy."

She thought of herself as deflowered for a moment and did not find favour in the term. Then she wondered about the entire devirgination process.

"What are men called after their first act of love, husband?"

"Spent."

At this, she laughed, deciding she had questioned him enough for one sitting. So little did she like him to have gone to such a place, yet she wanted to know it all. However, she knew it unwise to over use her "wheedle." She had the notion that this "house" he visited must be in town. They would leave for London after Easter.

Darcy would learn by spring he was not yet out of the woods of enquiry upon this subject.

For those royal and those not, clearly the least hazardous way out of France was the sea (the Pyrenees were not insurmountable, but they were a bit forbidding). From thence, the nearest port was in England. Forthwith of wriggling from beneath the besotted Lord High Executioner, Juliette Clisson fled.

She fled Paris and she fled France.

Tying the symbolic *le ruban rouge* about her neck, thus announcing what she had escaped, she took the most expeditious route to self-preservation. She came to London amongst the hoards of French *émigrés* whom, if they had left the means behind as they ran for their lives, still had the title to find consequence in England. For London did love titles, foreign well-nigh as much as their own. London was society, and, although it was not Paris, London was where English men of society played. Juliette had learnt at the foot of the scaffold that betimes serendipity sings.

Yet for the recently disavowed Juliette, no entrée into this society fell before her save for her mother's fallen rubric. Hence, she picked up the standard of Viscountess without compunction. Had she even a small fortune, she could have installed herself independently amongst society. However, as a woman with more pulchritude than cash, she traded upon those charms.

When young Mr. Darcy's path crossed hers, he was compleating his second decade of a very privileged life and Juliette had settled into a position of considerable pelf herself at Harcourt House. More than a few of the fine houses of Mayfair were financed through the annuities bestowed upon particularly accomplished courtesans. None were more prominent in this elite demimonde than Viscountess Juliette Clisson.

Other than that she was living in a country not her own, she had few vexations to burden her. It was true, inertia did rule most of her gentleman friends, but that was not necessarily a disadvantage. Accommodating elder effendi was a little tedious, but tolerable. It had been her study that weathering the disadvantages of dotage was preferable to putting up with their feckless heir presumptives (they could be a rowdy lot). Having secured her wealth, she no longer had absolute need to offer her services to anyone. Nevertheless, travelling in the circles of haute monde did require substantial cash outlays. Hence, she occasionally allowed herself a dalliance if one looked to be particularly lucrative or entertaining.

Either of which happened but seldom. Inevitably, men of wealth were not a particularly handsome or charming bunch. Therefore, when the considerable *italege* of young Mr. Darcy came under her gaze, she was, let us say, not uninterested. Indeed, a little sleuthing was in order. As Cyprian circles harboured a gossip mill more reliable than *The Times*, she prodded tongues. Evidently, the elegant bagnios of the West End had not entertained him. Other than his family connexions and rumour of fleeting affairs, she learnt little.

How he came by her name, she did not fancy to inquire.

Forthwith of their first meeting, an agreement with terms favourable to both was formed. He required exclusivity only when he was in town. When he was, he sent word. Clearly, he had distaste for frequenting ladies who chambered with more than one gentleman a night. (His fastidious nature revolting, no doubt, at the notion of putting into another man's leavings.) This punctiliousness hearkened back to his demeanour in general. For when he did call, he never stayed the night. Was that because he chose not to be espied leaving in the morning daylight? Perchance he chose not to have his horses stand in wait, and his coachmen in speculation, whilst he tarried. She had not an inkling of his motives. He remained aloof and enigmatic.

This recondite deportment did not exclude physical congress. Indeed, he was at once lusty and detached. His lovemaking was zealous and prolific, but silent. He spoke no words of desire and barely uttered a sound at achievement. Those sounds occasioned came unwillingly from Juliette's own lips, much to her professional mortification. She prided herself upon how well she feigned passion. Her rendition of it was, she fancied, provocatively demure, with little affectation. For in her vocation, allowing oneself carnal satisfaction was a dangerous practise. It led to attachments, and attachments were only a burden.

Yet upon the consummation of their inaugural exchange of flesh, she emitted a lengthy and sincere shriek of pleasure. In her defence, he did exact the economic (and noteworthy) feat of double *coitus* with the same genital tumescence, imposing it with uncommon vigour. Hence, she had little time to gather her wits, much less perfect a performance. Indeed, his fervour accounted for the repeated rapping of her head inflicted upon the headboard. A true gentleman, he apologised dutifully for perpetrating such imprudent mischief. Yet he said, "Forgive me," with all the formality had he stepped upon her toe at a dance. She found the entire occasion most disconcerting.

Despite all the confusing incongruity of ritual, she quite eagerly awaited his return. That should have alerted her to the possibility of emotional involvement in what should have been strictly a matter of business. With any other gentleman, she would have laughed at such indiscriminate doings and been mindful not to repeat them, not connive to continue. Nevertheless, she connived, continued to see him upon subsequent nights, and allowed him to satisfy her.

Their financial arrangement never altered.

Truth be known, she would have seen him without compensation. She fully believed he knew that. Therefore, that consideration was paid befit his notion of what characterised their relationship, not hers. Regardless, even after several years, he made no lasting provision for her. It would have been simpler to pay her an annual sum— the length of their acquaintanceship would have warranted it. However, he preferred not, perchance thinking it would be an indication of allegiance of some kind. An encumbrance. Howbeit his visits were sporadic and guarded, she knew she was in effect, but not in situation, his mistress.

In not daring to repeat that observation of her surrogate mistressdom to young Mr. Darcy, Juliette avoided a blunder in twofold measure. First, pointing out to him something he obviously did not want noted, and secondly, having him think she was suggesting he keep her. If that was what he wanted, she knew he would have offered.

Indeed, she did not believe he wanted the burden of fidelity to one woman in any manner. That, perchance, was a measure of his appeal. She had certainly accommodated more handsome lovers, some quite libidinous and equally well-timbered. Darcy, however, was entirely inexplicable. His courtliness disguised a fierce ardour that was, in itself, remarkable. Even she had not plumbed the depths of his passion. Was it ever excavated, she hoped to be the one to enjoy the eruption.

Which she knew to be a foolhardy fantasy.

Initially she told herself her interest in prestigious young Mr. Darcy was no more than a certain amused conceit that the most desirable bachelor in England chose to spend time with her. Even after she admitted to herself that it was more, she redoubled her efforts to appear, if not actually to be, dispassionate. She made certain she awaited him with a practised look of indifference and despised herself for her weakness. If anyone dared imply it, she knew enough to offer no protestations and let it pass.

Their association, however, came to a close in a most unsettling manner.

He appeared upon her doorstep without his card preceding him. As closely as he adhered to convention, to present himself unannounced was unprecedented. Yet, as it had been a half-year since their last encounter, she anticipated an inspirited, possibly rhapsodic, frolic. However, it was not to be. He was sullen and unusually withdrawn. It occurred to her that upon his previous visit, he had bestridden her perfunctorily. He arrived, came, and then left.

That night, she afforded him every seduction, every allurement, but all was for naught. Her every art was ineffectual. He refused to disrobe or appreciate her denudation. Thereupon, when she had nearly given up on amorous congress, he heaved himself upon her and heatedly, almost savagely kissed her. Then, quite abruptly, he rolled away and sat back against the headboard.

He looked at her rather solemnly, but made no other move toward her. Taking the vacant initiative, she moved atop him and ran her hand down his body, if only in reassurance that she had felt his arousal. Indeed, she had made no mistake. That in and of itself was confusing. It was not unheard of for a man to have the will, but not the means. However, Juliette had yet to encounter this specific manifestation. For his virile reflex was quite evident. He had the means but not the will.

Simultaneous to her deduction, he drew himself from beneath her and off the bed, then bid her good-bye.

As he took his leave, she reclaimed her detachment and placed it upon her face before the door had closed behind him. That, however, had been a useless, and then again, helpful exercise. Useless because he did not give her a backward glance, and helpful in that she saw, indeed, that she needed the practise.

In the weeks that followed, she often thought of that evening and pondered what provoked his departure from Harcourt and her life. The possibility that he was in unrequited love was given cursory consideration, and then abandoned. How could any woman Mr. Darcy fancied spurn him?

Nevertheless, she learnt in due time that he was engaged. He was engaged to a Miss Bennet of Hertfordshire. Through persistent query, Juliette uncovered that the lady in question was reputed to be quite a country beauty. She heard too, that she was not nearly so well-born as was Darcy. That was quite astonishing, for Juliette knew well of his dedication to his station. Men of rank always believed it unacceptable to marry for passion (hence, her very prosperous life).

It would have been an amusement to see just what sort of woman had pierced the froideur surrounding Mr. Darcy's heart so compleatly. Just a curiosity, of course.

One certainty was that their relationship had ended. She did not need to read the missive from his solicitor to know it. Married, he would not return to Harcourt. His scruples demanded such. And had they not, she felt certain that if he would not couple with her when in unrequited love, he would most assuredly not once it had been found.

If Miss Bennet had managed to make Mr. Darcy love her, once she tasted of the delight of his loins, she would know she had gained a husband of great fortune far beyond his wealth.

When questioned later why Mr. Darcy no longer called, Juliette would foster a brief smile and answer, *"C'est la vie."*

Ensconced as they were, a hundred miles apart, Elizabeth and Jane had been unable to manage more than a sedate correspondence by post. Bingley's townhouse was only a few blocks from Darcy's in London. Hence, by Easter the sisters would be unconditionally reunited. However, that winter, the Bingleys could only manage to come to Pemberley for the week of the ball.

And so the families gathered in Derbyshire.

As it was but a week, Maria and Kitty wanted to waste not a moment and begged a ride to Kympton, much in want of finding a milliner with ribbons in colours they had yet to discover. Mrs. Darcy was happy to have them out from underfoot, their pleasure compounded by knowing the livery of the carriage in which they rode bore the Pemberley colours.

As Mr. Gardiner was the favourite uncle of both their wives, Darcy and Bingley were inclined not to be displeased with his company. Nor would they have been despite that inducement, for he was a man of superior knowledge and his conversation marked his good manners. (Altogether, he was found to be the most superb of relations, one whose acquaintance was not a punishment.) Much taken with sport, particularly fishing, he was handsomely diverted at Pemberley. When he was not afield, he was most inquisitive of Pemberley's fine library. It was an astounding collection, the pride of the master of the house.

"I have often chided Darcy that he has no need, but for all of this, he is always buying books!" Bingley told Mr. Gardiner.

A happy marriage had not altered Mr. Darcy's disposition in so great a fashion that it now overflowed in mirth. He still smiled but little in company and conversed with not more ease, yet he was clearly pleased at their admiration of his library. He prest his company to avail themselves of the treatises, maps, charts, and memoirs to their hearts' content. Bingley, who very seldom found time to read, seemed happy at the prospect of investigating the books of Pemberley with someone who knew less of them than he.

After treating her Aunt Gardiner to the long-promised, much-anticipated pony cart tour of the little lake beyond Pemberley Manor, Elizabeth and the ladies took tea and biscuits in the small-parlour. Knowing their husbands fully occupied, Jane and Elizabeth were most anxious for a post-wedding *tete-a-tete*, one the bouncing cart did not accommodate. Their dear Aunt Gardiner, it would seem, was almost as happy for an accounting as her nieces.

Foremost, they laughed in sheer amazement at the scope of feminine gossip now rendered unto them.

"Yes," Elizabeth said to her aunt, who had not been privy to the chatter at the ball, "inducted into the guild of married women as we are, it seems the salacious gossip we can hear is limited only to the hours in the day."

Her aunt listened to their lively remarks with pleasure. They were both quite dear to her. But it was Elizabeth's happiness that she held with greater self-satisfaction, knowing what part she played in the Darcys' betrothal.

She did not know that she was not the first to notice Mr. Darcy's growing regard for her niece, however. Surprisingly, Charlotte Collins's pragmatic nature saw it first. It was on Elizabeth's visit to Kent that Charlotte suggested that a man of Mr. Darcy's stature would not call on the wife of a lowly vicar (particularly one as weak-headed as Mr. Collins) with such dedication if not for some further motive.

If Charlotte saw it first, she saw it not best. Astuteness in recognising true and abiding love fell to Mrs. Gardiner. From her first step onto the grounds of Pemberley and into her niece's waiting arms, her aunt detected a glow in Elizabeth's complexion even more pronounced than on her wedding day. Jane was sublimely happy, she could tell. Elizabeth, however, dwelt in the very lists of empowered love.

An afternoon spent in quiet reminisces and merry tales of household woes did not wear out the sisters' thirst for truly intimate discourse.

Therefore, when their aunt inveigled her husband away from the books to take a rest, Jane and Elizabeth wasted little time before they retreated atop the Darcys' bed (much as they had on their own at Longbourn) to talk at length.

As they had not truly confided since their weddings, they eyed each other cautiously, perhaps each waiting for the other to broach the single conversational topic that was of greatest interest to them both. However, this exchange of information demanded some delicate manoeuvring. For it necessitated sharing confidences of a physical act that neither entered into alone. Their bond as sisters was still just as strong, but their devotion to one another had been eclipsed by the vow of "forsaking all others" with first loyalty to their husbands.

Nevertheless, Elizabeth furiously schemed a way to talk about making love without mentioning her lover, thus protecting said lover's tenaciously held desire of privacy. However, before she managed such a feat, Jane (of all people) initiated the subject of The Marital Bed. She did so in true Jane fashion, fretting about Elizabeth's discomfort upon her first night as a wife without actually mentioning devirgination.

"Oh, Lizzy," Jane said, "are you well? In your first ardour, you were not...ill-used?"

Elizabeth reassured her forthrightly, "Yes, it was painful at first. But, of course, in repetition it was not."

She smiled, expecting Jane to return her knowing look. Jane, however, sighed with resignation.

"I suppose 'tis a woman's lot."

Elizabeth did not consider associating intimately with her husband as her "lot" in life. Rather, she considered it a considerable gift from heaven above. Hence, a bit puzzled, she attempted a little interrogation.

"After the initial act of love, the consecutive ones, were they not pleasurable? Did they not transport you to rapture?"

"I daresay, Lizzy, you sound like Lydia!"

Jane had exclaimed such before fully appreciating the breadth of that particular insult (or that it was an insult, for Jane would never deliberately say something unkind to Elizabeth). Fortunately, Elizabeth knew that and chose (only with great test of will) to overlook the unintentionally scurrilous comparison. Yet Elizabeth had to admit, though wrapped up in her hyperbole, Lydia's version of physical congress was not a fabrication. Availing oneself of a husband's love torch was quite glorious.

"I hope," said Elizabeth rather primly, "that I do not at all convey my sentiments with the same unwarranted embellishment as does Lydia. Nevertheless, I must confess, Jane, my sentiments are not dissimilar. Making love to one's husband is quite euphoric. Surely you have found this to be true."

With Elizabeth's concurrence before her, Jane believed she must reconsider and did so carefully.

"I do enjoy Charles's kissing me. However, I cannot say without a doubt that I have ever felt anything akin to *rapture* when he...becomes impassioned. But I truly have no complaint, for although he is quite diligent in his attentions, it does not last all that long."

Elizabeth was confounded. Charles Bingley was devoted to Jane. He held her hand constantly, kissed her incessantly, and showered her with every manner of compliment. Certainly, Bingley's affection was unquestioned. It does not last all that long? She and Darcy had whiled away hours whilst in such pursuits. Perhaps this was simply a matter of imperfection of technique. It must be addressed. Here, however, was where overlapping loyalties became a confusing issue. Elizabeth did not want to offer confidences of her own husband's love-making prowess, but was tempted to by reason of affording Jane connubial bliss. Gathering from what Jane said, Charles Bingley seemed utterly, well...staid. Or, at least unlearned.

Compromise of loyalty was found in the third person.

With a scholarly voice, Elizabeth began, "'Tis said, that if the husband takes time and caresses his wife properly, she should find the same pleasure as he, Jane. She should be brought the most..."

"Who said that, Lizzy?" Jane interrupted.

Exasperated, Elizabeth abandoned third person for bluntness. "I said it, Jane."

There were few euphemisms at her disposal and she despaired of having to become quite frank, but did.

"When Mr. Bingley has his—his 'activity' should excite you to great passion."

Jane looked at her as if she was certain her sister had run utterly mad.

"Lizzy, pray, whatever are you talking about?"

If bluntness was absolutely necessary, Elizabeth believed she could be blunt.

"I am talking about…that tingling and pulsing that you feel down there when your husband rubs your insides with his member. It fairly makes your eyeballs roll up into your head."

There. That should leave no room for misunderstanding. Absence of experience, however, did not allow Jane to appreciate the clarification and she blushed with embarrassment. Thereupon in reflection, she regained her composure enough to lower her voice and bid reassurance.

"I cannot say that I have ever felt that way. 'Tis truly possible?"

Elizabeth shook her head far more emphatically than was actually necessary.

"Yes, 'tis quite possible—every time, Jane! One can find indescribable bliss. Good heavens, yes!"

Jane shook her head as if not daring entry of such unimaginable thoughts.

"Lizzy, 'tis man's province to be served in such a manner. It is an act of generation, is it not? This is for procreation. Men must be inspirited to emit their seed. It falls to wives to have babies, not invite rapture."

"If a man is allowed pleasure whilst procreating, cannot therefore a woman?"

"But Lizzy, everyone speaks of it as a duty."

"You know as well as I many amongst our society did not marry for love. To them, perhaps, it is a duty. If I had no feeling for my husband beyond admiration of his character, I should think I would agree. As it is, I love him compleatly, just as you do Mr. Bingley."

Gripping the mattress, Jane sat very still for a few moments, as if pondering that possibility. Thereupon, she turned back to Elizabeth and lowered her voice to an even more confidential tone.

"'Tis true, I admire Charles. However, I believe I love him in all ways, for I would not be happy if we did not share affection. Sometimes after he has…been obliged, I feel that I should like him to hold me longer, kiss me more. Sometimes 'tis difficult to sleep after he has returned to his bed."

He returned to "his" bed? No wonder the lack of spontaneity. That was passion by appointment.

"Tell him of your discontent! For as a loving husband, he should want to please you. Tell him, Jane!"

"Tell him he must…titillate me? I could never say such a thing to him, Lizzy!" Jane gasped. "He might think me unhappy."

"You are discontented. He loves you, he should want to know."

Jane's horrified confoundment bid Elizabeth to abandon the notion of enlightening Bingley. She took an alternate route, by way of Jane's initiative.

"If you dare not speak of it, perchance it is the simple matter of situation…"

They had been married near a month, Elizabeth reasoned. Thus, if Bingley was too dim to figure this out, Jane must for him. However, Jane was not moved to forward this reasoning. Indeed, there was not a flicker of understanding.

Determined as she was for Jane to see the light, Elizabeth struggled with the notion that if Jane could just situate herself atop her husband, this manoeuvre would keep Bingley from escape long enough for Jane to…. Such a suggestion would surely scandalise them both. The sisters stood upon the precipice of absolute and irredeemable indecorousness, and Elizabeth was not quite ready to take the leap alone. Fortunately, she did not have the opportunity.

Jane announced with finality, "I could never injure Charles with criticism of his love. I am quite happy as I am."

Thusly, Jane dismissed the entire possibility of connubial achievement. Conversation moved on to the weather.

That night before sleep encroached, Elizabeth lay in a disgusted heap pondering her sister's marital impasse. Next to her, but beneath the bedcloth, her husband stretched out his full length and waggled his feet as if in invitation for her to join him. Rather, she enlisted his reluctant participation in a conversation of which he wanted no part.

"Jane and Bingley do not both share the same pleasure from physical connexion," Elizabeth said incredulously of Jane's dilemma. "This is intolerable. I encouraged her to confide in Mr. Bingley, for certainly he would want to know. But she worried it might cause him grief. She is too good."

Hitherto, Darcy lay quite passively, endeavouring, with great conviction, to believe he was not part of this particularly mortifying discussion. He pondered with great abhorrence the understanding that ladies even spoke of such matters to each other. Only when Elizabeth bade his opinion did he venture a comment.

"If your sister does not think herself unhappy, then perhaps you should not attempt to convince her otherwise."

That was not the desired response. Elizabeth took another course.

"You and Mr. Bingley are the very closest of friends, Darcy. Moreover, very close friends are almost as brothers. Perhaps you could suggest to Mr. Bingley that he…"

"No," he held up his hand. "Absolutely not."

"But why? Certainly, he would benefit from your expertise. How could you deny him your good advice when it is possible to help?"

"No."

"I believe you should not have to come right out with it. You could wait until an opportune time. Whilst breeding the mares, perhaps. Then with all due nonchalance…"

Aghast, he said, "I cannot begin to imagine how you think that conversation would ensue. Absolutely not."

She rolled onto her stomach and rested her chin petulantly in her hand.

"Well, I cannot say anything to Mr. Bingley…"

Darcy half-rose with a look of abject horror upon his face. Would she actually consider such a gambit?

"I said I could not!" she replied defensively to his unspoken reproach.

With an exaggerated sigh of relief, he dropped his head back upon the pillow. She, however, continued to ponder the problem for a few minutes longer. That was, until she realised all this talk of Jane's rapture—and her husband's nakedness underneath the sheet—was making her reflect quite intently upon her own. Recognising her expression, he drew her beneath him.

"I can ensure the happiness of only one woman, Lizzy. Let it be you."

At last, the evening found an unequivocal meeting of the minds.

That afternoon's coze left Jane quite as discomfited as her sister. Rarely did exchanging confidences with Lizzy leave her thus. Had anyone but Elizabeth—sensible, dependable Elizabeth—intimated that Jane's connubial necessities with Charles were left wanting, she would have been affronted to the core. Lydia's rantings about copulation could be dismissed as just that. But not Elizabeth. It must be true.

Jane, who would venture any lengths to spare others blame, worried. She worried it was she who was the culpable party in not allowing her husband to rouse her passion.

Such fretting led her to recollect her wedding-night. It was not a memory she liked to invoke, as it had not been the event to which some poets alluded. It was unthinkable to disappoint poets. It was undeniable, however, that when Charles Bingley came to her the first night of their marriage, angels did not sing.

Having inadvertently preceded him to the bed, she patiently awaited for some time. As it happened, so much time passed before he presented himself that she had begun to wonder if she had retired to the correct room. Her wait had not been unproductive, for she had busied herself. She readjusted the covers. Fluffed the pillows. Spread her hair just so. Tied and retied the satin bow at the neck of her gown. Fortuitously, Mary, her new lady-maid, left the door open leading to Bingley's dressing room. Hence, Jane was relieved of the possibility that he would knock upon the door and she would have to arise to answer it, thereby undoing all the adjusting of bed covers, hair, and bow.

Was she not uneasy enough, Mary was an intimidating woman, suffering not fools gladly, and her mistress' wishes with no great humour. (All of the Bingleys' female servants were called either Mary or Anne regardless had their parents, with all due contemplation, named them Beatrice, Elinor, or Phoebe. In the Bingleys' service, you were Mary or Anne. It was, of course, not discourtesy, simply expedience, for it did relieve the good ladies of the house the ghastly chore of learning the names of their all and sundry servants.) Even Jane knew it impolitic to be hectored by your own lady-maid and promised herself she would stand more firmly in the future. In the future, when she was not so otherwise anxious.

After the third retying of the bow upon her night-dress, Bingley finally appeared. He wore a night-shirt buttoned to the neck and a look of excited apprehension. Jane thought that top button looked uncomfortable for sleeping, but she did not want to initiate any comment that could be remotely construed as critical. His face managed a nervous smile, but she no more than caught sight of his bare feet before he hastily doused the candles and scrambled beneath the covers.

There in the dark, they lay side-by-side, shoulder-to-shoulder, not unlike had they been upon the settee in the parlour.

For every day of their engagement, Bingley had vowed his undying love, declared she was the most beautiful woman he had ever beheld, and lovingly kissed her hand. The darkness, however, apparently found him mute as well as paralysed. After some time had passed without the barest hint of movement, Jane finally reached over and placed her arm across his chest. A gesture that appeared to be in reassurance that he was, indeed, still there. Evidently, that broke the stalemate, thus unleashing from Bingley a torrent of affection. He gratefully kissed her cheeks and repeated every manner of accolade he had previously bestowed upon her.

Once the floodgates of love had opened, so flowed his fervour. He covered Jane's lips, her chin, her forehead, and both cheeks with quick little kisses (sometimes quantity overrides technique). Foreplay culminated, he bade her favours.

"May I raise your gown?"

Blushing in the dark, Jane allowed that she found that acceptable. That he raised her hem no higher than her knees did introduce more manoeuvring and less finesse in consummating their marriage than Bingley would have hoped of himself. He desired not to frighten the demure Jane with his ardency. That wish, coupled with the fact that the only practise he had experienced of a sexual nature was no more than some groping of a nubile young lass in a hayloft, left him keenly interested in the possibilities, but no less enlightened about the act. Moreover, it lent their first encounter less than a compleat success.

As it happened, Jane was not at all certain their marriage actually was consummated, however heavily Charles snored beside her. The prolificacy of bed covers and bedclothes made it hard to determine, but she did not believe herself transgressed. It was her understanding that her husband would enter her with an appendage and that it would be painful. It was not. Nor did she feel any intrusion upon her person. The only thing she felt was a sticky wetness upon and about her thighs. She dabbed at that with the corner of the bedcloth and, ever mindful of the laundry, lived in hope it would be over-looked by the help.

It took several nights and just as many attempts before Jane was certain she was, indeed, a wife. Charles seemed happily satisfied with himself if he managed to insinuate his member anywhere near her womanhood. Apparently a little uncertain of the actual whereabouts of the intended orifice, he chose not to intrude upon Jane's privacy any more than necessary in search of specifics.

Uncertain of the correct avenue herself, all this random prodding was a little disconcerting to Jane. Indeed, during their initial intimacies, she had raised her hands above her shoulders. This was not only to allow him free access to whatever he wanted to access, but because in his somewhat meandering explorations with his organ, she had once inadvertently grasped it. When she flung it hastily from her hand, it had startled Charles almost as much as his member had her. (She had not yet seen it and it had felt as if a separate entity, possibly amphibian, had accessed their bed.) It was altogether an unfortunate incident.

However, subsequently, Charles seemed quite happy with his performance and as he lent little imposition upon her time, Jane thought their coupling was of great success as well. At least insofar as the satisfaction of her husband, for was that not the duty of a wife? To make her husband happy?

Jane had assumed she had experienced all that a woman could ask of the act of love. Lizzy had always had a more adventuresome nature. It was likely that she would spend her life experiencing everything more fully than would Jane. Although Elizabeth was more willing to discover, Jane did not dismiss her own strong feelings of love, for she loved Charles Bingley deeply.

In Jane's opinion, both sisters had married men who were good. Although Charles was open, affectionate, and amiable, Mr. Darcy, conversely, appeared taciturn, staid, and remote. Yet Jane had realised sooner than had Elizabeth that the closely regulated Mr. Darcy knew himself to need that stern control. That he was of a passionate nature initially escaped Lizzy. Mr. Darcy's sentiments were found only in depth. By the standards he set for himself and others, it was as if he dared self-satisfaction. Charles Bingley was less ambiguous. He wanted everyone happy.

Jane's most salient joy in life came from the happiness of those she loved. She and Charles were of the same disposition. They were both amiable and agreeable. That the task of being wife to the frightfully complex Mr. Darcy fell to Elizabeth invited Jane's sympathy. It was only when Lizzy told Jane to what passionate heights her husband brought her that Jane bethought the possibility of envy. But if she was covetous, it was only momentarily. Jane judged her own happiness and satisfaction to be less important than that of others. If the man she loved were happy, she could find happiness in that as well. Everything else was inconsequential.

Elizabeth eventually gathered the courage to question Darcy about the family that had offended him so grievously by their very appearance at the Pemberley ball. His explanation was terse.

He told her that the man only recently had decided to promote his son in society. Elizabeth's raised eyebrow, which he now knew to mean she was not satisfied by his answer, forced him to expand upon the subject at hand.

Hence, he put down his newspaper and deigned to explain thusly: Mr. Howgrave's elderly father had taken a decided dislike to his oldest son for some distant misdeed, and refused to entail his rather extensive holdings upon him. Rather, he intended to leave the place to a grandson, or failing that, a nephew. Mr. Howgrave had no younger brothers who were father to a son, but there existed one male cousin in Aberdeen. In no way did Howgrave want to lose title to the family property, and most certainly not to a Gael. The matter of a child born of his housekeeper by him had lain unclaimed until the matter of entailment had arisen.

"In presenting the young man to society and giving him his name," Darcy said, "Howgrave hopes he will find favour and his grandfather will keep the property upon his behalf. Mrs. Howgrave is not affronted by standing next to the proof of her husband's infidelity in society. That makes it perfectly clear that she values herself no higher than does her husband."

It was a harsh assessment, but not unexpectedly so, when considering from whose sensibilities it sprang. Elizabeth longed to query Darcy as to just which indignation he found most objectionable: that Mr. Howgrave had a relationship outside his marriage, or outside his station, or that he had decided, upon merit of economics, to make it public.

However, she dared not. She let the matter drop, allowing her husband to return to his paper uninterrogated. Still, she wondered which was the man's greatest sin in Darcy's eyes. Knowing her husband as she had just begun to, she thought he probably saw the greatest damnation in that Howgrave had chosen not only to publicise a bastardy, but had done so at Pemberley.

Not to be outdone by man, woman, or biblical indiscretions, Elizabeth's mother arrived within a fortnight with as much folderol as she could muster (which was an impressive measure). Encapsulated in a coach with his wife for one hundred and fifty miles was the long-suffering Mr. Bennet, whose weary countenance announced he was inordinately ready to relinquish the office of martyr to his wife's ceaseless tongue.

Having new ears to afflict, Mrs. Bennet was not inside the door before she embarked upon a lengthy recitation of Lydia's labouring travails. Uncharacteristically, she had little to remark upon her new grandchild other than that he had an impressive head of hair. It was presumed that her lack of enthusiasm was equally due to the child's dearth of primogeniture expectations and that Mr. Bennet had taken to calling her in the third person, "Grandmother Bennet."

Howbeit the Gardiners and Bingleys had departed (Bingley saw quite enough of Mrs. Bennet in Hertfordshire), Kitty and Maria stayed. Yet with fifty bedchambers, bed-closets, and sitting rooms from which to choose, one would not have expected any accommodation complications. Regrettably, there was one.

Because Mr. Darcy simply did not want to hear Mrs. Bennet's blathering any more than necessary, he had Mrs. Reynolds situate the Bennets upon a higher floor. However, Mrs. Bennet would not be so easily eluded. She insisted two staircases were too many for her to climb and found a pretty prospect overlooking the lake. Alas, the room that manifested this view lay just down the hall from her daughter's bed of amour. As Mrs. Bennet's shrill cackle wafted down the corridor, Darcy chastised himself relentlessly that he had not thought of the staircase dilemma and frantically sought a duplicate prospect upon the ground floor. But to no avail.

Whilst her husband had been silently setting his own plans of installing Mrs. Bennet as far away as possible, Elizabeth agreed for reasons all her own.

With just her sisters in the house, her coronation as an exalted marital partner was not moderated. The only true alteration was the occasional giggle if she became too boisterous, imagining Jane and Bingley might hear from across the wide corridor. Having her parents under the same roof, however, was a far more imposing hindrance.

When the Bennets inadvertently ended up on the same floor, Darcy came to understand Mrs. Bennet's voice was not the only discomfiture he would suffer. For, although she admitted it quite unreasonable, Elizabeth found it was impossible to think of herself concurrently as a passionate vixen and daughter of a father just down the hall. She was convinced her parents would hear them making love. Had not Goodwin heard her small shriek in the bathtub? (Had she had any notion of the dog business, she would truly have been mortified.)

This was initially a nettlesome apprehension. However, it rapidly blossomed into full-fledged paranoia. Darcy insisted it was impossible to be overheard. They were half the house-length away, the doors were massive, the windows were closed, the passageways carpeted. Sound did not carry in Pemberley.

"But," Elizabeth reminded him, "Goodwin heard."

Not truly of a mind to deny herself or Darcy pleasure, Elizabeth did not consider abstaining from marital connexion, but their couplings were certainly more sedate. At her insistence, a few nights of love were endured beneath two quilts, a counterpane, and a bedcover. Drenched in sweat, Darcy finally threw off the padding in disgust.

"I will suffer for your love, Lizzy, but I refuse to suffocate!"

"Shush," was her only rejoinder.

Had not there been all this concern for silence, the other senses might not have been as compleatly investigated as they came to be. With their sounds of passion suppressed, the other four faculties became enhanced. Touch, taste, and scent had been fully explored and examined; perchance sight was slighted, if only by half. For, by reason of configuration, Elizabeth could only imagine what Darcy saw when they came together. This is what she whispered one night as she watched him watch himself do a kindness unto her person.

"Darcy, it has occurred to me that women are at a distinct disadvantage in the act of love. A man, evidently by nature's intent, is able to view what I, as a woman, can only feel and enjoy."

He did not stop, but glanced at her face as if considering her literal viewpoint, for this was not something over which he had ever puzzled. In a moment, he did stop. Her comment had been meant to be simply philosophical, just an observation. Nevertheless, Darcy was a man, and men tend to approach such inquiries as tests, not passive observances. Hence, he rose and purposefully strode to the far wall. This interruption was not an utter hardship. Indeed, his bare-buttocked stroll across the room was a significant treat. The thew his naked body exhibited as he strained to lift a heavy pier glass from its hooks well-nigh gave her the twitters.

Resting it against the bed board, he made a few adjustments to the lay of it. Thereupon he grabbed her ankles, drew her playfully about, the friction of the silk beneath her heating her back. She shrieked at that, and then clamped her hand over her own mouth.

He pointed at the image in the mirror, asking, "Do you approve?"

Looking at the enormous reflection of her own *feminus denudata*, she blushed, released her mouth, and covered her eyes in mortification. As curiosity is always a stronger force than embarrassment, it took very little coaxing for her to look with him and watch their bodies locked in conjugal union.

"It is really rather fascinating," she told him. "A voyeurism, but without any guilt."

Conversation withered away in absence of any true interest in talking, whispered or not. He had only glanced in the mirror to see what she had seen. As it bore no revelation for him, her ambitiously renewed fervour caught him unawares. (The few times he had seen mirrors above a bed, he had fancied it for titillation of the man, such was the catering.) Hence, he was amazed that the mirror aroused Elizabeth as it did. Amazed and gratified. And neither was particularly silent about it.

Knowing that she had reached new heights of carnal pleasure, both sensual and vocal, Elizabeth did not come down to breakfast the next forenoon, feigning illness. The lie only exacerbated circumstances, for when she finally appeared, her mother rushed to an outlandish conclusion.

"Perhaps you are with child, Lizzy! Oh, Mr. Bennet! A son for Mr. Darcy! Our Lizzy will give him a son!"

"We have not been married five weeks, Mama."

The mirror was stashed beneath their bed for the duration of the Bennets' stay. However, the dust had not settled from their departure before it was retrieved. (Thenceforward, that looking-glass witnessed more carnal pleasures than did a knocking-house piano player.) It was secreted again beneath the bed for convenience sake and, without question, another adornment found its place upon the wall. As far as Elizabeth knew, the looking-glass and its hiding place were their little secret. In time, she laughed at her own naïveté. For she eventually realised that each time they drew it from beneath the bed, the glass was always dusted.

26

The foxhunt Lady Millhouse had arm-twisted at the ball was scheduled within weeks. Hence, Elizabeth dedicated her days to improving her horsemanship. Leisurely rides with her husband were quite enjoyable, he upon Blackjack, she upon the plodding, dependable Lady, but she told him she longed to run.

"We must move more aggressively if I am to join you upon the hunt."

He was adamant that she should not.

"'Tis dangerous for an unpractised rider. I will not allow it."

That he would not allow it was a condition Elizabeth was tempted to address rather frankly. However, as his words were tempered by his obvious concern for her safety, she did not.

"I can stay astride a horse, even if 'tis demanded in so inefficient way as side-saddle."

Abruptly, she kicked Lady, who could manage only an indolent gallop. In one kick and two strides, he caught up to her side, both their horses finding an easier canter. It was her observance that her husband was a fit rider. Elizabeth's simple ambition was one day, if not to match him, to at least not be a disgrace as his equestrian companion.

Eyeing him as he rode along, she admired the figure he presented astride Blackjack, for he bore a high polish upon his boot and a handsome leg above it—one that she admired as they rode stirrup to stirrup. She fancied she could see the outline of thigh muscles tightening as he posted beside her. In want of disguising what she was certain was a discernible sigh at the sight, she lifted her skirt to reveal her own disreputable footwear. Her ankle-jacks were ridiculously inappropriate. She wished she could ride astride as did he and wear a tall boot as well.

Although few questioned it, horsewomen understood that the only way acceptable for a lady to ride a horse defied the laws of common sense, if not gravity. Even with that disadvantage, it was evident to her husband the horsewoman Elizabeth could become. He discerned a natural seat and instinct for her horse that could not be taught. Still, a natural seat was no substitute for experience. It would take more than leisurely rides with him to prepare her for the hunt and he explained that patiently to her.

One person's patience is another's condescension. Hence, Elizabeth was unconvinced. A small, single rail fence loomed in their path, an ideal stage to disabuse Darcy of the notion she was not practised enough to take a jump. She cantered Lady to the fence and the horse, quite nimbly, jumped it. There. How could he refuse her the hunt in the face of such a cunning display of horsemanship?

"I believe 'tis quite possible, Mr. Darcy, you have not heard the last from me upon the matter."

He smiled an inscrutable smile, knowing full well it was quite probable he had not.

They walked back to the house from the stables hand in hand, a triumph for her in that he rarely displayed affection if there was any possibility of an audience. He forsook her to the stairs and her feet assaulted them two at a time in jubilation before she managed to rein herself into a more ladylike step.

Even so lackadaisical a ride was a sweaty business. She peeled away her riding habit and took to her tub. Humming in satisfaction at her success at the rail, Elizabeth sat in the suds and marvelled at her own elation. Stretching out, she hooked her heels over its edge and waggled her feet, then wiggled her toes. As she looked at them, she pondered her most recent perspicacity. Why was it that, as impressive as her husband was when dressed, and compelling as he was when not, nothing was quite so arresting as seeing him in his riding boots?

As if by magic a pair of tall boots sat in her dressing room the very next morning. They were of fine, supple calf, but were not of that familiar masculine size that so incited her to lust. Nor were they black. They were Hessian in style, exactly the colour of butter as it just begins to bubble in the pan. Tooling of a little darker thread ran about the faux roll at the top and performed a tassel in front before curlicueing down the sides. The colour and size told Elizabeth they were for her. They had appeared just as mysteriously as her riding costume had a few weeks previous.

She picked one up and admired the workmanship, quite proud of a cobbler who could make a boot that could engulf the length of her generous foot with such brevity. She had not once said anything to her husband about boots. Truly, she had not even known that "Women Who Rode" wore such fine tall boots. Indeed, she had never been in the company of a serious female rider in her habit (and if she had, she would not have thought to lift the lady's skirt to peer upon what adorned her feet).

If anyone had watched her examining her new footgear, one might have inferred from her expression that she was not pleased with her husband's unanticipated gift. On the contrary, she was quite moved. It was the timing that caused the disorder. For at that very moment, she intended to embark upon an activity of a covert nature. The boots seemed almost an admonition. Her design yielded not to such grief. (However, she chose not to have them prick her conscience further and did not scruple to set them temporarily aside.)

Waiting until her husband rode out with Mr. Rhymes, Elizabeth approached the stables in her old shoes and with great apprehension. Knowing it was only a se'nnight until the hunt, she went there alone, determined to steal some time from beneath her husband's inhibiting gaze to practise her horsemanship. It was apparent that he was convinced she had not the time to become proficient enough to join the hunt. Possibly, she reasoned, because upon their joint rides he was far too solicitous. Hence she had no opportunity to stretch her abilities. He insisted she take her riding with deliberation. Elizabeth abhorred purposeless tedium; she was too impatient to creep when she could run.

In concluding that Darcy's conservatorship over her riding was repressive, she saw no recourse but to ride out alone. As she walked to the stables, she was anxious. However, not exclusively over her first solitary ride. She was in fear that their exceedingly indulgent staff would see her alone and converge upon her, insisting she accept their offers of assistance. With a mere flick of his head, Darcy could have the many servitors disperse as hastily as they had appeared. However, protestations from Elizabeth had the opposite effect. Evidently, they were deigned as insincere. The more firmly she protested to the servants her lack of the need, the more she was tended.

"Mrs. Darcy is unattended!"

If she dared to venture upon the landing in her dressing gown, "Mrs. Darcy is unattended!"

The cursed announcement echoed down the halls of Pemberley. Indeed, if she ventured anywhere alone, upon her heels would come a servant. Her complaint about such oversolicitousness went unheeded by her husband.

"They have been told to see to you."

She understood compleatly how seriously the servants undertook her husband's instructions by their sheer doggedness of her steps. Hence, she promised herself she would eventually perfect that little shake of the head that would send the servants away. Until then, she skulked. For Mrs. Darcy wanted to be unattended in her present employment. Her riding habit bade her look quite the horsewoman. Seldom, however, did appearance ever abuse reality quite so emphatically.

Elizabeth did not embrace this truth fully, but she did believe it was possible that the Mistress of Pemberley might find herself in less than dignified endeavours and wanted no witnesses at all.

The horse she had ridden each day was the very one Darcy had first chosen for her. Lady she was, in name as well as temperament. She certainly was well-bred and a great deal more spirited than fat old Nellie, hence preferable to ride. Having been atop few horses, Elizabeth believed the mare as safe as Nellie as well. Hence, having successfully eluded the house help and gotten to the stables quite upon her own, she had Lady saddled.

The journeyman groom allowed his second to leg her upon the horse. John, the young lad she very nearly caused to be turned out, did the honours and seemed quite pleased that he was allowed it. Elizabeth looked down at his young face, flushed with pride, and thought it quite probable he was as innocent a hostler as she was a horse-woman. Pursing her lips, she pressed her forefinger against them begging the boy's silence. He smiled. They were conspirators in ignorance.

With Darcy riding beside her, Lady had not seemed so tall. As Elizabeth looked down in lonely sentry from atop her saddle then, she wondered if she would ever be able to remount if she needed to rest. (She did not dare consider the other reason she might need to remount.) As she rode out, she assured herself, "I shall persevere."

When she found herself far enough away from the stables for no one to hear, she spoke to the mare, who responded by turning back first one ear, then the other.

"You shall be a good girl, now, will you not? We shall surprise Mr. Darcy with what we can do. Surely you too are tired of these plodding walks. We shall have a treat, just you and I."

Soon she was well enough along their oft-travelled path to see a small tree that had fallen across the way. Propitious fortune saw it exactly the height she needed. She patted the mare's neck, then urged her to walk over to the slim trunk. Lady put out her nose, and then deftly stepped over the obstacle. Satisfied, Elizabeth turned about and urged Lady into a little quicker walk. The horse stepped daintily over the tree once again. Relieved, Elizabeth decided that her first jump was perhaps less a fluke than she had granted. Darcy had told her she had a natural seat. Who was she to dispute his opinion?

She turned the mare about once again and, summoning up all her courage, nudged Lady into a trot. This time Lady balked, causing Elizabeth to tip precariously over her neck. Concluding they had not enough speed, she turned once more and kicked Lady's flanks, urging her forward. Again the horse balked, almost causing Elizabeth to lose her "natural" seat.

"You can step over this little log," she told the mare. "Why will you not jump it?"

Lady did not offer any enlightenment upon horse reckoning. In the horse's silence upon the matter, Elizabeth refused to accept caution rather than risk. Perhaps Lady had not enough time to build speed. She would give her a longer approach. Again, she turned at a greater distance and kicked her horse more firmly. Lady responded splen-didly and Elizabeth could feel her own heart take a leap just as they came to the tree trunk. Elizabeth, certain they would soar, leaned forward in preparation. This time, Lady halted, planting her feet in the turf at the very last moment. So decidedly did the horse stop, Elizabeth's person had no warning of it and continued on neck and crop. Not only did Lady stop, she turned away from the tree at the last moment, causing Elizabeth to catapult over the mare's shoulder and land upon the ground on her back. Hard.

Stunned, she lay there still holding tightly to the horse's reins. When she opened her eyes, she knew she was upon her back, for she saw nothing but the almost cloudless blue sky that somehow had been gifted with a scattering of glittering stars.

"Stars in the morning," she thought dumbly. "How odd."

Gradually the stars disappeared and she saw Lady take a step toward her and put her nose directly above her face as if to take her due.

"You could have let me know you so little liked taking this jump, Lady. We could have discussed it."

Although the horse did not actually reply, when Lady shook her head, Elizabeth understood the message. Lady was in obvious disgust at such a clumsy and unwise rider. Elizabeth was disposed to lie there a moment longer, trying to decide if she was impaired or not. Feebly, she moved her limbs about. It appeared no more ill had befallen her aside from possibly loosening all her teeth. Still undecided if she should simply repose as she was for a time or try to stand, she was suddenly confronted.

Col. Fitzwilliam ejaculated, "Elizabeth! Elizabeth! Are you injured?"

With no little amusement, he had been watching her attempts from the vantage of his own horse some distance away. However, when he saw her fall, he had raced over to her and jumped down, horrified that he had stood idly by and allowed her injury.

Understanding that he had witnessed all, her humiliation was compleat. She closed her eyes in defence of her mortification. First scorn from her horse; now this.

"How long did you have me in your eye?"

She started to laugh, but her body ached. She then liked not to laugh. Fitzwilliam pleaded with her not to move and insisted he would go for help. Call for a surgeon. Send for Darcy.

"No, no, I am fine, I assure you, sir."

She slowly rose whilst he continued to insist that she not.

"Allow me to demonstrate that I am fine."

He helped her up and she moved about a little slowly, but in perfect working order. The good colonel was certain that a gentlewoman such as herself could not possibly continue after such a spill. Elizabeth attempted to persuade him she had not the constitution of a frail, elderly aunt by changing the subject from herself to the mare.

"I cannot understand Lady, for we took a small jump yesterday with no problem. Today she is not of that mind. Darcy said she was even-tempered. Perhaps she likes me not at all."

Fitzwilliam looked the mare over.

"Lady? This is Lady?"

Elizabeth nodded. Fitzwilliam could not but contain his mirth.

"Lady might have jumped in her younger years, but she is far too stiff in the hocks to do so now."

"If so, why so near as yesterday did she take it in all good stead?"

"Perhaps she forgot she could not," he suggested.

"As simple as that?"

"I can explain it no further. If you managed to have Lady take a jump, then you are indeed a horsewoman of merit."

"Has she great age?"

"Well over twenty years, I dare say," Fitzwilliam said. "In fine shape for her age, but for riding, not jumping."

"Darcy gave me an old horse named Lady and did not tell me she could not jump," she said, unreasonably miffed.

"I think he intended for you not to jump," Fitzwilliam suggested.

"Obviously. But I shall not be deterred."

Quite adamant about that, she really did not know what recourse to take. It would seem her husband had foiled her. Thereupon, an idea occurred.

"Perhaps you could help me select a horse that will jump, Colonel. I know the stable is rich with them."

"Indeed. However, the hunters of Pemberley are far too high-spirited for an unpractised rider." Endeavouring not to dampen her spirit, he thereupon added encouragingly, "No matter how natural her talent."

Near tears with disappointment, she could not disguise her frustration. In the face of her acute distress, Fitzwilliam offered the reins of his own fine animal, Scimitar, whereupon Elizabeth looked at him in wonder.

"You would allow me to ride your horse?"

"There is no other I would trust you to than Scimitar."

After her fall, she felt cautious enough to accept his generosity. Generous it was, for she knew most men would begrudge anyone other than themselves to ride their horse. Men who rode to hounds were thought to be more parsimonious with their hunters than they would be with their wives.

Fitzwilliam and Elizabeth stayed in the field for the better part of an hour. Scimitar, indeed, proved a willing and safe jumper, carefully picking his way over the fallen tree trunk no matter what Elizabeth did or did not do. Fitzwilliam was not a superior teacher to Darcy, but as she was less intimidated whilst enlisting his correction, she found herself responding more easily to his instruction. In time, however, even the colonel was frustrated trying to give her more than the most rudimentary of schooling, for a side-saddle was foreign to him. Moreover, there was the impediment of the necessity of a gentleman speaking to a lady of body parts. However comfortable Fitzwilliam was with polite conversation, he was accustomed to giving explicit instructions to cavalrymen in his charge. The vocabulary of the two did not overlap.

("Elizabeth, keep your back straight and cup your…self forward. Good, now grip the horse's sides with your…limbs. Shoulders back, er…front out.")

Finally, finding nothing to request besides "toes up" that did not demand a euphemism, he declared, "I fear you need to have a real instructor, or at least the advice of someone who has mastered jumping in such a precarious balance. The best horsewoman I know is Lady Millhouse."

Patting Scimitar's neck, she explained she wanted to surprise Darcy, then asked, "Do you fancy Lady Millhouse would be willing to school me? And if she did, would she be discreet?"

"Of course she would be happy to help you, she despises idleness. Although I am quite certain there is not a discreet bone in her body, nothing diverts her so much as intrigue. Your secret will be safe with her."

Elizabeth returned Scimitar's reins with reluctance. He put up his hand in opposition.

"I would be honoured if you allowed my horse to help teach you. I would be happy to leave him here until the hunt and take another back to Whitemore."

Grateful he was there to leg her back upon Lady, Elizabeth did not want to think of the spectacle she would present if she had to walk the horse back on foot to the stables.

As they arrived back at the barns, young John met them. Elizabeth explained to Fitzwilliam that John was privy to her ruse. Hence, Fitzwilliam removed his saddle and left Scimitar's reins in the boy's hands with instructions for him to be saddled each time Elizabeth rode. She bade Fitzwilliam good-bye and left him to select a temporary mount.

She had not allowed herself to limp until she had returned indoors. Now, as her limbs were extremely sore, her thoughts begged, "Mrs. Darcy is unattended," but she could not make herself call it out however she might need attending. Upstairs, Hannah filled an invitingly hot tub for her. As she eased herself in, Hannah gasped and pointed to her bruised elbows. Elizabeth dared not inquire as to the colour of her derrière. Her husband had only just returned and though she would have liked to soak in the tub for hours, she forsook the water. Gowning herself in long cuffed sleeves, she lay back upon their bed trying not to emit a groan of pain. She felt as if she had fallen off a horse.

Seeing his wife in her gown so early in the eve led her husband to believe she was in a mood of affection. As to why this night of all nights he was most desirous of sharing this favour with her bestride him, Elizabeth could only inquire silently of God.

As she sat atop him, it was not his hands beneath her gown, but her aching point of collision that seized her thoughts. He instantly realised the moan from her was not born of desire.

"Lizzy, what is the matter? Are you ill? You should have spoken."

Found out, she gratefully fell to the side and groaned in relief.

"Are you ill, Lizzy?"

She shook her head decidedly. Her neck was sore and she moaned again.

"Your horse threw you!" he accused.

"I fell off my horse," she admitted.

She reconsidered. Perhaps she was thrown from her horse, that sounded more proficient, but his countenance did not appear to invite such specifics.

"How?" he demanded.

She replied defensively, "You put me upon a horse that would not jump!"

This accusation was met with silence.

Then, "Yes. You were not to jump."

He was maddeningly good at this, confronting her with facts as he did.

"You said I was not to jump. I did not choose it."

There, touché.

"You cannot learn to jump until you learn to ride."

Having no answer to that, she changed course, "Lady was her name. I should have guessed."

She huffily turned upon her side, her back to him. However, her side ached and the only position of comfort she could find was upon her stomach. She was too sore even to huff effectively.

Taking pity upon her, he sat up and begat a gentle massage of her shoulders.

"I pray this shall convince you to allow yourself to become more practised before attempting such a thing again. And please promise not to ride alone again until you are."

She considered it would not be deceitful to promise him this and did. The promise extracted, he raised her gown and saw her bruised backside. He winced. Looks of reproach were exchanged. A truce was called.

Hunt day began a little gloomy and cold, but by the time all the riders had converged upon the courtyard, the sun had burned away the chill. Pemberley was filled with guests, the most serious hunters having spent the night in order to get the best rest, and hence the keenest sense in pursuit of the fox. The field would consist of four-and-twenty hunters, not to mention a few unlikely riders (beyond the Mistress of Pemberley). In truth, Elizabeth was somewhat relieved about a turn of events she learnt of but the night before. For she believed if her own endeavour was ultimately untoward, a public show of other impolitic riders would dilute her infamy.

Eventually disabused of the notion that Elizabeth was already with child, Mrs. Bennet had turned her attention to the still unmarried Kitty, applying to Mr. Bennet to stay on for the weekend of the hunt. This application may well have been upon Kitty's behalf, but it was at her mother's behest. For Mrs. Bennet was riding the heady crest of three married daughters within the year. Her optimism bade her believe that Derbyshire society in general, and the auspices of Pemberley specifically, would offer Kitty more opportunity of matrimonial possibilities than Hertfordshire.

Mr. Bennet was not in favour of the extension of their visit, complaining he could not sleep well in any other bed but his own. That had always been his given reason for his reluctance to travel, but there was a truer one.

He had a keen interest in books, and Pemberley's vaunted library had held him captive for the first half of his visit. However, his love of literature fared a poor second to his admiration for independence. That was primary, and relished beyond any other possession. Once Mrs. Bennet found him hidden in a deep chair, twirling a glass of brandy, *The History of Rasselas, The Prince of Abyssinia* open in his lap, all joy of Pemberley evaporated. In the home of another he had not the opportunity to take his leave upon some solitary errand as he did when at Longbourn. Confinement with his wife was tolerable only when there was chance of escape.

Mrs. Bennet had a trying voice when at ease; in want of something she could be quite strident. Mr. Bennet thus now chose to listen to her at his leisure for a few days more, rather than deny her, only to hear of her unhappiness all the way home. Hence, stay they did.

Adding to the happy party at Pemberley was Georgiana (who did not ride, but loved to watch those who did). Accompanying her home from London was Newton Hinchcliffe, a nephew of the Millhouses. This young man was a pale, esoteric sort of fellow (not at all as one would expect a kinsman of the Millhouses) and an Easter term graduate of Oxford.

He was prone to brooding, but Lady Millhouse had misinterpreted his lugubrious expression as poor digestion, insisting he return to the country, for she was well aware that fresh air would cure any malady. ("One good feist is all he needs," she had announced to all.)

His despondency, however, was born not of gas, but of academia. As it happened, he had come precariously close, and then in the end, had failed to earn a coveted double first at Oxford. After suffering with him through this near miss, his family was left hanging precipitously the previous summer when, disappointed in matters educational, he had flirted with the possibility of renouncing High Church for Low. He was only rescued from this scandalous act by being reminded that did he do so, he would have to forgo not only dancing, but his impressive cerulean coat and satin waistcoat. Evangelism demanded black. Duly reprimanded (what was he thinking?), his reformist tendencies were set aside for sartorial splendour. Hence, he found consolation in self-expression.

Deciding whether to promote his soul in paint or verse tortured him for over a month, but ultimately the decision was made by merit of reason. Painting had the incentive of requiring a paid model (he did not favour landscape—the outdoors, you know), but suffered the misfortune of being untidy. This, along with the understanding that one could be staring out the window and still call oneself a writer, decided him in favour of a literary career. Once that decision was made, he only tore himself away from his London garret at the insistence of his aunt. Lady Millhouse was quite certain he should die was he never to leave town.

The imposition his window placed upon his time left little for writing and, in lieu of any from his own pen, he turned to the convenience of the published works of others. That this poet had never actually written a poem did not alter the admiration of the feminine sort. For he had a pronounced single blonde curl that just grazed a set of eyebrows over a pair of particularly soulful brown eyes. If that did not a poet bespeak, what else could? Thus saith Kitty and Maria.

Indeed, forefront in admiration of young Hinchcliffe were Miss Bennet and Miss Lucas, who, even though Elizabeth glared at them mightily, became faint in the presence of the poetic (if not poet) Newton Hinchcliffe.

The competition for young Hinchcliffe occasionally became a larger rivalry than Maria and Kitty's friendship could withstand (Kitty once, in a snit, yanked one of Maria's ringlets), but it was to no avail. As well-tended as was his blonde forelock, one might surmise that it was purposely upon display. But so intent was he upon examining his own angst, their swooning went for naught. Young Hinchcliffe was more quixotic in word than in deed. Thus their histrionics did not excite him to love, merely frightened him. And, much to their displeasure and Mr. Darcy's, he sought the becalming company of Georgiana, with whom he shared a common interest in the written word.

Darcy disliked the overwrought sensibilities of young Hinchcliffe in reverse pro-portion to Kitty and Maria's regard for that young man. The moment they would swoon, young Hinchcliffe took to the garden with Georgiana (which was quite as out-doors as he chose to go). The two strolled the grounds in deep conversation whilst Darcy frowned and Kitty and Maria sat glumly in the window, watching, united again in defeat.

That is, they sat there mooning over Mr. Hinchcliffe until they caught sight of a far too familiar figure emerging from a hired coach. Nothing could clear a room faster than the spectre of Mr. Collins.

It is a seldom-argued truth that events anticipated with dread occasion with much greater dispatch than those that do not. Thus, although Mr. Collins's visit was expected, Elizabeth had not properly steeled herself by the time he arrived. However, his wife accompanied him, and the chance to see Charlotte again occasioned Mr. Collins a more welcome guest (but just by the merest margin).

He and Charlotte had travelled to Derbyshire from Kent at a great deal of personal sac-rifice. As vicar to Hunsford, Mr. Collins explained to those who remained in the drawing room beyond his introduction (primarily those hitherto unacquainted with him), he rarely had time to draw himself away from his exceedingly important duties to make such a trip. He did so then only as a favour to his very favourite cousin, Mrs. Elizabeth Darcy.

"I, of course, come under the personal condescension of the Mistress of Rosings Park, Lady Catherine de Bourgh," Mr. Collins said, then ducking his chin in all due modesty, clarified, "Mr. Darcy's aunt."

Satisfied that all present were aware of his elevated connexions, he bowed ever so dramatically. So deep was his genuflection, a few there were confused as to whether or not to applaud. Lady Millhouse was not among them.

"I dare say sir, you are a goose, are you not?"

Obtuseness having been elevated to his own particular level of virtuosity, Mr. Collins bowed again in Lady Millhouse's direction to acknowledge the kind words.

Settled in the drawing room with teacups on their knees, Elizabeth engaged Char-lotte in conversation. (Mr. Darcy had to take care of urgent business in another part of the house—a far, far distant part of the house.) Thus, Mr. Collins looked about the room at his illustrious company. He saw his decision had been the correct one. There were far more persons of consequence in visit to Pemberley than Rosings Park. More-over, he was not cousin to Lady Catherine.

Yes, he was frightfully satisfied with his decision. Had he not allowed that self-satisfaction to inflate as he did, he could have saved himself a great deal of beleaguer-ment. As it was, he set about ingratiating himself with whomever he could. Mr. Bennet sat nearest, betwixt himself and Lady Millhouse. His uncle, Mr. Bennet, was a gentle-man, but as what little he had was already entailed to Mr. Collins by reason of five daughters, the good vicar looked to Lady Millhouse for opportunity to curry favour.

"Cousin Elizabeth tells me you are a horsewoman of unparalleled proficiency, Lady Millhouse. Nothing suits the constitution better than the fresh air and exercise of a good hunt!"

However, Lady Millhouse bested even Mr. Bennet when it came to enjoying a truly fallible being.

She addressed Mr. Collins, "You have come here to hunt, Mr. Collins?"

Lady Millhouse inquiring of him? Mr. Collins was delighted by her interest, and although he had not, the suggestion from a woman of her import bade it seem much more likely.

He said, "I am most honoured at the suggestion, Lady Millhouse. I do enjoy nothing more than a hunt. And I flatter myself that there are few who enjoy taking a fence more than myself." (He had not actually ever taken a fence, but he had been atop a horse which travelled past several.) "However, as a lowly clergyman, my wife and I were forced to travel by hired equipage. Hence, at the moment I am afoot. I fear I must," he bowed low again, "graciously decline."

"Nonsense! There are many horses here. I am certain Mr. Darcy will lend you one. The weather is superb! I must have you hunt!"

Hence it was decided. Elizabeth, not married to Mr. Collins, and therefore horrified at the possibly fatal consequences of his riding to the hunt, cut a look at Charlotte (who should have been). Mrs. Collins, however, betrayed nothing but benign indifference to the precariousness of her husband's immediate future.

Whilst Mr. Collins sat upon the edge of a chair attempting to gain Lady Millhouse's attention ("Ahem, Lady Millhouse? Lady Millhouse?") that good lady had turned to Mr. Bennet.

"And you sir? Do you hunt?"

Having been reduced to escaping from his wife's company to that of Mr. Collins, Mr. Bennet was in desperate enough straits to think he would like to do just that. Nothing sounded better than riding out all day with persons other than Mrs. Bennet. Indeed, if Mr. Collins truly mounted a horse, seeing that alone would be worth the trouble.

He answered, "I hunt, but it has been near a dozen years since I rode to hounds, dear Lady Millhouse. But I think it an excellent notion."

"Lady Millhouse. Oh, Lady Millhouse," Mr. Collins continued to try to regain her attention.

She shushed him, "Mr. Collins, do not fear, you are not imposing. Pray, he is not, is he, Elizabeth?"

Lady Millhouse had Mr. Collins by the hand and was out of the room before Elizabeth could stop either of them. Her father sat in his chair chuckling, but stopped when he looked at Charlotte. He observed the same disinterest as did Elizabeth.

Now seriously fretting, Elizabeth bade her, "He would not truly attempt such a thing, would he, Charlotte?"

Charlotte smiled a strange little smile, took another sip of tea with all the complacency of someone who saw no reason to be troubled. If Charlotte was not in fear for her husband, then Elizabeth decided it was not a burden that necessarily fell to her, and turned her worry toward her own horsemanship.

Early the next forenoon, whilst many a guest was still in their morning-gown, Lady Millhouse pounded upon Mr. Collins's door.

With much swilling of wine, the field of riders awaited the hounds to be put in. When the hubbub surrounding the pre-hunt toasting reached its apex, Elizabeth and Scimitar eased into their midst. None too boldly, she looked about waiting to be discovered. It took her a moment to descry her husband, for he was not astride Blackjack, but rode a blood-bay named Jupiter. That he eschewed his beloved mount for the best fence horse in the barn announced just how earnestly he took such a hunt.

He spotted her, and waved a greeting. Forthwith of occasioning that happy beckoning was his simultaneous recognition of Scimitar beneath her and what that betokened. He was quite unamused.

"Pray, what design do you propose? Where is Lady?"

"Under a guest who does not intend to jump, one must suppose," Elizabeth answered firmly.

He turned about in his saddle searching for Fitzwilliam. When he espied him upon an unfamiliar black gelding, he affixed him with an icy stare. Witnessing it, Fitzwilliam flicked the end of his reins against his palm, pursed his lips, and remained silent. Darcy redirected his ire to his wife. However, his voice remained very calm, in a curious, strained way.

"Pray, how do you come to ride Scimitar, Elizabeth?"

Fitzwilliam overcame his quiet to rise to her defence.

"A surprise for you, Darcy. She has been under instruction every day…"

However, his voice trailed off, as if not really determined to provoke Darcy further. Despite such consideration, his cousin's temper was roiling quite magnificently.

To Elizabeth, Darcy repeated, "Every day, indeed. I am all astonishment."

His anger surpassed any pique she might have imagined. His face overspread with a shade of hauteur rivalling the one that she had witnessed that fateful evening in Kent. Eventually, it took on a most peculiar and unpleasant rosy hue.

"Colonel Fitzwilliam declared me capable of handling Scimitar and that you would not deny me the hunt," she said sprightly.

Her attempt at a smile died a dismal death, however, and she felt a bit cowardly about ricocheting the blame back toward Fitzwilliam, the success of which exacerbated her guilt. Darcy returned his glare to Fitzwilliam, who sat very straight in his saddle and drew upon the reins of his horse, edging him away.

Still holding Fitzwilliam in his eye, Darcy said to Elizabeth, "How frightfully happy I am to know that Colonel Fitzwilliam knows my mind better than I myself. I shall be certain to confer with him in the future and ask him what is my will that day. It will save my mind a great deal of bother."

Fitzwilliam looked a bit disconcerted by Darcy's sarcasm. Elizabeth was shocked by it herself, for she was certain he was, for some reason, angrier at Fitzwilliam's complicity than at her covertness. The ill-conception of the entire scheme was falling readily apparent when Lady Millhouse turned her horse to join them.

Heartily, she said to the Master of Pemberley, "Wait until you see her perform, Darcy! You shall be quite astonished. I think in time your sweet wife will ride to covert as well as any gentleman here."

Darcy looked at Lady Millhouse without comprehension.

"You have seen Elizabeth ride?"

"It was Lady Millhouse who instructed me, for I promised you I would not ride out alone," Elizabeth told him.

Flustered, Darcy said, "I see. I see."

It took a moment for Elizabeth to understand that Darcy had believed that she had spent her time in Fitzwilliam's company. Evidently his anger had been whipped into a lather by indiscriminate jealousy. Upon the realisation of his misapprehension, his countenance crimsoned ever more.

He said, "Very good," several times more than necessary.

"Well," Elizabeth reflected to herself, "when it comes to his wife, the Master of Pemberley is as chary as any other man."

She would even have offered him that, had she the opportunity. However, upon the edge of the group a commotion commenced that stole everyone's attention.

For, indeed, Lady was under a rider who did not intend to jump.

The commandeered Mr. Collins was attempting to mount her with the help of one footman on all fours and a second to leg him up. The first attempt was but partially successful, in that Mr. Collins got his leg over, but Lady lowered her head and he slid down her neck, returning to the very spot from whence he had started.

Mr. Darcy, always impenetrably grave at social indiscretions and yet in high dudgeon over his misapprehension, had further reason to glower.

Mr. Collins was moderately tall, immoderately heavy, and somewhat ungainly. Hence, he was altogether amazed he had managed such a feat and was still standing. The footman, who had struggled mightily just to get him up, called for reinforcements for another go. Another footman joined him and this double effort almost prevailed. An additional heave actually raised Mr. Collins to saddle level again. However, quite fordone from the first attempt, as he endeavoured to fling his leg over, Mr. Collins's strength failed and he fell back.

This might not have been met with the laughter that it did, had not Mr. Collins, in the splayed position that he was, landed atop one footman's shoulders. Moreover, in an effort to right himself, Mr. Collins frantically grabbed the poor man's head. Regrettably, this grappling dislodged the footman's wig and it sagged over his eyes, thus rendering the poor man momentarily sightless. In his blind confusion, the be-Collinsed footman attempted to rid himself of his unwanted passenger by unloading him atop Lady. This, however, was all too successful, for while Mr. Collins was ejected from the footman's shoulders onto the back of the horse, momentum propelled him beyond.

Had there not been the good fortune of a portly wine servitor happening by right then, Elizabeth's premonition on behalf of Mr. Collins neck might have actually been realised before he was able to mount his horse.

As it was, there was only a great deal of noise and egregiously wounded dignities of the unwigged footman and flattened wine server. Mr. Collins apologised to the footman whilst atop his shoulders and he apologised further to the wine server whilst the man was underneath him. If Lady had not been startled by the clatter of silver and trotted for the barn, he most probably would have offered apology to her as well.

"Mr. Collins," Lady Millhouse explained, "you need a shorter horse!"

Mr. Collins was really not inclined to think he needed a horse at all, but Lady Millhouse seemed so very certain he did, he dared not argue. Moreover, very nearly actually getting atop a horse gave him more confidence than prudence would have allowed.

At that moment it was announced that Mrs. Bennet had but just discovered her husband's intent to ride, for her voice could be heard somewhere upon the other side of the toasting riders.

"Mr. Bennet! Mr. Bennet! You will be killed! Mr. Bennet!"

Concurrent of Mrs. Bennet's fears for Mr. Bennet's life was heard the call that the quarry had been flushed from the gorse. Hounds began to bay and the horses, well-attuned to the hunt, began to jig.

The excitement was infectious. Elizabeth was certain no heart raced with more anticipation than did hers (in particularly good spirits now that she saw Lady had escaped Mr. Collins and her father had eluded her mother). As they began to canter out, her excitement built. Darcy shadowed her persistently, but could not quite abandon the subject of how she came to ride Scimitar. She explained to his enquiry as best she could (whilst trying not to bounce more than post upon the cantering horse's back) how Fitzwilliam saw her fall.

In a bit of a chide, she asked, "How did you think I came to ride Scimitar, Darcy?"

It came as no surprise that he changed the subject.

"Let us catch up to the others."

He kicked Jupiter into an easy gallop and called to Elizabeth to stay with him and bade her not attempt anything untoward. In other circumstances, Elizabeth might have rebelled. She had, however, gained enough wisdom from her fall not to want to repeat the experience and so she did not promote Scimitar unduly.

Once the horn sounded, Lady Millhouse forsook any interest in Mr. Collins's equestrian attempts and left him to find another horse upon his own. Once it commenced, Lord and Lady Millhouse brooked little distraction from the hunt, heedless whether it was their hunt or someone else's. Lady Millhouse, however, catching sight of Elizabeth, insisted she be more aggressive and show Darcy how well she could ride.

In encouragement, she called, "Lie upon your oars, Elizabeth! The tide is with you." (Her father had been a navy man.)

The day was fine and crisp, spirits were exalted, and Elizabeth took a few low jumps. After his initial contretemps, Darcy manifested every sign of good humour. Indeed, with all due understanding of provocation, he challenged Elizabeth to prove her horsemanship, kicking Jupiter into a run. She countered with a kick of her own and their horses competed. Darcy's amusement at the idea of her contesting him was evident and she sought to show him up. Of course, even upon Scimitar she was no match, but he allowed her to think it a race for a time before he moved ahead of her.

Had he not been so smug, he might have been watching Jupiter's path more closely. But as exacting a bit of a gloat absorbed all his attention, he did not see the fox that had been the instigator of the entire day run directly into his path. Jupiter did, however, and swerved almost in a pivot. Decidedly.

Darcy, of course, did not swerve. After a momentary midair excursion, he fell hard to the ground. Jupiter, aware that something impolitic had occurred, first ran in circles and then stopped, shuddering slightly, and hung his head. Elizabeth did not see the horse's contrition, only Darcy down.

Tall as Scimitar was, she withstood no hesitation and leapt from him even before he had come to a full halt. Landing upon all fours, she scrambled to her feet and flew to her husband's side. He had initially sat up, having only wounded his dignity (which was in far greater abundance than that of the unwigged footman and flattened wine server). She fell to her knees, calling his name.

Well aware he suffered no injury, he allowed her concern to birth the possibility. As she hovered over him, he lay back and moaned. He portrayed great trauma with impressive melodrama, only to betray himself by a furtive peek to gauge her reaction.

She smote him on the shoulder with a closed fist.

"What mockery!" she cried and rose to leave.

He caught her arm and drew her down to a kiss.

"If you are to nurse me, begin with my lips."

"You, sir, shall be fortunate if I do not deliver you true impairment, for you deserve it!"

Once he was up and walking about, Elizabeth bade him assure her he was fine by operating all of his limbs, then he legged her back atop Scimitar. She took the horse's reins, looked down upon him, and made an announcement in feigned hauteur.

"I understand, Mr. Darcy, that horses tend to go where their riders are looking. Hence, perhaps you should be looking ahead, if that is where you hope to go."

She kicked her horse forward. Darcy understood that a line had been drawn in the sand. He leapt onto Jupiter and took off after her, and neither went in the direction of the fox.

Unbeknownst to them, they had a chance for him still. For as Darcy and Elizabeth set about their own frolic, the fox had been trailed and lost. Scattered about upon futile quest for the vixen, the sound of a second baying of the hounds bade the other hunters converge.

"Tally-Ho" was sounded.

All joined a headlong race toward the quarry that was high-tailing it to the far side of the hill. One-and-twenty riders had just gotten up to speed at the crest when they were startled by meeting a horse and rider (both terms could be used quite loosely) flying head-long in the direction whence they had just come.

The second commotion of the day had the same instigator, but different means. The initial dilemma involved Mr. Collins's attempt to mount a horse; the subsequent arose upon his attempt to stop one.

For some helpful person at Pemberley's stables had located a horse nearer to the ground for Mr. Collins to ride to the hunt. Due to its shorter stature, Mr. Collins pre-sumed his substitute ride was less of a risk to jump as well. However, the pony he rode was a Connemara and that Mr. Collins's feet hung below its belly did not convince the animal it was impossible to leap a fence with him aboard.

By the time he met the field, his pony was running full out, and Mr. Collins had abandoned his reins. Indeed, they flapped about behind him whilst he clung to the pommel of the saddle. The pony's strides were quick, which did not suppose them smooth to a rider who had never actually acquainted his posterior to a post. Thus, Mr. Collins flailed about quite impressively. It was apparent that a miscue had occurred when he and his mount passed the pack of hounds upon the other side of the hill. Evidently, the high-pitched squeal which Mr. Collins was emitting excited the dogs off the trail of the fox and onto him and his pony.

Because the dogs were plunging forth in the opposite direction behind Mr. Collins, the riders stopped in stunned disbelief, each taking his own counsel upon what to do next. Some commenced to follow the hounds after Mr. Collins; some held their ground. Eventually all came to an astonished halt, uncertain they believed their own eyes. For the Connemara pony, quite in a mind of its own (for lack of any other) took a wide turn, rounding the group, and headed back the other way with Mr. Collins still floundering atop him.

He disappeared back over the crest of the same hill whence he first came, the forty dogs baying upon his trail. As Mr. Collins's shrieks echoed off into the distance, each rider decided independently, yet synchronously, to follow.

They rode but a quarter of a mile before they came upon a fearful sight. A thorny thicket was warily being eyed by two-score silent hounds. Some sat looking into the brush; others shambled about in tongue-hanging exhaustion. The Connemara pony stood quivering, its saddle hanging ominously to one side. As the riders approached the thicket, the master of the hounds and the huntsman met them. All stopped in an informal semi-circle, silently peering into the tangled copse.

In a moment, Fitzwilliam and Mr. Bennet (it was his nephew after all) urged their horses forward a few feet, and then stepped down. Except for a slight rustling breeze and the heaving breaths of the winded animals, all was quiet. Both men looked first at the other, then to the bush. Thereupon, Mr. Bennet reached out, gingerly drew back a branch, and peered into the thick gorse.

There was movement. Upon hearing some unintelligible sound, the dogs began to bay again. Immediately, two more men jumped down in aid. The thorny branches were pulled back and Mr. Collins was removed scratched and gibbering from the thicket. The field stood in murmuring relief that he had not been killed, only rendered witless (no one saw that as a serious impediment for him).

It was only when Fitzwilliam investigated him for injuries that he found the point of his landing congruous with the highly sought fox (much more flattened than was the wine server). And fortune allowed Mr. Collins to leave the course virtually buggered, but senseless of it.

By late afternoon, when Darcy and Elizabeth eventually overtook the hunt, most of the hunters were in an odd mood, simply meandering toward Pemberley in polite wait for their host and hostess. When the Darcys caught up, the only notice that was made of their absence from the field was that there was no notice made of it at all. Elizabeth espied Mr. Collins lying upon his stomach across the saddle of a pretty little pony, grunting each time that the animal took a step. She turned to her father, a question upon her lips.

However, Mr. Bennet put up the flat of his hand and said, "Ask not."

Lady Millhouse, who took notice of everything, rode up next to Darcy, reached out, and grandly slapped him upon the back.

"I say, Darcy, as often as you plough that field, it will surely yield you a good crop soon."

Lord Millhouse was as silent as his wife was candid, yet laughed heartily at his wife's remark. Darcy had long accepted her earthy euphemisms, but until that day, only others had suffered them. If Elizabeth heard, she made a great pretence of being unwitting of it.

Hitherto, Darcy knew he should have taken offence at such a comment. His dignity was abused somewhat that day too, yet the sun-dappled grounds they trod bade him not to deny what he knew to be true. Protestation always invited further study.

Therefore, he simply spurred his horse up to Fitzwilliam's, and, in penitence, asked him of the hunt.

Within a month of first setting foot upon Pemberley soil, John Christie had allowed himself a very singular pleasure. He endured the unaccustomed sense of belonging. Yet the manor hold still rendered him in awe.

So imposing had the manor house and holdings been when first he had dared approach them, John had taken his first measure of them from a peek around the trunk of a sizeable oak. The beauteous sight had done much to excite his esteem.

Pemberley was a considerable eminence, one that included an enormous park with an untold variety of ground, all fetchingly framed by a wood. Pemberley House situated itself prettily on a rise beyond a lazy, but consequential, stream, one that swelled into a small lake at the bottom of a narrow valley.

A soft wash of dusk bathed the stables as John's eyes lit upon them, eliciting from him a swift intake of air at their beauty. His gaze ascertained that they were surrounded by hedges neatly trimmed and connected by a covered galley. The ground betwixt the outbuildings was not dirt, or even gravel. It was cobblestone. So well-tended was the place that nary a tussock sprang from between them, although a neat ring of turf surrounded the paddock. Beyond the carriage house was a trellised path that led to the great house itself.

Squatting within the concealment of some heretofore unfamiliar berried bushes, he gaped in wondrous awe. This shelter allowed him to take a more detailed inspection of what interested him most.

There were two horse barns, each large enough to lodge at least a dozen and a half horses. Several fine-looking mares were loose in the enclosure and nibbled at the winter grass whilst a foal capered about in a frisk. Whilst eyeing their doings, the boy idly plucked a berry from the bush, and then hastily spat it out. It was unexpectedly bitter.

So very little notice did he take of this, the offending fruit lay at his feet uninspected. He was much taken with the aroma of clover hay, which filled his nostrils with unerring seduction. Enthralled, he fancied taking a running leap onto the stack that tumbled out of the big doors at one end of one barn. Had he, he thought it quite probable that he could lie within it for a lifetime. It was a temptation to take a run even then, but there were too many people about to make it a serious consideration. In time, he edged out into the sunlight and a groom espied him.

"What d' ye want 'ere, boy?" said the man.

John thought to wrest his hat from his head and clutched it tightly before him.

"Work, sir," he answered.

The man made no effort to speak in response and dismissively waved him begone. John turned away quite reluctantly, disappointed he had not the opportunity to make his case for employment.

As he turned, the man called out, "Ain't ye that boy from the inn? The one what's ma died?"

Villages. Was nothing safe from gossip? Everyone knew everyone and everyone's business.

Pity he sought not. He sought honest work. Yet his situation was dire. Hence, he nodded in affirmation that indeed, he was. The man then asked his age. Understanding that he was too old for someone to take him in and too young to be expected to do a man's work, he weighed what answer best would increase his chances before responding. Thinking it more likely that he could be taken for older than younger, he stood tall and told a bald-faced lie.

"I'm sixteen, sir."

In fortune, the man did not blink at the prevarication.

"It's not likely ye are needed 'ere, but stay and talk to the man. He might 'ave somethin' for ye," was the reply.

Certainly, that was no absolute, but he had managed an audience. This was a considerable feat in that customarily, a stranger would be run off, as thievery was known to be the prevalent occupation of strangers in the countryside.

Finding a barrel, John settled upon it to wait for "The Man." He watched as the half dozen stable-hands fed the horses and raked what had been eliminated and shovelled it out the door. The odour of manure was not unwelcome, for it smelled of profit. Many an hour he had spent upon the handle end of a pitchfork and was paid, if not wages, at least a meal. There were far less worthy occupations than mucking out. Certainly, that was better than cleaning the floor of an alehouse (that was truly execrable). Indeed, he would much rather smell the stench of a horse.

It was several hours before a short, jowly man with chin whiskers arrived. He was pointed out to John Christie as the overseer of the estate. However, Mr. Rhymes had no more than begun their interview when a fine gentleman and his lady arrived. Rhymes immediately quit him and diverted all his attention to this obviously illustrious couple. The gentleman was impressively tall, even when he alit his horse. And the lady was beautiful, as befit a man of such prominence.

In all good time, the gentleman spoke to Rhymes, the lady spoke to the gentleman. Mr. Rhymes returned to John and shook his head with finality. John gathered his few belongings with resignation, not truly disappointed, just downcast. He had known he was unlikely to have found work at Pemberley. An estate such as it was could have service of the most practised of servitors. It had been folly to believe in his mother's omens and superstitions.

The groom to whom he had first spoken looked upon his crestfallen face and took pity upon him. He offered John to attend his own table, then allowed that the hayloft suited sleep most admirably.

"First light is soon enough t'go," he had said kindly.

Yet no sooner had John settled into his bed of hay when the harsh light of a lantern aroused him. Beyond the beacon was the face of Mr. Rhymes. His first thought was that he would be routed. He stood eyeing the man toe to toe, considering whether to offer that he was there by invitation or leave without a word.

Rhymes anticipated no explanation, he said, "We've been lookin' fer ye. Aye donno' know why ye be so fortunate, son. But Mr. Darcy 'imself has said for ye t'stay."

Mr. Darcy, it would seem, was the tall, imposing gentleman he had seen. It was his lady's horse to which he owed his employment (thus enhancing his previous thin regard of superstition). The Good Samaritan who offered supper introduced himself as Edward Hardin and his wife as "the missus." With a jerk of his head, he told John to follow him to see where he was to stay.

Never had John seen such luxurious lodgings. The grooms' quarters had windows. They had windows with glazing and beds with legs. (A pallet upon the floor was the best his mother could give him.) Moreover, even the stable-hands at Pemberley enjoyed muslin sheets. John had never seen a bed that actually had sheets. He had heard of such a thing, of course. He had seen bedclothes hanging out to dry, the Kympton Inn being of greater largesse of soap than many. Perhaps his intuition to come to Pemberley had not been a folly. The place was fine. The servants were evidently happy. If he was not so innocent as to believe a compleat farewell to disappointment and spleen was at hand, he held hope that it might well be nigh. Yet superstition and premonition held him prisoner, and the very delectation of the situation led him to expect something equally contrary to befall him.

It did. John Christie had but a day of respite before he espied, with utmost incredulity, none other than Tom Reed lounging against a door, cleaning his teeth with an obscenely large knife. A few other employees stood about, some in willful occupation of not hearing his disreputable remarks, others thanking them with harsh laughter. Dejectedly, John could not help but recall seeing him in Kympton on the eve of his mother's death.

Reed embodied every evil that a boy could conjure: sloth, greed, envy, gluttony, lust, and anger. (If he could have remembered the seventh, he may well have found Reed guilty of that, too.) Immediately upon Reed recognising Abigail's boy, he abandoned furthering the complaint that he was not allowed inside the great house to serve as footman (there was vanity). Edward Hardin had newly informed him that he was forthwith stricken from thence and relegated to riding upon the coach and to the stables. Reed had been convinced he should serve the table and was furious to be denied access to even the lowest floor of the manor-house. Of this, he complained with all the vehemence of an exceedingly vile vocabulary.

Great was John's horror upon seeing such a despicable apparition, and he jumped behind a wall and gave making himself thin full occupation. But all was for naught. Reed had espied him.

"Boy!" he had exclaimed. "Boy! Come 'ere!"

John stepped forward in quivering reluctance. Reed grabbed him by the nape of the neck with a hand so huge, the thumb and forefinger almost met beneath John's chin.

He said to the other men, "See this boy? There be no better wagtail than his ma. Am I right, boy?"

The other men who stood with him instituted a murmured disapproval, but none were of a notion to actually intercede. Displaying more gumption than prudence, John defiantly announced that his mother was not loose, and more specifically, was now dead.

"Pity," Reed said, his countenance contradicting the sentiment.

Thereupon, he turned to the other men there, saying, "She were a bit of a muck-suckle, but she could blow my bag-pipe good as any…"

Time upon the brutal streets of London was not without its education. Hence, John Christie imposed a quick feint, releasing Reed's stranglehold upon his neck. His instinctive reaction was to kick Reed in the danglers for good measure, but an innate wisdom told him this time he should invest all his energy in escape. As he broke free and ran, Reed angrily reached out after him. Seeing he had lost his quarry, he laughed the only way he knew how—meanly.

John eluded Reed that day and for many after. Other interests deflected Reed, for he was never in want of a scheme of some sort. John avoided him conscientiously. He knew no good would come of such an acquaintance. For the first time, John had pride of employment and did not want to jeopardise it. Reed was an impediment. A sorry impediment.

Winter did coldly pass and spring was beckoning when two days before Elizabeth's birthday, Darcy most unexpectedly announced that he and Fitzwilliam would be taking a short overnight trip. They would leave at first light. It was to be the first night spent out of each other's arms, and that it came upon the eve of her birthday was not the gift for which Elizabeth would have wished. As he otherwise paid her every attention, she thought it insupportable to complain about such a triviality. Hence, she did not ask why she could not accompany them. She presumed they could make shorter work of their business upon horseback than having to make their journey in the carriage with her.

Mr. Darcy eschewed travelling by coach when he was alone. Horseback offered a freedom of mind unobtainable from the seat of his fashionable six-horse coach. From thence, duty encroached. (On horseback he was not actually liberated from the weight of his position, but he bore it with better humour.) Albeit he enjoyed the power of doing what he pleased and had better means of having his will than many others, true liberty was his more infrequent guest than, say, even indecision or ambivalence. Decision and certainty ruled his life.

This lack of liberty, however, was of his own hand. Had he so wanted, the responsibility for Pemberley could be shirked without a second thought. For it was under the stern guidance of a good overseer in Mr. Rhymes.

With so many people under his guardianship, Mr. Darcy chose not to leave it to another. To him, that was almost as unthinkable as it was insupportable. Moreover, his one true love beyond his wife was of the soil of Derbyshire. Few people were witting of such a curious leaning.

Farming was technically the occupation of Pemberley, but propriety allowed Darcy no more than a very proprietary interest. Most men to the manor born rarely looked upon their land beyond the coverts. Mr. Darcy rode out daily as the overseer of heart, if not of record.

Once, in all the impulsivity of youth, he announced to Fitzwilliam that if he had one good horse and a hectare of land, his life would never be wanting. (For his part, Fitzwilliam allowed that he wanted but one good horse.) As insular as was his life, Darcy could hardly have been unaware of the bleak existence of those who worked the land. Not unlike most young men who had never actually suffered a day's true labour, he had an elevated notion of what it meant to spend one's days turning the earth and laying in crops. That he, upon particularly euphoric rides out, thought himself quite amenable to such a life, he admitted to not a soul. The ridicule would be unendurable.

Pragmatism ruled his life. Hence, that little fantasy kept company in the back of his mind along with a picture of Elizabeth at the door of a thatched-roof cottage, in muslin cap and apron, babe upon each hip. (Most likely, she would not find the notion utterly agreeable, but she was, albeit, the single woman he knew who would not laugh.)

Parallel to Darcy's love of the soil was Fitzwilliam's love of the army. Both men had been raised in similar privilege and indulgence. As a second son, Fitzwilliam had not the prospects of Darcy, but he could have led a comfortably idle life. He could have taken his commission in the Life Guard Greens. There he could have lifted a glass with the other un-entailed sons of the aristocracy. (At least, with those not carted off to toil in the East India Company.) There, he could have lolled at court, kissing the hands of smitten ladies with no greater fear than to marry badly.

Fitzwilliam despised idleness in general and life at court in London specifically. Rather, he took a commission in the cavalry. When he did, some of his fellow officers questioned his sanity; others had thought him a fool to submit to such discipline and deprivation. It was an error of their judgement upon either account. It took courage and skill to lead a charge of light cavalry. Fitzwilliam commanded these traits—and had his one good horse in Scimitar.

Their boyhood passions had been identical: the horse and the sword. Both were put upon horses before their third birthdays, and they jousted with birch limbs. It was not lost upon Darcy that Fitzwilliam alone stayed true to their early ambitions. While they both still rode, it was Fitzwilliam who traded his foil for the finely honed curve of a genuine sabre in his scabbard. Long before had Darcy put his away, now content to wear it but upon royal occasions. He had always admired Fitzwilliam's choice of mettle over indifference.

That day, the mission upon which they travelled was of great import, but one of a peculiarly happy nature, thus not hindering good humour. They enjoyed the charm of reminiscences of their childhood and commiserated fancied travails. Not unlike a declawed beast of prey, Darcy lay in quiet wait of an opportunity to broach a subject with his cousin, one with which he had been charged by his aunt, Fitzwilliam's mother.

The subject was of particular import to her.

The training of new cavalry recruits fell to Fitzwilliam's duty, yet he longed for battle himself. As none was so grieved as a soldier without a fight, the news of an able general seeking ambitious officers had engendered Fitzwilliam with a new determination to join the war with the French.

"It is what I have been trained for all my life," he had said.

However ready Fitzwilliam was for battle, not all shared his enthusiasm for jeopardy. Lady Matlock was exceedingly fond of her youngest child and had issued a mother's prerogative by bidding Darcy (brother James had little influence over Geoffrey) to dissuade Fitzwilliam of his notion of taking off in pursuit of Napoleon. Not an obligation he cared for, but as Darcy was the foremost male member of their family, it was his patriarchal duty.

Hence, upon their leisurely sojourn, he did speak to Fitzwilliam. However, they talked but of the sea trip, the fine weather expected, which generals were the most stupid, and how difficult it was keeping a uniform fit in the field.

The Iberian Peninsula and Wellesley were much too fierce an allurement. Fitzwilliam would go to Lisbon soon, his mother would be inconsolable, and Darcy had spoken to him about it.

Because no true dissent was offered, the trip was an amiable as well as a fruitful mission. Darcy enjoyed his horseback outing, Fitzwilliam was able to discuss the topic of war, and Elizabeth would have a gift for her birthday.

It was late afternoon, making their trip a long two days, when Elizabeth espied the grooms unsaddling Blackjack and Scimitar. She found the nearest entrance into the house and, in her hurry, bumped into Fitzwilliam in the back passageway. He took her hand and kissed it in greeting. She, almost shyly, bade enquiry of the success of their trip. Thus assured, a little impatiently did she cut short their conversation to take her leave to find her husband. Had she turned and looked, she would have been quite embarrassed, for a knowing little grin bechanced Fitzwilliam's countenance as she hurried upstairs. Her hastening feet told him more than her impatience with civilities.

Fitzwilliam went into Darcy's library, found a book and made himself comfortable in a high-backed chair. Darcy had told him that he would bring Elizabeth down

directly. However, Fitzwilliam was not unlearnt in matters of amour. Her quickening
steps foretold neither would be seen again in all that good time.

Upstairs, Elizabeth paused briefly as she passed Darcy's dressing room. Because she
saw but his man putting away her husband's belongings, she hurried on to their bedchamber door and flung it open. In the glow of the late afternoon sun, she espied a
sumptuous sight. It was one of considerable bare-chested glory. Still in his breeches
and boots, he had just washed the dust of the road from his face and tossed a towel
aside. Even after his trip, his boots had not lost their sheen and she could smell their
leather from the door.

Without consciously making a decision to do it, she crossed the room. So expeditiously did she move that he, intent upon rifling through the drawers of a chiffonier,
did not hear her come to him. Hence, when she literally leapt into his arms not unlike
a particularly precocious twelve-year-old, he gave vent to a slight grunt and took a
staggering step backward. By the time she embarked upon a siege against his lips, he
had recovered enough to return it in kind.

The perpendicular act that followed defied logic, for their bed was not a dozen feet
away. She had no idea why she was incited to climb his body and he evidently had no
interest in questioning it. She gripped her legs about him; he braced her against the door.
The explicit nature of their activity was announced with a resounding thud each time he
bore into her. Indeed, the noise reverberated down the hall. In a lifetime of reticent propriety, he never once deliberately defiled his own privacy. It all fell to this understanding:
if Elizabeth wanted him to take her fevered and hard there and then, he would do so. He
was big, he was strong, and he would use his size and strength to please her in any way
she so chose. Seldom did any event occasion that bade him less contemplation.

Because of its heat, their coupling blazed fiercely, but inherently, it did not last long.

Knees trembling, he still twirled her about and over to the bed. Thereupon, he
kissed her quite hungrily atop it. The one night they missed of each other's company
was possibly a little more enjoyable in that moment's impetuous fervour of requited
passion. Neither, however, took the time to compare the possibility. He let out a playful groan and rested his spent body upon hers for a fair moment before he rose.

Even buttoning his breeches, chivalry was not abandoned. He bowed low, and then
offered her his hand.

"I suppose I should say 'Hello, Mrs. Darcy, 'tis good to see you.'"

Elizabeth did not take his hand immediately. Her gaze, which rested first upon his
face, drifted down his body in retrospective appreciation. Perspiration began to trickle
down his breastbone and glistened in the hair just beneath his navel. Compleatly
sated, she did not fully understand why his soiled, sweaty breeches and turned down
boots still bade her savour the sight. She smiled up at him.

"I believe, sir, you just did. Rather emphatically."

The full extent of the unseemliness of her rash leap upon his person dawned upon
her with that statement.

She said, "You are away not two days and your wife greets you not unlike a lady of
the streets. You must think me an irredeemable tart."

It was a forgone conclusion that Elizabeth would not be aware had that particular assignation been performed upon the streets of London, she would have been a party to what was known amongst more common folk as a "thruppence upright." Hence, Darcy assumed she spoke of the impetuosity of her dash to him, not the method.

He said, "I was beginning to believe you would not come to me, that it should always be my duty."

"Should it not be the husband's duty?"

"I cannot speak for other husbands, just myself," he said, then he leaned down and whispered fetchingly in her ear. "Come to me, Lizzy. When you favour it, I want you to."

"Besides," he stood up, repaired his attire, cleared his throat, and said, "however miserably I missed you, I have something to show you, outside."

She took his proffered hand and he pulled her from the bed and toward the door.

"Wait, wait," she said, as she endeavoured to locate the shoes she had somehow lost.

Encouraging her toward his surprise, he insisted, "Come, come."

Shoes recovered, they finally reappeared downstairs, and Fitzwilliam, without comment upon their tardiness, accompanied them out to the courtyard. There, a little ceremony was enacted. Darcy bid Elizabeth close her eyes. He called to his man, Elizabeth hearing much scuffling. When given word, she opened her eyes to behold her groom, young John, proudly holding the lead rope that led to the halter of a beautiful dark bay mare.

Darcy told her, "I could not find a horse so fine as Nellie. However, when I saw this one, I knew you must have her. For she is the exact colour of your hair."

As Elizabeth stood for a moment in open-mouthed astonishment, her husband and his cousin stood to the side, arms folded in satisfaction. This self-aggrandisement was not arrested, merely solidified when she kissed the blaze upon the nose of the horse in emphasis of her appreciation. Any surfeit of gratitude she bestowed enthusiastically upon her husband's neck. Such was her delight, Fitzwilliam stood about beaming in reflected glory. If hitherto Mr. Darcy had not chosen to be the recipient of such affection in company, he certainly did not acknowledge that reservation then, for he kissed her full upon the mouth in return.

Immediately he and Fitzwilliam reclaimed solemnity to embark upon a lengthy detailing of the horse's lineage, in which she held no true interest. Yet such was their obvious pleasure in relating it that she smiled and nodded at the information as if she did.

Before they had long set about impressing Elizabeth with dam and sire, a commotion occurred outside the arched entrance to the courtyard. Loud voices ensued, and the squealing sound of horses. Fitzwilliam was closer than was Darcy and they both walked hastily in the direction of the noise.

Although Darcy turned and said to her in useless exercise, "Stay here," Elizabeth, much too curious, followed a short distance behind.

When all came through the gate, they saw a footman yanking upon the rein of one of two horses harnessed to a gig. He was tugging upon the bit cruelly, simultaneously striking the trembling horse with a coach whip. Frothy blood came from the horse's mouth, his eyes wild with terror. Involuntarily, Elizabeth put her hands to her face, horrified at the sight.

Before Fitzwilliam had taken many steps toward the man, Darcy's long legs over-strode him, and he reached the footman first. Whirling him about, he yanked the whip from the man's hand and brought it down across his shoulders.

"There, does that not encourage you to do my bidding?"

He spoke in a loud, angry voice, one Elizabeth had never heard. From the astonished look upon Fitzwilliam's face and those of the grooms, they had not either. All stood in petrified anticipation. John Christie, too, had followed and was standing behind the group, his mouth agape, unnoticed.

Casting the whip to the ground, Darcy turned his back upon the man and walked over to the still quivering horse. He raised his hand and spoke soothingly to the animal, which steadied but slightly, excitedly still attempting to back away. Taking hold of the bridle, he stroked the horse's nose and neck, talking softly to it. Gradually the horse was becalmed. When Darcy called for a groom to unharness it, several men jumped, and one came forward to take the poor, shivering, lashed horse to his stall.

Darcy turned back to the horse flagellant. Indeed, all eyes fell upon him. Tom Reed was standing glaring at the Master of Pemberley with fists clenched, his body recoiled into a near crouch. Curiously, as Darcy approached him, the man's eyes first darted to Elizabeth before returning to his advancing adversary with considerable malevolence. As Darcy advanced, Reed, who was quite as tall as Darcy and a stone heavier, backed up a full step.

Darcy said, "You have been warned before. Begone from this property and do not return."

As a man used to having his instructions obeyed, he turned his back and looked not back.

To the other footman who was better known to him, he said, "Stay if you wish, but your brother will not step upon my soil again."

When Mr. Darcy spoke to him, Reed's brother, Frank, was making a great point of inspecting his boots. He did not look up at Darcy, but nodded an acknowledgement before sneaking a pusillanimous glance at his brother.

Tom Reed spit upon the ground in Darcy's direction, then looked again directly at Elizabeth before he stomped away.

Shaken, Elizabeth stood in abject stupefaction. Sheltered as she had been, she had never witnessed an act of brutality or such a confrontation as had just played out before her. Rather than frightening her, however, the sight of her husband, in his shirt-sleeves and riding boots, standing up to a larger man and facing him down, bestirred her blood in what she knew was a decidedly unseemly fashion.

Once reclaiming his equanimity, Darcy seemed to remember himself. Addressing Fitzwilliam and Elizabeth, he murmured numerous apologies for his eruption. Trailed by John Christie, they walked back to the courtyard. Elizabeth took her husband's hand. It was an instinctual gesture of reassurance. Nevertheless, it was apparent it was she, not he, who needed restoration, for his grip was steady. Hers was the one that trembled.

The mare stood peacefully where her lead rope had dropped. John ran ahead of the others, sheepishly taking it in hand, realising that in all the excitement he had done the unthinkable of forsaking his post. He looked at Darcy fearfully, expecting a reproof. If Mr. Darcy intended one, he was deflected.

For just then, Elizabeth turned to Fitzwilliam (who looked a little shaken himself) and asked, far too merrily, "Has Darcy told you what I am to call my horse? He has not spoken of it to me."

Not able to rescue good humour in so swift a fashion as Elizabeth, Fitzwilliam looked at her a little dumbly, and then to Darcy, then back to Elizabeth.

"He said you were to name her yourself."

"Then she shall be called 'Boots,'" she announced with finality.

This garnered both Darcy and Fitzwilliam's attention, both making a point of not looking at each other in mutual disregard of Elizabeth's whimsical choice of appellation for such a fine specimen of a mare.

For both men believed that the horse was named but for her two stockinged feet.

The trio turned their thoughts toward supper, which was to be capped by champagne (from France—there was a war, but Portuguese wine was indefensible) and cake in honour of Elizabeth's twenty-first birthday. Because of the company and cake, their retirement was later than usual. Due to an imprudent enthusiasm for toasting, Fitzwilliam found himself a little in his cups. Darcy steered him up the stairs, insisting he stay the night.

There was little more that could be done with Fitzwilliam than to remove his boots and roll him face down onto the bed. That accomplished with bleary, if inept, co-operation from Fitzwilliam, Darcy returned to his dressing room to see to himself.

Expecting Elizabeth already to be asleep (unused to champagne as she was), he tip-toed into their room in want of not disturbing her. Elizabeth's eyes, however, had not found sleep. Be-gowned, she sat cross-legged upon the bed. It was well apparent that champagne was more an aphrodisiac than a sleep inducer to her. Never one to question, he immediately drew off his night-shirt and joined her upon the bed, happy to re-toast her birthday in any manner she chose. She chose something surprising. "Husband, I wonder if you might indulge me in a whim?"

He assured her that he would.

"I wonder if you would…pull on your boots?"

His countenance bore a quizzical expression.

"My boots?" he repeated.

"Yes, your tall boots."

"Now?"

She nodded her head emphatically. Looking a little bewildered, he did not question her more and went back to his dressing room. It was but when he closed the door that a flicker of understanding overspread his face.

He reopened the door, stuck his head around the corner and asked in reassurance he had heard her correctly, "My boots alone?"

"Perhaps those breeches you wore today, as well."

When he came to her clad but in his breeches and boots, she was looking out the door of the balcony onto the moonlit lawn. However, when she felt his presence, she turned to him and ran her hands across his bare chest, an invitation he would not ignore.

If this perpendicular embrace had not the heat of the one previous, no hesitation was brooked. Moreover, if their passion was birthed standing up, it did not expire that way, for this time their bed bade them come. The night might not have been particularly young, but there were many hours until dawn. And boots did give better traction.

When they had been gratified, Elizabeth rose and returned to the balcony door. The air was cold, hence he came up behind her, putting his arms around and beneath hers. Both gazed out at the moonlight.

Nestling his face against her hair, he asked, "Are you actually going to call that mare 'Boots'?"

"Certainly."

"'Tis a better name for a cat."

"I like it for my horse."

"I am not certain my countenance will not betray me each time I hear you say it."

"Why, Mr. Darcy, whatever do you mean?…"

When the moon drifted behind a cloud, the stone of the balcony reflected an odd glow. Elizabeth looked at it curiously, but before she could ask Darcy what it meant, he startled her by abruptly pushing her away and heading for the door.

He bellowed, "Make haste! Rouse Fitzwilliam! The stables are on fire!"

Fortunately, he had on his boots and breeches and needed but to grab a jacket as he raced for the stairs. Elizabeth ran the length of the corridor to Fitzwilliam's room and pounded both fists against his door. The shouted word, "Fire!" rendered him both awake and sober. Running back to their room, she grabbed Darcy's long coat, and, unable to find her shoes at all this time, gave up the search and ran back to the stairs just behind Fitzwilliam.

When they reached the esplanade the sharp rocks slowed her bare feet, hence, Fitzwilliam immediately out-distanced her. By the time she got to the first barn, flames were already licking at the roof from the hayloft. Swirling smoke and cinders filled the air. A dozen people had converged upon the site, the distant sound of neighing, frightened horses accentuating the shouts and confusion.

The immediate plan was to get the horses out before the ceiling caved, but that could not be initiated until the barrels blocking the main door were rolled away.

Darcy and Fitzwilliam alone dared enter the burning building to open stall doors for the horses nearest, slapping them upon the rump to encourage them out. The barn had filled with smoke, but no fire was yet in sight inside and the horses pounded out, greeting Elizabeth's tardy appearance. She had to leap aside lest she be trampled. When the loft burnt through, lumber and burning hay fell to the floor with a hissing crash, thereby alighting new fire along the floor betwixt Darcy and Fitzwilliam. When Elizabeth was able to enter, she could see but Fitzwilliam for the smoke.

He called out that the fire lay between Darcy and their exit.

Running back to the throng of people who had already initiated a water brigade, Elizabeth screamed to the men they must open the doors at the other end of the building. Several ran for them, Elizabeth in pursuit, the tail of Darcy's coat dragging upon the ground behind her. The weight of the coat and the stones upon her bare feet allowed Fitzwilliam to overtake her lead. By the time she got to the doors, the barrels that blocked them had already been rolled away.

When the doors were thrown back, they were greeted by a spewing cloud of smoke and five more freed horses galloping by. Not seeing Darcy, Elizabeth attempted to run in, but Fitzwilliam grabbed her arms and held her back. Hardly impeded, she hastily yanked her arms from the sleeves of the coat to free herself and started into the smoke again, screaming her husband's name.

Fitzwilliam knew well if Darcy survived but to learn that he had allowed Elizabeth to enter the flaming stable, he would never be forgiven. Hence, he ran and caught her again, this time by her night-gown, and held her fiercely to him. Impatiently, he shouted to her if she would just stay he could go, but, in hysteria, the reasonableness of this was lost upon her. She was still struggling thusly when Darcy emerged from the smoke. He had a rag over Boots' eyes, the singular way he could get the terrified mare through the fire. Smoke curled up from his figure and, thinking it was his hair, Elizabeth ran to him. As it was just his jacket that smouldered, she and Fitzwilliam both beat it out, Elizabeth with her bare hands, Fitzwilliam using the coat Elizabeth had escaped.

It was but when she clutched herself to him in relief that Darcy realised she was there. "Elizabeth! What are you doing out here? You should have stayed! Fitzwilliam, how could you have allowed her to come?"

Wrenching the greatcoat from his cousin's hands, Darcy wrapped Elizabeth in it. Fitzwilliam gifted him with a look of confounded exasperation. Thereupon, with a shake of the head, Darcy withdrew the reproach, both understanding the difficulty of thwarting Elizabeth. (If she was chagrined at being the culprit in this vexation, contrition did not visit her until later.)

The large stable in irreversible ruin, they re-routed the bucket brigade to wet down the roofs of the other buildings. Blessedly, dawn brought a soft shower of rain. It smothered the smouldering timbers, and the family sought refuge in the house.

Sitting in smut-stained faces around the informality of the big wooden kitchen table, they took assessment. It appeared just three horses were lost, one, the horse that Reed had beaten. Those three and Elizabeth's horse had been deliberately tied in their stalls. Darcy had but time to untie Boots. Such were the circumstances, all were convinced the fire had been set intentionally. Moreover, no one doubted that it was at Reed's hand. Elizabeth found it difficult to conceive of a heart so hard, even in a horse-beater. Could any man do such an inhuman thing? Certainly, someone had done it. She had to admit one thing to herself. In the face of the facts, although she might not be as naïve as was Jane, unquestionably, she would have to readjust her notion as to just what some individuals were capable of.

The certainty of Reed's guilt could not be proved, for eventual interviews with the servants and grooms could not place him upon the estate after he was dismissed. Nevertheless, when the sheriff set out to question Reed that next day, he would find no trace of him. That would be further reason to believe him the arsonist. However, in the early hours after the fire, all could see that nothing could be accomplished just then and returned upstairs to beg at least a few hours rest. Darcy and Elizabeth fell into the deep, black sleep of exhaustion.

If Darcy and Elizabeth found easy sleep, Fitzwilliam did not. He lay there for some time, tossing restlessly. Initially, he told himself his insomnia stemmed from extreme fatigue, the excitement of the fire, or a combination of the two.

Fitzwilliam had witnessed, although he knew Darcy did not, Reed's look as he directed it upon Elizabeth. Fitzwilliam had taken a step forward in her defence at such an ominous provocation, but in light of the man's banishment from Pemberley by Darcy, he had held his counterstroke to that single step. He did not then report to Darcy Reed's perceived insult, if not outright threat, to Elizabeth. For at the time, his cousin was labouriously trying to reclaim his thoroughly ruptured temper. Nor did Fitzwilliam think it wise to bring up such a minor affront in the light of the contemptuous crime perpetuated upon the stables.

It was a vile end to what had begun as a delightful diversion.

Fitzwilliam had happily accompanied Darcy upon his search for the perfect horse for his wife. As it happened, he held no little conceit of the fact of how well he knew horseflesh. His own horses numbered twelve, and he was happy to lend his animals and advise those favoured among his fellow officers. It was the single judgement Fitzwilliam would not find modesty to disclaim. He knew horses. It was perhaps a family trait, for Darcy's eye was thus discerning as well. Old Mr. Darcy did not have this virtue, for he thought if a horse had a high stepping gait and a nice coat it made him as much a horse as a man might want to draw his coach. Darcy's mother was the horse fancier of that couple. She was a prodigious rider and could recite the bloodlines of any horse in their stable.

Hence, it was reasonable that her brother, Fitzwilliam's father, had harboured the same love. Darcy inherited it from his mother, Fitzwilliam from his father. When Darcy went on a quest for a horse for Elizabeth, he trusted his own horse judgement, but did hesitate not at all to have Fitzwilliam's opinion as well. Betwixt the two of them, it would be impossible not to obtain the finest horse with which to gift Darcy's wife.

The dusky horse they chose was named Dulcinea. Fitzwilliam and Darcy thought that a coy enough name and in no need of changing. They asked Elizabeth's opinion but as a courtesy. That she named her new horse Boots had seemed rather odd to Fitzwilliam, expecting, if not something more sophisticated, at least a little more…more…horsy. Initially, Darcy had seemed puzzled by her choice, thereupon simply embarrassed that his wife had named her exceedingly well-bred horse something so "precious."

It was quite unlike her nature. That was one of the little quirks of Elizabeth's that Fitzwilliam had found endearing. She was so compleatly acerbic, witty, and arch, then, in turn, could do something so unfathomable as name her horse after its fetlocks.

Thus, when he closed his eyes seeking sleep, Fitzwilliam did not think of the horses, the fire, and the pandemonium, or even of Darcy nearly being killed. The single thing that unsettled him was more of a sensation than a conscious thought. And that wonderment was how it had felt when, clad but in her night-gown, he had held Elizabeth to him.

He dozed fitfully. In time, he awoke and sat upon the side of the bed, relinquishing any ambition to sleep. In his soldierly way, he endeavoured to embark upon the troubling employment of analysing the shades of his own mind.

Elizabeth was pretty and charming. What was there not to admire? Any man who possessed a heartbeat would look upon her with favour. Nor, he reasoned, was it improper to look upon Elizabeth with fondness, for she was Darcy's wife. Fitzwilliam considered that his unsettled feeling perchance told him it had been too long since he had been favoured with the attentions of a woman. Perhaps, when he returned to London, he would rectify the situation. That decision made, he laid back and closed his eyes, thinking of that woman, any woman. Yet, when her image came to him, her face was not anonymous. It was Elizabeth's.

Fitzwilliam sorely wished he had not been at the fire at the stable, for he would then not have held her. Nor would he have had to face that he was very much in love.

John Christie fell into a deep and abiding sleep each night. The work, although tedious and steady, had a rewarding symmetry. He lugged about heavy feed buckets and filled the mangers so the horses could have their oats. Those same horses he turned out onto the pasture for their exercise, then scooped up their dung and flung it onto the manure wagon to be cast upon the new crop. Order and rule.

That such a peaceable world existed, and that he had managed to insinuate himself in it, was an unending astonishment. Edward Hardin chuckled at the zealous diligence with which he undertook each and every chore. But then, Edward Hardin had never once been to London, nor seen the lodgings they had once kept on Buck's Row.

Hitherto, the horses John Christie had tended were tired and often ill-used, frightfully few offering any glimpse of past distinction. Inevitably, horses left overnight at an inn were either hired or recruited from a plough. They were nags, no denying that. Yet, the barmaid's boy indulged these disreputable animals with furtive currying and purloined sugar. It fell to reason that if he managed to dispense kindness to the inglorious, the fine horses at Pemberley were in respectful hands.

That was reasonable, but not the whole truth. The simple fact was that he had always taken affection, and bestowed it, where it was found.

As beauty of temperament and confirmation were not an impediment to fondness, the horses at Pemberley were not slighted. On the contrary, horses at the inn were not there long enough for John to build a true attachment. At Pemberley, he came to know them each by name. And if they did not know his name, they knew his presence. A gratifying orchestration of nickering began whenever he entered the barn. This was most pleasing, for it was a family of sorts. Something that he missed.

Was he called upon to name it, his Family Equus would have to include Edward Hardin who had taken to calling him, not John nor Christie, but "Johnny, me lad." The man was a little deaf, hence he always sounded a bit rankled when he doled out orders.

Yet he began every one, "Johnny, me lad…"

John Christie did understand there was a hierarchy at Pemberley—not hereditary, yet an oligarchy, nevertheless. The line of rule was rarely transgressed. John knew he answered to Edward Hardin, who answered to Mr. Rhymes. Mr. Rhymes answered to Mr. Darcy, and evidently, Mr. Darcy answered but to God.

It was fitting. John's life had been subjected to little but the bedlam and discord of Whitechapel, but also to the general chaos of his mother's love life. It was reassuring to know exactly where one stood. That one stood at the end of the line was not pertinent. At least there was a line in which to subsist. Order and rule.

He had even managed to elude Tom Reed.

Edward Hardin despised the man (no greater obligation of regard could be asked) and had complained to Mr. Rhymes about Reed abusing the horses. Why Reed was even at Pemberley, no one seemed to know. Reed was hired in London; his single recommendation had come from his brother, Frank. All the other footmen and grooms disliked him, even though, as do most men who are bullies, Reed seldom confronted other men. He turned his roughest hand toward the weaker: animals, women, and boys.

The single blight upon his tenure had come at Reed's hands, but John knew, ultimately, that it was his own fault. For he had the poor judgement to honour one of Reed's orders. That day of the hunt, Reed had told John to bring the shortest horse in the barn for that sweating, pear-shaped gourd of a vicar. And he had done it. He had delivered that innocent little chestnut pony unto the hands of that buffle-headed meacocke, Collins.

Of course, the vicar did end up the worse for wear.

Reed laughed uproariously at each retelling. John was convinced that the pony mistook his part in the whole debacle, for thenceforward, he looked at John maliciously every time he passed his stall. It was just another in the long line of Reed's wicked deeds.

The confrontation with Mr. Darcy was unexpected. It was not, however, unwarranted or unwelcome. Hitherto, Reed had been clever enough to hide his malevolence from those of higher rank behind a somewhat smirking amiability. Almost everyone who witnessed the public disclosure of his cruelty savoured it. (Frank Reed may have savoured it, too, one can but conjecture.) Regardless, John loathed that the horse that he beat had to suffer to expose him.

John liked that horse in particular. He was an Irish Draught called Farley, a bit long in the tooth, yet still spry. He was the horse of choice for the housekeeper upon her infrequent trips to Lambton. She liked him, not in spite of, but because he was plodding and slow. The old woman likened herself to that horse. When Mr. Hardin claimed he was getting too stiff, she reproached him.

"No, we are both old, yet we can get on with the work."

Normally quite placid, Farley always jumped about nervously when Reed approached. Having been given the employment of driving Mrs. Reynolds to Lambton that day, Reed was in his usual ill-humour. Like most of the other servants, he feared her. Yet, unlike them, he despised her as well. His hate exceeded his fear by half. She bade him sit up straight and not mutter curses under his breath, rapping him across the knuckles with a switch (one that she carried when he drove her just for that purpose) upon an expletive. Hence, when the horse that reminded Mrs. Reynolds of herself would not behave, Reed's pugnacious temperament exploded.

For fate to allow Mr. Darcy to hear the welter was not just propitious, for the horses it was providential. Indeed, had John not been so ungoverned as to drop the lead rope to Mrs. Darcy's new horse and follow, he might have missed the entire rumpus. Witnessing Reed's comeuppance at the stinging end of a carriage whip and by the hand of none other than Mr. Darcy was the single event for which John would have risked his employment.

John did not read, but he had heard of books that portrayed fearless figures performing heroic deeds. When Reed suffered the bastinado, John was convinced that was what he was witnessing. Weaponless, the valiant Mr. Darcy saved the horse and turned Reed out. Out of Pemberley he fled, tail betwixt his legs, like the feisting cur he was. Mr. Darcy was a noble warrior. He was just. He was courageous and he had the most beautiful and kind lady at his side. It was difficult not to become giddy with admiration of the man as well as the deed.

The entire valorous episode had lasted less than a minute. Reed was struck and banished. Quick as that. Struck and banished. Reed was gone and with his departure, John breathed a considerable sigh of relief. Yet, it amazed him how such a momentous event to him seemed not to alter anything else. Another man harnessed another horse to the gig in Farley's place. Mrs. Reynolds came and another man drove her to Lambton. Everyone dispersed. Poor, shuddering Farley was led back to his own stall. John returned Mrs. Darcy's new horse as well, whistling as he did.

After supper, everyone, including Frank Reed, sat tranquilly about the stove in the stable room, warming their feet against the cool night air, no one quite ready to retire. One man whittled, another beat some tune out on his knee with a spoon. Mr. Hardin came in and got a flame to light his pipe. Gradually, the men stretched, claimed weariness, and admired the thought of their beds.

John, however, was not ready for sleep. He was still beside himself with excitement over the afternoon's altercation. Such was his relish, he wanted to savour it a little longer. He found a shrivelled crab apple at the bottom of a barrel. Tossing it in the air, he determined that it was still good and took it to poor Farley. At the stall, he stepped up on the gate to lean out with the apple, talking quietly to the horse. He spoke in a soothing voice, not unlike that he had once used with his sisters.

"Did that man hurt yer, Farley? 'e got his due, din't 'e? 'e got what's comin'. Yer'll be fine, now. Yer'll be fine."

From behind, a hard hand gripped John just above his Adam's apple, lifting him back off the rail and hard against the wall. Instinctively Farley backed away, stamping his feet nervously, whirling, and looking for escape. John would have liked to find escape himself, but his feet could not achieve the ground. Using both hands, he frantically sought to pry loose Reed's hold on his neck.

Hysterically gasping for air, John squeaked out, "Mr. Darcy ran yer off! He'll see yer 'ere and do it agin!"

"Mr. Darcy! Mr. Darcy! That bastard's not gonna get 'is 'ands dirty. Save yer breath to cool yer porridge!" said Reed, using a strangely benign circumlocution.

"Yes 'e will! Yes 'e will!" squeaked John.

John struggled, wanting to believe it. Reed let him drop. John fell to the ground soundly with a loud "Uuh" as he landed. Reed laughed.

"Yer too stupid t'even know, do yer? Do yer?"

He kicked John in the knee and John looked back, uncomprehending.

"That rich bastard's the one whot poked yer ma. She tol' me. She tol' everybody. 'e's your pa and 'e don' even speak to yer! Does 'e? Well, does 'e?"

He kicked him again. John shook his head dumbly. Reed grabbed him up and yanked him so hard it rattled his teeth. More than life itself, he wanted to fight him, but his senses were far too compromised. He felt beaten, but not by Reed. Quite vociferously, Reed threatened that if he told anyone he had seen him, he would steal back and kill him. That seemed less a threat than a promise.

Unexpectedly, Reed relaxed his grip, allowing the boy to fall to the ground again.

Scrambling to his feet, John ran, not looking back. He ran hard and for a long time. Stumbling into the woods, he fell to the ground flat out. Then he sat up, out of breath, his mind unable to catch up with his thoughts. He put his head in his hands. All he could hear was his own chest heaving and Reed's words still echoing in his ears.

John shook his head as if to expel Reed from his mind. Yet the words remained, contributing more to the lump in his throat than the grip Reed had inflicted about his neck. Because he could not dislodge Reed's words, John gingerly examined them again, for he knew his mother had left Pemberley with child. He had but once asked her who his father was.

She had answered absently, "A man that 'as no use for either of us."

But she had been drunk and feeling sorrier than usual for her circumstance. Hence John never asked her again.

If what Reed said was true, and somehow John thought it was, Mr. Darcy was that man. For the past few hours, John had thought Mr. Darcy a courageous hero. Momentarily, he was elated. He was of Mr. Darcy's blood?

Hastily, reality abused elation.

Did Mr. Darcy acknowledge him? Even speak to him? Mr. Darcy spoke to Mr. Rhymes, Mr. Rhymes to Edward Hardin, and Edward Hardin to him. Mr. Darcy did not even speak to Edward Hardin. Did Mr. Darcy know John was Abigail Christie's boy, fathered by him? Reed did. Did anyone else? Did it matter?

Apparently not. His mother told him the man who fathered him did not want him or her. They were cast out. Rich men fathered bastards every day. Perchance, he was begat of Mr. Darcy, but John knew he was more truly the son of a whore.

John considered that for a moment, and for the first time thought of his mother's circumstances before she was a whore. No one was born a fallen woman. Perhaps her disposition had a predilection to be a bit light-heeled, but there certainly were more than a few feminine occupants of high station who could be accused of the same crime. When at Pemberley his mother was a respectable chambermaid. Ergo, she was seduced, cast out, and rendered a whore. By Mr. Darcy.

A rich and illustrious father was nothing of which to be proud. Particularly not one who was a seducer of innocent girls.

John reconsidered his position on the merit of Mr. Darcy's character.

"He's not so brave," he muttered, "just used to gettin' his own way. Like all rich men."

In the dark, John sat in sullen contemplation of rich men's ill-deeds until he heard yelling and saw the glow and ashes from the fire rise above the treetops. Duty called.

Reluctantly he stood and started back to Pemberley at a slow, deliberately unhurried pace. He began to run only when he heard the horses scream.

Part

Two

The gallery of Pemberley was undeniably august. Its majesty traversed the length of the house, halving it much like the spine of an open book. The preponderance of what was essentially a portrait hall in relation to the size of the great house itself was indicative of the importance of that room. Indeed, the Darcy antecedents' upon display there were revered with no less obeisance than the king himself.

Though not necessarily with reverence, Elizabeth did like to take the length of that hall and study the ancestral faces that paint had rendered unto perpetuity. If she fancied it was possible to draw from her husband's fore-fathers some family trait her own children might carry, she was to be disappointed. There were well-nigh as many distinct features as personages presented. Excepting for Darcy and his father, who favoured each other both in swarthiness and in stature, no two shared a duality. That is, of course, if one discounted the predisposition to adiposity, vibrissa, and wattles (those inclinations hardly peculiar but to the illustrious).

There stood Elizabeth, pondering those dissimilarities, when her husband bechanced upon her.

Up the wide staircase came a small procession. His party consisted of Mrs. Reynolds, who carried her ever-present red folio, and two burly footmen. All bore expressions of purposefulness.

"Elizabeth," Darcy said, announcing the obvious. "There you are."

So great was the length of the hall that, by the time they reached her, his words affected a slight echo. As his voice was more commanding than was hers, she did not attempt to return his greeting across the vastness of the hall. With well-rehearsed economy, she waited to speak until she met him midmost in the narrow room. Even when she did speak to him, he did not actually acknowledge it. He looked at her distractedly and thereupon to the portrait-laden walls. Without explanation, he turned back to Mrs. Reynolds and began issuing terse instructions upon the rearrangement of the massive portraits.

This upheaval was discombobulating to Elizabeth for no other reason than that the paintings appeared affixed to the house with much the same permanence as the windows and doors. What engendered such a disruption of kindred she could not fathom. Her sentiments upon the issue, however, were unbidden and she dutifully stepped back, watching raptly what was to unfold. It was obvious her husband intended for her to witness his endeavours. She studied what alterations were made intently (should she be quizzed upon it at a later time).

"I have just begun to know these people. You are not to move them now?"

Obviously, he was. And because that was obvious, he ignored, not his wife, but his wife's question. There was a great deal of shuffling about and disturbing of furniture as the footmen moved taboret, chiffonier, and benches. As they committed these sins of rearrangement, Mr. Darcy consulted what appeared to be a diagram.

Thereupon, he pointed to several paintings, directing their relocation; one he (gasp!) ordered to be removed entirely.

Such unceremonious disposal of an ancient painting bade Elizabeth wonder if the man depicted was the perpetrator of some newly discovered disgrace. If this was the case, his offence must have been heinous indeed, for by the outlandishness of the wig he wore, his portrait must have been hanging there since the War of the Roses. Elizabeth could not remember his history, only that Mrs. Reynolds told her he was the second duke of something-or-other. Hence, she watched dispassionately as Duke Something-or-Other's vainglorious countenance was carted from the room.

Compleatly baffled, she finally bid, "Pray, what are you doing?"

"I am making way for a new portrait," he said. "Yours."

"But, I have no…" she began.

She stood thenceforward in open-mouthed stupefaction upon the revelation of his plan. Had he concluded she came to this hall longing to have her own likeness amongst the others?

Hence, she countered a little defensively, "Do not suppose that I visit this room to beg for my own portrait."

"Of course not. However, in consequence of your birthday, I shall have it. As it happens, this painting is not for you. It is for me."

Yes. The compulsory portrait.

Elizabeth knew she should have anticipated this obligation, for howbeit Georgiana's portrait hung, fittingly, in the music room, every other member of the Darcys' last five generations hung in the gallery. As the co-procreator of the sixth, hers was to join them. Elizabeth realised all this rearranging exposed a large expanse of bare wall next to his own portrait.

He pointed to the space and said, "Yours shall hang here next to mine for all time."

The very stoutness of the walls of Pemberley announced that the paintings just might remain there well unto eternity.

"Yes," she said, "that is, until our descendants decide they favour other countenances and we are consigned to the farthest heights of the library to gather dust."

His most recent activity having announced that possibility, he well-nigh laughed.

But as he laughed but seldom, he caught himself before revealing to the help that, however covert, he, upon occasion, enjoyed a diversion.

"Ahem, yes. I suppose that is true."

Recognising he was perilously close to losing his countenance to diversion, she prodded him mercilessly.

"To contravene such an event, perhaps one or both of us could create a scandal. Nothing is so desirable as to have a portrait of a scurrilous ancestor to exhibit for the enjoyment of one's guests."

Her attempt to bid him laugh fell short. He gathered his considerable dignity and looked upon her with an air bearing all the condescension of one whose fore-fathers had not an infamy amongst them.

Quite unchastened, Elizabeth raised her eyebrow to him in silent suggestion he might do well to rethink his supercilious attitude now that the Darcy family name was at the mercy of her occasionally unguarded propriety. (She dared not speak of Lydia; that was less a tease than a threat.)

As he was acquainted with the occasional cheekiness of his wife and her occasional admonishment against undue pride, he took her unspoken disapproval under advisement by kissing her hand. She smiled up at him out of the corner of her eye, partly in affection and partly because it was amusing for her to think of herself (scandalous or scandal-less) in the sedate company she saw upon the wall.

Moreover, as accustomed as she was to looking upon the portraits there as an objective observer, it did not please her to envision future generations eyeing her portrait and reviewing her countenance.

A small stamp of her foot was the single indication of displeasure she allowed herself. This gesture was less at the necessity of a portrait than that she had no voice in the matter. Not only did she not want her image studied; the process of effecting that invasion demanded a series of tedious sittings. Other than slumber and prayers, she could not remember a time when she welcomed being still for more than a full quarter of an hour. Hence, she certainly did not look with anticipation upon the labourious tedium that a sitting entailed.

Alas, a painter had been already commissioned.

He would be there within the week.

Both of Darcy's parents sat for Thomas Gainsborough, who died but a year after compleating the elder Mrs. Darcy's portrait. It was a bit of a contest to determine just who held the grander coup, they to have obtained the service of that illustrious painter or he to be called upon to paint such eminent personages. Hence, the mutual happiness of the commissions was exquisite.

Beyond the very basis of his livelihood (that being homage and lucre), Gainsborough harboured an ulterior motive for coming to Derbyshire. The true reason being that their Chatsworth neighbour was the Duchess of Devonshire.

The duchess was known as one of the greatest beauties in England and every painter of any repute clamoured for the opportunity to capture her allure. During his lifetime, Gainsborough painted her thrice. His first portrait of her was as a child; the second as a young woman; and the last was effected during the year he spent in Derbyshire.

The great man suffered for that final painting. He painstakingly sketched her again and again before finally submitting paint to canvas. Once committed, he spent weeks just endeavouring to perfect the pout of her lips (that little *moue* of hers influenced any number of intrigues and one ultimately non-fatal duel). Gainsborough died yet unsatisfied that he had done her beauty justice.

For Georgiana Spencer was arguably the most famous enchantress in England. When she was but seventeen, Georgiana, daughter of John, the First Earl of Spencer, wed William Cavendish, the Fifth Duke of Devonshire. Many a gentleperson pronounced her far too young for him. But however old, a fifth duke far outranked a first earl, thus the overt quibbling over age disparity evaporated.

Nevertheless, it was an obstreperous match.

Her beauty was of legend. Unfortunately, her comportment was ruled by imprudence. She dressed flamboyantly, flirted flagrantly, drank with intemperance, and squandered her husband's considerable fortune. All of these acts were committed with a zealous deliberateness that could not utterly fall to the onus of youth.

Her questionable reputation, however, did not belay gentlemen from lusting after her. In spite of (or perhaps because of) her dubious repute, the ladies copied her manner, her voice, and her dress, whilst vehemently condemning her low morals. None of this might have caused the scandal it had, had not the duchess taken such a keen interest in politics (or more specifically politicians). As compelling a woman as she was, her campaigning skills were unparalleled. These gifts reached their apex when she perfected the tactic of obtaining a vote in exchange for a kiss, which, howbeit highly popular amongst the electorate, exposed her to the severest kind of criticism.

"It was an outrage against station!" decried the aristocracy. "Actually cavorting in the streets with common citizenry!"

They insisted it revealed a vulgarity of character unheard of in proper society. Whilst her equals spoke of her in whispered near-hysteria, there was a consensus amongst the clergy that was not so quiet. For every man of the cloth felt called upon to denounce the duchess as a wanton strumpet obviously suffering from rampant nymphomania. (When that particular sin was addressed from the pulpit, the pews were full—no man actually knew of a nymphomaniac, but the possibility was thrilling.)

The duchess went about her business heedless of the uproar and it most probably would have died down had not there been the untimely arrival of her love child by the future Prime Minister of England, Charles Grey. This indiscretion became quite public during the final year of Gainsborough's life. One might premise that such improvidence on the part of the lady with whom he was besotted might have hastened his demise.

Notwithstanding Gainsborough's consternation, Cavendish himself was in a bit of a snit. Busy as he was with his own *affairs d'amour*, he learnt of his wife's *faux pas* belatedly. But learn of it he did, and thereupon banished not just Georgiana and Charles Grey's son, but also the final Gainsborough portrait from Chatsworth compleatly.

After a year abroad, tempers had calmed and Georgiana returned to her ducal home. Little note might have been made of her re-entry to the neighbourhood had not an oddity occurred. Whilst the duchess was absent, the duke's mistress, Lady Elisabeth Foster, had moved, bag and baggage, script and scriptage, into Chatsworth. And upon the duchess' return, Lady Foster did not vacate. Indeed, the duke, the duchess, her children by the duke, her son by Charles Grey, Lady Elisabeth Foster, her children by (one must suppose) Lord Foster, and her children by the duke, all lived together in seeming harmony for another dozen years.

The Duchess of Devonshire's portrait, however, disappeared. A masterpiece lost, those who had beheld it attested. Gainsborough's finest. In absentia, its reputation swelled to adulation. Unfortunately, the same could not be said for its subject. The duchess' person merely bloated. Indeed, when the duchess died, her fondness for spirits had left her a dissipated shell of her once beautiful being.

In time, the stories of her excess faded along with the tales of her beauty. Without a backward glance, the old duke abandoned Chatsworth for London. He had been there but a year when he took kith and kin quite unawares by fathering yet another child with

Lady Foster (any number of wagers would have been covered that the old duke had no powder left in his pistol). Within a few years, Cavendish was dead as mutton. His numerous offspring (with all due bereavement and impenitent greed) embarked upon a vigorous jockeying for a position of prominence in the hierarchy of inheritance. The haggling was interminable. By the time of Elizabeth and Darcy's marriage, Chatsworth was largely unoccupied and the beautiful duchess rarely spoken of at all.

Any mention of her was removed from Mrs. Reynolds' recitation of Derbyshire history. The single remnant of the story that dogged Pemberley was a question that Darcy asked but of himself. And when he did, it was with great disquiet. He did not at all understand how, with all the opprobrium surrounding their former neighbour, the duchess, why a member of the dignified Darcy family carried her name. Moreover, who had chosen to name his sister Georgiana? His mother, or his father?

With a scud of dust worthy a particularly impertinent cyclone, Robert Morland's coach descended upon Pemberley. Protégé and heir apparent to Gainsborough, it was Morland who had won Mr. Darcy's commission to paint his wife's portrait.

Previously, nothing less than a request from St. James's Palace could lure Morland from his studio in Bath for a sitting. Beyond royalty, all who sought his services were bade come to him. Darcy, however, demanded, by means of polite request, that the painter bring himself to Derbyshire at Elizabeth's leisure. Morland seldom travelled from the healing waters of home and that city's simpering adulation of him, and never to the incivility of Derbyshire's fresh air. However, he had made haste to commence this work, understanding the portrait might well be the benchmark of his career.

Other than the King, the Queen, the Prince Regent, and sundry royal family members, few sittings were of more import than that of Mr. or Mrs. Darcy. As a young man, Mr. Darcy's likeness had been taken by Sir Thomas Lawrence (Reynolds should have, but the poor man died in the year of '92) and that gentleman was bid return for the honour of Miss Georgiana. Morland considered it quite a coup to wrest the Darcy commission from the courtly master.

Morland arrived at Pemberley with two assistants, five trunks, and an ill-temper. His poor disposition was a result of his most recent project, that of a bust of good King George. Not only did Morland's genius fail to flower successfully in the unfamiliar setting of the royal court, but dementia had already descended upon George and he continually called Morland by Thomas Gainsborough's name. Morland's self-regard could not allow himself to admire another's talent, even if poor Gainsborough was dead. By the very nature of the work, each artist competed (however each insisted not) with not just his contemporaries, but also the many who traversed the dicey water of artistic interpretation long before him. Thus there was reason aplenty to disparage, be it current or historical, competition.

Artistic integrity notwithstanding, Morland had a frightfully lucrative career emblazoning enormous canvases with the shamefully embellished countenances of the wealthy. That occupation demanded an artist straddle the sometimes perilously fine line betwixt likeness and flattery. It was always a relief to Morland if his client was not so unprepossessing as to frighten children. (There was one unfortunate aristocrat whose ill-fitting wooden teeth could not quite be contained by his lips. The pictorial results were disastrous. Morland tried not to think of it.)

It is not unusual for painters to become a bit enraptured with their clients. One must feel a certain fondness to do justice to a lady's face and figure. (Ah! The figure!) Gainsborough had been more than a little smitten with the Duchess of Devonshire, else he would not have made three attempts to capture her likeness.

An artist's predisposition to infatuation did not leave Morland's sensibilities untouched. (The man fell in and out of love with all the regularity of the tide.) Moreover, if artists often were bewitched with their subjects, it was conversely true that the time and intimacy such an undertaking demanded lured (with considerable encouragement from Morland) more than one woman's affection from a faithful path. Romantic intrigue was an exceedingly happy by-product of his profession, for seldom was there a man more taken with wenching. Even whilst under the very noses of their husbands, he was surprisingly successful upon eliciting these assignations. This phenomenon, no doubt, was the direct result of a widely held supposition that those of artistic sensibilities were a bit light in the slippers.

He adored women, women adored artists, and husbands dismissed said artists' threat of wifely seduction. And he was paid handsomely. Was not life grand?

Perhaps the most salient amongst the many inducements to Morland's accepting the Darcy commission was the reputed comeliness of the intended subject. As yet, her likeness had never been attempted (Mr. Darcy had a miniature, but that ilk was hardly worth noting). The notion spun Morland almost giddy. It was he who would be first to pluck the flower of her beauty for the world to savour. It was unto him that she would surrender her image. A union of souls. An exchange. A consummation.

So to speak.

By the time he arrived at Pemberley, Morland was so unstrung as to be almost prostrate with anticipation. He had tortured himself the length of the trip, alternately certain, then not, that Mrs. Darcy's handsomeness had been exaggerated.

Ushered into the grand salon, he espied her sitting next to Mr. Darcy. Neither rose, demanding Morland cross the room to perfect a bow. He issued a respectful dip of the head, but just enough of a slack-wristed brush with his hand to his heart to insist his genuflection but a courtesy and not a true statement of obeisance. This little pantomime compleated, only then did he allow himself to look fully upon the face he held in such hopeful apprehension. His reaction could be described no other way than confounded.

He was both disappointed and fascinated and he stared upon her quite blatantly.

So long did his gaze tarry, he feared it was obvious to Mr. Darcy that his usual professionalism had abandoned him. For the great man arose, shifted about uneasily, and put a protective hand upon his wife's shoulder. Mrs. Darcy, however, not in the least off-put, unsuccessfully contained a laugh. That she found amusement in his perusal of her countenance was, in and of itself, astounding. For even the grandest of ladies became flustered when he lavished his eye upon them in preparation of his rendering their likeness for eternity. Thus, he was immediately astounded, confounded, and roundly beguiled.

At first glance, he had dismissed those opinions that accused her of being a great beauty. He had seen many thus named, all more impressive than she. She was dressed demurely, wearing but a single strand of pearls. Her hair was quite dark, her face heart-shaped. Initial observation did not divulge a single feature that demanded the attention of a discerning eye. It was upon the second that he became enraptured. For when she did allow a laugh to escape, a slight rise of one eyebrow punctuated it. That little paraph of her countenance was undoubtedly the cause of a tantalising tickle in the pit of Morland's stomach.

Indeed, she was not truly beautiful, but very pretty, and her eyes literally danced when she gazed up at her husband. It would be difficult to capture such a presence.

Eager was Morland to commence. He very nearly startled the Darcys by abruptly demanding a room to set his easel and arrange his paints. ("And it must have northern light!")

Mr. Darcy may have harboured the prejudice that disparaged the masculinity of men of artistic bent, as it was one that was seldom questioned. But if he did, he was not so unenlightened as to believe it a universal truth. As his own appreciation of his wife's pulchritude was considerable, he understood other men admired her as well. This acknowledgement, however, weathered any overt display of this admiration not at all. Whilst Morland bestowed long looks upon Elizabeth, he was watched by her husband with all the generosity of a sheepdog eyeing a wolf circle his flock.

Before blows were thrown, heads broken, or an unnamed portraitist was cast out upon his…nether-end, Elizabeth made a fortuitous demand upon her husband. If she must submit to the tedium of a sitting, thereupon he must keep her company.

Under any other circumstances, remaining idle for that length of time should have been a trial for a man of Darcy's temperament. But her request meant he needed not to fabricate some excuse to stand sentry over her whilst she submitted to Morland's attention. He could thereupon level his gimlet-eyed glare upon the painter without prejudice—for he was under specific invitation from his wife.

Whilst exacting an air of uxoriousness heretofore unwitnessed by his wife (and making certain Morland heard him), he allowed, "There is no greater duty that I could find for myself than to sit with you, Elizabeth, dear."

The disingenuousness of his declaration was not lost upon her, but as it fell to her own advantage, she chose to ignore it. The request that followed atoned for that little treacling flummery. It bespoke an undiluted artlessness.

"I shall meet your demand so long as you meet my own," he told her. "I must have you wear a yellow dress."

Hence, in constant repose and a yellow dress, Elizabeth was captive for many hours of the day. But her subjugation was not to Morland. Whilst she was unable to do anything but sit idly upon a rather purgatorial sofa, it was her husband who ensnared her.

He used no strops to tether her, but she was trapped as surely as if he had. With studied nonchalance, he sat to the left of Morland. One happening upon this placid little scene might think nothing of it. But as Elizabeth was the recipient of her husband's exceedingly intimate and constant gaze, she would have argued his motive was not so benign as one might fancy.

Under his indefatigable scrutiny, inevitably a flush began deep within her bosom and crept upward. He might alter his position ever so slightly, perchance move one booted foot forward and rest his wrist insouciantly upon the arm of his chair. Her rubescence tingled up her throat. With a settling of his chin upon an upturned fist (and further shifting of his immense boots), she sensed his eyes trace her crimsoning (or at least staring from whence it flowed). Not unexpectedly, her pulse quickened.

Away she looked. Out the window to admire the fine weather, to the ceiling to count the tiles. She retraced piano concertos in her mind, fought to remember a flower for every letter of the alphabet, and counted sheep. But her thoughts eventually wafted back to her husband who sat in purported *dégagé*, mercilessly seducing her from across the room.

As it came to be, it was but Morland's romantic ambition that was thwarted. The poor man might have advanced his time at least upon the portrait project more economically were it not for an invariable interruption mid-afternoon. Upon those occasions, much to Morland's displeasure, Mr. Darcy rose and asserted that his wife was looking tired and must be escorted upstairs for a "rest."

After perhaps an hour, she returned upon his arm, moon-eyed and prepossessingly flushed, which was annoyance enough. Insufferably grating to Morland, however, was Mr. Darcy's indocile hubris about whatever had been wrought whilst "resting." Not understanding Mr. Darcy did not intend subtlety, Morland thought himself quite undeceived by such flimsy subterfuge. Hence, came his reluctant acceptance.

He would not find a romantic conquest at Pemberley. However, a handsome fee would at least amply compensate him. For even with such interference, the portrait was turning out even better than his considerable ego had ever hoped.

Morland toiled upon his work in early spring. The artist had been encamped at Pemberley but a week when Georgiana returned for a brief respite from the tribulations of town.

Through determined eavesdropping Morland learned that although young Miss Darcy was socially unambitious, at eighteen, it was time for her coming out. All the important engagements would begin immediately after Easter. The family's imminent decampment from the country to town instigated a great flurry of activity.

London! All and sundry could speak of nothing else. Even the word made Morland's heart take a scuttering little leap. For if his finishing strokes were made with the perfection of which he knew himself capable, the painting should be a masterpiece.

Succès d'estime. He would not return to Bath. He would take the painting with him to London. There, it would be shown at the Royal Academy of Art. In May was its Annual Exhibition of Contemporary Artists. And all the art community's naysayers and curmudgeons would fall to the ground and kiss the feet of Robert Morland as the most illustrious artist in England—in the world! (Dash those Dutch painters!)

A knighthood should follow.

Wresting his considerable ambition into some sort of order, he restrained Elizabeth from plans of presentation gowns long enough to make his final touches. In those few hours he made but a half dozen brush strokes. Thereupon he sat looking at the painting with all the intensity he had once bestowed upon Elizabeth's person. His transient infatuation with her had transfigured into compleat and unmitigated love for the painting he had created. Morland carelessly tossed his palette onto a table and with a melodramatic flourish, laid down his brush.

It was compleated.

"Voilà!" he announced.

A call rang out. Everyone was bid attend the unveiling. Mr. Darcy, Mrs. Darcy, Georgiana, Mrs. Reynolds, and as many upper-level servants as could fit were herded into a tight group. Some amongst their number inched forward, certain an event of historical proportions was to commence.

Morland sat in a chair, his elbows resting upon the arms, fingers forming a steeple that he tapped nervously against his lips. The painting was wet still, hence turned from view. Two assistants stood expectantly upon either side of it, awaiting the master's instruction.

He signaled with a single dramatic nod of his head.

After the cumbersome painting was wheeled about, the three Darcys and Mrs. Reynolds stood transfixed. A murmur arose from those within the second tier of onlookers. Elizabeth turned her head slightly to the left and narrowed her eyes. Georgiana and Mrs. Reynolds simultaneously let out a deep, appreciative sigh.

The reaction did not quite reach the level of true adulation in that neither of his feet was kissed, but it came near enough for Morland to believe he had not underestimated his work. Accolades were enthusiastic and plentiful.

Better schooled in the arts than either Elizabeth or her brother, Georgiana gushed forth her praise. Elizabeth said Morland flattered her countenance. Mrs. Reynolds wiped a tear from her eye.

Whilst these various congratulations occurred, Darcy stood quite still, eyeing the portrait intently. In a moment, the others realised the Master of Pemberley had not yet rendered a verdict and grew silent. The time he had spent omniscient of Mr. Darcy's reticent presence had taught Morland an eruption of gratitude from that man was unlikely.

Hence, when Darcy's attention finally quitted the painting and turned to the painter, Morland veritably trembled with anticipation.

Though Darcy said quite simply, "I thank you," he shook Morland's hand even more firmly than usual.

That slight increase of pressure was the extent of Mr. Darcy's praise. And so parsimonious was his reputation upon extending aggrandisement, even Morland was content.

Indeed, Morland breathed a sigh of relief that the painting he knew to be remarkable met with Mr. Darcy's approval. The obstacle of Mr. Darcy's curt opinion overcome, talk turned to how long to allow for the painting to ripen before it could be framed. Ten days was the allowance. Darcy announced a framer was to travel from London to mount it upon the premises.

"But," Morland interrupted, "I can take it with me. I shall have it framed in time for exhibition."

"Exhibition," Darcy repeated.

"Yes," Morland explained patiently, "The Royal Academy exhibits in May. The timing shall be perfect."

"I do not understand," Darcy said, endeavouring to make Morland cognisant of the fact it was he who did not understand.

That comprehension, however, escaped the painter. Alarmed that Mr. Darcy somehow did not fathom the importance of the work or the exhibition, Morland attempted to explain further.

"Your wife's portrait will hang as the best in England, reviewed by the king himself. There is no greater honour for Mrs. Darcy."

Darcy understood full well that any lionisation primarily benefited the artist. But, he knew, too, it was a great honour for Elizabeth. Truly, he did not want to deny her such a prestigious honour; thus, he was conflicted. Proud as he was of her beauty and happy for her to be admired, he, nonetheless, wanted any admiration of his wife to be couched from a distance. He had not commissioned the portrait for anyone to gaze upon but himself at Pemberley. The idea of any man off the street gawking at her as if she was an actress upon a playbill was detestable. Her painting might be engraved and printed in a book, or worse (heaven save us from perdition!), in a newspaper. No. It would not do.

Intractable as were his wishes upon the matter, he, nevertheless, looked to his wife to see if she favoured exhibition.

"The painting is yours," she said. "The choice is yours as well."

No hindrance stood in his way. Thus, Darcy was adamant in objecting. Morland cajoled, pleaded, and came perilously close to threatening violence, but to no avail. Finally convinced Mr. Darcy's mind could not be swayed, he stamped his foot in petulant embrace of his pertinacity. Trailed by his two assistants, he fled the room near tears, his fingers pinching the top of his nose as if to stanch his weeping. Those who remained in the room stood in embarrassed silence.

Georgiana, while not abandoning loyalty to her brother, found herself sympathetic to poor Morland and said so.

"Poor Mr. Morland."

Not so certain the pitiable Morland would not undertake a rash act, Darcy had his man stand guard over the painting that night. It was, of course, but the utmost of coincidence that "poor" Mr. Morland's assistants were found in the darkened corridor long after midnight, both insisting they were upon their way to the kitchen for a "late supper."

So poor Mr. Morland departed the next morning, slouched in despondence, more convinced than anyone else of his ill-treatment. He vowed to everyone whom he could inveigle to listen that he was never to paint again. His two servitors chose to ride in overcrowded congeniality with the coachman atop the carriage, whose coarse company was far preferable to the cultured but querulous Morland. His purse might have been amply moneyed, but his reputation was no more enriched than whence he came.

Elizabeth felt certain sympathy for him, but just that he had contrived to use a commissioned painting to advance his own reputation. Perhaps he should have been warned in advance that Mr. Darcy cared little for public acclaim, for himself or his family. Prestige was inherent in the Darcy name.

Of the consequence of such an illustrious name, Georgiana was all too witting. Indeed, the prestige one held as member of the Darcy family should have made self-confidence inherent.

Her brother's imperious presence was testament to that assumption. Contrariwise, save for her brother, those in her company often misinterpreted Georgiana's introspective nature as timidity. She struggled for a time to believe her lack of assertiveness was a result of a motherless upbringing, not an intrinsic trait peculiar but to her. But unassuming as well as shy, suspected diffidence eventually became a self-fulfilling prophecy.

Hence, she harboured the absurd notion that her dearth of self-consequence cast aspersion upon the House of Darcy in general and her beloved brother in particular. Being the culprit whose lack of grace, wit, and charm impugned her family name would have been a heavy burden in one so young had she not been so very anxious to suffer it.

Of the family's several homes, Georgiana loved Pemberley most. Not only was it the place of her birth, its fields and trails begat her fondest memories. Alas, she was often not free to enjoy such quiet.

Given free choice, both Darcy and Georgiana would have spent all four seasons in the country. However, before his marriage Darcy spent less than half a year there, allowing his sister but half of that (as a female, she had no autonomy over such decisions as where to domicile oneself). Georgiana was mindful that this arrangement was because of society's dictates, not by his own volition. Although it was never once spoken, she knew London to be as much a trial for her brother as for herself. An example of their differing temperament, however, was how each approached such a dilemma.

Compunction drove him to surrender his presence to society. Georgiana would have been quite happy to hide. Nevertheless, she did not grouse about his despotic bidding that she attend town from Candlemas to All Hallows. For his sacrifice to propriety engendered within her a bit of guilt. She knew what fuelled his determination to consort amongst the patriciate was to facilitate her eventual ingress into society.

Though they were both expected to make good marriages, as her brother and guardian, it was his duty to see that she did. He undertook that commission in all gravity and dedication. This was done exactly as he had undertaken every other commitment in his charge. And it was his belief that any lengthy sojourn by his sister at Pemberley did not serve the better good. That good being Georgiana gainfully married. She weathered London as much as she did but to please his notion that it was there that eligible young men were found in the greatest numbers. All society pundits insisted (her brother unquestionably in concurrence) that the larger the pool, the bigger the fish. Moreover, his belief that nothing less than a very large fish would suffice as marriage material for his sister was absolute.

Not only did she dislike piscine metaphors, Georgiana despised thinking of her fortune as bait.

But she loved her brother.

And as much as she loved him, she revered him even more. Albeit her sibling, he was more than ten years her senior. His paternal dedication to her well-being but enhanced his role as a father figure. Her earliest memories were of desperately running after him and his friends upon their rowdy pursuit of adventure. Slowed by petticoats, young legs, and a faulty constitution, she would call after him, beseeching him to wait. Not only did he await, if necessary he toted her upon his back. Neither Fitzwilliam nor Wickham dared to carp about him allowing her accompany them upon their seemingly aimless exploits.

When her brother married Elizabeth Bennet, she was delighted at last to have a sister. Delighted despite the whispers that the Bennet family had questionable connexions.

Even if her umbrageous aunt, Lady Catherine de Bourgh, had suffered a rather vociferous conniption (one that was but partially vented by throwing both shoes and an empty pint of Geneva at the parlour-maid) over the match, to Georgiana, her brother and his opinions were infallible. Above and beyond that, Elizabeth's obvious adoration of Darcy was reason enough to inflate Georgiana's esteem of her to the seraphic.

The saucy banter and relentless bedevilment Elizabeth inflicted upon the exceedingly formidable Mr. Darcy were initially quite alarming to Georgiana. But witnessing him weather his wife's liberties with superb humour demanded she re-examine her previous understanding of his sensibilities.

Indeed, Elizabeth's lack of prepossession about all things Darcy called into question all that Georgiana had spent a lifetime accepting as incontrovertible.

Accomplishing the considerable feat of embracing neither condescension nor hyperbole, Elizabeth assured the shy Georgiana that she needed but to be amongst company more to feel comfortable in it.

"Once there, you must suffer with good grace all the attention and flattery you shall receive as one of England's true beauties."

It was the approbation of a lifetime. Not because Georgiana was naïve enough to believe it true. That someone she admired gave such sentiments with all due sincerity was compliment enough.

Even holding her with substantially warm regard, Georgiana spoke but once to Elizabeth of her disastrous near-elopement with George Wickham. And then, it was quite obliquely. It was upon the occasion of Lydia's name coming up in conversation.

"Do you know Major Wickham well, Elizabeth?"

Knowing it a captious subject, Georgiana brought it up at some risk. In her quiet way, she managed to learn just who was in and out of favour at any particular time with any particular member of the household. Therefore, she was not unwitting that Elizabeth was irate yet over Wickham's seducement of Lydia. (Georgiana did not know, however, that Elizabeth was uncertain that she could candidly assess that man's character without using the word cur.) However, it lay quite undetermined to Georgiana whether Darcy had confided his sister's near-defilement to his wife.

Hence, such a simple question incited no little angst. As much as Elizabeth yearned to reassure Georgiana that she was hardly the singular young woman deceived by

Wickham's charm, she could not quite bring herself outright to vituperate the reputation of her sister's husband (however deserved). Therefore, when she waded into the treacherous waters of character analysis of a member of her family, she said the single thing that came to mind that was neither compleatly condemnatory nor untrue.

"Mr. Wickham's keenest virtue seems to be an absolute dedication to his looking-glass."

A smile had tempted the corners of Georgiana's mouth upon hearing Elizabeth's analysis. It was the first time Georgiana had been able to find any humour at all in any part of her humiliation. She had not lost her virginity, but the debacle left her innocence considerably fissured.

Whilst falling victim to Wickham's foul scheme was disastrous to her self-esteem, this violation of the heart was not left uninspected. It provoked a creative eruption within her of volcanic proportions. She wrote of it with passion and fervour, scribbling furiously in her journal. Time allowed these renderings to evolve into verse. And of them, Georgiana was as penurious as a bean counter with the Exchequer. Not only did she not leave them lying about, when they were not in her hand they were locked in the false bottom of the midmost drawer of her escritoire. And if Georgiana was bechanced whilst working upon some sonnet, she took to stuffing the papers beneath her chair cushion, it was difficult for the family not to suspect she was involved in some enterprise that she chose not to share.

Hence, it was a surprise when one day she did just that.

"Elizabeth," she said, thrusting forth several folded pages, "I have a composition that would benefit from your opinion."

Literary critique was hardly her long suit, and Elizabeth said so. Georgiana persisted.

"I value your judgement."

Elizabeth perched the pages upon her knees and carefully read each one. Thereupon, she reread them. With great solemnity, she arranged them in order and folded her hands atop them.

She looked directly at Georgiana and announced, "I have never read anything quite so touching in my life."

Georgiana beamed.

"You must share these, Georgiana."

"That I could not. It took all the courage I possess to show you."

"Any ambition to publish I shall pursue on your behalf."

A conspiracy commenced. In entering into this plot, Elizabeth exhibited substantial daring herself. There was no possibility that Darcy should look upon such an endeavour other than with extreme disfavour. They attempted to mitigate their offence by submitting Georgiana's work to the Poetic Registry publication. It was not considered a proper occupation for a woman to write novels, but Elizabeth intended to put forth the argument to her husband that society considered poetry less a transgression.

She practised her entreaties. There were women of consequence in the literary world (Fanny Burney, Lady Montague). But even as she plotted her debate, she did as Georgiana bid and did not yet tell Darcy their plan. She would delay that intimidating duty until the poetry was accepted. No good ever came from borrowing future bother.

Far more promptly than either expected, Georgiana received a post from the publisher accepting her verses. It would be necessary to meet with the publisher's representatives, sign papers, accept payment, et cetera. Georgiana's initial position was to believe a colossal error had been committed.

She insisted, "Certainly they have mistaken another's work for mine. They could not possibly have accepted what I sent them."

Convincing Georgiana that her work had indeed been accepted took no little persuasion. Once that was finally accomplished, Elizabeth was elected to the office of intermediary betwixt the poetess and her brother.

With the publisher's letter in hand, she went on an intrepid search for the soon-to-be beseeched Darcy. Placing the missive before him, she silently allowed his own eyes to be the messenger of the news. Which had been an excellent tactic, for his indignation thus was directed toward the publishing house and not his wife. At least there was no displeasure bestowed upon her until he heard Elizabeth say she had encouraged and aided Georgiana in her literary aspirations. Emboldened, she told him not just that, but that she favoured publication as well.

Elizabeth addressed the issue of Georgiana's station negating any need of an occupation with the argument upon behalf of her self-confidence. Any pecuniary advantage was to be put in the poor box at church. Therefore, the single remaining issue was of propriety. A large issue.

He stated flatly, "It is inappropriate for a gentlewoman to present herself as a public person."

Elizabeth's preparation paid her well, for she countered, "Fanny Burney is a novelist. Lady Montague, a Shakespearean critic. Both are gentlewomen and have kept their reputations intact."

"Lady Montague, indeed," he scoffed. "A lady should not even read Shakespeare."

"You should hear yourself."

"Whatever do you mean?"

"You, sir, read Shakespearean sonnets to me. Is your own wife thought by you as not a lady?"

He stood looking at her for a full minute, apparently finding no method of extrication from the noose he had fashioned himself.

As there were no words that could expose his irrational protection of his sister more clearly than his own, Elizabeth chose to remain silent. Defeated, he sat heavily in his chair and glumly put his chin in his hand.

Taking pity upon him, Elizabeth selected a leather bound volume from the side table and sat herself upon his lap. She opened the book midmost, moistened the tip of her middle finger, and with a dramatic flourish, turned several pages.

"Show me," she inveigled with a tickling whisper against his ear, "just what parts of Shakespeare a lady is not to read."

For a man who suffered defeat but rarely, Darcy decided that it was considerably less abhorrent to lose when the conqueror was his wife.

The invitation from the publisher occasioned the trip much more favourably anticipated by Georgiana, thus, they were quite a merry group when they set off for

London. (In truth, Georgiana and Elizabeth were merry; Darcy merely reflected their good humour.) The coaches were laden with manservant, lady-maids, foot-men, jewel cases, and trunks. It was thus the family Darcy departed to London for "The Season."

The season commenced with Parliament, and Parliament did not commence until after the frost was out of the ground. Only when they could burrow did vixens begin to breed, thereupon releasing the lords from the rigor of the hunt. Every year, government was in wait until vermin sought reproduction.

Gentlepeople returned to London with the opening of Parliament. However, the true season did not begin until after Easter. Fair weather thenceforward begat a stream of bounteous coaches trailing in from the countryside. It was thereupon that the opera opened its most impressive productions, the theatre its most anticipated plays. Soirées were graced and supper parties attended. And ball after ball after ball lay waste to more than one pair of slippers.

Owing to their prominence in the first circles, duty demanded that the Darcys make appearances upon these occasions with far greater frequency than practicality might have instructed. Never was duty shirked. Georgiana had been nurtured at the breast of family commitment; Elizabeth was still a novice. Unexamined as he kept his feel-ings, however, neither was compleatly aware of how very repugnant the entire process was to Mr. Darcy.

Eager as he was for Georgiana to be out, however, Darcy that year did brave the incumbent pomp more readily. His sister in society and Elizabeth gracing his arm was a duality of pleasure. Moreover, as he was no longer in want of a wife, he was relieved of the discomfiting necessity of deflecting the attentions of young ladies anxious to acquaint themselves with his wealth. An additional gratification would occur at court. For as part of her coming out, Georgiana was to be presented to the king, and by rea-son of her marriage to Mr. Darcy, Elizabeth was to meet him as well.

Mrs. Darcy was a bit more apprehensive than was her husband. However happy she was about Georgiana's formal introduction to the peerage, it betokened her inauguration as hostess to the aristocracy with far greater urgency. They could not entertain with casual affairs using past guest lists. Every family of their station was to be canvassed quite mer-cilessly to ferret out marriageable young men. Families inhabited by such prospects were to be invited regardless of traits of ill-character and uncongeniality infecting their ranks.

The "marriage market" was hardly unknown to Elizabeth. Marrying well was para-mount at all levels of society. However important it was in Meryton for her mother to marry off her daughters to men of income, in drawing rooms in the West End of London, it was a matter of no less importance than (and in many ways comparable to) Parliament enacting a declaration of war.

An additional anxiety was the sheer volume of curious looks Elizabeth was certain she would incite upon entering every room as Mr. Darcy's wife. Unswerving attention would be paid to her dress, her coiffure, her every word. All would be monitored and discussed, and with no particular generosity. She believed she could weather the sniping, but it would be disconcerting to be the cause of such an uproar.

As her resolve often solidified in the face of intimidation, Elizabeth eventually chose a contrary course. She would not cower in embarrassment upon the arm of her handsome husband. She intended to enter every ball, opera, or drawing room with one single intention: to draw as many eyes, excite as many whispers, and disturb as many people as she could. And try not to trip.

They arrived mid-afternoon, mid-week.

It had been long past evenfall when she and Darcy had first arrived in London after their wedding. Thus, as they entered his townhouse that spring, Elizabeth gazed upon its majestic facade with unadulterated awe. Once indoors, she had little time to look about. For they had little more than kicked off their shoes before thither came a maid bearing a tray over-flowing with cards. Elizabeth was interested in but one.

Her experiment amongst the gossipmongers must wait at least a day, for Bingley and Jane were already in London. Their inaugural engagement would be supper with the Bingleys. This, quite naturally, was of considerable relief for an anxious societal neophyte.

However highly Bingley esteemed the Gardiners and their company, Cheapside was not a hotbed of frivolity. With only the company of the Hursts and Miss Bingley at home (who were carted from residence to residence much like three extra trunks), the Bingleys had been languishing restlessly in town for more than a month.

At least Charles Bingley was restless. For Bingley was the bellwether of any forecasted festivity and he dearly loved the social season. Not for rank—beatific Bingley could find pleasure within any social strata. He loved bobbery of any nature; hence, he was quite impatient for the Darcys to arrive. Upon their greeting, he literally wrung Darcy's arm.

"Now that you are here, my friend, things shall surely quicken. London has been dead as deuces. The horses will not run for another fortnight and Jane and I have been reduced to attending readings to have any pastime at all!"

Letters were a poor substitute for actual conversation, limited in their ability to convey the nuance of any specific bit of information, hence, supper was a bit of a bobbery itself. For a short interval it sounded as if all talked at once before conversation settled into a low murmur.

So deeply did they sally into the exchange of news, it is not surprising that Elizabeth's recent portrait sitting was addressed, for she had written of it to Jane. These details were savoured more assiduously than their meal (for Bingley's cook came with the house).

Modesty did not permit Elizabeth to tell Jane in company of how Morland begged to exhibit the painting at the Royal Academy—nor would it keep her from sharing that little morsel once they were alone. Jane would find more pleasure in that honour than did Elizabeth.

Georgiana took everyone unawares by announcing it herself. So eloquently did she speak of the work, her pride in the honour overrode Elizabeth's repeated self-effacement. Even Darcy sat basking in the happy glow of contentment, glad Georgiana had relieved him of the duty to crow.

Proving the bonhomous rivalry he and Darcy had always enjoyed was not abandoned, Bingley announced to the table that Jane was to sit for her own portrait. Attention thus turned from Elizabeth's compleated portrait to Jane's upcoming one, and, his mission accomplished, Bingley sat with a satisfied smile. Jane took the coaxed congratulations graciously.

Not yet satisfied he had stolen all the available thunder, Charles added, "Ours shall be taken together."

Inevitable as the rain (and bidding similar consternation), Bingley's sisters attended their table. When their brother made his addendum, both sisters visibly cringed. They knew that he had just announced their lack of aristocratic ancestry. All young men of illustrious heritage had their portraits hung in the ancestral home by the time they reached majority. As their own fortune had been made only as recently as his father and by West Indies trade, at that juncture, they had yet to form an estate. Had Bingley not embarked upon that search, he would not have let Netherfield Park, danced at Meryton, nor married sweet Jane Bennet. Of this the Bingley sisters thought little, preferring not to dwell upon the mean turns life took.

No one else at the table made note of Bingley's lack of his own likeness, certainly not Elizabeth. She was pleased at the notion of a portrait of Mr. and Mrs. Bingley together.

Wishes be known, she would have preferred hers had been taken with her own husband. However, all of the other subjects in the Pemberley gallery were presented alone, or in large family groupings. Thus, there was a tradition. Through the glow of the candles, she gazed at her husband sitting across the table.

"One day, when our children have been born," she thought as she looked upon him, "I shall suggest our own family portrait."

She envisioned a canvas containing both their countenances. A gaggle of children with dark hair and the Darcy eyes would surround them, a kennel of dogs lying at their feet. It would be a lovely picture and the vision was a consolation.

That she had thought of children during the supper, Elizabeth believed was serendipitous. For beautiful, gracious Jane was even more radiant than usual that evening. She did hope that her sister's glow was due to the delight of Bingley's more educated attentions, and pondered if her own countenance betrayed a similar luminosity.

Just moments after leaving the table, Jane urgently drew Elizabeth aside and, sotto voce, revealed that her sister's suspicion was, indeed, correct. Jane's glow was from Bingley's ministrations, not necessarily from the delight, but the result. She and Bingley (motility of deposit having overcome the obstacle of ineptitude of delivery) were expecting a child by late fall.

In rapt attention did Bingley watch his wife and her sister, much aware that Jane would tell Elizabeth the news forthwith. His was anticipation rewarded, for forthwith of Jane and Elizabeth's heads in brief conference, Elizabeth turned, caught her husband's arm and whispered to him. If Darcy was taken unawares by this confidence, only one quite familiar with the shades of that man's inscrutability would have detected it in the expression of happiness that softened his countenance ever so subtly.

As the others took their chairs, Darcy stood. With all the dignity and none of the vapidity expected upon such a singular occasion, he held his glass before him and led a toast to the happy couple. Bingley's face flushed with joy, happy at last to have finally begotten a first to Darcy in something.

Congratulations flowed along with the wine, but as another always compounds the delight of one good bit of news, an announcement equally tumultuous and no less happy was submitted. For even Bingley's happy disposition had finally been trampled by the very near proximity of Netherfield Park to Longbourn and, invariably, the ever-rapacious Mrs. Bennet. They had made arrangements to quit their tenancy and were in the process of making final negotiations to move to Kirkland Hall in neighbouring Staffordshire.

That was but thirty miles from Pemberley! Darcy pronounced it a fine estate (it was he who had quietly written about the vacancy to Bingley). Upon hearing this assessment from someone whose opinion she valued, Jane looked consoled.

Her husband had purchased it upon impulse, sight unseen. When he told her about the place, his countenance bespoke the unmitigated happiness of a child seeking admiration of a new toy. Therefore, Jane could do nothing but assure him she loved the place sight unseen. It was a relief for her to learn she would not have to persuade herself sincere.

From the heights of new-borns and new homes, discourse waned. Bingley's newest obsession was the gentlemanly sport of boxing, and he regaled Darcy with tales of pugilistic exploits. As the ladies excused themselves, the lolling Mr. Hurst sat upright in his chair (which was as much animation as anyone had quite known of him).

"It is far more rousing than the races, Darcy. I must have you come," Bingley said.

As he inveigled, he walked about waving *Bell's Weekly,* which contained the outcomes of the latest matches, but Darcy's countenance did not reflect his friend's enthusiasm. Indeed, he looked quite dubious.

"I should not think watching two men batter each other with fisticuffs much of an amusement, even if one can wager upon the outcome," he replied rather dourly.

"If you do not favour watching the sport, one can be instructed in the art. It is quite beneficial to the constitution."

"I take my exercise with a foil, Bingley. You know that."

All avenues expended, Bingley sat dejectedly in a side chair, his bit of moroseness unquestionably inflated by a bit of playacting. Darcy successfully contained a laugh, allowing Bingley to continue to believe himself an object of pity.

"I have laid money down upon one boxer, Darcy. He is a fine pugilist. Savage Sam Cribb."

"Indubitably an *artiste* of unparalleled sensitivity."

Not so thick as not to understand that jibe, Bingley replied indignantly, "That is not the point."

"What is the point?"

"I have laid money down backing this boxer and I have yet to witness a match."

"Pray, why not?"

Bingley sat a moment and glanced at Mr. Hurst who was studying *Bell's* with great industry.

Satisfied that he would not be heard, he leaned toward Darcy, lowered his voice and uttered the unthinkable, "Jane refuses to allow it."

At this most mortifying admission, Darcy dared not even smile. Therefore, he frowned.

"Too unsavoury," Bingley added.

It was quite evident to Darcy why Bingley begged his company. If her sister's husband attended such an event, Jane would relent.

Friendship required certain…concessions, hence he reluctantly relented. To make certain the debt was understood, Darcy acquiesced with overt magnanimity.

The single obstacle Mr. Darcy saw that lay before him was convincing Mrs. Darcy. This was not a question of permission to do his own bidding. The difficulty would lie in persuading Elizabeth, who adored the excitement of the races, not to accompany them.

Upon the carriage ride home, Elizabeth experienced an unexpected attack of melancholia. She thought possibly seeing her beloved sister once again and talking of Longbourn had made her homesick. True, she did miss her father dreadfully. Her mother, not so keenly. Hence, she was perplexed from whence sprang her languor.

Accompanied by two individuals whose natures were not particularly effusive (and ignorant that her husband was plotting to divest himself of her company for an evening of sport), the mood in the coach was positively bleak. It was unfortunate that he had yet to devise his plan of attack. A little repartee would have been welcome.

Alone in her dressing room, the unfamiliarity of the London house quieted her further. Endeavouring to keep her nostalgia at bay, she recollected the profoundly pleasant remembrances of their first night together there as man and wife. As anxious as he had been to bring his wife to Pemberley, it was the only true honeymoon they had.

They had talked several times of travelling to Italy when the French conflicts had ended. Elizabeth truly believed, however, Darcy should be happy if he never left England.

She rested her head upon her arms and pushed the curtains away from the pane. The window overlooked the street and the sound of carriages passing beneath could be heard. It had misted and the cobblestones shone in the night, yellowed by the amber glow of the new-fangled gaslights. It was odd to look out expecting the darkness only to be greeted by illumination.

She thought of her husband, who most likely lay just beyond the door, and longed to speak to him of her low spirits. Believing his less than sentimental inclination was likely to make him an unsympathetic confidant to such a weakness in herself, she was reluctant. Nevertheless, she wished he would venture to come to her. He had come into her dressing room just the one time and not again, even in play. Wouldst he come for her if she sought him not? Would he enter her dressing room again then? In all probability he would, but then his dignity had sterner understanding of ridicule than did his wife's. She, who finds herself upended in his bath.

Recollecting how she had sat in anticipatory apprehension in that very dressing room the night of her devirgination, she could not but smile. Was it memory of her innocence that bade her recollect that night in such exquisite detail? Perchance she was an irredeemable romantic.

In a moment, she stood, went to the door of the bedchamber, and opened it. There were rose petals upon the bed.

The staff at the Darcys' London house was not much accustomed to commotion. Miss Georgiana was frequently in town with her companion, Mrs. Annesley, but as she was quiet and made few requests whilst she dwelt there, little disruption bechanced. Before he married, Mr. Darcy had been in town but seldom, often for but fortnights at a time. Howbeit much sought after as a guest of others, he was host to just a few entertainments himself. All of which had made for an unruffled, yet prestigious service.

The season after Mr. Darcy's marriage implemented a great deal of upheaval and resultant tumult amongst the servants. Some were not altogether happy about the extra work this hubbub instigated, but most were in excited anticipation. Most particularly vexed, however, was the house steward, Cyril Smeads.

Smeads, the family called him. Mr. Smeads to his underlings. General opinion of under-servants in the Darcy service gave grudging respect to crusty old Mrs. Reynolds at Pemberley. (That woman had outlived three husbands and four children, and sheer perseverance is always a highly admired virtue.) Smeads was Mrs. Reynolds' son and single living issue (nepotism a dearly held tradition in all walks of life). Nevertheless, dislike of him was earnest and universal. So ill was he regarded, wagging tongues rendered it unto lore that Smeads had beat his siblings to death in their cribs.

Most believed Mr. Darcy would have put Cyril Smeads out upon the street was it not for his mother. Most, if not all, hoped when old Mrs. Reynolds died, he would finally do it. Some said that was wishful thinking, but they all looked forward to the possibility.

Indeed, Mr. Smeads was not much beloved by those who toiled for him. It was undeniable, had someone chosen to defend his character, that he was prone to little snits of temper and laughable that he could not pass a looking-glass without at least a preening glance. Was all that not test enough upon their forebearance, at every turn he endeavoured to weave foul designs upon the women in his service. This, of course, was well-practised in many houses, but such schemes were, still and all, inexcusable.

Of all the man's many sins, why he hired that vile footman, Tom Reed, was the most inexplicable. Such a beast was that knave that even Smeads would not allow him to serve the table. When he took him on, Cyril Smeads did not question Reed's character, just that he had height and a good leg. For nothing mattered more to Cyril Smeads than appearances.

Within days of Reed's being taken into service was the momentous occasion of Mr. Darcy's wedding. In preparation, the great man had relegated very specific instructions upon what he wanted done when he brought his wife to the London house for his connubial consummation. Under usual circumstances, he consigned the menu to Smeads discretion (who found absolution in good taste, if condemnation in scruples). Upon that occasion, however, Mr. Darcy chose not to do so. His specifications for every one of the twelve courses were detailed to the point of the temperature of the soup and the choices of mustard. Additionally, a silver brush and hand glass set was to be laid upon a silk cloth in Mrs. Darcy's dressing room. In Mr. Darcy's was to be a silver bowl, filled with rose petals (deep pink). These petals were to be plucked from flowers in the hotbeds of Pemberley's conservatory and brought in fresh that afternoon. The balcony doors would be cracked one inch. A single five-stem girandole (six-inch candles) must stand next to the bed.

Hence, the house hung heavy in expectation of that visit. However, the couple had departed nearly as precipitously as they had arrived. Nevertheless, the two maids that were charged with stoking the fireplaces in the interim burst forth quite a bit of prattle upon their return downstairs. Speculation was rampant upon what the honeymooning couple did or did not wear beneath their conjugal covers. Of course, those bedclothes came into scrutiny when the soiled laundry was brought from the honeymoon chambers.

The wedding-night sheet told that the mattress quadrille was danced a half-dozen times, and the chambermaids tittered about it innocently enough with the washwomen.

The big footman Mr. Smeads had hired who spent far too much time slouched in the kitchen had grabbed it and laughed rather lasciviously. It would have been reported to Smeads that the man he hired to ride upon Mr. Darcy's coach for no better reason than he was the right size had pilfered it from the laundry, but no one dared. Reason why they did not was equally divided betwixt their disdain of Mr. Smeads and outright fear of the footman.

Tom Reed had earned a great deal of ill-will in that kitchen. There was no doubt he could not keep his hands off the scullery-maids' bottoms and a general belief he pinched the silverware as well. Therefore, no one could even enjoy a little bawdy talk about the newlyweds in the light of Reed's leering. Dislike of him was so unlimited, any pleasure of his cast sudden dissatisfaction upon their own.

There was a tremendous heave of relief when he and his brother, Frank, rode the coach back to Pemberley (even if the sheet was in Tom Reed's haversack).

Upon their return to London, Smeads was called immediately to stand before Mr. Darcy in his library. The servants saw nothing unusual in that, but when Smeads left their conference, several bechanced to see his countenance. And his expression led them to believe, not unhappily (perchance even gleefully), that Smeads had been upbraided in some manner. If it was because of the destination of the pilfered bedcloth, and that Mr. Darcy had seen it in some vile country tavern as gossip had reported, there was no clear conclusion. Regardless which of his many misdeeds found him retribution, those who worked under Mr. Smeads's petulant command found the gratification exquisite.

Word that the Pemberley stables were set afire had preceded the Darcys to London. But it was not learnt until the arrival of their retinue the additional news that Tom

Reed had actually been beaten from service. And that none other than Mr. Darcy himself inflicted those lashes. That disclosure was repeated until it passed through every room in the house. Once the news had made the rounds, it was pronounced by all who heard it as the plum in the pudding of their day.

Within two days, and with no undue reluctance, Darcy met with his solicitor to make arrangements for Georgiana's first publishing. Elizabeth and Georgiana, thick as two inkle-weavers, spent this same time in giddy decision of her pen name (a necessity by reason of her station). Georgiana favoured something French. Elizabeth looked to something droll. The decision in favour of "A Derbyshire Lady" came quite honestly from Georgiana with no influence from her sister-in-law. If Darcy was not convinced that she did not suggest it, Elizabeth thought that frightfully unfortunate.

Coincident to the pursuit of the finer arts was a venture unto the coarser, that in the manner of the eagerly anticipated, if wrangled, trip to the sparring ring. It ended, however, all too badly. That was most unfortunate, but to Darcy not without merit, for it terminated Bingley's induction into the spurious arena of boxing compleatly and unequivocally.

Indeed, Jack Lewis took out Savage Sam Cribb not a minute into the first round. This bastinadoing debacle might have occurred regardless of the half a horseshoe Lewis had hidden in his left glove. But the expulsion of Cribb's teeth would not have been quite so...expeditiously catapulted onto the onlookers had he not. This *tir de barrage* of Cribb's incisors fell mostly upon his benefactor, Bingley, who stood ringside along with Darcy and the ever-cupshotten Mr. Hurst.

Because the wagering was heavy upon this particular match, a few of the more cynical in attendance suspected possible pugilistic malfeasance. They beset Jack Lewis and gainsaid his win by tossing him through the front window of the boxing establishment. This defenestration of Lewis was unseen by Bingley, for he had swooned at the eruption of Savage Sam's mouth.

Had Bingley himself not reversed his admiration for the sport of his own volition, his wife most certainly would have persuaded it. For as it happened, a bicuspid persevered through swoon and carriage, nestled in his hatband. But when he doffed his hat at home, it spun off the brim and came to rest, most unfortunately, in the cleavage of Bingley's lovely wife Jane. As one might surmise, what happened next was unpretty. Therefore, it shall not be dwelt upon.

Cribb did get off rather well, for a contrite Bingley settled a sizeable annuity upon him. It was only because his affront did not cause Jane to miscarry (although she leapt quite enough to have kindled one) that Bingley was eventually forgiven by anyone.

Not so horrified as Jane (and initially even a little intrigued), Elizabeth little liked her husband's person being in so close a company with violence. As for Mr. Darcy, he needed not his wife's urging to tell Bingley he would sooner purchase a ticket to Vauxhall than share another escapade anywhere near the vicinity of Covent Garden.

London was not foreign to Elizabeth, for she had visited upon a number of occasions. When in town, she had always stayed with her Aunt and Uncle Gardiner in their quite handsome townhouse. Cheapside, however, was not the West End. Moreover, their home was a positive hovel compared to the size and tasteful elegance of Darcy's Park Lane residence.

Elizabeth's single glimpse of the place having been upon her wedding night (and architecture, at least of a metropolitan nature, not being her keenest interest), she had but caught a glance of the red brick and white columns as they departed.

Contrary to many of London's wealthier citizens, Darcy eschewed Greek and Egyptian exotica (exotica considered the most fashionable of statements to be made) in favour of an ambience of understated, if undeniably opulent, dignity.

Pemberley had been the Darcy family residence for centuries, but he had bought his London house himself. Therefore, Pemberley may have influenced Darcy, but his London home stood testament to his own particular taste and French ancestry.

If she did not appreciate exotica, the diversions of London excited Elizabeth more than she should have liked to confess. Having attended but one opera and nothing more, she hardly considered herself a patroness of the arts. Her sensibility found diversion more happily in the exhilaration of a horse race. She did suggest they attend a play featuring a particularly popular tragedienne. However, her husband demurred, commenting neither upon the play nor the playwright. He merely suggested a performance by a new composer in its stead. Although the Theatre Royal symphony hall was, as often as not, less a spot to see than to be seen, Darcy did enjoy actually listening (and, unbeknownst to his wife, he was happy to have reason to attend a concert and not a drama featuring a woman he had once found lacking).

He held but a single reluctance upon coming to London with Elizabeth. Nevertheless, it was not insignificant. For their life at Pemberley was unconnected from the indiscretions of his past. However, London was an entirely different matter. No doubt, their paths would cross former...acquaintances of his. Thus, he accepted the inevitable, vowing he would take each occasion as it came, each encounter as presented. If Elizabeth asked, he would answer. If she did not, he would not offer.

And notwithstanding Elizabeth was the centre of that particular dilemma, she was wholly unwitting of it.

Hence, his bygone paramours were not what came to mind when Elizabeth first set her eyes upon Darcy, dressed in full panoply, ready to escort Georgiana and herself to their court presentation. Hanging from his waist was a sword that swung down his thigh in a graceful arc. Court protocol demanded such regalia (he but rarely wore seals and chains), but Elizabeth had yet to see him thus. Unschooled in weaponry, she nonetheless raised her eyebrow in admiration. (Whether it was the sabre or the sabre bearer who most incited this regard, one can but conjecture.) The hilt was French. The gilded relief covering handle, knuckle guard, and quillions were worn smooth from centuries of use. Had she asked, he would have explained that the blade was not true to its hilt, for this had been replaced after some long past, bloody battle.

Tentatively, she reached out and touched it, letting her hand slide down the cold enamelled sheath. Suddenly, the double *entendre* of that particular gesture occurred to her and she dropped her hand free. But the sense of lewdness was not easy to shake.

Hastily, she took his arm and whispered to him, "Mr. Darcy, I hope your wife is not about, for I find myself quite at the mercy of your figure."

As they marched out the door, Elizabeth was quite impressed with herself (howbeit mightily she endeavoured not to be). Had it not been her misfortune that the same strict code of dress that demanded her husband wear his sword, required of her a three-foot feathered train, she should not have thought herself ridiculous at all.

The gallery of St. James's Court made even Pemberley seem small. The Darcys took their place in line upon the stairs as each personage was summoned to the king in the Presence Chamber. When she entered, Elizabeth released the heavy train folded over her arm. Its weight yanked her back, thus demanding she effect an awkward, hips forward, gait. From this position, she could not help but gaze at the huge columns that supported the cavernous room and follow their arched path overhead. It was so high and her train so heavy, when they were bid step forward, Elizabeth was certain the first glimpse King George would see of her was the underside of her chin.

Or possibly not. It was one of the last public appearances of the increasingly demented king, and one might opine that not all of his dogs were barking. Having heard the rumours, she half-expected poor George to be a drooling lunatic. His loss of reason this day, however, manifested itself merely in a vacant expression and the occasional queer remark. (He had asked Elizabeth how she favoured her shoes.)

Even Prinny attended, evidently an unusual occurrence. Gossip had it that he did not often venture onto the same stage as his father. Nevertheless, stand he did behind the king and queen. At his elbow was his own entourage.

This sycophantic contingent consisted of dandyish men and pretty (if heavily rouged) ladies, all posed in various postures of boredom.

When she first saw the prince, Elizabeth thought that in being described as handsome, it was not the outrageous violation of truth that description usually construed. But upon introduction, a closer inspection saw him less handsome than pretty and quite easily as amply rouged as his consort. (It appeared the mole upon his cheek was pencilled as well. Elizabeth thought that affectation had died with the last century.)

So enthralled was she by the prince's maquillage, she was quite unwitting that his notoriously roving eye alit upon her. Such notice, however, did not escape her husband. Because of that, he kept a tight hand upon her elbow as she departed her presentation. So firm was his grip, she presumed him concerned for her nerves.

"Upon the contrary," he later told her, "my solicitation was in defence of your honour rather than your knees. I believed myself to recognise from the prince a more than patriarchal interest in your person."

It had long been whispered that the king's lunacy was a result of the unlikely faithfulness of the monarch to his queen, rampant infidelity normally the most reliable trait amongst royalty. Marriage, however, did not dampen his son's libido. His reputation announced he clearly intended to regain promiscuity in the name of the monarchy. Not only did he take advantage of his own position, but devoured what was unused of his father's. A daily diet of compliance did nothing to discourage the increasingly corpulent Regent from propositioning ladies of the court with brash liberality.

However injudicious to his person were his vices, he could act upon a whim. For it was no secret that most ladies at court would happily be debauched if it was upon a royal mattress. That did not occur without their ambitious husbands' approval.

Therefore, forthwith of the commencement of the ball, a request did come for the Darcys to join the prince's party in his salon. Darcy dared to tell the courier they were unavailable, thinking it wisest to keep Elizabeth from beneath Prinny's gaze, lest the man solicit her company. It would be impolitic to call out the King's son. Elizabeth was taken aback and said so.

Darcy answered her qualms quite bluntly, "I do not choose to dine with a man who has spoken of consigning his father to Bedlam and appears to offer nothing more to the enrichment of England than the introduction of sea bathing."

That remark reminded Elizabeth, howbeit he was an untitled member of the landed gentry, when it came to rank the Darcys held lineage consanguineous to the crown. Hence, as one of the most illustrious men in England, his deference to those titled was more a matter of ritual politesse than subordination.

Elizabeth was grateful to know herself the wife of one of the few members of the elite circle who had no reason to inflate his importance (for to what could one of such eminence aspire?). The level of self-important pomposity amongst that group was staggering. The lavishness of St. James's Palace was bedazzling; Elizabeth, nevertheless, believed that the lifestyle she witnessed there was not endured without substantial cost to one's character. Position was not the only thing. It was everything.

Character and goodness had no weight, no merit. Position alone held realty. Of this, she did not speak to her husband. For she knew, although not by reason of measured contempt, but birthright, it was a point upon which he held no perspective.

They attended and were hosts to many suppers, teas, private concerts, and amateur theatricals whilst in London. They did not venture, however, to another court ball until near the end of their stay. By then, Elizabeth was quite weary of the constant whirl of socialising. Nevertheless, she could not find disfavour that final night, for it had not been totally without merit. There were far more couples than could comfortably be contained in the ballroom. Hence, she could steal more dances with her husband than propriety allowed.

After one particularly enthusiastic romp across the dance floor (this not with Darcy, for he never romped), she repaired to catch her breath in the gallery. She was amazed (howbeit in retrospect, perhaps she should not have been) to find her cousin, Mr. Collins, and Charlotte with Charlotte's father, Sir William Lucas, lurking there. Sir Lucas had finally managed to insinuate himself again at court, albeit in a lesser ballroom. They had strayed from thence to eye the first circles, a reluctant Charlotte in tow. It was a happy treat to see her friend, even mitigated, as it was, by the presence of her husband. Elizabeth wanted to have a moment to talk to Charlotte who, since her marriage (understandably), usually seemed to have a pained expression upon her face. However, Mr. Collins heard of Elizabeth's royal presentation and could not contain his enthusiasm for being a cousin to someone so close to the royal throne.

"And could Mr. Darcy possibly use his influence to submit a lowly clergy to the honour of an upper salon?" he inquired. "I flatter myself that I am a gentleman of some repute. With the correct patronage 'tis done, is it not?"

"I think not," Elizabeth said, desperately trying to remember the rules. "I think it done singularly for the peerage, cardinals and bishops."

"But I thought a man of Mr. Darcy's influence…"

She insisted, "Surely, you would not want to risk offending your archbishop, Mr. Collins."

Mr. Collins silently (and mercifully) weighed that transgression against the elevation in status of private presentation. All the while, Sir Lucas stood observing this encounter with pompous condescension (Sir Lucas often looked pompous, but in this instance it was more pronounced than usual). His own knighthood was by reason of a handsome fortune in trade, a distinction that had perhaps impressed himself more keenly than it did his acquaintances.

Charlotte's marriage to Mr. Collins was, Sir Lucas believed, a step down. But with Charlotte plain and seven years older than twenty, there was a paucity of prospects.

Mr. Collins's proposal had therefore been provident and welcome. Indeed, he and Mr. Collins were of the same mind upon the most important matters. One, that Charlotte could do no better than Mr. Collins as a husband, and second, that every person of station was worthy of the greatest possible sycophantism. In the light of these understandings, when Mr. Collins's toadying deserted him for Mrs. Darcy, it was hardly an offence to Sir Lucas. On the contrary, he marvelled at his son-in-law's determination. The failure of his entreaty to Elizabeth was almost as disappointing to Sir Lucas as it was mortifying to Charlotte.

Charlotte's own countenance had not duplicated her father's, for she looked upon all events as a seasoned observer. All things fell into simple categories. Elizabeth was her friend, not a social opportunity. Charlotte was uninterested in servility to anyone and hated being at court as much as it delighted her father and husband.

Charlotte was a simple woman, caring but for her hearth and home. Only great interrogation might uncover (Elizabeth had never dared to bring it up) that Charlotte would just as soon her husband did not attend either.

With Mr. Collins ruminating yet, Elizabeth made her apologies in order to escape. When she kissed Charlotte's cheek *adieu,* she recognised that strange little detached smile first evident at Pemberley. It gave Elizabeth a slight shiver down her back as she bid a hasty retreat. Her eyes searched for the reassurance of her husband as she wended her way through the throng.

Her survey of the room took in Georgiana, who was wedged tightly amongst the dancers. Rarely did Georgiana favour a caper across a ballroom. A quadrille was a test of endurance for her. Unfortunately, Miss Darcy beckoned only the most ambitious of young men (this, by reason of Miss Darcy's fortune), and of all young men, ambitious ones were those Georgiana cared for least. Therein lay the vexation. The company Georgiana was most likely to enjoy was the very one whose meekness kept him from her. Hitherto, whenever Elizabeth caught sight of her circling the dance floor, her partner's face would reflect fawning insincerity. Georgiana would merely look pained.

However, with Colonel Fitzwilliam in town, her dance card was full, her partners discerning. The colonel had taken her about the floor at least twice and Elizabeth saw he had a hand in her current partner. He was a fellow officer, one assigned to the royal family. It could be argued that if Fitzwilliam selected him to dance with Georgiana, she was safe from mendacity. Thus assured her sister-in-law was temporarily in good hands, Elizabeth again pushed her way through the press of bodies looking for Darcy, happy to share that information.

Thither she went and so intent was she upon searching for her husband, she was almost sent reeling a step backwards from coming so precipitously under the glare of Lady Catherine de Bourgh. (She should have known Mr. Collins would not stray far from her side.)

Her daughter, Lady Anne, suffered poor digestion, poor chest, and poor feet, and hence ventured not unto St. James. Accompanying Lady Catherine that evening was none other than the inimitably steatopygic Mrs. Dalrymple. That lady harboured the same fat back, diamond tiara, white shoes, and pink nephew that she had presented at Pemberley. Her Ladyship's always imposing figure, however, was dressed *cap-à-pied* in the black of mourning. An immense diamond choker circled her so tightly from larynx to shoulder blades it may have required the woman choose soup rather than veal for supper. Her face, however, bore an expression of such decided distaste that Elizabeth was almost moved to laugh. Fortunately, her better judgement overcame her diversion because she was not compleatly unsure the provocation might have moved Lady Catherine to violence. Lady Dalrymple swept her monocle to her eye.

Elizabeth was frightfully cognisant that the meeting to which she was a party hung heavily in the curiosity of the surrounding guests. Lady Catherine was known to have been exceedingly vocal in all quarters in disparaging her nephew's marriage. Such attention from the floor proved what Elizabeth had always suspected, that people of rank enjoyed holding witness to social drama just as dearly as their kitchen help. She overcame her stupefaction enough to nod politely to Lady Catherine, who stared at her and thereupon snorted in obvious disgust and turned her back.

Of this, Elizabeth took no unexpected affront. Nothing more would have come from the passing incident had not Lady Catherine, in her rude haste, turned about directly to her nephew, Mr. Darcy.

Elizabeth could see her husband's face over Lady Catherine's shoulder, and found great relief that it was not herself upon whom his gaze lit. For so very unamused was it, Lady Catherine was rendered silent and motionless. If it were not for the roaring in her ears, Elizabeth would have realised that everyone surrounding them had ceased their discourse, and all attention was bent to Darcy and his aunt. It was Darcy who spoke, breaking the stalemate. His voice was quite unremarkable.

"Lady Catherine. I see you did not recognise your niece, Mrs. Darcy, there behind you."

Gracefully, he gestured in Elizabeth's direction. Lady Catherine turned about. Her countenance was not merely grim. It had blanched.

Darcy said, "Elizabeth, you remember my aunt?"

Mrs. Dalrymple's mouth was not exactly agape, but she had dropped her monocle. Her brain had not yet transmitted that information to her hand, for it was yet upraised.

Ignoring the bestupified Mrs. Dalrymple, Elizabeth replied, "Why, yes, I have had the honour of visiting her home. It is quite good to see you again, Lady Catherine."

She curtsied as deeply as her trembling knees would allow. By then the thunder had quieted in her ears, but the silence about them was several decibels higher than deafening. All ears were awaiting Lady Catherine's response. After an uncomfortably long moment of strained study of her niece, Lady Catherine glanced again at Darcy's imperturbable aspect.

"Yes, Mrs. Darcy," she finally said, looking yet at her nephew whilst addressing Elizabeth, "How good to see you. I hope you and my nephew are well."

Thereupon, Darcy took Elizabeth's elbow and quitted Lady Catherine. Conversations and activity resumed.

Elizabeth could feel the heat of Lady Catherine's glare upon her as they moved away. Instinctively, she drew back her shoulders and straightened her spine. Her stomach might wamble and her knees give a bit, but she refused to expose any overt sign of impuissance to Darcy's wretched aunt. Elizabeth, indeed, felt weak. However, it was not Lady Catherine who had discombobulated her. It was her husband. He had willed Lady Catherine to be civil, and she had acquiesced. A feat of substantial magnitude. Witnessing it—well, frankly, it gave her the twitters.

Initially, and with considerable self-satisfaction, Elizabeth believed the entire confrontation with Lady Catherine fell to Darcy's supreme devotion to herself. A fleeting rumination upon the matter bade her reassess with a measure of indignation. Before they had crossed the room, a greater truth came to her. However devoted Darcy was, that drama was not strictly in defence of his wife, but for the benefit of society at large. Fitzwilliam Darcy was the head of the Darcy family; it was he, not Lady Catherine, who held the reins of power.

Darcy advised Elizabeth, who was yet in a bit of a pother, that she appeared pale. Forthwith, he set out to find her some refreshment. Abandoned, atwittered, and aggrieved in the throng of *bon vivants,* she stood first upon one foot then the other, trying to not look peeved. Her singular petulance lasted but a moment, for the crowd was thick with a gallimaufry of Darcy family friends, colleagues, and cohorts.

One of whom (Elizabeth had not quite ascertained the distinction) previously introduced as Lady Twisnodde, descried her alone and called out.

"TooRoo! Elizabeth! TooRoo!"

Although she bade Elizabeth join them, their group more or less engulfed her. Their party included her daughters. And notwithstanding one was introduced as a married woman, they were identically costumed. The indistinguishable sisters had a tight grip upon the arms of an elderly gentleman whom Elizabeth at first assumed was Lord Twisnodde. Upon his introduction, it became evident that the duo's clamp upon the old man was not necessarily in familial fear for his decrepitude.

Half-blind and mostly deaf, he was not their father. He was, however, an earl. As a titled man of considerable age and no heirs, he excited all the attention one might expect, regardless that his conversation consisted but of the interrogative, "Eh?"

Miss Twisnodde's diligent attention to removing lint from his jacket and smoothing his lapels was exceeded only by her married sister's. Apparently, they believed two heads better than one (or four hands better than two) in obtaining a match for the unmarried sister (who bore an expression of prognathous determination, not unlike Caroline Bingley's). Their ample display of arts and allurements was temporarily arrested upon introduction to Mrs. Darcy. After a polite curtsey to Elizabeth, both looked at each other, then spontaneously and synchronously giggled.

In light of having no clue why either of the ladies was incited to such merriment by her introduction, Elizabeth took mental inventory of any possible indiscretion of her costume. All accoutrements seemed in order. Hence, she prepared an insincere apology to excuse herself from such discourteous company. Thenceforward, her annoyance over her husband forsaking her to the mercy of a couple of coarse fisgigs escalated precariously. She would have instituted her departure quite promptly had not her attention been otherwise appropriated. For before Elizabeth could disengage herself, it fell apparent that the ill-manners she witnessed from the sisters may have been inflicted upon herself, but she was not the grounds, merely the whatever. Her husband was the wherefore.

She espied him heading in her direction. He carried two cups of negus high in defence of the jostling crowd. Raising her hand, she caught his eye. As his hands were full, hence he could but lift his eyebrows to indicate he saw her. Elizabeth realised the imminent addition of Mr. Darcy to their group had caused the sisters to abandon the poor, palsied earl. They nudged each other excitedly, and one commenced a high-pitched squeal.

In the near distance, Darcy stopped quite abruptly. His eyes narrowed. Even halfway across the room, Elizabeth could see his mouth tighten into a grimace and his nostrils flare (very nearly quivering). Obviously, he had seen something distasteful. So decided was his expression, Elizabeth made a quick look over her shoulder to see if she was about to have Lady Catherine beset her again. When she turned back about, Darcy had compleatly vanished. The flirtatious young women were twisting and straining upon tiptoes, obviously as curious as she about her husband's sudden disappearance. She caught sight of the crown of his head as it moved into the midst of the crowd.

Excusing herself, she went to overtake him, intending to remark upon her new acquaintances' unusual matching *ensembles* and common manners. But by the time she reached him, he was deep in conversation with Fitzwilliam, still holding the punch cups delicately by the handles. The dedication of this discourse fortunately outlasted Elizabeth's interest in her previous company and the Twisnoddes were eventually forgotten.

The carriage ride home was endured with wearied congeniality. Both Elizabeth and Darcy were far too tired by their own perplexities for gossip. This quiet allowed them to bear witness to Georgiana's unlikely enthusiasm of the occasion. Darcy listened to her societal rhapsody with particular pleasure. Upon most occasions, if he were to converse with his sister, it was his duty to initiate a topic. That was a chore few others could induce him to weather.

As Georgiana chattered on, Elizabeth listened to her in all good humour. But as she did, her mind wandered to Lady Catherine and the nagging feeling that her cunning would not allow her to rest at being so publicly chastened. Although Darcy had not seemed at all discomfited by that confrontation, Elizabeth knew his powerful aunt was as formidable an enemy as might be encountered.

Twitters aside, she hoped for no heinous repercussions.

In London, summer did not age with grace. The odour of desperation permeated the young ladies yet unattached. Thus, hitherto festive balls became not such gay affairs, but more mercenary. For unpromised damsels enduring their third season of society since presentation, it was positively grave. (For Miss Bingley, nearing thirty, the chances for a good match had dwindled disastrously.) It was then that the most imprudent conduct was exposed. Flirtations became more blatant.

Some young men, understanding that desperation fuels impetuosity, took advantage. Young ladies were compromised. Duels of honour were demanded, but few fought. Often accommodation was found in an engagement. (Fathers guarded their daughters fastidiously, but they were not unreasonable.)

It was in this contradictory air of futility and success that the peerage turned their thoughts toward the civility and serenity of the country. Before they realised it, the Darcys had but two days left in London and there were many loose ends to organise.

Properly, for Elizabeth one of those loose ends (so to speak) was the dressmaker's, for Georgiana was to return within the month and could have her final fittings then. Elizabeth, not anxious to return to London anytime soon, needed to compleat her shopping forthwith. Happy to make every arrangement so that they could take leave in a timely fashion, Darcy elected to escort Elizabeth to Bond Street. His haberdasher lay across the avenue. He saw convenience to all.

With that first venture into Mayfair with Georgiana and Hannah to select fabrics and lace, women of society had been happy (to the point of exhilaration) to share lurid tales with Mrs. Darcy of what betimes late at night upon Bond Street.

Evidently, after supper and the theatre, their blood up from the quest, many young men not of a mind to risk censure walked the few blocks south to Bond and Regent Streets. For there, ladies free from chaperones and anxious parents tarried. Elizabeth, for her part, was almost as titillated with the hearing of it as the ladies in the relating. Nevertheless, she found it difficult to believe a street that harboured such sedate shops during the day became a teeming catwalk once dusk descended.

Everyone had heard of London's disreputable red-light districts, the worst of which lay betwixt Whitechapel and Wapping. The streets of St. Giles were thick with harlots so desperate for a farthing that they would slit a man's gullet as willingly as drop their drawers. Just the most base of men dared venture there.

Contrariwise, the demimondaines of Mayfair did not walk the street hoping to be propositioned. Respectable young men instead dallied inside anonymous houses amongst luxurious furnishings with women quite free with their affection. Notwithstanding these structures overlooked Hyde Park rather than the Tower of London, it could not be denied that the men's clubs upon Pall Mall served the said same purpose as the streets of the East End (save for the throat slitting). However discreet gentlemen believed their carouses were, there was but one true secret. And that was how eager the speculation about it was amongst the feminine side of society.

It had been small vindication of her husband that the patronising of these houses of ill-repute was so pervasive amongst gentlemen. However, Elizabeth had been absolutely flabbergasted at the dispassion with which some wives accepted their husbands' dalliances. What came to pass in Darcy's life before he met her, she had chosen to set aside. Before he was married, she believed him guilty of nothing greater than possessing an unusually healthy libido. Nevertheless, that was where she drew the line.

If a man visited a woman not his wife after he married, that was adultery. A shooting offence.

Elizabeth had not taken much notice of the area initially, for it was quite a respectable street. However, once she heard all the rumours, her interest was certainly piqued. (It had to be labelled hearsay, she conjectured, for no lady of her acquaintance had first-hand knowledge.) One person of her intimate acquaintance, however, did.

She cast her eyes curiously upon certain houses upon Regent Street, howbeit not overtly. No undo attention would have been attracted had she not overheard the milliner's assistant sending a boy to deliver several hatboxes to a house upon the next block.

"Harcourt House," she said. "It is the large grey one. White shutters. You know the place."

The boy nodded and set off upon his errand. Titillated by such news, Elizabeth could hardly contain herself until Darcy returned to escort her home. With studied nonchalance, she took his arm and suggested a stroll before returning to the carriage.

"We are to take leave to-morrow and I have not yet had my fill of peering into shop windows. Do humour me."

It was unlikely that he thought her entirely innocent of gossip. Thus in not demurring she believed he was, indeed, humouring her. In want of convincing them both she truly wanted to see what the shop windows held, she stopped and admired several whilst steering him determinedly about the block. When they rounded the court, she saw a handsome stone house. As they took the corner, Elizabeth was studying the house so diligently, she did not notice the woman who passed. No note might have been taken had not Darcy done the improbable.

Almost imperceptibly, he touched the brim of his hat.

It was not done for a gentleman to acknowledge a lady not of his acquaintance. The woman did not appear to respond nor was there any attempt at introduction. Nevertheless, Elizabeth could not resist turning and looking at her as she took the steps to the grey house. There, the woman paused and returned her gaze. She was tastefully costumed. Beneath the satin ruffle of her bonnet, honey-coloured curls framed a patrician countenance. It was one of breathtaking beauty. Her figure could only be described as voluptuous, her costume, exquisite. She did not appear to be wearing rouge at all.

A more dismal moment was unimaginable. Could not her husband have had the good graces to commit carnal necessities with a woman who looked cheap? Ugly?

Obese? No, he had hockled about with possibly the most beautiful courtesan in England. That was indefensible.

Other than his subtle acknowledgement of the passer-by, Darcy had looked straight ahead, keeping a firm hold on Elizabeth's arm.

As he led her away, Elizabeth said simply, "She is very beautiful."

When Darcy responded neither in question of whom she spoke nor in agreement, Elizabeth knew there was little doubt of the identity of the woman. It would have been reasonable, even expected, for her to ask him if he knew the house or inquire about the woman. However, she did not. She too, did the improbable. She spoke not a word.

Upon their return to the carriage, a dejection descended upon her that she did not attempt to rescue. For she realised her being had just been usurped by a green-eyed, grasping, grudging, possessive monster. By the time they reached the townhouse, Elizabeth decided that of all her many injurious faults, curiosity might well rank higher than impatience. She would have been quite content to live out her life without ever once looking upon that beautiful woman, understanding the intimacy she must have once shared with Darcy.

Obviously, Darcy knew Elizabeth comprehended all the implications of what she had witnessed. Her silence told him that. Hence, it was with no little tenderness that he took her into his embrace that night. When she received him, she did so with generosity, but when their union was compleat, she had a whispered entreaty.

"I wish we were home."

Perchance it was the step of being formally introduced to society that had coaxed Georgiana from her diffidence. Perchance it was something more. Whatever it truly was, Darcy gave credit for Georgiana's new-found confidence to her work being published. As that came about at Elizabeth's insistence, his esteem for his wife and her opinion only grew. He did not say so in so many words, yet she knew it all the same. Elizabeth was quite happy to have her husband's praise in place of possible censure had it gone badly.

He told Elizabeth that he was inclined to believe that Georgiana's eighteenth year should see her happy at last.

That was the single pronouncement made of their season. The subject of their encounter upon the street with his past was avoided with superb dedication. All appeared content to recapture the quiet serenity at Pemberley, Elizabeth most of all. When she had told him she wanted to go home, he did not once fancy she meant

Longbourn. He had been long persuaded to understand that she, as did he, thought only of Pemberley as truly home.

When the day of decampment arrived, the trunks had been loaded into the coach boots, but Mrs. Annesley was tardy yet from her visit with her daughter. Having had his fill of London, Darcy was too impatient to delay for a single minute. One coach was to await her return, and accompanied by Goodwin, would take leave directly thereof, the other forthwith.

Elizabeth, Hannah, Georgiana, and her lady-maid, Anne, fit into the first coach quite easily, but their number gave Darcy an excuse to return to Pemberley astride Blackjack. If he could not ride with Elizabeth in privacy, he chose not to tuck in his knees for thirty leagues just to look at the bobbing heads of Hannah and Anne.

Moreover, it was much easier to breathe a deep sigh of relief from the independent seat of his saddle. The dreaded trip to London and his past was behind them. He did not feel unscathed (Juliette of all people, and the Twisnodde twins as well), but at least relieved. Every trip to London would be successively less trying. The worst was over.

Immoderately cautious when travelling, Mr. Darcy always examined the soundness of the four matched carriage horses for himself. He first inspected each head, then each wheeler, running his hand down all sixteen legs, lifting the hooves to check their shoeing. This ritual may have been looked upon with some amusement by his coachman and postilions, seeing the great gentleman in his fine clothing doing the chore of a smithy. Nevertheless, it was also with grudging respect. For if Mr. Darcy was that attentive to their duties, they undertook the commission of inspecting the worthiness of the coach with the same enterprise.

That understood, it came as a surprise when the coach became disabled some distance outside of London. It was conjectured that a cotterpin must have been loosened upon the cobblestones, for they had not gone but half their distance.

When no spares were found, Darcy could barely contain his disgust. The governing principle of such vigilance was to circumvent being stranded upon the road. Fortuitously, he was already upon Blackjack, thus, he had one of his postilions loose one horse with its defective harness to accompany him to find the smithy in a village they had passed a short way back. It was imperative not to tarry long, for much delay meant travelling the last miles to home after darkness stole dusk.

Coming to her window to explain the problem to Elizabeth, Darcy almost leaned over to kiss her a brief good-bye, but decided not to by reason of an audience. He simply assured her of a quick return. Upon observing Georgiana's uneasy countenance, he made a point of noting to her that two men stayed. A long gun lay in the leg well up top with their coachman. A pistol rode in the other postilion's waistband. This talk of weaponry was said in reassurance, but to Georgiana, it merely reminded her that there were miscreants about necessitating them.

The disrepair of their coach occasioned upon an isolated stretch of the road. However, it was bucolic, trees lining either side. There seemed nothing sinister upon the landscape save for the attention of some buzzing insect. Elizabeth thought to take the time to find a bit of rest, but could not. It was hot. She considered untying the ribbon to her bonnet, for her neck had begun to perspire. She was just reaching to draw the window shade down when she saw the remaining postilion pass by with his handgun drawn. Alarmed, she peered out and thereupon espied an even more dreadful sight. The postilion was pointing his handgun at their coachman. Clearly, the coachman took the threat seriously, for after surrendering his weapon he raised his hands high.

At that moment, two armed riders approached the carriage. One man, invoking far more blasphemous invectives than were necessary, ordered the women out. Whether because of the guns, the curses, or a combination of the two, the ladies all sat in stuporous fright in their seats, no one yet daring to move. Finally, Elizabeth, of the opinion it was unlikely anyone was going to hand them down, motioned to Anne to open the handle and kick back the door. Their exit might have proceeded more expeditiously had not Hannah, who was first out, thought it necessary to negotiate the steps of the coach with her hands upraised. Elizabeth was disposed to believe even desperados would forgive the use of the handrail.

An additional string of profanity encouraged them to move faster and, once Hannah was upon the ground, they did. Of the two men on horseback, Elizabeth recognised the man in front. But not by name. She knew him but by deed, as he was the one Darcy had fired for beating the horse. In all probability, he was the stable arsonist. It appeared the man was not content to be a murderer of horses. He was a bandit as well. Nor was it unlikely that their disabled carriage was but coincidental to their thievery for his brother rode their coach and held his gun yet on the coachman. Clearly, the blackguards had gone to a great deal of bother to rob them.

Indeed, they had gone to a great deal of bother. Thomas Reed had been lying in wait for four months to exact his revenge upon the impervious Mr. Darcy. So keen was his hatred, he went to the lengths of enlisting Jack (Iron-Mitts) Lewis as an accomplice (since being cashiered from boxing, the erstwhile pugilist had been somewhat tardy finding alternative employment). The scheme of their little band was a bit precarious, Frank Reed's wavering courage, not Jack Lewis' missing marbles, being the most unreliable link in their chain.

Tom Reed called out as to where was Mr. Darcy, "Aye thought 'e to be 'ere on this 'ere coach."

Frank told him the man had gone to the smithy, then timidly added, "Ye said t'weren't t'be no killin', Tom."

Tom cursed his unremitting ill-luck with a single expletive, then said, "Aye wanted to see 'is bloody face when we's to rob 'im's all."

Unable to imagine what Tom Reed might do to Darcy had he been in his sights, Elizabeth whispered a prayer of thanks he was not. Moreover, she was relieved she had not worn Darcy's mother's pearls, for Frank Reed demanded their jewellery and appropriated their reticules. Thereupon he rummaged for valuables and weapons through the baggage in the coach boot he had loaded in London. The bandbox in which the *bijouterie* was hidden he procured forthwith, the pearls along with it.

Ere long, Elizabeth's upraised hands betokened her fright in a tremble. She dearly wished she could hide them behind her, but dared not. Next to her, Georgiana quietly lost her wits. Uttering what sounded like snatches of the Lord's Prayer, Hannah's discomposure was a little louder. Anne, however, was quite silent, evidently of the persuasion that if she did not see it, it was not happening. Therefore, she stood with her eyes shut tight.

As deftly as the coach was disarmed, the bounty was loaded. But hope that the men would then take leave began to fade for the brigands commenced to eye the women. Knowing well if the worst happened it was a useless gesture, Elizabeth nonetheless edged Georgiana, who had begun a low keen, behind her.

A brief impasse was instituted when Frank called to Tom to make haste. Yet Tom Reed lingered.

Abruptly, he swung his leg over the saddle and dropped to the ground. Then, he stood full and commenced a glowering approach to the already terrified women.

He stopped. And for a man of congenitally transcribed ignobility, his countenance thereupon did the unlikely. It smiled. However, no one who witnessed what passed for mirth with Reed believed it issued good tidings. For, albeit his smile exposed several teeth, it was actually just an extended smirk. Clearly, just partial incentive for the robbery had been extracted. He walked directly in front of Georgiana and looked upon her from head to toe with menacing deliberation. Although that was, in all actuality, just a sadistic threat, Reed thought it a pity. It would have becalmed a great deal of his considerable loathing of Mr. Darcy to breach his sister's chastity.

However, as time and horses were at a premium, he just had time to steal his wife.

Thus, he caught Elizabeth by the wrist and yanked her roughly to him. She wrenched it from his grip and hit his hand away.

"Unhand me!"

At this insolence, the man invoked an eerily demonic cackle, the echo of which reverberated through the trees. His ejaculation quieted as abruptly as it began. He then drew back his hand and struck her brutally across the side of her head with his closed fist. So sound was the blow that as she was knocked from her feet, the bonnet was torn from her head.

Hannah shrieked. Whirling, Reed levelled his gun at the maid's face. She silenced herself mid-wail.

Stunned, Elizabeth could not find her feet before Reed reached her and drug her upright by her hair. She slapped furiously at his hands, thereby influencing him to draw a rather vile looking snickersnee. When she continued to struggle, he pressed the point against the base of her throat.

Reed's affection for knives was notorious. Frank Reed looked at Lewis and rolled his eyes. He did not relish the idea of what mayhem his brother might incite, but Lewis merely shrugged. Nevertheless, Frank was worried. Robbery was one thing, slicing up women another. Larceny, yea. Defilement, perchance. Blood, however, made him squeamish.

"Get on that horse," Reed told Elizabeth, "or you'll see sissy here gutted in front of ye."

He flicked his head in Georgiana's direction. Convinced that was not a bluff, Elizabeth ceased resisting. Thus, Reed forced her upon a horse of questionable lineage and suspect ownership. Frank jumped on behind Lewis and, with the horses straining and grunting under heavy loads, they all disappeared down a narrow lane off the main road.

Within the quarter hour, Darcy returned. His man carried the missing pin and some spares as well, the master's temper assuaged by happening upon an expedient forge. As they approached and Darcy saw the women standing yet outside the coach, his reclaimed humour vanished. From that distance, he could not see they that were crying. But the ransacked trunks were evident; their contents exposed and in disarray.

The infamy was obvious.

Kicking Blackjack into a fierce run, he drew him to a hard stop at the coach and leapt from the saddle, landing squarely upon both feet. The women appeared unhurt. However, when he did not see Elizabeth amongst them, the colour drained from his face. For upon that realisation, the magnitude of the outrage fell upon him like a flatiron.

The coachman had yet to move from his seat. He sat with a look of stunned dismay, his hands dangling purposelessly. However, the arrival of Mr. Darcy aroused him from his stupor. So decidedly was he inspirited, he took the six feet from his seat to the road in one jump and was met by Darcy before he reached the ground.

"Who was it?" Darcy asked him. "And where did they go?"

Although Mr. Darcy demanded this in a peculiarly calm voice, the man returned his gaze with compleat lack of comprehension. He had no idea who it was. Or where they went. That information had fled his mind, perchance keeping company with his recently discarded wits. With implausible patience, Darcy repeated the questions again, but grasped the man's lapel firmly in encouragement. Not a word was extracted. He shook him ever so slightly.

Perchance of a mind this gentle advocacy might escalate, the driver finally croaked out, "Three men, Reed…his brother—that one what you fired—and another," and pointed up the lane.

Barely acknowledging the information, Darcy motioned for his remaining postilion to toss the part to the coachman, who caught it. In the time it took the man to regain his senses enough to understand his duty was to repair the coach, Darcy was at the luggage searching for a weapon. Only then did he realise he had wrested a crested brass lapel button from the coachman, and flung it to the ground.

As he caught the reins to remount, his logical mind made a brief consideration in favour of not pursuing the three men alone. Should he remove his saddle from Blackjack and give it to the postilion who still sat atop the harnessed coach horse? He knew himself most likely the better rider. However, he decided he dared not spare the time. Let the man cling to the harness and try to keep up as best he could.

As he began to remount, he recognised his wife's bonnet as it lay in a heap in the road. A little beyond sat one shoe. He stopped and walked to the bonnet, took it in his hand and fingered it fleetingly. The torn ribbon was mute evidence of the brutality of the abduction.

Looking from thence, it appeared he studied the shoe for a moment, but he did not move to retrieve it. Instead, he silently handed the bonnet to Georgiana and remounted Blackjack.

Digging his heels fiercely into the horse's flank, he disappeared as quickly as that into the trees.

The cold placidity of his face was more horrific to those who saw it than any other expression they might have conjured.

Once entrenched in the woods some ways from the coach, Elizabeth had become a very disobliging kidnap victim. So much so, the bandits did not get on fast. Hence, Tom Reed pulled the horse up short when he saw smoke curling from the fireplace of an inn.

"The Strangled Goose," said the sign.

Frank Reed had hoped that ransom had been the impetus for Tom's seizure of Mrs. Darcy, but obviously, that was not the only thing he had in mind. Frank might risk hanging for some sovereigns. But not to allow his brother to have lewd rites with Mr. Darcy's wife. Bitterly did he complain to Tom that the stop might be costly.

"We can't stop, Tom! There's no time!" Frank bewailed.

His brother told him to shut his hole.

"Aye think Missus Darcy needs herself a nice lie-down," he leered at her, tweaking her cheek.

Elizabeth slapped his hand away. He clouted her in return. Tom drug her down from the lathered horse and by the time she landed upon the ground, she was swinging wildly at him. Undertaking the single handhold that would not pinch, kick, or bite, he grabbed her by the topknot and held her, flailing, at arms' length.

"She's a prime article, this one is. The 'orn-colic's a'callin' me loud."

The taproom reeked of stale ale and the few people partaking therein quieted when they entered. Elizabeth looked about in vain for a sympathetic face. She endeavoured to call out that she had been abducted. However, before she managed a syllable, Tom Reed hit her again across the face. Was there any question (and unfortunately, there seemed not), the savagery of Tom Reed's countenance was assurance that none of the basted patrons had an attack of pot-valour.

He demanded a room. Upon seeing their weapons, a man in an apron silently pointed to the back and stepped away. As Reed disappeared into a room with Elizabeth, the door slammed solidly behind him. Jack Lewis found a table, wrested a deck of cards from two groggers and motioned for Frank. Thereupon Lewis, whose personal philosophy demanded he never turn down a chance to drink or rut, proceeded to see who drew high card for being next on Elizabeth.

"A buttered bun is better than none," opined poet Lewis.

In the low-ceilinged alcove to which Reed drug her, he tossed her atop the mattress of a low cot that was not just stained, but one that emitted the unmistakable stench of urine. From thence, she crouched warily, simultaneously trying not to take a breath, and plotting both escape and defence. Initially, Reed made no move toward her. He did, however, with great deliberation, draw out his dagger. Admiringly, he laid it upon the table next to the bed.

"Shut ye mouf if ye knows what's good fer ye."

At this provocation, Elizabeth screamed with obvious deliberation. That rebellion accomplished, she added the lone oath she could recall. Howbeit Reed had been cursed widely and with some creativity, he had not once been called a chuff-nutted son of a doggie's wife, hence, he laughed uproariously. Then, he stopped laughing.

"That's 'ow it is, eh? 'ow 'd ye think yer rich 'usband'll like you tendin' me like a French whore?"

He unbuttoned his breeches, thus exposing a disinclination toward inexpressibles as well as his pillicock. The latter being in her direct eye line, it was difficult to ignore, so she took the only retaliatory road by endeavouring to bite him. Regrettably, the meaty hands he clamped upon either side of her face were not indicative of a similarly proportioned manhood, therefore her effort was for naught.

He slapped her hard, and exclaimed, "Watch out fer me whennymegs!"

She endeavoured to bite him again. Reed reconsidered. He was having a bit of trouble maintaining an erection in light of her attempts at emasculation. Hence, he withdrew her delivering him fellatio from his mental list of possible outrages to inflict and tossed her upon her back. Elizabeth was both disappointed and relieved at this manoeuvre, in that however she would have liked to exact that particular agony (a few mishaps in affection with Darcy had made her understand this was a sensitive spot upon a man), she did not necessarily want to clamp her teeth upon Reed's nasty "whennymegs."

She had little time to contemplate missed opportunities to ruin him. He leapt then upon her in a savage search beneath her petticoats, which incited an unexpectedly fierce grapple. Wriggling away, she left him holding nothing but a pair of empty stockings. Reed looked incredulously at what he held in his grip, then at Elizabeth.

Instantaneously, and with fury, he cast them aside and set after her in a mad scramble across the bed. Well-nigh clear of him, he caught her by the ankle. Dragging her back across the bed by her feet rendered her splayed and skirt up. The perfect position for violation. She kicked at him with her bare feet, but he just elicited a strange lewd giggle as he held her down.

"When aye'm done w' ye, d'ye think aye oughter 'ave mercy and kill ye with one cut or make it last longer?"

"Pig!" she spat at him.

He would make it last longer.

The roaring panic in Elizabeth's head almost drowned out the sound of the door as it was kicked open and smashed against the wall. But it startled Reed, who looked thither from attempting to pintle Mrs. Darcy, to be greeted by the unthinkably harrowing sight of Mr. Darcy himself. And he did not appear to be in a forgiving mood.

Instinct told Reed that this was a situation demanding immediate offensive. Expertly, he flung his beloved knife at Mr. Darcy's head. For a man unused to attack, Darcy parried the stroke quite adeptly. Hence, with a quivering thud, the dagger sank to its shank in the soft wood of the doorpost. As he rarely missed, Reed simultaneously reared and reached for his pistol, preparing to exact a *coup de grace*.

Instead, and to Reed's obvious and decided horror, Darcy drew a sabre. The stinging jangle it made as it was pulled from its scabbard made Reed's teeth hurt.

It was thus that the breadth betwixt them was cut in half.

With not a moment of contemplation, and in the space of two long steps, Darcy ran Reed through. With such force did he render the puncture, his sword by-passed Reed's backbone and pinned his body to the wall. His hand on the hilt, and the hilt at Reed's gut, Darcy looked directly in Reed's gaping eyes as he ground the blade deeper. The stabee opened his mouth as if to speak, but he produced nothing more than a trickle of frothy blood and a gagging sound.

Putting his boot against Reed's body, it took both hands for him to retrieve his sabre. He did not watch Reed's body fall to the floor, nor see it twitch in the spasms of death.

He saw not, for he had turned to Elizabeth.

Neither spoke. She did not by reason of dumbfounded astonishment. His silence came by way of yet unadulterated, heaving rage. But betwixt them passed a moment of satisfied concurrence.

At last, he reached out and clasped her to him. To do so, he used but one hand. The other yet encased the bloodied sword in an icy grip.

"Lizzy, Lizzy," he said, crushing his face to hers, "Thanks be to God."

She knew she was almost blubbering, but could not stop herself, "Darcy oh Darcy oh Darcy oh Darcy."

"Can you stand?"

She nodded her head, but when he lifted her from the filthy bed, her legs buckled. Hence, with him having not relinquished the sword, she wrapped her arms about his neck and he half carried her back into the tavern room. He surveyed the occupants surrounding Frank Reed (who had divested himself of his wig, but stood, in obvious ignominy, still wearing the Darcy livery).

"Who else was it, Lizzy?"

With a wavering hand, she pointed to Lewis. If Darcy recognised Lewis as the contemptible poltroon who de-toothed Bingley's boxer, it was not evident. The single reaction he had upon this introduction was outwardly benign. But for a man of Lewis' recent vocation, when Darcy lowered his chin, the gesture was not misunderstood.

A reckoning was to occur.

Both bandits stood taut, eyeing Darcy's blade. Abruptly, and with considerable ferocity, Darcy flung his bloodied sabre down. It hit with a clank, then rolled against the wall, leaving a splattering crimson trail across the floor. The discarding of that gruesome weapon, even in so violent a fashion, led Lewis and Frank Reed to hold the hope their fate would not be so immediate as Tom's. They clung to that faith even when Darcy recognised the gold encrusted handle of his father's Catalonian over-and-under pistol in Lewis' waistband.

But Lewis did take a little half-step backward when he yanked it out.

Retribution was not to wait. Hesitating just long enough to check the load, Darcy drew Elizabeth's face to his chest. He thereupon shot Lewis and then Frank Reed squarely in the head. So rapidly did he fire, neither man elected a reaction, save for the resultant mist of blood.

Without another word, followed resolutely by a postilion whose loyalty would evermore be incontrovertible, Darcy and Elizabeth quitted the tavern.

The people in the room stood in stunned silence for full half a minute. No one dared move until the horses pounded away. Then, one man alone walked over to the sword lying by the baseboard. He picked it up. The others in the room stood still as stones, their gapes not wrested from the two corpses at their feet. When the man raised the sword and drew his gaze the length of it, the other patrons in the room then did as well. Thereupon, they all, as if by pre-decision, turned to the room from whence Darcy and Elizabeth had come. However, it would be a few more minutes before any would venture a look.

Mrs. Annesley was nearly beside herself when the hack delivered her back from Bexley at half-past eleven when she knew the appointed time of departure for Pemberley was nine. The woman was horrified to be the perpetrator of any disruption of the Darcy plans and had readied a profusion of apologies, explanations, and excuses. However, she saw she had not to invoke any to the Darcys, for their coach had not waited. It was unnecessary for her even to enter the house, because Goodwin was sitting impatiently in the coach, thus emphasising her tardiness.

Gratefully he did not denounce her lack of punctuality, but his pursed lips announced his displeasure as surely as had he carped.

Goodwin was unhappy to have to wait for the old woman. He would have much preferred to travel with Mr. Darcy. However, Mrs. Annesley was an agreeable enough woman (she did not have much to say). Thus he harboured no extreme regret in the assignment of escorting her, save for the peculiarly mouldy odour she emitted. That scent abused the most easily offended of his five, finely-honed senses.

When bound for London, Mr. Darcy, Mrs. Darcy, Miss Darcy, and Mrs. Annesley had ridden in the first coach. Hannah Moorhouse, Anne Wright, and he rode in the second directly behind them. Mr. Darcy was thereupon a married man and Goodwin knew he had to accustom himself to their new mode of travel. But riding with mere maids sullied his also pronounced *amour propre*. (Goodwin had few subtle sensibilities.)

Though his supercilious demeanour intimidated Anne, Hannah was another matter. Since becoming lady-maid to Mrs. Darcy, she had become somewhat of a bother to him. She was far too garrulous and inquisitive. She inquired of his health. She inquired if he favoured the weather. The dinner. The...whatever. That his reply was seldom more than a grunt did nothing to deter her. Her loquacity, however, did not extend beyond mundane matters. She revealed not one iota of Mrs. Darcy's privacy.

This was a trial to Goodwin, for nothing would have given him greater pleasure than to report such a transgression to Mrs. Reynolds. Had that come to pass, Hannah Moorhouse would be gone from service within an hour. But that was her saving grace. Her discretion was compleat about the Darcys and their doings. He had never learned of a single utterance that betrayed their privacy. Hence, he had forgiven her need of conversation and continued to grunt disapproval and murmur his agreement to her endless inquiries.

Goodwin was a terse, solitary soul by inclination as well as occupation. As a manservant, he knew to keep his position he could never expect to marry. That had never presented any sort of disadvantage of employment for him. He had never had much interest in women. True, he loved his mother unequivocally. He admired his aunt's (Mrs. Reynolds) strength of mind. But the chambermaids were flighty and sometimes crude. He despised coarseness in women. He despised coarseness in men as well. He supposed he simply despised coarseness.

If he held her lady-maid as somewhat a nuisance, one might have fancied Goodwin had held additional resentment upon the intrusion of Mrs. Darcy into Mr. Darcy's life. On the contrary, he believed Mrs. Darcy to be quite beautiful and refined. Refined, but not exactly sedate. He admired sedateness, but not nearly as much as he despised coarseness. In his mind, sedateness could be disregarded altogether when it was replaced by such unaffected charm. Moreover, she never failed to speak to him. As he was used to being regarded by women as part of the wallpaper, it was not surprising he found himself somewhat besotted with her.

This esteem had unequivocally and absolutely nothing whatever to do with the glimpse he caught of her in a soaking night-dress. Indeed, the entire matter of that little incident in Mr. Darcy's dressing room was exceedingly unfortunate. Goodwin had been so mortified at his unpropitious entry to the bath that his heart did not return to a normal beat for days.

He and Mr. Darcy had acted alone and in concert for so long, he had quite instinctively responded to the sound of disorder. So far as Goodwin knew (and he should know better than anyone save Mr. Darcy himself), there had never, ever, been a lady in his master's bath. Clearly, what constituted Mr. Darcy's privacy had altered irrevocably.

They had been more than two hours leaving London behind the Darcy coach. A small, if bitter, pill to swallow was their lapse meant their coach's trip across the West End avenues was travelled singularly. Nothing was quite so satisfying to Goodwin as the looks of awe that identical coaches in tandem incited amongst the spectating minions. It was possible their driver had similar pretensions, for he urged the horses forward more vigorously than usual, as if to overtake the first coach upon the road.

Overtake them they did.

Not halfway to Pemberley, they came upon the disabled Darcy carriage. It was immediately clear there was very serious trouble.

Until that day, the one time Goodwin had met with undue adversity was at the hands of some particularly unruly boys. They had knocked off his hat with a rock. He had actually called them "ruffians." He had never used such a common term before, but he had been so affronted it had slipped out. Thus, the level of the affront the coachman related as had come to pass then was shocking to the point of exciting Goodwin into a fit of breathlessness. He sat in the same horrified frozen state as the elderly Mrs. Annesley. Both gaped out the window, neither daring to step upon the same ground as the perpetrators of such a barbarous act.

Goodwin was so outraged, in time he bested his breath and actually considered following Mr. Darcy in pursuit of those…those…ruffians. Those thieving, woman-stealing ruffians. However, that embarkation demanded he mount a horse (he disliked large animals, Troilus and Cressida alone were frightening) and ride it.

Was he ever to do such a thing, then would have been the occasion. It was unfortunate there was no other saddle, for there were four women (including that young Hannah woman) there to witness his heroics—his leaping upon a steed and galloping off to assist Mr. Darcy. Had there been a saddle, he would have done it. Indisputably.

The opportunity to aid Mr. Darcy in saving Mrs. Darcy was dearer than any other duty he could imagine.

Goodwin never doubted that Mr. Darcy would find success. Mr. Darcy would never allow anything to happen to Mrs. Darcy. Mr. Darcy would overtake those men and demand they unhand her. They would do so immediately and with apology. (This notion revealed that Goodwin kept in a locked box under his bed several well-read books that some might disparage as banal.) Mr. Darcy would return with Mrs. Darcy sitting in front of him upon his saddle, her hair, perchance, in slight disarray.

However, it was not to be. Their aborted party sat upon the road for hours awaiting the valorous return.

Mr. Darcy, of course, did return with Mrs. Darcy. There was no question of him ever returning without her. However, it was not the glorious and romantic return Goodwin had envisioned. She was injured. Clearly, she had been wounded egregiously. Very egregiously. This was not how things should be, Goodwin thought to himself as they made haste for Pemberley.

This was not how things should be.

Although they made on fast, the ride to Pemberley seemed like an eternity. Urging them ever faster, Mr. Darcy's incessant beating the roof of the coach with his walking stick further exacerbated everyone's shattered nerves.

He had climbed into the repaired carriage with Elizabeth in his arms and wrapped his jacket about her. The other three women sat across aghast. Hannah could not clearly see Elizabeth's bruised and scratched face, but her feet were bare and bleeding. She spread the lap rug over them.

Georgiana dared bid, "Pray, is she all right?"

He shook off her questions, keeping Elizabeth's face to his neck. One of her arms was about him, the other gripped tightly to his lapel. Although he kissed her gently upon the forehead and whispered reassurances to her as they strove headlong for Pemberley, no one else uttered a word.

They broke post but once, the horses exchanged in less than a minute. Thus when they finally reached the courtyard of home, even the new team was in shivering exhaustion. Howbeit no man was more solicitous of his horses, Darcy took no notice of their near collapse. He had no thought but to get Elizabeth into the house.

Though several footmen ran to open it, he kicked back the coach door before one could. As the master was not of a mind to have his door opened for him, not one suggested they help him carry his wife. She protested she could walk, yet he would not put her down. Lest she be attacked before reaching the safety of Pemberley's walls, he made a dash with her to the house, taking the steps two at a time.

Without being told, Hannah knew to prepare Elizabeth her bath and ran ahead calling loudly for hot water. She slowed a step, realising she had broken the absolute rule of never raising a voice in Pemberley and expected reproach. There was none, for Mrs. Reynolds trailed Darcy as he took the stairs with Elizabeth still in his arms. Two candle-wielding servants hustling to light the way overtook both.

Once to their bed, Elizabeth finally released her hold upon him. Nevertheless, he waited until they were alone to unfurl her from his coat. He could see the swollen bruises upon the side of her face and scratches upon her neck. Her lip was swollen and bore a deep cut. Taking out his pocket square, he dabbed at the blood on her lip. She winced.

He called for Mrs. Reynolds hovering at the door and issued orders for the physician to be called.

"No," Elizabeth interrupted, "No."

He told her she must be seen.

She repeated, "No. I will not be seen."

Tears welled in her eyes, hence, he did not have the wherewithal to insist.

The notion of a doctor deflected, she attempted to rise, insisting, "I must bathe."

Understanding that compulsion full well, he, however, endeavoured to keep her still, assuring her it was being drawn even then. That reminded her others were about, and, if she did not want the doctor to inspect her injuries, she most certainly did not want to see anxious faces darting inquiring looks in her direction. Indeed, she bid him tell Hannah to take leave once her bath was in ready. That was done expeditiously, for he thought that it was just as well if Hannah did not tend her lady.

He could sponge Elizabeth himself and inspect her injuries both thoroughly and in private. He withdrew his waistcoat, wadded it in a loose ball and threw it toward the corner. Then returning to fetch her, he rolled up his sleeves as if preparing for a particularly difficult duty. Which it would be. He knew if she was able to bear it to happen, he must be strong enough to witness the result.

When he sat her in the tub, she gasped, the hot water stinging the long red scratching welts that streaked her thighs. It was just with the sternest of wills that he could bring himself to look at them. Hence, whilst murmuring words of love to her, he silently tortured himself with recriminations.

As a man with considerable conceit of his own understanding of humanity's shortcomings, he was incredulous that he had been duped by such scurrilous trickery. How could he have kept the brother of a man he beat from service still in his employ? Of course, there would be bad blood. Mr. Rhymes should have dismissed them both. Had he allowed his overseer or the bailiff to see to the matter, as he should have in the first place, instead of taking it upon himself to…

He made himself cease. Self-recriminations were of no particular help to her repa-ration that he knew. Hence, he denied himself additional *mea culpas*. His mission was to see to his wife.

Not noting a wound that needed binding, he dried and gowned her, then carried her to the bed, covering her with the bedclothes. Outwardly, she appeared but to be bruised. He sat heavily upon the bed, his head in his hands, awash with relief.

But quickly, relief that her body was not mortally wounded was replaced by the memory at just what outrage had been perpetrated against her.

Telling her he should not be gone but a moment, he rose to seek the solitude of his own dressing room. There, suddenly very weary, he splashed water upon his face in vain attempt to restore his flagging strength. Before that day, the only death he had ever witnessed was the gentle passing of his father. Never had he seen a man killed. From that day forward, he would have to live with the knowledge that he had taken three lives. He had slain them without remorse.

That had not been a thought until he looked down at the water in the basin. It was tinged pink. He gave a silent prayer of thanksgiving it was not Elizabeth's blood he washed from his person.

Looking at himself in the pier glass, he felt not a twinge of regret. Awash yet with rage, his singular wish was that there were three more to kill.

He sank heavily onto a bench, hoping to find enough energy to remove his blood-bedecked shirt, whereupon he heard Goodwin at the door. (Thenceforward of his inopportune intrusion, Goodwin knocked before entering Mr. Darcy's dressing room.) Drawing his shirt off over his head, he hastily wiped his face and neck clean of any remnants of spattered blood with it.

Thereupon, he thrust the garment into Goodwin's hands through a mere crack in the door and silently motioned him away. Appalled at the state of the shirt and affronted to have it unceremoniously dumped in his hands, Goodwin looked with repugnance upon it, for he reckoned whose blood it was. Hence, he held the vile garment from his person with a thumb and forefinger and carried it off. Darcy tugged off his own boots, donned a fresh shirt, and then went back to Elizabeth. However, before he lay down upon the bed next to her, he released the tasselled rope cord holding back the baldachin that draped from the canopy. The soft folds of glistening fabric encapsulated their bed.

He was uncertain what she might need of him just then. He would have done any-thing, gone anywhere, brought her anything. He simply did not know the extent of her discomposure. She had allowed him to help her bathe, but otherwise she refused to be attended. A denial of the physician's ministrations was not unexpected. But refusing Hannah's was unprecedented.

He thought that if she would but allow him to hold her safely in his arms, he would be unable ever to let her go.

She had been lying upon her back, her arm across her face but she removed it as he sat beside her. Afraid to touch her face, he finally reached out and stroked her neck with the back of his fingers.

"Pray, if I take care, may I hold you?"

She nodded her head and pressed her face against his chest as he kissed the top of her head.

His lips imbedded amidst her tresses, he beseeched her, "How can you ever forgive me? I know I shall never be able to forgive myself for allowing this to happen…"

Reaching out, she pressed her fingertips to his lips, effectively shushing such entreaties.

"Where in this is your part? The fault is not with you—no one could have known that danger was about."

"But Lizzy, I should never have left you."

Telling him what she knew he feared but dare not ask, she said, "He did not defile me and my bruises shall heal. It was you, husband, who rescued me from them."

The serrying of her body against his relieved him of the necessity of hiding his relief. True, he had not wanted to inquire if Reed had penetrated her (the ogre's intentions were flagrantly exposed), lest she believe if the man had, her husband would find his own insult. He hoped himself most concerned for the degradation she, alone would feel. Nevertheless, when she told him that she had not been violated, he could not say unequivocally that the relief he felt was for her alone.

In time, he thought he might consider why it should be that the woman absorbs the assault and the husband somehow believes himself the affronted party.

He started to speak again, but held his tongue and stroked her hair instead. Her shoulders began to shake and he knew she was crying.

"Do not think of it," he bid her, knowing even then that was not possible.

Putting his fingers under her chin, he endeavoured to get her to look at him, but she hid her face as if ashamed.

"But shall you ever desire me again?"

"Lizzy, how could you even suggest…" he was speechless.

She hesitated, then spoke, not looking at him yet, "I fear each time you look upon me you will recollect…what you saw."

It was true that vision was seared now and forevermore into his memory, however, it just made him want to hold her more dearly. Softly, he took her face in his hand and turned it back to his.

"Every time I look upon you, I shall see my beautiful, intrepid Elizabeth and nothing more."

"Perhaps we are both beyond reason at this moment."

Then, as if in reassurance of that, she bid the astounding.

She did not cry again, but her voice began to quaver as she said, "I want you. I want you inside me. I want that man erased from me…I want you in me now."

With a strength that defied the extent of beating she had undergone, she gripped his shirt in her fists, cleaving against his chest. Having been frightfully reluctant even to lie next to her, the ferocity of her desire took him especially unawares. That and that she desired him at that moment at all. Had she never wanted to be touched again, he thought he would have understood. It was the first time he had ever had to rise to the occasion, so to speak, for he truly did not feel arousal. He felt exhausted, angry, guilt-ridden, horrified, and, yes, even frightened. Once she was safe, the wrenching fear he had felt for her had overtaken him.

No, he was not aroused. Nevertheless, he could be. He realised that when he felt her hands upon his body, urgently seeking which caress or stroke would bring the fever to his blood. So impelling was her touch, he cast everything else from his mind and he let himself think of nothing but his love of her. She needed his reassurance then, not the next day nor the day after. Then.

It was an unusually warm night, but he would not open the windows nor draw back the heavy drape that surrounded the bed. No breeze reached them. The air was humid and still in the bedchamber. Although there was a slight breeze in the air, they suffered the heat rather than open themselves to the night.

By morning, her gown and his shirt were drenched in shared perspiration, for neither allowed the other to leave their embrace.

Eventually he betook himself from Elizabeth's side, but it was midday before he did. When he came down, Georgiana was waiting at the bottom of the stairs. She had been sitting for hours upon a bench in the corridor waiting to hear his footsteps.

It was not until he saw her that he was reminded what trauma she had endured. Not entirely certain it true, he, nevertheless, answered her anxious enquiry that Elizabeth was well. Georgiana was insistent he heard the entire history of the event.

"What extraordinary bravery! Not only did Elizabeth put herself betwixt us and the highwaymen, she fought them! We were all struck with terror, but Elizabeth would not have it," she shook her head incredulously.

She wanted to talk more about it, but he could not bear to relive it so soon and shook his head.

"Yes, we were all terrified, Georgiana."

She looked at him a little quizzically. She had thought it probable, however bravely she behaved, that Elizabeth had been frightened. Not until that moment had she considered that her imperturbable brother was. Thereupon, she ascended the stairs and repaired to her room. No one knew she spent much of the next few days furiously scribbling once again in her journal.

Darcy watched Georgiana take the stairs and closed his eyes in a brief prayer of thanks that she appeared not to be permanently traumatised by the event. It was at that precise moment that the Derbyshire High Sheriff, accompanied by not just the constable, but the coroner as well, all bearing successively apprehensive countenances, arrived to interview Mr. Darcy, the women, and the servants.

Duelling in the face of a man's honour was still overlooked by the magistrate, but the killing of three men, even by such an illustrious personage as Mr. Darcy, could not be ignored.

"Mr. Darcy," began the High Sheriff, before uneasily clearing his throat, "you understand that it is not I, but the King, who demands an accounting of these unhappy events be delivered to the magistrate. It is imperative that we question you and Mrs. Darcy."

"You may query me. I do not deny my actions. However, under no circumstances shall you speak to Mrs. Darcy. I am quite implacable. I will not have it. She has been distressed enough."

"You must understand. We cannot compleat an investigation without her testimony of the offence."

Not remotely interested in entering into a test of wills with Mr. Darcy (who at that moment appeared to be quite ready to bestow a full understanding to the High Sheriff upon what implacability meant), the sheriff shifted about. Upon Elizabeth's abrupt appearance at the head of the stairs, all discourse ceased. Was there was any doubt of offence, it was cast aside by those witnessing her battered face.

Her descent of the stairs began a little shakily. Darcy took them two at a time, with each step entreating her to return to bed.

"I shall speak with the man in the library," she announced with firmness of voice not mirrored in her step. "Pray, alone."

With considerable reluctance, Darcy agreed, but stood sentry outside the door with his arms crossed glowering at the coroner and constable as if daring them to plague his wife. It was but a matter of minutes when the sheriff reappeared.

Ducking his head with even more deference than when he came, he thanked Darcy for his time and apologised for the intrusion upon his privacy.

Darcy went in forthwith to Elizabeth to help her regain the upstairs. He did not ask her what she said to the sheriff.

On the third day after their return, Elizabeth felt strong enough to join Darcy and Georgiana at breakfast. This did not actually elicit the response from them for which she hoped, for she wanted to reassure them she was just fine. They both graciously acknowledged this attempt, but it fell short.

Howbeit the swelling had ebbed and the cut upon her lip was healing, she was severely bruised yet.

Hence, breakfast commenced with Georgiana paying the one compliment she could honestly think of, "You do not look half so bad as you did, Elizabeth."

It was not lost upon Elizabeth how dreadful she looked, for her looking-glass did not lie. Even a generous dusting of powder did not hide the contusion upon the side of her face that had turned a rather royal shade of purple. However, she had been cooped up in her room for three days and she was desperate to breathe some fresh air. She bid her husband to escort her upon a stroll after their breakfast.

He had barely turned to her to assure her he would when her face suddenly drained of colour (save for the bruise). She said she felt dizzy.

Masking his concern, he addressed her in a mild husbandly scold, "You have, no doubt, left your sick bed too hastily, Elizabeth…"

In response, she stood as if to take his advice immediately. Before she took many steps, however, she dropped like a rock. Darcy, already moving in her direction, partially caught her fall. He hastily lifted her into his arms. Mrs. Reynolds and Georgiana were at his side when Mrs. Reynolds saw Georgiana's gaze alight on the floor with alarm.

When she followed her gaze, she caught Darcy's attention and said, "Look there!"

There was blood pooled upon the carpet. Horrified, he saw it bespattering Elizabeth's shoes and stockings. He clutched her tighter to him. Still in a faint, her dangling arms twirled slightly as he made a frantic half circle, uncertain whether to run to the carriage or take her to bed. His decision in favour of immediacy, he swept her up the stairs to their room.

With a great deal of pain (and an untidy mess, both of which Elizabeth disapproved of herself to present to her husband) she miscarried in her bed before the doctor arrived.

Once there, holding Elizabeth's wrist to take her pulse met Dr. Carothers' notion of patient examination. Few doctors took the liberty of invading a lady patient's privacy by actually inspecting their female parts unless a baby's head was actually protruding. Instead, he donned his spectacles for a close inspection of her bloody bedcloth.

Thereupon he went into the corridor and, with great solemnity, spoke with Mr. Darcy, pronouncing what everyone already knew to be true. Darcy inquired of the doctor if Elizabeth understood she had miscarried.

Nodding his head, Dr. Carothers asked Darcy with as delicate a sensibility as a man of his bluntness could muster, "Pray…does anyone know how Mrs. Darcy obtained her injuries?"

In the mayhem of the new emergency, Darcy had compleatly forgotten about Elizabeth's bruises. He wrestled fleetingly with having to reveal to the doctor what indignities Elizabeth suffered or have Dr. Carothers think he had beaten her himself.

His decision eventually fell to the simplicity of truth.

"My wife's party was accosted upon the road from London. Her injuries occurred at the hands of the robbers."

"I see," the doctor said. "She was not…eh…violated?"

"No, she said she was not."

"Thereupon this unhappy event, undoubtedly, owes to that fright," the good doctor (a man of great science) stated. Taking off his spectacles, he leaned closer to Mr. Darcy and whispered, "Ladies are an excitable lot, are they not Mr. Darcy?"

Glaring at Dr. Carothers, Darcy said, "I cannot speak for all ladies, but as for my wife, she is not 'excitable.'"

The doctor said, "I see," but Mr. Darcy did not hear him, for he had turned to go in to his wife and Dr. Carothers found himself staring at a soundly shut door. Darcy walked over to Elizabeth. Howbeit pale, she was sitting upright against some pillows. He began to fluff them unnecessarily, muttering to himself.

Moving aside in mute request that he cease and sit by her, she asked him what the doctor said to cause his consternation. He shook his head, said it was nothing of any use, not wanting to relate the doctor's exact words. She leaned back against the newly plumped pillow and gave a deep sigh, alarming him.

"'Tis me, is it not?" she said. "I fear I have failed you."

Darcy, baffled, "How so?"

"I was too stupid to realise I was with child. I thought it was merely the excitement of being in London. Had I been mindful of it, I should not so hastily have come downstairs."

"It was none of your doing," he countered. "The physician says it was owing to the fright caused by the attack."

"If that were so, I believe it should have bechanced when I was frightened, not days later. No," she insisted, "I did not take care of myself properly. I can fault nothing but my own ignorance. And because of that I fear I have failed you."

She produced a weak but knowing smile as if to reassure him that, although culpable, she sought no pity. However, tears welled in her eyes and as they began to creep down her cheeks, she turned her head.

"I think you are mistaken as to who has failed whom, Lizzy."

"I was with your child and was unawares. Jane knew she was with child for Bingley. Because of my own ignorance, I am no longer with child for you."

"For me?"

"Yes," she said stoically, "I know I must give you a child. A son. It is my duty as your wife. My body has failed me and because of that, I have failed Pemberley" (for to her, he and Pemberley were one and the same).

"You have not failed me. Surely you do not wish to have a child just because you think it your duty?"

"No."

That single admission allowed her to overcome her guilt, and, unable to hold back the tears, she began to cry anew. She abhorred such a display as self-indulgent. Still, she had striven hard to define her own culpability in their loss and, finally able to abandon gathering blame and the resultant satisfaction she received in cleaving it to her bosom, she grieved.

She allowed herself to keen just for the baby that was not to be.

Not entirely certain weeping was an improvement, he soothed her, "We have not yet been married a year. There is ample time for a family without you worrying that you must produce an heir."

She ceased crying and eventually slept. Her husband, however, could find no peace.

He sat in darkness upon the side of the bed. He was angry beyond words. He was angry with the men who abducted her and angry with himself for allowing it to happen. He was even angry at the position he held if it bade her believe she was useless to him if she did not bear him a son. Never, not once, had he felt impotent. Indeed, potency had ruled his life in one form or another. Yet, a sickening impuissance engulfed him then.

He abandoned her bedside just as far as the carpet. There he paced. He begat a relentless traverse of the length of the unlit room. To and fro, he walked. A brooding man, he repined thereupon with a tempestuousness even he would have not imagined possible. The dismal contemplation of her initial rejection seemed obscenely mild in comparison.

A grimace of outright pain crossed his face as he thought of that. Had he managed to secure her love just to have his own improvidence bring her to draconian disorder? What good were wealth and position if he could not even keep her safe?

Within the month, when Elizabeth was well enough to go outside, Darcy brought her a pistol. (Not his father's pistol, even he could not bear to look at that, and had locked the weapon of murder away.) The gun he purchased was brought to him all the way from Spain. It was light, yet powerful—easy for a lady to grip.

He went out onto the grounds and taught Elizabeth and Georgiana both how to use it.

Darcy had been undecided how to tell Elizabeth and Georgiana that the stolen jewellery had been returned by the innkeeper, not wanting to remind Elizabeth of that tavern.

The man had arrived at Pemberley alone and Mrs. Reynolds had been called. There upon his outstretched hands sat the Darcy jewellery. Nary a single piece was missing. Indeed, all were daintily wrapped in Elizabeth's ripped stockings, secured by her torn garters, and tucked inside the single slipper that persevered the fierce struggle upon Reed's horse.

Wisely, Mrs. Reynolds had the shoe, stockings, and garters burned. If it horrified her to see them and the violation that they represented, she could not imagine Mr. Darcy's reaction. In fortune, for just the sight of the recovered jewellery sent him into a renewed, if silent, fit of rage.

Because he did not know how, Darcy chose not to explain it to Elizabeth at all. He simply had the jewellery returned to her without accounting. When Elizabeth espied the jewel case mysteriously returned to her dressing table, she, of course, inquired about it. Hannah told her that the pub-keeper had brought it to them of his own volition.

Another servant announced, before Hannah could frown at her, "He said he din't want cause for Mr. Darcy to spite him."

Elizabeth thought, indeed, no, he does not.

For Darcy was unreasonably angry yet that not one man at the alehouse had come to her aid when it was obvious that she was captive and her abductors were bent upon her ravishment. Elizabeth, however, did not hold that same sentiment. For she had seen the fear upon the man's face and could grant his gallantry a little latitude.

Howbeit they had their jewellery and even her shoe and stockings returned, there was one possession that the pub-keeper did not carry to Pemberley. Neither Darcy nor Elizabeth ever returned to that inn to retrieve it.

For there, upon the stone floor, were bloodstains that diligent scrubbing could not remove. And in mute testimony to that day, in infamous honour over the fireplace, hung Mr. Darcy's sword.

Her husband insisted she rest. With reluctance, Elizabeth did as he bid, understanding that was her duty as his wife. His duty, it seemed, was to brush the curls back from her face whilst she did. All this recumbancy and unadulterated cosseting were largely silent, each lost in their own introspective conflict.

Blame, of course, has been a long and dearly held tradition in the wake of any tragedy. Rarely, however, had the grappling been so earnestly for the claiming of it rather than the laying as it was at that time for them.

Because she had not spoken again of her perceived guilt, Darcy thought she had ridded herself of it and savoured it as his own alone. But she had not. She had merely concealed it, compartmentalising the loss of the baby away in a place in her heart that she saved for her most purgatorial emotions. Only when she was alone would she think of it, worry it, probe it. She had no more regulation of these examinations than a tongue prodding a particularly grievous sore inside the cheek.

Darcy worried the sore inside his own cheek quite routinely. For he agonized over not only what Elizabeth had suffered at the hands of Reed at the inn, but how witnessing the bloody retribution he had exacted might also grieve her mind.

Had it been any other circumstance, death of another by his own hand might have lent him a great deal of contrition and begging of divine forgiveness. As it was, he held no other remorse than that it had happened at all and adamantly, almost defiantly, sought absolution from no one except Elizabeth.

Of course, he knew she had to have witnessed him kill Reed. That was undeniable. And unavoidable. What she beheld of the other two deaths was a bit more ambiguous. He had taken no more precaution to shield her from his rage than turning her face to his chest. Even in retrospect, that was the single act for which he held himself accountable during his savagely exacted vengeance—that she witnessed it. But just how much she saw, and how much she inferred, he had not yet determined.

He felt he must. The beating and attempted rape were horrific enough. To have inflicted larger trauma because of his rash retaliation was unconscionable.

Quite unwittingly, he stroked her face with the back of his fingers. In was an act he invariably undertook in times of great tenderness. This alerted her to an alteration in their wordless parlance. Therefore, when he spoke, she was not taken unawares.

"Lizzy," he said with great hesitation, "as much as I abhor speaking of it to you, there is something I must know."

She eyed him keenly and nodded once.

"What do you remember? What did you witness me do that day?"

(Thenceforward, "that day" would be a code entered into their common lexicon.)

It was her initial inclination to insist she remembered him committing murder not at all. In not wanting to be patronised, she concluded she should not be guilty of it either. She closed her eyes and allowed those horrifying events to replay themselves. Although she thought she might, she did not envision Reed's leering face. For some reason, she could not recall his face, nor did she try. Oddly, when she closed her eyes she saw the yellowing wall-paper of the room and upon it a faded, yet delicate, pink flower print. Queer what one notices at such grievous times; she should not have thought she even saw it.

When she answered, it was without hesitation and not about the wall-paper, "When you came through the door, I saw only you. I knew you slew him, but I did not look. I looked only at you."

She sat up, as if for added emphasis, "Had I seen, I should not have cared."

That bit of defiance granted him a small little twitch of a smile. Thereupon, he appeared to steel himself for some unnamed blow.

"What of the other?"

This answer, she took her time in constructing.

Finally, she said, "I know what came to pass, but you held me so tightly against you it was just a vague impression. The singular grief I feel is for you."

In a gesture he often bestowed upon her she took his distraught face in her hands and stroked his cheeks with her thumbs, telling him, "When I allow myself to think of any of it, the one vision that comes to mind is of you as you came through the door."

To her unasked enquiry, he said, "I remember nought but the fierce expression you bore. I have little doubt had you a weapon you would have taken the man out yourself."

"Did you know I become angry when I am frightened?"

He smiled in recognition and said, "Yes, I have noticed that."

"Once we were home safe, the thought of it all terrified me. At the time, I was too angry to feel anything else. I think I was not so afraid because I knew, somehow, you would come."

"I shall always come for you."

"I know."

Elizabeth had decided she must instruct herself not to remember Reed's face or that day, but this decision was hard fought. It would have grieved her husband to know that his enquiry did just what he feared it might, for it bade her investigate her memory.

Beyond the yellowing paper with pink flowers, if her recollection of that day did not reveal faces, her mind's eye brought forth a mural of colours. She did not remember seeing Darcy's sword obtruding from Reed's gut. However, if she did not recall his countenance, she did recall the exact shade of magenta upon his face when her husband ran him through.

Added to that recollection was the bulging whites of his eyes stamped with fixed black pupils. But, the colour red she recollected most of all: that which flowed from Reed, the splatter across the floor, that which filled the air and bespattered her husband's clothes. And the smell. The stench of the bed, but mostly the scent of blood. It was odd. She had no notion until that day that blood had such an odour.

No, she did not watch him run Reed through, nor see the other two men's heads explode. And if what she did see was gruesome in and of itself, she did not tell her husband. She would let him believe her in a stuporous shock through the entire ordeal if that gave him a single moment's peace.

It was, Elizabeth conjectured, unusual that her mind did not suffer more than it did as a result of such an attack. Her mind did suffer greatly, but not from that act. She had disassociated it from her miscarriage. That she dwelt upon in the privacy of her heart. Reed's demise, however, she belaboured quite consciously and with no little rancour. She did not feel truly traumatised by his brutality. Was it that she could find no more heinous retribution to the man than he, as it happened, received?

Her husband seemed to suffer her ordeal more than she did herself. She suffered for his anguish. That was what she held against that cur, Reed, above every other outrage. His act demanded Darcy do something that bade him suffer.

There was entirely too much suffering. The one person who had not suffered was Reed. His end was merciful. And just. She refused to think of him beyond that.

It was decided that even family members would be denied the knowledge that there had been more than a simple robbery attempt. It would be futile to keep word of the attack itself from circulating by reason of so many witnesses. The Darcys, however, would proffer officially that it was but a robbery. (Elizabeth refused to submit her father and especially the expectant Jane to the added distress of the indelicate matter of attempted rape.)

Her miscarriage was duly ignored. This information alone was under their compleat regulation, for the few who knew of it could be counted on for discretion.

On hearing of such a brutal robbery, Lady Matlock insisted the family (her mother-in-law could come or not) take up full-time residence in London. The lady never enjoyed country society, announcing it bestial. Thus, belabouring fear was as good an excuse as any to do what she wanted in the first place. James and Eugenia's immediate vacating of Derbyshire was usurped by another's arrival.

For, not unexpectedly, in a little over a fortnight Pemberley was visited by the Bingleys. It was just enough time for Elizabeth to regain sufficient inscrutability to assure Jane that the robbery was but that.

Darcy did not tell Elizabeth that Bingley, who had greater opportunity, had heard a great deal about what mayhem Darcy had wrought that day. It seemed the entire countryside, indeed, knew of what he had wrought. And Bingley knew it had not been by duel, thus, no insult was incurred. He understood that it had been an execution of sorts. As well as he knew his friend, the one thing of which Bingley was certain was that Darcy never reacted by overreaction. If he had the blood of three men upon his hands, extreme injury must have demanded it.

Though he was as close a friend as Darcy had, even Bingley hesitated to speak to him about the dastardly doings. He chose simply to repeat what he had been told and wait to see if Darcy corrected it. Darcy had remained silent. This information by silence from Darcy was not new to Bingley. He understood exactly what his friend was telling him and he did not revisit the subject again. Nor did Bingley speak of it to anyone else either, especially his wife. He knew had Elizabeth wanted her sister to know, she would have told her herself.

Elizabeth recovered her strength with dispatch after her miscarriage, but at her husband's request had waited a month before returning to the paddocks to take up with Boots. Actually, he argued for longer. (Indeed, had she allowed it, he may well have opted to have her toted about in a sedan chair for the better part of a year.) Although she knew herself perfectly healthy, in that he was guilt-ridden over the entire event she did not argue his solicitations for four weeks. She would do whatever she could to give his heart ease, be it invoking amnesia or keeping afoot.

But enough was enough.

The first time Elizabeth appeared at the stable, John Christie immediately brought her horse to her. ("Elizabeth, will you please reconsider that horse's name," Darcy continually bid her.) The entirety of this task was accomplished with the boy's gaze cast directly upon the ground. As he legged her up, young John deliberately averted his face. Clearly, it was not a genuflection. She thought him perhaps embarrassed to look upon her, having heard gossip of the abduction. She refused, however, to bear untoward distinction from an act not of her doing and questioned John about this and that until his eyes flickered to her, then hastily away.

Whether it was because he was an orphan, he was bashful, or perchance she often saw him sneaking sugar to Boots, Elizabeth had become fond of her young groom. She had heard him as he talked incessantly and softly to the horses in his charge, which was a bit of an incongruity for his voice retained the vestiges of his harsh east London accent.

Therefore, when, in that brief glimpse of his face full, Elizabeth saw a stricken expression far exceeding simple sympathy, she was taken aback. Concerned, she dismounted and drew him aside. He was taller than she was, and howbeit rangy in build, slight of figure yet. Maturity had not yet thickened his bones nor firmed his chin. Indeed, it undertook an independent wamble that announced his composure was about to collapse. Elizabeth thought Darcy correct to believe him younger than he attested, for at that moment he appeared very much a child.

Her initial attempt to cajole him into looking at her resulted just in his abandoning the mumbling he had bestowed upon his feet. Yet it was still an astonishment when he burst into tears. Before that day, she had seen him betray no emotion beyond the kindness of sugar for Boots.

"Mrs. Darcy, it was me own doin', it was me own fault alone!" he cried out.

"Pray, just what was your doing?"

"Whot 'appen' to yer was me own fault."

Assuring him he was quite innocent of the miscreant doings of highwaymen, she bid him to tell her of what he thought himself guilty.

"Reed! Aye knew 'e came back here that night. The night of the fire, and Aye din't speak."

Elizabeth exclaimed in surprise and disbelief. Clearly expecting it, John flinched all the same. They both knew that information would have led to Reed's imprisonment.

He began to cry again and then stopped himself. Grasping his cuff in his fingers, he wiped his nose with his shirtsleeve.

Quietly, he admitted, "'e said 'e'd kill me." He opened his mouth as if to say something else, but dropped his head repeating, "Them 'orses. Them 'orses."

"'Tis done," she calmed him, reaching out. "You should have told, 'tis true. Nevertheless, who among us can predict the future?"

"But that's nothin' to whot Aye caused by not tellin'. Them 'orses wouldn't 'ave died. Reed wouldn't 'ave been able to…rob yer 'ad Aye told Mr. 'ardin then."

Thereupon Mr. Darcy appeared in the lane, ready to accompany Elizabeth upon her inevitable, and in his mind, detestable, ride ("Recalcitrance, Lizzy. Utter recalcitrance," he had accused her). Upon seeing the master, John turned and bolted in a full-out run of terror. Innocent of the conversation, Darcy approached Elizabeth and looked in John's direction in all good humour.

"Where does your groom go in such haste?"

Elizabeth, still stunned, recounted what John had told her. At first, Darcy looked upon her incredulously. Then he stomped his foot in fury and whirled about to catch sight of which direction John had taken.

"He bloody well better run, for were I to catch him…"

Abruptly, he stopped himself, realising he had actually issued a curse in Elizabeth's presence. (He never cursed. Not even in the easy but often profane camaraderie of gentlemenly company.) Elizabeth, of course, did not think her virtue sullied by hearing the word. If anything, it was good that her husband had issued a profanity then, if just because it interrupted his anger long enough to reconsider the pursuit upon which he almost embarked. She raised an eyebrow at him and he shook his head a little, possibly to avert the ridiculous picture of himself that must have crossed his mind: running after a groom, ludicrously waving his crop.

He hastily apologised to Elizabeth who had put her hand upon his sleeve to calm his anger.

"Oh Darcy, he didn't have to tell us about it now. We should never have learnt of it had he not."

When Darcy turned and looked at her, her countenance reflected a level of sympathy that told him it would serve no purpose to speak further of the matter just then. He patted her hand with a reassuring calmness he did not feel. It was test enough upon her health that she insisted upon riding. Adding the apprehension that he might inflict a hiding upon her groom would not be advisable. He legged her back onto Boots and mounted his own horse.

They departed upon a leisurely ride that lent no more conversation of the errant John, nor reminders of "that day." Elizabeth knew no purpose would be gained by applying to Darcy for compassion upon John's behalf then. He was in festering anger yet over every aspect of her ordeal. Moreover, she was uncertain if she would even be able to find John, so relentlessly had he run. Thus, until that was addressed, she decided it best not to advance the matter.

Therefore, their ride passed with little more than innocuous conversation (and one more enquiry by Darcy, "Lizzy, will you not reconsider the name of that horse?"). It was a refrain she had begun to enjoy. Refusing to answer, she invariably patted Boots' neck in her negligence. It was a reassuring liturgy. He would implore. She would ignore. Yes, it was a reassuring remembrance of an easier time.

The next day John was not to be found at Pemberley and Elizabeth decided to ride alone to Kympton (eluding Darcy for this covert excursion was no easy task), where she knew his mother to have worked. As it would be unseemly for her to ride into town and up to the inn alone, she stopped at a short distance and bid a young boy to find the innkeeper's wife. The woman, Mrs. Turnpenny, upon hearing who bade application to see her, hastily rid her dirty apron from her ample bosom. When she came, Elizabeth stepped down from her horse so as not to converse from a position of officiousness.

The pursy woman had come with all amplitude and rush, her somewhat immense proportions placing an undue exertion upon her breath. But she had placed a welcoming expression of agreeability upon, what appeared to Elizabeth, a decidedly disagreeable face. Elizabeth told her she had come in search of the boy, John Christie, whose mother had once worked there. Had the woman seen him of late?

So nervous was Mrs. Turnpenny of speaking to Mrs. Darcy herself, this enquiry excited her into a conversational tailspin. She began a rapid monologue embracing every single tidbit of information of which she could think that might be of assistance to the grand lady. Eventually this discourse did actually cover what Elizabeth bid her, but only after she learnt of the good health and/or illness of every man, woman, child, or beast in the village.

Eventually, the woman volunteered, yes, John had come there the day before. Although she had not given him shelter, she knew that he had stayed in their stable the night past. She expected no better, the woman told Elizabeth, for his mother was known as a drunken whore ("Oh, mind your shoes ma'am of them trottles, the sheeps broke the hurdles!") and was not good enough to die in their establishment. Russet-haired trollop. Had Mrs. Darcy known that the boy John's mother had once worked at Pemberley? Or so she said, but who could trust such a fallen woman's declarations, certainly not she...

Exasperated, Elizabeth interrupted the woman to thank her with all due kindness and inquired as to the direction of their stable. That Mrs. Darcy had abandoned the conversation, it did not necessarily follow that the loquacious Mrs. Turnpenny would. Elizabeth could hear the woman babbling yet as a stableboy legged her up and she rode away. In that the stable was but a turn from the inn, Elizabeth was still within earshot when Mrs. Turnpenny quit her singsong conversational cadence for a more strident screech at her help.

The horse barn was a small, ramshackle affair that held the inescapable odour of sodden hay and manure. The hostler's room was easy to find, although nothing more than a lean-to upon the side. John was not there, but he was not far off. Not unexpectedly, Elizabeth found him sitting upon the wet ground in a stall, one arm wrapped morosely about his knees. The other petted the nose of a sway-backed, once-white horse. The screw quite obviously was only recently unhitched from a plough and was apparently very appreciative of a gentle hand.

John scrambled to his feet when he espied Mrs. Darcy. His obvious misery gave Elizabeth a twinge, but she knew instinctively that he sought no pity.

Without fanfare and with little ado, she announced, "You shall return to Pemberley if Mr. Darcy would but think so. Come this evening and we shall see what his decision will be."

John stood looking at her warily.

"Come, John," she added gently. "The worst that shall happen is that you will be let go...formally. Nothing else."

John looked up. He had reckoned few things in his life except that he could trust in no one. As to why he put his trust in Mrs. Darcy at that time could only be attributed to the same keen judgement of character that honed his mistrust of mankind in general. Mrs. Darcy was as kind as was her husband fearsome.

If there was any hesitation, John lost it when she smiled over her shoulder as she turned to take leave, saying, "If you do not, Boots will miss her sugar."

Reluctant she was to reveal to her husband what had transpired without his knowledge. But she did. Not unexpectedly, his ire toward poor John was intractable. Certain enough hurt had come from that sordid episode, Elizabeth persevered upon his behalf.

Eventually a bargain betwixt them was struck: John could stay, but no longer groom to Boots. Exile from the horses was a severe punishment, but it was better than a bastinadoing. Elizabeth was not of a mind to quibble with the decision. For she knew without the words being spoken that Darcy would be reminded of the hellish incident each time he looked upon the piteous boy.

In the aftermath, John was gradually readmitted to the stables, but kept his head down and made certain he stayed out of Mr. Darcy's eye.

Having managed to elude Lydia at least temporarily, Wickham located one of London's better grog houses. Trumbell's Gentlemen's Club was distinguished but not exclusive. It also boasted better gambling, faster wenches, and finer gins than any other and he expertly wended his way through the mass of patrons to locate which table emitted the unmistakable sound of dice.

After standing a few moments at the back of the crowd surrounding it, he moved on. Wickham favoured dice for pleasure, but this night he passed them by. The card tables were more lucrative and he was in need of some quick money.

In queer street yet again, Wickham was desperate. If funds could not be found to anoint the palms of the right people, Major Wickham was in fierce anxiety (if not outright panic) that he would find himself supporting the faltering British troops in the Peninsular War. True, there had been some heroics. However, unless Wellesley could re-supply his elite, but dwindling, troops, his great offensive against Napoleon's vast army would fail.

Wickham might have favoured visiting Madrid, but he was quite certain any endeavour that included the military tactic called "scorched earth policy" was not something of which he wanted any part.

He wished the British commander well in his quest of laying waste to the Spanish countryside. Most decidedly did he wish the commander well in combat against the French. For if Wellesley could not stop Napoleon in Spain, there would not be enough money nor enough palms to grease to keep Wickham's easily provoked sense of self-preservation becalmed.

Having no influence over Wellesley at that moment, Wickham reminded himself to address immediate needs first and he took quick assessment of the card players.

There were a number of well-dressed men. Wickham had learnt (from being left without a feather to fly with) that England could count amongst its citizens of rank and wealth at the gaming tables more than a few sons of smugglers and bootblacks. This second generation of new money had a veneer of refinement, but that gentility was often betrayed by an ever-so-slight coarseness in manner. If Wickham was to be successful at cards, he must cull those who gained position by sleuth rather than by birth. An advantage at cards would be found only amongst those who were in the happy circumstance of being wellborn and holding little sense.

Wickham expertly sized up the women as well. Practise told him that the two fetching chits eyeing him most zealously were likely to be much less interested in his countenance than the possibility of lifting his watch. He passed them by. Romance at that particular moment held little allure.

Having finally finagled his way into a company quartered in London and away from dreaded Newcastle, Major Wickham had looked forward to society again. Society did not quite reciprocate that happiness of acquaintance, for when he hied to London, his baggage included his wife.

Lydia, once merely a nettlesome flibbertigibbet, had somehow mutated into The Devil's Sister. The single most reliable trait she had was inciting mayhem. At the previous night's ball, he had dedicated his entire evening to the seduction of a rather comely young article only to have Lydia dash it all. Had he not been there to unfurl his wife's fingers, the poor girl might have been snatched bald-headed instead of merely having her turban deplumed. (What with Lydia bellowing and the young woman shrieking, the orchestra actually stopped playing mid-note and looked on incredulously at this exceedingly vociferous contretemps.) Knowing it was quite futile to reason with a witless woman, the attempt Wickham made at quieting her as he drug her outside was solely for appearances. Telling Lydia not to make a spectacle was much the same as telling a rooster he must not crow.

He had fled the ball with Lydia redirecting her wrath from the amorous woman to her husband. It was his brief consideration that a battlefield in Spain might be somewhat more peaceful. That he could neither quiet nor outsmart his dim-witted wife was becoming less a nuisance and more a humiliation to him day by day.

Indeed, Lydia had him by the short hairs. Hence, when the diversion of Trumbell's presented itself, he embraced it unequivocally.

Spying a slightly inebriated trio of red-faced, well-dressed men, Wickham bid to join them. He always wore his uniform in public houses, fancying it bought him a little unearned respect. Still able to charm those whom he pleased upon occasion, they immediately acquiesced and offered to buy him a drink as well.

"Drunk for a penny, dead drunk for tuppence, and straw for nothing!" Wickham recited with congeniality.

This nigh worn-out chestnut was met with semi-inebriated guffaws, which influenced Wickham that the group was full to the bung and ripe for a little fleecing.

Although a faro box sat upon the table, Wickham took the liberty of suggesting a game of commerce instead. The men were in fine, if not exuberant spirits, thus, they saw no reason not to accommodate someone they, if sober, would have considered a bit of a cock-a-hoop.

Wickham won steadily, losing just often enough and so amiably his fellow gamblers could feel no ill-will. As the drink took greater hold, they bantered heartily and one of the men, clear-headed enough to know him not from town, inquired after his home county.

"Pemberley in Derbyshire," Wickham told him, never one to seek false modesty. "I went to school at Cambridge…"

One man made the aside, "A tuft-hunter, no doubt."

Wickham wavered over whether to take active offence at the insult or let it pass.

Cravenness more a learnt response than inborn trait, he deduced he was out-manned, out-moneyed, and possibly outwitted. He ignored the aspersion. And he considered that perchance the men were not as dim as he thought if they nailed him for the truckler of the well-born that he was. He did not have time to ponder the problem long, somewhat grateful that the third man interrupted his unhappy deliberation.

"Derbyshire? Pemberley, you say?"

"Yes, indeed," answered Wickham.

"Then, no doubt, you know of it?"

Confused, Wickham shook his head he did not.

"It was quite a row, I heard. Quite a row."

Wickham did not have to encourage the man for more information. The other two did for him.

"Why, yes. Surely, you have heard of it. That family at Pemberley? What is their name?"

"Darcy," Wickham told him.

"Yes, that is it. Darcy. He dispatched them all, you know. Three men. Killed them all. Unaided."

"Darcy killed three men?" Wickham repeated, incredulous.

"You know the man then? I say, I would stay in his good graces. Pray, see you there what befell those who did not!"

The man thereupon shook his head at such audacity.

Astonished, Wickham bid the particulars. The man said he heard it was a robbery. He heard it might have been more than merely a robbery, for there was no formal hearing.

"He killed one by blade, but it was not a duel. Shot the other two. I fancy the man was put to anger in some fashion."

"Angered, indeed!" another pronounced and they all laughed.

Wickham, too. He laughed, but he was not amused. He felt uneasy and lost the next three hands. He knew his mind would not find further interest in the game. Hence, he took his sparse winnings and excused himself from the table. Pocketing the money, he kept out a coin, walked to the bar, and asked for another drink.

Nursing it, he stood there for a time thinking about his good friend Darcy. He simply could not imagine composed, collected Darcy killing three men. That gambler must have been mistaken. Talk is loose. Exaggerations occur. Surely that must be what bechanced. An exaggeration occurred. Perchance Darcy was merely present when three men were murdered. No. That seemed hardly more likely than Darcy doing the deed himself.

A slight, but unseemly, shudder fled down Wickham's spine. For he recollected that Darcy had more than a little wrath against himself (that unfortunate Georgiana matter). If the punctilious Darcy could actually become incensed to murder, was anyone safe?

Yet, Wickham reconsidered the facts carefully. Darcy was ill-tempered. He was ill-tempered and unyielding. But murder? A proud man, Darcy prided keeping himself under good regulation beyond any other conceit. Even in his anger at Wickham over Georgiana, he had not been enraged. Not visibly enraged. He had not drawn his blade.

In his contemplation, Wickham idly flipped a bob, but he espied a familiar reflection in the ornate looking-glass over the bar.

Col. Geoffrey Fitzwilliam sat alone at a table upon the far side of the room. His back was to the wall, but he did not look about. Dishevelled and drawn, he stared, with great concentration, into the half-empty glass of clear liquid sitting before him. Accompanying that glass were a half-dozen others, identical except that they had already been drained.

From the bung-eyed look of him, his sheets had been flapping in the wind for some time. It was an odd sight to see Fitzwilliam unkempt, much less sozzled. The man was never known to bend his elbow immoderately.

Fitzwilliam was not yet blind-drunk, but near enough that Wickham was not afraid to turn about and look at him directly. He wondered just what could have precipitated Fitzwilliam embarking upon a gin binge. It occurred to him that the history about Darcy might be linked to Fitzwilliam so suddenly taking to drink. Perhaps it was Fitzwilliam who killed three men rather than Darcy. But that seemed little more likely than the first premise.

In spite of Wickham's certainty that Fitzwilliam, as her co-guardian, knew of his attempted seduction of Georgiana, Wickham thought it safe to approach his table. Georgiana was not his sister and, most important, he appeared to be unarmed.

Wickham set his glass down and drew out a chair, taking a seat before Fitzwilliam's unsteady gaze focused upon him. Under the circumstances, Wickham forsook pleasantries.

He leaned forward conspiratorially and said, "There is a great deal of hearsay about the doings of our friend Darcy…"

Enlisting a steely-eyed (if slightly unfocused) glare, Fitzwilliam stared at Wickham. Was it that it took that long to identify who sat before him or to process what he said, one can but conjecture. Nevertheless, he did blink several times. Quite abruptly, he stood, grasping the edge of the table, his knuckles white under the pressure.

Thereupon, with a single, violent motion, he upended it, sending all of the many glasses crashing to the floor.

At the ruckus, whoever was tinkling upon the piano stopped. The dice ceased to roll, the card players quit shuffling, and a barman stopped pouring mid-drink.

Trumbell's was a respectable gaming house; brawls rarely occurred. To Wickham, it was an eerie repetition of the previous night's mortification, but at that time, he had not feared mortal retribution.

However, Fitzwilliam did not make a move to call Wickham out. He stood there frozen, staring at Wickham (whose mouth had become suddenly quite dry). Then, with the same dispatch as his fury had erupted, it vanished. Fitzwilliam tossed some coins down and stomped from the establishment.

When Fitzwilliam hurled the table, Wickham had instinctively picked up his own glass, thus saving it from being dashed. With it yet in his hand, he gathered what tattered dignity he could muster and walked back to the bar. Music began to play and talk gradually resumed. Once out of scrutiny, Wickham tossed the remainder of his rescued drink down his throat and called for another.

"Perhaps," he thought, "speaking to Fitzwilliam was a misjudgement. The colonel was obviously piqued yet about that Georgiana business."

As to why he was so roundly ploughed, Wickham had little notion. So long as he had escaped injury, he had no particular interest in uncovering the reason. He dismissed Fitzwilliam from his mind. When he thought again of the scuttlebutt about Darcy killing three men, he disregarded that matter as well. No, it simply was not possible. Darcy was far too disciplined, far too punctilious to dirty his hands by such a base act. If he wanted murder done, he would hire it. It was all an enormous exaggeration. It was simply not possible.

That was how Wickham had always found favour in a situation. He gave no consequence to that which did not conform to his own reasonableness.

He would learn to side-step Lydia more adeptly. He would manage to scrounge enough to bribe his way safe from battle. However, he would not see what he did not want to see.

Wickham was, and ever would be, true to himself alone.

With Jane's confinement speeding toward fruition, the Darcys had become an increasing presence at Kirkland Hall. Elizabeth would not allow her sister's delicate constitution to go unguarded during such a perilous time and Darcy would not allow Elizabeth's person to be without watch, either. Thus, it was necessary for him to concoct a series of convoluted excuses to accompany her every single time she visited.

It had taken several weeks for Darcy to allow Elizabeth out of his sight, invariably trailing her into her dressing room. After a time Hannah had become positively *blasé* about Mr. Darcy perching himself behind a folding screen whilst Mrs. Darcy compleated her toilette. She never once faulted Mr. Darcy's relentless monitoring of his wife's whereabouts, for Mrs. Darcy seemed to have little qualm about it herself. They moved about as if joined at the hip.

Hannah did not know it for fact, but believed nonetheless, that Mrs. Darcy was humouring her husband's necessity of keeping her under close scrutiny. As independent in spirit as she knew Mrs. Darcy to be, the forbearance with which Mrs. Darcy withstood her husband's smothering protectiveness was indicative of their esteem for each other.

In truth, although Elizabeth protested she harboured no emotional trauma from her abduction, her husband's constant presence was a comfort. She was not yet so collected as to ride in the carriage alone.

When they stayed at Kirkland, Darcy was afield during the day with Bingley and Mr. Hurst after black grouse. Thus, he was diverted with game and Elizabeth could enjoy company with Jane, both able to enjoy a respite from trepidation.

Kirkland Hall was quite beautiful. It was not quite so fine as Pemberley, but sumptuous all the same. Elizabeth and Darcy knew it well for they had visited Bingley there before Jane had come to stay permanently. He encamped early because, still anxious for her approval, Bingley wanted everything to be in order before she arrived.

Bingley's sisters were still much in tow—Miss Bingley and Mrs. Hurst understood that Jane was carrying either the Bingley heir apparent or presumptive. Whichever she bore, if they wanted to continue enjoying the largesse of their brother, their single guarantee of tenancy insisted upon a reconsideration of their haughtiness to his wife.

Elizabeth did not speak a word of her own miscarriage to Jane.

"I did not even know I carried a child," she explained her reticence of the matter to her husband. "Excessive sorrow would be self-indulgent."

With that rationalisation, Elizabeth continued to bury her misfortune in the dark recesses of her mind. She stalwartly refused to let it haunt her (except upon the occasions of being introspective, self-critical, self-pitying, or alone). As deeply as her martyrdom was imbedded in her subconscious, another niggling disturbance was welcomed to be her surrogate *idée fix.*

Jane told Elizabeth that she and Charles no longer shared a bed. This was not a disbandment by reason of the general annoyance of sharing one's sleeping space. It was biblical. They copulated not. (Nor did they fondle, finger, mousle, nor grope. But as they had not employed these particular variations of love previously, they must be dismissed as irrelevant.) They had ventured not into amorous embrace since Jane had first determined herself in a maternal condition. The door betwixt their bedrooms was locked.

Aghast at such a notion, Elizabeth, with no undue disconcertion, inquired of the reason.

"So Charles will not walk in his sleep and come to me accidentally," Jane said using her own peculiar logic.

"I mean," Elizabeth said patiently, "why do you not share a bed?"

Jane told her their mother had advised her that it was not good for the baby. Elizabeth countered (with a little more acerbity than she intended) that she did not think it particularly wise to take marital advice from one whose own marriage was so unhappy.

"Lizzy, you are speaking of the woman who gave you birth!"

Jane's scolding did tweak her conscience, howbeit the timing was most unfortunate. It was easier to observe the fifth commandment from a distance. With Mrs. Bennet under her roof, the sixth (proscribing homicide) was problematic enough for Elizabeth.

The Family Bennet had arrived a week before Michaelmas. Mrs. Bennet, Mr. Bennet, Mary, Kitty, Maria Lucas, and even Lydia Bennet Wickham. Albeit when Lydia applied for the visit, Elizabeth made certain it was understood her husband was unwelcome. It was, unequivocally. There was no inveigling from Lydia, for she thought Darcy's displeasure a perfectly good reason to holiday without Wickham (who became exponentially less charming a husband with each year of their marriage).

Lydia accompanied the Bennet Family unescorted by Wickham and, once again, quite pregnant.

Fortunately, Georgiana had returned to London chaperoned by four armed, exceedingly trustworthy footmen. Darcy had argued vehemently against her leaving the safety of Pemberley, but Elizabeth persuaded him that Georgiana's peace of mind would be better served by not disrupting her usual routine. (And she presumed Georgiana could do worse than bandits with Lydia in visit.) He would have escorted Georgiana himself, but his loyalty was divided betwixt his wife at Pemberley and his sister in London. It was a cruel dilemma. Because it was Elizabeth who was most grievously attacked, ultimately his reasoning told him that his place was with her.

With her family in attendance, Elizabeth thought it might have been less of a strain upon her husband had he accompanied his sister to London. For Mrs. Bennet contained her gushing admiration for Pemberley just long enough to belabour the matter of the robbery.

She took Elizabeth's hand and held it to her bosom, almost keening, "Oh, Lizzy! Oh, my dear, dear Lizzy! Beset by highwaymen!"

"There, there, Mrs. Bennet," comforted Mr. Bennet, who winked at Elizabeth, "you can see our Lizzy is just fine."

"But, Mr. Bennet! What good is it for her to marry such a very rich man if he cannot guard her! Ten thousand a year has he and he cannot protect her! She could have been killed! Or worse!"

Her distress appeared to be escalating at the excitement of her own words (and no one was of a mind to inquire what was a worse fate than death to Mrs. Bennet).

"Mr. Darcy! Oh, Mr. Darcy! How could you have let this happen to our own, dear Lizzy?!"

As was his habit when anything untoward was occurring in the room (this included anytime Mrs. Bennet was present), Darcy stood looking out the window endeavouring to ignore the upheaval. Therefore, Elizabeth cringed upon his behalf.

Overwrought in the only manner he would allow himself, that of silent self-condemnation, her husband suffered yet. However, her mother simply would not hush about it. However little he cared for Mrs. Bennet's opinion, Elizabeth knew her mother's abuse was not inconsequential.

Weary of his wife's outbursts, Mr. Bennet took her arm with husbandly courtesy and led her to a chair. Mrs. Bennet blathered on, fluttering a lovely, lace-trimmed, cambric handkerchief from forehead to breast. Elizabeth found herself contemplating just how long it might take to render her mother silent if she squeezed her hands tightly enough about her neck. She fancied she could see her jugular pulsating enticingly.

"Oh Mr. Darcy! Mr. Darcy! Will our Lizzy ever be safe again?!"

Perchance it might be more expedient to simply slit her throat. When pigs were slaughtered, they were hoisted by their hind legs. Elizabeth espied a heavy beam near the ceiling and thought it quite sturdy enough for a winch. It was only when she looked about to see if a penknife was handy that she was returned to her senses. Matricide was a major sin, no matter the provocation. She gave an inward shake of her head, supposing her decidedly intemperate flight of fancy due to "recent events."

Unaware that her second-eldest daughter was eyeing her neck malevolently, Mrs. Bennet fortuitously ceased her shrill harangue, continuing on with the insistent fluttering of her handkerchief. She was not yet ready to abandon such a prop, for it was an impressively melodramatic touch, reminding everyone in the room it was she who suffered the event most keenly.

Over her shoulder, Elizabeth looked at Darcy, who stood absolutely still, his mask of reserve firmly in place.

Temporarily spent, Mrs. Bennet rested her head against the back of the winged chair. Elizabeth feared this lull would merely allow her mother time to gather a second wind. Blessed be for Mr. Bennet, for he wrested the conversational topic from his wife, inquiring of Mr. Darcy how he favoured the weather. Realising the effects of her histrionics were fading, she sat bolt upright and regained the floor by abruptly changing tack.

"Mr. Darcy! Forgive me! A mother cannot but help herself! I compleatly disremembered what an exquisite home you have! Such refinement! Such beauty! Such elegance!" (Mrs. Bennet rarely spoke in other than the exclamatory and always in repetition.)

Fortunately for the Darcys, Pemberley's beauty, refinement, and elegance would be honoured with the good lady's presence but for the first half of their visit, owing to the need to share the second with Kirkland Hall's beauty, refinement, and elegance ("But not half so grand as Pemberley, Mr. Darcy!" Mrs. Bennet had assured him).

Shared office of host with the Bingleys was another benefit of Jane's imminent delivery. But whilst her family tarried at Pemberley, Elizabeth weathered them as best she could. It was not an easy duty. In light of recent events, Elizabeth and Darcy were in no mind to entertain, finding nothing celebratory in robbery and death. Hence, Elizabeth pointedly ignored Lydia's frequent whining about the dearth of society in her life and her need for the diversion of a ball. Not of a mood to endure the prospect of her family (particularly Lydia) being foisted upon well-placed members of the local gentry, Elizabeth insisted propriety demanded they remain in seclusion—the Darcys because of traumatic events, the Bingleys because Jane was great with child. Laudable intentions upon Elizabeth's part, but to no avail.

In honour of the visiting Bennets, the Millhouses arranged a ball at Pennyswope for them. At his wife's encouragement, Lord Millhouse persuaded Elizabeth that it would just cause more talk if she and Darcy refused society. Thus, she tried to assuage her impending mortification by reminding herself that the mistress of Pennyswope bore eccentricity well and hoped her family's bouts of unseemly behaviour might be considered such.

The favoured Millhouse nephew, Newton Hinchcliffe, was in residence, and with writing tablet in hand, mused in his room most days. Lady Millhouse thought a ball just the occasion to lure him to exercise, as fresh air was evidently an impossibility.

At the news that the eligible young Hinchcliffe was in Derbyshire and their archrival for his affections (unbeknownst to her), Georgiana, was in London, Maria and Kitty trilled in impenitent excitement.

As they dressed upon the appointed evening, the obviously pregnant Lydia tightened her corset recklessly, impending motherhood be damned. She refused to let so minor an issue as a coming baby infringe upon her participation in society.

For having bested her sisters by marrying first, that coup was negated by their much more advantageous matches. She was not about to relinquish her position of superiority with the impressionable Kitty and Maria. (The current arena of competition was the race to produce grandchildren. Although Lydia had given birth to the first son, and saw herself at match point, Jane was already *enceinte*. Hence, Lydia knew her position was in jeopardy. The importance of a child who had expectations far out-stripped that of a child of an army officer. All might not be lost, for Lydia knew well that if her sisters did not produce heirs for their rich husbands, their fortunes *could* fall to a cousin. Longbourn was entailed to Mr. Collins. It was conceivable.)

In Maria and Kitty's eyes, Lydia's infamy as a *femme fatale* was unparalleled. She went to Brighton, she wanted Wickham and she got Wickham. (More accurately, Wickham had her, but semantics are rarely questioned under some circumstances.) They, unfortunately, looked to her as an expert upon allurement and she counselled them both in their quest of Newton Hinchcliffe specifically and romance in general. When Elizabeth overheard Lydia whispering to Kitty that was she to have any success in attracting young men ("You do not have the face for it, Kitty, so you must use other wiles") she must begin by dampening her chemise, thereby more advantageously exhibiting said "wiles" beneath her muslin, Elizabeth could be a silent observer no longer.

"Lydia, to advise your sister to do such as that just to reveal her figure to young men is beyond mere vulgarity. It will announce to them she is loose."

"Of course, Lizzy," Lydia was exasperated at Elizabeth's denseness, "that is how one attracts lovers. One does not have actually to be loose. One must only appear to be."

Elizabeth very nearly reminded Lydia that in her case, actually being loose did attract one rather unsavoury lover. However, since Wickham ultimately became Lydia's husband, Elizabeth decided not to stir that particular kettle of fish. And knowing any reproof would be laughed at, Elizabeth offered a simple statement of fact.

"As it happens, if either of these girls attempts repair from this house with wetted slips, I shall feel myself falling ill and give our regrets to the Millhouses. Am I understood?"

Lydia pursed her lips and made a face, but did not argue.

The ball was barely tolerable. Only a few guests dared venture a comment about "recent events." The one person Elizabeth might have thought to do just that, Lady Millhouse, had remained staunchly silent upon the matter and when others alluded to it at the ball, she pointedly altered the subject. Thus, she was spared all but the dereliction of decorum in play in her own family. By the time they took their leave, her cheeks were in quivering weariness from the smile that she had determinedly fastened upon her face all evening.

As gauged by the listless remarks of disappointed celebrants the next morning, the ball was not a resounding success to others either. But as it was not rendered an unmitigated disaster by a misdeed of a relative of hers, the morning saw Elizabeth looking upon it more favourably than most.

There was but little time for Elizabeth to breathe that sigh of relief before she was set upon once again by her mother's carping. This time, however, the subject her mother chose to abuse delivered her daughter mute. This not was by reason of fancying heinous methods to disengage her mother's tongue, but because she was absolutely speechless.

For Mrs. Bennet sat upon the side of the bed and took Elizabeth's hand, patting it sympathetically, "Oh, Lizzy, Jane has been so fortunate to be with child of Mr. Bingley so soon after the wedding."

"Yes," Elizabeth cautiously agreed.

Shaking her head woefully, Mrs. Bennet looked at her quite pitiably, "But you, Lizzy!" Elizabeth sat in wait.

Mrs. Bennet took her arm and, looking first to her right, then left, to be certain they were free of eavesdroppers, shared a conspiratorial whisper.

"Mr. Darcy's fortune is far too vast for him to be in want of a son. You must lure him now, Lizzy. Now, whilst his interest is keen."

"Lure him?" Elizabeth repeated.

"Yes. If you are to become with child as Jane, you must now. If not, he shall find other pursuits and your chances of giving him a son will diminish post-haste."

With a look blank of any true emotion, Elizabeth stared at her mother. Not a single comment came into her mind in response to such a remark. Silence, however, was a commodity Mrs. Bennet refused to leave at peace.

"Yes, yes," she consoled Elizabeth of the unspoken undeniability of Jane's husband's preferable temperament. "I know Mr. Darcy has not the happy disposition of Mr. Bingley, but he is a man. Certainly, you can interest him. You must deliver him a son, Lizzy. 'Tis imperative!"

"I do not think…" Elizabeth began.

"Pray, do not despair, Lizzy. Perhaps you can ask Jane's advice upon these matters. She has been successful. She might offer you some suggestions."

The eyebrow Mrs. Bennet raised intending to be provocative was, to Elizabeth, possibly the most lewd expression she had ever witnessed.

"Yes, Mama," Elizabeth said. "Perhaps."

When Jane's labour commenced, Bingley, a father-to-be of considerable means and no little anxiety, summoned not one, but two midwives and a physician to see to his wife's laying-in. Perchance wanting to assure Mr. Bingley they were, indeed, all needed, they hovered busily about Jane's bed, causing Elizabeth to fear for her feet.

However, Jane did not want two midwives and a physician, just Elizabeth. Jane's ever-intimidating lady-maid, Mary (Jane had never been able to summon enough courage to dismiss her), stood before Jane's door. With an officiousness peculiar to an unchallenged servant, she told Elizabeth that, howbeit married, a woman who had not borne children would not be allowed to witness a delivery.

Before Elizabeth could explain that what she would be allowed to do fell to her own will not Jane's lady-maid, she was interrupted by Jane, already in hard labour.

It was the first time Elizabeth had ever heard Jane raise her voice.

"My sister *will* stay with me," she said, as if daring anyone to keep Elizabeth from her side.

Was her adamancy initiated by the perturbation of childbirth, no one was willing to reckon and Elizabeth did, indeed, second the physician with the birth. And, howbeit hers was an easy labour and swift delivery, Elizabeth was quite surprised with the aplomb with which Jane dealt with it, for she did not call out ("Charles might hear me," she worried), not wanting to be a bother.

Elizabeth told her, "Jane, if you are ever to be a bother, now is the time."

At the onset of this event, Mrs. Bennet took to her bed in a dress rehearsal for the impending delivery of her favourite daughter, Lydia. Mr. Bennet hid in the Pemberley library, and Lydia waddled off to shop.

Bingley spent the hours of Jane's labour in his own library, alternately pacing and sitting uneasily in a wing chair in the company of Darcy and Mr. Hurst. Neither of those men having had acquaintance with impending fatherhood, they knew nothing but to keep the glass Bingley clenched tightly in his fist filled with brandy.

Bingley's pointer, Hap, attempted to comfort him by resting his head upon his knee when he sat and following him upon his cursory trips the length of the room. Alternatively, Bingley lifted a hand to his ear listening for the initial wail of an infant.

By the time Elizabeth appeared to tell him he had a thoroughly undistressed (and therefore silent) daughter, Bingley was quite unable to stand unaided. Unwilling to wait for sobriety, he had two burly housemen carry him in an armchair up the stairs to have Elizabeth Jane Bingley introduced to her father.

It was the first time that Darcy and Elizabeth had been apart from each other since their ill-fated return from London the summer past. Hence, no one should have been surprised that he cut short his business trip to Exeter with Matlock rather abruptly.

So abruptly did he forsake Matlock's coach for horseback (saving a half-day), he arrived in the early morning hours. Hence, his home-coming was with compleat absence of the fanfare upon which they had departed. Indeed, hardly was an eye awake to see him appear. However, for a house compleatly asleep, it came to life with considerable rapidity.

Fatigue notwithstanding, he quite uncharacteristically bounded up the stairway, scattering hastily assembled footmen and servants as he went. Hearing the commotion, the dogs began to yelp, thus awakening Elizabeth. She was to her feet and at their bedroom door before he made his way up half the staircase.

Their reunion was lengthy and undertaken with considerable vehemence, very nearly consummating there in the corridor. Instead of scandalising them both, he exuberantly picked her up and carried her into their bedchamber, kicking the door closed behind them with a thud.

However, by the time they reached the bed, exhaustion reclaimed him. He heaved her upon it and sank with a groan beside her.

Moving astride him, she began to undo his cravat, chastising him, "Your strength could better serve you than carrying me about."

"I want nothing more than to lie here next to you."

Both entered into, and perpetuated, the charade that the trip, return, and reunion were unextraordinary—a commonplace occurrence of no particular note. Nevertheless, it was not.

That he had even embarked upon a trip was a high-water mark in reclaiming a dauntless existence. Thus, that it was conceived and consummated without incident was of far greater relief than one unfamiliar with their history might have understood.

"At least pull off your boots," she insisted.

He leaned back against the headboard allowing her to attempt what heretofore had been Goodwin's chore. As she was unschooled in the particulars of the removal of a gentleman's boots, it came as a surprise that he braced one boot-clad foot against her hinder-end for a support as she tugged off the other. The look she bestowed him over her shoulder at this affront set him to laughing and he would actually have guffawed had he not been so very weary. He quieted. And in that quiet, he realised that she did not wear a gown.

She wore his incongruously oversized night-shirt. The sleeves were turned back several revolutions just to clear her wrists.

"Pray, is your husband so ungenerous as not to buy you a night-gown?"

"As you see, he is a cruel and stingy man."

His boots conquered, she ignored the abuse to her dignity (his stockinged foot not nearly the affront the booted one was), then turned and undid the buttons at the knees of his small clothes. With a bit of exaggerated coquetry, she began to massage his legs whilst issuing sympathies upon the excessive weariness he suffered.

"If your concern is for my weariness, you are not serving your purpose, Mrs. Darcy."

In answer, she raised her eyes to him in a manner so provocative it gifted him a slight tingle in the area of his recently horse-wearied nether regions.

"Am I not?" she said in all innocence.

He might have conjectured that when she brought her hands from beneath his pants legs, but let them rest tantalisingly upon his knees that she truly did not know she had provoked considerable husbandly lust. Whatever the case may have been, any speculation upon his part was soon abandoned. When her hands undertook a tantalizing trip, sliding lazily up his legs toward his torso, he knew she felt the unmistakable evidence that he was not so very weary after all.

She felt it twice more (one must not leave some things to wonder) before she gripped the knees of his pants and drew them off. There, exposed, was an exceedingly generous example of masculine arousal.

Raising one eyebrow, she reminded him, "I believe you said, sir, that you just wanted to 'lie next to me.'"

"A blatant prevarication."

"Very blatant."

Thereupon she shed his nightshift and bade him be still. Quite happily, she undertook the singular office of inflicting a rather pleasurable penance upon his body for perjuring his intent. He bore this chastening with the utmost of perseverance. And when his reparation was exacted with a shuddering moan, he turned her upon her back and repeated the process with the enthusiasm of a man who had not relished his wife in two fortnights.

Thus spent consecutively and unequivocally, he said, "Lizzy, at this moment I am grateful twice you are my wife. For I should have to steal you if you were not, and I do not know where I might find the strength just now."

Sleep claimed him almost as he made that declaration and morning came and well-nigh fled before they finally awoke.

To her drowsy supine figure, he murmured, "Far, far too long, Lizzy."

"Darcy," she sighed, as if reassuring herself that he was, indeed, home.

He drew her closer, buried his face in her hair and let his hand gently search her curves, his body announcing there would be an imminent recapitulation of the previous night's passion. This preparatory exploration led his hand over her breasts and down her abdomen. There, it came to an abrupt and baffled halt. He slid his hand back across her stomach and left it there, cupped.

She looked over to him as his hand rested thus. His eyes were still closed, yet a bit of puzzlement overspread his countenance. He flattened his hand and ran it first across, then thither, then yon.

Much like one who had lost his way, his hand re-inspected her, from the beginning.

This reiteration confirmed the tumescence of her breasts and a pronounced swell in her belly. As closely as he had investigated her the night before, he could not imagine how he had missed it. He let his hand tarry, lightly caressing it.

Obliquely, he looked at her.

"Pray, you feel it as well?" she asked.

"I believe I do. Yes."

"Thus, it is not my imagination," sounding relieved, she then confided, "I have told no one, not even Jane, for fear it just a wish."

"If it is true," he chose his words carefully, "when will your confinement end?"

"Before All Saints."

Yes. That was little more than five months hence. It was certain. Overtaken by an unprecedented giddiness, he made a gesture as to ring a celebratory bell. Jubilation re-routed his ardour, thus, when he kissed her they rolled across the bed laughing. With that merriment yet tickling their innards, he became quite solemn, stroking her cheek with the back of his fingertips.

Then, in a voice husky with emotion he said simply, "Lizzy," before he leaned down to kiss her belly and thereupon repaid the debt to her lips.

Gratitude and relief flooded his senses, as much for the timing as the event itself. The decision he dreaded would not have to be made at all. Elizabeth's condition would be justification not to travel to London for the season. They would not have to take the road to town as an armed convoy, nor pass the place where the abduction occurred. He would have a year's reprieve before he would have to take his family upon the road again. Elizabeth would remain within the sheltering walls of Pemberley.

Their breakfast had become a luncheon due to the hour. By the time he came downstairs to join her, Darcy found Elizabeth at her favourite window. He came to her there and surprised her by, in full view of Mrs. Reynolds, putting his arms about her and placing his hands upon her stomach, caressing the fullness there.

Elizabeth could but guess, but fancied he did that in lieu of initiating guessing-games amongst the staff. If he did, owing that his chief vice was that of abiding reticence, she was quite delighted to learn he thenceforward appeared to own no faults at all.

Elizabeth's ever-growing belly had become cumbersome to her by autumn. As was expected of her, she kept herself cloaked in great folds of clothing and withdrew from society once her condition became obvious. Seldom did she venture beyond the immediate demesne. The single time she ventured to the stables to visit Boots, her husband scolded that the uneven ground was too treacherous for her. He even feared her negotiating the stairs and suggested they room downstairs until after her confinement.

Exasperated, she reminded him, "I am merely with child. I am not suffering from dropsy!"

In the presence of company (the very narrow circle that her confinement allowed), Mr. Darcy never spoke of Mrs. Darcy's health or the impending *accouchement*. It might have been presumed that he chose to ignore it, as it was a woman's province and not a subject on which gentlemen concerned themselves.

However, as Elizabeth had come to understand, the more detached from a topic Darcy appeared to others, the greater was his private emotion. For when they were alone he was immersed in pleasure and overwhelming pride. In the privacy of their bedroom, he uncovered her stomach, marvelled at its girth, and bedevilled her about her protruding navel.

"If you get much larger, I fear it will explode," he said to her with such seriousness, it took her a minute to know it was a tease.

Weeks were spent summoning him to her side in anticipation of foetal activity. And for weeks, all went for naught. Their shy child became still as a mouse the moment its father laid his hand upon her stomach. ("Are you certain you are with child and it is not simply gas?") However, after the initial kick, the baby gyrated relentlessly whenever Darcy was near. So rambunctious a bundle was it, Elizabeth complained she had been undoubtedly impregnated with a whirligig.

As blithesome as were most of their days, all was not frivolity. For some reason her husband did not fully understand, Elizabeth favoured wearing his night-shirts yet. And, although she did not tell Jane, she and Darcy continued to share a bed. If their desire for intimacy was not discouraged by her menses, neither would it be by the lack of them nor the resultant child. Even so, they were not so certain that such intrusion in her body would not harm the baby as to risk it. However, they did continue to find methods of pleasure not hitherto discovered (and both firmly believed it was but with practise that perfection could be achieved).

A particular delight was to lie amidst tousled bed-covers long after all decent folk had arisen to meet the day. Upon these occasions, he undertook a preoccupation with her maternally-enhanced trinity of breasts and belly. These mounds were kissed, massaged, and caressed assiduously. This relentless manipulation eventually resulted in his discovery that her belly was not the only part of her person that was fecund. Her gown became wet.

She laughed at his expression as he turned and looked to her saying, "Madam, pray, just where did you acquire that? I thought there was milk but after the baby was born."

"'Tis not milk, just the preparation for it," she explained.

Had Jane not gone through the process first and enlightened Elizabeth, she knew she might have been as surprised as was Darcy. And because she witnessed baby Eliza's birth, Darcy insisted she describe it in messy, bloody detail. He listened intently, but with great abhorrence. Having seen any number of animals give birth, he did not quite want to envision such messy disorder of his dear Elizabeth.

"I do not think it fair for me to have enjoyed such pleasure putting the baby in you while you should have to endure such pain to get it out."

"Fairness has nothing to do with it, for if it did, men would certainly give birth to half of the babies."

Daintily, he touched the end of his tongue to her nipple and then took it into his mouth. Although he had pressed his lips to her and suckled before, never had he expected to taste the fruit of her body. He was all astonishment at the achievement.

His lips' insistent drawing of her breast bestowed upon her an odd sensation. Much in fascination of this new ability of hers, he was unwitting of her rumination.

He mused, "It does not taste of milk."

Thereupon he tried it again, looking puzzled, as if it was demanded that he assign it a flavour.

She nestled against him, then sighed and said, "My mother says I need to find a wet-nurse now. I am to begin interviews."

He stopped the investigation of her colostrum-in-the-making and, with all due consideration, asked, "I wonder if my wet-nurse is yet about here. What was her name...?"

"If she is, and by some miracle producing milk yet, I think we must have her. But you no doubt drained the poor woman dry."

She laughed, but was soon overtaken by a bit of melancholia. Happy in all other aspects, she was not happy about this. Thus, a small annoyance inflated to unreasonable proportions. He sensed her unease and gave her his full attention.

She sighed and said, "Mama says modesty demands that a lady must have a wet-nurse. Perchance you shall think ill of me, but I do not wish to think of our baby feeding from another woman. She says it is common to be suckled. But I know mothers who nurse their own babies. The doctor says men of medicine today believe it is good, if I so choose it. But Mama is adamant."

The more she thought of it, the more senseless it seemed.

"Jane listened to Mamma and had to bind herself to belay her milk. The pain was unbearable..."

She looked at her husband. He appeared to have heard of more womanly distress than he could bear at one sitting.

"You will not have to do anything you do not wish. You will not," he stated emphatically.

There existed within him yet a serious lack of humility in understanding how little Providence fell under his sway.

That he refused she endure any distress was of particular pleasure to her. However, he was unburdened by much other bother on her behalf. For her pregnancy was an easy one, with no more concern than musing over nursery and nursings. The doctor pronounced her indecently sturdy for a woman with child.

Nonetheless, Georgiana was banished for the duration of Elizabeth's term. Her brother was adamant that being under the same roof as a knapped woman would sully her virtue. When this pronouncement was made (using those exact words), Elizabeth had to slap both hands over her mouth to keep from sniggering out loud.

By that time, Jane was knapped again herself, and her frequent visits bade Darcy, with considerable self-righteousness, point out that Georgiana must be unwitting of such unseemly doings.

"Yes," Elizabeth agreed in overt facetiousness, "she might wonder just how these babies were deposited in the first place."

As was often when he believed himself accused of overindulged compunction, he chose to rise above it. This forbearance was suffered in pitiable silence. Usually he allowed himself to be cajoled from it within the half-hour.

With Jane often came her youngling, Eliza, who drooled constantly and jabbered incomprehensibly. Her namesake, however, pronounced her adorable and interpreted every syllable for her somewhat sceptical uncle.

"She said my name, Darcy! Jane, did you not hear her? She said 'Elizabeth.'"

"No lack of affection for you upon her part I am sure, but I do not believe 'Elizabeth' will be her first word," Darcy said a bit too dourly.

"Here, Mr. Darcy, you must practise this," Elizabeth announced, unceremoniously plopping Eliza in his lap.

He made a face of great imposition and said, "I have no intention of practising something which I intend not to do." Thereupon he added, "I shall look upon your baby, Elizabeth, but just from a distance sufficiently safe from any unexpected discharges."

Jane and Elizabeth sat with their arms folded, unswayed by his profession of distaste of babies. He held Eliza up before his face and talked to her quite seriously.

"You did not say Aunt Elizabeth, did you Eliza? You were trying to say Uncle Darcy, were you not?"

Enthralled, Eliza put her fingers against his lips as he spoke and giggled when he pretended to nibble them. Glancing at Elizabeth and Jane watching this exchange, he stood and awkwardly handed Eliza back to her mother. He checked his pocket watch. Noting that there were any number of manly things to which he must attend, he said he had no further time to spend with expectant women and babies. Pausing to kiss Elizabeth's cheek before he departed, she whispered that his ruse was ineffectual.

"You have been quite unsuccessful at disguising yourself a curmudgeon."

"I fancy I shall have to practise that as well," he said as he strode away.

As early autumn brought a chill to the air, Elizabeth awoke one morning with a cramp. She thought nothing of it, for it was weeks until her expected laying-in. With that in mind, Darcy planned to ride out with Mr. Rhymes to inspect the fields, for a wet spring had delayed harvest and the scythes had just begun to reap. The nearer the calendar drew to All Saints, the more he would limit how far he ventured.

When he came to her to bid her good-bye, she was yet atop the bed. To her husband, her stomach looked as if it was one more voluminous pillow amongst the covers and he gave a slight tug of affection to her braid and kissed her forehead. (Darcy had told Elizabeth that her body was mimicking the land, sown in the spring and ripened in the fall. He thought that a fit analogy and she was grateful she was not to deliver in the spring, lest he liken her to a cow.) With a promise that he would return before the gloaming, he departed.

Early afternoon saw Darcy a number of miles away overlooking a just-harvested field. The measure of the crop was reckoned by counting the ricks in each meadow. By the number upon which they gazed, it was an abundant year. Already those in the pinch of want had moved in behind the reapers, womenfolk and children scavenging for what was left of the corn. Some of the more penurious landowners imposed a levy upon what the poor winnowed from the soil, but Pemberley did not. If a family was so poor as to seek relief from the parish, they were free to take all they could find.

A billowing cloud of dust announced a rider coming fast down the lane. He rode with such haste that it stole Mr. Darcy's attention from the gleaners. He recognised one of his own horses and upon it, Edward Hardin. He did not wait to be told.

He turned Blackjack and spurred him hard toward Pemberley.

Skidding into the courtyard, he slid off Blackjack before the horse stopped compleatly and tossed the reins and his crop in the direction of whoever happened to be standing by the entrance. He burst through the doors with such force, it sent them vibrating backwards, which startled even Mrs. Reynolds, who stood in anticipation of his entrance.

"Where?" he demanded.

She pointed up the stairs, to the room that had just recently been prepared for labour. He took the stairs two at a time, his boots hitting them loudly.

Over his shoulder he inquired, "Is this not early?" Then to no one, "This is early."

When he reached the door to the birthing room he stopped and hesitated. The voice he heard told him he had arrived tardy to Jane. Hannah, literally wringing her hands in anxiety, stood outside. When he asked if the doctor was in with Elizabeth, she shook her head.

"Get him here!" he demanded, almost startling Hannah into tears, for she had never heard him raise his voice.

His outburst notified Jane of his presence. She came to the door to apprise him of Elizabeth's situation. Calmly, Jane said yes, it was a little early, but assured him it was not too early. In that Jane was not one to alarm anyone unduly, he listened to that reassurance without compleatly embracing it. She warned him that Elizabeth was in some discomfort, but that was to be expected. He nodded his understanding, but steeled himself for her suffering as he entered the room. He wished for a reprieve to prepare himself for it.

Her eyes were closed and she looked pale. Stopping just inside the door, he wet his fingers and smoothed down his hair in an attempt to present a composure he did not feel.

Walking stealthily, he approached her bed and carefully perched upon the edge. He pushed an imaginary curl away from her face, an excuse to stroke her. She smiled and grasped his hand.

"Pray, why did you allow me to take leave?" he asked.

"You are here now and that is all that matters," she smiled. "They should have let you be and you could have come home to sup and been handed a baby."

"I want to be here with you," he kissed her hands.

Her smile of encouragement deepened into a grimace as a contraction began to do its work upon her. It was clear she was endeavouring to disguise its strength, but it eclipsed her will. She clutched his hand, but turned her face from him, biting upon the edge of the pillowslip to keep from crying out. Perspiration broke out upon her forehead and upper lip. He felt ill.

After what seemed an eternity, it began to recede.

"I fear this will not transpire with haste," she gasped. "In time, Jane shall come to you with word of the birth."

Her indirect request for him to withdraw for the duration of her labour was taken as neither a rebuff nor a reminder of propriety. He knew he was unsuccessful at masking his horror at her suffering. His discomposure was one more burden for her. Thus, he knew he would do as she bid.

"Do you recollect once telling me how unfair it was that men are not allowed to see what their wives endure to bring their children into the world?" he inquired.

"Yes, but I also remember you reminding me that for every person in the world, there had been an act of love. I remind you that for every said same person there had to be a childbirth. My mother endured it for me, yours for you, and I shall for our child."

With that declaration, Dr. Carothers arrived, clearing his throat and tugging at the neck of his shirt. A fubsy, fleshy looking man, he had the good sense to appear a bit unkempt (a toff for a doctor was indefensible). Jane escorted him to Elizabeth's bedside to "have a look."

Darcy fled the room, face averted, stationing himself just outside the door in an impatient wait of the foetal examination. He did not abide the pause well, for he could hear lengthy murmurings and moans upon the other side of the door. Eventually, after perhaps an hour, the doctor reappeared with Jane shadowing his elbow.

Both countenances were sombre.

Dr. Carothers explained his grave face thusly, "Mrs. Darcy's labour is early...As often is in such cases, the baby is not positioned correctly. I have tried to exact an external cephalic version to turn it but it will not budge. Determined little cusser."

However obscure the terminology, his meaning was hardly unfathomable. The danger was clear.

"Pray, is that it then?" Darcy demanded far more loudly than he intended, thus he reiterated more softly, "There will be no further attempt?"

"Of course. Of course there shall. You must know, though, I hold little hope of success."

Darcy asked the unthinkable, "And if it cannot be turned?"

Dr. Carothers chose his words carefully, "I have delivered a number of breech babies with little more vexation than a lengthier duration of labour. But those were babies born of mothers who had birthed previously. This, of course, is Mrs. Darcy's first. She has a narrow...she is narrow. It is difficult to predict the outcome."

The look of frightened despair upon Darcy's face caused Jane to soothe, "Do not lose hope."

It was difficult not to be terrified when the best outcome they could hope for was grievously long labour. Darcy had assisted enough foaling mares to know just how perilous a breech delivery was. He had spent many a harried night watching Edward Hardin attempt to realign a foal. As hardy as was the lineage of Pemberley horses, these were bloody, long, painful affairs. When fillies were involved, not one in ten was successful. The unseemliness of comparing his wife to one of his horses was not lost upon him, but it was, quite simply, his single sphere of reference.

He could not bring himself to imagine Elizabeth attempting to expel an infant buttocks first. So little faith did he hold in Dr. Carothers capabilities just then, he fleetingly considered dragging Edward Hardin from the stables to attempt to turn the baby, but collected his wits long enough to discard that notion.

In preparation of the wait and the battle that he would be unable to fight for her, he removed his jacket and tie and loosed his collar. He drew a straight-backed chair from across the hall and set it firmly next to the door to Elizabeth's room. It was upon that seat that he braced himself for what would come to pass.

The afternoon sun grew long and then disappeared.

Upon hearing of the impending happy event, Bingley and Fitzwilliam rode to Pemberley in grand humour to offer their company and ply spirits into the expectant father. When Bingley learnt where Darcy waited, he went to coax him into joining them downstairs. However, Darcy refused to relinquish the chair by Elizabeth's labour room, for her pains had increased but progress had not.

Bingley said cheerfully, "You serve no purpose sitting here. Fitzwilliam has brought a superior cognac. I can tell you it helps one not to think of it."

"How could I not?" Darcy snapped.

Jane arrived forthwith to explain away Bingley's confoundment, telling him of the dire predicament. Nodding his understanding, he ceased his cajoling of the father-to-be.

Touching Darcy's sleeve, he did urge him to reconsider, "I do think it best if you come downstairs, Darcy. Truly, you can do nothing here."

Darcy just shook his head and stared with great intensity at the floor. The single entreaty refused, Bingley knew better than to beseech further. He returned to Fitzwilliam and they commenced to splash down the "superior cognac" without tasting it.

Periodically, Darcy left his post in the corridor and came in to see Elizabeth, but when she caught sight of him hovering over her, invariably she smiled and shooed him away. He would heed her wishes and take leave, but even so diligently as was it offered, her feigned nonchalance was pitiably inept. He despised having to participate in the farce when he wanted so fervently to stay with her.

With the baby imbedded in the birth canal, refusing to turn and unable to come out, the hours of the night stole even indomitable Elizabeth's strength. As dawn arose, a wearied Jane appeared in the corridor. Darcy knew well that her dedication to Elizabeth's labour room was risking her own health. She looked at Darcy, put her hands to her face and began to cry.

Never had he more than kissed Jane's hand, but neither hesitated to share a woeful embrace. So wretched was she, he could think of nothing but to pat her upon the back, assuring her Elizabeth would be all right.

Dr. Carothers had the poor timing to appear at that moment, dashing to pieces what little solace they gathered.

His message was succinct, "I am not at all certain the baby is yet alive. If Mrs. Darcy cannot rally, I fear for her as well."

The stricken look upon Darcy's face was duplicated by Jane's. A vision of a dead baby and dying Elizabeth bade Jane betray a promise she had made to Elizabeth.

"Mr. Darcy, you must know this. Elizabeth does not want you in with her for fear that it will excite your apprehension. She knows you are outside the door. She has stifled her cries in defence of your disorder. It is what she wants, but it is not good. She must push to get the baby out and she cannot push hard enough unless she wails."

From his perch outside her door, he had heard only muffled moans emitting from Elizabeth, not the strong screams of childbirth lore. When his sister was born, he was not yet twelve. Yet, he remembered quite vividly his mother's searing cries during Georgiana's birth. Elizabeth had told him Jane would not scream out in her pain because she knew Bingley could not bear to hear her. He knew Elizabeth would do no less.

Doctor Carothers would but think as Jane, "It is the only way she can draw upon the strength she must."

At this, Darcy closed his eyes and turned away, the back of his hand to his lips. He put his other hand upon his hip and stood motionless for what to Jane seemed an eternity. Then, perchance the words finally obtained, he went into Elizabeth's room alone.

She lay upon her side facing the door. Pale, her hair soaked with perspiration, she raised her hand as if to shoo him away once more, but it dropped uselessly back to the bed. Kneeling, he took her enfeebled hand and kissed it.

"I am told that if you do not cry out, you cannot push the baby out, Lizzy. Be not stoic in defence of me. I will not have it. Do you hear me, Lizzy? I will not have it."

At this well-used demand, she looked at him and very nearly smiled. Recognising his own ridiculousness, he might have as well, but the peril of the situation reclaimed such a notion with dispatch.

"You are too weak to push the baby out unless you scream. I shall be outside your door. I beg of you, howl, beshrew, anything. I promise you, I shall not be affronted."

At the notion of him bidding her to curse, she did smile and gathered enough strength to squeeze his hand. He kissed her forehead and, only with the utmost reluctance, took leave.

Although she cried out as he bid, whatever the temptation, "Mouse-foot!" was her most explicit profanity.

Her screams were weak, but he could hear her. And when he could not, in his own private agony, he called encouragement to her.

"Scream so I can hear you, Lizzy!"

And once again, he could hear her calling his name.

In the library, Bingley and Fitzwilliam sat mute. They listened to the screams that even Pemberley's thick walls could not muffle. In time, Bingley took notice that Fitzwilliam had gone. Although his senses too begged him flee, he could not. As long as Jane stayed with Elizabeth, so did he abide. However, it was not with compleat composure. For as he paced the room, he looked through the open door across the corridor. There Mrs. Reynolds sat at the great table, her hands over her ears.

Jane sat in torturous disquiet next to her sister's bed. Betwixt Elizabeth at her side and Darcy in the passageway, it was compleatly indiscernible which wailing bore the greatest pain.

Sometime before dusk, Elizabeth's cries silenced. Darcy sat in frozen horror in his chair until Jane came out to tell him a baby had been borne dead of Elizabeth.

"Lizzy survives," she said quietly.

Jane followed him into her room and placed the baby boy in his arms. He held their child on behalf of his wife.

In time, Jane gently but firmly lifted the lifeless baby from him. Hannah changed the bloody linens beneath Elizabeth and brought a basin of water. Jane returned, intending to cleanse her sister.

Darcy motioned both Hannah and Jane aside, and with tender strokes, sponged the blood from her himself. Jane retreated to the corner of the room, for she believed herself intruding upon a moment of uncommon intimacy.

Thus tended, Elizabeth lay there in the freshly made bed, stomach then vacant, hair brushed smooth and spread out across her pillow. As he sat next to her, his fist yet gripping the hairbrush, it seemed to him an almost perverse serenity, as if nothing horrific had come to pass. But that tragedy had befallen was betrayed by the shallow, shuddering breaths she took. And then, for one, agonisingly extended moment her slow, rhythmic respiration became indiscernible.

The stifled weeping Jane and Hannah had been issuing from the cranny beyond the chimneypiece ceased. All held their breath and feared the worst.

"Lizzy!" he cried, and shook the mattress fiercely as if to awaken her from the clutch of eternal sleep.

Jane and Hannah both ran to the end of the bed. He thought to put his ear to her heart. As if in answer to the percussion his fit of anguish incited, her chest again struggled to rise. Then again. He held her hand, laid his head next to hers, and began to sob.

Jane sank to the floor. Hannah fled the room.

The house was deathly quiet, befitting the circumstance. Bingley and Jane occupied a bed in a guestroom, lying across it fully dressed save for their shoes. Fearing to move her, Darcy lay by Elizabeth's side in the room of labour and held her hand to his cheek. But sleep was denied him, for every time he closed his eyes he dreamed, and his dreams were nightmares of screams: Elizabeth's, his mother's. They became indistinguishable and unbearable. He awoke, and then dozed, and in his exhaustion, he began to think he might be going mad.

Near dawn, his dreams again awoke him. He reached out for her only to find Elizabeth was not beside him. In a panic, he blinked his eyes wildly in an attempt to see her in the darkened room.

Where she had found the strength to rise, he could not imagine. Nevertheless, he saw the door ajar, rose, and peered out. His heart leapt into his throat when he saw her in a bloodied gown swaying unsteadily at the head of the stairs. Heart pounding, he walked to her quietly, fearing he might startle her. He took her hand.

Elizabeth turned and, her voice echoing eerily, bid him, "Darcy, where is our baby?"

In a choked voice, he said softly, "Come with me, dearest Lizzy. Come with me."

Gently, he lifted her into his arms and carried her back to bed. Then, a precautionary arm firmly draped across her, he lay down beside her once again, but dared not to enter even a tenuous slumber.

When morning came and Elizabeth did not open her eyes, it puzzled the doctor. He intoned dire possibilities to Darcy. Much to the surprise of all, Darcy refused to listen to calamitous predictions.

He knew her breathing to be shallow, but it was steady. He believed she simply could not bear to face what had yet to be reckoned, and waited for time to render her strong enough to accept what she could not change.

The baby was to be buried in the private cemetery next to the Pemberley Chapel used but for baptisms, funerals, and silent reflection. Thither came Elizabeth's family. Unrehearsed in the rituals of sorrow as they were, the entire Bennet clan was uncharacteristically subdued. Obtuse as she sometimes could be, even Mrs. Bennet knew not to impose her position of grieving grandmother and solicitous mother upon those about her. Indeed, her lawn handkerchief remained unfluttered and consigned to her dress sleeve (except upon the occasions it was used to dab at the corner of her eyes).

The dolorous climate of the house was unrelenting. Elizabeth was yet unconscious, and her husband stood tenacious watch over her. Other than to offer the briefest condolences, no one but Jane ventured conversation with him. It was only Jane who dared to embrace that impenetrable man. It was she alone who was admitted.

The cemetery had rested the Darcy family members for centuries. But until that cold morning, few would have described its tree-canopied, vine-entwined location as desolate. When the baby's tiny coffin was laid to rest there, however, that was the single description that came to those who sought to characterise it. The ritual was brief, but not just because of the chill. Words were spoken, prayers offered, the more ostentatious accoutrements of death having been eschewed by Mr. Darcy. Just a single death knell sounded. Nevertheless, it echoed an interminably long time.

When the service concluded, all but Mr. Bennet and Darcy returned to the house. They paused at the lych-gate. The baby had been named Bennet Fitzwilliam Darcy and it was not lost upon Mr. Bennet that his daughter's condition required such a decision to have been consigned to her husband. Mr. Bennet's usual detachment abandoned, they stood silently for a time alone, the wind causing a chill far beyond what it should.

In time, Elizabeth's father spoke, but could not bring himself to look upon his son-in-law as he did, "I trust you to do whatever my Lizzy requires of you."

Mr. Bennet's shoulders betrayed a strong intake of breath, then he continued, stammering, "Elizabeth is a singular young woman…she loves you dearly."

Upon recollecting what Elizabeth had said to him when he questioned whether a man of such unpleasant temperament was a suitable husband for her, Mr. Bennet issued a brief smile.

Turning to Darcy, he explained his unexpected humour, "She assured me once I came to know you as she did, I should find you perfectly amiable. I dare say she was right." It was barely audible when he turned his gaze back to the small barrow and said, "Lizzy is always right."

Darcy felt a particular bond with Mr. Bennet, one beyond their shared love of his daughter. For he was certain that the aloofness so ingrained in Mr. Bennet's character was a defence to buffer himself from the intemperate doings of certain members of his family. Detachment and restraint as a defence was something of which Darcy had intimate acquaintance.

Mr. Bennet personified the man he might have become had he married injudiciously. Just richer and more arrogant. The thought infected him with an unlikely wave of empathy. The single man he had ever embraced had been his own father, but Darcy impulsively embraced Mr. Bennet then. His father-in-law returned it, then coughed, obviously flustered by the unexpected gesture. Both stood in awkward silence for another half-minute, thereupon Mr. Bennet coughed again and then patted Darcy upon the back.

"Come along then, son," he said. "We must return."

Dismal days, small comfort.

Elizabeth's continued lack of improvement set Dr. Carothers talking of leeches or searing. Having remained peculiarly collected until this notion seized the doctor, Darcy resisted with considerable vehemence, denouncing such measures as barbaric. He would not allow her to be bled nor burned.

"Elizabeth will heal in her own good time."

Hence, it was less jubilation than a profound relief to him when Elizabeth awakened but a few mornings later. She announced her re-admittance into consciousness and harsh reality with a simple act. She grasped her husband's fingers as they held her hand.

The Bennet family, with all good intentions, planned to stay at Pemberley until Elizabeth's health was no longer in jeopardy. Once she was awake, Darcy was inclined to believe that Elizabeth would recuperate more quickly in quiet, for she was still quite weak. With Jane's assurance that she would not forsake her sister's side, Mr. Bennet reluctantly agreed. Darcy and Jane both knew Mrs. Bennet's shrill presence would not benefit Elizabeth's recuperation.

The members of her family Elizabeth held dearest, Darcy found esteem for as well. Jane was a jewel, precious to his wife and therefore to himself. He had grown to be fond of her father, regardless of the breach of conjugal obligation Mr. Bennet displayed toward his wife—for his wife was, after all, Mrs. Bennet.

It was a trial, but he had even come to accept Mrs. Bennet (he did so only by employing the proverb about teaching a pig to sing). Mrs. Bennet was to be endured. Mary was plain and didactic, but almost tolerable. Catherine was still silly, but becoming more promising in Lydia's absence.

Lydia, however, was a young woman for whom he could find no redeeming quality whatsoever. And that assessment was not reached only for her being the wife of Wickham. This stern judgement was not to diminish.

Amidst the considerable dither, fuss, and ado engendered by the organising of the Bennets' trunks, Lydia's grating voice could be heard. So insistent was her whine, it caught the attention of someone quite determined not to listen.

Darcy had been striding down the corridor, head down, hands clasped behind his back, staring diligently at the pattern upon the carpet he followed. Lydia's peevish complaints and Mrs. Bennet's grating responses wafted out upon the landing and unto his ears.

He stopped abruptly. As a personal rule, his step would have quickened under the threat of imminent convergence with Lydia or Mrs. Bennet. Therefore, it is understood that it was the nature of the discourse that compelled him to halt.

"Mama," pouted Lydia, "this simply is so unfair! I have just spent far too much upon confinement gowns [for Lydia was with child again] and now I have to have more made in black. Even if one may wear white weepers, I look horrid in black. And for what? 'Tisn't as if my father has died, or my own child. The baby was not even really a baby, being born dead as it was, so why must we mourn so unrelentingly? Lizzy gives me hardly any money to help us as it is and you know we are always beyond our means. She probably will not even be well enough to see to funds for me and I have to dress in black as well! 'Tis all so unfair!"

Mrs. Bennet responded, "Dear Lydia! You look quite lovely in black! And now that Lizzy has returned to her senses, she will see to your stipend! Do not fret so, dear. It will leave you with a wrinkle betwixt your brows!"

It was abhorrence aplenty merely to learn that Wickham's loins and Lydia's womb had united in begetting yet another offspring. But to overhear the additional vituperation clearly rattled Darcy's notion of what physical harm a gentleman would or would not impose upon a female—even a female relation of his wife. As he stood in glowering contemplation of the possibility of throttling them both, he was espied by Lydia. The deterioration of the expression upon her countenance when she realised she had been overheard was swift. And to Darcy, quite exquisite.

It was violence enough. He strode on.

However, as he did, he shook his head. Lydia had revealed not just her condition, but that Elizabeth had been giving her money surreptitiously. This was of no particular vexation to him, for he knew well it came from her own modest income and not by way of Pemberley coffers. Elizabeth often had chastised herself for lacking Jane's Christian charity. Although Elizabeth despised Lydia's husband and knew well that her financial shortfall did not come by way of capricious chance, she helped her nevertheless.

It displayed a level of generosity far grander than he knew he could have mustered.

With considerable restraint of temper by their host, the house cleared of most of the guests without incidental bloodshed. Jane, of course, stayed on, accompanied by Bingley. Fitzwilliam too felt the need to remain close at hand.

Col. Fitzwilliam stayed on at Pemberley in spite of the fact that Whitemore was but an hour away. It was as if he had lost his own will in the matter. It was clear he was not particularly needed. He stayed because of his own need, not another's.

Since his return from his sojourn in the Spanish peninsula, a debilitating gloom had overtaken him.

The ferocity of the fight against the French in Portugal was successful, but the countryside and its people had paid a hefty toll. Under the pall of that misery, and suffering a lead ball imbedded in his rib cage, he had been anxious to return to the peace of Derbyshire County. There he meant to repair from both his physical trauma and the emotional tax of witnessing so much death and destruction. The peccability of surviving war when many fellow officers had not was intolerable.

To return unwhole of body and mind, only to learn of the murder and mayhem that had occurred at home whilst he was gone, was devastating. And to come to understand that those he held most dear had been terrorised because of his inaction, lay waste to what little heartsease he yet had managed to squirrel away.

In time, the piece of shrapnel worked its way out. Too, he eventually understood from whence his melancholia brewed. Such wisdom, however, was not obtained with dispatch. First, he would have to suffer considerable self-recrimination because he alone had seen the ogre Reed's lascivious leer at Elizabeth and had not called him out.

Elizabeth's convalescence was not brisk. The restoration of her health demanded she keep to her bed. Had it not, Darcy guessed she would have hibernated there regardless.

Unable to mourn for her child, she did not once inquire of him. It took no professor of philosophy to convince her husband that she was still in emotional jeopardy because of that refusal. He knew they needed to talk of it, but had not the slightest notion of how to broach the subject, nor any words of comfort if he did. In his uncertainty, he reverted to the familiarity of reticence. He stayed close, but quiet, despairing for his failing.

Gradually, her body grew stronger. Her spirit, however, did not. The eyes that had once danced so provocatively when they had lit upon him had turned leaden.

Most frightening was the solemnity that had engulfed her. She sat in silence, staring through the lattice of the casement into the distance. She did not smile, nor did she weep. The one revelation of despair was the handkerchief she knotted ceaselessly about her fingers.

With each of Jane's attempts to draw conversation from her about the tragedy, she simply turned her head to the window as if she did not hear.

As if he somehow refused Elizabeth's mind to suffer more than his own, Darcy found new territory upon which to agonise.

The baby had been large even for a month early. Dr. Carothers had said those very words. Darcy saw his own impressive height and frame, of which he had held himself quite proud, as accusation that he was the perpetrator of Elizabeth's torment.

Hence, he tortured himself unremittingly with the notion he had impregnated her with a baby too large for her to deliver. For the first time, he thought of Elizabeth as not simply the woman he loved, but the woman who had to bear his children. He had always thought of her as nothing less than healthy and robust. Her rosy complexion and full bosom might suggest her hardy and nubile, but he knew well too, she was also fine-boned and narrow-hipped. The succulent tightness of her womanhood from which he had so revelled in pleasure should have forewarned them of this danger. But he had been too blinded by desire. Would he have had the self-constraint to practise withdrawal or even abstinence had he known the future? That was not a question he pondered, for regret and remorse demanded all his time. He was terrified yet that having another baby might kill her. He could not bear to query the physician if Elizabeth might have been able to have born the baby safely had it not been breech.

Eventually Darcy understood that Jane's solicitous attentions, not his, engendered a more expeditious convalescence for Elizabeth. The hovering spectre of his private anguish aided her recovery no better than it had her labour. Thus, for a few hours at a time, he allowed himself coaxed from her bedside. Bingley and Fitzwilliam were bent upon a little sport in the field upon his behalf.

They knew little else to do. Even in the knowledge of how deeply Darcy loved Elizabeth, neither would have believed that Darcy, a man of strength and fortitude beyond any other they could name, could be so broken by the tragedy.

Whilst they awaited his company one evening, they talked of it.

Bingley said, "'Tis not that this is not the most grievous of all life's many sorrows, for it certainly is. But Elizabeth survives, and they shall have other children."

Only he and his brother had survived from their mother's four births, hence Fitzwilliam hesitantly agreed, "True, no one knows of a family, neither earl nor cottager, that has not lost children."

It was unspoken, but both knew as perilous as infancy was to a baby, childbirth was to the mother. It could be surmised that Darcy and Elizabeth might look upon it as fortunate, under the circumstances, that Elizabeth was not taken too. In a particularly philosophical turn, Bingley very nearly remarked that Darcy's seeming obsession about the loss of the baby and Elizabeth's health, which was obviously improving, might stem from never having been deprived of anything he had ever wanted. Fortune allowed him to glance to the darkened doorway. Darcy's visage was shadowed, but discernible. Bingley held his tongue.

Fitzwilliam observed the alteration in Bingley's expression and his eyes moved from Bingley to the door at his back. Darcy stepped into the room. The men were silent. Darcy did not reveal whether he heard their remarks or not, but spoke just of the weather, Bingley's daughter's latest words, and asked Fitzwilliam when he might be well enough to return to his regiment. After a leisurely partaking of a glass or two of claret, the gentlemen decided to retire. Fitzwilliam took the stairs but Bingley had not yet quit the room, howbeit he had taken steps in that direction, when Darcy called after him. When Bingley turned, the look upon his friend's face very nearly made him flee. But not in fear.

"You are right, Bingley, I have Elizabeth, or at least she is alive. However, unless you have had to endure what we have, I should think it most impolitic to make judgement to what lengths grief should be taken. I pray you and Jane never have reason for better understanding that the frequency of a tragedy does not diminish the wound when it is your own."

Bingley was shaken. He did not fear his friend's wrath, not really fear it. But to know something could so easily overtake a couple's happiness, as it had for a union as strong as that of Elizabeth and Darcy, made him shiver in apprehension for Jane and the next birth she would face.

"What was it?" Elizabeth bid matter-of-factly.

"What was it?" Darcy repeated, uncertain he had heard her correctly.

"Boy or girl?" she asked.

"A boy," he answered quietly, "named for your father."

With studied deliberation, she replaced her teacup into its saucer. The censored subject was finally accessed. Daring not let it slip away, he asked if she wanted him to carry her to the gravesite. She nodded once, thereupon the wall of composure she had so diligently maintained shattered into a maelstrom of tears. As she fell face down upon the mattress, sobs began to rack her body. She was heaving as he picked her up and turned her to him, holding her tightly to his chest.

It was a not an unwelcome phenomenon. Anything was welcome to release her from her relentless melancholia. As she clung to him, Elizabeth had no notion that the weeping was not hers singularly.

"I could not do it. I let your baby die…" she sobbed again and again.

He soothed and shushed. In time, she listened.

In the hour they lay, a measure of healing took place. Eventually, her tears were exhausted, emotion spent. With her heaviest cloak about her, he carried her down the stairs and out of the house. The servants observing this sight stopped their chores and went to the windows in silence as the master carried the mistress up the path to the baby's grave. Unbeknownst to him, the stone had just been set. Thus, they saw it first together.

He knelt, allowing her to place a small bouquet of winter roses at the base of the marble. Neither cried nor spoke. There seemed nothing to be said.

That first spring after Hannah came into Mrs. Darcy's employ was a heady propo-
sition, indeed. She had never once ventured beyond Derbyshire in her brief life.
London had always seemed an impossibility. Nevertheless, when the time came she
boarded the second coach with Anne, Mrs. Annesley, and Goodwin without hesitation. Albeit she did not quite release a full breath until after they had reached the out-
skirts of the fabled town.

She had heard tales of London from her third brother, who had once travelled
there. He claimed it so harsh a place that fine people stepped over dead ones upon the
sidewalk without even looking down. The streets of London upon which they travelled to reach the Darcy house were quite wide and inviting. They bore no dead bodies that Hannah could see. There were, however, a few darker concourses leading away
from this main avenue that might possibly contain these reputed corpses.

She narrowed her eyes as they passed each shaded street, telling herself she did not
want to spot one. She peered quite conscientiously in want of not, regardless.

Interrupting her inspection, Goodwin asked her just what she was trying to spy.
That startled her from her contemplation, and she shook her head stupidly. She could
not recollect Goodwin ever initiating a conversation with her.

Those were to be the first and last words she heard from him for a time; the disembarkation in London sent them all into a tailspin of activity. Within this household maelstrom, a comeuppance occurred, the recipient none other than the houseman, Mr. Smeads.

As Hannah held Mrs. Reynolds in less than close affection, it was of no great surprise to her that she was even less enamoured of the son. For a reason unbeknownst
to Hannah, London staff literally smirked upon invoking his name.

It appeared Mr. Darcy was unhappy with him for some misdeed. Hannah asked
Goodwin if he knew what had come to pass. Goodwin answered in the negative (a
grunt, meaning either "no" or "I refuse to answer," which one Hannah could but surmise). If Goodwin's curiosity did not coincide with her own, she found more willing
mouths amongst the chambermaids to tell the history of the bedcloth.

Admittedly, it was Hannah who, much in want of repaying such salacious information, told them about the coachman Reed and that Mr. Darcy had thrashed him
and cast him out. She was a little guilt-ridden for enlarging this tale from a single
strike to a thrashing, but her audience was so in want of Reed being thrashed, she
feared she simply could not disappoint them. (And she would have repaid the rather
rude look Goodwin gifted her for gossiping by her sticking out her tongue at him, had
not her conscience already been grieving her.)

Having situated herself in the good graces of the London staff with her tale of Reed,
Hannah basked in the fineness of the city house. In time, the newness of her adventure

wore off and she begot a bit of homesickness. But if she busied herself inside and did not look out upon the bustling streets, she could convince her mind she was not far from home. If she did look up from her chores and out the window, however, it was a tremendous task to retrieve her attention from the fine carriages and distinguished-looking people.

At first, her sleep suffered from the excitement, but her appetite was unaffected. As at Pemberley, the town help partook their meals just a little less grandly than did family. But at Pemberley, Hannah remembered longingly, no one stood about checking to see how much food one had taken upon one's plate. In Derbyshire, people partook until they were full, period. One might think Mr. Smeads fancied their dinner had been pilfered from his own plate, as parsimonious as the man was with a potato. She huffed about it diligently, but in silence.

If Mr. Smeads was an impediment to Hannah's culinary consumption, he had no weight in other matters. For she was lady-maid to Mrs. Darcy and it was Mrs. Darcy and no other who gave Hannah instruction. Hannah had not taken up any airs even in so high a position as she held whilst in the country, but town affected her pride. Was it born of the very impressive coach in which they rode, or the looks that coach affected from passers-by, she did not question. She knew only she felt quite the fine lady in London, the distinction lessened just by her country frocks. And that small consternation was put to rest upon the trip to the dressmakers with the Darcy ladies.

Whilst they were fitted, Hannah sat in a straight-backed chair observing for a time. But the expected hour turned into two and she rose to stretch her legs by wandering about the shop.

There was a drapery in Lambton. Or more accurately, a shop that sold fabric. But Hannah had never seen, nor even imagined, a place such as the one they now visited. Great bolts of fine fabric lined one wall; another appeared to bear nothing but lace. She fingered one of the prettier pillow-laces, saw one of the clerks frown at her, and put it down, suddenly certain she had been found out a fraud. Clearly, that was what she must be. For her life seemed far too chimerical not to be a fairy tale. In such a store as she was, in the employ of Mrs. Darcy, and in London.

The clerk continued to frown at her so decidedly, Hannah lifted her arms and looked about herself wondering just what manner of disorder she had caused to invite such a look. Finally, the clerk said, "Ahem," and motioned toward the activity. Mrs. Darcy was calling Hannah's name and in her idleness, she had not heard her. Penitent, she hurried to her mistress.

Mrs. Darcy and Georgiana had dressed and stood waiting for her to move betwixt them. The dressmaker told her to stand upon the stool and two assistants started to unbutton her dress, at which Hannah grabbed her bodice to wrest it from their unexpected assault.

"Aye don't 'low no diddlin' with me corset buttons!" she exclaimed.

Realising Hannah had never been helped from her clothes before, Mrs. Darcy assured her it was all quite proper. Hence, Hannah dropped her hands and reclaimed her regard for her position.

Mrs. Darcy had the frowning clerk retrieve the lace that Hannah had fingered, announcing it would adorn Hannah's new dress. As a matter of convenience, Mrs.

Darcy suggested Hannah select a half dozen muslin fabrics to be transformed into day dresses (and one black worsted, for Hannah did not own a mourning dress and death occasionally struck when one was unavailed of a seamstress).

Hannah no longer had any doubt of her gentility. It was one conceit to be lady-maid to the wife of the most illustrious person in Derbyshire, quite another to be the same in London.

When they returned home burdened with hatboxes (Hannah had two new bonnets herself), her exalted state of mind led her to order Smeads a little too disdainfully to have the boxes carried upstairs. His response made her reconsider whether she would want him to tell his mother how she had spoken to him. She hastily picked up two boxes, as if she intended to carry them up all along.

Tossing her head gaily, she trilled, "If you please."

Smeads frowned at her much as had the clerk in the store, but he did have a man carry the boxes for her. Hannah thought, with practise, she might just be able to carry off this hoax of position. Perhaps she would never, ever be uncovered as the country charlatan that she knew she was. It would have seemed there was no word or deed that could have disturbed her happiness once she had thwarted Smeads even in so small a deception as the bandboxes. London invited a smugness in her demeanour she began to believe was unchristian. Hence, summer's end saw Hannah's pretension of grandeur fall away as well.

She would have returned to Pemberley just as she had left it, a happy country girl of great luck, had not such violence and outrage transgressed their party.

The closest Hannah had been to evil was witnessing a thief swipe a shoat. Or so she would once have said was anyone interested in hearing what passed for evil to Hannah. At the moment he levelled his gun at her, she had seen evil personified in the face of Tom Reed.

It was not a great leap to believe that man of the devil even before he stole Mrs. Darcy. When Hannah looked down the sight of his gun, her eyes first focused on his. It was possible they glowed yellow. It seemed an eternity before the black hole of the business end of the gun barrel became clear. But when it did, a mad scream, shrill enough to shimmy the leaves, reverberated through the trees. And, then, in that heart-beat, ceased. Hannah could not recollect from whence it had come.

If her scream had been frightened from her mind, she most surely wished the rest had been with it. She, Anne, and Miss Darcy stood in the road and wept. They had no choice but to cry. They could not will themselves otherwise.

Hannah did not stop crying until they had reached Pemberley, only stifling her tears in occupation of tending Mrs. Darcy. She had thought that such tribulations had been conquered until Mr. Darcy banished her once the bath had been drawn. That was the absolute nadir, she had believed then. But times yet to be endured showed her she only thought she understood grief.

When her lady's baby was dead-born, Hannah stayed in the room as long as she must. But the strain of the hours spent, the pain endured, and the recognition of pain to come was more than she could bear. Mrs. Bingley repaired to Mr. Bingley's embrace. Hannah, however, felt frightfully alone.

When she came onto the landing, she saw Goodwin standing opposite. His weight was resting upon his hands and those gripped the railing with white knuckled ferocity. Even so, she started to walk toward him. But he turned away.

In time, she would wonder why he had turned. Was it to deny her, or to deny his own sentiments? At that time, she did not think of it. She blindly and loudly ran down the stairs heading for the door. Possibly, she sought her mother, but it was just a feeling, not a conscious thought.

Had Mrs. Reynolds not caught her and hugged her to her bosom, and had Hannah not felt the tears upon the old woman's face, she was uncertain how far she might have fled, for her mother had been dead six years.

When Jane's second child was born, Elizabeth, as she had before, went to Kirkland Hall for her sister's laying-in. Yet in self-proclaimed ward and watch of his emotionally fragile wife, Mr. Darcy joined the small party of relatives awaiting the birth.

It was a fecund environment, for Bingley's second sister, Mrs. Hurst, had finally wrested enough of her husband's attention from drink, food, and the hunt to have a lap-full herself. Ever vigilant for future worry, she flittered nervously about Jane, collecting her every murmur of discomfort as a knell for her own anticipated suffering.

Jane, even when in the midst of full labour, patted her sister-in-law's hand in reassurance, "There, there, Louisa, all will be well."

If the happy circumstances of wedlock and motherhood for Jane and Louisa chagrined Bingley's elder sister, Caroline, she did not overtly betray it. For during the parturient watch at Kirkland, Caroline Bingley paid Jane every attention and lamented her every twinge of pain. However, the very vehemence of her professed devotion persuaded Elizabeth that Caroline's fondness for Jane was less than genuine.

For unmarried yet, Miss Bingley sluiced about her company—consisting of three married men, two expectant women, and Elizabeth—in full husband-hunting regalia. Bedecked she was with a cherry-coloured, tabby dress, all furbelow and brocatelle (announcing more *de trop* than *au courant*). With every passing year, it appeared she added another adornment to her already festooned-to-the-gills costume (at some point Elizabeth fully expected her accoutrements to keep her from heaving about at all). Ever in the want of social opportunity to promote herself, she appeared for all the world ready to pounce upon the first titled, or at least landed, nabob who accidented through the door.

All her folderol went for naught. With Jane in confinement, the balls that Bingley loved to accommodate had ceased. What few gentlemen were about were out for a little sport in the field and none ever seemed to be bachelors (or even had sickly wives). Indeed, the entire length of Jane's pregnancy must have been interminable for a bedizened *poseur* like Caroline Bingley. Pretending affectionate concern whilst enduring a seeming disinterest over an ever-lengthening spinster-hood must have been a dogged test for her, indeed.

As the time drew nearer for Jane's delivery, Caroline took up an impatient pace to and fro the room even before Bingley instituted his own measured, if nervous, stride. Caroline's abrupt little steps sounded to Elizabeth less of familial solicitude than social frustration. Ever benign, Bingley, however, saw it differently.

"Caroline is so very fond of Jane," he announced. "Perhaps not as much as yourself, Elizabeth. But as dearly as a sister."

At this little treacling colloquy, Darcy looked over at Elizabeth. She had been slicing dessert, but stopped and stood poised with a cake knife in her hand. They both looked at the devoted Caroline, who hummed as she inspected her nails. Then Darcy's gaze leapt back to his wife, possibly expecting to see Caroline's trepanned cranium creating a crimson stain upon the carpet at their feet.

Surprisingly, Elizabeth was not considering mortal retribution for Caroline Bingley. Nor did she intend to gainsay Bingley's misapprehension of his sister's heart. Although Elizabeth believed Caroline was cold as charity, she had begun to feel some sympathy for her. If she had found no one to love her, it was because she had no love to offer. It was likely she might eventually find a titled husband in need of her funds and a match would be made. It was a shame, really. Caroline's mission was a needless one, for she did not own the usual argument in favour of affectionless matrimony, that of being poor.

Jane's labour was brief and fruitful, and mid-morning Sunday, she did, indeed, produce an heir. Fittingly, the boy-child would be called after his father. Little Charles was blonde as was Eliza, and, in proof of Bingley's pronouncement that he was the heartiest child that had ever been born, screamed loud and long.

"Well, I will agree he has the finest set of lungs of any child I have ever heard," said Darcy, slapping Bingley upon the back.

Mr. Hurst inquired if there was to be any sport at all that day and Louisa took to her bed in exhaustion of Jane's ordeal. Caroline clucked at the baby several times then sat in a side chair, finding ample entertainment in playing with her multitude of bracelets.

Jane was weak from the birth, and Elizabeth was anxious to have her rest. However, she could not, for Bingley insisted upon carrying his new son about. Although not as roundly soused as when Eliza was born, he had sustained far too much fortification for there to be no worry of him dropping little Charles. Working in concert, the Darcys finally corralled Bingley in a sitting room long enough for Elizabeth to rescue the baby.

"I say Darcy, have you ever seen such a handsome manikin in your life?" Bingley slurred.

Wresting his attention, Darcy assured him that he had not, whilst Elizabeth fled with the youngling. Elizabeth repaired the baby to his mother's arms, jesting about Bingley's inebriated celebration of fatherhood. Notwithstanding her seemingly good spirits, Jane fretted yet that memories of her dead-born child might be reawakened. Inevitably, Jane's countenance betokened her heedfulness of such a possibility. Hence, Elizabeth felt compelled to reassure her such was not the case. In the course of the many repetitions of this declaration, Elizabeth began to believe it herself.

Looking upon the red, squirming newborn, it was not of loss and death she pondered, but of all the possibilities of life. So engrossed was she in revelation, she peered into the newborn's face with a keenness that was neither immoderate nor cursory. This was scrutinised by those about her with well-nigh the same intensity as she looked upon the babe.

All of which engendered several misconceptions.

Firstly, that she was unsettled by the birth; secondly, that she was unawares that everyone was eyeing her so closely; and lastly, that when she said she wanted to take leave for Pemberley, it was because of her disquiet, not theirs. All these misty, inchoate suspicions that all was not well in the household of Elizabeth's emotions were most unfortunate.

The ride home was oddly silent. This muzziness about why she wanted to take leave led her husband to believe it was because she was despondent. Elizabeth, however, worried why everyone looked upon her so peculiarly. Darcy spent the entire trip in quiet despair over his wife's seeming melancholia, Elizabeth in bewattled contemplation of why all and sundry seemed to believe she was dicked-in-the-nob.

By the time they arrived at Pemberley, the incessant wambling of the coach and his irredeemable wretchedness had rendered Darcy both morose and ill. All the jouncing about had simply made Elizabeth, well—randy.

Instead of following his wife upstairs, Darcy went to the wine cabinet, filled a glass and sat glumly at the end of the fully set great table. He partook first one sip, and then another. He tossed off his jacket, tore loose his collar. Gradually, his stomach was becalmed, but not his unease.

He had been considering returning to sleep in the bedroom of his bachelorhood. This not because he did not want to lie with Elizabeth, but because he did.

However, lying beside her each night yet not in her embrace was becoming not only more difficult, but physically excruciating.

It was not that she denied him. She had not. He had not asked.

Connubial pleasures seemed an unconscionable request by one nagged as relentlessly as he by the reasonable fear that another baby might kill her. Given the choice of her life or her passion, there was little indecision. He would rather remain celibate and childless than lose her.

Alternatively, he could use withdrawal, that time-honoured test of a gentleman's mettle. He understood it successful if used diligently. Could he trust himself to withdraw from the lush confines of her womanhood at the very brink of achievement?

Each and every time?

As a matter of life or death, he probably could.

That was not certain enough. It would not do. To insure her safety, he must not chance what was probable. They must abstain entirely. He must not only be strong, he must be impervious to the temptation. Thus, he sat in an uncharacteristic slump pondering these harsh truths in the same large chair from whence he presided, with considerable stature, over their supper parties.

The light was dim. The central candelabra had only a few candles yet burning, the rest had flamed out. He slouched there in the shadows, staring into the glass in his hand as if it were a quartz sphere. Finding his fortune untold, he emptied it, reached for the decanter and filled it again.

Elizabeth was barefoot; hence, he did not hear her walk up behind him. When she put her arm across his chest, he was so surprised as to slosh some wine from his glass.

"My intention was not to catch you so unawares," she apologized, then asked, "Shall you retire soon?"

"In a bit," he said as he set down his glass.

With a spontaneity he had not witnessed for some time, she plopped down upon his lap. Her legs draped over the arm of the chair, and she dangled them fetchingly.

Very fetchingly.

As he buried his face in her hair for the first time in months, a small little soughing sound came from the back of his throat. Not understanding that it was a moan born of a superb attempt to frustrate lust, not an announcement of its unleashing, she pressed her lips against his throat. This time his groan was more pronounced and convoluted in motive.

"Did I ever tell you how very much I love your neck?" she asked in what could only be described as a purr.

Not trusting his voice, he could do no better than give a shake of his head. His voice might have been suspect, but nothing else about him was. For he tangled her hair about his fingers and slowly drew her head back, determined to expose the lips that issued that exceedingly seductive utterance. Thereupon he, perhaps unwisely, endeavoured to cease their seduction by kissing them deeply. All the while, her fingers ploughed furrows in his hair.

Good intentions losing a hard fought battle with proud flesh, he drew himself from their kiss long enough to hear his own ragged breath. Elizabeth used this fleeting respite to tug his shirttail loose, sneak her hand beneath it, and up across his chest. Seeking to belay its tantalising waltz, he grasped her hand through his shirt and held it still. He knew if she did not cease, there would not be enough blood remaining in his brain (he was quite certain it had all pooled in his groin) to say what he knew he must.

"Lizzy, I fear if I give in to desire…"

"You do not fancy my father will call you out…?"

"I am quite serious, Lizzy!"

She became quiet. And still.

"Another baby might take your life," he said solemnly. "I simply could not bear it if…"

He started to say more, but fell silent. It was not a great leap for her to understand what he was telling her. Had he been able to look, he might have seen her countenance reflect that she, indeed, did know precisely what he meant and all that it implied.

Carefully considering all that he had said, it was a long moment before she spoke. "I think you must agree that a choice of that nature should be mine and mine alone."

She stood up, facing him, her hips and hands resting upon the edge of the table.

Thereupon, she reached out, gently stroking his cheek with the back of her fingers as if to soften what she said.

"Surely, even you, Mr. Darcy, do not possess such wanton hubris as to question God's will?"

Not really expecting an answer, she waited a moment regardless, and then looked into his eyes.

"I should sooner die than not be a wife to you."

He, however, could not hold such a gaze, so much was at stake and she gave him so little choice. As he thought of that, his hands found her thighs, then slid to her hips. Those his embrace engulfed and he pressed his face against her abdomen.

The only warning he issued that a decision had been reached was the nip he took at her stomach. Thereupon, he stood up full. Her gaze devoured the length of that not inconsequential sight.

Had the choice been celibacy, it would have had to have been endured. But if their love was to be relished, time was a-wasting.

One swipe of his arm cleared away the crystal, rendering the table a jackleg love-bed. He pressed her back upon it. So hastily was she upended, her head barely missed a rather ornate candelabra. (It only escaped the carnage by taking a precarious tottering trip down the length of the table.)

She said, "Should we not go upstairs?"

"Yes."

That was in apparent concurrence with what they should do, but not what they would. For he did not release her.

Instead, his hands slid beneath her gown, glided over her again, and then drew her to him. By the time that he struggled his inflamed member free from his nether garments (the rigidity of his arousal and tautness of his breeches had rendered him temporarily trapped), he was in such a state of heat that prudence for possible infirmity of her innards did not come to mind. Which was perchance fortunate, in that once he obtruded them with a substantial degree of vigour, the moan she elicited was not misidentified as pain.

Rather, that sound from her was as familiar to him as her voice. Hearing it again inspirited him well-nigh to the point of pain himself. Upon such a fevered union, the rather sturdy Chippendale table began to tremble. What little crystal that had persevered through the initial assault of his long arm began to fall. Even so, the crescendo that ensued was from their passion, not the breaking glasses. However, that was not clear to a servant who transgressed onto the scene until it was too late to go undetected.

Without a pause, Darcy managed to choke out the gruff command, "Begone!"

Whoever had been there hastily retreated. As they were in great distraction, neither participant of this exceedingly well-explored act of passion cared to conjecture it might have been anyone other than old Morton.

Indeed, it was only after this fit of fever was spent that they discovered mahogany was not comfortable. He drew her back down off the table, her bottom sliding rather smoothly in their common pool of perspiration. With Elizabeth atop him, they sank back into the relative comfort of the armchair. Technically, they had been sated, but affection reigned yet. They continued to kiss until her wine-saturated gown was discovered to be a bit sticky. With a groan that this time was unmistakably exertion, he gathered her in his arms and carried her upstairs.

He did not think again of leaving her bed.

Fittingly, the first sunlight to be seen for many weeks awoke him as it streamed into the room. He raised upon one elbow and unabashedly drew the sheet from his wife's naked form.

She stirred.

At first, he smiled at such impenetrable somnolence, thereupon, quite involuntarily, recoiled as he gazed upon her. Not only was she thin, but well-nigh diaphanous. He had been sensible of her loss of appetite (he covertly inspected her half-eaten trays). But this.

Even lying in such close quarters, he had not seen how ravaged she had been in both body and soul. She looked so frail, his chastening was compleat.

How could he have ravished such a fragile flower with such vehemence?

A fluttering of eyelids announced her awakening. As he looked down upon her, she opened her eyes full and a happy dance of a smile began at the corner of her mouth. She, however, did not see happiness upon his countenance as he gazed upon her spindly frame. He looked nothing less than appalled. And he realised that directly.

Retrieving the sheet, she drew it up to her chin and stared sullenly at the ceiling, saying, "Could you not have contained your revulsion even a little?"

"Lizzy," he said, drawing her close, "how you have suffered."

Well aware that being the object of pity was possibly her least favourite pastime, he knew he bestowed it upon her at some risk.

"Are you now to return from this devastating hegira you have been thrust upon?" he asked her.

That utterance both quieted her resentment and invoked love.

"I fear my restoration demands less of me than of you."

As she said this, she stroked him in a manner that persuaded him that however weighty was his duty, it would not be remotely objectionable. Moreover, he thought he might commence this reparation forthwith. Laying himself more against her than upon, he tenderly stroked her limbs.

"You finger me as if I shall shatter at your touch. You had no such compunction last night."

"Forgive me that."

Betimes obtuseness afflicted him more keenly than at others.

It became necessary for her to disabuse him of the notion of her fragility. There were several ways she could have made him witting. She could have told him outright. But she did not.

Rather, she chose to show him.

This was accomplished by embarking an assault of his body that befitted a love-starved Amazon. Admittedly, his purblindness bade him weather this siege for a moment before he understood it was, indeed, a siege. However, when enlightment came, it was compleat.

The coupling to which he found himself party had all the single-minded intensity of their tabletop savagery, but with the benefit of no glassware. Too, the additional advantage of a soft foundation should have suppositioned. But as their passion came to fruition on the floor upon the far side of the room (and halfway under a chiffonier), that luxury must be discounted.

Finally spent once again, they both lay there upon the floor in a quivering heap. It was a few minutes before he regained his breath enough to inquire (his wits not yet gifting his senses the information that his partner in love was exceedingly hardy) of the unlikely injury to Elizabeth's health. Reasonably, but breathlessly, she assured him she was quite well, thank you.

Civilities rendered, they lay there for a few minutes more. He was unable to find any additional comment in his yet misfiring brain. Indeed, his senses had rendered no further contemplation than that the friction from the wool rug might issue a resultant rash upon his hindquarters. (He abhorred itching.)

In his silence, she reminded him, "You said you favour me coming to you."

This prompting allowed him to re-enter the realm of the functioning mind. He agreed, indeed, yes he did.

Eventually, they made an attempt to quit the floor. But this initial effort was aborted when Darcy (perchance senses yet altered) slightly misaligned their position, reared his head and struck it forthwith upon the overhanging bureau. They lay there another fifteen minutes, before venturing upright. Upon the second, the unsteadiness of their legs suggested a duo of drunken sailors but managed, nonetheless, to deposit them atop the bed. There, limbs akimbo, they collapsed in slumber.

When she awoke, she found herself quite alone. It was unusual for him to rise before her under such circumstances, coitus most often rendering him more drained (literally) than she. Hence, she allowed herself to consider that perhaps she was not so strong as she had professed. Then, as the act that had incited her fatigue came to mind, a mischievous smile overspread her face.

Indeed, it was hard for her not to think of him without overt carnality just then.

For months, he had showered her with endless and tender attention. She had been so disquieted by recent events, she had been happy just to have that. Once it had been rediscovered, however, her passion was in high colour.

Lying in resplendent satisfaction, she could think of nothing but the man and his manhood. His manhood and its lather betwixt her legs. It was glorious to be totally witting of when he spent inside her. Not once had she thought of it an act of generation. Just one of shared pleasure. If repeated carnal infusions rendered her with child, so be it. She just wanted him near. And if in that closeness, he was inside her, all the better.

She had lounged about, mooning and musing, for the better part of an hour when she heard a whistle from outside. A very loud whistle, a skirl unlike any she had ever heard from the interior of Pemberley. Indeed, it came from outside and sounded exactly the same as the two-fingered whistle of someone calling a dog.

Holding curiosity only minutely less dear than venturing outside in the all-together, she grabbed the first item of clothing discernible in the mess of covers. Prancing to the double doors of the balcony, she peered out. Again, she heard the whistle.

Eagerness to uncover just who perpetrated such an intrusion beneath her room bade her to the stone railing and look down. Whereupon, she espied her husband upon Blackjack on the turf below. He put his fingers to his mouth and let out another shrill whistle. Her countenance accomplished the considerable feat of raising one eyebrow, dropping her jaw, and shaking her head concurrently.

Of all the many and diverse talents she knew he possessed, this was the most outrageous.

Only then did she realise he had Boots saddled for her to join him. They had not ridden since…before.

She rose upon her tiptoes to lean across the wide balustrade quite unwittingly revealing to him a bedazzling sight. It would have been her premise that she looked quite silly, be-robed in his oversized shirt and her hair an unkempt scandal. All that he saw was the sun glinting off a vision in white. One whose dark hair tousled and tumbled down her shoulder as if directing his attention to just how thin the gauze of his shirt was. The darkness of her hair and the shadow of her breasts contrasted against the brilliance of the shirt in the sun. All conspired to make the healthy glow she wore from a night of love-making even rosier.

From below, his eyes made the triangular trip down her hair, across her breasts and back to her face more than once. If he cleared his throat before he entreated her to join him, it could be understood.

"Come," he beckoned hoarsely.

In answer, she put one bare leg over the rail as if she meant to jump down then and there. He put his hands over his face in feigned mortification. Thereupon, forsaking that tease, he urged Blackjack and Boots up the incline directly beneath the low balcony.

"Pray, would you dare do such a thing, Mrs. Darcy?"

A challenge such as that could not be ignored. So leap she did. He could just reach her outstretched arms and drew her onto Blackjack in front of him then over to Boots. Such was the nature of their ride that she threw one leg across Boots' withers and sat astraddle.

In defence of such daring (though he truly did not look as if to protest), she said, "At this moment, I think my costume defies any attempt at propriety. Would you not agree?"

Aiming Blackjack toward a crown of wood atop a small rise at the back of the house, their little party trailed to it. Thereupon they dismounted. In a small clearing at the crest of the hill, they sat, she betwixt his legs. Drawing her knees up to her breasts beneath his shirt she wore, she let it cover her legs and rested her fingers upon his knees. There, they crept beneath the tops of his boots.

She said, "I shall never rename my horse."

He put his arms about her and rested his chin upon her shoulder.

"I know."

This was how they sat as they looked across at the great house, the stream, the lake and beyond. Neither spoke for some time. It was never said in so many words, but both felt as if they had crossed some darkened, fiery land and had managed to come out alive, if only by each other's help.

They were scarred, but unbowed.

Georgiana leapt from poetess to novelist with such ease, it was unbeknownst to her family. Thus, Elizabeth was taken quite unawares when she set a compleated manuscript in her lap. It was not a thin work. Moreover, the publication of a novel entailed a great deal more fuss and bother than sending verse to a magazine. For this weighty endeavour, Newton Hinchcliffe was contacted.

Having forsaken his own purple prose, he thenceforward sought loftier service as a scribe for a news publication (a vocation that did not improve his standing with Mr. Darcy). His writing inclinations bent more in the direction of the inflammatory, but his connexions were impeccable. And as the single common trait he shared with his aunt was the allurement of subterfuge of any kind, he hand-carried the manuscript to a publishing house of repute. Not seeking to borrow future bother (which was by that time well-nigh a mantra for Georgiana and Elizabeth when it came to putting certain matters before Darcy), the Darcy women reasoned it best to wait for it to be accepted before assaulting the will of the Master of Pemberley.

It was a toe-tapping time of wait for both of them. Georgiana awaited word from a publisher; Elizabeth, her body. For, although it had been more than two years since the loss of the baby, Elizabeth had not yet conceived again. She did not speak of it to her husband, for he produced worry lines yet betwixt his eyebrows upon any allusion to her begetting another baby. As each fallow month passed, however, so escalated her fear that the difficulty of the breech birth had somehow rendered her barren. The physician told her only time might tell, and time seemed to be telling her naught.

As close as she and her sister were, Jane knew Elizabeth fretted for her unfruitfulness and, as was her nature, worried excessively upon her behalf. When she became *enceinte* for the third time, Jane had been disinclined even to tell Elizabeth. That, of course, would be folly, for even if she could disguise her blossoming form, she could not conceal how many children she had. Elizabeth could count.

Jane was not moved to consider such an elabourate charade because she believed her sister to be envious. Coveting was a sin and, in Jane's eyes, her dear sister Elizabeth was simply incapable of peccavi of any kind.

It was capricious nature to blame. It had bestowed an overabundance of fertility upon her (indeed, it seemed she and Charles only needed to breathe the same air for her to become with child) and cruelly slighted Elizabeth. Jane could find no way to share her good fortune with her sister save one. As she was twice, soon thrice, successfully a mother, Jane reasoned that her method of confinement must be superior to Elizabeth's. But loathe was she to speak of it. For Elizabeth had always remained peculiarly silent about the loss of her baby, this pattern having been instituted from the inception of their bereavement. Jane had respected her wishes. Nothing other than her sincerest concern would have moved Jane to broach that delicate subject to her.

She prayed upon the matter relentlessly. Finally, the decision was made. However difficult, Jane knew she could not shirk a responsibility. If it might benefit her dear sister, she would yield what wisdom she held. This decided, it was with some trepidation (and a wavering voice) that Jane embarked upon the conversation.

"Lizzy, do you suppose…I know you have your own mind about such things…but, do you suppose it was not best during your confinement to have…"

Jane's vocabulary upon this subject was even more limited than most ladies of the day, hence she (resorting to the universally accepted euphemism) gave a wag of her head in place of the unknown verb, "…uh, 'been' with your husband when you were with child?"

Jane sat hunched awkwardly, looking steadfastly at her knees, cheeks florid. It took her sister but a brief rumination before she understood what she meant.

Nonetheless, that is exactly what she asked Jane.

"Whatever do you mean?"

Even with the head waggle, both knew what she asked was not what Jane meant by "been with your husband," but why it was not best.

"Well Lizzy, 'tis said that it is bad for the baby."

"Too much jostling about?"

Elizabeth was highly amused that Jane should even bring up the subject, modest as she was about such matters.

"That," Jane said, but added, "but it is said, if a woman's insides are excited she might suffer a miscarriage."

"If her insides are excited," Elizabeth repeated. "But I did not miscarry, I was delivered of a dead child."

Saying the words chased any humour from her.

"Yes. Owing to a fright," Jane said.

Thereupon, sitting up very straight, Jane raised both eyebrows.

Elizabeth repeated these words too, if only to assure herself she was hearing correctly.

The physician had said that was why she had miscarried, owing to the fright of the "robbery." But Jane did not know that and Elizabeth could not remember being frightened once during her second confinement. The tutored sat silently waiting for the tutoress to continue.

The appointed hour had arrived for Jane finally to reveal to Elizabeth the secret she had held with such dread for so long: She Knew the Reason Elizabeth Had Lost Her Baby. She held her breath (unschooled in theatrics, Jane had no idea she had just taken a pregnant pause) until she could muster courage to expel her revelation.

"I am told that if you do 'that' when you are with child, the baby will see your husband's…" thereupon stumped for a noun, Jane paused, again instituted the head wag, then continued, "your husband's…and be frightened to be born! That is why your baby would not come out."

There. She had said it. Scientific fact.

"Oh," Elizabeth replied, quite genuinely unable to think of any additional response.

Elizabeth was, however, certain that it was the most ludicrous supposition she had ever heard. The only births she had witnessed were Jane's babies', true, but those infants' eyes came into the world quite firmly shut. Moreover, it was too dark in there for the baby to see anything if its eyes were open. Nevertheless, there sat Jane before her. And from the superior position of success, she bore the profound expression of A Woman Who Knows.

Which bade Elizabeth's consideration of absurdity begin to waffle. Perchance it was possible. Perchance carnal indulgence did cause their baby's death. Suddenly, Elizabeth felt a pang of guilt in the pit of her stomach. It subsided, but not with dispatch.

Not long after Jane quitted Pemberley for the day, Darcy espied Elizabeth sitting dejectedly in her sitting-room. He entered, walked to a chair, and sat.

"What is wrong?"

Elizabeth shook her head, less in denying anything wrong than in disbelief of what she had heard.

"Jane has told me that she knows why our baby died."

It was the first time they had spoken of it for some time. These were murky waters that even he would just as soon not wade.

"As a mere mortal, I had believed it was because he was turned breech. If Jane has uncovered something of which we were not privy, I am grateful she has decided to confide in us."

His usual laconism was dredged in more than a tinge of sarcasm. Upon some occasions, a little acrimony is understandable. Therefore, Elizabeth did not even consider reproof. Nevertheless, she felt impelled to defend Jane's motives whilst he muttered something about Jane taking up office as Job's comforter.

"She said she spoke only in caution for the next child we will have," she glanced at Darcy. His brow had furrowed. "She thinks we lost the baby because we shared a bed during my confinement."

"How might she know that, Lizzy?"

"If you think I told her, I advise you I did not. When she was first expecting Elizabeth, she said she and Bingley...did not..." she did not realise she mimicked Jane's head wag. "I was all astonishment and told her thus. She could only fancy what I chose."

"Why does good Doctor Jane think that proximity should cause you to lose the baby? We did not..." he wagged his head, "when you were near due."

Taking a deep breath, she relaunched the story.

"Jane says that if a woman's insides are 'excited' when with child, she will miscarry."

"You did not miscarry."

"True. But she also cautions, that if we...do that..." she started to smile, abandoning any attempt to relate the story with solemnity, "the baby will see your..." she wagged her head again, "and be frightened of it. Afraid to come out. And that is why ours could not be born. He had seen your...you and was frightened from birth."

His eyes narrowed, lips tightened, nostrils flared. Substantially.

"That is the most preposterous thing I have ever heard!"

When he spat that out, he sounded somewhat defensive. It occurred to her that was this story true, the culprit in the birthing fiasco was his manhood, not her narrow birth canal. But this retelling rendered that from unlikely to ludicrous.

"Yes."

"Then why do you repeat it. For humour?"

"No…I know it must sound ridiculous, but yet…in light of no other notion as to why 'it' happened, I fear I am coming to consider even the most absurd of tales…"

"I cannot speak for a woman's 'excited insides,' but if that second tale was true, Lizzy, there would not be a child born in Derbyshire. Country-folk call it 'steg month' not 'steg three-quarter-year.' And for all the talk of steg widows, as it happens, husbands upon the land investigate their impregnated wives until they are met with the protruding infant's head!"

"That is a gross exaggeration."

"Not entirely. The country folk certainly lose no more children than the gentry. You know the man, Piddlenot, who tends the cattle south?"

She nodded.

"From his own lips I heard the story. When his good wife relinquished the herd relating herself in labour, he inquired of her if she had time for him to 'dip his wick' before she had the baby."

"Even he would not confess such a thing!"

"I believe it was more in the manner of complaint. It seems she denied him."

"Whatever did you say?"

"I cannot remember committing myself to a comment."

"Was I that baby, I daresay the sight of that man's privates might have frightened me from delivery."

(It would not be unkind to say Piddlenot was an ugly man. To say that he was disgustingly ugly would be unkind, but not untrue.)

She perched herself upon her husband's lap and sighed. It had been a dotty notion to attempt to enlighten Jane in matters conjugal.

"Have I disabused you of such an outrageous suggestion?"

"She was honestly trying to be helpful," Elizabeth assured him.

"But you do not believe it?"

"Not truly. How could I? The story you fashioned to seal your debate was far too illuminating. 'Dip his wick?' I shall never look upon a candle quite so innocently again."

Vast estates across the countryside harboured countless duties, some overseers upon them more conscientious than were others. Although it had traditionally fallen to Pemberley's mistress to visit the ill amongst the tenantry upon their lands, Elizabeth's self-perceived idleness eventually embraced it as her mission. Her own privilege in the face of illness and misery she witnessed was unconscionable. There was certainly no starvation, but deprivation was rampant.

The necessitous existed to varying degrees all over England. But neediness as seen from the middling vantage of Longbourn was not near so grim as that same view from the height of Pemberley. Compared to many landowners the Darcy family had a finer honed sense of *noblesse oblige*. (Generous to a fault, a few of similar station had remarked, their own parsimony exposed in comparison.)

If she lived in splendour, Elizabeth knew well that it was through her husband's largesse, not her own. It would have been exceedingly presumptuous of her to suggest that the Darcy fortune be dispersed across the countryside any differently than it had for generations. Had it been hers by birth, she might have had a struggle of conscience. But it was not. And that it was not, released her to contribute the only thing she had that was truly her own—her time. And of that she gave unsparingly.

In the deadlier days of winter, Elizabeth's weekly visits to the sick became daily. So determined was she not to be a mere condescending dilettante, she enlisted Georgiana's assistance when she was about. The need was great. Dropsy and consumption threatened adults. Quinsy and the croup menaced the children. They brought soup, bread, and occasionally a foot-dragging Dr. Carothers to see to a particularly sick child.

"The apothecary is good enough to see to these people, Mrs. Darcy," he told her stiffly, but did what she bid nonetheless.

Repetitious acquaintance eventually overcame Georgiana's inborn squeamishness. (Furuncles, carbuncles, and chancres not a particular inducement to reform.) Once this vertiginous tendency was conquered, she set upon the ailing with a ferociousness none might have suspected of her. She stoked bitters, calomel, various poultices, and embrocations in a miniature portmanteau. Cobwebs she tucked in surreptitiously. It was unlikely they might happen upon a severed appendage, but if the improbable occurred, those little spider toilings were excellent to stanch the bleeding (one must be prepared).

Collywobblers, she fed asafoetida, and the dyspeptics were encouraged to belch. In so little time and with such aplomb was she issuing her advice, Elizabeth was quite astonished. Amidst all the eructation, kecking, and coughing, Georgiana and Elizabeth became quite a merry pair. And, inevitably, upon this indecorous turn of events, Darcy announced a dictum.

"It is quite inappropriate for a maiden to be exposed to…humanity so injudiciously."

Elizabeth knew full well that this was a Janus-faced accusation. He may not have been any less pleased that his sister was cavorting about the unwashed masses than his wife, but he was most decidedly affronted that Georgiana might be exposed to said unwashed masses' anatomies.

Elizabeth assured him, "You can be certain her eyes are protected from anything so vulgar as bodily functions. We only touch children's foreheads for fever and pour broth into elderly women's mouths. Surely you cannot deny those poor souls that?"

No, he could not. Nor could he quite leave the subject be.

"It is my understanding that nursing is indisputably a cabalistic calling. I beg not to suggest your sound nature would fall to such allurement, Lizzy. However, Georgiana is not so commonsensical."

"Are you suggesting that because your sister has found an enthusiasm, she is in danger of becoming an hysteric?"

"Enthusiasms are well and good, but unrebuked they can be as intoxicating as any liqueur."

"Pray, where do you read such absurdities?"

He drew upon his considerable hauteur to reply, "I do not find it necessary to enjoy an observation under instruction of someone else's opinion."

"Very well. But fear not, Georgiana's interest is merely piqued, not obsessed. I promise you, she shall not abscond in a gingham dress and white cap to St. Bart's."

Stymied upon the long-abused battleground of decorum, he reasoned, "These people are proud, Lizzy. You do not want them to think themselves pitied?"

"We do not aid the able-bodied, only the ill."

Reason overcome by logic, it was time for a full frontal assault.

"You shall become ill yourself."

"I am indecently healthy. Dr. Carothers said as much."

He circled the flank.

"You shall bring disease back to us."

Capitulating that point, she said she would not tend the contagious so closely.

"I shall not enter a house sick with consumption. We shall just take them what they need and leave it upon the stoop."

Elizabeth knew Darcy had perfected his tactics for such a campaign and that he was quite pleased with himself for it. No ultimatums were given, no shots fired, so to speak. He, obviously, did not even feel a twinge of guilt at using her love for him as a weapon. It was a victory worthy of Elizabeth's own powers of persuasion. Given enough time, she thought he might actually rival her in these contests of reason.

He added, "And two footmen shall accompany you."

This, perhaps, was revealing a bit of overconfidence upon his part. For she was halfway to the door and stopped when he said that, turned and stood looking at him in silent study. She did not appear to be reflecting kindly upon the wisdom of his demand (and particularly that it was obviously a demand). He had learnt, after much practise, to couch his demands to Elizabeth to appear as requests, but she saw then he had suffered a lapse.

In a moment she said, "'Tis far too pompous to ride about the lands of Pemberley in a coach waited upon by a gaggle of footmen. A waggon and driver will suffice."

"I shall not have you out alone."

There was an uncomfortable silence, to which he added prudently, "Please. For me."

"For you, anything."

And thereupon a compromise was struck. Or so he thought. Actually, she capitulated only to that of which she had already predestined. This was not pointed out to him. One should not wag the bloodstained flag of defeat beneath the victim's nose. That was indefensible.

Of course, she knew it only prudent not to expose her family to illness. And the footmen would be quite helpful in carrying the pots of soup. They could nurse much more efficiently with such sturdy help as that.

Sovereign power of persuasion had not yet passed.

Indeed, Elizabeth thought them quite the spectacle riding about the countryside trailing maids and servants visiting poor sick, and the sick poor. Others amongst their acquaintance thought them quite unseemly (if not outright mad). Georgiana thought this well-nigh hilarious, for she had never had the opportunity nor gumption to do something denounced as truly improper. It was a giddy freedom to be thought unconventional.

"Soon my reputation shall be sullied enough to be known a novelist will lend me credit!" she whispered excitedly to Elizabeth, in obvious anticipation of such an event.

The assignment of mercy waggon driving duty fell to Edward Hardin. That her husband forsook his most dependable man (the linchpin for the entire estate, he often said) to cart her about was not lost upon Elizabeth. It was a fortuitous coupling. Hardin offered the kindly suggestion that a non-liveried intermediary should ride with them to the cottages. The people therein were much more likely to confide their need to a simply dressed and soft-spoken one of their own.

Thereupon John Christie was brought into this fold. It was he who was delegated to approach a ramshackle home. Time had not obliterated Darcy's abhorrence of John, but it had waned to the extent that John quit leaping behind a tree if Mr. Darcy came into sight. Nevertheless, the boy was a little uneasy yet the first time he rode upon the waggon. Before long, however, he collected himself, finally believing it unlikely that Mr. Darcy might accost them and yank him from his seat.

John was considered good help by Elizabeth and Georgiana, staying at their elbows getting water, silently retrieving needed supplies from the coach. Endeavouring to coax conversation from the boy, Elizabeth told him he had missed his calling, that he might have made an excellent doctor.

He beamed at the suggestion, but said nary a word.

Hardin said, "Yer'll not get that boy to say boo to a goose, Mrs. Darcy. Lor' knows me and me wife have tried."

As if taking that as a verbal gauntlet cast at his feet, John did first the expected, he crimsoned. Then the unlikely. He spoke.

"No ma'am. Not me. No. Yer needs learnin' fer the likes of that. Aye got no learnin'."

His candour incited the demure Georgiana to object.

"'Learning' is a derivation of a verb," she announced.

He looked at her blankly.

"Learning is a derivative of the verb to learn, with the addition of a non-inflectional affixed."

If she somehow believed this had cleared his confusion, he did not. He looked at her, for all the world, as if a toad had crawled out of her mouth. She tried once again.

"Learning is just that. To learn. An action verb. One can learn."

Thereupon, they were at least, literally, speaking the same language again. Nonetheless, he shook his head at the absurdity of the idea and laughed nervously.

"No ma'am. Yer got ter have brains ter learn too. Don't got that neither."

Ignorance (as differentiated from stupidity) was rampant upon the countryside and to be unlearnt should not have shamed John. None of the grooms could read. Only those amongst the upper level servants could: Mrs. Reynolds, of course, Goodwin, and Hannah. (It was Hannah alone, though, who spent a portion of her prayers each day addressing the shortcoming of owning excessive pride in such an achievement.) Even with that understanding, upon their next missionary trip Georgiana brought a book of the alphabet and a slate.

Their lesson began by obtaining the information that John could sign his name, hence he knew those letters. From thence, the learning commenced. She compiled a list of words—anagrams—containing the letters of his full name, John Christie.

Those anagrams were to be his first lesson. He was to sound out the simple words— toe, sit, hot, tie—and read them to her the next time she saw him.

Gazed upon in fatherly pride by Edward Hardin, John recited his assignment to Georgiana.

"Smart lad, he!" said Hardin.

This entire journey of uncovering the mystery of words delighted them all. That same day he picked up a tin in one cottage and inspected it. When he read, unprompted, the word "tea" from its label, they all leapt in joy at his ingenuity. Observing that, the poor family in the house set to quivering with fright beneath their covers, never quite certain they were not being ministered by lunatics. Upon the heels of such success, Georgiana brought John primers. He devoured them all.

It was a contest of just who had more pride in her success of schooling him, Georgiana, John Christie, or Edward Hardin.

Had not Georgiana befriended another young man that same spring, nothing might ever have been said. But, as could be surmised from her enthusiasm for tending the ill and tutoring the illiterate, Georgiana had a penchant and a heart for outcast souls.

Young Henry Howgrave was hardly needy, but an outcast of sorts all the same. He was well-educated, mannerly, and not at all unattractive of face and figure. True, it might have been suggested he dressed to remind those to whom he was introduced that, howbeit left-handed, he was a gentleman's son. A bit of a dandy he was, but his particular circumstances could offer him some justification for foppery.

The terse explanation given to Elizabeth by her husband about the notorious Howgraves suggested it was no great leap to assume that he had not spoken to his sister of their situation at all. Nor did he suspect she had heard the gossip. He had reckoned that when he had taken her onto the dance floor in lieu of the hand of Henry Howgrave at the Pemberley ball, she had not understood the implication.

However mindful was she of just why her brother had interfered, Georgiana had been mortified upon young Howgrave's behalf at the time.

As his opposition to her nursing the sick implied, Darcy's presumption of his sister's innocence was compleat. Included in this conjecture of ignorance were infidelity, promiscuity, and carnal lust in general. Indeed, it extended to all elements of reproduction. Had he not shielded her at every turn from accouchement?

If queried upon the point, he most likely would have insisted she was quite oblivious to anatomical differences betwixt the male and the female as well. (There were rutting animals about, but surely she had not noticed.) This was probably the single subject upon which he looked blindly.

Which is why Elizabeth never questioned Darcy about Georgiana's liaison with Wickham. Actually, it had never been addressed in open conversation. He had written of it in a single letter and it was never brought into conversation. Whatever abhorrence he held for the affair, in his letter he had purported it as fleeting and chaste.

Nor did Georgiana imply otherwise.

Because he held the presumption of Georgiana's sexual innocence, Elizabeth knew her husband would not have asked Georgiana The Question. It was reasonable to presume her honour was not outraged. She had been but fifteen years old. A very naïve fifteen. Notwithstanding, Elizabeth's own sister, Lydia, had been fifteen when she ran off with Wickham. Lydia was not particularly naïve, but when she ran off to London with Wickham, she had been a virgin. Georgiana and Lydia were two separate understandings of young womanhood. Withal, Elizabeth did upon occasion wonder if Georgiana's seduction had been more than emotional.

Never would she have ventured to conjecture that to Darcy, let alone Georgiana. Darcy was a man of considerable worldliness. Nonetheless, he had chosen to believe that his sister was not compromised beyond her emotions. Had he believed the affair had progressed beyond professed love, Elizabeth knew blood would have been drawn.

Uninitiated or not, Georgiana was far too intelligent to be wholly insensible to life. Hence, when she had seen Henry Howgrave in the village and he asked if she might favour a visit by him, she fully understood the implication when she answered in the affirmative.

Henry Howgrave weathered more than his share of disdain. Cuts were not unknown to him. And he was well aware of Mr. Darcy's ill-regard. Georgiana might not have been naïve, but she was not so seasoned as to understand that when Henry Howgrave ventured to Pemberley to seek her company, he was uncovered as not some hapless knave. It revealed a calculating ambition of considerable gall.

Ambitious, but not foolhardy. The day of his visit, Darcy and Elizabeth had not been at home. Georgiana and Mr. Howgrave were accompanied upon their stroll by Mrs. Annesley. (That good lady held the most advantageous of claims that one could want of a chaperone—that of being severely nearsighted and compleatly deaf.)

A common interest in literature was discovered and from thence came most of their conversation. A few possible future meetings were suggested but nothing absolute.

It was all quite proper.

She might have been ingenuous to his enterprise, but Georgiana understood and accepted that most young men would be as attracted to her wealth as to her scintillating conversation. Not wanting to be secretive (that an improbability at Pemberley regardless) she announced his visit at supper.

Elizabeth did not lift her head from her soup, but glanced at her husband from the corner of her eye. But upon hearing that the infamous Henry Howgrave had stood upon Pemberley ground and in the company of his sister, his expression did not alter. That was alarming. Elizabeth lay down her spoon, awaiting the detonation of his temper. However, he held only the mildest of queries.

"Is he to return?"

In a wide-eyed expression of innocence, one that Georgiana perfected for just such inquiries from her brother, she replied (not untruthfully), "No."

Conversation moved on.

That same week Darcy espied Georgiana sitting with John Christie, their heads almost touching in conference. Albeit they were in close conversation, it was in the innocence of education, for they pored over a slim book. This scene was descried upon a walk as Elizabeth held her husband's arm. He paused thereupon and scowled. She urged his attention back to their walk, not waiting for him to speak his displeasure.

"She has been teaching him to read. He is frightfully bright."

Darcy, however, was not so easily becalmed. "It is not proper for her to school a manservant."

His position was that personal interest in a male in service over the age of twelve by a lady of the house, however innocent, was to be abhorred. Elizabeth believed it merely a kindness extended by Georgiana to which Darcy should see himself as over-reacting. But, Darcy beheld this sight upon the heels of learning young Howgrave had appeared again at Pemberley that day. He came thither only to leave a misdirected copy of the Quarterly Review, but that was not a particular pacification.

Little else was said about the matter, but later Darcy called Georgiana before him in his library. Elizabeth did not have to inquire what was said or the tone. She saw Georgiana immediately after, near tears.

Georgiana was alternately incensed and hurt. And expressed it vehemently.

"He does not trust me to make my life my own! I am to spend my time as he thinks I should, take company with those that he chooses! In his eyes I shall ever be a *naïve* and should look to him for my every decision!"

Her rant vented, she looked at Elizabeth who made no becalming assurances that her brother's intentions were not all that unreasonable. Neither did she offer qualifications to soften his dicta. No apologies, no excuses.

"That, I should say," Elizabeth said, "is exactly correct."

Hence, Georgiana stood looking petulant for a moment until she and Elizabeth both began to smile and eventually laugh.

Georgiana finally asked Elizabeth, "Then, how shall he ever react to this?"

Out of the folds of her dress, she produced a letter. It was addressed to Georgiana and the seal had been broken. Newton Hinchcliffe had fulfilled his promise. A publisher wrote inquiring if it might be agreeable that the first printing of her book be at least fifteen hundred copies.

Their collective delight exceeded the joy at the word "tea." After a jubilant, if silent pantomime of euphoria, they sat in a laughing heap. Her bosom heaving with merriment, Georgiana shook her head in defeat.

"Brother will never allow it."

Elizabeth plucked the letter from her fingers as she swept passed Georgiana and out the door.

Over her shoulder as she went in search of Brother, she trilled, "We will see, will we not?"

Darcy sat behind his desk in his library, ledgers open. But he was not at them, intent as he was upon mending his pen. However busy he made himself look, Elizabeth was certain he was still trying to justify his stern ultimatums. His affection for Georgiana was deep. He would regret wounding her, no matter how righteous he thought his position. Guilt, his wife believed, might just be the most advantageous chain to yank for this particular application.

"You have made your sister weep," she accused.

"I expected no less than for you to come, Lizzy," he said, then hurried toward absolution, "You know I cannot allow her to see such a man as Henry Howgrave. He is an affront. His entire family is an affront…"

"'Tis not only that. You tell her she must not see to the sick. She must not school a groom. She must not speak to those who offer her friendship. What of her own will have you left to her? You have thwarted her every interest, her every pursuit. Will you not be satisfied until she ends up a Miss Bingley?"

That stung, she knew. Contrition nibbled at her a little, but not unduly. He did not reply, but sighed. Apparently, this was expended in dejected martyrdom. It fell upon his abused shoulders alone to make Georgiana unhappy. If compunction be served, who else would do the deed?

In silence, Elizabeth unfolded the letter from the publisher and set it before him. He read it, but did not look up.

"You must allow her something. Which shall it be? The poor? A groom? Mr. Howgrave? Or the anonymity of 'A Derbyshire Lady'?"

Darcy sat there a moment longer. She cringed ever so slightly and even gave a start when he abruptly reached out. Unnecessarily, for he grabbed her by the wrists only to draw her onto his lap. Wrapping his arms about her waist, he kissed her wetly upon the neck. Her entreaty was going better than she ever anticipated.

Quite solemnly, he thereupon asked, "Do you fancy Georgiana has any idea the intrepid ally she has in you?"

Georgiana's alliance with Elizabeth was endangered by only the mildest of complaint. It was not spoken of, however, for it was one in which Elizabeth had no voice. Does not all mankind suffer under the inability to select whom one has as relations?

Georgiana's book was published to modest acclaim. Word quickly circled of the identity of "A Derbyshire Lady" unwittingly by way of Elizabeth. For she told Jane, who told Mrs. Bennet, who told everyone including Lady Lucas, who told her daughter, Charlotte Collins. Charlotte, always in search of conversational topics in her husband's company (or he would hold the floor relentlessly), told him. Georgiana was by turns pleased, skittish, and mortified by all the clamouring attention.

Far too often mortification and fear overwhelmed her, and Elizabeth fretted the fame (even in so small a dose) might frighten her from society compleatly. This, unknowingly, was preparation for collision, for soon one May day, providence was so unkind as to find Georgiana with Elizabeth at Kirkland Hall when the Collinses' visit to Jane overlapped theirs. It could be appreciated, owing to a good understanding of Mr. Collins obsequious nature, that coming into company with the exceedingly well-stationed (and thereupon prominent) authoress, Georgiana Darcy, he was almost prostrate with admiration.

Cornered in the parlour partaking of afternoon tea, Georgiana sat captive in a chair. For facing her on the sofa opposite was Mr. Collins. Thus, so suddenly in need, Mr. Collins newly applauded himself that he had taken the necessary time to rehearse. For he entertained many a carefully thought-out tribute to those of station and bestowed them most generously upon Miss Darcy. (Betimes he did have to draw a tiny, judiciously pre-folded piece of paper from his pocket with the proffered compliment to remind himself of the exact wording. But otherwise, such enterprise must be congratulated.)

Marshalling these snippets was a more complicated endeavour than the casual observer might suspect. For his compliments were divided not only by gender, but social strata as well. Left waistcoat upper pocket, men of rank. Left lower, men of lesser. Upper waistcoat right, ladies of rank. Lower waistcoat right, other ladies in general. The waistband of his breeches he saved for all-purpose adulations, mostly about the superb weather. (There was that unfortunate incident when one compliment upon the cloudless sky did work free of his waistband and insinuated itself in many-cornered discomfort in Mr. Collins nether region, thus initiating a provocative leg-waggling jig from him that incited a great deal of mortification amongst those in his company at the time.)

After expending all other notion of laudatory statement upon Georgiana's behalf in regards to her beauty and refinement, he hastened also to effusive praise for her new occupation as a woman of letters. Those exhausted, Mr. Collins leaned over and lowered his voice to a conspiratorial whisper.

"Not many know this Miss Darcy, but, I also have had pretensions to publish. Alas, my Christian work has left me little time to pursue such a worthy pursuit."

From her seat upon the far side of the sofa, Elizabeth had been talking to Charlotte, but her attention was snatched as soon as Collins lowered his voice.

Elizabeth had issued a somewhat blanket apology to Darcy's family about her cousin, the vicar, but was more than usually concerned when she could not hear what he was saying in such a secretive manner. (Those mortifications of which one is witting pale in the presence of those imagined.)

She excused herself to Charlotte, stood, walked to the tea table to refill her half-empty cup, and returned only as far as to the left of Georgiana's chair. This manoeuvre was preparatory in defence of the expected onslaught to her sister-in-law's delicate sensibilities.

Mr. Collins barely glanced at his cousin, so enthralled was he in his confidences with Miss Darcy. (His profuse adulations for the wife of Mr. Darcy were abandoned as soon as he espied, shall we say, new opportunistic waters to troll.)

He said, "I cannot tell you what fortune it is, Miss Darcy, that indeed, I just happen to have upon my person a few story notes I had once considered elabourating upon myself. I should not flatter myself to think, had I the time, that I might do them the justice as one of your talent. But I should be most honoured if you did me the honour of taking them under advisement for your own use." (Occasionally, Mr. Collins's enthusiasm for station lapsed into repetitious use of gratitude.)

Until only recently blessed with a mere nodding acquaintance with the vicar, Georgiana said politely, "I thank you, Mr. Collins, how kind."

Had she known him better, she might well have fled the room. As it was, she sat still as a stone, betrayed only by her eyes, which commenced to blink with rapidity. Mr. Collins pressed a handkerchief to his perpetually moist upper lip and glanced to either side before continuing, perchance to make certain there was no nefarious blackguard skulking about Kirkland in employment of stealing his plots.

With great foreboding, Elizabeth put a hand of reassurance upon Georgiana's shoulder. For Mr. Collins pulled a stack of notepaper thick enough to pad a sofa from beneath his waistcoat (scattering a few tiny little tributes to men of rank as he did). Did he, Elizabeth wondered, actually carry these about in the unlikely hope of finding such an opportunity? Apparently. And she could not argue his perseverance, for opportunity was surely thrust before him.

Holding the first page up, he announced, "My first is a story of a virtuous but poor vicar, of chaste heart and pure thoughts, who falls in love with the daughter of a villainous earl."

He took that paper from the top of the stack and moved it with an impressively silly flourish to beneath. At that, Elizabeth's fingers dug ever-so-slightly into her sister-in-law's shoulder in obvious mortification of her cousin's unceasing, and newly appreciated, gall.

"How nice," Georgiana said.

A keen lack of interest from his audience was understood by Mr. Collins to mean he should lengthen his recitation rather than desist. This, because he was under the profound misconception (one of many it would seem) that if one is operating at a loss, doubling one's effort will increase one's profit, not double one's depletion.

He read from the next, "This one tells of a poor but virtuous" (as opposed to virtuous but poor) "vicar who is thwarted from literary aspirations by a depraved plagiarist, persecuted by society envious of his refinement, and forced to flee civilised society..."

Mr. Collins had to take a breath here, for his chest was actually obliged to heave as his words conjured for him the vision of the aggrieved, virtuous, and literate clergyman of his story.

There were many, many more. As he read from each and every single piece of paper, it was obvious, had one had the poor judgement to hope otherwise, that there was a profound similarity betwixt his heroes and heroines. Beyond honour, valour, virtue, beauty, and abhorrence of the tithe system, they all had an unrelenting deficit of wit. This was undoubtedly inherited by them from their author who had the same deficit, but, alas, none other of those sterling qualities he bequeathed his characters (save objection to the tithe question).

"And this one!"

Mr. Collins's voice raised an octave in his excitement of having, after three-quarters of an hour, reached his favourite.

"This one is about a devout, modest, and unusually handsome vicar who is forced to take leave of his of home to save England in some manner. There are a few story details to be worked upon that one, of course."

"I do beg your pardon, Mr. Collins. Could you possibly forgive me? I have just come down with a most excruciating head-ache."

Attempting to quit the room, Georgiana pressed the back of her fingers to her forehead in true distressed heroine fashion.

Elizabeth had let go of her shoulder as she stood and stepped back. But she had the good sense to keep the chair betwixt herself and Mr. Collins, uncertain she could overcome the intense need she had to strike him.

"Oh, I am so sorry," Mr. Collins said as he stood and bowed. "Perhaps I have bestowed too much anticipation upon you. Could I just entrust these memoranda with you? Do use them at your convenience."

"No, no," he insisted when she demurred. "Take them. I have several copies."

Georgiana retreated from the room clutching the papers. As she did, Elizabeth turned away and gulped down half a cup of hot tea. (And whether that peculiar little noise she emitted was from searing the roof of her mouth or perturbation, we shall never quite know.)

Mr. Collins sat down and looked about to the others in the room (which had been forsaken within the previous half-hour by all but Jane, Bingley, Charlotte, and Elizabeth), oblivious to their silence. With an expression of satisfied benevolence upon his face, he gazed about the room. Whilst he looked about, he could not quite contain his glee. Nudging Charlotte, he whispered excitely to her.

"I wonder which of my stories she will choose."

His wandering musings drawing his attention to the far corners of the room, he did not see Charlotte gift him a look of stifled mortification (one she had perfected by reason of a great deal of practise).

Hence, he asided to her again, "Perhaps she will dedicate the book to me!"

Thereupon, he set about a low conversation, more with himself than Charlotte, "Perhaps I shall send Miss Darcy a note suggesting just that. It will save her the trouble of thinking of it."

Because he was not yet looking at Charlotte, he did not see her eyes had not left him, but her usual complacent gaze had mutated into a stare of confounded incredulity.

Yet contemplating, he said, "If she offers me compensation, I shall certainly refuse it."

Charlotte eyes widened when, upon reconsideration, he said, "Perhaps a small gift of money. That would not be unchristian, would it?"

He looked at his wife for her Christian assurances. Because her face was just inches from his, it startled him. He turned his head carefully about to face the others in the room, drew his handkerchief from his sleeve, and mopped his forehead and upper lip. If his wife's look was cautionary, it did not find its duty for long. For he reached down to retrieve the little pieces of paper that had fallen from his lap to the floor.

Thereupon, he dropped them, one at a time, onto his outstretched, upturned palm. Moreover, as he did, he was already composing Miss Darcy's note in his mind.

This Collins encounter was mercifully brief, Elizabeth and Georgiana immediately conjuring a reason to return to Pemberley. The excuse had something to do with Georgiana's extended head-ache, and if it was somewhat convoluted, no one at Kirkland (save Vicar Collins) questioned it.

Elizabeth knew she had abandoned Jane, but Pemberley had weathered a purgatorial visit from her cousin once that year. She had a strongly held belief that had God chosen to punish her in some fashion, Mr. Collins would again be upon her own doorstep instead of her sister's. (Even in so strong as their sisterly bond, it was unspoken that in some matters, 'tis every sister for herself.)

The full humour of this entire episode had been lost upon Elizabeth, until, under the protectiveness of distance, the retelling exposed it. The audience for this was Darcy, who had begged stay behind at Pemberley to oversee construction of a small dam. Missing company with Mr. Collins was fortune in itself; Elizabeth's droll retelling merely compounded his felicity.

This conversation came from horseback. They had ridden out west of the house to give Elizabeth opportunity to admire the work, which she did as effusively as recent company of Mr. Collins would allow.

"I fancy I was far too much in fear of your sister's sensibilities, but I truly thought it possible such an encounter with Mr. Collins might frighten her from ever entering society again. Her poise was more than admirable and far better than my own."

"We have finally found one meritorious quality of your cousin, Lizzy. He can rid a home of extended guests more hastily than the threat of the plague. We should remember that if we have any visitors to overstay their welcome. We shall but tell them that we are entertaining the notion of inviting Mr. Collins. Pemberley will become suddenly deserted."

Upon returning their horses mid-afternoon, they espied Georgiana sitting in the shade with several youngsters (including John Christie, who looked quite conspicuous amongst the other prepubescent lads).

"There seems to be no end to my sister's ambitions. She writes the books and teaches the illiterate to read them," Darcy said as he alit from Blackjack.

Although he did not say it particularly meanly, Elizabeth (obviously not recollecting what one should do with sleeping dogs) thought to further his sister's argument in favour of teaching at least so large a charge as John Christie to read.

"I cannot speak for the other boys, but John is surprisingly bright. He grew up in London and has told us that we only think we have seen misery in this county."

Elizabeth had been to London, yet Darcy knew she had never come close to seeing the squalor that existed in certain sections of that city. Even he had not seen the worst, but could remember some sights he passed that he wished he had not.

As he helped her down from Boots, he said, "If this London boy tells you many more of ghastly stories you shall no doubt be opening alms houses there, Lizzy."

Laughing at the perspicuity of that particular truth, she reassured him there was no such possibility.

She added, "Though he did live in town before he came here, he's not truly a London boy. I understand that his mother once worked at Pemberley. Perchance you remember her. What was her name? I do not recall. It is said she was of red hair. Can you imagine that swarthy boy's mother being of such colouring? It was Agnes or Abby. A chambermaid, I believe."

Startled at hearing the reference from Elizabeth, of all people, he corrected her automatically, "Abigail."

Thereupon, his countenance crimsoned, realising it would be unusual for him to have remembered something so well, for so long. Even with the understanding, be it lady or gentleman, it is rarely forgotten to whom one sacrificed one's virginity, he certainly did not want to announce to Elizabeth a connexion substantially greater than the one she supposed. It was fortunate that her thoughts had drifted, for she turned and bid him to repeat himself.

He cleared his throat and asked mildly, "You say she had a situation here?"

She nodded, but as he had nothing else to add to her colloquies, the subject was rested. Yet he felt a certain unease. One he did not understand.

By the next day, a feeling of impending doom had overtaken him so compleatly, he looked heavenward upon occasion to catch sight of the cloud. After vacillating upon it for several hours, he decided to go to the one person whose mind kept meticulous record of such things.

Mrs. Reynolds was seated in the dining-room with the second best set of silver in front of her. Half lay in a velvet-lined, rosewood box, the others in a newly polished row upon the table.

It was awkward to bring up. He laboured upon just how to do it before finally coming right out with it.

"Is it your understanding that the mother of the foot-boy, John Christie, was once in service here?"

Mrs. Reynolds replied matter-of-factly that, indeed, she knew of the boy's mother, for she had worked there as a chambermaid for six months. Her Christian name was Abigail, maiden name Christie. She departed Pemberley with child and in disgrace. This recited, she exhaled upon a serving spoon and polished away the vapour of her breath before making a cryptic addendum.

"That boy is not the twenty years he claims. For 'tis said he is the child she carried and it was not eighteen summers ago she left."

As he listened, Darcy turned to the window. In the hollow silence that followed this revelation, he could hear her as she carefully set down one fork, selected another and rubbed it with her felt cloth, put that one down and repeated the process.

If there was one thing for which the old woman had an uncanny knack, Darcy knew, it was remembering dates.

Another was second sight upon the doings of the other servants. If she said it, it was thus. And with that understanding, his thoughts began to race, returning him to a time of which he had not thought for many years.

It was initially indistinct. Then, gradually, a few aspects drew clearer. As those were ruled by immoderate libido, he endeavoured to concentrate upon the more nebulous ones. Specifically time in conjunction with events.

The one thing that was inescapable, Abigail's dismissal was immediately upon the heels of his father uncovering they were engaging in carnal rites. He imperceptibly shook his head, not wanting to admit what appeared to be a certainty. In that denial came a recollection. When she first looked upon the boy, Elizabeth had made a remark about his countenance. Odd that such a small comment would have stayed with him. But he remembered quite clearly. She had said the boy reminded her of how he might have looked at that age. And if he were honest with himself, he could see a similarity of colour and build even then.

Somewhere in the distance, he heard Mrs. Reynolds' voice yet speaking, but he did not hear what she said. He was desperately trying to recall the events of that year, the year he lay with Abigail. He endeavoured to remember what year it was, how old he had been. Thereupon, he reminded himself it did not matter what year, for it was the year Abigail departed Pemberley and no other.

Elizabeth found him late that afternoon sitting in his library. He was at his desk, but his chair was half turned toward the waning light of the window. His elbows rested upon the arms of his chair, his forefingers steepled against his lips. Slowly, they tapped.

Evenfall was upon them and she almost overlooked his presence there, for he had made no effort to light the room. She asked him if he was well. He turned to her, lost in thought, not answering for a moment. Thereupon he stood, and with a slight shake of his head, gave her his attention, declared himself quite well, and inquired only as to the supper menu.

In a few days' time, he saw a repetition of the impromptu schoolroom under a spreading oak, this time more at sunder. For it was just Georgiana there—and John Christie. She laughed at some jest he had made at his own expense. Darcy spoke sharply to her, her name, nothing more. But it was called much more sharply than he intended.

At his side walked Elizabeth, who at this eruption turned upon her husband's face with puzzlement troubling her brow. And, because of his outburst, she could only believe her husband intractable about whom his sister befriended. If she thought him implacable and severe, it was not as he wished, but he saw no choice. The expression upon Georgiana's face did pain him, but the spectre of John Christie's paternity was a haunting one. To see his dear, good sister consorting with proof of his own lascivious conduct was unacceptable. He would not have it.

At his reproof, Georgiana's distress was obvious. However, Darcy did not witness John Christie's. For, if he had, he might have seen the boy's fallen countenance betray full understanding of the master's implication of tone and hastily turn away.

48

In his very few years of living at Pemberley, John had altered a great deal, and then again, not at all.

His declared years of twenty were not betrayed by the truth of mere ten and seven, for he was the tallest of the grooms by nearly a quarter-foot. He had a far better view of Edward Hardin's sandy hair than of that man's dimpled chin. There was even talk he might be promoted to footman, if Mrs. Hardin could but put some flesh on his bones, for he was yet quite slim.

So lean was he, Mrs. Hardin teased him that he cast no greater shadow at four than noon. This jest was usually in encouragement of him to take a second helping, for he often partook of meals with them.

He had grown in height if not breadth and had to shave three times a week, but had not changed one smidgen in demeanour. His expression was still deliberately bland. Indeed, it might have been no bother at all to convince others of his placidity was it not for his eyes. Those denuding culprits were accentuated with an unruly tangle of dark lashes, but that was not why they were remarkable. They were farouche and fierce in one fell swoop. His countenance exposed nothing of him, but his eyes manifested all. Had he known that, he would have been most displeased.

His posture spoke him shy, not because of a stoop, for he stood quite straight. However, he walked, stood, partook, and in all likelihood, slept, with his face cast down, rarely holding anyone in his gaze. Hence, his eyes had little opportunity to forecast the shades of his mind. Nor did his voice. He rarely spoke. And never if a head-shake, nod, or shrug might suffice. Upon those occasions when he was provoked to speak, even the keenest of ears strained to hear him.

As he grew, his voice did not strengthen, only deepened, and never did its softness quite escape the incongruity of east London's rough dialect. That was how he might have been described was someone moved to do it: tall, head down, silent. For the first few years at Pemberley, little scrutiny was paid to him at all. That suited him very well, thank you. For never had he allowed himself to escape penitence for the horses that died in the stable fire. Albeit it was not public dishonour he bore, for it was never told. However, that no one knew of his part in it did not keep him from taking a firm seat in his own purgatorial house of guilt.

Head down, he did his work, partook of his food, and slept in his bed. When girls began to take notice of him and call his name, he did not look back, only reddened. This embarrassed pigment enhancement in his cheeks was unbeknownst to him, for he never looked in a mirror past scraping at his whiskers. He had not a clue as to why the girls giggled and nudged each other when he bechanced by them. It was not that he had no interest, for his body reminded him frequently that his interest was keen. But the girls seemed always to be about in pairs and he had not the conversational wherewithal to breach the twittering gap betwixt himself and feminine company.

His social activity embraced only meals with the Hardins and the taking of treats to some of his favourite horses (which was not technically a social activity, but well-nigh as good, horses being more convivial to him than people).

His circumstances of birth were more unstable and insubstantial than even the lowest of servants at Pemberley. This is perchance why he had maintained a cynicism of human-kind that would have befitted a moneylender. It might be fancied he trusted the Hardins, howbeit that supposition had not yet been rendered under fire. Hence, there was one indisputable sentiment he harboured beyond misanthropy. And that was an unmitigated infatuation with his employer's wife.

Beautiful, brave, and propitious, it was Mrs. Darcy alone who was his preserver in the wake of the fire and robbery. (He ranked Mrs. Darcy even higher than Mrs. Hardin, who cooked for him.) When Mr. Hardin bid him ride atop the coach when that good lady went upon her sick visits, John was desperately pleased with himself. The insecurity of a childhood transgressed by bastardy, uncertainty, and the loss of his mother, not to speak of the abuse of poverty in general, had not particularly inflated his ego. Riding upon the waggon, escorting Mrs. Darcy and Miss Darcy, did not unnecessarily inflate his ego then, but plumped it enough to call it middling.

The footmen came and went with food and blankets, eventually waiting at the coach. Indeed, it was he alone who stayed in the house of illness the entire time with the Darcy ladies. That understanding of the zenith of pride was cast out and a new criteria instated when Mrs. Darcy suggested he might have made a good doctor. That elevated her to his notion of sainthood.

Therefore, it could be understood how, compared to the sanctification to which John Christie held Mrs. Darcy, the girls about Pemberley fared somewhat poorly. Suspicious as he was of others, his own character was quite without guile. Thus, he did not realise his deification of Mrs. Darcy was used as a pretext to excuse himself from the troubling undertaking of conversing with those of the opposite sex. Moreover, he certainly did not understand, however virtuous his feelings toward Mrs. Darcy were, they tread treacherous waters. For in the grander realm of his mind's circumstance, he believed her husband to be his father.

John was bright, even astute, but, true, he was utterly unsophisticated in matters of the heart. When Miss Darcy began to teach him to read, he should have ducked his head and reinstated his hermeticism. He did not. She was pretty and kind, and the supposition that, was Mr. Darcy his father, she was his relation as well was shoved to the farthest reaches of his mind. It stayed right there until the day Mr. Darcy spoke so uncharitably to them both.

Because Georgiana was to return to London upon the heels of that encounter, John did not have to agonise over whether to weather Mr. Darcy's disdain, or to tell Miss Darcy he no longer had any interest in letters.

Nevertheless, he did go to Edward Hardin forthwith, begging off riding upon the waggon altogether. Mr. Hardin neither encouraged him to stay nor questioned him why he no longer chose to go. Wordlessly, he took another boy on in his place. One might suggest it, but John believed he never once felt a twinge of regret. The burden of her husband's disapproval had usurped the pride and, ultimately, the pleasure of being in Mrs. Darcy's company. That, above all things wrested from him in his ignominious existence, was unpardonable.

Hence, that summer's solstice saw the primers Georgiana had given him shoved beneath the batting of his bed. Moreover, John retreated with renewed determination into his protective shell of silence. However diligently he guarded it, his little fortress of taciturnity was betimes transgressed. For those who were of more congenial nature than he, his quiet invited discourse. Which presented him a conundrum. Idle conversation always included a little idle prattle. Usually these tidbits were quite innocuous. But he was most adamant in his dislike of gossip. Was this because his mother was once the brunt of a great deal of it, perchance? It was undeniable that he had suffered keenly upon the altar of human foibles, hence they were no particular amusement to him.

Yet even John found it a little diverting that Mrs. Hardin would carry on a conversation with him without him once having to look up, much less respond. These little discourses were mostly about the village and country doings, in which he held little interest. One day, however, one particular piece of information caught his attention and had it not come from Mrs. Hardin, he would not have looked up from his soup to listen even then.

Mrs. Hardin had made it a personal objective to find him company of the feminine persuasion (as she thought him a rather late-blooming twenty-year-old) and never ceased putting forth first one hearty girl, then another. But this day, as she went about her work chatting both case and canard, she grumbled more than usual.

For it seemed the girl she had set her eye most doggedly upon for him had fallen into disrepute.

"Whot's there t'say when a gerl from a good family falls for the wiles of a man just because he's rich," she groused.

John stopped eating, his spoon suspended midway to his mouth.

"That man's not going to see t'her," she fussed on. "The best she ken hope is if he gits'r with child he'll marry her off to some lad for a quid and he'll treat'r like the doxy she is!"

Abruptly, Mrs. Hardin ceased her diatribe, the collop beneath her chin still quivering with indignation. She looked at John and saw she had his full audience for the first time in her recollection. Not one to waste anything, especially the peerless occasion of having John Christie's ear, she offered him some motherly advice.

"Don't ye go havin' no time for no gerls that'll waste theyselves 'pon a few trinkets from a rich man, John."

He shook his head he would not. Satisfied, she had turned back to her work when she heard something unlikely. John asked her a question.

"Who is 'e?"

She looked at John, dumbfounded. John took it that she did not understand his question, not that she was dumbfounded he had asked one.

He repeated, "Who's the rich man?"

Recovering from her astonishment, she grumbled to herself again, and thereupon said, "Who'd yer think? There's not that many rich men about here. It sure ain't no squire."

(She did not actually know who the rich man was, but having the floor, she did not want to relinquish it for want of information.)

John only knew one rich man about and that one sat in a very big house a near cry from the small one where he sat partaking of his meal. Before he could digest that particular, he heard Edward Hardin's urgent call. Giving his usual mumbled thanks to Mrs. Hardin, he ran out the door.

His instruction was implicit. Make haste to fetch Colonel Fitzwilliam's horse. That gentleman had appeared unexpectedly; Scimitar was not yet saddled. The horse's imminent departure was a mild disappointment to John. The humble equine fancier deemed him a handsome one indeed. Mr. Darcy's horse was probably finer, but Scimitar had more…John thought about it and searched for the word…spirit. Yes, he had more spirit, which was truly an indefinable point in a horse. Either they had it or they did not. John thought Scimitar had more of that indefinable something than any he had seen. Smooth of gait and fine of spirit. What more could you ask of a horse than that it be honest?

Working with meticulous dexterity, he bridled and saddled Scimitar. Hastily, he grabbed the reins and slung back the gate to lead him out. Too hastily.

Unpropitious fate allowed the gate to hit the post and bounce against it just as he attempted to take Scimitar through.

That set the stage for a horrifying occurrence.

The gate sprang betwixt him and Scimitar, exciting the horse to bolt. One flaying hoof glanced off the gate and wedged betwixt two boards. Spooked beyond all reclamation, the near two hundred stone of horse reared and thrashed at the gate in a frenzy to free himself. All this clattering fury of a nightmare unfolded as if in slow motion before John's disbelieving eyes.

Momentarily, he stood in petrified terror, a cold sickness in his stomach. He had no doubt he was about to witness that fine horse shatter a leg. Some deep will wrested him from his shock, and he leapt about frantically trying to catch a handhold upon the bridle. That, however, only made the horse flail more. The more the horse thrashed, the more desperately John endeavoured to catch him. They were locked into an ever-escalating trial of panic.

Even amidst such bedlam, John heard a calm voice behind him.

"There, Scimitar, there."

Rather than run to the fracas, Colonel Fitzwilliam strode up with little more effort than a saunter. One observing him might have believed the man not rushed at all. So quietly did he approach, John did not realise he was there until Fitzwilliam firmly grasped his arm, thus thwarting his fruitless quest for Scimitar's bridle.

"Be still," he cautioned. "Be still."

The voice was one that made John do just that. Save for the trembling that afflicted every muscle in his body, he stood perfectly still. Fitzwilliam commenced to talk in a soothing tone to the horse whose thrashing had de-escalated but not yet abated. Gradually the horse stopped lurching and heaving about. Fitzwilliam picked up the reins and made a gentle clicking noise with his tongue. The horse stepped forward on three feet and stood with great patience whilst the colonel managed to extricate his hoof from the gate.

Drained, John sank with a dull thud to the ground in relief. Forthwith, he leapt up, ready for his well-deserved dressing down. Any rant or criticism he would accept without complaint. For if the horse was unhurt, it was not because of—but in spite of—his own ministrations.

Nonetheless, Fitzwilliam did not look at the mortified groom, intent as he was upon examining the horse for injuries. Gently, he traced his hand down Scimitar's hock. No blood was evident. Scimitar stood fully upon all four feet, not favouring the recently imprisoned hoof. The horse was evidently uninjured.

Standing tall and straight during this inspection, John waited with forbearance for its completion to receive his due. The only fervent hope he held (and it was niggardly indeed) was that as the horse was ultimately unhurt, the colonel would only keel-haul him, not have him turned out. But when Fitzwilliam finally turned to him, he did not speak in reproach.

"I see your instinct is in defence of the horse. When I was your age, I am certain I should not have jeopardised myself in such a manner. I thank you."

He thanked him? He had almost caused mortal injury to the man's horse and he thanked him? John could say nothing; he just stood there, stupefied.

Clearly aware of the groom's surprise, Fitzwilliam adopted a scholarly tone, "Whatever you do when a horse is trapped, show no alarm. Move with care, speak quietly. If the horse is to be extricated, that will be the only way to prevent injury. To either of you."

With the last remark, he turned to John and smiled. John nodded his head eagerly. Then he watched raptly as Fitzwilliam walked Scimitar about. Slowly, he led the horse in a wide circle, allowing him to calm. Once satisfied of that, he bid John to unsaddle him.

"I shall let him settle a half-hour before I take him out."

Instructions compleated, John climbed atop the fence as Fitzwilliam personally loosed him in a paddock. Odd to be sitting there whilst the gentleman saw to the horse. Had John's notion of absoluteness not been so roundly shaken, it was additionally abused when the good colonel climbed upon the fence and sat next to him.

With the merest flick of his hands, the colonel tossed the tails of his jacket from beneath him as he perched upon the top rail. John admired that flick. He thought he might like to have a jacket with brass buttons, epaulets, and tails to flick aside when he sat.

They sat there a few moments in silence. John cut his eyes over to Fitzwilliam several times then to his excellent steed.

Of Scimitar, he asked, "'e's a charger, ain't 'e?"

Fitzwilliam nodded. John knew quite well who the colonel was, for he came to Pemberley often. He was a cavalry officer. Scimitar was the horse he rode upon those courageous cavalry charges. Until then, John had never had opportunity to scrutinise him, only his horse. But he had always been impressed with his caped uniform and choice of mounts. Sitting as near as he did, John could see an impressive scar upon the colonel's cheek. It was deep. Curling his lip slightly at the sight, he wondered if a sabre had rendered that scar and if it did, in what battle. He was eyeing it so closely, he did not realise Fitzwilliam was watching himself be inspected.

"Are you appalled by my scar?"

Startled, John looked to the ground and said, "No, sire."

In a voice he reserved for the greenest of trooper, Fitzwilliam demanded that he speak up, "What?"

John said louder, "No, sire." Thereupon he impetuously added, "It is an admirable scar."

Fitzwilliam smiled, "Admirable, is it?"

The bonhomous company of a man of such substantial rank rendered him profoundly spellbound, else John might have never blurted out, "Yes. Aye have never seen a scar so fine. Was it from battle?"

"No," he said, "Not from battle, just in practise for battle."

"But yer been to battle?"

Fitzwilliam nodded.

Swept thither by the throes instituted of such manly camaraderie, John said, conspiratorially, "Aye 'ear ladies swoon at such scars! The worse the better. Proves you a fine man wi' a blade!"

"I have heard such things," Fitzwilliam allowed, "but all I can see is that a scar announces at least one man bested your defences."

John did not actually register this aside, for his attention had wandered from the scar to the weapon which might inflict such. Indeed, the sabre that hung from the colonel's waist was long and curved.

Seeing his awe-struck countenance, Fitzwilliam inquired rather disingenuously, "Do you care to take it in your hand?"

Jubilantly, John jumped down. With a slithering swoosh, Fitzwilliam drew the sword from its scabbard, then tossed it hilt up in John's direction. Seeing the glinting metal barrelling toward his head, John instinctively reached out, as much to deflect as to catch it. Nevertheless, catch it he did.

Flicking it several times, he appreciated its weight and battle-marred pommel. Thereupon, he jousted the air, puncturing any number of Napoleon's *Vieille Garde*. Giddily, he looked from the sword to Fitzwilliam, who sat yet upon the fence, to see if the colonel demanded it back (he not exactly ready, but at least willing to return him his sword). His gaze settled behind the colonel though, upon Georgiana who was watching from the vantage above them.

He was mortified to be caught in such flagrant play and meekly relinquished Fitzwilliam his weapon with a genuflecting duck of his head. Taking notice of the young man's obvious alteration in demeanour, Fitzwilliam turned to see what incited such a reversal. He almost laughed, then caught himself, perchance having been the victim of boyish humiliation himself at one time.

The innocent provocateur of this discombobulation walked down the incline to the fence and spoke to Fitzwilliam. John busied himself resaddling Scimitar, but he heard Georgiana tell the colonel she was to repair to London.

In less than a quarter-hour, the colonel was upon his way and Georgiana returned to the house. In that good time, John's body returned to routine, but his thoughts returned to the mundane quite unwillingly. As he went methodically about his chores, he hummed when he thought about the colonel, the colonel's horse, the colonel's sword, and most of all, the colonel's impressive scar. So enthralled was he in all that was the colonel's, it took him a time before his thoughts rambled back to his meal at Mrs. Hardin's table.

Remembering then just what she had said, his humming stopped, as did his chores. The bucket he held was emptied and he upended it for an impromptu seat. It was better to ponder from a sitting position, for one could prop one's chin upon one's palm in thoughtful contemplation. From thence, he recollected what Mrs. Hardin had said and replayed it carefully in his mind.

Undoubtedly, the contemptible scoundrel of whom she spoke was Mr. Darcy. There could be little doubt. First John sneered at the very thought, then became quite wretched upon Mrs. Darcy's behalf. Would that Mr. Darcy were of Colonel Fitzwilliam's character, for Mrs. Darcy deserved better. Certainly, Colonel Fitzwilliam would never compromise a young woman. Mr. Darcy was an unrepentant debaucher.

Fitzwilliam was almost as rich as Mr. Darcy was, but he was not a defiler of virgins. He was a hero. Or certainly heroic. He was not above talking to a groom. He did not father children then abandon them. Colonel Fitzwilliam wore a red uniform and cape.

Colonel Fitzwilliam had a truly fine scar upon his cheek.

Betimes it did not cross Mr. Darcy's mind to think of John Christie's paternity. Those occasions, unfortunately, were infrequent and fleeting. Not surprisingly, this preoccupation led to an obvious distancing of his attention.

If he thought his inattention was unheeded, he was mistaken. For it was obvious to his wife. Moreover, Elizabeth laboured under the misapprehension that his distraction was indicative of a misgiving upon her behalf. She had heretofore been persuaded that his foremost fear was for her to bear another child. This supposition was abandoned. In its place, she instituted an alternate presumption. She became quite convinced he thereupon feared she would not.

For they were no longer newlyweds. She was expected, demanded—yes, required to be with child (not only be with child but said baby must be male). And did she ever escape this ever-increasing worry, she was reminded of it twice monthly. Once, when her courses came and second, when her mother's post arrived inquiring had she yet conceived (indeed, her mother's letters arrived with more regularity than did her menses).

As time went on, that she had not was glaringly obvious, for children abounded. In addition to Jane's ever-increasing family (she was expecting yet again), Lydia also had begat three boys, howbeit Wickham seemed to be in her company only long enough to impregnate her.

Even Charlotte Collins had become the semi-proud mother of a toddler. Of course, in order to have produced Chauncey Charlemagne Collins, Charlotte had to suffer the unenviable task of engaging her husband in conjugal embrace. At least once. (No one actually made a retching sound at the idea of such a union, but several made audible gasps of abhorrence.) This sacrificial act of generation had resulted in a child whose eyes insistently gazed independently of each other and, in his third year, had only a wisp of hair and not yet produced any teeth. However, that was overlooked as politely and solicitously as possible. For after all, regardless of his shortcomings, he had a male appendage.

It had been just two springs previous when in great excitement, Jane brought Lady Lucas' letter proclaiming that unceremonious birth. Apparently, Charlotte was brought to the straw quite unexpectedly. Jane related the details to Elizabeth.

"Her mother was all astonishment and thought Charlotte delivered so hastily owing to a fright."

"I suppose she happened unawares to look upon her husband," Elizabeth concluded.

Even kind Jane did not argue that.

Ever obliging, Jane ended her fourth confinement by mid-November exactly as partridge season overlapped that of pheasant. Owning no undue pride, Bingley, who loved to be host to shooting parties for friends and neighbours, believed a new baby boy as good a reason as any to celebrate in that manner. The men could make a perfunctory inspection of the new infant, then go out for sport, leaving the ladies in peace to talk of feminine pursuits.

Amongst the ladies in attendance to admire the Baby Bingley came the longsuffering Charlotte wagging her myopic, bread-gumming child with her. Because of the boy's double-vision, he stumbled into furniture, but other than a few broken bric-a-bracs, was no particular bother. The same, of course, could not be said for his father.

Mr. Collins accompanied Charlotte to Netherfield, but he was more than usually out of sorts. For in the close company such a lengthy journey demanded of its travellers, Mr. Collins had broken out in a rash. Quite intemperately, he blamed poor Charlotte for his torment, certain that Chauncey was the culprit responsible for his itch and Charlotte did beget him.

It was most probable that Bingley sought to relieve the ladies of Mr. Collins's constant whines of affliction when he invited the cleric to join the gentlemen for the day's shoot. Good intentions aside, Bingley most likely did not think the matter through, else he might never have suggested arming him.

Any man who went afield with Mr. Collins resting a weapon upon his shoulder, unless a fool, knew full well what possibilities lay in wait. Hence, a brief conference betwixt the other shooters exacted a plan. At no time might Mr. Collins be allowed to trek alone. Each man would take a turn to walk with the vicar and keep watch upon which direction his barrel pointed. (In defence of life and limb was probably the single impetus that could have persuaded anyone to take that duty.) So jittery was their group to have a loose cannon in its midst little game was taken, for the few times a shot was fired, they collectively flinched.

It was during Mr. Hurst's watch that disaster struck.

In the merest flick of a moment, a dog burst upon a covey and sent it flying skyward with a flurry of flapping wings. Before anyone had chanced to duck, Collins whirled and fired blindly in that direction. The dog yelped loudly, but was fortunate to be hit by only a pellet or two (Mr. Collins having been blessed with aim as poor as his judgement).

It was not fortunate, however, that Darcy stood ahead and to the left of Mr. Collins. But had he been more to the right, he would have certainly been fatally wounded instead of, as he was, rendered only temporarily deaf. This misjudgement left the bumbling Mr. Collins exceedingly apologetic and Darcy might have been more favourably inclined to accept his many felicitous solicitations were he able to hear them.

No fingers were pointed, but it was unavoidable to mistake upon whom the unspoken reproof rested. The Collinses retreated from Netherfield with such dispatch, they very nearly collided with the physician rushing forth to examine Mr. Darcy's ears.

In less than a week's time, the post brought a letter from Charlotte to Elizabeth. After mindfully inquiring as to Mr. Darcy's recovery and remarking upon the fine weather so late in the year, Charlotte added a lengthy, but carefully written, addendum to her letter:

My dear husband's misadventure upon the shoot, I fear, left him more bewattled than usual. Dear husband sat about fidgeting for half a day until I, in sincerest concern for his nerves, suggested he take some fresh air. Whilst I do not fault that advice, for it has served mankind well for lo these many centuries, I should not have offered it had I known its eventual outcome. For Mr. Collins, who believed idleness as grievous a sin as any other I can recall, sought occupation in replenishing our honey stores before winter set in.

One can only conjecture why his bees rose to such unjust fury. I, for one, believe bees have an innate sense of purposefulness. Mr. Collins always believed so too. Perchance the indocility of his nerves that day incited them to take umbrage when he attempted to rob their hives. But I shan't speak of what I do not know.

But I do know their splenetic attack found entry beneath his wimple and forced him to flee. Had God, in his wisdom, bestowed upon my dear husband a more agile figure, in the aforementioned panic to escape the bees, when he leapt into our pond he might not have had the misfortune to become upended. And had he not chosen to wear my canvas joseph rather than his doublet, it might not have filled with water, much like an inverted umbrella, I should think. Which caused him to drown.

The fortuitous lack of autumn rain did, however, allow the pond to reveal his stockinged feet protruding above the water (panicked from his shoes he was), lest dear Mr. Collins might never have been located at all.

The apothecary said that save Mr. Fillingham's gilt, he had never seen man nor beast stung so many times by so many bees. (I believe he related that the gilt survived, but then she did not wear a canvas joseph.) Indeed, this was the reason the mortician gave for the look of absolute incredulity that went with dear Mr. Collins to his coffin.

Allow me to explain, dearest Elizabeth, that although the weather cool, the rancidity to which dear Mr. Collins's corpse was lent by measure of the venom of the bees made it necessary to inter him as hastily as possible. Hence, there is no need to hurry to Hunsford. Dear Mr. Collins has been given back to God. Earth to earth, ashes to ashes, dust to dust. That has always been one of my favourite passages. We must obtain solace from whence we can. Do you not agree?

I have written you forthwith, my sincerest concern for your deep and abiding love for your cousin mitigated only so briefly for the visit from my seamstress. I say, have you priced bombazine of late, dear Elizabeth? It is ghastly expensive.

I hereby submit to you my account of your beloved cousin, my beloved husband, Mr. Collins's untimely and unlikely demise.

I am always your affectionate friend,
Charlotte

As Elizabeth read Charlotte's letter, Darcy and Georgiana sat before her watching her countenance carefully. This scrutiny was ultimately unsuccessful, for they could not quite make out by her expression alone just what information the letter revealed.

Initially her face beheld astonishment, followed quickly by disbelief, horror, then yes, they were certain they saw (however she endeavoured to stifle it) a look of confounded amusement. Thereupon, just as hastily her features arranged themselves into a look of solemn and reverent sadness.

When Darcy inquired just what the mysterious letter contained, his usual firm voice was considerably more stentorian than one nescient of his recent infirmity might expect. Owing to his afflicted ears, however, his misapplication of modulation remained unbeknownst to him. Therefore, Elizabeth chose not to tell him he spoke too loudly; she knew it would abuse his dignity. Reminding herself to speak more firmly (understanding one insensible of the circumstance might well think they were witnessing a shouting match), she declared a summarisation of what she had just learnt.

"I think Mr. Collins has, in dying, done the only thing he could possibly do to make one cease to loathe him."

"What?"

It might have been inferred that he did not hear her, nevertheless, in this case it was not merely auricular, more a matter of comprehension. The echoing of their voices in the cavernous room persuaded Elizabeth to hand him the letter. Thereupon, she watched his countenance take the exact trip of emotions had her own.

When at last the letter was finished, he set it aside. They looked at each other a long moment. There was a thoughtful consideration before he ventured a comment.

When he did, it was not particularly profound.

"I see."

The sympathy Elizabeth harboured for such an untimely leave-taking had various shadings. It was her Christian duty to pray for Mr. Collins's soul (and pray fervently she did). However, she could not help but suspect that Charlotte might find the office of Widow Collins a far more felicitous occupation than that of wife.

Georgiana was only given to muse, "I am in a quandary, Elizabeth. Does this mean I will or will not have to dedicate my next book to him?"

Forthwith of learning of Mr. Collins's departure from this earth, Elizabeth and Jane journeyed to Hunsford to console the bereaved Charlotte. It was upon this altruistic trek that Elizabeth reminded Jane that their father's estate would thenceforth be entailed to Mr. Collins's unfortunate son. (Charlotte was always "Poor Charlotte." Chauncey was always spoken of as the "unfortunate son.") Both were quite content that they had not to weather their mother's company when she heard this perverse turn of events.

If Jane and Elizabeth were saved from their mother's unhappy eruption initially, they were not ultimately, for she was yet in a barely contained snit when they all gathered at the vicarage upon Charlotte's behalf. And Chauncey Charlemagne Collins's now three-year-old bald pate was of no particular consolation.

"Perhaps I should knit him a cap," Jane wondered solicitously.

Indeed, it was an inglorious sojourn. The Bennet family all travelled together from Longbourn and although Mary made the trip with her Bible pressed to her bosom, Kitty was bored senseless in Hunsford. Lydia too had come, but without Wickham.

It was a mystery of sorts just why the egocentric Lydia felt the need to comfort Charlotte, but that was eventually unravelled. Initially, it was presumed she merely wanted to be out of society for at least a part of the six weeks that the death of a cousin demanded. (Black, she believed, made her skin look sallow.)

Lydia's motives, however, were often as well-layered as an onionskin and just as transparent. For, howbeit Elizabeth made a concerted effort to avoid Lydia's company, they had not been there but two days when she suggested an exceedingly ill-advised visit upon Lady Catherine. Having heard Mr. Collins's lengthy description, she was quite curious to see the fabled decorations of Rosings.

"You are her niece, Lizzy," she cajoled, "Surely she will offer us an invitation if you request it, even if she does not like you."

Subtlety a much abused product in the face of Lydia's obtuse sensibilities, Elizabeth spoke to her plainly and with no little vehemence.

"Out of the question."

Knowing it would be added bother, Jane did not even consider bringing other than her newborn and wet-nurse to Hunsford with her. It was of no great surprise that such heedfulness did not enter Lydia's mind. Her three boys were handsome, but she was too impatient to mother them properly. Rambunctious and ill-mannered, they partook of far too much cake ("It's the only way I can quiet them," Lydia said defensively) and absolutely refused to bathe. The Collinses' unfortunate son was frightened of their rowdy behaviour and insisted upon standing in a chair when any of the three were in the room. Mrs. Bennet was, as always, her favourite daughter's most loyal supporter and did little to corral them.

After they played with a dog that had chosen to acquaint himself with his surroundings by rolling in the remains of a long dead animal, the stench was overwhelming.

This distasteful adventure was uncovered when the boys came to the supper table ready to partake. Everyone threw down their silverware to hold their noses in disgust. Lydia remedied the affront by sending them off with their plates to the kitchen.

Unhappy to be the proprietress of decorum under any circumstance, Elizabeth took it on nonetheless.

"I hardly think it fair to make the help ruin their suppers to spare our own."

At this rebuke, Lydia flung down her napkin in a huff.

"What would you have me do, Lizzy?"

"I would have you bathe them."

Lydia gave a heaving sigh, tilted her head, and gave her mother an imploring look,

"Oh Mama! You know what bother it is to get them clean. I have no nurse. What am I to do?"

Brightening under the influence of a notion, Mrs. Bennet said, "Perchance Chauncey's nurse could do it."

With the exact same tilt to the head, Lydia and Mrs. Bennet turned in synchronic query to Elizabeth upon this possibility.

"They are not her children to bathe."

As always, Jane was the peacemaker. "I shall go."

Knowing full well the entire contretemps was escalating into an outright squabble, Elizabeth nonetheless held firm. There were times when one must simply stand one's ground lest no one be safe.

"No, Jane, they are Lydia's children, she should see to them herself."

Lydia, annoyed, "Mother!"

Elizabeth looked at her father. He sat at the head of the table, his spectacles upon the end of his nose, reading (more than likely rereading) a letter. It was a pose quite familiar in him. He always seemed to have something to take his attention when bickering commenced. Often he would simply remove himself. Rarely did he abandon his food. A previously read letter was ideal in this specific situation. He was present but otherwise occupied.

Elizabeth looked upon him with exasperated affection. In spite of the semi-grievous (she knew it should be wholly grievous, but could only grant Mr. Collins's passing a limited amount of sorrow) circumstances, she was happy to be able to spend some time with her father.

He looked to her quite thin. Was it lack of seeing him more regularly or a sincere dissipation of his constitution, she had no objective opinion, for Darcy had not accompanied them, decrying his hearing deficiency. Elizabeth thought it a perfectly good excuse, for she despaired of him having to deal with her relatives and loss of hearing concurrently. That Rosings Park was across the hedge from the Collinses' was reason enough to plead infirmity. (Neither did Bingley come. His reason was not quite so grave, and a little suspect. Elizabeth concluded it was a matter of Bingley refusing to weather Mrs. Bennet if Darcy did not have to.)

The entire bath confrontation was solved by Jane "helping" Lydia bathe her children.

"You have servants for such things, Jane. We are too poor," Lydia complained pitifully.

Upon hearing this lament, Elizabeth made a mental note to query Jane if she was slipping Lydia money, then hastily dismissed it. If she was giving Lydia help, certainly kind-hearted Jane was. Elizabeth came perilously close to reminding Lydia she was in no worse circumstance than her own parents. And she might be in better had she been even a little prudent with money. But she did not. It would begin an even greater argument and round of rebuke, reproof, and complaint.

Elizabeth had simply had enough for one meal and was certain her father's stomach was paying him as well.

In an unusual attack of poor judgement, Elizabeth inquired of her mother about their father's health. A hypochondriac of unrivalled eminence, Mrs. Bennet plaintively enumerated her own many ills (for she enjoyed her own nerves and spasms more than any other diversion). Sourly, Elizabeth held her tongue. She believed, nevertheless, if her mother truly was in fear of loss of circumstance upon her husband's death, she might do a better job of looking after him.

After a week of unremitting solicitude, the Family Bennet took their leave. Lord and Lady Lucas were yet at Hunsford, hence there were enough condolences remaining.

Lady Lucas, for one, was quite happy to have them go. For, although one of her dearest friends, Mrs. Bennet caused her considerable consternation. Not a day passed without that lady reminding her at least once how well her own daughters had married. This, always couched midmost in a statement of sympathy for Charlotte (e.g., "Poor Charlotte, had she married half so well as Lizzy or Jane, she might not have such worry now!").

Lady Lucas, in turn, and with the identical measure of sincerity, pitied Mrs. Bennet's situation at the death of her husband, thus reminding Mrs. Bennet that her grandson (the unfortunate son) was to inherit Longbourn (e.g., "But at least, dear Mrs. Bennet, her son shall have a nice entailment coming to him in time.").

This tender compassion very nearly came to blows.

In light of this thinly veiled animosity, any respite was welcome. The Bennets fled and the Lucases waved tear-stained pocket squares as they did.

As Elizabeth and Jane were actual friends of Charlotte's and not merely unwilling relatives of her late husband, they stayed on. It was a compleat bafflement as to why Lydia wanted to stay also. Lydia, so far as Elizabeth had known, had never harboured any particular regard for Charlotte. Indeed, Lydia mocked her linen cap.

"She ties it under her chin! I shall not wear one until I am thirty!"

"Charlotte is thirty," Elizabeth dryly apprised her.

But Lydia was not of a mind to return home forthwith, for her boys were going to visit Longbourn.

Not that Mrs. Bennet was a particularly attentive grandmother. Quite the opposite, looking after them would be relegated to the servants. Mrs. Bennet would merely take to her room and complain to Mr. Bennet of the inconvenience when that opportunity arose. But for Lydia, a holiday was a holiday.

When Lydia made the announcement that she was to stay on, it was not mitigated by the understanding that her children would not. Therefore, Charlotte's countenance overspread with a look of barely concealed horror. So profound was her expression of distaste, Elizabeth was not certain it did not rival one she might have presented at the apparition of her dead husband risen from the grave.

In that Lydia stayed, the Lucases quit Hunsford as well (Lady Lucas unable to tolerate the Bennets' youngest).

Hence, the first order of business for Charlotte in this respite from unrelenting sympathy was to take to her bed to recuperate.

Thereupon, save for Chauncey, the three sisters had the house to themselves. And that dear boy was not about long. Forthwith of displaying the unique talent of inserting his entire right hand inside his mouth, the nurse took him to his nap.

Which was just as well. Although Lydia did say "ick," no one else had a comment upon that lad's proclivities other than those that were best not shared.

In the silence that followed his leave-taking, Jane was moved to note that it was the first quiet they had enjoyed for a fortnight. Evidently, this comment reminded Lydia of the true motive she had for remaining at Charlotte's.

"Lizzy! I thought I would burst lest Mama and Papa not take their leave!"

Elizabeth surmised this exclamation did not introduce a subject upon which she would look with favour. She was not to be disappointed.

"I have only just learnt that when your coach was robbed that day, the bandits stole you! You related it was merely highwaymen bent on thievery! But Wickham says not. He says he learnt Mr. Darcy murdered them for it!" She turned to Jane and repeated for her benefit, "Murdered three men!"

The lace Jane was working upon fell to the floor in a dainty clump.

No, Elizabeth did not favour this discourse. She peeked at Jane, not unwitting of what she would witness. Had her forsaken handwork not, Jane's astonished expression betrayed her innocence of the unabridged story of the attack. That dastardly Wickham. Bingley had kept his silence with his wife. Why could not have Wickham?

"They stole Lizzy, Jane! And Darcy killed them for it! Is that not the most dramatic and romantic doing you could ever fathom? And our own sister!" she nearly screeched that exclamation, but lowered her voice conspiratorially as she turned back to Elizabeth, "Lizzy, were you defiled? You are so lucky!"

Well. It had taken ever so long a time, but the story had finally made its way the length and breadth of England and thus unto her sister's eager ears. Elizabeth was grateful that Lydia had been struck with an unlikely attack of good judgement and had not told their parents. But as it had been quite some time since anyone dared to speak of it in her presence, she was in a quandary what notion of Lydia's to quash first. That there were bandits (indeed), manslaughter (undeniably), that it was dramatic (regrettably), romantic (not at all), and that she was lucky (hardly). Elizabeth was almost moved to apologise to Lydia that she was not violated.

Howbeit Elizabeth silently blessed Bingley's discretion, she realised that it was no longer germane. In light of the terrified look upon Jane's countenance, Elizabeth worried she might swoon even then. Had she heard it direct of its occurrence, Jane might not have recovered. However impregnable Lydia's hyperbole appeared, she knew she must convince Jane it was not quite as horrifying as it sounded.

"Lydia, being accosted by thieves is frightening, not romantic. Only fables name it thus. I was not defiled and I shall not discuss it with you beyond that. If you continue to press the matter, I shall vacate the room."

Lydia bestowed her a profound look of disgust.

"I merely want to ascertain the particulars, Lizzy. Wickham boasted that he knew all, but he did not. Do tell!"

This beseechment was denied. In defiance of her sister's prying, Elizabeth stood and folded her arms. In response to her implacability, Lydia instituted a lengthy and grating whine, one that she accentuated with a petulant a stamp of her foot.

"Lizz-e-e-e, you are so-o-o-o selfish! Can you not even share such an exploit with your own sisters?"

This tactic unfruitful, Lydia embarked upon an alternative, "It is my understanding Darcy behaved valiantly in saving you. Thus, it is not as if there was cowardice to shield. Darcy was heroic, was he not? You must tell all!"

The oblique strategy revealed that years of practise had refined Lydia's inveiglement skills. Elizabeth, however, was still disinclined to respond. Her husband's heroism was beyond any telling. Particularly to her present company. Moreover, Lydia's abuse of familiarity bade Elizabeth suffer an attack of sanctimony unrecollected of herself.

Hence, rather sniffily, Elizabeth corrected her, "*Mister* Darcy did only what he had to do, Lydia, no more."

Still snagged in the drama of Elizabeth's long past kidnapping, Jane interrupted them both, "Pray Lizzy, why did you not speak of this to me!"

"There was nothing I chose to relate, Jane. 'Tis done. It is long over. If only others will let it be."

Pointedly, her eyes rested upon Lydia.

"You, Lizzy, think of no one but yourself," Lydia pouted again. "As extraordinary a story as that and you refuse to share it. What can I do but enjoy another's adventures? I, who have nothing. Only Wickham. Not once has he rescued me. He is utterly worthless."

With her lower lip protruding significantly, Lydia sat in a disgusted heap. Jane stood, thoroughly aghast and categorically appalled at all that she had heard. To suffer learning that highwaymen had beset dearest Lizzy only to be subjected to hearing Lydia casting aspersion upon the father of her children made her feel faint.

Swooning, however, was out of the question. If Wickham's character was indefensible, Lydia's defamation still had to be protested.

"Lydia! How can you speak so contemptuously of your own husband?"

Elizabeth nodded in agreement. Albeit she thought quite contemptuously of the wastrel Wickham, even she was appalled to hear such unadulterated disparagement from his wife.

Lydia responded to them both with a snort, "Well of course, you, sisters, have greater reason to amuse your husbands than I do Wickham. If he were in the circumstance of Mr. Darcy or Mr. Bingley, I dare say I could find him more affection. As it is, Wickham is poor and cannot even diddle long enough for me to come, so what good is he as a husband?"

Agape yet over Lydia's ridicule of her husband, it was clear Jane's sensibilities were further sullied upon her uttering the word "diddle." Hitherto, Elizabeth would have been in concern for Jane's discombobulation. But in that it otherwise spared the conversation her dear sister's enquiry as to whither Lydia journeyed during coition, she fretted not.

Jane was diverted from that query by ascertaining just which of Lydia's indignities demanded reproach first. Unable to come to a decision, she used a non-specific, all-purpose announcement.

"Lydia, I am shocked!"

Lydia rolled her eyes. Thereupon, she continued to enumerate Wickham's shortcomings.

"Be not astonished, Jane. Wickham does not deserve your sympathy. He has lifted more skirts than…" She searched a moment for an example, "…Casanova! And I for one say good riddance. When he is at home he wheedles me into submitting to him, then cannot remember to withdraw. He leaves me high in the belly, then takes his foul weapon elsewhere."

Jane firmly believed that all God's creatures were fundamentally good, howbeit it had been a particularly demanding search to find a redeeming quality belonging to Wickham. He had proven himself unreliable, duplicitous, and vain. In absence of any obvious virtue, Jane had fancied him at least an ardent husband. Thus, it was particularly difficult for her to encounter the dual revelation that not only was he unfaithful, he was absent-minded as well.

Elizabeth, however, had long concluded that Wickham was nothing less than a simpering Lothario. Therefore, she was not particularly astounded to learn he was guilty of gross marital misconduct. Ergo, it was not difficult to find sympathy for someone who had partaken her wedding vows with him. Even if she was a twit.

Thus, Elizabeth patted Lydia's hand, whilst saying, "Perchance you are mistaken. You have children. A husband would not forsake his family thusly."

Other than shopping, self-pity was Lydia's favourite pastime. Thus, it was seldom necessary to coax it from her. Moreover, she often found consolation (if not out-right delight) in shared misery.

Lydia grimaced, "Open your eyes, Lizzy, all men stray. 'Tis their nature."

Thereupon, she sighed with exaggerated resignation. Elizabeth was not of a mind to carry the marital standard of fidelity upon behalf of all husbands, but she felt compelled to disabuse Lydia of the notion that every husband cavorted outside marriage.

"Condemning all husbands because you believe Wickham has caroused about is ill-considered."

"'Tis not! Look about you, Lizzy. Men get their oats when and where they can and marriage is no impediment. They are beasts once they get the scent. Some more relentless than others. Be not smug. You may believe your husband constant, but I have heard those dogs howl outside your door. His blood is hot."

At this obscure reference, Jane looked baffled. So confused did she look, Lydia felt it necessary to aside an explanation, "He is at her night and day, Jane."

As Elizabeth sat in open-mouthed fury, Lydia obliviously continued her harangue.

"I too obliged Wickham regularly. Yet he forsook me. Think of it, Lizzy. If a man who has nothing but his charms to promote him can find willing arms, what of a man as rich as Darcy? Unquestionably, wanton wenches fling themselves at his feet..."

With all due restraint (she did not coldcock her with a girandole), Elizabeth spluttered briefly. Then, voice escalating, she said, "Is there no limit to your slander? Do not defame my husband as a blackguard by virtue of Wickham's sins!"

Realising she had over-stepped a rather strict boundary, Lydia regrouped and then cajoled, "Oh, Lizzy, true, I know not of your husband, I only conjecture. But if our mother says our own father did not stay faithful to their marriage, how can we fancy our own husbands would do better?"

"Mama could never have said such a thing!"

Knowing she then had the whip-hand, Lydia inspected her nails whilst saying, "She did. Ask her."

Elizabeth and Jane both sat in dumbfounded confoundment. Their silence bid Lydia to suspect victory and take her leave. In fortune, for Elizabeth was still in a barely contained rage. The double affront first to defame Darcy, then their father, was beyond reprehensible. It was unforgivable.

Finally, her face possibly the colour of stewed beets, Elizabeth spit out, "I cannot believe even Lydia would speak so..."

Words failed her. Born of unequivocal ignorance, Lydia's comments about Darcy, though despised, could be dismissed. Hence Elizabeth's wrath toward Lydia descended upon and engulfed her defamation of their father. She knew that he was not of a disposition to seek comfort in any of those pleasures that too often console those disappointed by conjugal infelicity.

"How could she repeat such a thing, Jane? How could our mother tell her such a thing? There is no finer man anywhere, no better husband, no better father!"

Jane sat quite still for a moment before agreeing, "I cannot bear to hear him labelled a philanderer either, Lizzy."

"Libelled, you mean," responded Elizabeth.

Ignoring the clarification, Jane hesitated a moment, then added, "But as dearly as we hold Papa, we had daily proof that our parents' marriage was not a happy one. Moreover, as I sit here I wonder why our mother would have told such a fiction to Lydia—it would lend her no service as a wife."

It was Elizabeth's considered opinion that their mother was capable of uttering such a blasphemy simply to reassure Lydia that Wickham's betrayal was not her fault. Nevertheless, she did not say so to Jane. She simply shook her head in denial of Lydia's allegations and vowed not to think of it again.

Upon the trip home, Jane sat napping upright, thereupon giving Elizabeth time to ponder her father's fidelity. The possibility that it was compromised was far too painful; hence, she thought of it no more.

Darcy weathered his auricular plight with considerable ill-humour. Silence would have been vexation enough, but his injury instituted a profound ringing noise that drove him to distraction. Hence, an eminent auditory specialist was called from Edinburgh to see to his malady. Had not Sir Malcolm MacFarqhuar been knighted by King George himself, Darcy might have refused his counsel. Nevertheless, he harrumphed at the notion of being seen by any other than an English physician.

Darcy's Anglophilia well-entrenched, Sir MacFarqhuar's person did little to placate it. For howbeit he arrived at Pemberley with all due haste, his russet beard, pleated kilt, and melodious burr were a profound reminder from whence he came. Already agitated at the repeated prodding of his ears, Darcy did not suffer the Scot with forbearance.

Not only did he despise being inspected, the infliction of the sight of the doctor's hairy knees did nothing to becalm him. But as the doctor was quite efficient and not particularly wordy, he suffered his examination in peevish silence.

Elizabeth stood by her husband witnessing his dour countenance and issuing just enough commiseration to keep his temper at bay. After an extensive consultation with an odd assortment of peculiar instruments, the prestigious doctor made his diagnosis.

"Mr. Darcy shall regain his hearing," he pronounced. Then cautioned, "Although his eardrums are not ruptured, they are severely inflamed. It is a precarious situation. Another assault upon them might render him permanently deaf."

Because of his deafness, this warning was issued to Mrs. Darcy, whose own countenance did not belie her alarm at such an ominous declaration. With studied patience (and an annoyed expression) Darcy awaited whilst his dismayed wife wrote the doctor's judgement out and handed the paper to him. Upon reading it, he seemed little concerned beyond the eminent physician's suggestion of the use of an ear trumpet. ("My great-aunt!" Mr. Darcy had responded indignantly, and those present took this as a negative.) The possibility of auricular foredoom was of no particular consequence to one who is both pragmatic and not easily unnerved.

Such insouciance is seldom the reaction of a loved one, however stout-hearted. Elizabeth was unnerved, and she cared little who knew it.

Not wanting to unduly distress illustrious Mr. Darcy's illustrious wife, the doctor attempted to mollify his diagnosis thusly, "It is true Mr. Darcy's hearing has suffered grievously and Aye fear that another loud noise might take it from him permanently. But that is unlikely. Aye understand that poor Mr. Collins is newly departed?"

The nature of the accident and culprit responsible had obviously been explained to the doctor.

It was indisputable that few who walked the earth could have rivalled her cousin's ineptitude, but the doctor regretted his small slander against kin of the Darcys as soon as he realised he had committed it. He announced he understood his *faux pas* in a fit of coughing.

Amused, for Sir MacFarqhuar had revealed himself a ceaseless toadeater (not even close in rank to the Vicar Collins, but then no one was), Elizabeth answered his question with deliberate obtuseness.

"Well, Mr. Collins did make a hasty retreat to Kent. Hence, depart he did, but forthwith dropped dead."

Having been of Mrs. Darcy's acquaintance only a brief time, Sir MacFarqhuar was taken aback by her lack of politesse. As a man whose occupation demanded considerable pussyfooting when rendering an opinion of an unfavourable nature (and who never, ever spoke any variation of the word death), he was rendered somewhat befuddled by Elizabeth's bluntness.

"Yes, yes," he muttered, but found himself unable to quit the subject in such frank disorder.

Thus he intoned (leaving nary an "r" untrilled), "Plucked he was from your midst to wing his flight from this merciful world. How very regrettable. But we must all pay nature's last debt. Aye hope his passing was peaceful."

"I fear it was not," announced Elizabeth.

At these words, the doctor's eyes widened in anticipation of a harrowing tale of death and dying (his delicacy extended to circumlocution of one's demise and not, apparently, the gory details). Albeit Elizabeth's verbal inclinations strayed from the metaphorical, neither was she of a mind to feed another's imprudent curiosity.

Thus, she abandoned candour and resorted to the tergiversation of one raised eyebrow.

"Bees," said she.

This single, cryptic word was enough to ignite the good doctor's imagination and he nodded his head as if he had heard the entire, bloodcurdling account. Because this exchange was denied him, the humour of it was begrudged Darcy as well. And this silent purgatory was endured by him only because there was no choice.

Volition was something that had rarely been denied a man of his literal and figurative stature and (was other expected?) he did not submit to this revocation with resignation. So ill was his temper during this epoch, few dared to traverse his path. Bingley made perfunctory visits if only because his Christian duty demanded he not abandon a friend in time of adversity, no matter how sour said friend's disposition.

Fitzwilliam ventured thither for the same motive (the word "family" substituted for Christian).

Most of Darcy's days, however, were spent upon solitary rides astride Blackjack. Evidently, in lieu of hearing of it, he intended to inspect every foot of earth under the auspices of Pemberley. Although he spent a perfunctory morning visit with his wife, he set out before noon, partaking only of a Spartan midday meal and often not returning until darkness overtook him. Moreover, he did not consume his supper with particular gusto. His lean frame had always camouflaged a build of substantial thew. His withered appetite began to take its toll upon his weight, but it was only his wife (and probably Goodwin) who knew it. Other than to entice him with his favourite dishes, Elizabeth had not a clue how to counter melancholic malnourishment. It was her personal understanding that if one had not the inclination to eat, it could not be coaxed. Furthermore, howbeit she truly did not believe his sense of taste was physically affected by his hearing impairment, she was certain that they would both return simultaneously.

His lone figure, however, was still a sombre sight. Not only did he forsake Elizabeth's company, he refused to be attended at all. Silently, she fretted for his despondency. Aloud, she insisted that it was unsafe for him to ride about thus.

"Pray, should your path be crossed by some misfortune…"

"Misfortunes occur to the most healthy of souls, Lizzy. I should think I would be merely saved the ordeal of hearing it befall me."

Though she was miffed that he disregarded her upon that matter, she was recompensed.

For within his disability, they did discover a previous delight. By reason of opportunity, an ancient adage was proven true. The absence of one of the five senses did enhance the others. Two impaired was an exultation of sensory riches. The pier glass was unearthed from its hiding place beneath their bed and put to good use reflecting innumerable capital acts. Conversation was not needed for any of them.

Beyond those connubial, however, pleasure was not his companion. Tolerance for his self-perceived ridicule made him increasingly fractious. Alas, the inadvertent gun blast and resultant injury could not have happened more incommodiously. In his cotton-headed vulnerability, he had little to do but stew. And of the vast pool of possible vexations a man of Mr. Darcy's standing could select to gnaw upon, his mind seized upon but a single perplexity. That of the paternity of John Christie.

Other than once wanting rather dearly to wring his neck, Darcy had not given the lad a thought. He cowered about so, had Georgiana not taken the notion to school him, Darcy was uncertain he would have recognised his visage. Perchance that is why no one ever remarked upon a resemblance. John rarely allowed himself within the same eye-line as his employer.

Upon Darcy's commencement of a surreptitious study of the boy, a disconcerting revelation was uncovered. Clearly, John Christie was a tall, dark-haired, taciturn fellow and carried himself with a graceful amble of a walk. Even Darcy could not deny that, except for a more purposeful gait, it was the very description that might have been used to particturalise himself. Once one accomplished the feat of overlooking grimy fingers, crude garb, and common speech, it could be noted that John's features and figure were remarkably regular and straight. Even noble. Close observation and cautious interrogation of Edward Hardin revealed to Darcy that John was also industrious, honest, and bright.

Imperceptibly, Darcy began to feel a swell of pride. Many men of station (and almost all those royal) could not claim such fine attributes. Breeding will out, he concluded. The august Darcy blood overcame all manner of nurturing deprivation.

Few men would be able to compleatly abandon a certain conceit on behalf of the potency of their loins. It was the most primitive of instincts. However he might have wanted to believe otherwise, Darcy was no exception. Who should not want to bask in the glow of begetting a strong, handsome boy-child? Even in silent self-satisfaction, Darcy would not. When he realised he had leapt from speculation to acceptance, the smugness of those particular deliberations were roundly quashed in favour of less heady ones.

If it were true that the boy was of his seed, it was his duty to acknowledge him. Was he to do just that, it might well be the most shocking thing to come to pass in Derbyshire since the passing of the Duchess of Devonshire. Howbeit to Darcy's way of thinking a significant scandal it would be, as far as aristocratic indiscretions were concerned, it was rather minor. More gentlemen than he cared to name had harboured intrigues or kept paramours. If discreet, offspring resulting from such liaisons were tolerated amongst society. Seldom, however, were they acknowledged.

There lay the infamy.

Gentlemen dallied and society turned a blind eye so long as such peccadilloes did not become public. Darcy respected the lessons of the station to which he was born; however, his notion of honour was a little weightier in scruples than most. Holding the generally unpopular belief that public and private disgrace were one and the same, he wrestled relentlessly with his conscience. Could he cast all decorum aside and openly claim a bastard child of his chambermaid as his own son? Give him the Darcy name? His father's name?

Notoriety, particularly for sins of the flesh, was indefensible. As abhorrent as he held a rupture of his privacy, Darcy's private mortification eclipsed even that. There was nothing upon which he prided himself more than self-discipline. Although he had never quite reached a reckoning with his unequivocal surrendering to the fever of his youth, he had believed it was an ancient imprudence. Admittedly, when he married Elizabeth, he was not an innocent. But if he had once succumbed to the call of his libido, he had truly believed his reputation was unsullied by any, shall we say, lasting evidence of it. Except for that unguarded initial frolic into carnality, he had been meticulous about how and with whom he bedded. Hence, the appearance of this particular misbegotten bairn thrust unknowingly upon his doorstep (if memory served, literally upon the inception of his wedding), proclaimed itself unto Darcy as a harbinger of judgement. He saw it clearly as a condemnation of his early sins of the flesh. And if it was not divine, the difference was indiscernible.

Tormented with guilt, he wrestled with how best to announce to his wife, his family, his friends, and society in general that he was no better that Henry Howgrave's father. How could he find the moral courage to deliberately besmirch his father's memory in such a vulgar manner? After weeks of vacillating, he knew he must make a move, for he was out of humour far too frequently. However, he wanted to reach a decision uncluttered by sentiment before burdening Elizabeth with his public disgrace.

Ere that opinion could be reasoned, fate intervened.

It was a perfectly lovely afternoon for midwinter. Not a finer day had been had for weeks. It was then Mrs. Reynolds chose to board a waggon for Kympton to personally berate the costermonger for the unacceptability of their most recent delivery.

The old woman issued orders to bring the waggon about whilst complaining bitterly about the necessity of having to endure the fallowness of winter at all.

"Was it not such a dry autumn, the cellars would be full. There would be no need for such flummery as this!"

Just outside the steps of the house, Mrs. Reynolds checked a sheet of paper with her index finger, methodically reviewing what appeared to anyone else as hen-scratching. Evidently, the costermonger's sins were so numerous as to need explicit delineation. Once that was accomplished, she was impatient to light into the man and stood about in irascible wait for the waggon.

The footmen scurried about, none anxious to invoke her wrath, which led to undue hastiness in preparation. The harness needed adjusting. But as Mrs. Reynolds was getting testier by the minute, a dirk that was both too long and too dull was produced. It fell to John Christie to employ it. Had Mrs. Reynolds glowered less relentlessly or the wielder been more experienced, greater caution would have been observed. But as it was not, the knife slipped, gouging John's hand nearly to the bone just below his index finger.

The geyser of blood that erupted caused the usually unflappable Mrs. Reynolds to shriek, thus alerting the house of the accident.

Georgiana and Elizabeth rushed to the scene, then ordered John whisked into the kitchen. Most knife wounds occurred there and, as a veteran of such mishaps, cook was charged with repairing this one. This was neither a solemn nor a solitary procedure.

Surrounded by an assortment of scullery help, cook still set about this task with all the aplomb of a surgeon.

Howbeit Mrs. Reynolds covered her eyes, Georgiana observed the doings closely. So carefully did she watch, it appeared she might actually take the needle and thread from cook's hand and compleat the operation herself.

Elizabeth was both mesmerised and repulsed by the ordeal. She noticed that the victim, however, was astonishingly stoic (the ladies were quite unwitting that it was their presence that bid John's denial of pain). Indeed, during the close scrutiny of this process, Elizabeth considered howling upon his behalf. But as screaming in empathy was not an acceptable option and a chorus of "o-o-ohs" erupted with each stitch taken, she busied herself shooing out unnecessary observers.

After the cut had been closed, Georgiana took over. She patted some cobwebs upon the wound, then swaddled his hand in muslin batting (in all honesty, it was a little overly swaddled) and led him outside. From thence, Elizabeth could hear her issuing strict instructions to Edward Hardin about keeping John's hand elevated and dry. This instituted some stifled laughter amongst the other footmen, and it wafted indoors.

Elizabeth smiled to herself as she imagined John Christie's mortification.

"Noble blood, to be so brave," she remarked.

Mrs. Reynolds replied "As well he should."

Cook had returned to her oven, and this inexplicable comment seemed to dangle in the air inexorably.

"He should?" Elizabeth bid.

"Why yes, I thought you knew, 'though I'm not so sure if the boy does."

A profound sense of foreboding compelled Elizabeth to ask a question that she was not certain she wanted answered.

"Knows of what?"

"It was under this roof, it was, where she got with child."

Elizabeth nodded patiently, anxiousness betrayed only by the rapid tapping one foot undertook. Knowing it a redundancy, she could think of no other query to further the conversation.

"His mother?" she asked.

"Yes. Abigail Christie. She was all of nineteen and should have known better. But she was quite an article. Flounced about beckoning every attention, she did. No wonder a young master's head was turned. I ask you now, if grown men can't resist such doings, how can a mere boy?"

At this revelation, Elizabeth felt the blood rushing to her head. At the resultant crimson of her face, she turned away, her heart racing.

"A mere boy?" she repeated, beginning, for all the world, to feel like a parrot.

"Yes. Although, I suppose, not that so much of a boy. Mr. Wickham."

Momentarily, Elizabeth had half expected to hear the old woman speak Darcy's name, but that notion vanished with the same dispatch whence it had come.

Incredulous, she asked witlessly, "Wickham is his father?"

"Yes, and wild Wickham turned out to be. I guess he began his life of dissolution with that strumpet."

Interminable as the story was, Mrs. Reynolds' loquacity was quite unwitting of its longevity and she chatted on.

"Abigail Christie was half-term gone when she left here. I told old Mr. Darcy that young George Wickham laid with her, but he did not want to believe it. Something bechanced later, I know not what, and he altered his opinion and dismissed her."

Mrs. Reynolds looked out upon John walking out of the courtyard. Elizabeth's gaze followed hers.

"He does favour Mr. Wickham, does he not? I always wondered if he knew of him."

Elizabeth agreed indeed he did favour Wickham, but could find no opinion upon merit of the major's information. However, she did have a notion as to who would.

Taking the most direct path from the kitchen to Darcy's library wherein she knew him to be engrossed in a ledger, Elizabeth endeavoured not to run. Once there, she quieted, for she truly did not want to appear as anxious as she was to pass on gossip. Settling herself upon a sofa, she bade her husband come sit by her.

Her excitement was obvious, thoroughly intriguing his attention. Thus, he abandoned his figures. But he did not come and sit. Although his hearing had returned to a tolerable degree (though not yet his appetite), he stood before her, hands folded behind his back in wait. As soon as she saw that she had his full heedfulness, she launched her tale.

"You cannot imagine the startling news I have just learnt from Mrs. Reynolds."

"The pigs are loose in the garden."

"No, the pigs are not in the garden!" she said with mock irritation.

"A disappointment. It has been a quiet day…"

"Not in the kitchen. There was an accident, but that is all forgot now," she brushed off the details of an incident that did not serve her story. "It was John, the groom. But his injury is not of what I came to tell."

Darcy's alteration in temper was immediate, but undetectable to Elizabeth. Hence, there was no hesitation before she made her announcement.

"Mrs. Reynolds told me that he was fathered by George Wickham!"

Never expecting any untoward display of astonishment from her husband, Elizabeth was not entirely surprised that at that pronouncement Darcy only emitted a mild, "Oh."

He had turned away, highly engrossed in prodding the waning fire back to life. To his back, Elizabeth continued, "I knew the boy's mother once worked here, but I had no idea Wickham was her lover. Did you?"

A lack of response influenced Elizabeth to believe he had not heard her enquiry and she waited patiently as he kicked some scattered wood back upon the hearth. Though his countenance was turned away from her, to Elizabeth his unease was obvious. As the conveyor of his disquiet, she harboured a certain amount of contrition that her own eager curiosity provoked the mention of despicable Wickham in the first place. But because that subject was already before them and could not be reclaimed with any facility, she quite shamelessly advanced her own investigation. The details would be entirely too salacious not to be savoured.

"Do you fancy Wickham knows he fathered a child here?"

In answer, Darcy shrugged his shoulders. The illogic that he had not heard her first question, but did the second, was lost upon Elizabeth. For, quite abruptly, she was embroiled in her own machinations of relation.

Had she not long felt affection for John, bashful and motherless as he was, romanticism might not have overtaken her sensible nature. In a flight of fancy worthy of Jane, she imagined John a love-bairn left undiscovered by his true father.

Certainly, his true father was a walking muckheap, but he was married to her sister. That this particular misbegotten son ended up working at Pemberley under her auspices, she believed fell to serendipitous chance.

A wrong to be righted.

Elizabeth's speculation about this little peripeteia was relentless. Only by instituting the utmost self-restraint was she able to keep it to herself until they retired for the eve.

As they lay in bed, the flickering candlelight revealed Darcy resting the back of his hand across his eyes, seeming to block out some vision he did not want to see.

For his thoughts were not so illusory as Elizabeth's. He had implied to her he did not know if Wickham had knowledge of his son (the shrug, which technically indicated uncertainty but upon occasion he used one in place of "I choose not to take part in this conversation"). The gesture was implemented at that time in both definitions, for Darcy did not know absolutely. Notion was another matter.

Wickham had to have known of the baby Abigail carried when she vacated Pemberley. Darcy had no doubt. He believed that Wickham had a hand in her hasty departure as well. Elizabeth's words had much the same impact upon him had he been struck full in the stomach with a closed fist. It was impossible that Mrs. Reynolds was mistaken. That woman knew all. He shook his head at his own naïveté. His penitence had been so thoroughly embraced, he had not instituted his usually dependable logic upon the matter. Guilt, compounded by time, had beclouded his recollection of the relative briefness of the affair and the swiftness of Abigail's departure. For only then did it occur to him that their assignations all befell within a se'nnight. His father spoke to him upon the seventh day and upon the eighth, she was gone. Had Abigail been impregnated by him, she would not have known it yet and neither would Mrs. Reynolds.

It was doubtful any man was of a more cynical nature than he. Yet, howbeit he understood Abigail had not been a virgin, he never once considered the possibility that her child had been fathered by another. Had fate not intervened, he might have committed a blunder of near biblical proportions. He would have given Wickham's bastard son the Darcy name. It was the single most mortifying misapprehension a man could make. Indeed, his notion of his own infallibility was mocked irrevocably. That his humiliation was evident only to himself was of no particular comfort. For it was by virtue of Wickham, he whose very name invoked treachery.

He was caught in a maelstrom of conflicted emotions. Unmitigated self-abasement was foremost, but the profound relief he should have experienced was compromised by guilt. For his conscience was not so kind as to allow him to dismiss the episode as a nerve-racking, but ultimately harmless, misunderstanding.

When another might have seen some amusement in being saved from such colossal misapprehension, Darcy did not. Suffice it to say he weathered his misjudgement not well.

But it was to be some time before he wearied of self-flagellation and concentrated on outrage at the reprehensible Wickham for abandoning Abigail and the baby he begat. As he did, Elizabeth lay so quietly at his side he had thought her asleep. Thus, it startled him when she spoke.

"Darcy, if Wickham is his father, John Christie is family."

"Not of my family!" Darcy spit out before he could check the vehemence of his words.

"True. Not of your family, but of my own. For, if you recall," she reminded him, "Wickham is married to my sister."

Darcy removed his hand from his eyes and looked at her, anticipating just what she was thinking, "Certainly you do not intend to further this?"

Elizabeth's silence told him it was quite probable she would. Knowing when she resolved to take action, rarely was she swayed, he nonetheless implored her to reconsider.

"Lizzy, I do not think you understand just how despicable Wickham is. It would be a kindness to keep from the boy just what measure of man fathered him."

She rolled over, half atop him and queried in all earnestness, "Do you truly think knowing Wickham to be his father is more cruel than to have him believe he has no father at all?"

"Yes," he said unequivocally and without hesitation.

"This opinion, of course, comes from a man who had a fine father, does it not? How can we say what is best for another?"

In the dark, she heard him say he agreed with her without mitigation. In light of his concession, she hooked her leg affectionately over both of his, changing the subject quite effectively. Which was most regrettable.

However much Mrs. Darcy relished her husband that night, had their conversation reached a less…ardent conclusion, a great deal of vexation might have been prevented. For she might have realised that, although he was in concurrence that no one should suppose to act upon another's behalf, he did not imply it was his own judgement that was suspect.

Knowing her philanthropic bent, he advised her, "Do not interfere in this matter, Lizzy. This boy is grown. Some things must be forsaken to find their own end."

As well-intentioned as it was, the wisdom of his admonition was most probably lost upon her. And if it was, it was he who should have borne the responsibility. For it was he who embarked upon a particularly pleasurable violation of her person, dowsing any opportunity for logical thought.

But if thoughts of orphaned grooms and happy endings danced in Elizabeth's dreams that night, they were dashed by morning. For the dawn brought a reminder that not all troubles were within her power to right.

For light was barely creeping into the room when Darcy awakened and saw Elizabeth had taken leave of their bed. When he drew back the bed cloth, he saw the bloody evidence from which she had taken flight. The search for her was brief. He did not have to venture beyond her dressing room and tub. The water had long lost its warmth and there, in shivering misery, she sat. He walked to her and took a bath cloth, urging her out.

"Come out, Lizzy, you shall become ill."

She turned and looked at him wordlessly. As he bade her stand, he swathed the soft folds about her cold body, rubbing her briskly to create some warmth.

"Do not despair," he said. "Do not despair."

In only a few years, the Wickhams' marriage had disintegrated into a bickering, loveless test of endurance. Lydia's trial was suffering Wickham's limitless infidelity, Wickham's was weathering Lydia's merciless nagging about it. For, he reasoned, had she not kept at her relentless carping, he might not have caroused half so much as he did. Therefore, a goodly portion of his debauchery was all her fault.

Life as Major Wickham's wife might have been quite vexing had Lydia not invented her own little diversions.

In the beginning, it was not at all amusing.

The first time she found Wickham compromised with a notorious piece of baggage, Lydia had been furious. Her fury was vented upon that strumpet's costume and the hair upon Wickham's head. As vain as Wickham was about his appearance, he was mortified the entire quarter of year it took for the bald spot upon his scalp to disappear (he had to institute an elabourate comb-over which usurped half the curls he liked to spiral down onto his forehead). The young woman was simply grateful to have escaped with her life.

However, repetition eventually jaded Lydia's indignation and it soon became a bit of a game to catch Wickham *in flagrante delicto,* the more flagrant the better. This did incur some bother, for Lydia knew well that what Wickham enjoyed was pursuit; endurance in bed was not his strong suit. Timing was of the utmost. She must burst upon the liaison betwixt initiation and emission. Five minutes maximum.

Despite the vexation to her, observing the expression upon Wickham's countenance as his...ardour succumbed to humiliation was exquisite. In that efficiency is not of particular merit in matters amorous, Wickham might not have been asked for an encore by the ladies he conquered regardless that his wife had a penchant for surprise. And, unwitting as he was that his wife was ferreting out his amorous liaisons with considerable merriment, Wickham had become a desperate philanderer. This desperation, of course, merely fed Lydia's glee.

The mirth of her marriage did not come without, at least in Lydia's estimation, considerable cost. This came by way of three children born in five years. The initial bliss Lydia had enjoyed in carnal union was usurped by the discomfort of pregnancy specifically and the annoyance of motherhood in general.

She renewed her sleuthing efforts upon Wickham's dalliances, but flatly denied him his conjugal rights at home. This was a monumental conundrum for Wickham. It had been some time since he had desired Lydia's...favours (his lack of interest inversely proportionate to the length of their marriage). He had done his husbandly duty and begat three sons, which had served the dual purpose of proving his own masculinity and keeping Lydia sick in bed (she did not suffer her pregnancies with good humour).

There was the rub. He had no interest in pintling his own wife and she petulantly announced she would not let him.

Dash it all.

He had to demand marital rights that he was not remotely interested in enjoying. It was into this environment of recrimination and retribution that a post arrived addressed to Major Wickham bearing the Pemberley seal.

U nder the specific circumstances, no one else might have been. Elizabeth, however, was astonished when she espied Wickham standing in her foyer awaiting to be announced.

Astounded dismay temporarily immobilised her.

It had been several years since last she had seen him. Time had not altered him in appearance or demeanour. He stood with one hip cocked, one hand resting upon the hilt of his sword. His cape was tossed with studied rakishness over one shoulder, and whilst tapping the toe of his highly polished boot, his eyes expertly took measure of the lobby. Twice he twaddled the tips of his fingers in his mahogany curls as his gaze paused at the tall entry mirror. Much as in Hertfordshire, Wickham's uniform was still more a prop for his vanity than an announcement of his occupation. His pose allowed the shine of his boots to be fully appreciated by whoever might chance to gaze upon his figure.

Before Elizabeth could react, either by hiding or outright fleeing, Wickham caught her in his eye.

"Elizabeth!" called he, "how good to see you! It has been far too long!"

"No, it has not," Elizabeth thought meanly, but replied a reluctant, yet mild, "Indeed."

The scheme that she and Jane had hatched appeared to be taking a rather startlingly ill turn. They had merely hoped to apprise Wickham that he had a son in preparation for the sisters taking upon the highly anticipated office of John Christie's long-lost aunts. Never once did Elizabeth consider Wickham might come to meet his son himself.

Immediate of discovering that John was their brother-in-law's illegitimate son, Elizabeth had hied to Kirkland Hall. With all due diligence, the sisters carefully explored the implications of his heredity. Forthwith, Jane returned to Pemberley to have her newly discovered nephew pointed out. They both admired the young man's heretofore unremarked upon handsome features, whilst Elizabeth expounded upon his innate intelligence, kindness, and lack of family. It was during an extended conversation about their Christian duty to humanity that the plan was concocted for Elizabeth to write to Wickham and tell him of his son.

If there was a particular protocol in introducing bastardy into the family fold, both sisters reasoned the first step was to notify the father.

As a result of their collabouration, Wickham stood unexpectedly in her foyer. Thereby, Elizabeth concluded, for them, collective reasoning was not necessarily an improvement. (Elizabeth would happily share the blame with her sister for their blunder.)

Indeed, Lydia's husband bowed, inquiring if Darcy was about before quite compleating his flourish. At hearing he was not, Wickham visibly exhaled a sigh of relief, one that was synchronous to Elizabeth's. Neither evidently wanted that particular confrontation. Thereupon, Wickham took Elizabeth's unoffered hand mid-curtsy and kissed it. So distasteful was this affectation, she reclaimed her hand.

The withdrawal of her hand was exacted with such dispatch, she very nearly gave him a labial abrasion.

Her haste bade him look askance, and from his upturned countenance, she discerned a likeness to John Christie so strong, it struck her dumb.

Quite unbeknownst to her, Elizabeth was overtly staring into Wickham's face. She was searching it, exploring it for markers of similarity betwixt his countenance and John's. They were there. How could she have mistaken the similarity for that of Darcy?

The nose was straight like her husband, but John's was longer. Wickham had an aquiline nose. But none had quite the same smile, for Wickham smiled incessantly, Darcy rarely and John not at all. The chin was familiar. She had once thought the cleft in John's chin reminded her of Darcy's, but she saw then that it was Wickham's.

Wickham had a cleft in his chin, as did John. The area that lay uncompared were the eyes, for John had usually kept his cast away. When Elizabeth's eyes finally rested upon Wickham's to take their measure, she was almost startled. For his two orbs stared back at her with unexpected licentiousness.

If that distracted her, it was but fleetingly, for her chief concern was that of privacy.

Of the belief that any frank talk of their groom's parentage should best be done in private, Elizabeth reluctantly invited Wickham into the drawing room. They crossed its width and so smoothly did he slide onto the satin settee next to her, she well-nigh landed in his lap. She settled at the far end and folded her hands primly upon her knees. Imperceptibly, Wickham leaned toward her. Just as imperceptibly, she drew away.

If Wickham looked upon Elizabeth as the object of a seduction, as the manipulated party of Elizabeth and Jane's faltering strategy, he too was a victim of events.

He was this, of course, as much as the result of his own self-deception than at the hands of anyone else. For as it might be suspected, Wickham did not come to Pemberley in search of reuniting with his lost son born of Abigail Christie. His reason was two-fold and representative of his objective in life in general. He hoped to partake of an intrigue and get rich in the process.

However, Wickham was labouring under several misconceptions. Primarily because he could not imagine that Elizabeth would write to him personally only to tell him about a long forgotten bush-begotten baby. If he had no interest in such an event, he did not fathom her own. Therefore, why she initiated contact with him was a mystery to be uncovered.

The second involved the widespread partnering of people of wealth into marriages of convenience and the rampant belief that was an exclusivity. Wickham had never reconciled within himself that Darcy had married Elizabeth for love. He believed it was inevitable that Elizabeth Bennet Darcy was bored and lonely. Upon the fringes of good society, Wickham had serviced the occasional unhappily married baroness. He was only one of a contingent of Lotharios who undertook these aristocratic assignations. Thus when Elizabeth looked with trepidation into Wickham's seriously lascivious gaze, he thought he saw chance befall him. The opportunity seemed ripe for a rare triple success of seduction, bribery, and revenge.

His very favourite things.

"You look particularly lovely, Elizabeth."

"I thank you," she said, and sought to alter the subject. "If you have come all this way, you must be impatient to see your son. But I am not certain he is about."

She struggled frantically with what to do, for nothing yet had been said to John about his parentage. She certainly did not want to introduce him to Wickham without warning. But at the mention of his overgrown misbegotten, Wickham seemed taken aback, as if he had forgotten why he was there in the first place.

Elizabeth looked at him curiously, but he quickly recovered.

He said, "You understand, this is embarrassing. We men do have our youthful indiscretions. Better, I fancy, to have too many sons than none at all."

The remark was far too pointed, and Wickham far too conniving, for it to have been a slip of the tongue.

She said (a little sarcastically), "One must suppose."

"Lydia has told me of your disappointment, Elizabeth. My heartfelt sympathy." His eyes batted several times before continuing, "The silence of this large house must be quite unbearable." (Commiserating loneliness seldom failed him.)

She was uncertain whether first to disabuse him of the notion of her forlornness, explain implicitly that their "disappointment" was not to be spoken of by a man with the morals and sexual appetite of a particularly libidinous goat, or simply smite him across the forehead with the fireplace poker. This deliberation was not lengthy, but during the time her mind took her upon that fanciful trip of possibilities, her breath grew heavy with rage and her face flushed.

A misfortune. For in her reluctance to tell her sister's husband that she was considering violence upon his person, he continued to believe her heaving bosom and heightened colour resulted from the employment of his considerable charms. He continued to speak, but in a low murmur.

"You are far too enchanting to be without company, Elizabeth. 'Tis no fault of yours, of course, this I know well. You recall your husband and I were once exceedingly close friends."

Careful not to speak his name, Wickham continued, coaxing, "He was of a somewhat priggish nature when it came to…love. A passionate woman such as yourself deserves better, Elizabeth…"

Incredulous, Elizabeth interrupted and asked him bluntly, "Are you offering to avail yourself of me?"

"Well, I should not put it so plainly," he said, pressing her back, his puckered lips making little kissing sounds up the length of her neck.

Compleatly flabbergasted and the poker out of reach, she brought her hand upward to slap his face but he caught it by the wrist.

"You always were a saucy wench, Miss Eliza!"

It came to Wickham at the exact moment he realised Elizabeth was seriously not interested in his attentions, that when she said Darcy was "not there," she might have meant he was "not in the house," not he was "not in Derbyshire." This premonition struck him a little tardy, for he had time neither to rise from her nor to release his hold upon her wrist. Hence, when he felt the cold metal tip of a blade beneath his chin, it sent a shuddering chill of naked fear down his spine.

"Step back now, Wickham, or I shall spill your blood upon this floor."

Having been apprehended in mid-inveiglement, not only by Lydia, but by more than one irate husband, Wickham had been threatened all manner of retribution. Nevertheless, he had never once had a blade drawn upon him and that Darcy held the other end led him to believe the warning of bloodshed not just a threat. With the blade yet beneath his chin, Wickham, with all due care, rose from Elizabeth.

Knowing the merest flick of the blade would render Wickham a second leer, Elizabeth held her breath. Under it, she implored her husband to contain his rage.

"Do not do it. Do not do it," she repeated silently. "Dear God. Do not do it."

As Wickham backed the length of the room, the sheath at his waist dangled loosely. He felt it empty, thus allowed himself a considerable relief. Few might have felt reprieve at that moment, but versed as he was in such reckoning, Wickham realised the blade poised at his throat was his own. No duel had been called. Yet his armpits produced a cold clammy sweat so copiously that it was discernible under the sleeves of his wool jacket.

If Wickham had a momentary palliation of dread, it was fleeting. For Darcy's voice betrayed an icy calm, one reflected by his countenance. That was what was most unsettling to all who saw it. His face reflected no emotion whatsoever. There was a time when Wickham had totally dismissed the possibility that Darcy had taken three lives by his own hand. But as he stood within that cold, placid stare, the furtive little darting of his eyes announced Wickham was just then reconsidering his position. Thus, he made a prudent backward retreat whilst endeavouring a less judicious attempt at convincing Darcy not to believe what he had seen.

"I am afraid you are quite mistaken, for I am here upon invitation of your wife."

Evidently hearing nothing to induce him to expand upon his initial statement to Wickham, Darcy silently advanced upon him. Wickham backed through the double doors. A small crowd of footmen and maids stood motionless in the foyer as he edged his way out. Once upon the doorstep, Darcy lowered the blade and a slight spot of blood could be seen upon Wickham's neck just above his Adam's apple.

Wickham brought his fingers to the nick, wiped it with his middle finger. He looked at the blood before turning and taking a careful but brisk leave down the steps.

With a fierce fling of his wrist, Darcy sent the sword sailing toward Wickham's back. A whirring sound directed at him caused Wickham to take a galloping leap into the air. When the blade imbedded in the gravel-covered dirt of the drive just to the left of Wickham's feet, the handle was bobbing yet.

With a sheepish look about, Wickham retrieved his weapon and redeposited it in his scabbard. Mustering more dignity than some might have produced under similar circumstances, he haughtily snapped his fingers to the man who held the reins of his horse. Once mounted, he felt secure enough bestow upon Darcy a derisive laugh before he dug his spurs into his horse's flank, speeding them upon their way.

Wickham's laugh was an impotent one, for no one saw or heard it save for the man holding the reins to his horse. Darcy was already re-entering the house. Elizabeth did not witness the fling of the sword nor Wickham's last insult either, for she had not moved from the settee whence Darcy ejected Wickham.

Her husband returned to her alone and carefully closed the door behind him. She sensed Wickham was done no harm.

Regardless, she asked, "Pray, has Wickham departed?"

He nodded.

Overcome with relief, Elizabeth rushed to her husband, grateful his fury over Wickham's advances was not lethal. Clutching him to her, she began to babble, "The unmitigated gall…how could that man believe…what brass cheek…"

But she trailed off when she realised his arms hung woodenly at his sides. The colour had drained from his face and his chest still heaved with rage. She looked at him, but he waited a moment, perchance allowing himself to tether his temper, before he spoke.

In the clipped intonation that he always used to announce his displeasure, he asked a nonquestion, "You invited Wickham here when I bid you not?"

Trembling, she endeavoured to keep her countenance.

"I did send him a post, because I believed he should know of his son. I did not invite him to come here."

"Your letter was invitation enough. When I bid you to desist of the matter, I expected you to follow my wishes, not contact Wickham clandestinely. There are things of which you do not know, Elizabeth."

"I did not contact him in secrecy," she insisted, certain at that moment she had not.

"You did not do it openly. Anything other is furtive."

Of course, he was right. She had not meant to act surreptitiously, simply independently.

It ended badly. Before she was ready to concede that point, she accused his own secrecy, for if there were "things of which she did not know," he had kept them from her.

"If you expect me to follow your wishes implicitly, you must make them known. Pray allow me the privilege of knowing your motives if I am to understand."

"Is it not enough that I ask it of you? Must I share of everything? Some things are too harsh of which to think, much less palaver them incessantly."

The magnitude of her inadvertent injury to his meticulously guarded *amour proper* was evident, even if she was not quite witting of just how she had brought it about. She reached out to him, but he stepped away. As he stood with his back to her, she observed that his shoulders rose and fell yet in the shudder of anger.

In a voice more bitter than resigned, he said to her, "If you will excuse me, I must take my leave. Because of Wickham's visit to this county I must now canvas the shopkeepers in three villages to see what debts he has incurred that must be discharged."

When he quitted the room, he did not look back. Elizabeth reached out behind her to seek a chair and gratefully took the first one she found. He had never, in the life of their marriage, left her company so abruptly. Her chin quivered and it angered her that her own countenance was questioning her too.

As for Wickham, she thought of what Lydia said of him that eve in Hunsford and thought her not so senseless as she had once been accused. Lydia was heedless and marriage had bestowed her no restoration of character, but no woman deserved such a husband.

Forlorn, Elizabeth pondered the life Lydia had chosen, but her sympathy was not overly employed. She saved the greater part of it for John Christie, for that hapless lad had no voice in what lot he was assigned.

In time, her thoughts turned to what she believed were the mundane. Cook would need to reappraise the supper preparations. A nice *poularde*, perhaps. Some damsons.

Mr. Darcy favoured brandied damsons.

These alternative dishes were not to placate an angry husband. Nothing quite so coquettish as that. It was more medicinal. He had only just begun to devour his food again. Intuition told her his appetite was again going to need some coaxing.

Elizabeth was certain that she had never been warned that tribulations came in pairs.

As to why Pemberley had the misfortune to receive a visit from Lady Catherine de Bourgh directly upon the heels of Wickham's unceremonious departure was an outright bafflement.

For it was only a few days more than a week later when Elizabeth's rewarding afternoon amidst the conservatory directing the repotting of a particularly healthy growth of aspidistra came to a disharmonious end.

She heard the rattle of a coach. Expecting more felicitous company, she discarded her gardening smock and made a dash back to the house to see to her hair.

She flinched involuntarily at the sight of Lady Catherine's chaise and four at leisure in the courtyard. Because Lady Catherine had not once visited Pemberley (nor stepped one tasselled toe into the county of Derbyshire) since their wedding, Elizabeth presumed the good lady's presence was not of simple sociable congeniality.

Whatever her reason for being there, Elizabeth was happy it would fall to Darcy to deal with her.

Howbeit she knew him about the property, he was not coming to the house directly. Yet, Elizabeth avoided the lobby by way of the postern stairs, uncertain she could muster enough civility to greet such a disagreeable visitor. Her attempt to camouflage her entrance was foiled (with her escape so imminent, she had one hand poised upon the stair rail) by a servant anxiously beckoning her.

"Lady Catherine de Bourgh here to see you, madam."

Elizabeth made a mental stamp of her foot at her stymied bolt for freedom, but could not fault the servants if they dared not reply negatively to Lady Catherine. It was poor luck and added bother that Pemberley had ridded itself of a pest only to be sent a plague.

Much to her surprise, Elizabeth learnt that Lady Catherine had come, indeed, not to seek audience with her nephew, but with her nephew's wife. Elizabeth entered the lobby with no undue reluctance and curtsied politely. Thereupon, she led her into the increasingly infringed-upon drawing room. Lady Catherine did not acknowledge her curtsy with so much as a nod and somehow managed to find her way into the room ahead of her hostess.

"You honour us with your visit, Lady Catherine. I hope you and Lady Anne are well. Is she with you?" (It was a fair question. Sometimes that young lady's sickly chest demanded she wait in the carriage.)

Waving away her enquiry with her walking stick, Lady Catherine seated herself with fatuous regality. As that lady arranged her considerable…self upon her chair, Elizabeth allowed herself an involuntary roll of her eyes. Expeditiously, she found a seat a respectable, if distant, ways from her. Thereupon, she sat in determined silence, hands folded primly in her lap. If that mimicked her demeanour with Wickham, she did not recollect it.

With an arch of one eyebrow, Lady Catherine announced, "You, of course, know why I am here."

"No, I cannot account for your visit," was the honest reply.

Before that disavowal left her lips, Lady Catherine initiated her assault.

"I cannot undo the most unfortunate marriage my nephew has made, but it is my duty to make certain there is no room for misunderstanding. It is because of your impecunious birthright that the name of Darcy will be stricken from these halls into perpetuity."

She paused, but as Elizabeth sat in open-mouthed astonishment, she continued, "Darcy is an only son. He must have a son to carry the name. It has been five years since you worked your wiles upon him. Five years you have denied an heir to Pemberley. Twice you have failed. I knew no good would come from his alliance with such an inferior and I have been proven true. For God has sought penance from you by denying you a son."

Elizabeth was astounded by her pronouncement. Not because the woman accused her of tarnishing the halls of Pemberley because of the Bennet's middling familial connexions. That insult had been hurled more times than Lucifer's dinner. Nor was she astonished to hear Lady Catherine admit to finally accepting the fact of their marriage (albeit that was a considerable surprise). But she was very much interested in knowing how the Lady of Rosings Park had come to have intimate information about the workings of her reproductive organs.

The stillbirth was public knowledge, but no one knew of her miscarriage, not even Jane.

"Yes, yes," Elizabeth said impatiently. "Sullied the halls of Pemberley, worked my wiles, inferior of birth…a sorry tune that has been played many a time. But I dare say I am all astonishment to learn that God Above seeks personal vengeance upon behalf of even so illustrious a person as yourself, Lady Catherine."

"Impertinent young woman! I am not accustomed to such disrespect!"

"Nor am I. If you have only come here to wound our misfortune, Lady Catherine, you must be advised your visit is not welcome."

Elizabeth stood. But Lady Catherine did not. She snorted a laugh so mocking, Elizabeth understood her tirade had not yet subsided.

"Our misfortune you say? Our misfortune? Indeed! 'Tis no fault of my nephew!"

She stood and raised a fist at her announcement. Elizabeth might have been more intimidated by the gesticulation had not Lady Catherine inadvertently mimicked a familiar depiction of *Moses Upon Mount Sinai* by de Vos the Elder which adorned the Book of Genesis in her Bible. She strove to concentrate upon the matter at hand. But, because, save for the tendrils, she realised Lady Catherine was, indeed, indistinguishable from Moses, it was difficult to do so.

Unwitting that her niece's thoughts had wandered from her diatribe to her earlocks, Lady Catherine continued, "I have learnt that Darcy is father to a son. A babe born this year! My nephew's loins have not failed him. You are the barren party! Was it not for your shrivelled womb Darcy would have several legitimate sons by now and Pemberley would be assured of its lineage."

That regained Elizabeth's attention forthwith.

The sheer heartlessness of the censure and the severity of the slander that spewed forth from Lady Catherine was reprehensible (the gravity of which was mitigated ever so briefly when Elizabeth realised the woman had, rather indelicately, referred to Darcy's loins). Quickly though, any reaction other than outrage evaporated and Elizabeth's indignation exploded.

"My husband has no such son! He shall be here directly. Should you favour repeating your accusation to him? I think not! No doubt he would cast you body and bonnet from his home!"

Elizabeth knew her countenance betrayed her astonishment, thus allowing Lady Catherine to believe she had found her trump card. Hence, the lady lowered her voice to a harsh whisper.

"I see you are unawares your husband has not been faithful to your bed. Of course, he would not speak of it to you. It would not be something of which a gentleman would speak. He has forsaken your fallowness for a more fertile womb."

Elizabeth's mouth opened to speak, but Lady Catherine cut her off.

"I speak no mendacity! It is common knowledge! I have my spies. This nurseling was born before Candlemas right under your nose. That male-child is proof that it is you who has deprived Pemberley of an heir, not my nephew!"

If Lady Catherine had been a cat, she would have licked her own nose.

Veritably shaking with anger, Elizabeth endeavoured to calm herself and said, "You shall importune this house no longer. You must take your leave. I shall watch you quit this house, and thereupon I shall think of you no more."

"No more denials? You are not so certain of my nephew's devotion as you profess. I do not intend to visit these halls again. In time, my nephew shall know the righteousness of my position and see you for what you are, undescended in rank and inferior of birth."

The lady started out but paused in the doorway to remind Elizabeth, "When I first learnt of your ambition to marry my nephew, I told you I was most seriously displeased. You can believe it of me now."

She turned and without further comment repaired to her carriage.

In trembling, righteous indignation, Elizabeth shook her head in new appreciation of Lady Catherine's considerable crust. She began to pace the floor with quick angry steps anticipating Darcy's imminent return.

Silently, she replayed Lady Catherine's invectives in preparation for repeating them verbatim to him. Upon hearing an explicit account of his aunt's visit, his own wrath would bring vindication. And however Elizabeth might deny it, she needed his exoneration. Lady Catherine's words stung her more than she could ever admit even to herself.

Barren. She despised Lady Catherine speaking of her womb, fallow or otherwise (or for that matter, Darcy's loins), but the word "barren" was painful. For that was the fear that haunted her.

Repetition of the accusation against Darcy echoed annoyingly in her head. It brought her disquiet. Initially it was not under even the briefest of consideration as to whether Lady Catherine's allegation was true or not. Of course, it was a falsehood. However, vindictive as she was, Lady Catherine was never known to bluff.

Her design may have been to inflict injury, but she must truly believe herself privy to an infidelity by Darcy to say it. Intrigues and liaisons abounded even in the country. Was some rumour about? But everyone knew Darcy despised men who dishonoured their wives. Did they not?

However, she did not understand just how Lady Catherine might profit in telling her such a lie, or for that matter, such a truth. The answer was the same for both. Nothing. The only possible thing she could glean was grief. For Lady Catherine that alone might be motive enough to send her upon a trip across three counties.

Scheming shrew! No, she refused to allow herself to be drawn in by Lady Catherine's ploy. She refused to be baited. Her trust in her husband was implicit. Questioning his fidelity would play right into the evil provocateur's scheme. Indeed, when she uncorked Lady Catherine's temper by marrying Darcy, she had loosed a serpent. The more she thought of it, the more irate she became and angry tears welled up in her eyes.

Which made her even more irate, for she hated that she cried when she was angry.

Seated in the library, Fitzwilliam had, unbeknownst to Elizabeth, been waiting for Darcy to return for the better part of an hour when he heard the unmistakable skirl of his aunt's voice.

Having no more inclination than the average person to bask in the glow of his aunt's trying company, he tarried, feigning great attention to a very boring book. Once Darcy's hitherto grey funk had lifted, Fitzwilliam had once again become a fixture about Pemberley. Howbeit unspoken, his attendance bespoke a return to the norm. The reclamation of Darcy's hearing did not alleviate his solitary treks, but it was accompanied by better humour and appetite. Of this, all were roundly relieved. Darcy's disturbances bid house-wide disruption. Fitzwilliam could not bear to witness Elizabeth's distress, regardless whence it came.

However, during these abundant visits it had not been betrayed once, in word or action, the yearning he suffered for his cousin's wife.

Under Fitzwilliam's stern regulation (a family trait, it would seem), it simmered quietly beneath the confines of his heart. Only upon the occasional witnessing of some covert touch or look betwixt Darcy and Elizabeth did it begin to seethe. Because of this, he chose to frequent Pemberley only as a sort of test, as if to prove to himself he was stalwart enough to do it. This reasoning, of course, allowed him to gaze upon Elizabeth and avoid further introspection. For had he examined himself more closely, even he would have had to admit he had entered into a pattern of self-torture.

It might have been easier to eschew Derbyshire compleatly. There was ample opportunity to find the company of other ladies had he stayed in London. Whatever he was of a mind, be it circumspect courtship or a little helmet polishing south of Bond, town was thick with ladies, by turn virtuous or of accommodating morals.

Marriage should have been a temptation for Fitzwilliam. Although he was but a second son, his family was illustrious. Therefore, he was considered an exceedingly desirable match for a lady who had her own fortune but sought prestige. His chief reluctance in taking a bride was the eternal vexation that she would not be Elizabeth. For that lady and no other had the beauty, vivacity, and wit that he believed was the absolute perfection of womanhood. Elizabeth had not only withstood near ravishment and bandits, she was the only lady who hitherto had dared to stand up to his exceedingly intimidating aunt. It was unconscionable to take a wife when his mind had seized upon another.

Elizabeth's bravery in the face of his aunt was that of legend. Even Darcy simply avoided Lady Catherine when he could. Perchance as then. His aunt's intonation was of a sort that carried. When she was in ill-humour (which was not infrequently), it was even more distinct. Hence, if he could not make out all of what she said, he could certainly hear the contempt in her voice from down the passage-way. Unsure as to just whom she spoke so uncivilly, curiosity got the best of him and he entered the corridor just in time to see her as she stormed out. From the doorway, he realised upon whom Lady Catherine's considerable truculence was directed. Albeit she was turned away, it was unmistakably Elizabeth who appeared to be standing alone in the drawing room. Fitzwilliam saw her knees begin to buckle and made a mad dash for her. She righted herself before he got farther than the doorway.

From thence, Fitzwilliam gazed upon the woman he had loved from afar. Courageous Elizabeth. Weathering a vicious assault from the dowager supreme of Kent, she was in desperate need of comfort then. No other decision could be made. He went to her.

Hearing someone else enter the room, Elizabeth turned toward the door. The subtle expression of disappointment she birthed gave him a twinge, for it told Fitzwilliam she expected Darcy. Tears had just begun the trip down her face. When she caught sight of him, she immediately turned her face away and blotted her cheeks with the back of her hand, feigning composure. For Fitzwilliam, her tears invoked the agonising recollection of her abduction. The abduction for which he carried guilt yet. And his self-reproach had ebbed not at all. But that horror was in the past; the distress Elizabeth suffered then was immediate.

He crossed the room, "Pray, is there anything I can do?"

Her face turned from him, she shook her head. He reached out and took her trembling elbow, turning her to face him.

"I shall never forgive my aunt."

She opened her mouth to respond but began to cry instead, stamping her foot in frustration.

"It is absurd to be in such disorder at Lady Catherine's hand," she said. "She is an irredeemable shrew."

Suddenly, the realisation that she had maligned not only Darcy's aunt but Fitzwilliam's as well claimed her and she covered her mouth in self-censure.

"Forgive me, Geoffrey. I am not myself."

"There are those who have invoked far more perverse invectives than that against my aunt, Elizabeth, and with much less provocation. She is a tyrannical ogress."

"You heard what she said," which was a statement of fact.

He nodded, "A little. I cannot imagine what compels her to such evil."

"It can only be the ghastly fear that someone, somewhere might be happy and the unrelenting need to put an end to it," she said bitterly. Then, "Oh! You must think me mad, for you always seem to witness my worst humiliations."

Her mortification was obvious, but Fitzwilliam was uncertain how much of her disconcertion was from his aunt's cruel words, or his having overheard them.

"Why did she call, Elizabeth? I heard her speak of Darcy. Where is he? What did she say of him to distress you so?"

She looked worriedly at the door as if in fear that Darcy might happen upon her. Deferring to her want of privacy, Fitzwilliam closed it upon her behalf. He returned and immediately implored her to confide what had made her so desperately troubled.

Reluctantly, she began the story, "She told me that Darcy…"

Abruptly, she grasped Fitzwilliam's coat sleeve, "Do not speak of this to Darcy, please. He must not know!"

"He must not know what?"

"Any of it!" she said, and thereupon she burst into tears once again.

Her misery wrenched his heart so violently he drew her to his chest as if to relieve the pain. He did so quite unwittingly and some small portion of his consciousness reminded him it was he that was to comfort her, not contrariwise.

"There, there," he soothed.

In her wretchedness, Elizabeth clung to the comfort of his lapels with a renewed round of weeping. Perchance (and he was to wonder this relentlessly in days to come) he was caught up in some chimerical state, some illusory trance. Certainly he was usurped by some phenomenon not of his control. For there was no other reason he could account for why he said what he did then.

"Elizabeth dearest, I love you. I would do anything to ease your distress."

At that, the weeping halted. Fitzwilliam stood perfectly still, endeavouring to decide whether should he drop his hands from her, or continue to pat her back and pretend he did not say what he had. The choice was made by Elizabeth, for she drew back and, having ceased to cry, commenced to hiccup. Abandoning all hope that she did not hear, he clung to the slim prospect that she might have possibly believed the love he just professed was familial.

But alas. Her countenance announced a confounded incredulity that did not suffer the suggestion of anything but a compleat acknowledgement of the extent of the imprudence of his declaration. Having spoken the unspeakable, Fitzwilliam dared not try to appease his affront with added comment (God only knew what other confession he might blurt out!), hence, he opted for silent, abject mortification.

Not surprisingly, Elizabeth endeavoured to fill this deafening void, but each time she tried to speak, she hiccupped.

Finally, she managed to say, "Water!"

Provoked from his self-imposed inertia, Fitzwilliam rushed to the sideboard, sloshed some water from the pitcher into a glass and hurried it back to her. She downed it by gulps, but when she opened her mouth, she hiccupped again. And again he repeated his trip to the side-board and she gulped the second glass.

Again she hiccupped and managed to say, "Perhaps some wine?"

He duplicated the water brigade with that of wine and she upended it before he could say, "I do not think you should drink that so hastily."

This absurd ruckus did circumnavigate the entire subject of Fitzwilliam's unprecedented declaration of love. Thus, once satisfied she was situated non-weeping and un-hiccupping into a chair (with another glass of wine in her hand), he undertook a stiff, formal, kind of bow.

"If I cannot serve you in any other way, you can be sure of my secrecy of your meeting with Lady Catherine today. Darcy shall not hear of it from me."

"No," Elizabeth said, "Darcy shall not hear of it."

It was not a leap of imagination to believe she did not refer only to Lady Catherine's visit. Fitzwilliam took a leave so brisk, a small sheaf of papers scattered to the floor in his wake. He did not, however, stop to pick them up.

So distracted was Fitzwilliam and so hastily did he depart, he did not see Georgiana standing just beyond the doorway. Had he looked her direction, he might have seen her expression of profound disorder. One remarkably similar to the one he bore.

Quite tardy of all the brouhaha, Darcy entered a house so laden with portent it was almost visible upon the walls. When he asked, everyone was quite unenlightened as to why Fitzwilliam had departed without waiting to speak to him, almost in the dust of Lady Catherine de Bourgh's carriage.

Elizabeth explained simply of his aunt, "She did not stay when she learnt you were not about the house."

Having long disavowed any interest in his aunt's pursuits, Elizabeth believed Darcy thought little of her precipitous visit or post-haste leave-taking. Elizabeth's still trembling hands did not escape his notice. She insisted that it was due to her extended afternoon amongst the rose beds without her hat (and did not offer she had belted down several glasses of wine). As if all that was not intrigue enough, Georgiana too seemed oddly out of sorts. She kept her gaze lowered to her plate through supper and quit the table without touching her food.

It was understood that Georgiana was never a hearty partaker, but when alone with her brother and sister-in-law she was usually, if not effusive, at least a cordial conversationalist. Had Elizabeth not been quite so intent upon hiding her own disconcertion, she might have noticed Georgiana's.

Even in the absence of that heedfulness, Elizabeth knew it must all seem quite odd to her husband.

It did.

Thus when they retired, Darcy endeavoured to pry out of Elizabeth what might have come to pass that day. However, as he was less determined to unearth than she was to evade, he uncovered nothing.

Elizabeth admitted to herself that her motive for not revealing Lady Catherine's visit with Darcy was selfish. In the aftermath of Wickham's visit, it had taken a day or two of coolness betwixt them before an implied truce was called. Gradually, the tension was, if not eliminated, at least diminished. Having not quite repaired that breach, Elizabeth was determined not to provoke any other upheaval. Hence, she weathered Darcy's questions about what bechanced that day with semi-pious solemnity, vowing to herself not to allow Lady Catherine victory over her spirit. Darcy's love was for her as inexorable as his all and sundry opinions (which was not a particularly romantic way to think of it, but it was true).

Supper was no problem, but her resolve began to waver as she laid beside him that night unable to sleep. She rose and quietly opened the door to their balcony and walked to the balustraude. The breeze rustled her gown and as she felt the silk billow about her legs, Lydia's voice trespassed her thoughts.

"All men stray. 'Tis their nature. Even Papa."

Though she knew there was little measure of respect by Mr. Bennet for his wife, any rancour he held for her was couched with humour. Elizabeth had always believed (or wanted to believe) that they had once been in love. It was easy to perceive him seeking a refuge from her mother, he always disappeared into his library after supper. But with another woman? Ghastly thought! Her own father! A philanderer?

Her mind canvassed the Meryton possibilities for a lady that might fill her mind's personification of her father's mistress. Few were plausible (the Widow Cadwallader was neither morbidly obese, blind, nor stupid, which made her a feasibility until Elizabeth recalled she had the laugh of a she-ass). No, there was not a wellspring of prospective paramours for her father. As dear a man as she believed him to be, it was unlikely Mr. Bennet actually had ladies queuing up for his company.

Mr. Darcy, however, was another matter entirely.

Handsome, wealthy, worldly, and his time was his own. If her sweet, homely father had managed to find a woman with whom to hockle, Darcy should have little trouble at all. If a temptress importuned him, would he walk away? Would any man?

Despondent over the thought, the spring chill persuaded Elizabeth to seek the warmth of her covers. Thinking Darcy asleep, she tiptoed to the bed and nestled against him. As quiet as she had crept, she was convinced at first that it was her cold feet that must have awakened him. To her delighted surprise, sleep was not from whence he was aroused. He had been watching her as she gazed upon the lawn. Her gown had rippled about her body so enticingly, he had an unexpected gift for her beneath the multitude of bedclothes. The reassurance of his desire was precisely what she was most in need of just then.

As if in gratitude, she drew her gown over her head and impetuously tossed it aside. The removal of her night-dress, however, was not in obligation, but preparation. For she intended to exact a kindness upon his person of considerable magnitude. She sat atop him and stretched her arms seductively over her head.

Thereupon fully limbered, she inquired, "Shall we give the ferret a run?"

He laughed softly, "Where did you hear such a term?"

She smiled mysteriously (partly for allurement and partly because she could not remember where she heard it, and the question was quite beside the point). From her perch, she laced her fingers through his and pressed his hands back against the bed, allowing him to understand she was to be the aggressor. For she wanted to overpower him in some fashion, but was uncertain exactly why. Vagueness of motive, however, did not alter her intentions. Thus, it was from a position of dominance she sat astride him, riding him with relentless vigour, demanding his love to come to achievement. His blood fevered, he took her beneath him, denying his own passion's release until he gratified hers.

Both in sweaty exhaustion, she unwisely attempted to bring him to arousal once more. He halted her.

"Lizzy, a moment please. Wait."

He said that gently, yet (and quite unreasonably) she felt herself rebuffed and drew away.

"Your passion for me is lost?" she asked far more petulantly than she intended.

"My passion for you has yielded me too weak in the knees to stand."

"There was a time when you would have come about again."

"I have been in the saddle most of the day, Lizzy. I beg you, have pity upon me."

The smile he bestowed as a punctuation to his entreaty was most enticing. It was difficult to be miffed at him when he smiled at her as he did (especially when she did not truly want to be out of humour).

In a solemn turn, he bid, "What is it, Lizzy?"

As difficult as it was to stay angry with him, it was even harder to hide her desperation. But she did not answer his question immediately, for she did not know what "it" was. She did not know if she were demanding reassurance that his passion for her had not abated, or—she asked herself—was she trying to render him unable to be with any other by reason of sheer exhaustion? She smiled at her own recklessness. A sudden weariness overtook her and she laid back.

"'Tis simply your wife who loves you more than you can ever know. Forgive my rashness."

Unknowing what birthed it, he seemed relieved by her smile. And, satisfied with her denial, he hooked his chin over her shoulder and snuggled behind her. Within minutes, she heard the inevitable soft snore that told he was sound asleep. She, however, could not sleep. For steadfastly as she tried, she could not keep herself from a persistent speculation:

In light of his inability to effect a second coitus, in just whose saddle did her husband spend that day?

In the next few days, she wavered. She knew that to doubt her husband's character was despicable. However, that severe self-reproof did nothing to calm her bedevilment. Lady Catherine's unwavering conceit of information and her own father's marital disloyalty made her increasingly uncertain. Quite simply, too many unsettling events had occurred in a small frame of time to ignore. Darcy's recent need for solitary horseback rides, his distraction, his fury at her over Wickham's advances. All would have been curious doings in and of themselves. Collectively, they added up to outright mystery.

Initially, she had tried to reason them away. His anger at Wickham seemed fitting. Or was it? If Lady Catherine heard rumours, could Wickham have as well? Did Wickham come because he believed Darcy dallied, thus would she? And Fitzwilliam. He comforted her tenderly. Fitzwilliam, above all others, knew shades of Darcy's mind, and he offered her his love. Did he believe she had lost her husband's?

She finally decided she must quit self-torture and learn the absolute truth to whatever ends it led.

Hence, reassuring Edward Hardin (and herself) it was but temporarily, she relinquished the waggon and the care of the ill to him. There were many hands to help him. Her own endeavour, however pressing, she embarked upon alone.

The first order of business in Elizabeth Bennet Darcy's Investigation of Marital Infidelity was to identify the parentage of any babies born both within a day's riding distance of Pemberley and within the past half-year. Boots saddled, she aimed her directly toward the rectory in hope of finding it empty. After an hour's wait, the noon meal for the rector at the parsonage presented itself. Once he had gone, she looked to and fro for the curate or beadle, then slipped into the church office.

Therein she found the heavy registry of marriages, christenings, and deaths. A ribbon marked the last entry, from thence she retraced each.

The half-year saw seven deaths, four marriages, and five births within a reasonable radius of Pemberley. Small print upon one line registered the date of both the birth and death of one baby causing her a pang in the pit of her stomach. She shook off such a mawkish vagary, for she could not allow distraction from her mission.

Of the five live births, two were girls, three boys. She hastily scribbled the names and departed, not wanting to account for her curiosity to anyone. None of the names were known to her, but she had good notion of where each lived. With as much insouciance as she could project, she set about to take her ride in due course to each location.

The first was a handsome cottage, one that she had admired before, its inhabitants unknown to her. However, there she observed, not a young woman, but a man leaving the house and entering a carriage. He was accompanied by an elderly woman carrying a baby swathed in a shawl. It was upon this observation that Elizabeth realised she should have checked to see who was listed amongst the dead.

Whatever sadness she felt for the household, it made her enterprise simpler. As did the next. For at the second and more dilapidated cottage laboured a portly woman with at least six other children (possibly five, possibly seven, they were far too lively to count with any accuracy). This also seemed unlikely for she could not picture her husband committing carnal acts atop so corpulent a mistress nor with so many offspring to witness the union.

Beginning to think herself quite ridiculous, nonetheless, Elizabeth persevered the day after to the third location, one that was somewhat isolated. Nothing but a narrow path twisted its way from the road to the house. There appeared no discretionary access. However, there was a promontory overlooking it. Loosing Boots to graze the down, she climbed upon the small tor and settled in for a stay. She sat there that day and returned the next and, thereupon, the day after that. Her pattern did not alter for a week, save Sunday church. When Darcy rode out each day, she never questioned him. She even waited patiently for the coach to depart carrying Hardin and the footmen. Only then did she mount her horse.

As she rode her horse out, it was Boots' name that bade her make an unhappy consideration.

Darcy wore his boots, of course, each day when he rode. She weathered the welter of wondering if his boots reposed beneath another woman's bed. Or, she pondered, was it protocol to keep on one's boots whilst carrying on an assignation?

More than once she had hoisted her skirt to him and they enjoyed a fast and furious physical congress. Yet, it was somehow more comforting for her to believe that if he was with another, he did not remove his boots. Bare feet seemed more intimate.

Niggling matter, she supposed, but small comfort was better than none.

She realised ruminating about the intricacies of how this affair was conducted announced a subtle, but certain, metamorphosis from suspicion into outright condemnation. However, in her defence, she told herself she was merely steeling for whatever she might learn. No practise was needed for exoneration.

Therefore, she travelled to the point each day, sat, and waited, her only diversion torturing herself with images of Darcy in another woman's embrace. By the time that a man finally appeared, she was certain she had girded herself adequately for the inevitable.

For five days, the hours she sat there had been unproductive. There was no activity save a small wisp of smoke from the chimney and occasionally an anonymous toss of water out the back door. (If who lived there went to the well, it was after dusk.) Upon the sixth day, a chilly wind made her sentry increasingly disagreeable and, howbeit disgusted at her lack of sufferance, she rose in decision to take leave. Under the old "watched pot" theory of occurring events, that would be the very moment when a rider approached.

Which he did.

Elizabeth ducked hastily out of sight; thereupon furtively peered over the top of a rock. A woman came to the door holding a baby. The rider alit, walked to the woman and kissed her full upon the mouth. All three disappeared inside. If the rider was depicted simply as a finely tailored man upon a handsome ride, the summarisation might have fit Darcy. But the man was neither tall nor dark, and he most certainly was not Darcy.

Bathed in relief, Elizabeth did then quit her post, deeply chagrined (at what would evermore be recollected by her as Elizabeth Bennet Darcy's Idiotic Quest), when she felt a moment of intense queasiness. So intense was this indisposition, she knelt and put her head to her knees (just as she always counselled faint patients in her care). She took several deep breaths but they did nothing to relieve her. For she realised, howbeit he was not her husband, she did recognise the man who had come to the house just then. He had been at her supper table the very night before.

She almost wished it had been Darcy, for she knew herself able to weather the pain of such a betrayal with greater fortitude than her kind and trusting sister Jane.

She found her way back to Boots, silently cursing herself for ever undertaking such an odyssey. Benightedness might have been a blessing just then, for she would have been happy all the days of her life to be blissfully nescient of Bingley's philandering.

Her father could be, if not condoned, at least forgiven if he sought affection from a more agreeable woman than her mother. But, Bingley! Bingley's devotion to her sister had always been unquestioned. There was no sweeter, more beautiful and good wife than Jane. Jane, who bore Bingley four children in five years. He could certainly not claim denial of affection.

From a stump, she attempted to draw herself upon Boots but fell back impotently. Still gripping the saddle, she leaned against the horse and rested her forehead against the sun-warmed leather. Had she not been so sickened, she might have found her abrupt alteration from a wife scorned to an indignant sister-in-law amusing. Truly, she wished she could have had the time to enjoy a little diversion at her own foolishness.

It took her the better part of an hour to find her way home. Upon her arrival, she espied Blackjack, lathered and steaming, being unsaddled. It told her that evidently Darcy had ridden in only moments before. The only groom about was the still parentally-unenlightened John Christie. When she handed Boots' reins to him, he looked at her curiously.

Her face, as always, betrayed her. Hence, when she entered the house she took the precaution of surveying her countenance in a pier glass. Yes, she appeared quite out of sorts. Time to practise severely limited, she settled what she believed was a more inscrutable expression upon her countenance by furrowing her brow (this, however, did not affect placidity as she intended, but rather a possible intestinal disorder) and headed for the stairs.

Stopping in the passageway, she stood very still and listened to see if she could hear Darcy downstairs. She might hoodwink the servants by her charade, but not her husband.

The time it had taken her to return from her little espionage excursion could have been better utilised than only conjuring expletive epithets to hurl at Bingley. Instead, she should have taken time for sober reflection upon whether to tell Darcy what she had seen. For did she, it would be difficult to explain just how she came about her information.

Her hand found the banister. She took a step thither when she first heard the ominous sound of Darcy's boots behind her.

"Lizzy."

Cautiously, she turned. Only to be confronted with the seriously conflicted countenance of her husband. Indeed, his mien was so sombre, she knew its gravity could mean only one of two things. Either a servant had unknowingly exposed the true nature of Lady Catherine's visit, or someone had died. It was with some self-reproach that she realised she was more willing to deal with someone's demise.

As he escorted her to his library, she frantically began to formulate a speech. Her position for not telling him was to be thus: she was protecting her husband from knowledge of Lady Catherine's diatribe so he would not be upset about his aunt's cruelty to her. Thus, she would present herself as both unjustly persecuted and selfless. Certainly, he could not fault her for that.

They seated themselves in quite proper opposition. After several minutes of an uncomfortably silent stand-off, he spoke.

"I followed you today."

She sat open-mouthed, speech having deserted her. He waited for a moment and when she said nothing, continued.

"It is an egregiously deceitful thing to do, but I have been quite anxious on your behalf. You have been quite out of sorts."

Yes, she most definitely had. Her cheeks reddened in shame, for if he thought it designing to follow her, her own suspicions were exposed as undeniably duplicitous. When she did not speak nor look at him still, he walked over to her, knelt on one knee, and took her hands in his.

"My stealth did not serve me, Lizzy, for I have no idea what brought you to that croft or why you stayed and looked upon it so long. It was a pretty prospect, but not all that beguiling. I am confounded. Pray, will you tell me?"

She closed her eyes and lowered her face to his hands yet holding hers. When she could bear to gaze upon him, she tenderly brushed his cheek with the back of her fingers. He gathered those fingers in his and kissed them.

Unquestionably, she knew herself a mistrustful wretch. And a coward as well because all she could say was but one thing.

"I love you so very much."

He cupped her face in his hands, wiping away her tears with his thumbs. In a moment, she began again, with no bravery and little resolve.

"I have gone to watch that house every day for a week, because I was told you had intimate association with the woman who lived there." Staring at her knees, she finished, "And had a child with her. A son."

It was likely that she visibly cringed. He sat back, literally upon his heels. She, however, kept her eyes shut tight, unable to bear witness to his expression. A pause allowed him to overcome his obvious astonishment.

Finally, he said, "You believed that of me?"

"No," she said.

She knew that a lie, but at that moment she desperately wanted to think she had not.

"I told myself I only travelled there to prove you innocent, but..." honesty began to overcome denial.

"Have I given reason for you to doubt me? Have I done you some hurt unknowingly? Pray, tell me I have not," said he.

She came perilously close to telling him his unreasonable anger at her over Wickham's ignominious visit hurt her deeply. But she knew, though true, it was not relevant to their particular conversation. Hence, she desperately delved about her memory for some long buried misdeed of his that she could recount to justify herself. But she found none.

She acknowledged, "You have never given me reason to doubt you."

It was with substantial relief upon her part that he reacted with an empathetic embrace. She allowed herself his consolation, for she had the unhappy notion that she might not have it after she told him just how her faith in him had become so fragile. He remained silent and she knew he was awaiting her explanation, thus she abandoned the possibility that they could sit as they were, eventually consigning the entire incident to oblivion. Gathering herself together, she sat back and began at the beginning.

"I did not tell you that Lydia was with us in Hunsford when we stayed with Charlotte. I know you do not wish to be reminded of Wickham." (She would lay culpability at her husband's feet anywhere she could at that moment.) "It was there that Lydia told us that she was full-witting of Wickham's faithlessness."

At the mere mention of Wickham's name, she could see Darcy stiffen. That disquiet granted her a little credibility of position as an injured party.

"That he is a lecherous scoundrel is of no surprise. But Lydia also told us, in defence of her own husband's infidelity, that all men were faithless and in proof of that announced that Papa..." here her voice faltered and she studied her knees again.

She swallowed, and then went on, "...harbours a mistress. Or mistresses, I know not which," which was digressing, so she got back to the point. "The intelligence of this infidelity having come from our own mother's lips!"

She looked up at Darcy and saw conflict in his eyes as clearly as had it been written upon a page. There, looking back at her, was a contest of sympathy and indignation. Sympathy upon behalf of her learning such an abhorrent thing about her father and the demand for an explanation of just how that condemned him. There might have been no condemnation, of course, without his aunt's visit.

"Lady Catherine came here week last, not seeking you, but to speak to me."

He waited.

Unable to repeat her other insults, Elizabeth said, "She was the one who told me she knew you fathered a child by this woman because I could not..."

"What!" he exclaimed, causing her to give a start. "You listened to an accusation by Lady Catherine! Lizzy, I thought you of all people could not be drawn into a plot she devised."

Actually, Elizabeth still wanted to believe she could not have, either. However, her manipulation at Lady Catherine's hands was undeniable.

Softly, she said, "It seemed reasonable at the time."

His voice did not mimic hers. Indeed, he spoke angrily.

"Why did you not tell me of Lady Catherine's lies unless you thought them possible? You did think it possible, for you spent—what, an entire week—seeking to find it true!"

"There is no excuse, of course, but I have endeavoured to explain…if you do not understand, I can say no more other than I was wrong. Wrong to listen to Lady Catherine. Wrong to mistrust you. Wrong to believe that if my own father does not honour his wife, it thereupon questions all men. I was wrong. W-R-O-N-G. Wrong."

With each successive "wrong" her voice escalated from the bowels of penitence until it reached the summit of rather impressive martyrdom. She had folded her arms and her face mirrored a myriad of emotions. Fortunately, the most salient was regret.

"Lizzy, you must promise me now. No more secrets. Ever."

She nodded her head emphatically, happy that he was going to let the matter drop. In all the relieved magnanimity of one who has survived calamity, she told him, "Undoubtedly, had our positions been reversed, had you listened to such a ridiculous accusation of me at the hands of your aunt…well, I can only admit that it is unlikely that you would have ever heard the end of it from me. I hope you are more generous."

A tentative smile from Elizabeth coaxed his.

"I am always more generous than you," he said.

And with his tease came a liberal sigh of relief from Elizabeth. In the embrace that followed, she truly wanted no secrets betwixt them, agonising whether to tell him what she had seen of Bingley. But she had no such doubts about his cousin.

There could be no good come of telling Darcy that Fitzwilliam had professed his love.

In light of their newly declared candidness, Darcy managed to persuade Elizabeth to give him a compleat relating of all that was said to her by both Lydia and Wickham.

She told him, "Wickham said he knew that you were 'priggish' in matters pertaining to love. In your defence, I considered disabusing him of such a notion, I but could not think of a way to say it that would not have been scandalous."

It was with a bit of a laugh that Darcy heard himself described as a prude by Wickham. The subject was not furthered conversationally.

Having a little time to think about it, though, Darcy came to the conclusion he must attempt to explain himself to Elizabeth. He had vigorously avoided ever revealing such specifics because it demanded he speak to her of his life previous to their love. So abhorrent was that recollection to them both that he did not want to think of it, much less speak of it to her.

Undoubtedly Wickham believed him a stiff-rumped prig. And, if compared to the standard set by Wickham's morals, he admitted he most likely was. Feminine conquests, however, were not something he needed for a better conceit of himself. Brash although it might sound, he knew himself quite unsusceptible to the allurements of other women.

Once he had fallen in love with Elizabeth, passion and settled affection were united. He needed nothing else. His exceedingly warm constitution was the only reason he had ever had other dalliances at all. He renounced the notion of a mistress because he sought neither company nor affection. It was his body that made demands of him, not his heart. And because he had accepted the favours of women for whom he cared nothing, his privacy had been forever breached. He had abhorred such carnal need, and despised himself yet for surrendering to it.

The first true contentment in his life had been with the exchange of his and Elizabeth's love. His trust was charged only to her. To assure her that he was not disposed to indulge in trysts simply because he was content with her was a prodigious understatement. Contentment was too passive a noun, for his love for her was not complaisant. She needed to know he had no interest in other women. He would not do as other men. He had no need. He had her. But he did not have the words.

Hence, he abandoned all hope of telling her what he wanted. Instead, he whispered but one thing in her ear that night.

"I want nothing more from this life than to lie here next to you, Lizzy."

It was not the clarification of the shadings of his soul he might have liked to offer, but it was the essence.

Even without that endearment, Elizabeth would have happily repaid her husband every debt of doubt. And Darcy decided that if he were to expect her to be totally forthcoming to him, he must be thus to her. One day he would find the words he must to tell her the entire story of Abigail, John, and Wickham.

There had been little time to wrestle with the decision to tell Darcy about seeing Bingley and little more to fret for Jane.

The thirty miles betwixt Pemberley and Kirkland were usually traversed twice a week, once by Jane, once by Elizabeth. The seven days preceding Elizabeth's last visit to her croft were spent upon horseback, hence she was long overdue for a visit with her sister. Wanting more time to weigh the matter and gather a perspective, still Elizabeth did not go.

Two days later, Jane came to Pemberley alone. Seeing her arrive without her children gave Elizabeth a sense of foreboding that was not to be unsatisfied.

The pleasant weather brought them outside to take tea and sweet biscuits; both remarked it a fine day. Admiration of the cloudless sky and slight breeze was cursory. In want of not thinking, and particularly not speaking about Bingley, Elizabeth at last shared with Jane the tale of Wickham's infamous visit and unceremonious retreat (any port in the conversational storm). After Elizabeth told Jane about Wickham's advances, Jane was properly aghast. Thereupon, Jane did the unlikely. She suggested the use of violence upon him.

"Lizzy, did you not smite him? I should have thought you would have."

Elizabeth thought she should have throttled him too, and full curious as to how Jane might exact this comeuppance, inquired just that.

"With what should I have smote him, Jane?"

Without hesitation, Jane answered, "A fireplace poker."

Not telling her that had, indeed, been under serious consideration and might have been employed had it not been out of reach, she said, "I shan't have opportunity to smite Wickham with anything, for Darcy influenced Wickham of his disaffection for me."

Having winnowed from Elizabeth a truer accounting of the long past bandit incident, Jane had since worried incessantly about safety, suggesting to her upon this occasion, "If not to use upon Wickham, Lizzy, perhaps you should carry a poker in the coach with you as I now do."

Elizabeth thought about it for a moment, thereupon opined, "I fancy a poker is easier to wield than a gun."

Sitting in the sun, it seemed a contradiction for two refined ladies to be discussing the merits of weaponry and upon whom to use them. When Elizabeth pointed that out, they both had a hearty laugh. Had Elizabeth been so inclined, from thence she might have embarked upon the telling of Lady Catherine's visit.

She knew, however, the examination of that topic would cause more evasion than conversation, and in silence, searched her mind for another. Jane, however, had one quite all her own.

"Pray, Lizzy," she said in her hesitant, soft voice, "there is something of which I must speak to you."

Jane stood and paced about before she spoke. That foreshadowing bade Elizabeth's attention. Jane sat before she continued, resting folded hands upon her knees, almost in supplication. At this, the premonition of ill-tidings Elizabeth had attempted to quash since her sister's arrival reared its ugly head.

"Lizzy," Jane started again, "I must tell you something in the severest of confidence."

Jane looked up at her sister then, and not at all certain she wanted to hear what Jane was going to say, Elizabeth nodded her head once in irresolute encouragement. Without additional exposition, Jane made a rather firm announcement.

"Charles has begotten a child of another woman."

This divulgement originating from Jane rather than herself, begat of Elizabeth a conflict of emotions. The utmost was undoubtedly the relief that she would not have to keep that secret, but it was closely seconded by astonishment that her sister rendered it not a secret at all. She feared for her countenance only a moment, for she was certain astonishment quite overwhelmed the subtlety of relief upon her face. Jane did not suspect she already knew.

"You are astonished to learn this I know, for your strong protest at Lydia's tales when we were gone to Charlotte's told me you find such indiscretions difficult to accept as true."

Elizabeth knew her mouth was slightly agape, closed it, looked away, and then returned her gaze to Jane. Jane reached out and placed her hand upon Elizabeth's, and gave it a comforting pat.

Elizabeth thought, "Jane is reassuring me? 'Tis I who should be offering her comfort."

"The baby is but a half-year old," Jane continued. "The...mother is consumptive and is not expected to live out the year."

Even more earnestly, she explained why she was confiding then, "Lizzy, I cannot bear to think of a child of Charles's to be handed to strangers. I want to have the baby with us, but Charles does not know I know of it. It might grieve him to know that I do. I could not bear that."

Elizabeth stifled a highly inappropriate snort of a laugh. Not that she thought anything at all humorous. But the incongruity of Jane's concern for Bingley's feelings, and that she weathered his betrayal with such restraint, assaulted Elizabeth's every notion of the verity of love. Elizabeth swept rationale and solicitude of Bingley aside.

She wanted to take the flat side of a shovel across Charles Bingley's head, but prudently kept that inclination to herself. For the manner of Jane's remarks told her that she had reason more for speaking of it than just sharing a confidence.

The vexed expression that overspread Elizabeth's countenance did not take Jane unawares. She knew well that would be her sister's initial reaction.

Hastily, she went on, "I must ask something of you that will take great generosity. The bother is not lost to me, thus you know how important it is."

Elizabeth took a deep breath, for until that moment, Jane had not once asked anything weighty of her. Without hesitation (but with no little trepidation), Elizabeth assured Jane that there was nothing she would not do for her.

"I want you to bring the baby to Pemberley."

Dumbstruck, Elizabeth said only, "But why?"

"If I could I would take the baby myself, but Charles must not know I know. Yet I cannot bear a son of my husband not knowing love, nor, in time, his father. I know that a more loving home than yours cannot be found. Charles should see him here frequently. The woman is tenant to Pemberley, he would not question you taking the baby in light of you having none of your own thus far."

Pemberley was great, servants abounded. The baby would be of little physical trouble, but one did not take on a human life without serious consideration. Yet Elizabeth made no hesitation.

"Of course, Jane. I shall apply to Darcy. The decision shall be his as much as mine."

Jane nodded, thereupon embraced her sister, "I thank you, Lizzy. There is no other of whom I could ask such a undertaking."

Elizabeth could not help but worry the issue, "But Jane, how can you forgive Bingley for such a betrayal? I thought no man more in love than Mr. Bingley with you. How could he do this to you? How can you simply submit to it?"

"Lizzy, it is a knotty thing for you to comprehend, this I know. Charles's love for me has not altered, this I know as well. But as I have been confined much of our marriage and Charles is...he needs...attention. If he called upon another woman, it was for other than affection."

Clearly, Jane could pardon a weakness of the flesh in her husband, however, she could not share his love. Her sister's generosity in this matter was only astonishing to Elizabeth because it came from Jane. Many a gentlewoman accepted her husband's transgressions so long as they were exercised with lessers. There was no perceived threat to position or marriage there. As Jane had no interest in position, she apparently found no undue injury so long as her marriage was sound. Elizabeth recognised that she, quite profoundly, was not of the same mind.

Elizabeth squeezed her sister's arm in reassurance, nonetheless, and said nothing. Her resentment was so ample, however, she found quite enough to compleatly drown Bingley and lap at the hem of her mother's skirt as well. Because of Mrs. Bennet's ill-advice, Jane had denied her husband consolation for much of her marriage. (That was no excuse for Bingley, of course, but the poor man's ballocks were probably a bright shade of blue more often than not.) Her ire fully piqued, she reckoned she should be angry at herself as well, for had she pursued the subject of Jane pleasing her husband and herself more relentlessly, perchance things might have been different…But Elizabeth made herself not think of it.

The afternoon waned and Elizabeth accompanied Jane to her coach, not daring to query her more. In time, she might address those questions to Jane, but for then, she bid her good-bye. Jane waved a little wearily out the window of her coach, unquestionably as relieved as Elizabeth that they did not have to keep any more skeletons in the cupboard. And as she stood and watched her sister take leave, Elizabeth silently pondered just how she and Georgiana had actually overlooked a consumptive person to nurse upon Pemberley lands.

Solitude was necessary for Elizabeth fully to appreciate what had just come to pass. With her chin resting in her palm, she deliberated upon her sister's nature from a window seat in the music room.

Each of the five Bennet sisters had their attributes assigned almost from babyhood. Mary was prim, Kitty flighty. Lydia was outlandish, and Elizabeth, bold. Jane was, and always had been, gentle, kind, and naïve. Was Elizabeth to admit it, however kind, she also thought Jane to be fragile. Strength had been her own trait, not Jane's. She was the Bennet sister who was forthright and strong. However, had their positions in this sordid mess been reversed, Elizabeth could not ascribe to herself the benevolent fortitude to see to the well-being of all those involved as had Jane.

Soon her thoughts drifted to the dreaded mission of telling her husband of Bingley's sin against his wife. And she dreaded what lay before her as much as any anticipated event she could recall. She methodically went over several times in her mind what she must tell him, giving each version contemplation, deciding the exact approach she wanted to employ to cite the facts.

However pleasant the possibility of reprieve, Elizabeth knew telling Darcy about Jane's entreaty and Bingley's extramarital "bonus" could not be put off for long, thus she stood and aimed herself for Darcy's library. He was seated at his desk in all good humour of unprecluded ignorance. Blissfully, he studied his books, unaware that his wife peeked at him with trepidation from behind the door. Elizabeth pushed open the door and took a deep breath. Looking up, he smiled when he saw her, thereupon leaned back in his chair and turned to her in welcome.

She knew he expected her to come to him as she always had, but after taking only a few steps in his direction, she altered her course. Once at the window, she stood silently looking out. He watched her mute contemplation with a hesitant concern that was betrayed only by a worrying of his ring. She realised he must be in some disorder, wondering what surprise next lay in store. Wickham. Another woman. Now this.

"My poor husband," she thought, "how I do try your patience."

She walked to him, knelt beside his chair and, sighing, rested her head upon the arm. She thought this sigh a little too melodramatic, however she could not help but do it once more in preparation for her plea. He reached out to draw her onto his lap, and whatever temptation it was to whisper her shocking disclosure in his ear, she decided to take a chair facing and moved it close to his. Knee to knee, eye to eye, she would say what had to be said.

"We promised to keep nothing from each other ever again. I have been waiting for the right moment to tell you this, but now the moment has chosen me."

Elizabeth sighed once more before continuing, "Jane visited me today…no, I must begin before then."

Taking both his hands in hers, she looked away for a moment, for her practised speech had vanished. Desperately, she endeavoured to find a kind way to tell him his dearest friend was a…detestable scourge and blight upon humanity. An execrable, letching infidel. A scurrilous, walking dung heap. A…

Taking a gulp of air, she started again, "What I withheld from you of my observations of the woman your aunt bade me visit, was that, I, of course, did not see you there, but I did see a man visit that cottage that last day."

Darcy gave her his full attention.

"I espied a man ride thither, kiss the woman, and hold the baby." She did not prolong the drama, "It was Charles Bingley."

His astonishment at the revelation was obvious.

Elizabeth had once dared to ask him if Bingley ever went with him to the infamous house of accommodation he visited in London. Darcy had responded with the emphatic announcement that it was exceedingly dishonourable to speak in violation of a friend's privacy.

That pronouncement made, he nonetheless said, "No, he did not," apparently believing defence of repute not a transgression of privacy.

It was obvious he had not thought this of Bingley, or at least did not know of it. Not until seeing surprise upon her husband's face did Elizabeth consider Bingley might have told Darcy. Surely men talk of such things, and Bingley was his closest friend. Elizabeth saw this a positive for her own husband's devotion, for if Bingley did not tell him, he must have expected disapproval. This train of thought was abandoned, for Elizabeth did not want to obtain any sort of self-satisfaction from her sister's circumstance.

In a moment he bid, "Are you certain, Lizzy? Bingley has never given me reason to question his character in word or deed for as long as I have known him. Perchance you mistook him."

Elizabeth told him, regrettably, there was no mistake, "When I espied Mr. Bingley that day, I was so astonished and appalled I had no notion as how to tell you, or if it was in my province to speak of it. My concern I lent to Jane. I was certain was she to learn of such business as this, it would wound her gravely."

For assurance, she added, "Did I doubt my own eyes, Jane came today bearing the story."

Thereupon she told him of Jane's knowledge of the baby and upon the heels of that, her own promise to seek his approval of bringing the child to live with them. Thinking it merely a formality in asking, she began to assure him how little inconvenience would be brought about, where the baby might sleep, who might attend it. Overtaken as she was by the necessity of preparation, she mused upon these matters almost to herself. Therefore, she did not see his eyes darken nor his mood alter.

But so decisively did he stand, his chair was forced back several feet.

Had this not startled her enough, he said, quite scornfully, "Yes, why do we not populate all of Pemberley with bastard sons?"

Thereupon he turned and angrily walked to the window she had so recently vacated.

She did not move. She did not think she could will herself to move. Her face flushed crimson. Tears threatened her, but she refused them. Cheeks blazing in fury, her hands clutched the arms of the chair as if to keep her from fleeing, either after him or from the room. Immediate upon his unreasonable umbrage at her for Wickham's unexpected appearance, he spoke to her in this manner. It was his friend who had done the despicable, not her sister!

Righteous indignation fully employed, she desperately sought some sharp reply to him, but was visited by nothing but a fleeting vision of the shovel she had conjured for Charles Bingley.

Something made her stay and hold her tongue as well. It was decidedly not in character for him to treat an appeal from her so churlishly. Hence, she rose and went to him, putting her arms under his and about his waist, resting her cheek against the soft back of his coat. From the valley between his shoulder blades she detected the furious beating of a tortured heart.

As steadfastly as he held his pose, one might have supposed it would have taken no little persuasion for her to coax him from it. But it did not. When she reached up and turned his face to hers, it was not anger she saw. In that instant, he gripped her to him. At that moment, she could not see his face but she heard his words.

He repeated, "Lizzy, Lizzy, forgive me, forgive me."

She kissed him, if not in understanding, at least in empathy, salted with a great deal of apprehension. Whatever caused him to lash out at her was far beyond the bounds of what he had just learnt of Bingley.

"I have already forgiven you, but please tell me."

Taking her hand, he led her to the side chair by the window and cradled her upon his lap. It was only in that intimate embrace that he was able to embark upon the telling of his history with Abigail and Wickham.

"As you know," he cleared his throat, "Wickham came to live in the house as an adolescent."

She nodded.

"We were quite competitive as we raced and played at war. There were rivalries. Some were overt, some unwitting. It was during this time I was initiated into intimate rites with a young woman who worked here. As it happened, Wickham shared her favours first."

As he spoke, she sat in bewilderment as to why he was telling her of this ancient story from his youth. He said he had an early dalliance with the same servant girl as

Wickham. How droll. Her husband's gravity was the only thing that kept her from smiling as she thought of the two young men chasing the same young woman. Lusty, exuberant youths!

Playfully, she asked, "So this was the lady who worked foul designs upon your innocence!"

"I freely admit any pollutions committed were done with my absolute consent," he smiled fleetingly (or at least turned up the corners of his mouth). That cheered her. So much so, it occurred to her to quiz him about specifics, but that ill-conceived notion was immediately cast aside with his very next revelation.

"The girl's name was Abigail. Abigail Christie. John Christie's mother."

Elizabeth sat bolt upright and any notion of amusement deserted her. John Christie was born of this woman and Wickham fathered him. She blinked repeatedly.

"You and Wickham both lay with her?"

Which was not her true question, only the one she asked. Thus, he answered the one she had not inquired.

"Wickham is the boy's father, not I."

"You are convinced?"

"Not until Mrs. Reynolds related it to you did I know that Wickham had…been availed of her before me. She was well on with his child and, in my ignorance, I knew not of it."

A flash of lightning could not have rendered it more blindingly clear: Darcy had first thought the young man was a son of his own, owing to her own loquacious dispensation months previous that John was the son of Abigail.

"Why do you speak of this only now?"

As he often did, he almost spoke, then retreated into silence. Invariably, quiet overcame him at the most precipitous moment possible. Betimes, this was only mildly frustrating. But not then. Elizabeth had to fight the urge to clutch his lapels and shout at him to speak to her. He had turned his face to the window. His silence allowed her to contemplate what he had just told her. Immediately, she understood the full complexity of his opposition to Georgiana's friendship with John Christie. But she wondered why he was not relieved to learn that the boy was not his, for the possibility would have wounded his dignity. Most importantly, why did he not tell her?

Was he mortified at even a possibility that he fathered the boy? And why did he become angry? All of these questions begged answers, but he offered none.

To her husband, it would be substantial loss of face to have to admit to a misbegotten child. But Elizabeth could not help feeling a small disappointment that John was not truly Darcy's, for the thought of being able to mother even a near-grown lad was far more inviting than the office of step-aunt. Thereupon, her own disappointment did the unlikely. It announced the crux of Darcy's disorder, and that truth settled over her so heavily her shoulders visibly sagged.

Darcy too was disappointed.

And it was at her hand. It was she who took all due pleasure in announcing Wickham's paternity to him, thus dashing his belief that the boy was his son. The only son, the only child he might beget. Another woman's son. Of course, he could not tell her that.

The answer to every question, Elizabeth realised, was herself. It was she who could not give him a child. It was she who brought Wickham to his house, the true father of the son he thought was his. She was the one who spied upon Bingley, and she was the one who wanted him to take in Bingley's child. In defeat, she dropped her hands from him. Only then did he look at her. He reached out and touched her face, thereupon he drew her to him again.

"Of course, we shall take the baby," he said.

"We need not decide it now," she said, unhappy that she had asked at all.

She had begun to be excited about the baby. Thenceforward and forever, that happiness was polluted. She was certain each time that she looked into the little boy's face, it would hark back to her own failing.

Unable to tell Darcy that she had grasped the magnitude of her own role in his unhappiness, the next few days saw her spending far too much time ruminating upon Jane's husband's misdeeds.

For if Bingley could not keep his breeches buttoned and another child of his appeared thither upon the countryside, Elizabeth intended to hatch some heinous scheme to teach him a lesson. This was a delicate matter and engendered a great deal of malicious thought. One particularly delightful one she imagined involved a leather thong, a dead cat, and some pepper sauce.

Eventually, this obsession was abandoned and Mr. Bingley was granted temporary, if unknown, amnesty.

In the few years since that first fateful trip to London, the Darcys had not returned as often as society dictated. And when they did, each excursion there took upon all the preparation and caution of impending battle. And, in some sense, it was.

Mr. Darcy did not ride in the coach with his wife, even if it was occupied by only his wife, Hannah, and Goodwin. He rode his horse beside it, a gun beneath his coat and sword hugging his leg. Hannah knew it was not what her mistress might have chosen, for she had heard her attempt to cajole her husband to keep her company in the carriage. He had steadfastly and adamantly refused her (to Hannah's understanding, a rare occurrence). Mrs. Darcy did not argue beyond that first brief endeavour. No one questioned why he chose to ride as he did, for it was quite accepted that his vigilance was rewarded far better from the saddle than in the leather seat of a barouche.

As the Darcys' visits were infrequent, Cyril Smeads enjoyed almost unlimited autonomy amongst the servants in London even though Mistress Georgiana was often in residence. But her attention was employed by her writing and, regardless, she was not inclined to find fault with the running of the household. Absence of the Darcys in town announced they spent most of their time at Pemberley. Mrs. Reynolds (although she certainly would have been allowed) did not often take herself away from her duties to visit her son; hence, he was quite happy, upon occasion, to travel to see her in Derbyshire.

He brought with him (excess baggage of sorts) the very traits that alienated general regard of him in town. Pompous and petulant as his mother was humble and firm, they bore little similarity in character. Hannah thought that peculiar, but reminded herself that Goodwin was nephew and cousin, his own understanding of comportment distancing him from them both.

That abused Hannah's own notion of familial similarity, for her four brothers, in manner as well as countenance, seemed almost interchangeable (so much so, neighbours often confused them). And, except for more generous waistline and a rather decided hair loss (his, not theirs), the brothers favoured their father as well. Although Hannah did harbour a few fanciful notions, her hand glass allowed her to entertain none about her own person. She knew her figure reflected a feminine interpretation of the familial sturdy build that predicted time would burden them all with more weight than a person of vanity might desire.

The single thing she hoped was left wanting. For she dearly wished she favoured her mother. Even though Hannah had been sixteen when she died, she could not remember her face. Her father's somewhat taciturn disposition denied him comment upon the matter, hence Hannah was left to ponder that herself. When she consulted the looking-glass, she fancied she did favour her mother; for most mourners, memorial retrospection grows kinder with the years. She dared not seek her brothers' counsel upon this, for they had never ceased to mock her for her elevation of position. Because of that, her visits home were a bit trying. Her pleasant nature, however, believed that in teasing they were simply dutifully fulfilling the office demanded of brothers, and did not complain.

But then Hannah rarely complained about anything. And it was unusual when she had curt words with Cyril Smeads for she was quite in fear of inciting his wrath even when he was no more than a visitor of the house. Cyril Smeads had little weight at Pemberley. There, his mother was in charge.

If Hannah was yet frightened of the son, she was no longer of his mother. Since the day the Darcys' baby died and Mrs. Reynolds stopped her from running away, Hannah had readjusted her opinion of the old lady. For where once she had found her coldly critical, she now realised she was merely capable and strong with nothing but the best interest of the Darcys as her motive.

Hannah's devotion to Elizabeth and exceedingly high regard for Mr. Darcy cemented Mrs. Reynolds' opinion of Hannah as well. That day she ran from Mrs. Darcy's childbirth in vain quest of her late mother, Hannah thought Providence had found her a second in Mrs. Reynolds. Mrs. Reynolds still spoke sternly to her, just as she did the other servants. Yet underneath that terse cadence of instruction was undeniable affection. Hannah accepted that gift and returned it.

Her son was another matter compleatly. It was the single thing she found unforgivable in Mrs. Reynolds. She begat Cyril. The only positive that anyone could locate of him was that when his ill-temper was unemployed, he could be an interesting conversationalist, for he did not limit his discourse to the weather and price of eggs. It might well be described as gossip, but only by those who did not have the benefit of hearing it first-hand.

Notwithstanding Hannah's exceedingly well-husbanded maintenance of Mr. and Mrs. Darcy's privacy, she did confess to an avid interest in listening to unsubstantiated rumours about others (the questioning of substantiation being, by far, the most enjoyable part). This did grieve her conscience, and upon Sundays, a better part of her prayers addressed this failing. However, she had far greater success at chastising herself subsequently rather than denying the opportunity, rationalising that it was not possible to determine it actually gossip until she had heard the entire tale.

Hannah was able to keep the confidences of Mrs. Darcy so diligently by reminding herself that the information she held was exceedingly valuable and she alone was entrusted with it. Well, she allowed, Goodwin was also entrusted. However, she opined that Mrs. Darcy's confidences were in much greater number and importance than any Goodwin held of Mr. Darcy's. It was a conversation she might have favoured engaging in with Goodwin. That of the similarity and importance of their confidences. They did have that in common. But Goodwin had steadfastly refrained from just such an exchange. Hannah had thought herself successful did she elicit from him the concession that it was favourable weather.

She had never quite resigned herself to his unforthcoming nature, no matter how conscientiously he practised it. Hannah believed him perhaps uncertain in the company of a woman, possibly reticent and shy. As it happened, she even harboured the notion that Goodwin was truly of the same temperament as his employer. Hannah was well aware that Mr. Darcy was considered proud and aloof. Hannah, however, knew too (rather than only guessed, as did the rest of the servants) that Mr. and Mrs. Darcy had an exceedingly passionate marriage. It followed (at least to Hannah's supposition) that Goodwin's still waters ran as deep as did Mr. Darcy's.

As she watched him move about his duties, she often thought of that and could not help but admire his small hands and the fine hair upon them she could see just below his ruffled knuckledabs. It did not trouble her mind to wonder why, as such a big girl, she was attracted to such a meagre little mite of a man.

Passion aside, their respective positions denied them (had Goodwin been inclined) any kind of romantic involvement. The office of lady-maid and manservant were occupied only by unmarried persons. Hannah was not so certain of Goodwin's possible intrigue as a paramour to risk her employment. (There was far greater pleasure from imagining Goodwin ripping his shirt from his body and drawing her and her heaving bosom to his chest than to learn belatedly that he had not the strength nor the chest to do either.)

Thus roundly unrequited in romance and much in admiration of it, Hannah was probably far more susceptible to flattery than another might have been.

When Cyril Smeads did the unlikely by complimenting her disposition, she ignored previous warnings she had received in regard to liberties he had taken with the London maids. (And if she disregarded those warnings, she hoped no one noticed the spontaneity with which he was rendered from demonic to celestial to her through the very mildest of flattery.) She had noticed that one of Cyril Smeads's more reliable traits (aside from rather impressive temper fits) was an uncanny ability to locate the most vulnerable of feminine opportunity. She did not consider herself particularly vulnerable, but could assign herself thus if it served her greater good. Hannah decided that if Goodwin happened to see her giggling at one of Cyril Smeads jokes and did not approve, that was just very unfortunate.

Goodwin noticed Smeads's guile toward Hannah more sharply than did others. He took notice too of Hannah's giggling. He protested not, however, abhorring the possibility of divulging more interest than provident. Normally he might have discussed such unseemliness with Mrs. Reynolds, but in this specific instance he knew his own influence with the Pemberley housekeeper had not the weight of the London houseman. Thus, as cousin to her son, he kept his silence and watched in trepidation as Hannah was enticed his by wiles, her allurements to him suddenly more pronounced in light of another's interest.

Hence, flirtations became more vested and tensions a little greater when Cyril Smeads was in visit. Hannah was the not-unknowing pawn in a subtle game of influence. Into this delicate but intricate web of flirtation came the unseemly intrusion of adultery and deceit.

Indeed, if the origin of this infidelity and deception was a little muddled, it was fathomable. For Elizabeth Darcy often became so entwined in problems within her family, she did not remember that their private lives were not all that confidential. Hannah was trusted implicitly. Goodwin as well. But when she went upon her rides seeking to determine of her husband's fidelity, it was not in the privacy she thought. The Darcy household was centre-stage of the entire county. When one of their household made any visit or spoke any comment, it was noted. It was noted widely. When Mrs. Darcy's routine of visiting the ailing altered, it was scrutinised. The cessation of these visits was scrutinised more profoundly than whence they had commenced. Because she had finally become accustomed to the intrusion of servants and they with her disinclination of assistance, she thought herself unobserved.

She was not. Nor was she mindful that she was generally admired amongst the population, as much for her unassuming manner and good deeds as the fairness of her face. But that admiration did not belay whispers about her activities, it merely incited more curiosity by the public. Darcy, having been born into his position, had a greater appreciation of the interest he held. He even knew that he was thought a rather unfriendly, proud man. Knowing that there were far more dishonourable appellations bestowed upon men of his station by the populace, he accepted that pronouncement as not untrue and was happy to be known also as a man of his word.

Darcy had no interest in his reputation beyond the concern that his name not be brought to ridicule. Having not had the same upbringing, it was impossible for Elizabeth to think of herself in the third person. If she thought of her persona, she knew herself to be who she had always been, she was simply a wife also. She had a fair notion of the public regard of her husband, but none of her own.

She was well aware, even appalled, at the level of romantic indiscretion amongst ranking members of society. So prevalent was the phenomenon, it had been cheerfully euphemised as "gallantry." Thus, of course, those who dabbled in it and those who made it their life's work could eschew that unsavoury little word "fornication." The ladies and gentlemen of the royal court held the dubious honour of being thought of as the least chaste and most gallant in the country. Of course, these of the aristocracy gave themselves absolution by reasoning that most married to unite fortunes, not for love. Their lessers knew this as well, hence it was as much a scandal to them when Mr. Darcy married Miss Bennet as had he taken a mistress. They were viewed a bit of an oddity yet as a couple, if not in countenance, at least in circumstance. Some of all levels of society looked upon them in admiration, just as some believed them nothing other than anomalies.

Had it not been widely known the Darcy marriage was one of mutual love, Elizabeth might have been inundated with any number of invitations for adulterous affairs. Wholly unconscious of this, she certainly did not miss what she did not seek. But had she been, she might have understood that in Wickham's proposal of liaison, however distasteful, he was operating upon a less unlikely presumption than she understood.

It took less than a day for every man and woman, and half the children, to know Mr. Wickham had been invited to take his leave from Pemberley *at the point of a blade.* Just what led to this was wildly speculated upon, for who could resist such intrigue? Beautiful people, great wealth, the threat of death. It was the greatest point for gossip since the time Mr. Darcy slew ten men simultaneously in a duel protesting his wife's honour. (There had been a bewildering variation of explanations as to the exact nature of this event, but the fundamental facts varied not at all: ten men, killed single-handedly by Mr. Darcy's sword. Some more hardy souls even made a pilgrimage to The Strangled Goose, ogled the blood-stained floor, and stood in awe of the blade.)

Given this level of interest, the manner of George Wickham's departure was speculated upon as well. Particularly since there was that other matter about Abigail Christie's boy. There was great interest in her assertion upon the eve of her death that she had once bedded with young Mr. Darcy because it was the only time anyone in the county could actually have almost first-hand knowledge of such an occurrence. There had been many rumours, mostly about someone who knew someone who had been with Mr. Darcy. In the light of no hard evidence, it had begun to be believed that Mr. Darcy rarely dallied. Talk of him soon abated, for no diversion is found in integrity.

Therefore, when Elizabeth began to take her rides each day, abandoning the county's sick, it did not go unnoticed. It was noticed where she went as well. If it was confused that the man who visited the house that Mrs. Darcy watched was Mr. Darcy, it was understandable. What other rich man would Mrs. Darcy follow? Thus, it was quite logically surmised that the baby from that woman was begat by none other than Mr. Darcy. Why else would Mrs. Darcy adopt him? Mr. Darcy had no sons. He must have one to entail Pemberley. There was no other explanation. In the time it took for word to reach Bingley's woman requesting the adoption of the baby, it had come full circle back to Pemberley that Mr. Darcy had an illegitimate son.

It was chatty Cyril Smeads who announced it to Hannah. He said he knew it was true, for when Mr. Darcy had lived in London before his marriage, his coach made regular trips to a bordello (he had used the term "House of Lewdness"). Hannah should have liked to hear more about this "house" in London, but she was so indignant over Smeads's accusation of Mr. Darcy, she could only sputter her protestation.

"What Mr. Darcy did when he weren't married means nothin' now!" she said hotly.

Cyril Smeads looked upon her with an expression he often used in recognition of the ignorance of a lesser and said, "Were you more in knowledge of gentlemanly pursuits, you might understand that age and circumstance do not alter one's proclivities."

Hannah thought Cyril Smead's proclivities were most probably shrivelled from disuse and he had no business speaking in an unsavoury manner about Mr. Darcy's. This, of course, remained a thought and not a comment, for Hannah was incensed but not so irate as to jeopardise her position. Simultaneously, Cyril Smeads as a romantic feint was rendered obsolete. She simply folded her arms and watched him waddle (there was no kinder way to describe his large-bottomed walk) up the corridor.

It was only thereupon that she noticed Goodwin across the landing. He was quite openly eavesdropping upon their conversation. Hannah might have allowed her anger to spill onto his obvious snooping had he not stood mimicking her exact stance, arms folded, brow furrowed, and jaw clenched. It was the very first time Hannah knew that she and Goodwin had an utter meeting of the minds. They might have found additional duplication of emotion had they heard Smeads stop upon the stairs just as a woman was leaving an interview with Mrs. Darcy. A quidnunc of unparalleled curiosity, he punctiliously inquired of her business within the household. The woman told him she was seeking a position as a baby nurse. Cyril Smeads did not query her more, but his raised eyebrows told the woman that the baby in question was of notorious origin.

Hence, if there was doubt in Derbyshire whether it truth or rumour that the baby that was to come to live at Pemberley was Mr. Darcy's, it was decided in favour of truth at Cyril Smeads's silent but unmistakable instruction. But if he remained mute at Pemberley, as he hied to London he was not so inconversable. Indeed, he took a short excursion into Kent. But he tarried neither at the Hunsford Inn nor at the home of Mrs. Darcy's late cousin's wife.

The woman who sought the situation of nurse was none other than Mrs. Hardin's sister, Bessie.

Forthwith of her employment interview (and thus proving herself indisputably a truly good sister), Bessie made haste to Mrs. Hardin's kitchen to give an accounting of the entire episode. Ignoring her cook-pot, Mrs. Hardin settled in to hear her sister tell the particulars regarding the infant come to stay in the House of Pemberley.

When Mrs. Hardin learnt from Bessie that the young woman who had the glaring fall from grace was the very one she had eyed for John Christie, she was undeniably vexed. Although neither Mrs. Hardin nor Bessie said a further word on the matter, they exchanged significantly indignant looks. Their attempt at discretion, however, was for naught. Quite beyond their notice, the disapproving discourse incited the avid interest of John Christie, who sat at the far end of the table seemingly in rapt attention to a bowl of bread and onions.

But he had taken notice. Keen notice. For what Mrs. Hardin foretold had truly come to pass. This time, however, Mrs. Darcy was there to save the baby Mr. Darcy begat and cast aside. This ruined woman had it easier than his own mother. Her death would be swift. Not a long, slow descent into the bowels of hell. Mrs. Darcy should be avenged of her sorry husband. If he had a sword like Colonel Fitzwilliam, John fancied he just might be able to do it. Especially if he had that red cape as well.

For the first time in his brief life, John had found a duty strictly of himself. And he wondered, when the time presented itself, would he ever have the courage to do it?

It was uncustomary for Fitzwilliam to spend the winter months in town and even more peculiar for him to return to Derbyshire just when London society was in full bloom.

However, after his confession of love to Elizabeth, to London he went. And there he endured months of tortuous, self-imposed exile. When he returned in late May, as one might suspect, his reason was of the utmost importance. He had an announcement to make, and much to his mother's displeasure, it was matters political, not matrimonial, that brought him home.

The day of Fitzwilliam's very impolitic baring of soul to his cousin's wife, he had come strictly because he had heard of Wickham's call upon Pemberley and that man's near violent ouster. Gossip was rife about the event, thus he wanted to hear a first-hand accounting of it from Darcy. Of course, that conversation never came to pass. He aborted his call and hied to London, his tail cupped protectively betwixt his legs.

Elizabeth's terse comment as he removed himself that day assured him of her silence regarding his stupendously ill-conceived declaration to her. She would not divulge a word of it to Darcy. A considerable relief. For even as well as he knew him, Fitzwilliam could not say unequivocally that Darcy would not call him out for such an act, tantamount to blasphemy. Had it come from any other man, a presumption of attempted cuckoldry might be taken without question. Fitzwilliam was not so certain of Darcy's temper to believe himself beyond such condemnation regardless of the strength of their friendship.

Free of such censure, Fitzwilliam concentrated upon mortification. His dignity was humiliated beyond redemption to have suffered such a lapse in self-restraint. And he wavered betwixt worrying that Elizabeth thought him a lascivious cad and regretting the loss of the easy acquaintanceship they had enjoyed. He simply could not face her again. Her opprobrium would be unendurable.

Though he fled from Elizabeth, he would not compleatly rupture his relationship with Darcy. This, the outcome of two understandings. The first was a rationale, the second a matter of platonic esteem. If he severed his connexion with his friend utterly, it might invite enquiry and Fitzwilliam did not want to have to account for a discontinuity betwixt them. Additionally, and most importantly, breach himself if he must from his home county, he could not weather the loss of Darcy's friendship. Particularly as a result of his own dishonourable feelings. Hence, he bartered himself a compromise by maintaining communication by post.

Endeavouring to accomplish his arrested visit to Pemberley by letter (what he should have done in the first place, he scolded himself), Fitzwilliam carefully composed a missive. Making only the most cursory attempt at remarking upon the mundane (roads, weather, his boots, and the poor state of all three), he thereupon inquired specifically of Wickham and the call he paid to Pemberley.

Darcy's reply was prompt but succinct, which was the way of all letters betwixt them, thus betraying no knowledge of any indiscretion upon Fitzwilliam's part. (Had he been angry, his response would have been more eloquent, always a flag of displeasure in Darcy's correspondence.) With Darcy supplying the gist of Wickham's visit, Fitzwilliam was able to glean the truth of the matter. And that it involved Wickham and bastardy was not an astonishment.

Darcy's retelling did not, however, include Wickham's advances upon Elizabeth. Had it, Fitzwilliam's perplexity over the subsequent visit of Lady Catherine would have escalated into outright bafflement. He might have leapt to the same incorrect conclusion as had Elizabeth, believing the two occurrences were not coincidental. His rescue from misconception was unbeknownst to Fitzwilliam. Thus, he could not reap any comfort from it.

Consolation he needed in abundance, for his misery was very nearly making him ill. In desperation, he forsook his exceedingly advantageous assignment with the Household Cavalry and took to loitering about the Horse Guards building in Whitehall reading the latest missives about the doings across the Channel. Most of these were penned by Wellesley, whose defeat of Napoleon's marshals in the Iberian Peninsula demanded a dukedom. Hence, he signed his dispatch announcing Napoleon's banishment from France as "Wellington." (So exalted was Wellington's reputation in England, one might have believed the duke had personally annihilated Napoleon's battalions upon the frozen Russian tundra himself.)

With their French nemesis exiled in despotic petulance upon the tiny island of Elba, Fitzwilliam's cronies revelled in the victory. However happy they were to have Napoleon upon his knees, few were quite ready to forgo all chance of glorious rencontre and many groused about their spate of medals.

Fitzwilliam, however, fretted, "That slyboots has two strings to his bow. He cannot be counted *hors d'combat* until we see his head on a spike."

Prophetic words.

After the initial triumph of Napoleon's expulsion, the successive dispatches from the continent were of a tiresome political nature, nothing at all to excite an Iberian veteran. Fitzwilliam and his Whitehall colleagues read each of the increasingly tedious reports with dispassion. They had most probably reached their apex of monotony upon the day of the arrival of the improbable (to the point of hilarity) news that Napoleon had escaped and was marching upon Paris with an army only six hundred strong.

To those not quite willing to give up the sword, interest, to say the least, was piqued. As each subsequent day brought new revelations (and less jocularity), the number of officers who listened in disbelief at the Horse Guard Offices grew into a jostling, impatient mob.

Most promptly, news arrived that Napoleon's discharged army officers (unhappily thrust into civilian oblivion with only half-pay) had developed sudden amnesia of the Russian debacle they had experienced at their former emperor's command and flocked to his leadership once again. If he was to be stopped, immediacy was all.

By mid-March the Petite Usurper had amassed a battle-hardened army of two hundred thousand soldiers. Thus, when Wellington arrived in Brussels to man a stand to check the aggression, he was disheartened to find a few Hanover units buttressed by only ten thousand British troops. The duke was desperate for brigades, regiments, companies, yea, any allied man with a weapon or a horse.

It was within this call to arms that Fitzwilliam found absolution. Experience was crucial, for the fight would be to the death. With that understanding, Fitzwilliam volunteered for Belgium duty and returned to Derbyshire to say good-bye to those he loved.

Unsuspecting of the nature of Fitzwilliam's reappearance, Darcy was quite happy to see him again, insisting upon hosting a small celebration. Their group was small, a family gathering. Lady Matlock was not present, for she refused country life yet, necessitating Matlock to winter alone. Her absence, however, did not preclude Fitzwilliam's farewells. With Georgiana, Jane and Bingley, Bingley's sisters, and the increasingly dissipated Mr. Hurst all forsaking London for a leisurely spring in the country, theirs made a tolerable number to mark the occasion festive.

When Fitzwilliam had decamped from the county immediately after his impetuous confession to her, Elizabeth had been both relieved and bothered. She had hoped to have the opportunity to make light of the incident, fancy it a jest. It might be awkward, but she could think of no other way in which to handle it. The precipitousness of his departure eliminated that possibility, and the longer he stayed away, the more severe seemed the gaffe.

Hence, the family supper was most uncomfortable for not only the guest of honour, but the hostess as well. An additional irritant was the presence of Caroline Bingley. Possibly in preparation for the season in London, possibly because there was simply no other unattached man about, Caroline Bingley had taken to dipping her interminable chin and batting her stubby eyelashes at Fitzwilliam. It was unlikely that Caroline was so desperate as to seek a match with title-less, fortune-less Fitzwilliam when she had once set her cap for Darcy, but he did present a dashing figure.

Elizabeth watched Caroline rearrange the place cards to seat herself next to her latest flirtation with less than forbearance. Under the best of circumstances Caroline tended to be a bit crabby, which led Elizabeth to conjecture she had not yet (or at least not regularly) had her pleasure garden ploughed. But as much as she would have favoured seeing an improvement in dear Caroline's disposition, Elizabeth was not so unkind as to wish Fitzwilliam's manhood sacrificed upon her particular *pudendum femininum.* His disappearance to London had pronounced him spooked of Pemberley and Caroline's blatant coquetry was not an inducement to tarry.

Nevertheless, Elizabeth concluded it best not to reason another's desires. Perchance Fitzwilliam might be happy to accommodate Miss Bingley. It was her understanding a woman had to be truly offensive for an unoccupied man to absolutely refuse to copulate. However disagreeable Elizabeth thought Caroline, she must not presume Fitzwilliam's mind. He had taught that lesson to her well.

After supper, Fitzwilliam patiently unwound Caroline's arm from his and the men departed for tobacco and port in the library. Before the ladies had time to arrange their dresses about their ankles and pick up their sewing, firm, even strident, voices drifted into the air of the drawing room. That was most unusual, for indocile exchanges were rarely heard (Lady Catherine had been there only the one time) inside Pemberley. Above the din of the Bingley and Hurst children's complaints as they were corralled for bed, Elizabeth heard the unaccustomedly stern voice of her husband.

There was an argument ensuing amongst the gentlemen, but only Elizabeth and Georgiana seemed conscious of it. They sat side by side upon a sofa centred in the room. Thus, the disagreement echoed through the double doors and wafted upon their ears. What they heard was alarming, although the debate had not escalated into a row. There were no truly cross words, but opinions were unquestionably vehement.

Elizabeth glanced nervously at Georgiana. Her countenance did not betray if she was eavesdropping upon what was being said across the hall. Full curious herself, Elizabeth considered making a casual stroll to the door in the hope she could hear enough from that vantage to determine what was at odds. But Caroline Bingley sat across the room and Elizabeth was afraid her retreat to eavesdrop at the doorway might invite her scrutiny. If she were to be a busybody, Elizabeth preferred not to have it noted.

"How can you believe that, Fitzwilliam?" Bingley demanded, "Napoleon fled France disguised as his own postilion to escape his own countrymen who called for his head. None but the *Vieille Garde* will follow him again."

"As badly as we want to believe they will not, it is true. French officers were discharged from service at half-pay. They are flocking back to him by the tens of thousands. Even Marshal Ney, who vowed to recapture him, fell to his knees and kissed the little man's feet. A considerable battle is upon us."

The men-folk were all seated in chairs near the fireplace; Matlock, Fitzwilliam, and Bingley each held a brandy snifter in their hands. Well-fortified at supper, Mr. Hurst had judiciously abdicated the conversation by reason of being incoherent. Darcy had set his glass down. The men, save Mr. Hurst, sat upon the edge of their wing chairs. (Mr. Hurst, who was more or less lolling, was having difficulty keeping his glass upright. A servant, stationed behind him just for this purpose, took the linen from his arm and dabbed at the fabric of the chair with each slosh of Mr. Hurst's glass.)

"I thought the French were happy with Louis," Matlock puled.

Morosely, he peered into his wineglass, utterly perplexed by the capricious nature of the Gaul.

Ignoring his brother's innocuous complaint, Fitzwilliam said with finality, "The Leopard merely had his tail removed; he is a dangerous animal yet. Wellington has advised that we must refortify our army now or be content to have the threat of Napoleon's bravado for another decade. I, for one, intend to take leave to-morrow. My regiment will depart from Portsmouth."

"Your superior officers, of course, will be happy to have your expertise amongst them.

But your service in the peninsula was at great personal expense," Darcy reasoned. "You have been wounded once, you were lucky to survive. Even the King does not demand you go into battle once again, Fitzwilliam. You are needed here to train the officers who take the place of those lost in Spain and Portugal. Is that not service enough?"

"Indeed, that is just the point," Fitzwilliam countered. "Many of the troops allied with us are ill-trained, the Dutch, the Belgians…"

"Yes," agreed Darcy, "that is just the point. Napoleon's army may be small, but you say they are seasoned veterans and fiercely loyal. Except for Wellesley and Blucher amongst the allied military, there are no true leaders, only courtiers and politicians. Csar Alexander is a joke as a general and determined to interfere with strategy. Even a British victory will still be annihilation. A bloody mess!"

"Am I not to engage in battle because of the possibility of bloodshed?" Fitzwilliam retorted. "Or am I to desist because I am needed here?"

"Whichever argument will keep you at home, I fancy," Darcy replied miserably, knowing he had blundered with his rebuttal.

Matlock interjected, "Young Howgrave has purchased a commission in the Fourteenth Hussars."

"Indubitably favours their hats," Darcy said with a sardonic sniff. If his conscience demanded him to cease despising that young man's connexions, he would heap his considerable contempt yet upon Howgrave's sartorial exuberance. (In his defence, Hussar uniforms did consist of an impressively tall beaver hat with a brush. Most others just had plumes.)

"He is quite keen on hats, is he not?" Matlock agreed, happy to find a point that he understood.

Fitzwilliam's brother was uncomfortable with political debate and matters foreign. So long as Nappy and his Frenchies were not espied descending upon Whitemore, Matlock would be quite happy to spend his time doing nothing but fretting over the price of keeping up an earldom.

"Young Hinchcliffe has gone, too," Bingley ventured timorously.

Thus far, the only thing of Bingley's endangered by the endless monstrosity of war were the manufactured goods from which his own fortune was claimed then piling up on British docks. The wavering blockade by France loosened those monetary fears and beyond that, he held no personal ideology. He had told Jane he was grateful the decision to join the fight against France was not his. (The long held British hatred for France was in reverse proportion to the wealth of the British citizen in question. Perversely, those who had the least to lose, bore the greatest malice.)

The reminder of the scurrilous pool of which officer material was drawn to support Fitzwilliam was of no particular comfort and Darcy begat a pace about the room. "A bloody mess," he muttered, then louder, "A bloody massacre."

Flabbergasted to hear Darcy actually curse, Elizabeth had set down her sewing, giving up any pretense of needlework. By that time, their nurses finally had the various nieces and nephews in hand and the children began a reluctant tramp up the stairs, thus effectively drowning out what little Elizabeth could hear.

"Bloody bother," she muttered, then hastily glanced about to see if she had been overheard.

It was additional frustration for her husband's profanity to have encouraged her to exercise her own. So intent upon her eavesdropping, Elizabeth had not paid due attention to Georgiana who, as always, sat quietly at her elbow. Beyond the brief prayer that Darcy's sister had not overheard her curse, she had not given her notice. Hence, when Georgiana finally spoke, even in so soft a voice, Elizabeth was startled.

"You understand what is happening, Elizabeth?"

Astonished, Elizabeth turned to Georgiana and shook her head, for she was not certain, only suspicious, and that Georgiana was not asking her for information but offering it was an amazement.

"Fitzwilliam is going to Belgium to join Wellington," Georgiana stated. "I fancy he is to depart immediately."

Elizabeth furrowed her brow, "Wellington?"

"Wellesley. He is now a duke."

She knew that Wellesley had been made a duke. The newspapers were full of it. It had slipped her mind momentarily. Darcy shared his gazettes with her, even the most scurrilous. She devoured them voraciously. She fancied there were few ladies more informed about public events than she. Unless conversing with her husband, she spoke of matters foreign but seldom, so rarely did she find any interest or knowledge of it in her society of gentlewomen. It was a mild irritation upon the very first occasion she had to speak intelligently about intelligent matters she sounded thick as a post.

In Paris, ladies sat smoking amongst gentlemen in grand salons dedicated to affairs of state, not just affairs. In London, they were certainly less prevalent, if not absolutely nonexistent. Just how an innocent such as Georgiana came in possession of information so esoteric to men was a considerable mystery to Elizabeth. Obviously, she did not spend all her time cloistered amongst her books.

Knowing it sounded patronising even as she said it, Elizabeth offered, "How can you be so certain, Georgiana? We best wait and see, perchance it is only a possibility."

She patted Georgiana's hand reassuringly.

"No, Elizabeth, he will go. I know he shall. I know why he shall, as do you," Georgiana said, and said no more.

Elizabeth sat silently also, looking directly at Georgiana, whose gaze held hers without faltering. Glancing covertly about the room to make certain she would not be overheard, she spoke.

"What do you know of this, Georgiana?"

"I came upon you the day my aunt called."

Elizabeth nodded once.

"Go on," she bid.

"I overheard her harsh words to you and hurried to your defence. But I was preceded."

Elizabeth dropped her head and touched her forehead with her fingertips. The reason for Georgiana's own disconcertion that day was uncovered. She overheard Lady Catherine's accusations against her brother, and from the look upon her countenance, Elizabeth was certain she was about to hear Georgiana announce she heard Fitzwilliam's vow of love as well. Elizabeth's foremost fear was that one more person knew of it. That bade it one step closer toward Darcy hearing of it. Truly, she did not want to come betwixt her husband and his cousin. That simple wish was soon forgot.

"Colonel Fitzwilliam has chosen to put himself in harm's way rather than cause a cleft in our family. He shall submit himself to a *felo-de-se*," Georgiana deduced, thus eliminating any other possible interpretation of events.

"I would do anything to undo this," Elizabeth said.

When Georgiana did not respond, Elizabeth asked, "Do you see any way out? I truly believe the colonel's regard is merely an infatuation, not true love. I believe him misguided…"

Before she could say more, her husband burst into the room indignant and angry. Discreetly, Georgiana withdrew. And after Darcy gave them a pronounced glare, she was followed hastily by Mrs. Hurst, Miss Bingley, and Jane. Had she not been so utterly confounded by Georgiana's revelations, Elizabeth might well have fled after them. Darcy seemed not to notice the flight he incited, but walked to the fireplace and hit it with his closed fist causing the bric-a-brac upon it to shimmy.

"Fitzwilliam has decided to take leave at dawn to-morrow to go to Portsmouth and join a regiment bound for Brussels," he announced. "He knows with his connexions he will not be turned away. Wellington remembers Fitzwilliam from the Portuguese encounter and will be most happy to have a man of his ilk to join him."

Elizabeth raised her forefinger in an attempt to interject a question, but it was not significant enough a gesture to be noticed.

"Fitzwilliam is an excellent horseman. Well-schooled. His men admire him. Every manner of a man that the King's army should want in an officer. But however courageous, however laudatory his horsemanship, he will be but fodder for the amateur leadership of the great British army."

He took a heavy breath at this and Elizabeth leapt into the brief pause to becalm him.

"But Darcy, Fitzwilliam came home from the peninsula with honour. He survived that war."

"Fortune was with him there. The need to stop Napoleon has reached desperate proportions. Fitzwilliam is courageous, but he does not have the guile nor the perversity to survive in this coming Armageddon, Lizzy. He will put nobility and selflessness before his own well-being and shall not last a single campaign more. I know it. I know it!"

His anguish was expressed in fury, and that was not lost upon his wife.

When he continued to rant, "He knows what I have said is true, we have talked of it often. Why has he decided to go now? I know it is not for him to find glory for himself. He is not of that sort. Why is he going Lizzy? Why?"

A fair question. Elizabeth hid her face in her hands rather than risk answering him. Her mind moiled about, what with her husband's indirect wrath and knowing herself to be the reason for possible loss of life or limb. Should she go to Fitzwilliam that night and tell him he need not take leave? She practised that speech in her mind; she would assure him the matter betwixt them forgot. It would not be spoken of again. If he would only not go.

Unable to find words of comfort, she went to the fireplace where Darcy stood making angry jabs at the ashes. She put her arms beneath his. Howbeit it was fleeting, he patted her reassuringly. Momentarily, he let her go to poke at the fire and to vent his ire upon the mantelpiece.

"Fitzwilliam will be gone before first light," he said dejectedly, acceptance of the inevitable gradually sapping his anger.

That decided her quandary. There would be no time for entreaties from her, Elizabeth knew. She made a hasty consideration that perhaps if Darcy knew why Fitzwilliam was so determined to go to Belgium he could reason with him...no. No, if Darcy knew of Fitzwilliam's declaration of love for her and told him thus, Fitzwilliam would still take leave. And his return, was he to return, might be all the more difficult.

With daybreak yet only a promise, Darcy rose from a sleepless bed. It was imperative to go to Whitemore and intercept Fitzwilliam before he left for the sea. At that moment, there was nothing of greater importance to him than that their last words not be spoken in disagreement.

For some unfamiliar reason of sentiment, Darcy took Blackjack, not by the road, but by way of a shortcut through the chase. It was once a well-travelled route. The hedgerow twenty years later showed yet the effects of when, as young boys, he and Fitzwilliam had regularly trod through them. Maturity and civilisation eventually influenced them to traverse more sedately via the road. Thus, the gaps had over-grown to a mere cleft betwixt the hawthorn, the locals having more respect for greenery than the young bucks of station.

Hence, Darcy spurred Blackjack and leapt each one. And as each stile, each hedge brought him closer to Whitemore, their youth too seemed close at hand.

By the time Darcy arrived at Whitemore, day had broken and his canonising of lost boyhood had ripened his already low spirits into full-fledged melancholia. This farewell was to be very different from that when Fitzwilliam had departed for Spain. That leave-taking had invoked a raw jubilation, an excitation born of innocence of just what lay ahead. At that time, Darcy had felt the anticipation almost as acutely as Fitzwilliam. Thenceforward, neither had any illusions.

When Fitzwilliam saw Darcy had come, he stopped his preparations and forsook Scimitar's reins to his groom. The expression Fitzwilliam bore as he walked over was strange, one that Darcy could never recall of him. It might have been perceived, appropriately, as one of apprehension. But misgiving was not what Darcy believed it was. He thought it was a look of loss.

"You shall take Scimitar?" Darcy asked.

"A good mount is essential."

"Undoubtedly."

Only a few more terse comments were made. Those were the obligatory ones about the expected weather, the possible conditions of the roads; it did not truly matter. That Darcy had come was the statement, the words were irrelevant.

"Fitzwilliam," Darcy reached into his breast pocket and removed a sealed letter, "here are a few names of family in France. A vouchsafement should you need it."

Fitzwilliam smiled ever so briefly and tucked the paper, warm yet from Darcy's waist-coat, beneath his own. He knew regardless of the political situation, family would rise above anything else. He mounted Scimitar.

"And Fitzwilliam," Darcy took the reins from the groom to hand to him, "do cover your ballocks."

Smiling more openly at his cousin's improbable vulgarity, Fitzwilliam said, "I thank you for the sentiment, Darcy. I shall indeed look out for them."

With that, he removed his hat with a flourish and a bow. Thereupon, man and mount wheeled about and cantered away. Darcy watched as he rode off, his figure and horse gradually being swallowed by the early morning fog.

By the time Darcy returned to Pemberley, the morning sun had disintegrated the fog into the merest of haze. His sleepless night and the exercise of his seldom-used sentimentality had rendered him quite fatigued. It was a relief to step down and hand off Blackjack's reins. As he dropped to the ground his knees almost buckled so great was the weight of the morning. Shoulders sagging, he started for the house and he could not will them back in place.

Just as he entered the stone arch leading to the courtyard, John Christie stepped out in front of him.

So abruptly did he appear, Darcy stopped in his tracks. He eyed him a little warily, so precipitous was the encounter and so truculent was the expression the young man bore. Mr. Darcy was never confronted, partly because of his position and partly because of his size. That his own shirt-sleeved servant accosted him in such a hostile manner did not improve his ill-humour.

His lethargy lost in ire, he automatically reclaimed his stature and exercised a posture particular only to him. This bearing was one which allowed him to look down upon anyone in his eye, regardless of their height, with an exceedingly keen gaze (a vexatious position, indeed, and no one once escaping from thence wanted to return). He impatiently slapped his crop against the top of his boot.

"Yes?" he said, and nothing more.

His master's displeasure was obvious. If John recoiled at the sight, it was only inwardly.

"Aye must speak to yer, Mr. Darcy. Aye must speak to yer now."

Placing his hand upon his hip, Darcy tapped his crop a few more times whilst he considered whether to grant the lad some time. Then, with a curt nod, he agreed.

Another groom stood holding the reins to Blackjack and John's eyes flicked nervously to the audience then back to Mr. Darcy.

With even more brazenness, he insisted, "Private."

Having already abused his patience, at this additional demand Darcy gave a slight shake of his head in incredulity at the impertinence. However, he begrudged himself of his gloves, handed them and his crop to the groom, and walked with John toward an arbour a few yards away. It was not with a countenance of civility that he looked upon the young man as he awaited to hear why this servant son of Wickham was plaguing him.

John uneasily shifted from one foot to another for a few moments before speaking.

"Me ma worked at Pemberley before Aye was born, did yer know that, sir?"

Darcy heaved a sigh of disgust at the horizon. Here was the reason for such effrontery. No doubt, Wickham's visit had stirred talk. The boy wanted money. Another of Wickham's debts to discharge. It was a moment Darcy had thought might come, thus such a demand had been considered. However, just how many pounds should he lay upon Wickham's child, he had not yet decided.

"Yes. I know that," he finally answered.

It would be best to await the demand. See how much the boy thought himself worth and thus be relieved of the unpleasant duty of determining a monetary value to put upon a human life.

"As well yer might," John said bitterly, "though many such men as yerself might find it hard to recall what servants they lay with. Was me ma among many? Aye would guess most likely."

Not only was this scoundrel demanding surreptitious *pourboire*, he had the brass cheek to heap additional insult. Clearly, he knew the amplitude of his impertinence. Yet, when Darcy's face coloured, it was of such a peculiar hue that the boy retreated a step.

The irate flush of Darcy's face was tempered with the humiliation of recognition, for he knew what John said was true by intent if not actuality. Had his father not chastised him, his youthful libido might have led him to bound from atop one servant girl to the next. Truth or no, however, he was not so generous to hear it from his own groom.

Though both knew John's days at Pemberley were ended, John did not cease with that one accusation. He strove on.

"Me ma's life was 'arsh, Mr. Darcy, 'arsher than Aye think a man like yer could imagine. Me own 'as been nothing to what she…" his voice cracked, he swallowed, then continued, "and it is because of yer."

By the time John launched into the tale of his mother's woe, Darcy's forbearance had long past peaked. Thus, he was quite astonished to hear John lay the blame for his mother's dissolute life at his feet. Perplexed, he was curious enough to know how he came to this rather daft conclusion to continue to listen, albeit with considerable scepticism.

"When she died, Aye came thinkin' there was something for me 'ere. Me ma tol' me she got with child with me 'ere and Aye heard she lay with yer," John said.

Darcy's stern countenance began to fail him. He blinked once, then again.

"Yer're thinkin' I'm wantin' somethin' from yer. Not true, though Aye guess yer owe it. Aye wanted to see what a man my father was. Aye heard 'im a great man, but that was wrong. 'e's a man who gives no quarter to kindness, a man who spends 'is life havin' 'is way with gerls and throwin' 'em out when 'e gets 'em wi' child. Aye see no greatness, Aye see a rich man who knows nothin' but richness and cares fer nothin' else."

By the end of his oration, Darcy understood that the boy believed that he had ruined his mother. He did not understand, however, the plurality of the condemnation. Before he could disabuse him of the notion he had fathered him, John interrupted, yet at full moil.

"The only cause Aye have to look to yer is that two ladies find yer a finer man than me. Mrs. Darcy and Miss Darcy is fine ladies. That they find some reason to give yer regard gives me the only doubt Aye 'ave of yer being nothing more than a bastard's father."

Upon hurling this last vilification, John pulled a vicious-looking dagger from his belt. He exacted this manoeuvre with an effortlessness that decried the infrequency of its occurrence, thus giving his quarry pause. Yet it was so ridiculously large a snicker-snee and of such obvious mediæval origins, Darcy was almost moved to laugh at the incongruity of it being in the possession of his groom.

However old, the glint of the blade told it quite lethal. That understanding chased any semblance of humour from the situation. In the speck of time it took for him to see John held it by its tip and intended to fling it, Darcy made a decision. He folded his arms and made no move to run or feint.

Laudable as was his valour, had his wife witnessed it, she might have preferred discretion. Mr. Darcy, however, would rather have been murdered by his own servant than been known to have fled from him. This blade, though, imbedded itself where it was intended, in the dirt betwixt Darcy's steadfast feet.

"That is what Aye intended to give me father, Mr. Darcy. The same yer gave my ma. The same yer gave me. It would just come to yer faster's all. Yea, Aye know it would find me gibbeted in chains at the Kympton crossroads, but at least there'd be…" he searched for the word, "revenge…yea, revenge. But your ladies will not mourn because of me. I'm done wi' yer. 'ang me for the attempt, Aye don't care no more."

Dejectedly, he turned and walked away. Darcy looked down at the ancient knife resting betwixt his boots. Pulling it from the ground, he turned it over in his hand, noticing the elk horn peeking beneath the unravelling leather of the grip. It was an indefensibly crude weapon, yet certainly deadly. He let the dirk hang loosely at his side and watched as John's back straightened in defiance of his dampened outrage.

Darcy knew happenstance was the only thing that stood betwixt what John believed and that which was true. Though he was not his father, he could have been. He mounted Abigail not out of love or even infatuation, but from the sheer innocence of lust. There was no affection (if anything, it could have been more truthfully identified as gratitude).

The incorrigible indocility of his adolescent libido notwithstanding, Darcy did not want John to believe him his father when it was not true. Loath as he was to mention the name, he thought he should tell the boy who did father him. Let him curse Wickham. Let John curse Wickham as well and let that cad share the damnation. Any young man deserved the truth, even one bent upon patricide. Although it was a temptation to sic John on Wickham, he did not. Nevertheless, he called out for him to stop.

John did stop, almost mid-step. He put his foot firmly down and turned, almost in a military about-face. His attention, too, was military. So military was it, he might well have been facing a firing squad. Nonetheless, his countenance betrayed not fear, but considerable contempt.

"Did he fancy I would shoot him?" Darcy wondered silently before it occurred to him that John just might have had that foreboding, so insistent had been the gossip since his infamous slaughter at the inn. Yet dangling the knife, Darcy walked toward thereupon stopped at a distance, not wanting to present menace.

"Young man, I fathered you not. Had I, I should not deny it."

Hatred did not abandon John's face entirely, but it was tempered by belief. Still, it was a half-minute before he spoke.

"If not yer, who?"

It was here that Darcy's decision to leave Wickham's name unrevealed wavered in the face of such a direct question. He very nearly defended himself by relating Abigail was with child when he lay with her. Prudently, he reconsidered. He could not bring himself to speak of having intimate relations with one's mother. A gentleman should never speak of such indecorous matters. Particularly to a son. Highly improper. The courage Darcy had shown when threatened with the knife did not reassert itself in the murky waters of his own guilt. Wickham was not pardoned, just postponed. Thus, Darcy dodged the entire issue with a statement of evasive rationalisation that was worthy of a seat in Parliament.

"Only your mother had answer to that question for certain."

John closed his eyes in frustrated anger. Turning, he stomped away and said to no one, yet to everyone.

"Damn yer," he said. "Damn yer all."

With leaden feet, Darcy trudged up the postern steps. When he had deserted their bed before dawn, he had thought Elizabeth asleep. She was sitting mid-most in the bed when he returned, her knees tucked under her gown. The drawn look about her eyes told him she had slept no better than he.

"You went to Fitzwilliam?"

It was not actually a question.

Pulling off his jacket and tossing it down, he did not answer her nonquestion.

Instead, he said rather stiffly, "Your groom (Darcy had been unable to bring himself to call John by his name) has, as well he might, accused me of his paternity. I told him I was not his father, but I could not tell him it was Wickham."

Quite astonished, for John had never given a hint that he thought Darcy his father, she bid, "How did John come by this misinformation?"

Darcy shook his head that he did not know.

"Has he thought this all along?"

"Perhaps. But that it has only come up now leads me to believe Wickham's visit prodded memories, instigated talk. I really have no idea."

"And you had to tell him he was not your son? Poor John," she fretted, then queried, "But why did he ask? Did he want something from you?"

"My life, it would seem." Darcy said sardonically, tossing the decrepit knife upon the bed.

From Elizabeth's vantage, the dagger looked appallingly deadly and she pulled herself to her knees with alarm. Thus, Darcy hastily assured her that he had not actually been attacked and made light of the knife.

Explaining thus, he said, "He was armed, as you see. However, had he been serious, I should not be standing before you. He thought I had fathered him and cast out his mother. What son would not want to defend his mother? Had you heard what he said of my character, you might question your esteem for your husband."

He smiled, but it was mirthless. A verbal assault upon that which was so hotly contested in Darcy's conscience, Elizabeth knew to be as painful a wound as any bodily one inflicted. Having begun to think of herself as the young man's surrogate aunt, she felt sympathy for the despair such confusion must demand of one so young. Nevertheless, no hurt to her husband could be compleatly forgiven. And she held a considerable reservoir of indignation for anyone who did.

"You have more goodness, more character, more love and righteousness than any man I have ever known…"

He walked to her yet mid-sputter and lovingly put his forehead to hers. Her defence of his honour was the single effort that could actually becalm his substantial disorder. He endeavoured to smile. That attempt failed miserably, thus he kissed her on her forehead instead. It was not spoken, but they both knew if he were not John's father, it fell only to chance.

Such was the day, it could be understood if it was not realised that Georgiana was not about until late afternoon. Had Elizabeth not gone in search of her to continue their interrupted conversation of the night before, it might not have been discovered even then. The disquiet of her absence notwithstanding, Elizabeth at first believed she had simply sought some solitude from the tumult of events. Respite from the turbulent spin their lives had taken was something she might have favoured to find herself.

Darcy's early morning farewell to Fitzwilliam and the subsequent near assault upon his person and injury to his integrity had left him unusually cheerless. His despondency was always Elizabeth's as well, and quite aware that she was the culprit responsible for Fitzwilliam's departure, Wickham's visit, thus John's onslaught, her own conscience was troubling her relentlessly.

Fitzwilliam had obviously departed without incident, but that was hardly a concession. If the reason he quit England (if she was indeed the reason) ever came to light, there would be considerable tribulation. Elizabeth dared not let her mind envision the worst that might befall Fitzwilliam in France, for the even the best outcome might be fraught with disorder. If he were to survive the war and return home, it would be to the same untenable situation he had fled.

And John Christie. Regardless of the wrath he earned because of his unmitigated, and ultimately unfounded, ill-will toward Darcy, she felt a twinge.

"He's probably back at the stable of the Kympton Inn, morosely petting some pony's nose whilst awaiting the constable who will not come."

She shook her head sadly at the thought of it. Perhaps she should send a messenger to tell him he would not be hung for his offence. This plan was not set into place for dusk and no Georgiana began to make Elizabeth seriously uneasy.

At one time Georgiana's whereabouts would never be in question, for she had always been accompanied by Mrs. Annesley. Eventually age took its toll upon that poor woman and her remaining senses did not necessarily include her wits. Even Darcy admitted the *non compos mentis* lady not to be an adequate companion for his sister. Hence, to Georgiana's delight and her brother's consternation, Georgiana was released from the necessity of her elderly companion.

However, just what to do with the old woman was a bit of a problem. She could have been packed off ignominiously to her daughter's, but tradition at Pemberley demanded that any employee who served the house well should not be put out by reason of infirmity. Mrs. Annesley was an industrious lady, insisting upon being of some use. However, near-blindness and compleat deafness left few options open in the way of occupying her time.

Her visual deficiency had rendered the old woman quite frightened of the dark, hence, when she began her candle-lighting fetish, it precipitated a slight reorganisation of the staff. And that is how the little train of night-travellers was instituted. The footman once charged with re-lighting the candles old Morton put out was newly directed to steer Mrs. Annesley in that path. Hence, when Morton, extinguisher upon his shoulder and wig slightly askew, wandered the corridors snuffing each candle, the torch-bearing Mrs. Annesley was directly upon his trail. In defence of the sensibilities of those under the roof of Pemberley unacquainted with the idiosyncrasies of the house, one footman accompanied their party to make certain they did not accident into a guest's room.

Whilst the house basked in the laurels of this particularly happy arrangement, the interview for a suitable companion for Georgiana progressed slowly. Had that position been filled in a more timely fashion, a great deal of vexation might have been prevented. For the lack of a companion allowed Georgiana to wander about quite at will, a freedom highly treasured by her, but one that did not make her brother happy.

And upon this particular eve, it was a freedom that did not make her usually quite sympathetic sister-in-law happy, either. For, in absence of a governess or companion, there was no one to note Georgiana's doings. Thus, Elizabeth's search for her led to her rooms and interrogation of Anne, her lady-maid. Anne had no notion of Georgiana's activities save those that were incompleat; she had not seen her since that morning. A quick inventory revealed a portmanteau bag missing along with several of her dresses.

That revelation set Elizabeth aghast. It appeared Georgiana had not only taken leave, but had left no note of explanation.

"Has everyone gone mad?" Elizabeth exclaimed to herself as she headed to the stairs to pass this horrifying information to Darcy.

Her mission, however, stopped at the head of the stairs. For there in the vestibule stood Edward Hardin with Mr. Rhymes talking to Darcy. Hardin had his hat wadded nervously in his fist.

"Aye can't believe that boy to steal, Mr. Darcy. It aren't like him at all. Johnny's a good lad. But that gig and him are both gone. Aye don't know what else to think."

"There is nothing on this day that I cannot believe," Darcy assured him wearily. "If he has them, let him be. I want no retribution."

Mr. Rhymes looked surprised that Mr. Darcy was not angry at the idea of thievery. Stealing something as valuable as a horse and gig was a hanging offence, which was most probably the reason for Edward Hardin's nervous wringing of his hat.

"He means to be a soldier, he's been drillin' regular," Hardin said.

"No matter," replied Darcy.

"You might have thought if he wanted to go off to war, he would've just walked," Edward Hardin could not yet believe the foolhardiness of John's apparent act.

As soon as the door closed behind Rhymes and Hardin, Elizabeth descended the stairs.

With her first step upon the floor, and breathless from the scurry as well as fright, she announced, "Georgiana has gone."

"Gone?" he repeated.

Elizabeth nodded.

"Where?"

"I know not."

Albeit it was not remarked upon, it was immediately recognised by those witnessing the alteration in his countenance that the missing groom, gig, and sister added up to kidnapping to Darcy. As he began to heave with rage, his face did not flush, it blanched. The pallor he bore was eerily familiar. It was a lividity Elizabeth had not seen upon his countenance since the day he burst through the door and skewered Reed.

Elizabeth knew it might be a matter of only a few moments before he demanded John's head on a stick and sought a gun to run him down himself. Piercing his ever-increasing high dudgeon was no easy task, but her reasoning was sound.

"If John had abducted Georgiana, she would not have packed her bag. Hence, if she went, she must have gone of her own volition."

That reasoning may have mollified his murderous rage, but it did not answer the rather large issue of why. Such an impenetrable question was set temporarily aside whilst Darcy issued orders. In his usual logical manner, he dismissed the notion of setting out after Georgiana himself, for he could ride in but one direction.

Thus, ten men were charged to investigate all routes from Pemberley to trace both John and Georgiana, presuming they had absconded together. A half-dozen more were hied to as many towns to enlist constables in their search. All were laden with gold to make certain they met with no hesitation to cooperate.

There was a brief consideration of what to do with John was Georgiana in his company. Darcy might have favoured having him thrashed, possibly drawn and quartered, but Elizabeth insisted it best to wait before inflicting mortal consequence.

They could be jumping to a conclusion of monumental error.

After watching all the riders pound away, Elizabeth and Darcy sat in miserable inaction upon the step. It most likely looked peculiar for the master and mistress to plop themselves down unceremoniously upon their stoop with all manner of servants standing about in wait for instructions. But Darcy and Elizabeth were baffled.

In a moment, Darcy stood decisively and announced he would look for clues again in Georgiana's room. Thinking that was more profitable employment than sitting with her chin in her hands, Elizabeth accompanied him to research her room.

Her room, however, was just as neat and undisturbed as Elizabeth had seen it that afternoon. Her dresses hung in the armoire, her jewellery lay in her case. The dressing stool was set precisely at a right angle to her dressing table. Upon it were only a few perfumes (most of them early gifts from a brother who had no idea whatsoever to buy his sister as a birthday gift), for she did not favour scents. Elizabeth interrogated Anne again about Georgiana's demeanour the last time she was seen.

As they were speaking, Darcy walked to the secretary and touched a leather-bound book that was sitting at a precise right angle upon it.

"Pray, what is this?"

Elizabeth walked over and looked at it as it sat perpendicular to the corner of the desk. Very precisely perpendicular. They both stood looking at it wordlessly, neither making a move to pick it up. Thereupon, as if by prearranged decision, they both reached for it at the same time.

"It is Georgiana's journal," Elizabeth said.

Darcy stood impatiently as Elizabeth flipped the pages to find the last entry. She read it silently. She turned back a page and read it, then turned page after page each more urgently than before.

"What?" he said, again impatiently, "What?"

Not wanting to give interpretation, she handed it to him, and he sank upon the satin counterpane and bestowed upon it his full attention. His hands took the same trip as did hers, for page after page contained not a single line of her own composition.

They were filled with unattributed quotations, the Bible, Bacon, Blake, and Shakespeare again and again as well as many others. The theme, however, was ominously similar.

"It is impossible to love and to be wise."

"There is no fear in love,
but perfect love casteth out fear."

"If thou rememberst not the slightest folly
that ever love did make thee run into,
thou has not loved."

"Set me as a seal upon thy heart,
As a seal upon thine arm:
for love is strong as death."

Neither Darcy nor Elizabeth much liked the sound of it, and as he read the last word of the last entry, Darcy's only recently regained colour lost ground.

Elizabeth thought it possible, even probable, Georgiana was unhappy. But until that moment, she had not considered the magnitude of her loneliness. She believed it unforgivable that she had not recognised it. Very few emotions in life could move a person to drastic action and love was one of those few.

An incredulous possibility moved him to ask, "Has she eloped with that boy?" The contemplation of such an execrable possibility caused his face to crimson to such a degree, Elizabeth feared he might well be felled by apoplexy before the day played out.

"Not necessarily," she soothed.

"Not necessarily eloped, or not necessarily eloped with your groom?"

"Either or neither. This could be symbolic love of which she recites."

"You are suggesting she intends to enter a nunnery and bid that boy to take her?" he demanded.

"I am saying perhaps she too has a commitment to love mankind. Perchance in service. Her love of nursing the ill is profound."

"Surely she has not followed her flight of fancy off to war. What flummery!" he exploded. "This entire thing is preposterous!"

She was eternally grateful he chose not to repeat her now infamous assurances that hysterical obsession would not overtake Georgiana. If he did not, it was quite possibly because, outrageous as that possibility was, it was far better than the one that included elopement and John Christie. Certainly, he prayed, the gods could not be so cruel as to allow his sister to run off with a lowly groom.

"If only a nurse, Lizzy," he reconsidered, "but what if not? Then she has run off with a groom! A bastard groom! Wickham's bastard!"

With that fit of temper, enlightenment descended upon them both. Only that morning John still believed Darcy to be his father. The unlikelihood of a romance betwixt Georgiana and John grew as they thought of it.

"Perchance it was not he with whom she eloped. He was not the reason, just the means," Elizabeth suggested.

"Has she been seeing the Howgrave son, Lizzy?"

Elizabeth shook her head, "I know not. Quite obviously, however, I know not everything."

Grasping at straws (at least a more acceptable straw), she offered, "Newton Hinchcliffe?"

"The fatuous, dim-witted one?"

"You had best be more circumspect in what aspersions you cast until we have unravelled this mystery," she said.

"With all the eligible gentlemen we have thrown into her path, could she have not befriended one sensible young man?" he lamented.

They had no idea if Georgiana was with or followed John. Even if she had, he may well not be in knowledge of it.

"She did not know he thought himself my son. Or at least I hope she did not know," he fretted, yet disquieted by the notion of his sister learning of her brother's infallibility.

"We know not yet if she did indeed elope. It may be as simple as a need to aid and comfort."

"Or as complicated as the possibility of being killed," he replied and Elizabeth could find no words of comfort.

Thereupon, he asked with no humour intended whatsoever, "Your cousin Mr. Collins did not offer her a story of a vicar fighting Napoleon, did he?"

She shook her head, but smiled briefly at the recollection of a time when their most formidable trial was Mr. Collins's company.

It was decided that, in all probability and for whatever reason, Georgiana was en route to the continent. Such an understanding did not have the makings for a restful night. Darcy could not rid himself of the notion that his sister had run after a young man of the lowest order (John Christie, Howgrave, the dim-witted Hinchcliffe). Elizabeth believed he had seized upon that possibility simply because it was one that gave him the most grief. For he had assigned himself guilt that he had not foreseen his sister's unhappiness.

The night lasted longer than a night, but by morning Darcy had decided he must trace Georgiana's trail himself. To see where she had gone. To see if he could help her. He had been given guardianship of his sister. That responsibility was not something he took lightly. She had always been his to look after; he could not just stand and do nothing.

He assured Elizabeth, "I do not mean to deny her decision of will, only to try to ease what way she has chosen. And see her safe."

Elizabeth believed most profoundly, just as he adamantly denied it, that he did intend to deny Georgiana her will. Darcy would never stand by and let his sister run about the English countryside, or French for that matter, flaunting convention and risking ruin. Certainly not with a groom. Or even Mr. Howgrave. She was not certain he would not throttle the dim-witted Hinchcliffe. "Seeing her safe" meant different things to different people. Darcy's "safe" was the severest of all.

One of his riders returned with word that Georgiana's gig had been seen upon the road south toward Portsmouth. Until that moment, Elizabeth had somehow believed Georgiana's disappearance was a fluke, a frivolity. She could no longer. If Georgiana did board a ship for the war, undoubtedly as a nurse, Elizabeth knew there was no concern too extreme, no fear for her safety too great. Darcy intended to embark upon her retrieval as quickly as his coach could be readied.

If John had entered the army and Georgiana had gone with him or after him, they would end up on the continent and in Napoleon's path. If it happened, Darcy intended to find Georgiana and bring her home. War or no war.

Most men of Mr. Darcy's rank would have enlisted an emissary to search for his sister. But, as Elizabeth had once enjoyed reminding herself, her husband's personal courage was far greater than most men's, both of rank and lesser. And as Elizabeth again repeated that proudly to herself, she hoped she could be forgiven for grousing about it as well. For if the army were endangered across the Channel, she wondered what chance lay for a lone Englishman, whatever his merit. That same danger, of course, was tenfold for Georgiana. Thus, Elizabeth could not truly expect Darcy not to seek her.

It was difficult not to be angry with Georgiana for endangering them both, for surely she should have known her brother would move heaven and earth to find her.

What was she thinking? Of course, the answer was that she was not thinking. She was in love. Although Elizabeth had not shared that conviction with Darcy, she was certain it correct. Had Georgiana gone to war upon some quest of salvation of the wounded masses, she might have hesitated to announce it in advance, but she would have left word. Only love, either unrequited or unacceptable, would have made her surreptitious.

Georgiana's departure already a *fait accompli,* Darcy's anticipated one loomed before Elizabeth like a gaping behemoth, for it was immediate. There was to be no private time to hold each other in close embrace before he left, no special caresses to remember, no words to comfort. She was to be bereft and alone at Pemberley whilst he went into a raging war to seek his sister.

His intention was to search for Georgiana, if not incognito, at least in stealth. The men he had sent in pursuit of her were withdrawn in favour of private agents gifted in the nuance of discretion. Darcy feared for Georgiana's reputation, but also that word not spread more than it already had that she was alone and vulnerable. For if that be known, every scoundrel in England would have their nose to the ground seeking her trail as well. Hence, Darcy refused Elizabeth to accompany him. Not only had she asked, she had wheedled, beseeched, and deliberately wept.

Darcy was unmoved. He would not even consider it.

"I can travel with much greater dispatch alone, by horseback if necessary," he had told her.

"I can ride horseback!" she answered petulantly knowing that was hardly the point.

He must go in stealth, alone, and unaided. And she must wait. Alone as well. Elizabeth did not argue when her tears could not move him (and chastised herself for resorting to such a feminine weapon); his resolve was in place and thus additional entreaties were quite useless. There were certain times, when he used a specific voice, that she knew her powers of persuasion had peaked.

His preparations were methodical and calm. So unruffled did he appear, so disciplined, it was forbidding. Had Elizabeth not been already in a state of profound fright, that alone might have daunted her witless. Thus, when his stoicism included a reminder of where his important papers were in the library and just what arrangements he had made for her were he to die, she did not hear him. The moment he spoke of the possibility of not returning, she ceased to listen and began to tremble.

Unlocking the top drawer of his writing table, he opened it and removed a gun. The very gun he had taught her to use upon the lawn. Holding it for her inspection, he showed her again how to cock it.

"Remember, pull it all the way back, Lizzy." The hammer clicked twice.

No answer.

"Lizzy?" he turned.

In times of crisis, his decisive reserve had always paid him well, but that day it demanded Elizabeth weather a struggle to maintain her composure. This was not lost upon his attention and it wrested him from the orderly delineation of details.

He carefully put the gun back in the drawer and closed it. Thereupon, he rose and drew her to his chest.

"Do not despair, Lizzy. These are but precautions. To ease my mind. Will you not allow me this?"

Because he caressed her neck reassuringly, she obediently nodded. It was with reluctance, but she did nod her concurrence. She understood her duty. If she could not accompany him, she would find the benevolence to ease his way. A wife must not make her husband's tasks more arduous than necessary. One must acquiesce happily. Dutifully. Suddenly, she tore herself from his embrace and, with all the strength she could muster, struck him across the face. His look of stunned hurt incited her to slap him again. She brought her hand back a third time, but he grasped her wrists and drew her into his arms to soothe her. Her strength spent in a fit of wretchedness, she harmlessly pounded his shoulders with impotent fists and might have fallen to the floor had he not held her so tightly.

"Pray, do not leave me," she wailed desperately. "Please do not. Take me with you! I shall be no trouble. I shall not complain. Please," she begged, "take me with you for I cannot bear for you to leave me, for I know I shall never see you again."

He held her face in his hands and looked upon her so long and so deeply that she began to cry anew.

But he said simply, "Help me bear to go, Lizzy."

Slowly, they slid in a heap upon the floor. The intimacy they had not had time for was found there upon the carpet, but not by kiss or embrace. She cupped his face in her hand and he kissed her palm. They sat thus for only a very few moments. In that time, Elizabeth realised she had not thought to write him a letter. It seemed an insurmountable oversight. She might have favoured hiding one in his trunk, reminding him of all the ways she loved him. It would have been lengthy.

The coach was called ready. They rose to go outside. Elizabeth realised there was not another word to be spoken.

By the time they reached the portico, they had both adopted their appropriately dispassionate masks. She stood aside as he, ever methodical, checked the horses one by one. When the task was compleated, he turned his attention to his trip and she saw upon his face the look of determination she had seen many times before.

Turning to her in reassurance, he said, "I shall be back before you realise me gone."

He kissed her once upon the lips. She grasped his lapel as she returned it, then held on, pretending to straighten his jacket. Thereupon, she made her hands drop from him. It was the most difficult task she had ever asked of herself. He kissed her once again, took hold of the grip to step into the coach, turned and looked directly at her.

She mouthed the words, "I love you."

He wordlessly said, "I know."

Then, he pulled himself into the carriage and the door slammed shut. As Elizabeth watched his coach take the gravel lane away from Pemberley, she wondered was she right not to tell him before he left the one thing that might have made him stay.

No, she thought and shook her head imperceptibly but to herself. She could not put the burden of decision upon him: should he save his sister or remain with his wife? His wife, who was quite certain that she was again with child.

Part Three

Fitzwilliam's regiment gathered at Portsmouth. General conscripts were amassing there also. And for once, the usual military "decision by absurdity" had a favourable outcome for at least one man.

To have the army travel south half the length of England to take leave by ship to travel half the length of England north by way of the Strait of Dover made little practical sense for the army. However, it certainly made Darcy's trip more expeditious.

He headed his coach directly south-east to Dover.

So relentlessly did the hooves of his four matched horses pound the road, it appeared they were trailed by a tornadic tail of dust. The beauty of the team was indisputable. But they had been bred for stamina as well. In another circumstance the endurance of his horses, whose lineage he had carefully nurtured, would have been a substantial point of pride for horse-conscious Mr. Darcy. However, the very reason their fortitude was so critical at that moment kept him from giving any thought to self-congratulations.

His sister had already spent one night from beneath the shelter of her home, he dared not imagine in what manner. As he made haste, Darcy fingered the letter of credit in his waistband and fretted he had not taken the time to inventory Georgiana's jewellery. When they had taken measure of her room, they searched for nothing other than motive. A *bijouterie* had been evident, but she could easily have taken a few pieces of jewellery with her. Several were worth the proverbial king's ransom. Clearly, a single stone would fund whatever design she sought. Initially he had worried that she would be taken advantage of because of her impoverished flight. Thereupon, he commenced to fear quite the opposite.

It was an embarrassing admission, but he had to concede that his fragile sister had totally flummoxed him. Involuntarily, he shook his head in renewed appreciation of the sheer impertinence of her daring. When she was recovered, he vowed he would not make the error of underestimating her again.

Amongst his many concessions, he refused to acknowledge that Elizabeth's caution against thwarting Georgiana's many pursuits was providential. (In return, she chose not to recollect his adamancy that untethered enthusiasms resulted in either judgemental anarchy or fainting fits.) He had always conceded the fact of Georgiana's keen mind, but an imaginative sensibility meant to him that she might truly be lured to seek adventure.

"If adventure was what she sought, why could she not have travelled to Greece to sketch the ruins as do other young artistically disposed gentlewomen?" he groused to himself (contrition evidently not giving him leave to accept the probability that he would have faulted Greece for her as well).

In self-righteous defence of his implacability, he reminded himself that Georgiana had a literary career. He had not denied her that. He had not liked it, but he had not denied it. His sister had family, position, and she was published. What more could a young woman desire that she would have to go off in the most imprudent manner...

The answer to that silent harrumph was quite obvious and he wisely endeavoured to draw his thoughts elsewhere. But to little avail, for he could do nothing but chastise himself for his lack of brotherly attention. Something nagged her so fiercely that she had taken a drastic and injudicious measure. He realised quite clearly that he had been far too obsessed with his own quandaries to see hers. Independently from Elizabeth, Darcy had ultimately reached much the same conclusion as had she. As much as he would have liked to believe it, he thought it quite unlikely his sister would take leave clandestinely only to share her meagre nursing skills with the British army. But she might use them as a means to reach someone in the British army.

If those previously identified unacceptable romances (the groom, Howgrave, Hinchcliffe) left him feeling decidedly uneasy, those of which he had not yet thought worried him even more. A young woman of wealth in her own right, wealth of thirty thousand pounds, was ten times that which would normally tempt the least avaricious of blackguards. The more he considered his sister's situation, the more fearful for her he became.

Fitzwilliam was Georgiana's second guardian and there were few others with whom Darcy would confide his sister's flight. Confidentiality of Georgiana's decidedly unguarded act was foremost in his mind. Protection of their standing was imperative. He would have to tread carefully. If he were successful, he would return her to Pemberley unsoiled in deed, and if at all possible, in repute as well.

In the hope that Fitzwilliam's ship was delayed at Portsmouth, Darcy had sent off a messenger to warn him of Georgiana's disappearance. If he was not reached in time there, most ships were stopping at Dover to take on more provisions. Darcy intended to intercept him and seek his counsel. For at that moment, Fitzwilliam was Darcy's most trusted ally in finding Georgiana.

If he missed Fitzwilliam at Dover, a brief but profitable conference with Bingley before he left gave Darcy the name of a specific merchantman for him to board to make the crossing. Bingley's good authority advised the ship would not be seized. That particular captain could provide a licence or not, as each situation demanded. The French demanded a licence, the British would confiscate the ship was one presented. In such times as these, ambiguity was all.

To take leave of England would be a drastic measure, and hope played far too prominent a role in the outcome. Nevertheless, he believed the safest course was, rather than follow, to try to overtake Georgiana. If she stayed in England, indubitably she would be located by the agents he had upon her trail. Alone in England she was not really safe, but certainly safer than in France.

His plan was less precise and more sparse than he would have liked. He would make certain she had not joined a medical unit, thereupon, retrace her. He prayed she stayed in England. Trifling with gouty toes and upset stomachs could not prepare her for the horrors she would find in the wake of battle. Was there any doubt, Fitzwilliam's recounting of his Spanish engagements were testament enough to the carnage. War was not adventuresome. It was not romantic. It was perdition.

Such a recollection led him to accept that the Darcy reputation was the very least of concerns.

His journey was broken but once, the respite embracing all the recumbence men and animals could engender whilst Mr. Darcy paced menacingly about, obviously under his own counsel. His Herculean determination was looked upon with wonder by his weary coachmen. However, by the time his carriage finally drew to a stop near the wharf at Dover, even Darcy had begun to feel the fatigue of the road.

Thick with soldiers and longshoremen, the bustling wharves, however, newly invigorated him. Then, all too soon, his renewed spirits were dashed. He learnt Fitzwilliam's ship was not to stop at Dover. He saw no other choice. He must depart for the continent. The beleaguerment his departure had bestowed upon Elizabeth nagged him and he was most unhappy to have to extend it.

When he located Bingley's ship, the *Barrett*, he learnt it was to set sail under the cover of darkness only six hours hence. Bingley's information was that it would attempt a landing near Bolougne sur Mer. Howbeit the name and departure were accurate, Darcy learnt the ship did not carry cargo. Now the H.M.S. *Barrett*, it had been fitted with cannons.

If it was now His Majesty's ship, it was only recently thus, for the flaking paint and foetid smell of the vessel told of its neglect. Such laxity would not be allowed by the Royal Navy for long. Darcy had not the smallest notion of that which constituted seaworthiness. His only hope was that the vessel could stay afloat until they crossed the Channel.

Without hesitation, he had his name added to its manifest.

Sending his footmen and coach on their way, he weathered the wait for embarkation with his back to the wall of a public house. Travelling incognito demanded he not board any sooner than necessary (even if he had to sit in a taproom as an alternative). The last thing he did upon English soil was to send an express to Elizabeth to advise her that he sailed and the name of the ship.

It was evenfall before he finally boarded. He took no more than a single step upon the gangplank before he was jostled roughly aside by a group of midshipmen. His initial response at such inexcusable rudeness was a rebuke. However, he realised the perpetrators of such discourtesy were too busy with their immediate task to listen to a lesson upon civility. For betwixt them they were dragging two men, both of whom were groaning with inebriation. Onto the ship they climbed, and into service in the Royal Navy.

"Two more 'volunteers' for the sea duty?" was Darcy's mild, if facetious, enquiry.

This remark was generally ignored by the sailors, for they had their hands full when the victims of their press-gang suddenly realised their predicament and began to resist. As he watched these doings, Darcy was reminded of the pride the general populace of England had in their navy.

"The most loyal navy in the world," Lady Millhouse was wont to remind everyone whenever her father, the Admiral's name came up in conversation.

The sea was a seductive mistress and Darcy did not doubt that many men were subjugated to her mystique. Nonetheless, he was not particularly blinded by patriotism.

Clearly, there was little chance for desertion aboard a ship once it set sail (one man's loyalty is another's prison). In another time, another place, he might have interceded upon the purloined men's behalf. But for then, he only stood to the side and let the flailing men be brought aboard. He would not interfere in another's quarrel. He faced far too many of his own. It was only by reason of his considerable connexions and Bingley's name that he was even on this sorry excuse for a battleship.

When at last the mighty H.M.S. *Barrett* literally creaked out of the harbour, everyone aboard knew its destination fell at chance's feet. Albeit Boulogne was their port-of-call, in truth, they had none, for the coast of northern France was fortified with six-inch guns. Their captain (no admiral would set foot upon smaller than a ninety-gun boat) had a simple mission. He was to land where the guns were not. Thus, wind against them and rough seas were not the greatest vexation, simply the most immediately uncomfortable.

The wamble of the ship influenced Darcy to find a secluded spot on deck to practise his seldom-used French. It was a bright, if cold, night for spring; the air was clear, but as always in the Channel, the water was choppy. Even his sound constitution became a little queasy as he stood at the stern and looked at the roiling water churned by the rudder. The fresh sea air was a meagre reward.

Contemplating the murky brine, his attention was caught by a fellow rail-hugger. A young man, his face so fresh it did not appear to have seen seventeen years, was retching violently. With each turn of his stomach, he was upended ever farther over the side and in danger of plunging overboard all together.

Darcy abandoned his French long enough to grab the boy by the seat of his pants and haul him back. The lad sank moaning onto the deck, simultaneously begging for his mother and the deliverance of death.

"This weather will soon settle, as shall your stomach, I grant you," Darcy assured him.

"Aye thank you sir, Aye hope you're right."

The young man eyes were wide with fright and red from hurling his supper.

"First time out?"

A nod from the boy was punctuated by another moan of nausea.

Darcy said, "You shall get your sea legs soon. Just be glad you are in the King's Navy. It is the mightiest to sail the sea. Your mother shall see you again."

The boy replied, "Aye wish, indeed, a navy man Aye was, sire, but Aye cannot confess to be. Aye am in the infantry. So my ma may have to remember the last time she saw me and be satisfied."

The boy's words were true as any spoken, thus Darcy had nothing to add. He nodded once and moved away. It would be prudent, he decided, not to venture into consoling any more anxious lads lest he fare again no better than he just had. It had been an enlightenment to speak to him, however. For it was that boy's words that uncovered the true naval nature of the *Barrett*.

It was a camouflaged troop ship. The hull was undoubtedly filled with soldiers. The single fortune that young lad could count was that he was up on deck and not in its squalid hold. As that was not his predicament, Darcy, however, held a single hope—that the forty miles across the Channel would be only that long.

As their ship cut its inky path, he turned his face toward the blackness of the water once again. There had been a time when he would have thought it beneath his company to speak to a seasick knave. Though it was a bust, he had tried. Some ventures, he concluded, brought all humankind to parity.

His countenance toward France, again he began to chant, "*Bonjour. Comment allez-vous? S'il vous plait. Je m'appelle Monsieur D'arcy.*"

With Darcy already on his way to France, John and Georgiana, even with a day's head start, were yet in Portsmouth. Edward Hardin had been correct, John did intend to join the army in the only capacity he could, as an infantryman. Conscription had been in progress for some months, but John had drawn a high lottery number. It was no feat to find a Derbyshire boy of single digit luck who was not yet prepared to repair from his home and a trade was made, thus ensuring John of a legitimate uniform.

Once in Portsmouth, they had to wait for a full contingent of their county levy to sail. (Some were not as anxious as others to fight and a little foot dragging did occur.) John's plan had been in place long before he confronted Mr. Darcy the morning before at Pemberley. His resentment had been building daily and exponentially since he heard Mrs. Hardin and her sister talk about the bastard child that Mr. Darcy had sired. That gentleman's perceived defilement of innocent girls festered in John's mind until his resentment mutated into absolute loathing. He wanted to render Mr. Darcy unable to beget another baby to abandon. He wanted Mr. Darcy dead.

For weeks he struggled unsuccessfully with just how to avenge, not only his mother, but all the many women Mr. Darcy had ruined (and infidelity to Mrs. Darcy as well). Finally, he asked himself what good Colonel Fitzwilliam would do in the face of such outrage.

The answer was obvious. Colonel Fitzwilliam would have challenged Mr. Darcy to a duel. Of course, Colonel Fitzwilliam had quite the sword for that. It was perchance fortuitous that weapon was denied John. For not only did he have little notion how to use a sabre, save for attempting to run one's opponent through, he had little idea of how to conduct a duel in the first place. A great deal of ritual and decorum was involved. He was quite certain he had heard the event had to be endured with both contestants' chests bared to prove they harboured no armour. Moreover, it was to commence with the slapping of the offender's cheek with a pair of kid gloves. As it happened, John's collar button was always undone in that he had no cravat to begin with, hence that requirement was of no bother. But not only was he not in possession of a sword, he did not own a pair of gloves. Thus, he concluded a more efficient means of confronting Mr. Darcy must be found.

A duel of honour out of the question, the next surest way to exact his death was by gun. Regrettably, John had no more access to that than a sword. The only weapon available to him was a knife. (One of the few possessions he had brought with him to Pemberley, he had pilfered it from Archie Arbuthnot, who had pilfered it from some long-forgotten port.) He knew it would be dangerous, but, with righteousness upon his side, a knife would surely inflict a mortal wound. The only drawback to his plan was that there was nothing proverbial about stabbing a man. John cast that objection aside. He wanted Mr. Darcy dead, biblical retribution or not.

Once the deed was done, he intended to make his escape by changing his name and joining the army. With his experience, he hoped he would be assigned to the cavalry, if not to ride, at least to see to their horses. And in the heady fantasy that he had constructed of Mr. Darcy's execution (he never once thought of it as murder) and his own escape, John was certain divine intervention would render him assigned to Fitzwilliam's regiment. There, he would follow the colonel into glorious battle. (It did not occur to him that Fitzwilliam might not think kindly of the person who slew his cousin.)

But his plan was circumvented. That nettlesome little matter of actuality obtruded betwixt him and his mission.

When John hurled the accusation of paternity at him, Mr. Darcy's face first reflected anger and incredulity. That was a considerable reward, but John could not quite muster his resolve for a *coup de grâce*. The notion of actually drawing blood was just too heinous. He had thrown down the knife that he intended to use to slay Mr. Darcy in disgust. Vengeance might not be exacted that day, but he vowed to himself that it would one day soon. As he stalked away burdened by his own lack of grit, at first he did not hear Mr. Darcy deny he was his father. Nor did he see the sympathy that overspread that man's features as he did.

However, when he stopped and turned around, John saw it quite clearly. No other expression would have bade John accept the truth more earnestly. Immediately upon Mr. Darcy's repudiation and his own realisation of its authenticity, John felt sick. Forthwith, an overwhelming bitterness overtook him. When he cursed Mr. Darcy, then everyone in general, it included himself.

His conviction that Mr. Darcy was his father had been so strong for so long, it was not easily abandoned. Nor was he anxious to liberate it. Injury is savoured more than most might be inclined to confess, in that injustice requires little of one save indignation. Fate requires a lengthy contemplation of philosophy.

Was he by nature disposed, John was hardly in contemplative humour. He should have been humiliated at such an embarrassing misapprehension. But whilst in such high dudgeon, there is little room for mortification. John's version of objectivity rendered Mr. Darcy, if innocent of his mother's particular defilement, certainly guilty of many others. Thus, though his father may have been technically rendered faceless, an anonym he was not. The begetter yet, and ever would be, conjured by John as an icon of Mr. Darcy.

With that understanding, John strode resolutely away, not once looking back. For there was one certainty. Even if his murderous scheme did not play out as he planned, it was nonetheless necessary to take leave of Pemberley forthwith. His meagre belongings had already been packed in anticipation of a felonious flight. (He thought it imprudent to ask for his knife back.)

He had a makeshift knapsack on his shoulder when he encountered Georgiana. Yet enraged, he stared at the ground and barely grunted in acknowledgement as he passed her. She called after him. The meanness of his spirit did not harbour pleasantries, thus he probably just stopped by rote when she asked where he was going. He told her where, but not the whole truth as to why. She asked him to wait, for she intended to take leave of Pemberley as well and bid him to drive her gig.

Initially he was reluctant, but he reconsidered. It was a long walk unto Portsmouth. Other than learning of a common interest in passage to France, he queried not.

Once at Portsmouth, they needed the gig only for some hasty cash. Georgiana and John conferred about what would be a good price. Neither had a notion of the monetary value of the rig, John, because he never had as much as a sovereign in his life, and Georgiana, because she never had as little. When they settled for two tenners with a beefy man (wearing a waistcoat that announced what he had had for dinner), Georgiana thought it a fine trade.

John, however, observed dourly, "That codger's too jolly with the price. If yer donno leave 'em screamin' they're robbed, it weren't a good bargain."

Separate rooms were found over an alehouse near the Portsmouth harbour. Georgiana turned up her nose at the stench; to John it was not a novelty. Indeed, the clinking of mugs below them was the lullaby of his youth. They stayed close that next day, having exacted a promise from each other to board a ship together (this was in defence of Georgiana's sensibility, not John's). As he waited for his company to depart, she waited as well. The ship would carry medical personnel and Georgiana knew that would be the only way to find passage.

When it finally came time for her to apply, she was nervous at the deception and nearly gave up on the scheme. Yet, she persevered. The captain looked at her keenly. Howbeit she steadfastly claimed to be a nurse and wife of an officer, he was hesitant. His qualms, however, were overcome. Whilst feigning ignorance of military custom, Georgiana offered to pay for her passage. With two five-pound notes proffered upon her outstretched palm, her inexperience and marital status were of little importance.

For a young woman believed to be an innocent, Georgiana was not naïve. Once underway, the headiness of freedom made everyone giddy, but Georgiana was one of the few too excited to be seasick. Aligning herself with a hearty girl in the hospital corps, they gaily strolled the deck arm in arm. John, however, glowered at her oceanic savoir-faire from atop a pile of rigging. There, he and some other recruits huddled in a clump. That is, when they were not taking a turn visiting the rail to lose their dinner. So sick was John, he had not the wherewithal to check the crew for the likes of Archie Arbuthnot.

When land was found, it was rather precipitously (it was only a makeshift wharf), and those who had found their sea legs endeavoured to travel down the gangplank with dignity. Those unrecovered from the crossing staggered ashore. A few of the less stalwart passengers threw themselves upon the seastrand and kissed dry land. John, who was not inclined to kiss any earth but England's no matter how severe the trip, looked upon such doings disdainfully.

As it happens, disdain often dissolves in the harsh reality of cold, naked fear. John was handed a gun. From the precarious vantage of foreign soil, and holding a weapon he was to use to personally kill Nappy, John's courage did not exactly collapse. But it did buckle ever so slightly. For he could not stop himself from recalling the stories about the Frogs he had been told as a child. They might not all be mindless, rug-chewing bogeyman, but John thought it probable far too many were suspect. Hence, being upon the same ground as the Frenchies was unnerving.

If morning saw him revisiting his childhood, the distribution of a uniform and his assignment to a company elevated him unto manhood by mid-morning. He had been disappointed that he was not given his uniform whilst yet in England. The powers that be, however, must have reasoned that they did not want to waste a uniform upon some soul that fell overboard during the trip.

He donned his uniform and, affecting a raffish swagger, looked about. Eyeing the other new recruits, he hoped he did not look half as green as they. Of course, this hope was negated each and every time he looked admiringly down at his new uniform and fingered the brass buttons (his uniform was missing only one, others did worse). Such a fine uniform was abundant compensation for the seasick voyage.

It boosted his morale as well to finally at least look like a Brother of the Blade. For upon the ship they had nothing to do but listen to tales of the trials of war. The stories he had heard in Derbyshire were triumphant. Those that were told shipboard by the veterans amongst them were just as vivid, but bloody. Visceral. Each one besting the last. There was no motive for the stories save frightening raw, young soldiers and of that, they were unconditionally successful. Tall stories or no, John thought far too many had a ring of truth. He would have congratulated the storytellers for their success at scaring the bejeezus out of him had he any humour left at all.

As cargo was being unloaded, he espied Georgiana. But their conversation did not include stories of war. Somehow, he knew she would learn soon enough. Instead, he stood before her displaying all the limited frippery of his uniform.

"Me and that other tall feller been asked into the Grenadiers," he announced.

Unwitting of such a distinction, Georgiana said, nonetheless, "How excellent for you."

Only those soldiers of the most commanding build were mustered into the Grenadiers. It was important to John that she understood that.

Thus, he explained, "Me and 'im are both bigger 'n the others. Tall, yer know?"

"Tall," Georgiana repeated, endeavouring to understand.

"Yea. Tall. To throw the grenades. So as yer won't hit yer own men in the back of the 'ead wi' 'em."

"Oh! I see! Tall. One must be of impressive height to be asked unto the Grenadiers!"

Albeit her admiration was both belated and prompted, it was still sincere and inflated John's pride more than he would have liked.

At the reminder of battles he would fight, John warned Georgiana, "Aye heard plenty from those boys over there. They tol' me about this fight. It's not a pretty war,

Miss Georgiana. It's not a pretty war."

She allowed that few wars were and thanked him for his aid and company, "Words to thank you are quite beyond me."

Tersely, he replied, "Hope we're both alive later for yer to say 'em."

In defence of the affection that crossed her face, he furrowed his brow trying to look severe. Regardless of his purported disdain, Georgiana took notice of his deliberately exposed cheek and bestowed it a kiss. Other soldiers witnessed that endearment and began to whistle and hoot. Georgiana blushed and apologised for opening him unto ridicule. He did not seem all that miffed. He merely touched the spot on his cheek where she had kissed him and gave her a half-smile before turning away.

Once he had walked a short distance, John had looked back and located Georgiana's figure disappearing into the crowd of soldiers and weaponry. On his own for so long, he had the conceit to believe himself world-weary. He was just beginning to see how truly little he himself knew.

In the less than two days since they left, John had not thought of what danger his aid had found Georgiana, having no true way of understanding how little of the world she knew. Her vulnerable visage as she commenced her mysterious odyssey made him recollect the particulars of how it had all come about in the first place.

Initially, it had not seemed at all arbitrary. When he encountered her subsequent of his confrontation with her brother, both were in low spirits. The little gem of a scheme was set into play when she saw him stalking off with his meagre possessions wrapped in a roll, tied with a string and hanging from his shoulder.

Over it, he said, "I'm goin' to war, Miss Georgiana, I'd rather be a dead soldier than a man with nothin'."

So heavy were his own travails, it took him six hours on the road to Portsmouth to remember to inquire just why she had wanted to come. Certain it was only recklessness that she risked, John accepted her one word answer.

"Love."

His mother had always said he was the least curious person she had ever known.

The dust had not settled from Darcy's coach's departure before Jane and Bingley were upon their way to Pemberley. The oblique conversation about ships and passage that had come to pass between the friends had alerted Bingley that trouble was afoot.

Their visit was a boon to Elizabeth in that she had, for the sake of appearances, been feigning composure, but with ever-increasing desperation. When they arrived, her resolve crumbled with the extraordinary gesture of embracing not only Jane (who was only mildly surprised at the greeting), but also Bingley (who was utterly astonished). The dam of suppressed hysteria burst and in a torrent, she poured out the history of Georgiana's mysterious leave-taking and her fear that Darcy's hasty pursuit might well tangle them both irretrievably in the tentacles of impending battle.

The entirety of Elizabeth's explanation took place midmost in the floor, and that they stood upon a rather lovely Persian carpet notwithstanding, it did not lend substantiation unto the absurdity of the tumultuous doings. Hence, Jane led Elizabeth to be seated and bid hear the whole story again from beginning to end, possibly believing it would not sound quite so dire was it related from the sedateness of a settee. Bingley, however, stood frozen exactly where he was. Evidently, his shock was compounded by the news.

Voice trembling, Elizabeth patiently gave an orderly retelling of the occurrences (omitting the particulars of the leave-taking of John Christie). By that time, Jane was mute. But Bingley was stricken with an unlikely case of logical enquiry. Successively, he asked: How did Darcy travel unto France? With whom did he travel? How could he find Georgiana once there?

The answers, of course, were: By whatever means he could find. Alone. And, not a clue. Which was precisely why Elizabeth was near panic.

She said, however, "I can give you no account of any of it."

Observing her increasing alarm, Bingley summoned considerable ingenuity in a lengthy answering of all of his own questions, registering a more reasonable rationale than one would suspect of him.

He concluded his recitation with the reassurance, "As you tell this, Elizabeth, it may not be necessary for Darcy to leave England at all. Georgiana may well be safe even as we speak."

In the face of little alternative, Jane concurred with her husband, "Yes, Lizzy, he may well be returning with Georgiana this minute. Do not give way to fright."

Somehow, Elizabeth did not really believe that it could all end so simply. The situation was unquestionably calamitous. But she gave leave to Jane and Bingley to think that they had cheered her.

Much in want of believing that they had, Jane assured her further, "If there is any man who is able to be successful in such a quest, it is Mr. Darcy. I cannot forget that he found Lydia and Mr. Wickham when they ran away. He rescued Lydia and saw them married. He is a man of just duty and much enterprise. He shall put everything to right this time as well."

Elizabeth thought Graetna Green and battle wastelands were hardly similar undertakings and impatiently worried just who would see after Mr. Darcy whilst he was "putting everything to right." She knew her husband was resourceful and ever cautious. But fear for one's sister could put the most provident man in harm's way. Too, she prayed for Georgiana's sake that she was yet in England. If Darcy was endangered in seeking her, it could only recommend her jeopardy tenfold.

Bingley insisted upon making inquiries upon Darcy's behalf and, had he expected protocol reckoned by her declining the initial offer, she did no such thing. Hence, he came to a right understanding of the depth of her fright.

He assured her, "I shall repair to Portsmouth immediately."

Before pulling on his gloves, Bingley took Elizabeth's hands in his. He spoke in a voice troubled by apprehension.

"I do wish Darcy had confided more to me. I would have much rather gone with him than to think of him alone."

Any inexpressible vexation toward her brother-in-law was dashed with that sentiment and Elizabeth squeezed his hands in return.

"He was quite certain he could move with more dispatch alone. As much as I would be comforted to know he had the company of such a good friend as yourself, it is probably best that no one else is imperilled by this business than must be."

Bingley almost spoke again, but there was a catch in his throat. Instead, he nodded his reluctant acceptance of Darcy's decision and the wisdom of it. Thereupon, he tapped his hat firmly down upon his head and swiftly took his leave.

Over her objections (which were but a formality), Jane insisted upon remaining with Elizabeth.

With the sincere vow to excite Jane no further with her own discomposure, Elizabeth willed herself to be calm. Such strength of will did this endeavour employ, however, that the room began to spin. Deducing that she was about to be felled by a swoon, with great economy of motion Elizabeth tucked her head neatly in her lap.

This manoeuvre did not encourage Jane's own composure, thus all the colour that had so recently taken hold of her countenance drained.

"Lizzy!"

So precipitously did Jane lose her hue, upon her exclamation, she followed suit, lest she swoon herself.

"Lizzy, you must cease your fright, lest you fall ill," was Jane's advice from the vantage of her own disorder.

With seeming synchronicity, they both sat up and looked at the other in sisterly consolation.

Regaining her senses, Elizabeth saw that the vow of silence she had only recently taken on the matter of her condition could be cast happily aside in defence of her sister's own well-being.

"Fear not for me, Jane," Elizabeth said, not unmindful of the complexities that request would entail.

The remark was unexceptional, but her sister's tone was not. Jane's countenance was a bit wary, quite apprehensive of what calamity might yet befall.

"Pray, allow me to tell you one happy bit of news," Elizabeth said.

"Pray, do."

Elizabeth then both enlightened and burdened her sister with the news of her impending confinement.

The first tumult of joy and subsequent turmoil of trepidation that such news provoked nearly brought Jane to a swoon once again.

"Oh Lizzy! That is the most happy news!" Jane said as she finally reclaimed her senses, "Mr. Darcy must be so very..."

"I have not told him, Jane," Elizabeth said and then spoke what Jane could not, "I could not burden his trip with so uncertain a business as this."

"He does not know?"

"No. I have only told you. I want no one more to know of it until I can tell my husband myself," thus, reinstating her recently abandoned vow.

The duration of Darcy's absence quite uncertain, Jane did not query the feasibility of Elizabeth's wish. Hence, their evening was spent alternately laughing and weeping. By midnight, they were both quite foredone, Elizabeth from the ordeal she was enduring, and Jane by the forced pretence that there was no question that all would be well.

Jane insisted Elizabeth must retire. Nevertheless, Elizabeth was reluctant to dress for bed. Knowing it unreasonable, she held the unlikely hope that lengthening her days would shorten the nights she would have to sleep alone. Jane offered to take sleep with her, but Elizabeth shook her head. Their bedchamber had always been hers and Darcy's sanctuary. It was theirs alone. Elizabeth did not want to share that with anyone, not even Jane.

Yet, thither did she go, only to find even greater disconcertion once she gained the room. For both sides of the bed had been turned back as if in readiness for them both. Elizabeth walked to it and sat, not on the side she claimed, but upon Darcy's. There, she lay back, closed her eyes and placed the flat of her hand upon her stomach, feeling the small swell there.

Thus, reassured she was not mistaken, she wondered for the hundredth time if she should have told him of the coming baby before he left. Would it have caused him more concern or less? She weighed it in her mind and could not be certain. He could be very single-minded, it was one of his strengths. And he would need all the single-mindedness he could prevail upon for what he had to do. Now that it was done, Elizabeth was disposed to think it indeed provident that she had not told him. At that moment, however, that was of little consolation.

Albeit it was a serious (if indecorous) consideration, she decided that she could not sleep in her clothes the entire time Darcy was away and she rose to go to her dressing room. Yet, she tarried in obstinate procrastination. If she sat dressed upon the edge of the bed, it was yet the day he left and not the night he was gone. At her feet, she glimpsed a bit of white fabric peeking from beneath the bed. Raising the bed-skirt (and trying not to notice the mirror yet beneath their bed), she took a garment hiding from thence and held it before her. She recognised it as the shirt Darcy had worn the day before. In his haste to leave, it had been very nearly kicked out of sight. Goodwin would have been contrite at his lapse of diligence with the laundry.

He would have had he learnt of it. But that knowledge would be refused him. For Elizabeth thought it a gift of greater worth than any jewels Darcy had bestowed upon her. She lay back and held it to her face, taking a deep breath of her husband's scent. It brought her to tears. But they were not the tears of dismay, but of exultation. For his aroma reminded her that though he was not with her, he was yet alive, and, somehow, it made her believe that he would return.

Nothing could make her relinquish such a treasure to the wash.

The second day was no easier to endure than the one before, but with the covert aid of her husband's soiled shirt, eventually Elizabeth made herself cease her obsessive contemplation of what was and stopped brooding, at least aloud, upon that over which she had no control. Jane, perchance in want of diverting Elizabeth, or possibly because it could be put off no longer, recommended that they make final arrangements for the baby that Bingley's woman (Elizabeth could not think of that loose woman in a less derogatory term) had birthed to be brought to Pemberley.

Logistics were a quandary, but in time, it was decided that Elizabeth, Mrs. Reynolds and Georgiana's lady-maid, Anne (nervously idle since Georgiana's disappearance), would go to get the baby. Approval of the arrangement had already been obtained, hence, the formality of bringing the bantling to Pemberley was all that was left to do. As Jane waited anxiously at the house, the other women set out in the coach.

It was less than a half-hour's ride by road, but it was uncertain terrain and the bouncing of the coach made Elizabeth queasy. As they arrived and the others were handed out of the carriage, Elizabeth fled upon her own out the opposite side and very nearly retched upon her shoes. Her discretion was for naught, for when she raised her head from her knees, there stood Mrs. Reynolds proffering a handkerchief. The look the old woman bore supposed she did not believe her mistress was suffering from simple dyspepsia.

Elizabeth gratefully took the handkerchief and allowed, "Perhaps it was best that Mr. Darcy travelled without my company."

Mrs. Reynolds only gave a single nod. But Elizabeth knew if a short coach trip made her ill, the rough waters of the Channel might well be lethal. Thus, her husband's resolve to have her stay was re-evaluated. (Elizabeth found it was much easier to acquiesce in his absence.) Even the contemplation of the sea encouraged her nausea; hence, she turned her attention to the house.

When she gazed upon the cottage, she was reminded of the days she had spent at the crest of the hill overlooking it and its inhabitant. From a distance, it had looked neat, even pretty. But distance had lent its only beauty. In truth it was dingy and in disrepair, with fowl wandering in and out of a broken door. A vision of Bingley upon that dilapidated threshold crossed Elizabeth's mind, but that thought was more upsetting to her stomach than open water and she hastily dismissed it.

It was an unspoken assumption that a woman of her station need not go into the cottage herself. However, Elizabeth abhorred the presumption of taking a baby from its mother without giving her leave to look upon the person who undertook her child's life. Inside, various family members of the woman had gathered and stood in a reverent semicircle in front of the fireplace. Her father, hat in hand, introduced himself and his wife and then merely pointed to the room where his daughter lay. The young woman's mother opened the low door to the bed-closet and Elizabeth dutifully followed her in.

Lying under a faded quilt was the woman that Elizabeth had seen from the promontory. Beside her was the baby. Much like the cottage, at a distance Bingley's woman was pretty. But even in the dim light of the room, Elizabeth could see her shrunken skin and the incongruous glittering of the eyes that announced her lungs were stealing her life. Elizabeth was shocked at her appearance even though she knew her to be ill, somehow expecting her yet to look the part of a scarlet woman. She was really only a girl and the only thing obscene about her was the handkerchief spotted with blood that she had held to her mouth.

The baby sat solemnly next to his mother, eyes wide, looking at Elizabeth. Contradicting his mother's sickly pallor, the baby was rosy-cheeked and hefty. The girl's mother lifted him from the bed and handed him to Elizabeth with an announcement.

"The boy's name is Charles."

"Charles?" Elizabeth repeated.

"Yes, ma'am."

Mortified, Elizabeth was faced with yet another quandary. Her governing principle was not to cause any undo distress, but there was no way she was going to introduce this infant to her household under the name of "Charles," even if it was a common name.

"Pray, does he have another forename?"

In fortune, he did.

"Hello, Charles Alexander," Elizabeth said.

In answer, the baby reached out and took a firm hold upon her earring. At this audacity, his grandmother gasped. But Elizabeth only smiled tolerantly and unfurled his tiny fingers one by one until she was free from his grasp. Elizabeth did not know if Alexander's mother or her family knew of her connexion with Bingley, but thought it probable (especially after the name conundrum). And they all appeared both terrified and heartbroken, so if they were resentful, too, it was difficult to determine. An awkward silence ensued and as all other topics were threadbare, Elizabeth inquired of the girl her name. She said her name was Mary.

Happy to rid the room of the lingering sound of the name "Charles," Elizabeth told her, "My sister's name is Mary."

But their discourse was abbreviated, for when the young woman managed a smile at the coincidence, she was excited into a fit of coughing. That reminded Elizabeth how small the room and how dense the contamination of the air. Knowing they must take leave, not only in defence of their health, but so as not to prolong a grievous farewell, Elizabeth bid Mary adieu.

Careful not to employ past-tense, she said, "I shall make certain he knows how much his mother loves him."

Mary wiped tears away with the back of her hand and tried to smile, but Elizabeth was too overcome with grief upon her behalf to return it. Business taken care of, Mary's mother herded Elizabeth back out the door, but at the doorway Elizabeth stopped. Impulsively, she pulled both her earrings free and put them upon the table by Mary's bed. She feared it could have been construed as a crass gesture, buying a baby if you will, but the look upon Mary's face was one of gratitude not offence. Albeit they were modest by Darcy standards (and once belonged to Darcy's grandmother), the earrings were worth a great deal. They could provide for a family for a long time. And they were the last things the baby's mother saw him touch.

Having been contemptuous of her morals at one time, Elizabeth could no longer. The family's destitution was obvious. Elizabeth could not say with absolute certainty that had their positions been reversed she would have lived with more circumspection. The only contempt she felt at that moment was for Bingley. If he had given the woman and baby any support, it was niggardly indeed.

Elizabeth relinquished the baby to Anne's needy hands and as mightily as she tried not, tears burned her eyes. She blinked them back and reminded herself that it was a kindness to Mary for her not to worry for her child. Nevertheless, she entered the carriage not unburdened, for the ache of the loss of a child was one with which she was all too familiar.

Once upon their way, Elizabeth chanced to look upon Alexander's face (already the detested appellation of Charles was forgotten) more fully than she could in the darkened cottage. The bright daylight revealed him to be blonde, but of darker colour than Jane's children. If there was a Bingley family resemblance, it was not profound. Hence, she breathed a small sigh of relief. Any scandal resulting from this entire event at least would not be embarrassingly overt.

The boy looked healthy, but sat very still on Anne's lap with a lost look upon his face. Elizabeth put out her hands, waggling her fingers and smiling encouragement for him to come to her. He sat determinedly sucking on his two middle fingers and did not make a decision at first. Thereupon, as if he had taken her due, he slowly reached out. She took him upon her lap and kissed the top of his head. It would be good to have a baby upon whom to shower attention and love. At least this chance-bairn would have a home, she told herself, and endeavoured not to think about the lot fate drew for poor John Christie.

Elizabeth expected Jane to be waiting in the vestibule when they returned, but she was not. Hence, Elizabeth sent Mrs. Reynolds to find her whilst she and Anne took the baby up to the nursery.

Mrs. Reynolds search was to be fruitless, for there in the nursery sat Jane anxiously fingering a tiny lace bonnet. Looking neither at Elizabeth nor Anne, Jane's eyes lit upon the baby and, arms extended in acceptance, went directly to him. With an instinct known only to babies, Alexander immediately reached out for Jane, whose countenance reflected an expression of anguished love that was difficult to witness.

Elizabeth and Anne quietly left Jane to have her time with Charles Bingley's son without benefit of audience.

Late that day, a rider coming fast was called. Before the *estafette* could pull his horse to a lathered, skidding stop, Elizabeth met him in the courtyard. The express was from Mr. Darcy and was characteristically brief. He had found a ship, and by the time Elizabeth received the information, would have set sail. That he was upon a ship bound for hostilities was trepidation enough. However, Bingley returned from Portsmouth with the news of neither time nor place but that the *Barrett* was one of the ships shot from the water by French cannons. Thitherward, the house of Pemberley was shrouded with an impenetrable foreboding.

Elizabeth drew her shawl about her, set her jaw and waited.

The *Barrett's* outward-bound voyage was uneventful except for briefly becoming entangled in an unusual influx of sea-wrack. The only true engagement with the enemy was upon the *Barrett's* approach to land, necessitating the dodging of a bombardment of cannon fire from French ships anchored along the shore.

It had taken six hours and the cover of darkness to find even so dangerous a place to dock as they had north of Calais. As chancy as was their landing, had Darcy known the *Barrett's* fate upon its return it would have been no great surprise. Their disembarkation was no more expeditious than a regiment of untrained infantrymen could manage. Darcy edged around the chaos, hoping to find a horse to buy or hire before it was conscripted into military service. The possibility that a horse lurked about seemed unlikely. There was but a small fishing village adjacent to the wharf, quite empty of animals save for a few bleating goats. Determined to find some sort of transportation, he walked up the slight incline that led away from the hubbub of the men and ship. Once cresting the hill, he heard the unmistakable nicker of a horse.

That propitious sound granted him renewed gratitude that if he had to chase Georgiana to the ends of the earth, it was with his hearing intact. Whilst he took the time to give that thanks, he included one, too, for the fortuitous stabling of a horse. (Conducting his search for Georgiana upon foot would be neither efficient nor agreeable.) He rapped upon the door of the nearest house, rousing the owner from his slumber. The man (apparently slumbering through a rather noisy enemy invasion) was unhappy to be kindled from his bed and issued several colourful Gallic curses as he bumped into furniture upon his trip to see who incited such a late-night disturbance. Flinging back the door, he hurled a few more invectives in Darcy's direction for good measure.

Adopting a deliberately hoarse voice (hoping, ultimately in folly, to disguise the imperfection of his French), Darcy ignored the insults and inquired politely as to the possibility of buying his horse. With little civility, the man shook his head in noncomprehension and slammed the door shut in his face. In the hope that the man was obtuse from somnolence rather than misunderstanding his deplorable French, Darcy decided not to risk conversing in a language foreign to him again. Thereupon, he employed the time-honoured signal of a willingness to do business and jingled a bag of gold coins, then waited. Odd how such a timid sound could be heard from such seemingly impenetrable depths. The door was reopened forthwith by the recently irate man, his humour much improved.

"*Oui! Oui! Un cheval! J'ai un bon cheval! Bon marché!*"

With all due haste, the man showed him to *le bon cheval*, which was indefensibly sway-backed. But as his stirrups did not drag the ground, Darcy tried not to be unduly critical of the poor nag's confirmation. The horse, quite unawares of his less than impressive configuration, pranced about as if he was taking a lap at Ascot, necessitating Darcy to remind him otherwise with a crop. They took to the road a little gingerly, Darcy attempting to rein his steed into some sort of identifiable gait whilst hoping most fervently the man from whom he bought the horse was indeed its owner.

His destination was Lille. As de Bourghs and D'arcys, an arm of Darcy's family had lived and prospered in Normandy since the Hundred Years War. Because of political upheaval, he had not visited his French relations since he graduated from Cambridge and set out upon his grand tour. He and Fitzwilliam had travelled there a decade before, for war or no war, an English gentleman worthy of the name was not properly turned out into society until he had visited the continent.

At Darcy's father's specific request, the young men had spent a fortnight under the auspices of their cousin, Viscount Charles Roux. Roux (a misnomer of a surname, for his forefathers may have been, but Roux was not red-headed) and Darcy's father had been close friends until the revolution forced the Roux family into hiding. When the *auto-da-fe* slowed to a mere trickle, Roux wasted little time in reclaiming his villa and reinstating himself and his family to the sumptuous lifestyle they had previously enjoyed. Though not the highest of station, Roux was closer in proximity than blood to those relatives the Darcys had in France and that served Darcy's purpose this trip. He sought his uncle out for convenience, not conviviality.

Upon seeing the *Chateau de Roux* again after its housing successively a monastery, a brothel, and several garrisons, Darcy saw the lovely mansion had altered but little. The place may have been abused, but it had recovered its previous splendour with remarkable rapidity. He forsook his animal at the gate and when he gave his name (presenting a card seemed superfluous) the servant went scurrying into the house. Immediately, and with arms upraised and extended in effusive greeting, came Roux himself. Waving aside Darcy's formal bow, he drew him into an ursine hug, enthusiastically (and wetly) kissing him upon both cheeks.

This osculation was a little awkward, for Roux was the better part of a foot shorter than Darcy. Nothing about the man, as it happened, suggested their shared heredity, for Roux was not only of limited height, but also of short legs and large head, not unlike a particularly elegant dwarf. Though he moved with grace, his physique suggested a life of epicurean overindulgence.

As if in corroboration of that assumption, Roux settled them in with a carafe of wine and splashed a generous portion of burgundy into Darcy's glass.

"To your good health," toasted Roux.

"*A votre sante.*"

Even oiled by spirits, their conversation began a little stilted. This, not because of the company, but because, howbeit Roux spoke nearly flawless English, Darcy insisted upon conversing in French. (His attempted exchange with the man with the horse told him he needed to practise. If he were to stumble in French, he would rather it be with Roux and not when lives were at stake.) Offering only that Fitzwilliam had arrived ahead of himself ready for battle, Darcy unbosomed as little else as possible of his own reason for being there. (He was astute enough to offer some information, if only in politeness of seeking it.) What he sought to learn of the coming clash was in regard to time and place (the British officers aboard the *Barrett* had been no better informed than he was). He hoped to hear the battle was not imminent, for he needed time to locate the commanders and their hospitals to search for Georgiana. He was disappointed.

Roux told him, "The Prussians are just north-east of here. *Le Fou Emperour* is in Paris amassing what French troops are left. Word is rampant that the Belgian levies are untrained. *Nouveaux*. Napoleon's soldiers are not many in number, but they are veterans of many conflicts and fiercely loyal to him."

Howbeit that was not a great surprise, it was yet unsettling to hear. Thus, Darcy changed the discourse. He looked about his opulent surroundings.

"I am happy to see you and your household were spared vengeance."

"Oh that," Roux said, dismissing the carnage of beheadings with a graceful wave of the hand. "Revolution is simply another word for readjustment. This, a little violent of course, but nothing catastrophic."

Darcy thought it probable that those who met the guillotine might well consider it catastrophic and wondered how his cousin could remain so unflappable in the bedlam of relentless insurrection and anarchy. He could only attribute Roux's attitude to irrepressible Gallic forbearance and two decades of getting used to it.

Recognising Darcy's confoundment, his cousin explained, "We are happily some distance from Paris. People here believe themselves of Flanders or France as the situation warrants. And fortunately, we have only a few relatives amongst the Bourbons. Just enough to favour us if they are in rule and few enough to ignore if they are not."

"I was unaware we had any connexion at all."

Roux said, "My mother's sister bore a child by a Bourbon. But it was not *de consentement.*"

Aghast, Darcy demanded clarification, "Pray, I do not take your meaning. Are you saying that a member of the royal household violated her?"

"She was a lovely woman, but a little indiscriminate with her affection," said Roux. "I think the accusation could be no greater than…'surprised.'"

Roux guffawed at his own story, and although Darcy did not find the anecdote particularly amusing, he smiled almost as if he did. If ever he were to serve hypocrisy, he reasoned, this was the single time he would forgive himself. He wanted and needed Roux's good graces. They talked into the small hours of the night, Darcy gleaning bits of political gossip amidst Roux's witty quips and barbs. Finally, eighteen hours in the saddle and two days without sleep overcame him. He made his apologies and fell into bed fully clothed.

The next morning rose with more dispatch than did Darcy and he chastised himself when he saw it would be noon before he could be upon his way. However, when he readied to leave, Roux insisted upon fitting him with a rather fine dun. As that would certainly make his travel to Brussels all the better for not having to dicker with his horse over a vacillating lead, he thanked him prodigiously.

Albeit he carried with him only a single satchel, it was cumbersome on horseback and Darcy left it with Roux, wrapping up only a change of shirt and two miniatures (one of Elizabeth and one he had brought of Georgiana to prod faulty memories as he sought her) before tying the roll to his saddle. With that, he donned the sword he rarely wore and stowed his pistol in his waistband. Thereupon, with a look of resolve that gave Roux pause, he mounted his horse and headed east.

He had not expected his odyssey to be easy. And that expectation was not denied that day nor for weeks after. It became a long and frustratingly fruitless search. Regiments were pouring into Brussels heavy with artillery. Dozens of cavalry companies had been lent to the Prussians and Dutch-Belgium commanders. Fitzwilliam's regiment had been divided, but no muster carried names, only a list of units. Individual rosters were with each sergeant-major. Even more frustrating, all hospital corps were stalled en route, no one much of a mind to worry about where they were until actual casualties occurred. He was stymied at every turn.

By the first of June, word had reached the British that Napoleon was preparing to march northward. It was then that word reached Darcy from one of the four men he had searching for Georgiana that she had been positively identified as boarding a troop ship for France. As they had suspicioned, she had obtained passage with a hospital corps. The account he received told that she had not used her real name, but it was most certainly Georgiana. She had claimed to be the wife of an officer. If he believed she would have been thwarted in her quest of hospital duty, Darcy saw he had underestimated his sister. He had no notion of whether she was travelling under an assumed name or if she truly was the wife of an officer. Regardless of her circumstance, if he could not find her before war commenced, he feared he would not be able to find her at all.

Major George Wickham's colonel had advanced him to a new regiment. Reassignment without demotion usually meant advancement in the military. This was true particularly during wartime, when careers were made upon one good skirmish. Exhausting all evasive action, Wickham had resigned himself to assignment *outre-mer* and thought a few medals would garnish his uniform quite nicely. A quiet adjutant position, possibly doing correspondence for his commanding officer in Brussels, would be no strain upon his nerves. Brussels in the spring was said to be lovely.

But Major Wickham had never been less pleased. Albeit, in all good conscience, even he should not have been surprised. For the colonel reassigning him was also a cuckolded husband—cuckolded by Major Wickham—and the said same major found his newly reassigned person right in the midst of a most distressing battlefield.

As long as he had been encamped near society, the army had not been unbearable for Wickham. Actual combat upon a filthy countryside, however, was entirely insupportable. He believed a demotion might have been an improvement (howbeit that was perilously close to being cashiered altogether). Was this dubious advancement not insult enough, the reason given for it came by way of one of his many vanities, his height. Yes, tall he was. Hence, the Grenadiers called.

This was an assignment where he could not prosper and had a high probability of physical harm. Moreover, the Grenadiers had decidedly unfashionable uniforms. His least favourite things.

He was in an undeniably unmerry pinch. Not only endangered and sartorially affronted, prosperity had been most unkind. That last little business at his previous post with those pesky gambling debts meant he was yet signing his lamentations to Lydia for more money with no higher rank than major. In light of some of his more provocative peccadilloes (even only those of which his army superiors were aware, which, of course, would be the only way to find a manageable number from which to gauge his greater body of works), it would be highly unlikely that he could expect to receive a promotion in the near, or even distant future. Even was that possible, the next step up from Major would be Lieutenant Colonel. And that was a rank that would expect of him some actual effort of occupation.

No one weathered one's own predicament with less forbearance than Wickham. It was evident that his superiors had hoped to corner him. Actually, he knew if they could legally use him for cannon fodder, there would have been a number who would have suggested it. To Wickham, they, in effect, had.

"This," he asked himself petulantly, "is what I am delivered of an army composed of dilettante officers and failed sons of the aristocracy?" (That he was very much a dilettante and might even be considered a failed son was lost upon him. Inferiority of connexion had always fed the greatest injury.)

Hence, Major George Wickham, who had spent his life in pursuit of pleasure and aggressively avoiding even the most meagre hint of danger, was exceedingly displeased to be sitting upon the edge of the Belgian frontier. (One can only conjecture how additionally peeved he was to be looking into the hulking face of Napoleon's army bulwarked only by a bunch of gangly grenade-lobbers.)

The only possible positive of his situation was that he was not upon the same continent as his wife. In light of that good tiding, Wickham did not surrender to despair. He could not remember a time when he could not find one more shot in his locker of schemes. Hence, when he was not bemoaning his fate, he spent every spare moment conniving how to pull the hat-trick of staying in Europe—but out of the war—and getting rich in the process.

Possibilities abounded.

He saw no advantage in Brussels society, what with all the war business. But he longed to see Vienna! Now there was a city worthy of his talents (both honed and those yet untapped). He would have to find resources, of course. A possibility would be to sell his commission. If, that is, he was not killed where he stood. If Napoleon did not retake Belgium, if he was not captured by the French...

It was difficult to maintain his ever-optimistic perspective, but he endeavoured to do so. In the interminable boredom of waiting to be shot out of his boots, however, he was hard-pressed to maintain his sanguinity. His most recent grand plan had failed miserably and his ego was stinging yet from being so decidedly rejected at Pemberley. (He disliked critiquing himself, but knew that betimes one must suffer harsh examination to perfect one's technique.) Thinking back upon that visit, he endeavoured to determine just where he went wrong.

He had been in desperate straits when he received Elizabeth's letter. He had just been given orders assigning him to a battle-ready regiment and he was frantic for funds to buy himself free. A notification in her hand of some long-forgotten bush child (...What was it? A son? Yes, a son by that chamber wench...whatever she was called) seemed a perfectly good excuse to presume himself welcome unto the bosom of his boyhood home. Wickham had made an art of avoiding the pointing finger of woman with child, but if he could see an advantage of the situation in it, he could become as in want of family as needed.

The letter arrived from Elizabeth yet at Pemberley in early spring. Wickham would have wagered a year's salary (however little a major's pay might be) that Elizabeth would not have written to him was not Darcy ensconced in London. Undoubtedly yet-lovely Mrs. Darcy would be quite alone and quite vulnerable in her want of company. Perhaps, he told himself, it was only because her husband was about that Elizabeth did not find herself felled under his considerable charms that day. Wooing unhappy wives had always been one of his particularly reliable abilities.

That Elizabeth must be discontented, he never questioned. Darcy was certainly not of more handsome countenance than himself, nor was it in his surly nature to provide a woman the flattery and attention necessary to secure her...eh, affection. Thus, it was all quite vexing.

A half-dozen years and he could yet not comprehend how Darcy and Elizabeth's alliance came about in the first place. He would have wagered another year's salary that Darcy would never have lowered himself to Elizabeth's station to marry. Obviously she had not been with child, but of course a man of Darcy's fortune could have easily side-stepped that responsibility had it been the case. He shook his head yet at Darcy's arrogance. Wickham knew him fastidious, but he thought Darcy's self-regard a trifle too meticulous to so roundly disdain the hoards of women swooning at his wealthy feet. For that reason, if no other, Wickham had been determined to take another measure of Elizabeth. For he surmised she held allurement far beyond simple fairness of face if she managed to snare the punctilious Darcy.

As a man who prided himself upon appraising feminine attributes in a single glance, Wickham no more than cast his eyes upon Elizabeth that day than he assessed her nubile and ripe. If she was barren, it could fall to nothing but Darcy's indifference. Which was fortune to him. Elizabeth was ripe, in need of an heir, and undoubtedly lonely. He had the dark hair and, of course, the height of Darcy. Hence, no one would suspect the difference in paternity when he impregnated her with the needed son (Wickham's ego gave him no doubt he would father a son, such were his son-begetting credentials). Thereupon, when things were set in place, he would be able to live more than comfortably upon the money Elizabeth would bestow upon him to buy his silence.

Or, the other possibility. He almost smirked at the thought of Darcy being informed his son was not his own blood (for that was the one drawback to his first plan; he could not throw that in Darcy's face or there would be no silence to be bought). Darcy's pride would never allow that he was a cuckold be cast about. There could be no more satisfying revenge for Wickham than to do just that. Yes, it was a grand scheme. There was no way it should have failed. If Elizabeth would not buy his silence, her husband certainly would. Wickham would have wagered a year's salary on it. And he could have lived in comfort in Europe, in Vienna. Not sitting upon the edge of the Belgian frontier facing Napoleon's army.

In all of his mental machinations, however, the one thing Wickham kept forgetting was that he was an abominable gambler.

68

Servants took Bingley's hat and walking stick at the door. He was told that his wife was upstairs with Mrs. Darcy. Quite at home in the Darcy household, he went in search of them unaccompanied. He followed voices up the staircase and to a room at the end of the corridor. Both his wife and her sister were laughing and, the door open, he took a step into room. His easy smile in place, he was quite ready to appreciate what amusement caused theirs.

"Good day, ladies," he said jovially, "I see you are in finer spirits to-day…"

But his voice trailed off and his smile was lost when he saw the baby that sat betwixt them upon the floor.

Concurrently, Elizabeth and Jane looked up at Bingley, their expression mocking his somewhat. Both sisters' countenances bore the additional burden of guilt, but for decidedly different reasons. Jane was contrite, for she knew that she had not scrupled to scheme behind her husband's back. Elizabeth was mentally chastising herself for not having the courage to warn Jane that she had seen Bingley holding his baby not all that long ago and he would undoubtedly recognise him.

Obvious recognition of the baby was upon his face then, but worse, the realisation as well that Elizabeth and Jane both knew of his own complicity. The plan she and her sister had so labouriously hatched had not lasted a fortnight before it went off the rails by way of their own scrutable faces. Lacking incumbent guile, the sisters obviously needed more practise at subterfuge.

"Dash it all!" Elizabeth exclaimed to no one but herself, "Jane and I are hopeless connivers."

There was an exceedingly uncomfortable silence, broken only by baby Alexander. He reached out and grabbed a string of wooden beads that dangled from Jane's hand and noisily put them in his mouth. All three watched him do that, then an uncomfortable silence engulfed them once again. Seeing it quite impossible to reinstate their planned fiction that the baby being at Pemberley was a great coincidence, Elizabeth stood, and thereupon eased by Bingley who yet stood in the doorway.

She escaped the room but halted at the nearest doorway and entered, leaving the door ajar. She drew a chair next to it and sat, trying to hear what was being said above the pounding of her heart. The door closed behind Bingley and was followed by an agonising quiet. She believed Darcy right when he assured her so long ago that no one in an adjoining room at Pemberley could hear their lovemaking, the walls were that tight. She would have given up every claim of privacy to be able to hear what Jane and Bingley were saying then.

The shock and disbelief she had felt the day she saw Bingley with Alexander and his mother had revisited her like a thunderclap and made the blood in her temples throb. So much had bechanced since then, it had, until that moment, faded into the haze of some far distant past. No more. Her outrage restored as well, she knew she was finding more vengeful satisfaction that Bingley would have to answer to his betrayal in his lifetime than a practising Christian should. (That had been the most galling thing about the entire affair Elizabeth believed; Bingley being spared penance before Jane.)

But she knew her vengeance would be better appeased if she could hear what was being said. She opened the door wider and peered back down the hall at the thick oak door betwixt herself and Jane. Still hearing nothing, she boldly stepped out into the hall, leaned back against the doorpost and folded her arms. Her position improved, she heard muffled voices. Thereupon she heard weeping. Her anger boiled. This would not do!

Her hands firmly upon her hips (and a slight jutting of her chin announcing a pugnacity that was not particularly flattering), she marched down the hall. How dare Bingley make Jane cry! She was the injured party! He should be upon his knees begging Jane's forgiveness! Looking to either side, she searched wildly for some object to inflict retribution upon Bingley's person, becoming angrier with each step she took. Not finding anything handy by the time she reached the door, she decided she was irate enough to take a pound of flesh from his hide without a weapon.

She flung the door back and burst into the room. She wished she had not. At her sister's intrusion, Jane looked up.

It was not she who was crying.

It was unsettling to Elizabeth to have intruded into so private a moment, and the only consolation she had was that, in view of the fact that Bingley was weeping wretchedly into Jane's lap, he had not known she had witnessed it. She supposed he was suffering from his own misdeeds enough to satisfy her own righteous indignation. Pity was an emotion Elizabeth seldom found reason to summon, but she drew it forth in a measure large enough to keep herself from judging Bingley.

Albeit Bingley was in ignorance of her encroachment upon his privacy, there was, nevertheless, the no small matter of the rather flagrant proof of his indiscretion. The giggling, squirming, cooing proof of his indiscretion. It was difficult to step about it at first, Bingley behaving rather cowed in Elizabeth's presence. But soon, howbeit she knew their previous understanding of normalcy was forever altered, a precarious symmetry was eventually obtained. Conversation eventually abandoned wearying civility and flowed more easily, the self-conscious shuffling of Bingley's feet stopped, and the days returned to their maddening monotony of fear and dread.

And when Jane and Bingley took Alexander home to Kirkland, the folk of Derbyshire were thrown into a confusion of paternity supposition of gargantuan proportions.

For several days after Mr. Darcy took leave, Hannah drew Elizabeth's bath faithfully. Nevertheless, she ignored it. At first, it was not a conscious decision, Elizabeth merely stepped around the tub and donned fresh clothes. Gradually, it dawned upon her why she was neglecting so fundamental a part of her toilette. It was for the very same reason that she sat looking at, rather than sitting in, her steaming tub after their wedding night.

She did not want to wash her husband from her body.

In a time when one of average means did well to wash before church each Sunday, it took clearly a week for Elizabeth to suspect her own odour might be giving offence. To her it was a banner of loyalty to Darcy, but she chose not to explain herself, sparing the necessity of sharing that particular logic with anyone.

Another rationale for not bathing was Baby Alexander. He was a happy diversion and Elizabeth fancied that it made him feel more acclimated hugging the neck of an unperfumed woman. One who smelled more like his mother. (If the average man bathed but once a week, those of meagre circumstance could only pray for a good rain.) He may have been comforted thusly, but that was unclear. The thing that was clear was that Alexander had a happy disposition. Some traits will out; Elizabeth supposed he inherited his from Bingley. Moreover, he had shown no signs of his mother's disease.

When Jane took Alexander home to Kirkland, Elizabeth missed his company but lectured herself that it was as it should be. His relocation and Darcy's extended absence convinced her to give up her absurd determination not to bathe, but she sat in the tub and sobbed inconsolably when she finally did. If others were happy she came to the conclusion of finally surrendering to soap, no one spoke of it.

Thus, the days were more patient than Elizabeth was and she struggled to fill them. She was "not at home" for most people, seeing only the Bingleys and Lady Millhouse. She was determined word not reach her father, for she knew he would not be able to elude her mother long enough to come to her side alone.

Although she did not keep to her room, she rarely took to the outdoors unless to count off paces to the gate. There she would pause and look longingly for the mail-coach, thereupon trudge slowly back to the house. Even there her routine was strict, and she was unable to steel herself to visit the gallery. At one time, she was comforted during her husband's brief absences by sitting beneath his likeness. Elizabeth did not want to investigate her heart to understand why even the thought of his portrait was so painful then.

Recognising Elizabeth's despondency and knowing the reason for it, Lady Millhouse obliged her to do just that. She suggested they stroll the length of the gallery and make sport of some of the more ludicrous wigs worn in the ancient paintings. Knowing it imprudent to admit an extravagance of sentimentality to her, Elizabeth nevertheless demurred, saying it saddened her to look at Darcy's portrait. As expected, Lady Millhouse pronounced it maudlin to pine over an absence.

"It is insipid to sit about like a vapid flower moping over Darcy! He shall return with Georgiana within a fortnight. I shall not worry for Newton, God shall protect him. You must keep yourself busy! Come, let us walk."

Elizabeth listened to her reassurance with perfect indifference, for Lady Millhouse's bravado was quite suspect. That lady's will was not to be denied, however, She took Elizabeth firmly in hand and led her reluctantly to confront the source of her melancholia.

Darcy's portrait hung at the far end of the room, thus they were able to work their way to it slowly. Again, Elizabeth pondered the ancestors of her unborn child. Seldom did these countenances fail to amuse her, for they were all in the happy circumstances of riches, and all but a few seemed quite dour about it. (Was it simply bad teeth? She could only guess.) This thought of tooth-loss renewed her gratitude that her own were yet in her head and that Darcy's were sound as well. Perchance their children would inherit their parents' strong teeth.

Eventually their tour took them to the portrait of Darcy's mother. For, howbeit none of the portraits beheld smiling countenances, hers was not only unsmiling, but also seemingly forlorn. That thought had always nagged at Elizabeth, but she believed it an observation only of her own.

Darcy had told her this painting of his mother was done after his birth. It was ten years later that she would die bearing Georgiana, and Elizabeth wondered if she had some infirmity that grieved her even then (and hoped it was not her teeth). Lady Millhouse walked up and stood silently next to her as she gazed upon the elder Mrs. Darcy.

"Georgiana does favour Elinor, does she not, Elizabeth?"

Grateful she spoke of Georgiana in the present tense, Elizabeth was taken unawares at hearing Mrs. Darcy called by her Christian name. "Elinor. Yes, she does." Indeed, Georgiana did favour her mother, for she was blonde and slight. And howbeit there was a resemblance, Elinor Darcy would be much more likely to be described as handsome than beautiful. Georgiana had her colouring and slim figure, but her features were more delicate than her mother's, her chin not as pronounced.

"She was lovely," Elizabeth said diplomatically, knowing an outright fabrication would invite correction from Lady Millhouse. "But I wonder if she was ill when her likeness was taken. She looks a bit drawn about the eyes."

"What grieved her was not her health, I am afraid," said Lady Millhouse without further clarification.

It was the first time Elizabeth could remember her making such a deliberately abstruse comment. But she did not question it, knowing the lady would elaborate in her own good time. As if by prearrangement, both their gazes turned to the late Mr. Darcy's portrait. His countenance smiled down upon them from just to the left of his wife's. He had been a handsome man and did not appear to have the ability to brood as did his son.

"No question of that gentleman's health, he must have been quite a robust man," Elizabeth observed.

"Gerard was very robust," Lady Millhouse said, but it was not spoken in admiration. "Elinor was five years his senior, yet he outlived her by ten. I fancy she might have lived longer had her heart not borne a disappointment."

It was unlikely Lady Millhouse intended that remark to go unquestioned. Elizabeth obliged.

"Pray, did she not die in childbirth with Georgiana?"

"That is merely when she died, not why."

"You shall, of course," Elizabeth put her hand upon her hip, "tell me the why."

"I would not have brought it up otherwise."

No, she would not, Elizabeth knew that well.

"Gerard Darcy was much beloved in this county, not only by his son, but everyone of his acquaintance. He was of handsome figure, amiable disposition, and benevolent heart. Robust as well. Albeit your husband inherited his father's countenance, his temperament and scruples are those of his mother."

Elizabeth nodded her head in concurrence, for she had believed that to be true, but never heard it put so frankly.

"As you learnt quite expeditiously, Elizabeth, marriage within Darcy's presumed society is not often a match where love or even affection is a consideration. The fortunes of Elinor and Gerard were far too vast to leave to the whim of passion. Their marriage was arranged. Though it was not born of love, I believe, as often happens, eventually mutual regard developed. That esteem was perhaps felt more firmly by Elinor."

Lady Millhouse turned her back to the Darcy portraits and Elizabeth as well, possibly in apology of the story she intended to relate.

"Lizzy," (it was the first time Lady Millhouse had addressed her thus, and Elizabeth took it as an endearment) "have you heard the tales of the late Duchess of Devonshire? She and the Duke resided at Chatsworth."

"Of course."

"Difficult to avoid, I suppose. She did invite a great deal of gossip, not only in Derbyshire, but also across England. Georgiana was very beautiful. Very flirtatious. She drank like a sailor and gambled like a lord."

Lady Millhouse laughed at the memory.

Turning to look at Elizabeth, she assured her, "The reverse would have been better, for when it came to games of chance, luck was the thing that eschewed her company."

"In time her gambling debts became so great, she feared the Duke would refuse to pay them. Come she did then to the benevolent, rich, and robust Gerard Darcy, bewailing her sad tale of woe. At first, she merely sought his counsel. It blossomed into more."

Hardly unsuspecting of the direction this story was taking, Elizabeth nonetheless took a slight gasp at hearing it spoken.

"Mrs. Darcy learnt of it?"

"Oh yes."

Lady Millhouse turned about directly facing Elizabeth and folded her arms.

"I believe you know Elinor was a sister to Lady Catherine de Bourgh?"

Elizabeth nodded and resorted to the emphasis of a raised an eyebrow.

"Yes. Of course you do. Lady Catherine...I never had any use for that woman..." Lady Millhouse groused before continuing, "Lady Catherine made certain Elinor learnt of it. Her motive being yet unearthed. Most probably, she desired everyone to be as unhappy as herself. She always has had a nose for who was getting a leg over whom."

Getting up a head of steam over Lady Catherine's many personal inadequacies, Lady Millhouse's story was redirected, "I always believed the sour look upon her puss was from her marriage to old Lord Lewis. They say that milksop could not get his cock into a gallop if he whipped the beast with both hands. There was always a question of just who sired Lady Anne. It is said Catherine always favoured one buck-toothed footman and Lady Anne's teeth are a disgrace, if that lends the story any credibility. I dare say if you saw a man clinging to a Rosing's coach looking particularly abused, he would be the one who got the odious duty of lathering that woman's saddle..."

As much as Elizabeth enjoyed being shocked at Lady Millhouse's narrative about Darcy's aunt (her colourful euphemisms alone were worth the listen), Elizabeth was dangling yet over what bechanced with Mr. and Mrs. Darcy.

"Thus, Lady Catherine told Elinor about Mr. Darcy's affair. Pray, what happened? Did she confront him? Was there a row?"

"Nothing so dramatic, I am afraid." Lady Millhouse tsked several times. "Albeit, in a manner of speaking she did confront him. She was near term when she learnt of the affair. She died only days after the birth. But with her dying breath she told the rector what name she wanted her daughter christened."

"Georgiana."

"Indeed. I dare say Gerard suffered every time he spoke his daughter's name. I know he behaved more circumspectly. A little too late for his wife, however."

"I do not believe Darcy knows any of this."

"Few do. The liaison was discreet. Gerard was always discreet in his assignations."

"He had others?"

"Not after Elinor died. Though the Duchess of Devonshire is in her grave and that chapter ended, others are not so compleat. It is best to let them lie. Do you not agree?"

Elizabeth knew had she been otherwise inclined she had no choice but to think so too. In a less than facile change of discourse, she looked upon Darcy's likeness and thereupon to his father's.

"How tall was Mr. Darcy? I mean Gerard Darcy?"

"I believe that he was as tall as your husband and when young, his hair was dark as well. Odd, how some traits are stronger than are others. Should we not breed as we do horses? Weed out the ill characteristics, dishonesty, hypocrisy—was that done, we would not have any Lady Catherines about at all."

They both laughed.

"That is a thought, but are we not bred in a sense now? Land to marry land, title to title, position to position, and produce a son above all else?"

As she spoke, Elizabeth endeavoured unsuccessfully not to sound bitter. If she did, Lady Millhouse did not acknowledge it, and Elizabeth peered at Gerard Darcy's face and saw beyond his resemblance to her husband. Was it the story she had just heard that bade him oddly familiar to her? Or something else. She tried to pinpoint it in her mind, but before she mulled it long, Lady Millhouse startled her.

"Did our good Darcy know you were with child before he left?"

"Pray, how...?"

"Nothing mysterious. You have not ridden. I would have thought you would have ridden every day in your husband's absence. Moreover, as often as he butters your bun you were bound to have one in the oven again sooner or later."

Lady Millhouse's explicit delineation of her marital activities obliged Elizabeth to crimson and hastily redirect the discourse once again, "I had once hoped my husband would be the first to learn of this baby. If he does not hurry home, I fear he may well be the last."

With that small attempt at mirth, Lady Millhouse was cheered to know that Elizabeth had not compleatly given in to despair. Moreover, a little family history would give her more to chew upon than just fretting over her travails.

By mid-June, Wickham's company had an influx of raw recruits come in a day behind Napoleon's advance. Happy to get through his first battle alive and with the seat of his breeches unsoiled, Wickham, nevertheless, had not been pleased to see reinforcements. His company had lost thirty men upon the first flurry of artillery fire. They had been stacked up like so much cord-wood and carted away upon a groaning tumbrel only that dawn. Under such circumstances, most officers would have fallen upon their knees in gratitude for more soldiers. Wickham only saw them as more work, more responsibility and, most importantly, more reason to have to hold their position instead of retreating.

The newcomers all stood about looking apprehensive and green. He absently glanced at their anxious faces and waved to his sergeant-major to tell the sergeant (Wickham did not choose to speak to mere sergeants) to drill them. That done, he stayed in sullen petulance in his tent most of that day pondering his pitiable fate and the dispatch that announced it. For with his company numbers cut in half, his superiors had ordered Wickham's company to man a stand against Napoleon's cannons as the French's debouchment crossed into Belgium. There was a gap in allied defences betwixt Charleroi and Mons. It was crucial that it be stanched.

Man a stand? Were they mad? That he had survived the first murderous assault should have been heartening. Rather, his brief reprieve merely fed Wickham's festering ill-temper. Customarily, he took his meals in his tent, but in his anxious boredom, he was disposed to take some fresh (if humid) air and stretch a bit. He threw back the flap and looked warily about. Hearing no sniper fire, he gingerly stepped out and extended his arms over his head.

His men were sitting about a fire and he walked over to get his ration of saltless biscuits and dried pork. He picked a bit of bacon off a young corporal's tin, broke it in two, tossed half in his mouth and the other back upon the soldier's dish. It hit with a clink and then slid to the ground. The corporal cut a rather impudent sneer at Wickham's back as he picked up the meat, flicked it several times to divest it of sand, then popped it in his mouth. Wickham was busy sizing up the lot he was sent. It was not a particularly rewarding sight.

The new men were all young, all lanky and very tall. And because of that, all displayed half a forearm out the end of their cuffs, which further insulted Wickham's overly employed *lèse-majesté*. They sat in a group upon the ground, their knees sticking up like grasshopper legs. The war dogs, anxious of word from home, were grilling them as to what county they represented. Wickham heard one young man, who sat a little aloof from the others, say he hailed from Derbyshire, thus it caught Wickham's attention.

His men had moved about uneasily as Major Wickham joined them. The major's surliness had been much in display and no man dared hazard a misdeed to incite his wrath. The disquiet of the veterans alerted the more trenchant recruits that their major was prone to splenetics.

Either oblivious to, or ignoring, the disquiet of his men, Wickham sought a seat near the Derbyshire lad. At his appearance, conversation dwindled into only a cough or two, thereupon a gradual disbandment of the enclave of talk commenced. If Wickham noticed this either, it was unapparent. John Christie had risen to move away with the others when Wickham stopped him with a query.

"Where in Derbyshire do you call home, lad?"

Wickham's was forced congeniality. But was John uneasy about possible incarceration (his knife threat of a gentleman for certain, possible theft of the rig, and perchance even kidnapping), the young recruit admitted only Kympton as his home.

"Kympton!" Wickham exclaimed, "Now, that is an astonishing coincidence. For I am from Derbyshire and that is the living I should have had."

He thereupon relaunched the story of the cruel young Mr. Darcy who had denied him the living that old Mr. Darcy had promised him. In his ennui, Wickham's spirits improved remarkably by having an audience (however low) before whom to air his grievances. For the only thing Wickham enjoyed nearly as well as bedding other men's wives was to be the sympathetic centre of a tale of treachery. Particularly this one.

The young lad's face did not betray any understanding of the mendacity in Wickhams' claims. He told Major Wickham nothing more than that he knew of Pemberley and the Darcys. Wickham was pleased. Having been exceedingly bored for weeks, thereupon stricken with anxiety, he effortlessly slipped into his amiable social patter. It was a diversion to be in the company of someone who was both familiar with Pemberley and naïve enough to believe his tales. He sat and regaled the young man with all things Darcy until the insects eventually drove him back to his tent.

Once Wickham was out of earshot, an older soldier commented snidely upon the young grenadier's presumed alliance with their truculent commanding officer. Their umbrage was understandable. Wickham had scarcely shown his face to them but to berate. One seen as befriending their tormentor was considered a traitor to their ranks. The only reaction culled from the knave at such a blatant mockery was a shrug of his shoulders. Hence, unrequited by pique and with little else to do, the soldiers soon found another victim to needle.

Far too fleetingly; the men would soon long for the torturous tedium of waiting. For as the sun was at its apex the next day, the first report of gunfire was heard. It was but one soldier who heard that initial shot. He stopped eating, his spoon suspended halfway to his mouth. Another soldier heard the second shot and stopped chewing. By the time a volley of gunfire erupted, food went flying into the air whilst every man not squatting in the latrine made a wild dash for his weapons. (The man in the latrine was tardy only as he could not run very fast with his smallclothes hugging his ankles.)

Several soldiers squabbled over who would be first to look through the spyglass at the coming Armageddon. All were frantic to see, for they had heard the main body of Napoleon's Army was one hundred thousand men strong. It would be an awesome sight.

Wickham heard the melee if not the gunfire, and strode over to his bickering men. Bestrewing them to damnation, he wrested his spyglass from their trembling hands. As he put it to his eye, the ground began to rumble beneath them. The soldiers watched as their major looked through the lens once, then attempted to clean it with his sleeve before looking through it again. But he could not wipe away what he saw. An endless line of French battle *carre* approached their placement, and they were sixteen men wide and sixteen deep.

"Men to your positions!" Wickham screamed.

At this command, a flurry of activity commenced amongst the Grenadiers, not all of it military in nature. A few relieved themselves of their rations by various orifices and the literate amongst those not stricken with intestinal distress commenced composing their wills upon whatever bits of paper they could find.

That his company stood in the path of this great army forthwith was not information Wickham held early on. For if he had, the Prussian-Anglo forces would not have been able to count Major George Wickham still amongst them. Wickham had no intention of facing fire again. Abject terror did unspeakable things to a man's mettle, was one possessed of any in the first place. Wickham had joined the army to wear the uniform, not to earn it. One battle was one too many.

He bade his time, for the cost of desertion was death. Possible death by hanging if he were caught or certain death upon the battlefield, however, seemed to Wickham to be his choice. Betwixt the possible and the certain was a hair's breadth chance of escape. Wickham knew when he acted, he must act decisively. He was not certain how, but opportunity had an uncanny knack of calling his name when needed.

Whether the constant drilling Wickham had demanded was out of peevishness or perfection, it nevertheless served his men well. The Grenadiers were bombarded with cannon fire, but stood firm for some time launching their lethal pomegranates. It was the first action of any type John Christie had seen. Until they had gotten to the front, he had only looked at a grenade. None of the recruits had been given leave to touch one. They had practised with stones.

He had been impressed at their instructors' precision the first time he picked up a real one. The rocks they had launched replicated the weight of the grenades. He gave one a little toss in the air to test it again and saw the man next to him flinch. John looked at him queerly for the fuse was not yet lit. (The previous fight had left a few men jumpy.)

Before the battle, he had spent a bit of time wondering (in light of his failed attempt at murdering Mr. Darcy) had he the courage to actually kill anyone. It fell apparent that neither enemy faces, nor the mothers that love them, come to mind when one is thinking of nothing but endeavouring to survive. Philosophising about war, he deduced, is useless under fire.

A cadence of launch was hastily (and a bit awkwardly) established. He watched the grenades dwindle, his arms aching in reverse proportion to size of their store. It took just over an hour to shoot their bolt. The firepower of veteran French troops created a bastinado unparalleled in John's imagination. None of the Grenadiers could stand under such an assault, much less see in the acrid air. By snaking along upon his belly, he found a shallow ditch already inhabited by two fellow grenadiers. Implausible under the circumstances, none could keep themselves from curling into a foetal position and covering their heads in defence of incoming cannonballs. Yet, when the *tir de barrage* ceased, it was rather ominously.

The sultry air hung heavy with smoke, but John poked his head timidly from the trench. In such close fighting and resultant confusion, a general, friend or foe, would be hard-pressed to tell his own men from the enemy, therefore, the cannons were silenced (this not a decision born necessarily of humanity, but of economy). John had slaughtered pigs, decapitated chickens. He had once seen two men hanged. But he had never imagined such carnage.

Hands shaking violently, John wrestled with spiriting a bayonet upon a long gun, certain the French infantry was upon him. Miraculously, they did not come in to his depth. Their victory of this position evident, the French rolled on. A fugato of cannons rattling away and their own drums beating a retreat gradually influenced him to understand this particular battle was over. He had not been victorious, but he was alive. At that moment, survival was not the most important thing. It was the only thing that mattered.

John rolled upon his back, awash with relief whilst clutching the gun to his chest. Only a moment did he allow himself repose to savour life. He groaned to a sitting position and looked about to see what was next to be done. Every instruction they had been given was in anticipation of battle. Not a word what to do in its wake.

In the smoking stench, John espied Major Wickham's riderless horse running about randomly. His reins dangled dangerously, nearly tripping him once. John crawled upon his knees, then staggered to his feet. The major was most likely down. Yet another victim of Mr. Darcy's perfidy. Compatriots at the hands of such villainy had to aid each other, lest none survive. Stumbling over bodies and gear, John lurched toward the terrified horse.

"Halt," he reminded himself. "Speak quietly. Move with care."

He held out his hand and cooed in a low voice. The horse slowed and then stopped, his head hanging, but eyes keen. Grasping the reins, John looked about for either the major or the major's body. He then espied Major Wickham. He was, indeed, down, just upon the other side of a rise. But he was not dead.

It was not until he and the horse were almost upon Wickham that John saw him clear. He was not wounded as first thought. He was engrossed in the most incongruous activity. A corporal, rendered faceless and a corpse by reason of a horrific head wound, lay at his feet, and he was jerking violently at the man's jacket. John stopped some twenty feet away in disbelief. Obviously, the major had run mad. Spellbound, he watched as the major exchanged uniform coats with the dead corporal. It was not until Wickham finished his grisly task that he saw John staring at him. The gaze that passed between was so deep as to envelop the soul. And with it, all due revelation.

Wickham may have had no feel for battle, but when he saw his deceit mirrored upon the solemn face of a soldier in his command, he did not hesitate. He tugged the gun from his belt and deliberately discharged a single round into John's stomach. The impact of the shot tossed him backward upon the ground. Only from thence did the searing pain announce itself. And it was from thence that he watched the Major approach him, for he still clutched the horse's reins in his hand. Wickham yanked them free. Thereupon, he mounted the horse and dug his spurs deep into his flank to speed his departure.

Wickham did not look over his shoulder as he rode away.

71

The single blessing Elizabeth could find of her husband's absence was that Jane would not worry relentlessly that their unborn child would see its father's...*membrum virile*. Being unavailed of conjugal pleasures, however, was not foremost in Elizabeth's mind. As she became increasingly heavy with child, their bed may have grown more incommodious, but it did not seem less empty to her.

As time wore on, Elizabeth's funk deepened. It was only rarely that she spoke of her multitude of fears to Jane. Truly, she knew Georgiana was in the greatest danger, but she could not will herself to fear for her husband less than anyone else. Newspapers were rampant with rumours of the ever-looming war. She read them voraciously, far too often allowing the hyperbole of the press to sweep her away with fright. It was no compensation to understand that danger was relative. Fitzwilliam, Newton Hinch-cliffe, and young Howgrave would actually fight the war. But she kept a special place in her prayers for poor John Christie. To have been begat by George Wickham was test enough. To be a hapless cog in the ever-turning wheels of war was ill, indeed.

Sitting and brooding alone, Elizabeth could not reconcile her conscience against the notion that the entire tumult of their family had been instigated, however unintention-ally, by her own mismanagement. She had handled Fitzwilliam's declaration of love badly. When she learnt he intended to rejoin Wellington she should have intervened. Had Fitzwilliam not departed, John Christie would not have taken his lead and gone as well. It was an horrendous train of events, for had he not gone, Georgiana might not have left on her own. That was the most perplexing thing. Why did Georgiana go?

Having not the remotest notion of that circumstance was exceedingly troubling. Though she had no clue as to Georgiana's motive, Elizabeth only knew that, had she been a better sister to her, she might have anticipated it. A full circle of self-recrimination.

It was when she was packing up some baby items that Elizabeth came across the quilt Alexander's mother had sewn for him. She wrapped it in a scarf and tied it with a ribbon. In time, she would send it to Kirkland, for the baby must know his mother loved him. It had only been the day before that they had received word of Mary's *quietus*. Elizabeth fancied she could hear the tolling of the passing bell in the morning's stillness.

That quiet was resoundingly broken by a tremendous yawp downstairs. It sounded as if an army had just been encamped in their lobby and Elizabeth, in the direst dregs of pessimism, hurried to see what had next claimed misery. And as she should have known, if one expects the worst, one is rarely disappointed. From the top of the stairs, Elizabeth saw misery itself standing in their vestibule. Wearing a bonnet with an obscenely large ostrich plume and a nose for the affliction of others, Lady Catherine de Bourgh had come to call once more.

At the sight of the Detestable Doyenne of Distress, Elizabeth could feel herself droop. For Lady Catherine to arrive upon her threshold this early in the day, she must have left Rosings well before sunrise. It did not betoken a pleasant encounter. But Eliz-abeth wrapped her shawl resolutely about her and came down the stairs with as much dignity as she could invoke. This time, she attempted little civility, but she would not deny Darcy's aunt entrance into his house (no matter how vehemently she had threat-ened to do just that).

Lady Catherine's admittance, however, was not couched with anything more than rudimentary courtesy. Elizabeth did not speak in greeting, merely nodded blandly in Lady Catherine's direction. She intended to lead her into the grand salon, but in the considerable disdain that lady could muster, she pushed past her and into Darcy's library. Elizabeth did not particularly mind the affront, for that room afforded more privacy and she was certain words would be spoken that she did not want overheard. Indeed, Lady Catherine did not take a seat when Elizabeth motioned politely in the direction of a chair, but claimed her ground in the midmost of the carpet. Defensively,

Elizabeth crossed the study to Darcy's desk, turned and stood as well, folding her arms in front of her. Lady Catherine at first did not speak, possibly awaiting Elizabeth. Unaware of Lady Catherine's drama, Elizabeth merely raised her eyebrow at the woman, silent. Lady Catherine came to her, it was she who must ask.

But Lady de Bourgh did not come in query, for she had her own resources and she had heard. And that was what she announced.

"Young woman, I have had word."

Thereupon she added the odd demand, "You will take leave of this house."

Elizabeth knew it was inevitable she exposed an expression of dumbfounded incredulity and hastily reclaimed it. Seeing she had caught her off guard, Lady Catherine moved in post-haste to mark a coup.

"Yes, I know it all," she said. "My nephew is dead, my niece lost. What you have wrought upon this house!"

The declaration of her husband's death hit her like a slap in the face. She refused, however, to allow Lady Catherine to have the whip-hand over any part of her. Elizabeth might worry about it prodigiously, but no one would declare her husband dead until she stood over his cold, dead body. It was a point from which she would not waver.

Presenting a somewhat wavering facade of unflappability, Elizabeth, nevertheless, said evenly, "I am sorry you have been caused undue distress. My husband is in good health. My sister-in-law is well. You have no reason for concern."

"Play no parlour games with me, young woman! With Darcy's death, I am his closest blood-relative. This house will be entailed to me and whatever you may think, I can make you remove yourself. There is no heir and you shall not be welcome as his widow!"

Again, and with even more resolve, Elizabeth repeated, "My husband is in good health, madam. My sister-in-law is in good health as well."

Lady Catherine began to wail, "They are dead! Darcy is dead! Had he married my daughter none of this would have bechanced!"

"No," Elizabeth thought meanly, "he would have a bunch of sickly, bucktoothed children."

Lady Catherine began to keen, "Now he is dead! What you have wrought! What you have wrought!"

The plume upon the woman's bonnet bobbed incessantly back and forth, to and fro with each belaboured pronouncement. Finally, Elizabeth quite lost herself.

Slamming open the top drawer of Darcy's desk, she picked up the pistol, the very pistol that Darcy had so recently reminded her how to cock. It was heavier than she remembered, and she held it with both hands, in fortune, for they were both needed to draw back the hammer and take aim just above Lady Catherine's nose.

As Elizabeth's bead was drawn, Lady Catherine's eyes came into focus beyond the sight. They had widened profoundly. Furious yet, Elizabeth did not find enough satisfaction in this. Thus, she took her aim slightly higher, and squeezed both triggers at once.

In the relatively large library, the gun sounded much louder than it had those days in practise upon the lawn. Too, the smoke and powder had disappeared with more dispatch in the outdoor air. Hence, there were a few seconds when Elizabeth could not see Lady Catherine and thought her to have swooned. Waving one hand in front of her to clear her eye-line, Elizabeth's vision gradually claimed sight of Lady Catherine standing yet exactly where she had. Elizabeth was impressed with the old crone's fortitude, for the resounding boom of the gun had frightened her from its grip, and she was not the one at whom it had been aimed.

The smoke cleared, enabling Elizabeth to have a better view of Darcy's aunt. She had stood her ground, but her face betrayed more mortified terror than Elizabeth might have ever found for her in her sweetest of daydreams. Lady Catherine yet clung to her walking stick, but her bonnet had stopped bobbing, possibly because the plume upon her hat had been cut in two. The top half was only then wafting to the floor at her feet.

If being fired upon was not shock enough for the lady, Elizabeth had dropped her shawl to take aim. Thus, when her unsteady gaze finally rested, it was upon the decided bulge in Elizabeth's midsection.

Lady Catherine did not take her leave with any courtesies, but she did take leave in haste and Elizabeth desired nothing else. By the time she had reached the door, it was flung open for her by two burly Pemberley footmen, and just behind them stood Mrs. Reynolds. It was at that moment Elizabeth knew Darcy had laid instructions for them upon bechancing a visit by his aunt.

One of the men said, "Mrs. Darcy, ma'am, pray, is everything well?"

Knowing it was useless to deny the gunpowder in the air, Elizabeth nonetheless did not leave her position from behind Darcy's desk before kicking the yet smoking gun out of sight.

"Yes. Yes, it is quite all-right, just a slight accident. Everything is quite well."

She walked from behind Darcy's desk. The men backed out, following in the wake of Darcy's aunt's hastily retreating heels. (It was at this point that Elizabeth considered making a run for the window to gauge the overbites upon Lady Catherine's coachmen, but restrained herself.) Instead, Mrs. Reynolds entered and she and Elizabeth met midmost in the room. They both looked at the floor at the same time. It was the most difficult decision Elizabeth had been called upon to make for several weeks.

Should she tell Mrs. Reynolds that the puddle at their feet where the feather rested was the result of Lady Catherine's excited incontinence, or give blame to the dogs?

72

But a day later and a few miles away from the Charleroi debacle a slow, low drum roll was heard. It kept eerie beat and lent even greater menace to a dark line of advancing French infantry. The British held fast to the top of a small ridge at Quatre-Bras. From his vantage atop Scimitar, Fitzwilliam stood in his stirrups and could see the feet of British soldiers in front of him begin to shift in anticipation of the clash only minutes away. Scimitar began his own skittish dance and jigged in place. Fitzwilliam leaned down and patted the horse's neck, speaking to him in murmuring reassurance.

For most soldiers, this was the moment of greatest dread: that of the brief, agonising wait with the enemy in sight, but not near enough to engage. These few minutes of delay were crucial that day, for the half-dozen cannons that would be their only true means of defence had only just arrived and were creaking far too slowly into position. The massive column of Napoleon's army began their assent of the hill. Scimitar danced in place again.

Fitzwilliam's company had endeavoured with feverish haste to shore up the allied line at this point. And as always, as if as much by an unseemly evil intuition as military astuteness, Napoleon's generals seemed to know just where to drive their wedge to breach the enemy position. Covering this weak spot was only a brief and miserly triumph for the allied. As the weakest link, it was there that they would bear the brunt of the assault of this particular battle. The French artillery behind their troops was now within a half mile and Fitzwilliam could hear the first salvos that landed short of the British line.

Finally, theirs could respond and did, but only sporadically, for the ammunition had arrived tardy of the cannons.

Their own volleys were falling short of the French and Fitzwilliam could see the men make scurried correction to the lay of the cannons. He eyed one cannon specifically and watched the rhythm closely as it was loaded, primed, aimed, then fired. The power of the shot lifted the heavy gun upward, then hard backward with the percussion, as even the cannoneers cringed away. Hastily it was loaded, primed, aimed, and fired once more. Fitzwilliam made a mental calculation. First, one blast was shot off a minute, then two, then, blessedly, three. Their own cannons up to speed bestowed precious little time for self-congratulation, for they were immediately assaulted by incoming fire. The assault decimated their tightly packed ranks, mangling both bodies and equipment.

By the time the enemy had been engaged, the single shot had been expended from every soldier's rifle, and the bayonet rendered the weapon an unwieldy sword. Howbeit Fitzwilliam knew himself to be a particularly conspicuous target atop Scimitar and wearing the plumed hat of regimental leader, he had not drawn the most jeopardous undertaking. That fell to the lead infantrymen. It was they who had the poor prospect and unjust duty of meeting, bayonet to bayonet, the first of Napoleon's finest. These demonically hungry and worse, foolhardy, French soldiers were not ordered, but chose, to bloody themselves upon British knives.

As these frontiersmen began to bludgeon and stab, the cannon fire yet crossing landed upon enemy and defender without discrimination (victory being more urgent than economy in this particular battle). At one time Napoleon's weighty army would have deployed right through a position as slim as theirs, but politics and desertion had taken away what leverage greater numbers afforded the French.

This fight was a face-to-face encounter and the blood that splattered from it was an odious and unseemly repetition of the earlier rain. Had not every soldier's ears been deafened by the cacophony of arms, the screams of agony and rage would have been indiscernible of origin.

The first waves of French were repelled by the incline as much as military might, but the sight of these ferocious troops falling back lured some amongst the allied to move forward to crush them. But that was not the battle plan. They held and waited to be assaulted again. When it came, the next movement of French troops had again to fight the incline, but were now also hindered by the obstacle of dead bodies and abandoned equipment already fallen victim to the fight.

The French cannons volleyed yet into the British and Belgian troops, yet the second attempt by Napoleon's army took even greater toll upon both sides. Three British cannons had been silenced, hence, the throat-razing sting of gunpowder that filled every man's lungs came mostly from below.

Seeing the artillery might fight victory for them, the French cavalry poised at the side chosen for encounter. It was what Fitzwilliam had come to France to find. As ranking officer, all eyes were upon him. It would be at his signal, and not before, that they would draw their swords. A few horses shuddered, reflecting the anxiousness of their riders, not a good sign when coolness in the face of a charge meant all.

"Steady, lads. Show no hurry," Fitzwilliam called out in a low, reassuring voice.

With that admonition, he drew his sword and held it first high, thereupon rested it upon his shoulder. The order was followed with such precision, the blades of three hundred men made but a single sound as they were drawn. It was Scimitar who took the first step into battle; the regiment followed suit, first into a barely contained trot, from thence, a slow canter.

As they rode their horses shoulder to shoulder, the regiment of horse soldiers awaited the bellowing of the one word that would send them to their destiny. When it was sounded, it was Fitzwilliam who issued the command.

Every cavalryman raised his sword high above his head, and as each kicked their horses into a hard run, they stood forward in their stirrups and pointed their sabres toward the enemy.

"Charge!"

After the battle had been decided, the allied demarche demanded those who could to strive on to Paris behind the Prussians as occupation troops. Those injured were pouring back toward the English Channel to return home. Those men whose wounds demanded they not travel farther were cared for at the makeshift hospitals. If they had two legs upon which to hobble, they were directed on to Boulogne. The war was over more quickly than it began. Darcy had not yet found Georgiana, but was heartened. For if his information was correct, he was certain she would be at the abandoned villa that lay upon the road he trod.

Initially, he had chastised himself for the two weeks he spent getting to Brussels. However, they proved to be not so unproductive after all. Once there, he had a chance conversation with the wife of an attaché to Wellington, who had the good fortune to accompany her husband from Vienna to Brussels. (Anticipating fighting the next day, the general and his wife made the curious choice to attend the duchess of Richmond's heralded ball. She and her husband invited Darcy to join them, but he decried lack of evening attire in his bedroll, and declined.) However, before they departed the general's wife told Darcy that she had been struck by one young woman within a retinue of nurses.

"She was quite unlike the other young ladies with the hospital. Very demure, very ladylike," she said.

Then, from the discretion of her fan, she asided, "I am told many of the young nurses we have brought are no better than common trollops."

That his sister was in such despicable company was not a particular comfort. But just then, her companions were the least of his concerns. The young woman the general's wife described was to be in the hospital ahead. It must be her. There could not be two such gentlewomen toiling in such an execrable place.

And if it was not she, he was not certain he could bear the disappointment.

On the heels of learning the disrepute of the nursing corps, Darcy had also heard a troubling report that Fitzwilliam's cavalry regiment had been assaulted by heavy losses,

"Barely a horse left standing," another colonel had said to him.

It was of a nagging worry, but he saw little recourse to gain information. Casualty lists were nonexistent—even deaths were only in round figures. Generals killed in battle were immediately lauded as heroes, but the individual names of the lower ranks would be long in coming.

By skirting the remaining pockets of resistance and travelling horseback, Darcy was within sight of the once-grand house by late afternoon. Progress was slow. The animal he rode was not Roux's dun and, being flay-footed and wall-eyed, owned no quality save for four legs and tail to promote himself as, indeed, a horse. But in a war such as this, Darcy thought himself lucky to have him. Two days earlier, Roux's gelding was expropriated by the military at gunpoint. It took him a day to find another (and he would never admit to anyone how much he had to pay for him).

The house had not been hard to locate. He simply followed the ever-increasing stream of dying and injured Brothers of the Blade. Thitherward, the structure was demolished and it lay open to accept the line of wounded humanity as if a giant maw.

Wellington's forces had suffered heavy losses. That was a given. However, hearing of such losses and seeing them were two entirely separate understandings. At first glance, it was easy to identify the injured as British, for all seemed to wear their red uniform jackets yet. But, in closer inspection, what appeared to be their scarlet uniform was, indeed, a uniform, not of wool, but of blood. As he rode his horse past the endless trail of mangled men, Darcy felt the appropriateness of the colour chosen for His Majesty's army. He could only draw his eyes away from the horror of the spectacle by sheer will.

He was within earshot of Wellington when the duke spoke the soon-to-be-famous words, "Nothing except a battle lost is half so melancholy as a battle won." A truly Pyrrhic victory, indeed.

Darcy kicked his horse to move ahead in order to wrest sight and mind from the hopeless vista. Ultimately overtaking the trail of injured and dying soldiers, Darcy managed to get into the court of the hospital. Having some time to perfect it, he had planned a subterfuge to gain entrance. He had decided to claim himself not a surgeon, but a civilian physician (surgeons were known to be a tatty bunch; if he were to inhabit a masquerade, it would be one of dignity). All the folderol of disguise was of little use. When presenting his assertion, no one questioned him (for what reason would someone make such a claim who was not?). He was thrust an apron and a rather dull knife. Eyeing it, he issued the considerable hope that the dirk was used to slice bandages, not men.

Once inside, chaos reigned and he tossed aside the accoutrements of his assumed profession. No questions were asked of him, only an occasional demand to step aside by someone who did not glance up.

One side of the building had been felled by cannon fire. The majestic columns yet standing cast shadows across the men who lay head to foot in rows across the marble floor of what was once a grand-ballroom, exposing a peculiarly inappropriate harlequin pattern. He estimated one hundred men in that room alone, and from what he could see, one thousand stood in line for aid. Seeing few people offering help, he walked slowly about, hoping to spot Georgiana. With each succeeding minute that passed without locating her, desperation expanded in the pit of his stomach.

At long last, he espied her.

His relief was so intense, he very nearly grasped a granite column for support. But he did not. He did what he always did. He reclaimed his countenance and his bearing before anyone had a chance to notice he had lost them. Thus restored, he watched his sister silently and from a distance.

She knelt next to a bed and held a soldier's hand in hers. Thereupon, she lifted it against her cheek. So reverently did she attend this task, it occurred to him that she might have joined a convent. But her sleeves were rolled back and her hair was tucked under a handkerchief tied at the back of her head. No blue faille, no wimple. If she were a nun, it was of no order known to England.

Wiping her hands upon her long dirty apron, she rose. Then, methodically, she made her way across the line of beds. She looked at several patients, offering a word here, patting another. Once she stopped to summon a surgeon. Thereupon, she returned to her place and took the soldier's hand in hers again.

Eventually, and reluctantly, her gaze lifted from the soldier at her side. Her eyes expertly took in the ward, evidently in quest of any new emergency. The fidelity of her assessment was stolen when her eyes chanced upon her brother. No disrespect to her dedication; he was hard to miss, standing tall and comparatively pristine as he did midmost in a palliasse-strewn room filled with bodies of filthy, suffering men. Indeed, she shook her head as if in disbelief.

There was an initial stand-off, for he stood in paternal self-consequence awaiting her to come to him. But she did not. Once he realised she would not, he closed the gap betwixt them himself in several long strides. With the understanding that she had won a considerable concession, she rose and turned to him. Her countenance, nonetheless, was somewhat belligerent.

He had not come all that distance to be thwarted by a less than inviting mien. Folding her in an embrace of far greater vehemence than either could recollect sharing, he made himself not scold her. Words of love and reassurance poured from him with such ease, one would have never guessed it was the first time he had said them to her. He did not query her except of her health, for she looked tired. She shook off such inquiries and initiated a truly terse exchange.

"Pray, did you come for me or Geoffrey?"

"Fitzwilliam?"

"He is here."

"Wounded?"

"Yes."

"Badly?"

"Yes."

Upon inquiry as to where Fitzwilliam lay, she looked at her own hand and said, simply, "Here." In her grip, she still held the bandaged man's hand.

Fitzwilliam was unrecognisable. An involuntary gasp escaped Darcy, for he had not steeled himself for what he would see. Fitzwilliam's head was swathed in bandages, obscuring most of his face. His leg too looked ghastly, wrapped and bloodied as well. Georgiana knelt again and talked to him in a whispered voice.

"Darcy is here, Geoffrey. All is well."

Darcy could see Fitzwilliam nod feebly; he moved closer and knelt. Advised by Nurse Darcy to put his lips near Fitzwilliam's ear, Darcy did as he was told. At the sound of his voice, he raised his hand and Darcy grasped it. They spoke only a few moments. Most of those were spent offering impotent words of reassurance to each other.

He rose, cleared his throat, and then busied himself asking Nurse Darcy the exact nature of the colonel's wounds.

"His sight is questionable…" Her voice shook, so she calmed herself before continuing, "His eyes are burned in some manner, maybe by a cannon—no one knows."

Thereupon, she pointed to his leg and whispered, "'Tis desperate, I am afraid."

Now that his sister was found and a determination made of Fitzwilliam's condition, he was of the opinion everything was manageable. Provided, thenceforward, that he was the manager.

"The filth here is insupportable. He must be moved."

Her face brightened at the possibility, "Do we have the means?"

In any other circumstances that would have been an absurd query, the Darcys had the means for anything they so chose. At that moment, he had only an exceedingly unworthy mount, but it was, technically, a means. They counselled about it.

Darcy talked of fashioning a drag upon which to lay Fitzwilliam. (It would be undeniably crude, for Darcy had not fashioned anything for himself since he was a child, but they could not throw him over the saddle.) Georgiana bid a surgeon's opinion. He announced it not only crude, but also unfeasible. He said if they attempted to move Fitzwilliam in such a manner, he was more than likely to die.

"Every day you do not move him will better prepare him for when you do," but under his breath he muttered, "if the man lives at all."

Hitherto of no particular regard of surgeons, Darcy's disdain was unmitigated by this one questioning his plans. Somewhat imperiously, he insisted that a hospital such as this would not aid in anyone's recovery.

"And what do you suggest as an alternative?" Darcy inquired.

Clearly exasperated (and a bit imperious, himself), the surgeon said, "You move this man, it is at risk of his life. Forgive me, I have many others to whom I must attend."

Having abused the surgeon's good-will irreparably, Georgiana glared at her brother. He, however, was unmoved. He cared little for a lowly surgeon's good opinion. Nor should she. Employing questionable logic, he endeavoured to convince her to leave Fitzwilliam at the hospital and venture home. If she would go, he would stay. But she would not have it.

She said, "As long as Geoffrey is not repaired, I shall stay with him. I did not come all this way to take leave of him when he needs someone most."

He looked at his sister queerly for a moment, but only a moment.

Ultimately, they reached, if not an agreement, at least a meeting of the minds. He would find a way for them all to repair to England together, otherwise no one would leave. It was only within that conversation that Darcy learnt (for if horses were scarce commodities, maps were even more so) that Lille was but a few miles away. Lille and Cousin Roux's villa. And Cousin Roux's teeming stables.

The answer to their dilemma was at hand! He kissed Georgiana's forehead and told her he would be back from Roux's villa with a waggon as expeditiously as possible.

His every thought since leaving Pemberley had been to find his sister. As frantic as he was, he had thought little of how they would return home, presuming only that it would be the same way whence they had come. He had not begun to consider taking a wounded man with them. Allowing his sister, or even Fitzwilliam, to stay in that appalling ward was unconscionable. If he had to, he would move mountains and kings to get them both home.

He located his detestable excuse for a horse and, with more precision than elegance, turned him toward Lille. So cheered had Georgiana been by the notion of getting Fitzwilliam home, he dared not tell her there was a possibility that Roux's house might have been pillaged. It was with that apprehension foremost in mind that he travelled the distance to his cousin's villa.

But that did not discourage his plans. He would borrow a waggon, load Fitzwilliam and Georgiana. Thereupon make haste for Calais. If he had to, he would purchase a schooner. He would christen it *The Elizabeth*. All would be well once they were upon their way to England.

So grand were his schemes, it would only gradually occur to him that his sister's reason for coming to battle was, indeed, for love, but not for any of the suitors he had feared.

"Was Fitzwilliam a suitor?" Darcy wondered ever so fleetingly, thereupon dismissed it.

Certainly, such esteem was not returned. Unsuitable suitors, or unrequited love— neither were what he would have chosen for her. Sequentially, he began to chew upon a particularly tough nut. For he had to admit to himself that if he was so blind as to not recognise his sister's regard for Fitzwilliam, he could not truly account for Fitzwilliam, either. It was all too confounding.

In the face of life and death, Darcy's pragmatic mind put the impracticality of romance aside and concentrated upon something more in his control. A waggon.

When the war erupted, Georgiana and the *corps d'elite* of nurses were unceremoniously dumped into a semi-demolished house. Thereupon, they were influenced to ready themselves for work. As soldiers were hauling branches to fashion cots and litters, Georgiana tore bandages and continually stole looks at the gate to the courtyard, consumed with fear for what she would soon see come through it. She relaxed her guard somewhat when their first patient was a soldier who had no more complaint than a belly-ache from being reconnoitred beneath a heavily burdened crab-apple tree.

As she sat ripping cloth into narrow strips, it dawned upon her just how far from Derbyshire she was. And the entire endeavour had begun with a very sudden scheme. She had toyed with the idea upon overhearing the raging discussion in her brother's library. But she did not believe it feasible until she saw John Christie stalking angrily away from Pemberley. He did not tell her, and she dared not inquire, what had angered him into leaving. His demeanour suggested some sort of bad blood.

When she saw it took no more effort from him than to simply walk down the road to go, she suddenly heard herself calling out to him to wait. Not surprisingly, John had been disinclined of her company, so she resorted to the bribery of expeditious transportation. The decision to take her life upon her own course was made in that good time.

The magnitude of the change in her circumstances was apparent to her from that first night. As someone who drifted off to sleep upon the comfort of silk sheets and by the tinkling of a music box, Georgiana was kept awake as much by the clamouring noise that accompanied their accommodations as the smell. She lay her shawl daintily atop the batting cot and reminded herself such accommodations might be the best she enjoyed for some time. Thus, she practised not noticing the noise or the lumpy bed. Of lice, she dared not ponder.

Had it not been for John's friendship and his coincidental decision to take leave of Pemberley, she was certain she would not have had the courage to do what she had. Getting to Portsmouth had been relatively simple. Getting to the continent had been difficult, but hardly the severest obstacle she faced.

Forthwith, the whimsical start to her nursing career was hastily forgotten. That soldier with the collywobbles was soon usurped by scores of others. These were grievously wounded. Thus, he was remanded into service as an orderly by Georgiana. Now that she had not the time, she handed him a stack of fabric with the admonition to start tearing bandages. For having been the recipient of barked orders from the onset, Georgiana had mindlessly found a stronger voice herself. And mindlessness would be her only retreat.

Field nurses were desperately needed, but that did not keep the overworked doctors from overworking the ones they had, perchance knowing there was nowhere for them to flee from service. That they were in such need was fortunate for Georgiana, who could diagnose the croup but, at first, had no notion as to how to mend gunshot victims.

Fortuitously, she found a medical niche. It was one of her gifts. She had always needled delicate, lovely screens. All her life, everyone had told her she handled a needle with greater finesse than did any other lady. Hence, the surgeons learnt to call upon Georgiana when it was time to sew wounds together. The needles were similar in curvature to her embroidery ones, but heavier. She had only to alter her technique slightly to accommodate the weight of the catgut through skin. Her stitches were universally admired, when there was time. But ordinarily there was not and she soon abandoned her small, neat stitch for a longer one that embraced speed.

The sight and smell of blood eventually became mundane. It was a very specific moment in time when she realised that as fact. It came the minute of the hour of the day when she, with no qualm, put her knee in the back of a struggling man to still him so she could sew his oozing cheek—his oozing *gluteus maximus* cheek—she knew it was all routine. She also understood fully why she had to claim to be a wife to have this duty, for whatever their need of assistance, as an innocent she would never be given leave to witness the intimacy of the soldiers' bodies.

And as mundane as blood had become, so had men's bodies. After she had seen the first one, she saw no reason for all the mystery. Were they not all, more or less, the same? What silliness, she had thought, society thinking that it must protect women from this intelligence. She certainly did not feel tainted by the sight of a man's body, just the sight of what another man's weapon had done to it. The glory of war was certainly lost to her.

Indifference to the gore was one understanding, indifference to death was quite another matter. Regardless how familiar the premortal gasp became to her, she could not witness the *quietus* with any degree of froideur.

Death was ghastly. However, not dying was occasionally worse.

The one area of service she avoided was the area near an opening in a wall where the amputations were committed. The screams of the wounded held nothing to those who had to be held down to have a limb severed. (Those surgeons most appreciated were ones whose expertise with the saw made their amputation most brief. One gentleman was so adept, he could sever a leg with six strokes in less than half a minute.) It was understandable, therefore, when a surgeon called to her to aid them with a delirious soldier in that area, she hesitated. But only for a moment. There was but one way to do what she had to do. That was to do it. She went thither with no more contemplation.

A soldier lay upon a cot, his eyes bandaged, his leg mangled. The surgeons intended to amputate, but the man was struggling with such vociferous insistence, he could not be reasoned with. Before she had a chance to learn the surgeon's bidding, she recognised her cousin's voice.

He was repeating, "You shan't take my leg. You shall not take my bloody leg!" She stopped at the end of Fitzwilliam's bed and told the others there, "I know this man."

In only those few words, Fitzwilliam, far more lucid than they had supposed, recognised her voice. Automatically, he reverted to his drawing room tone, "Georgiana? Georgiana. Forgive me, I thought we were yet in France."

So relieved did he sound, Georgiana abhorred having to tell him he was not home. But again, as she had become accustomed, she did what had to be done.

"Yes, Fitzwilliam, 'tis I, but you are yet in France. Fear not, you are not alone anymore," and took his hand reassuringly.

The surgeon interrupted, "You know this man? Tell him his leg must come off now. We have not time for this."

Georgiana stood and told him, "Pray, can you not take the time? For there are many others here who await your knife."

The man turned away in frustration and Georgiana gave her attention back to Fitzwilliam.

"Can you see?"

He said, "The light causes fierce pain. I am not certain I can see. My eyes have been covered for days. But that will heal or not. They must not take my leg! It is imperative, Georgiana!"

She lifted the bloody muslin from his wound. It had begun to fester and redden, a very bad sign. She sighed. There was no time for the niceties.

"I see no alternative. If they do not take your leg, you will surely die. They do not need your permission. They shall do it without it, for they think you delirious."

"Delirious? Delirious? My denial of their taking my leg is proof enough of my lucidity, is it not?"

Evidently, he was not delirious. However, she could see he was fighting for consciousness. A bit of blood had dried on his ears, but not much. Perhaps it was from a percussion.

Hesitantly, she let her eyes light upon the pile of mis-mated and thus useless boots lying in the corner. All had been culled from severed feet and legs. There simply were no words of comfort for such an ordeal. She allowed herself to rest her cheek lightly against his shoulder. Her breath wafted softly against his. Sensing it, he reached out and stroked her face once. But he let his fingers tarry.

"Georgiana," he implored, "you must not let them take my leg. I am a cavalryman. It is not what I do. It is who I am. I will not be who I am if they take my leg."

His voice had weakened and she could barely hear his last words as he drifted off. His fingers dropped away from her face.

Terror-stricken that he would not reawaken, she was grateful too for what peace he found. If they were to take his leg, they best do it, for his sake, whilst unconscious. If they were to take it. She wondered if Fitzwilliam understood the magnitude of what he asked of her. How could she assign him death? But how could she let them take his leg and his will from him? The surgeon was returning with two other men again with a determined look upon his face.

Again, she did what had to be done. She pointed to a location on the far side of the ward.

"This man will be moved."

The beleaguered surgeon said, "Madam, you said you know this man. If this true, you must know that he is not just any colonel. I shall not be held responsible for his death when he could be saved."

"My good doctor, I am this man's family. I shall sign any paper you might want. I shall bear responsibility to the others in his family."

Her resolve was somewhat humbled, but held steadfast as the doctor looked at her suspiciously, for this was not what she had claimed as her circumstance.

"My name is Georgiana Darcy."

The doctor blinked several times.

"I came here to see to this man. My name is Georgiana Darcy," she repeated.

"Of the Pemberley Darcys?" The doctor spoke more a statement than a query.

"Yes."

"I see."

They left to find Fitzwilliam room against the far wall, and Georgiana leaned down next to him again to wait. Endeavouring with all her might not to cry, she took his hand and held it to her face. Thinking him yet unconscious, he surprised her when he took her hand and pressed the back of it to his lips.

It was with a sizeable sigh of deliverance that Darcy approached Roux's house and saw it had been neither abandoned nor ransacked. A half dozen horses milled about in a paddock. Twilight approached, and he could see a glow through the windows announcing the house had been lit for the evening.

It occurred to him to dismount away from the house and walk up. His pride was mortified by having to hand the reins of his disreputable ride to a groom. The man did look oddly at him. Of this, Darcy took notice and admitted his vanity should be ignored. If his mount lent him ridicule, his person fared him little better. He suspected his figure presented quite the spectacle. Even in a time and country of only sporadic baths. His face and hands were but the only parts of his body to be acquainted with water for better than a fortnight. His costume fared yet little better. Whilst in Brussels, he simply bought new shirts as they were needed (for not only did he refuse to wash his own laundry, it was an affront to have to locate a laundress). By the time he reached Roux's, this persistence of station reckoned him only one change of shirt in his saddlebag and that one had more grime from the road than the one he wore.

However ignoble his attire, his arrival was lauded exuberantly as Roux came rushing onto the portico to greet him. Not questioning whence he came or why, Roux immediately clapped his hands and shouted, thereby sending servants scurrying to see to Mr. Darcy.

But Darcy impatiently waved their ministrations aside. He turned to Roux and, in his anxiety, well-nigh grasped the man's lapel, keeping from it only by reason of an inborn, and thus unshakeable, sense of propriety. Collected, he made enquiry in his most sedate *comme il faut* voice (and quite incongruous to the disrepute of his aspect).

"Viscount, could I possibly impose upon you for the use of a waggon?"

Having no further need for French, Darcy spoke in English. When Roux assured him that was no bother, Darcy asked to be shown to it immediately.

"Now?" Roux asked, in English as well. "Surely you do not mean to take leave again at once? Crepuscule is upon us. You are tired. You must eat and rest. I insist you must. Nothing can be accomplished this evening. I insist."

With that, Roux hastened his servants again and Darcy did not protest more, for night was quickly descending. By the time the waggon was hitched, it would be totally dark and a sky endowed with only an old crescent moon would render it unsafe not to wait until morning. Hence, he acquiesced to Roux's exhortations. It would be an insult if he did not allow him to be a generous host. Nevertheless, he felt a prickly irritation overtaking him. He was so precipitously near to rescuing Georgiana, only to have darkness confine him.

Surrendering to his better judgement, he reluctantly followed a servant up the spiralling staircase. Once in the sumptuous chamber, he threw his dusty bedroll in a chair and sat heavily upon the embroidered bedcover whilst fleetingly wondering if his soiled breeches would stain it. Not truly a salient issue at that point, he set his full attention to tugging off his boots. (Under the best of circumstance, this duty was a difficult manoeuvre, made even more labourious, as it happened, by the fact they had not been removed for the better part of a week.) Accepting a footman's presented backside, he placed his foot thence, allowing himself help in divesting one tall boot. That effort sapped the last bit of vigour he possessed, and with success of only the one, he lay back upon the bed.

The sound of the copper tub being filled in the next room did not wake him from his sleep.

When a manservant rapped upon his door calling him to supper, Darcy sat up with a start and an unintended expletive. In the darkened room, he needed a moment to remember where he was. When he did, he also was reminded he had not partaken of food since morning. His appetite had returned with a vengeance. Gathering his bearings, he noticed his bedroll where he had tossed it upon the chair and retrieved it.

Laying it upon the bed, he carefully unfurled it, picked up his soiled shirt, and unwrapped that with care as well. Inside the shirt were the two miniatures he had carried with him from England. Elizabeth's was yet wrapped in the bobbin lace he had impetuously bought for her after seeing it in a window in a Brussels shop. (It was suggested *Ville d'Lille* had finer, but he was not cooling his heels in that town.)

Unwinding the lace, he gazed at her likeness nestled in the palm of his hand. He stroked it affectionately for a moment and then set it upon the table next to the bed. Only then did he go to the dressing room and plunge his hand into the tub's water. It was cold, but that was not a barrier to bathing. Gingerly, he slid into the water, gradually acquainting his skin with its temperature until he submerged his head. When he came up, he slung the water from his face.

Before him, he saw a fresh set of clothes and the retrieved bag that had divested them. After months of inhumane existence, Darcy thought it curious how easily his body surrendered to civility.

He was already buttoning his waistcoat when the manservant returned to help him dress. Quite contrite to have been tardy of his task, the man fussed unnecessarily with Darcy's costume. Darcy waved him away, realising he had become quite used to tending himself.

Hungry as he was, when he entered the hall, the tinkle of forks to china and the murmur of voices in the distance below announced Roux was entertaining other guests. The idea of company almost bade him ask for something to be brought up to partake in the silence of his room. But Roux's hospitality required more of him. As he intended to ask additional imposition upon his cousin, he tried not to think of the circumstances of Georgiana and Fitzwilliam. It was prudent to attempt to repay his host's kindness by being, if charming was an impossibility, at least a pleasant guest. Preparing a speech of apology of tardiness on the way, he went downstairs.

The doors to the dining-room were flung back with considerable flourish upon his arrival. At the announcement of his presence, all twelve sets of eyes turned uniformly in his direction. To the person, all were *grand parure*. Their attention was disconcerting. His *deshabille* in the face of their formal-wear even more off-putting (he was quite happy to have gotten the grime from beneath his fingernails). It had been a monumental misjudgement to think he should join company for dinner. He was far too committed to the room, however, to flee then.

Roux rose and motioned him to a seat of honour. Other than somewhat mumbling his apologies, however, he took the chair evincing all punctilious regard. Albeit he appeared self-possessed, he was not. Notwithstanding the lack of proper costume, it had been a long time since he had entered a room such as this without Elizabeth upon his arm. His unease of society reasserted itself. Regrettably, the distinction of his seating included the company of Roux's daughter, Celeste, to his right.

With Darcy's first glance at her, he caught himself in a sharp intake of air. For he glimpsed Roux's daughter in profile, and she had the same dark hair and round cheek as Elizabeth. The spell was broken when she returned his stare with a little snort of a giggle. She was exceedingly pretty, but her face was narrow, her eyes deep set. And though those eyes batted provocatively at him, they were not like Elizabeth's. It was a fleeting moment, but it left him unsettled.

Celeste may well have misinterpreted Darcy's expression, for she embarked upon an assault of flirtation with him that would have been worthy of Lydia Bennet Wickham.

Light conversation never came easily to him, but he did not want to offend his host's daughter (whom he immediately deduced had more hair than sense), thus gave his own understanding of politeness and nodded noncommittally to her comments. His dinner neighbour had no intention of being slighted, and supposing her initial efforts were too modest, she gushed ever more grandly. She induced from Darcy, however, nothing but his infamous monosyllabic replies.

This bombardment of Celeste Roux's romantic arrows was not quieted until she finally relented and put a spoonful of soup in her mouth. The conversational lull was usurped by their other dinner companions. All were French, and all had been politely waiting for their host's daughter to desist before querying *Monsieur D'arcy*. He was asked what were the British intentions in light of their rout of Napoleon.

Not so fluent as Roux, his guests peppered Darcy with rapid French. Having to field questions of a political nature, in a language not his first, certainly did not remove his unease. Had he expected his cousin to shield him in some manner, he would have been disappointed. For it was apparent that the guests were under the misapprehension that Darcy was some sort of government emissary. Roux sat at the head of his table in beaming pride, obviously the producer of this misinformation of his relation's appointment to government. (Darcy saw he should have been more forthcoming with his reason for being in France.) Another time he would have been amused (or possibly insulted, for though Roux might, Darcy hardly thought the label diplomat an elevation of his own status). This evening's interrogation was the last thing he would have hoped for and he looked at his wineglass in gratitude.

Grateful too he would have been to find reprieve with his fork, but the entrée was *cochon de lait* and he despised pork. Hence, he made great pretence of moving the meat about his plate and imprudently swilled his wine. It was only over it that he took the time or had the inclination to glance down the table at the other guests.

Across the table, four persons down, sat Juliette Clisson.

She looked almost exactly as she had upon the walk in front of Harcourt. She did not look at him, listening in apparent raptness as she was to the dinner guest just to her left. Darcy dropped his eyes back to his plate (in such disorder he partook of several bites of pork before he realised his error). He could not stop himself from stealing a glance again just to make certain his eyes had not deceived him.

Certainly she had recognised his name, if not his countenance, when he was introduced. But the discretion that she had always exhibited upon his behalf had not abandoned her. That was most probably the reason he once had sought her company solely—her discretion. He knew she would not acknowledge his acquaintance in company. With Juliette Clisson dining with his cousin, Darcy looked about the table taking measure of the other guests. He knew Roux to be married, but after two trips to the continent, he had yet to meet Viscountess Roux. She was absent this night as well. In her place, even with his daughter present, were a number of women who appeared to be *filles de joie*. He had to wonder, in the light of the chateau's lack of plunder when all around his were devastated, just what sort of home he had. A demimonde with vacillating politics?

The dinner companion to Darcy's left (he did not catch her name, simply understood it as something with many vowels) he knew well, too, was a lady of expansive sensibilities. In his lengthy silences, she and Celeste Roux chose to parry each other's overtures to him. When the endless dinner ended, neither had truly deflected the other, thus each took possessively of an arm and escorted him into the drawing room. If he thought he would find respite with smoke, cognac, and the company of men in serious query of the most expeditious way to England, he was disappointed. French custom did not divorce the ladies from the gentlemen in after-dinner discourse.

Whilst demurring, Roux ushered him into the drawing room. Darcy dropped his arms, the motion insisting both women release him, and headed for the fireplace. It had always been his most useful ploy, this keen interest in the fire (the window, his shoes), by which manner he was normally successful in disassociating himself from his company. But not that night. When he reached the mantel, he turned abruptly, causing a chain reaction betwixt the closely ensuing females.

All told, it was all quite unnerving.

Roux, however, only refilled his wineglass. Resolving to fend for himself, Darcy took a generous swallow from his newly replenished glass, thereupon gingerly removed from his person the hand (which she was running lovingly beneath his lapel) of the woman with the unintelligible name. And, trying not to sound too prim, he did as courtesy demanded (stating the reverse) and thanked her for her attention.

"I am here upon a mission for my family, and have neither the time nor the inclination for diversion."

She stamped her foot in petulance, and lamented, "The first handsome man I have seen in six months and I cannot entice him."

Roux roared with laughter at this, "I see you denigrate your host as not handsome. I fancy I am too old to be thought that by such a young woman."

The woman rethought her remark to Roux and offered, "You do not count, Viscount, for I have already enticed you!"

Roux roared again. His daughter apparently thought Darcy's rebuff to the "woman to his left" in her own favour and smiled at him fetchingly, obviously not insulted by, or more possibly, oblivious to, the woman's remark to her mother's husband. Alas, it was difficult to think entirely unkindly of a man who did not mind a jest at his own expense. Roux was indubitably an irredeemable reprobate, but a charming one.

The woman stamped her foot again, "There are no men here, they have all been killed or are playing at battle. Even the footmen have maimed themselves in order to avoid conscription."

Without compunction or further comment, the meretriciously inclined woman chose to plumb more inviting waters about the room. The Viscount smiled ruefully at Darcy, tapping his forefinger upon his wineglass as he did. Motioning toward Darcy's just divested admirer, he inquired, "Are you all that weary from your sojourn?"

"I am fatigued from my trip, but that is not why I declined."

Roux seemed taken unawares.

"Our Marie-Therese does not incite your ardour? Perchance you see another here to warm your bed."

With Celeste gazing upon him with open devotion, Darcy was quite unable to determine if Roux included his daughter as part of his hospitality. Darcy decided he must declare his position as perspicuously as possible.

"I am quite happily married, Viscount."

Roux guffawed, "What does that have to do with tonight, Monsieur Darcy?"

Despite the provocation to pontificate, Darcy said mildly, "You, of course, have not met my wife, Viscount, or you would not have expected otherwise."

"Our Voltaire said, 'The gloomy Englishman, even in his loves always wants to reason.' We in France fall less to reason and more to desire. You seem not to be your father's son in that respect, for I am certain you have heard stories of his conquests."

It took a moment for the spurious nature of this information to register to Darcy. When it did, he said rather stiffly, "Youth has its indiscretions."

Roux laughed again, "I find it so amusing that our sons think their fathers have no desires of the flesh. They think us aging eunuchs. "

"Certainly not."

"Of course you do! Gerard was not inconsolable, I assure you." Resorting to *sotto voce*, Roux continued, "I must confess though, I cannot imagine how he only came to have but a single *batard*; I myself can count at least six and I was not so successful in amour as he!"

In defence of his father's honour, Darcy very nearly made the mistake of letting loose his temper. He successfully contained it, taking another swallow of his wine (to busy his tongue lest it be otherwise inclined) knowing some men had need of assigning their own weaknesses to those about them.

Seeing the severity of Darcy's expression, Roux realised he had trespassed, laughed charmingly again, and said offhandedly, "*On dit*, a rumour, of course. Only a rumour, *Mon D'arcy*."

In occupation of wanting the matter to fall, Darcy checked his watch and saw he had spent enough time after dinner to reckon courtesy served. He almost made his apologies to Roux when he espied Juliette yet in the company of the man from dinner (who bore a seriously lubricious smile) and a notion set to work upon him.

He had posted letters to Elizabeth religiously, but at every turn was told it unlikely that they would find their way to England. Nothing other than military missives was accepted. Useless as the effort might have been, he nevertheless continued to write. This, only partly for the small chance of them reaching her; it made him feel a sense of propinquity to home. *Billets doux* to Elizabeth soothed his saturnine turns.

His presumption was that Juliette's home was yet London. It was puzzling that she bechanced to be in the north of France, but implausible or not, for his purposes, he prayed she was going, not coming. In another time, he would never have considered entering into a conversation with her in such a situation. But it was not another time, another situation. He made his apologies, but only of immediate company, and thither he went.

When he excused himself from Roux and his daughter and made his way toward the lovely Miss Clisson, it occurred to Darcy that they might believe he was impugning his own declarations. As did her oily companion, who retreated forthwith of Darcy's ingress to their group. Seeing this, Darcy hoped he had not interfered with any previous scheme Juliette might have laid, if only because he hoped to have her cooperate in a favour. To the contrary, she did not appear thwarted, but turned and held out her hand for him to kiss. As she did, she raised one eyebrow slightly and Darcy chose not to be reminded it was an expression he had often seen Elizabeth present him.

He took her fingers and kissed the back of her hand. The familiar redolence of her skin evoked memories that he would just as soon not be recalled.

"It has been a long time," he offered.

Her agreement was only by way of a slight nod, and he wondered if she remembered the day he and Elizabeth saw her upon the street in Mayfair. If she did, she did not speak of it, she only stood in silence, perchance waiting to see what brought him over to her. He had never spoken to her in a strictly social situation and he shifted uncomfortably, a demeanour, nonetheless, she knew well.

Finally he said (a little stupidly, he was certain), "It is a great surprise to bechance you here."

"Indeed, for myself as well," she answered.

"What finds you here in the face of war?"

"I might bid you the same," she countered.

Not inclined to banter, Darcy leapt directly to the point, "Do you fancy to return to England soon?"

She seemed taken unawares at this enquiry. However, she said that her overnight stop at Viscount Roux's villa with friends was not simply an entertainment, for she was travelling even then to find passage to return to London. She did not say if Roux was an acquaintance of hers or her friends. His single-minded quest of her itinerary did not include why she was in his cousin's house, just where she would go from there.

"I have only come from Verdun. I had hoped to persuade *mon pére* to return to England, for he has only me. Both of my brothers died with the emperor upon his great conquest of Russia," she gave a rueful laugh, "but Papa would not repair from my mother's grave. There is only death here and he chooses to stay with the dead."

Darcy said what he thought were the proper condolences, but found it difficult to make idle chatter when he had a specific reason to seek her conversation.

He bid, "Pray, are you returning to England directly?"

She said, "As soon as is possible."

"I wonder…" he began and then uncharacteristically hesitated. Thereupon, he began again, "I beg you to grant me a very generous favour."

"*Oui*. Of course."

"With the chaos about, I fear I have been unsuccessful in getting a letter posted to my wife. Do you think it possible for you to take one to England with you?"

"*Oui*, of course."

"It will be no trouble? I would not want to impose…"

The possibility of imposition compleatly explored, she told him she was to depart the next morning. He assured her he would have the letter for her before she took her leave. As he was preparing to excuse himself, Juliette initiated further conversation. This by way of announcing a false motive for his relinquishment.

"Please, I do not want to keep you from your companion," she said, and motioned toward the company he had just left.

Across the room, Marie-Therese was eyeing Juliette with open hostility. Rarely feeling the need to explain himself, he, however, found himself doing just that.

"The woman is a friend to my cousin, not of myself."

"I was not speaking of that *fatua mulier*, but the *vierge*, Mademoiselle Roux. She seems quite taken with you."

Taken aback by Juliette's frank and somewhat coarse denunciation of Marie-Therese, Darcy glanced toward Roux's daughter who was, indeed, looking at him in unadulterated devotion, and sputtered, "She is just a girl. Surely you do not suggest…"

"Look there. Speak but a word and I assure you she will happily surrender her virtue-knot unto you."

Heretofore quite unused to hearing virginal hymens addressed in the drawing room, he reddened and glanced about to see if they were overheard before remembering he was in French company. Hence, he did not immediately take flight, and discarded Juliette's notion.

"The girl is an innocent flirt."

"I cannot fault the girl for her acumen. If she wants to be delivered of her chastity, she could do worse than to avail herself of your amorous favours."

His crimson deepened, not only because of the nature of the praise, but that she was in a position to opine it in the first place.

Gathering together his considerable hauteur, he bowed formally, "If you will excuse me."

It was perchance fortunate that he did not see the mischievous glint in Juliette's eyes as he left her side, lest her amusement at his expense further sully his already sorely abused dignity.

Customarily the most cautious of men, Darcy knew it was unorthodox, but did not question the wisdom of requesting a woman from his past—a woman of decided intimacy from his past—to deliver a message to his wife. For he was desperate to contact Elizabeth. He must get word to her, to let her know he had found Georgiana safe, if nothing else. And that he would be home to her soon.

Seeking out Roux, he excused himself, begging his early departure the next morning. Roux, however, was not ready to let his guest leave company without a further toasting. He drank to the future, the British, the French, the weather, and eventually, simply to excess.

After only picking at his meal, and downing far more wine than he knew was wise, the inevitable occurred. The wine Darcy rarely partook befriended him far too acutely and he felt himself in his cups.

Making every effort to appear not to be, and with all the gravity of an undertaker, he bowed goodnight to Roux and his guests.

Charging down a hill would seem inordinately easier than an upward onslaught. In reality, it was more dangerous, gravity and momentum lessening manoeuvrability. If a horse was not surefooted, his rider usually plunged to the ground, as often as not being crushed beneath his (or someone else's) mount. After the initial charge whence protocol and aesthetics demanded sabres pointed heavenward, cavalrymen such as Fitzwilliam pursued the enemy in not so *recherché* a fashion. Often they wielded a pistol in their other hand, reins clutched betwixt gritted teeth.

Hence, if there was one accommodation certain to be afforded the cavalry, it was that each officer was allowed to supply his own mount. Whatever the cost in time and trouble, they brought their own horses. If cavalry was integral to success in war, and it was, the trust in one's seat in battle was an inviolate part of that success. Of course the horse Fitzwilliam rode was Scimitar; he was as much a part of Fitzwilliam's perception of himself as a cavalryman as his uniform. The horse and Fitzwilliam were in such close concert, Fitzwilliam was secure enough to abandon his reins altogether, knowing Scimitar would respond instantly to no more than the subtlest of pressure from his jack-booted knees.

By mid-battle, it became a pounding match and many of those horses along with their riders had been lost, for there was little but mangle and mess. Few infantrymen were yet fighting and horse soldiers were the only true defence remaining. The standard bearer was a stern rider who stood his ground through strong assault, but he was soon victim to the murderous cannon barrage. The standard drooped to the ground just as another man leapt from his horse to rescue it. It was essential for it to remain upright, for the yellow standard of their horse company was the symbol to which all rallied. As long as it stood, they knew from whence to regroup. Fitzwilliam did so as rote, and all able amassed to their flag, thereupon besieged the enemy once more. Each time they regrouped, their number grew fewer.

The fusillade continued, cannonball after cannonball fell like monolithic hailstones, and the horses were spooked to consider wild dashes to escape the melee. It was a separate battle just to keep them from bolting. Scimitar jumped about nervously but did not flee, his confidence in Fitzwilliam that keen. His master, however, was not compleatly undaunted, for the enemy onslaught was so savage there was not time to reload his pistol, thus his sword was given no reprieve from blood.

The French upon horseback were few, too; many horses had been dispatched. The cavalrymen not killed fought with sabre and gun from the ground. Scimitar's surefootedness had kept Fitzwilliam mounted long after others had fallen, thus giving him a height advantage, but also rendering him a blatant target. Thus, it was not the sword or the gun that brought him down, but a cannon. The shot landed to the right of Scimitar, who reared up at the explosion, the percussion finally dislodging his footing. Having no time to jump clear, the dying horse collapsed onto Fitzwilliam's leg. Knowing him mortally wounded, Fitzwilliam had little time to grieve, for as the eviscerated horse flailed in his death throes, he struggled frantically to scramble from beneath some eighty stone of horseflesh.

Before he could wriggle free, a French cavalry officer approached, his sabre resting upon his shoulder. This man too was already dead (he had a ghastly wound), but he did not know it and raised his sword. It was as if in half-time that Fitzwilliam watched the French soldier's approach and the proffering of his weapon. Desperately, he tugged at Scimitar's reins.

"Scimitar, until now you have never once given me reason to curse you."

With a moaning groan deep from his chest, the horse made one last valiant lunge and freed Fitzwilliam's crushed leg. If Fitzwilliam's decision to join Wellington had been more than simple reckless risking of his neck, possibly even suicidal, his will to live was fiercer than self-destruction. With the preternatural strength of a man not yet ready to be carried from the field upon his shield, he stood upon his one good leg and plunged his sabre into the Frenchman's beckoning chest. There was but a brief moment to savour his success before he heard the eerie whistle announcing the imminent arrival of yet another cannonball.

The missile, in fortune, did not strike him directly, but ignited a powder horn at what would have been at his feet was he yet standing. However, a burning flash seared his eyes and the force knocked Fitzwilliam backward. He tried to rise, fell, tried again, and fell once more. From thence, he heard himself scream out in pain and anger.

Lying amongst the mass of dead and writhing men and horses for an ungodly long time, he began to realise it was quite possible he would die where he was. Not from the enemy, for the battle either was over or fighting elsewhere. He could hear yet occasional salvos in the distance. But death would come as surely as the sunset, could he not stanch the blood seeping from his leg.

There was a tinkling and murmuring in the distance as unknown persons approached. He prayed they were British, not French come to finish off the wounded.

It would appear, however, the colour of the uniform was the single thing of no import to the hoards that scampered across the gore-strewn battlefield that day. They were the ragged camp-followers, both alien and allied, who were as relentless in scavenging as any London mud-lark. Without the tedious nicety of making certain their benefactors dead, they methodically stripped the bodies of their weapons, coats, boots, whatever they could heist. One inventive fellow carrying a bucket brandished a formidable pair of pinchers and inspected mouths often conveniently rendered opened by the throes of death. If he saw no gold, with the utmost delicacy, he appropriated front teeth (an incisor in good condition brought two guineas in London; not every dental deficient could afford ivory or gold).

Auspiciously, Fitzwilliam was spared this particular desecration, yet another vulture beset him for his fine boots. Someone, man or woman, he had no notion, tugged at one heel. Fortune or misfortune, the one they chose first to pilfer encased his wounded leg and at the resultant pain, he rose up wildly swinging the blade he clutched yet in his hand.

"Get back! Get back, I say!"

The unidentified despoilers promptly retreated, for there were innumerable other victims far less resistant. Of this, Fitzwilliam was not truly cognisant. For the pain and exertion of his rebellion robbed him of what little strength he had. He fell back, his arm across Scimitar's lifeless neck.

Thenceforward, he was rewarded with an unconsciousness that would take days for him to thank.

As Darcy perambulated up the stairs, they swayed unsteadily beneath him and he was grateful to have the railing to cling to. By the time he stumbled into his room and collapsed upon the bed, perspiration had broken out upon his forehead, causing him to fear he was becoming ill. That would be a mortification. It was abominable enough to admit to a little inebriation, but to be so conspicuously subjugated by intoxicants was indefensible. It was never acceptable to be out of one's wits. Especially amongst strangers. In another country. In war.

He eschewed the dressing room, for he had a matter upon which to attend (this is what he told himself, but actually he feared he might stumble and did not want even an anonymous servant to observe him in such a condition). Therefore, tossing off his jacket and wrenching free of his collar, he sat at the *escritoire* and fumbled for some parchment in a drawer, yet of the mind if he behaved soberly it would demand it of his body. But as he unsuccessfully endeavoured to focus upon the paper to write, he realised his lucidity was far too compromised to produce a coherent letter and he decided to abandon it until morning.

Picking up Elizabeth's picture, he attempted to focus upon that. When he failed at that as well, he ceded defeat. However unwise, he poured another glass of wine and lay back against the pillows, promising it was just for a minute. To let his head clear. That minute and several more did not improve his mind. His head swam. When the headiness of the drink rendered him into sleep, the glass he held dropped from his fingers and the wine spilled across his stomach and ran down his side, soaking the bedclothes. The wetness did not awaken him from his desultory dreams. Or what he thought were dreams. In some percipient limbo, he was uncertain what was conscious thought and which were actual dreams; they became confused in the tumult of his mind. He slept, awoke, thereupon slept again.

It was not surprising he thought (or dreamed) of Juliette, for he fancied he could yet smell the fragrance from her skin. Although she had crossed his mind, he had not truly thought of her since he fell in love with Elizabeth. He should have, for as much as he would like not to recollect it, she once played a particularly provocative role in his life.

It had not been an affair of the heart. There may have been some fondness, but he never once forgot his own station or hers. She was a lover but not a mistress, for exclusivity would be required. It was, was he to admit it to himself, a friendship. One in which a great deal of flesh was exchanged.

He suspected that she would have seen him without compensation. It was he who insisted upon it. For without compensation, an attachment might have occurred. He enjoyed her time, but he did not want the attachment. He wanted to be able to do what he had done when he fell in love with Elizabeth. He walked away. No promises were broken, no attachment was there to linger on.

Thenceforward of the morning he had confessed his past connexion with Juliette to Elizabeth, he was ridded of the necessity of guilt over it. That burden was given to Elizabeth to carry. It was she who must find reason and understanding, not he. In fortune he knew, for had Elizabeth been with another before she met him, to think of it might provoke him to run mad. Unreasonable. Unconscionable. But true.

With that understanding, the magnitude of the blunder he had just committed overtook him like a sudden cloudburst. He had just bid a former lover of his to carry a letter to Elizabeth. It had seemed so reasonable at the time. But how might he feel if a former lover of Elizabeth's brought him a letter from her? The thought, though muddled, incited him to consider violence. He shook his head, trying to find reason and did. Juliette would post the letter from London. She would not take it to Elizabeth. He had not blundered.

When he thought back upon their conversation, it was lost upon him that Juliette's remarks about little Celeste Roux were an indirect means to broach the chasm of time and station betwixt them. Her bit of coquetry had been an unconditional success. For it bade him think back upon their lusty (and lengthy) assignations. It would have taken him many years and many lovers to learn half what he had upon Juliette's pillow. By reason of that, her *aperçu* of Roux's daughter's maidenhood he dared not argue, for he thought her opinion upon such a matter inviolate. And if he accepted that truism, he would have to suppose her correct that the girl was intent upon him to be the one to deflower her.

Celeste's attention had been an annoyance, but he considered he could have unintentionally encouraged her. In her resemblance to Elizabeth, he may have looked upon her more often than he should have. Indeed, Celeste had that look of excited invitation one might fancy from the uninitiated. Women of experience invited much more deliberately, an understanding he knew quite well. Perchance she was a virgin, but he knew merely professing such did not necessarily mean it thus. In his youth, he had held women who had claimed he was their first, and he was certain he was not. For that had been an absolute rule. He refused to violate chastity, no matter how industriously it was begged.

Not George Wickham. Before that final breech with Wickham, the steps to thence had been laid stone by stone. A large one was placed when Wickham regaled him relentlessly with the notion that plucking a virgin was bliss *nonpareil*. Had he looked at it objectively, he would but think it almost absurd that he so adamantly refused to lay with a virgin and Wickham sought nothing else. Most probably, the nefarious Wickham found the innocent the most easily seduced (or else disliked exposing his performance to criticism).

But whether it was borne in protest of Wickham's method or an independent decision, he would simply not take a woman if he suspicioned she was unknown to men. And, in the dicey business of deducing virginity (some women mocked worldliness, others purity) he thought it a tribute to his discretion that he never actually came into introduction to an intact maiden-flower until Elizabeth.

Until Elizabeth.

Elizabeth. Her name invoked was a mournful susurration in his mind. All this thought of virginity, of course, made him think of her. He had discouraged himself from that indulgence, for with it he fell prey to melancholy, which was, in his mind, far too akin to self-pity. However, as much as he endeavoured not to think of her, an hour did not pass that he did not. Even in light of how frequently she was upon his mind, rarely did he relive their first union, as it tormented him yet.

But he thought of that night and of her virginity then.

This entry into the past was granted because of a single touching detail. Of course, he did not think of it as touching at the time. He had been mortified.

When they had compleated their wedding supper, they had each departed to their respective dressing rooms. To his chagrin, he had actually found his mien ruffled (fumbling with his cuffs until Goodwin reminded him that was his man's duty). He sat in determined recumbence in his bath, vowing to stay there until he could reclaim his nerves. It would be most untoward to appear eager. As he sat in the tub, Goodwin picked up a silver bowl and inquired what he wanted done with the rose petals.

They had compleatly escaped his mind. An unprecedented attack of sentimentality had led him to believe their wedding bed must be anointed with pink rose petals. He had not yet rationalised why he was sent akilter over Elizabeth in such an immoderate manner, and vowed, once he had regained control of his disconcertion, that he would quit behaving like an infatuated elk. But thereupon Goodwin intended to call a maid to have the petals scattered, and Darcy did not much like the idea of a maid scattering them. If they were to be dispersed, they would be with his hand. He climbed dripping from the tub, and drew on his shirt and trousers intending to steal into their boudoir with dispatch, lay the petals, and return to his bath unnoticed.

However.

His feet bare, hair dripping, clothes clinging to his damp body, he was up to his elbows in rose petals as he scattered them across her pillow when Elizabeth opened her door. It was not how he had wanted to greet her upon their wedding night. He hastily divested himself of the bowl and began a mad rectification of his costume, slowed by the disobliging tail of his shirt. Embarrassed as he was at the sight he presented, it took him a moment fully to look at her.

She had stopped, possibly startled, at the door. The light from her dressing chamber illuminated her gown, which did the kindness of revealing to him the beguiling outline of her bare figure. Her hair was loose upon her shoulders and he did not know if she realised that she had raised one eyebrow. Moreover, he did not know if she understood that raised eyebrow excited him to lust far beyond his previous adumbration of that desire.

It also sent him to her with such dispatch that he did not realise he had crossed the room until he picked her up. It was unprecedented for him to carry a woman to the bed. (Had he not taken Elizabeth thusly then, he felt certain he would have leapt upon her right there, on the floor.) Indeed, every aspect of her being conspired to usurp his reason.

For the filminess of her gown was little barrier to her body, but little was too much. As he drew it from her, it did not occur to him to fear for her modesty, for he was drowning in the sensation of his fingertips against her skin. Had she not enticed him from thence, he was uncertain he would have survived at all. But it was a most firm hold she took upon his slippery, wet hair, and she returned his kiss as deeply as he gave it.

Stricken with concupiscence, he felt himself turgid with desire. Knowing that, he nevertheless had moved betwixt her legs unguardedly. And although he wanted, with all his being, to kiss her tenderly and enter her slowly, he had not. When he found the moist cache of her womanhood, he lost all will. Her very tightness excited him to thrust into her again and again. She had never given of herself and he could not show her the gentleness he wanted, nor could he respond to her muffled cry of pain. She was a virgin and he was a beast. No better than Wickham.

His eyes shut tightly against the memory. Had his unmitigated passion been driven by her virginity or his desire for Elizabeth alone? Hers was the only virginity he had ever experienced, hence, he had no answer. Perchance he feared the answer. Would Celeste's virginity drive him to the farthest reaches of passion as had Elizabeth's? He allowed himself to imagine Celeste's comely young body beneath him. He thought about it briefly, turned it over in his mind, and felt nothing. However beautiful her countenance, however tight and new her womanhood, he had no desire for her. His desire was for the woman, not her *feminus pudendum.*

It was remedy to his soul to realise his loss of reason that night owed to his love for Elizabeth, not merely lust. Hence, he granted himself the luxury of clemency. If virginity fuelled his appetence that night, it was only because it was Elizabeth's. However overcome he had been, it had been born of love. The heat of the moment may have overwhelmed him, but at least he was not the swine that Wickham was.

Creeping off into intoxicated sleep, he could not stop himself from thinking of Elizabeth and felt aroused. He ached to hold her again. He had felt nothing but anger and anxiety for months, it was odd to feel arousal. He thought it most probably the drink.

In the darkened room, he was awakened from his sodden sleep. Her body was soft and full atop him. He reached out for her. How had Elizabeth found him? How had she come here? Her gown was soft, her body supple. Rolling her beneath him, his hands found the bottom of her gown and slid upwards. His only thought was how much he wanted to find the reassurance of her embrace. Already of a mind, the merest touch of her hand persuaded his blood to full cry. 'Twas but a dream he knew full well, but he could not bear it to end.

"Lizzy, oh, Lizzy."

78

Waiting had become Elizabeth's occupation, and she thought herself becoming quite the expert. As it happened, she began to take perverse delight in waiting, waiting, waiting. Waiting to hear. Waiting to see. Waiting to have their baby. If she did not run mad, she fancied she would open a school and teach the skill of waiting to those in want of mastering it.

As she waited, she paced. She traipsed about the halls of Pemberley quite without plan but with a pleasant countenance, assuring those about her that she was perfectly well, and thank you, no, she was not in need of comfort. Yes, she knew Mr. Darcy would be back any day now. No, she did not need to sit down, thank you. No, Jane did not need to stay with her, she preferred to be alone. Yes, Papa, I am quite well, no, I would not like to visit at Longbourn until I hear from my husband.

For ten weeks she had heard nothing. Ten weeks of uninterrupted disconsolation. She began to believe she might truly go mad; indeed, she thought madness might be a diversion. Hence, that conclusion decided it.

"If I want to go mad, I must certainly be mad, or at least half-mad."

That gave her some employment to her thoughts. Was she half-mad, one-quarter mad, or three-quarters mad? If she went mad, would their child be mad, also? Her rumination had become so ridiculous that she began to laugh and those around looked at her as if they knew she was mad, so she willed herself to stop. And she began to pace once more.

By mid-June, the greater part of the fighting was decided in British favour. That news was grand, but word had come that the war was won at ghastly cost. And that cost was in reverse proportion to each country's victory. Many soldiers died where they fell for want of so small a need as water. Her sense of apprehension was usurped by dread.

Each night she lay upon Darcy's side of the bed, her head upon his pillow, and sought a respite from the present trepidation in the past.

For this journey into her memory, keepsakes were needed. The most reassuring was the shirt of Darcy's she had rescued from the laundress, for from it she imagined she could yet catch his scent. A green velvet box contained her second most treasured comfort, an azure satin ribbon. That was the gift from her husband she cherished most. Of course, the ribbon had not been his intended gift. That had been the extravagant necklace the green velvet box had contained. But he had tied the ribbon around the box himself, and tied it rather badly. She knew, quite possibly, it was the only bow he had ever tied himself. And he had tied it for her. Odd how, in a lifetime of august moments, something so small signified so very much.

Her dauntless defence of her wedded remembrances bore the weight of additional tragedy. For in the hasty disembarkation of Lady Catherine's coach, the aging Troilus, possibly caught up in his own rancour, was crushed beneath its wheels. Thus, as Elizabeth paced nervously from one window to the next, it was with the equally decrepit Cressida mournfully matching her step for step.

When Elizabeth could make herself be still, it was in an upstairs sitting-room, one that held a particularly good view of the courtyard gate. That oriel became her daylight domain. If she stood at that window, she could see down to the lane for almost a mile. It was her post. Cressida's nose smeared the glaze of the window as her mistress diligently watched the road. She and the dog were sentries to the house (Elizabeth could only pray she had greater chance of seeing Darcy return than Cressida would have of Troilus).

Hence, the dust from the heels of an unknown rider did not escape notice when he came fast up the lane. Elizabeth gave a silent prayer that it was a messenger and hurried downstairs. Her prayers were only partially answered, for he did bear a letter. But it was not from Darcy. It was posted from London and she did not recognise the hand. Trembling, she impatiently tore it open only to find an odd message:

"Mrs. Darcy, I have been entrusted with a message from your husband. If you will be so kind as to advise me of a time, I shall meet you here. And if you will, please come alone."

It was signed only "J.C.," with a London West End address. The note was cryptic, but it told her the single thing she needed most to hear. Darcy was alive. He had sent her a message, and this man had it. Literally racing down the steps, Cressida yipping excitedly at her heels, she suddenly felt dizzy and stopped at the landing. Determined not to allow her condition to keep her from his message, she willed herself to composure and proceeded at a more deliberate pace. If she moved more slowly, she did not allow it of anyone else, ordering the coach readied, post-haste.

When those instructed did not move with enough dispatch, she almost bellowed, "Do not dangle about!"

She sought a messenger to advise J.C. that she was upon her way as directly as possible and hurried back upstairs calling to Hannah. It was at that moment that she spied Goodwin in the corridor.

He rarely came under her eye, staying out of sight, no doubt, because his presence at Pemberley was a reminder that Mr. Darcy was quite alone upon his mission. His face in the passage meant he knew she had heard from Darcy; however, he did not presume to inquire. Hence, she told him she was on her way to London, which incited from him an unprecedented display of emotion. He nodded, clasped his hands together and brought them to his chest, but his face displayed not a sign. Frantic with excitement, this subtle exhibition, however, made her pause and shake her head slightly. Indeed, Darcy could trust Goodwin not to disclose anything to anyone.

Thither into the midst of this melee of readying came Bingley. Albeit he was always of some excuse for his frequent visits, Elizabeth knew that by reason of her insistence upon solitude, he called upon her at Jane's behest. When he beheld her, so ecstatic was Elizabeth, one would but fancy a homecoming was imminent.

"Mr. Bingley, 'tis so good you have come just now! I have word from Darcy! He is well!"

Charles Bingley's closest friend was Darcy, and he was Darcy's—Elizabeth had never forgotten that. Bingley's countenance was counterpoint to Goodwin's, portraying his every emotion just as he experienced them. Elizabeth saw tears of relief in his eyes. In the moment of mutual assuagement, he reached out for her and almost hugged, would have hugged her, but the amplitude of her ever enlarging midsection obstructed him. He made several attempts to circumnavigate this predicament and his befuddlement caused Elizabeth to let out a laugh. Thereupon she hurried on, pointing and giving instruction to the footmen.

Bingley was puzzled by the commotion and inquired, "Elizabeth (he had never called her Mrs. Darcy), where are you going? Is Darcy back in England? Are you to fetch him?"

"No, he is not, or at least I think he is not, but the message from him is in London. I am going there to fetch the message. A post came today," she said, merrily waving the letter.

This explanation and reading the missive did not relieve Bingley's bafflement, "I do not understand why a message from Darcy was sent by way of this person, who has not signed his name. Why did he not pass on the message? Why do they not come here? Why must you go to London alone? It all seems quite irregular!"

Elizabeth knew that if Charles Bingley was the voice of reason, she was behaving far too impetuously. Nevertheless, she cast reason aside.

And as she could not answer any of his questions, she told him thus, "I cannot account for any of it, I can only hope to find answer in his message."

As she climbed into her coach, Bingley insisted she let him accompany her. She would not have it.

"The letter said come alone."

It did not escape Bingley's notice that Elizabeth's carriage sported not only two postilions and a coachman, but two liveried outriders as well. He concluded this was not at Elizabeth's instruction, but most likely Darcy's before he left. Darcy had never told Bingley the more lurid details of what had bechanced when their coach had been attacked that day. But he had explained that he had given orders to his footmen to shoot to kill anyone—man, woman, or child—who attempted to enter the coach if either Elizabeth or Georgiana was inside. Bingley had never spoken a word of it to Jane and thus she had been spared the beleaguerment.

When Jane heard of this, however, Bingley knew she was not going to be consoled that her beloved sister was upon the road alone, six and one-half months great with child, however dedicated her footmen. But he could not force his company upon Elizabeth. He rode along with the coach until the crossroads and then watched it travel out of sight.

The therapeutic value of spirits has long been held in high esteem. These benefits, of course, are conversely proportionate with adverse circumstances if said spirits are consumed immoderately. Thus, the next morning after his inadvertent attendance at Roux's *bonne soirée*, Darcy suffered cruelly under the truth of that particular principle of medicine.

He awoke with a start and a blinding head-ache. Immediately uncertain of his whereabouts, the uncovering of this mystery would have taken place with more dispatch could he bear to open his eyes to the daylight. Upon a meticulous (if squinted) inventory of his surrounding he recollected, not only where he was, but where he was to be. Staggering to the window, he threw back the sash, cursing the lost daylight. And the jouncing, clattering ride atop the waggon all the way to the infirmary was not a comfort.

The hospital was in the same bedlam as the day previous. Georgiana hovered yet over Fitzwilliam and reported he had not developed a fever, hence his prospects of recovery brightened ever so little. The daylight had made Darcy a little more reasonable to the understanding that it was unlikely Fitzwilliam would be able to be transported to the Channel. Upon being advised of the situation, Roux (who rebounded from the imbibing with considerably more resilience than did Darcy) had insisted to his young cousin that Fitzwilliam be brought to his villa to repair.

In no mind to set his sister in for a stay at the *"Chateau de Joie de Vivre,"* Darcy took note of a cottage upon the property and sought temporary shelter for them there. With all the sincerity of a host truly reluctant to lose his guests, Roux agreed. That settled, Darcy's head-ache and angst were greatly mollified. Fitzwilliam's wounds would take time to heal, but it appeared there was a good chance they would, indeed, heal. Though he could not make the trip to England, he could more likely survive a waggon trip of a few miles than the filth of the hospital. However happy she was to have Fitzwilliam rescued from thence, Georgiana was conflicted about abandoning the other patients in the hospital.

Much to his consternation, she told her brother, "They have scarce enough help, as you can see. Albeit Fitzwilliam deserves better, I am torn for the other men who will have nothing."

Darcy began the inevitable tap of his toe that announced his lack of forebearance at the complication of Georgiana's again-provoked conscience. Doing his version of not glowering at her, he nonetheless looked quite grim as she, quite unperturbed by his unhappy countenance, tried further to explain her dilemma.

With considerable impatience, he interrupted, insisting, "Come with me now. That is all I ask. If you must, you can return. I only ask that you take leave with us now."

"Now" was the only disagreement. Georgiana told him, "You see the men yet outside, I must see of them what I can. Once that is done, we shall take our leave."

In no manner accustomed to be given instruction by his sister, Darcy had little choice but to allow her that and nodded silent agreement. This lack of choice was becoming an increasing bother to him. He thought he did not like it.

Was the loss of his own election not vexation enough, Darcy's own compunction was becoming agitated in the face of all the ungodly misery before him. His choices were few. He could return to Roux's villa, but that would demand weathering that gentleman's guests. Or he could simply sit in the waggon. Or.

Georgiana had gone about the difficult business of stealing souls from death when she bechanced to see a very unlikely sight. Her brother, who had taken off his jacket and rolled up his sleeves, was helping carry stretchers into the hospital. Shaking her head at the marvel, she wondered if any of the poor, wretched men knew they had such an illustrious bearer.

In time, Darcy saw her watching him and looked hastily away, either mortified by it or not wanting to answer for his magnanimity.

Although he could not remember it ever being a consideration before, Mr. Darcy had decided that if he was there, he should make himself useful (propriety bade ladies busy themselves; in gentlemen, however, it demanded only leisure). As the extent of insult to his own station was substantial, he rationalised that he laboured thus because the greater the dispatch with which the patients could be brought in, the hastier would be Georgiana's departure. But in truth, economy of time was not his motive. The cries of the wounded were pitiful and he wanted not to hear them. Yet he wanted less to have to remember them (he had a notion they would not easily be forgot) and know himself to have stood idly by and done nothing in aid. The single consolation he saw in his service was that he acquired the duty of bringing in the newly arrived injured and not carting out the newly declared dead. Necessary as it was, he was not yet sufficiently hardened to the sight of death to be able to bear that.

Short of help, the hospital used its resources with efficiency. Before a wounded soldier could be brought inside, he had to be inspected by a surgeon to assess his injury. There were three classifications in this appraisal. If the wound appeared too grievous from which to recover, the soldier was set aside to find peace in his own time. Was he likely to live even without medical intervention, he was turned away.

Within the third category was the hospital's work: he who needed a limb severed, a laceration sutured, or a fracture set (and only then if the gash was more than a hand span or a bone protruded from the break).

Darcy observed the young surgeon, himself not more than a schoolboy, making the decisions (each excruciating judgement worthy of King Solomon) with a single nod, shake, or flick of his head. Darcy could but think that he was much more disposed to carry out the dead than be charged with naming who would live and who would die.

Stretcher-bearer was test enough. For he found himself teamed with a half-witted Brobdingnagian named Mott, who, though several pence shy of a shilling, nevertheless had more sense than teeth. The simpleton knew enough to understand, regardless of birth, he was the senior conveyor and took great delight in issuing instruction to Darcy, each command punctuated with a gap-toothed grin.

Though not death duty, theirs was yet grim. For the men they loaded were very much alive, conscious, and all in great pain. No matter how gingerly they were lifted upon and off the litter, all screamed in agony at the agitation, and Mott grinned stupidly each time they did. (As it happened, Mott grinned at just about everything.)

The happy circumstance of his life had demanded Darcy to carry nothing heavier than his walking stick, thus his back ached with unrelenting ferocity by mid-afternoon. Long believing himself to be quite fit (and, for a gentleman, indubitably he was), his ego was somewhat abused to learn that only a few hours of strenuous labour could so thoroughly undo him. As if to attest to that particularly unkind truth, he stopped after the delivery of one rather fleshy son of the British Empire, dropped the handles of their litter and stretched his throbbing back, unintentionally eliciting a groan as he did.

"Need t'rest, Guv'nor?" asked Mott with a smirk.

Obstinate in the conceit of his own strength, Darcy was hence determined that the imbecile Mott best him in neither brawn nor fortitude. Thus, he reclaimed his end of the stretcher and office of beast of burden with renewed vigour (and chose to ignore that he was engaged in the considerable folly of competing in a test of wills with a cabbage-headed behemoth).

He and Mott worked mechanically, lifting on, carrying, and lifting off. Soldier after soldier. Some heavy, some not, but all, by necessity of a defence of sensibility, faceless and nameless. Hence, it was of great coincidence that Darcy happened to pause to stretch his arms over his head before regrasping the litter that beheld to him the wounded body of John Christie.

Taken aback in recognition, Darcy very nearly gasped. Nonchalantly, the surgeon flipped back John's uniform jacket, observed the gaping hole in his gut and with a flick of his head pronounced him irredeemable. Abruptly, Darcy put out a restraining hand.

He announced with such finality, "This one goes inside," that the young surgeon looked at him queerly.

Shrugging, the weary doctor said, "As you wish," which was less in deference to Mr. Darcy than in lack of will to debate.

Darcy had not interrogated Georgiana about her method of travel to the continent. Once he had found her safe and understood her quest was Fitzwilliam and no other, curiosity of the matter was set aside. Until he saw John's face, smudged with sweat and gunpowder, he had not once thought of his danger. Even though John had aided Georgiana in eluding her family, now that she was found unharmed, it was far easier to find compassion for him. Mott helped carry John inside to a cot, allowing Darcy to wave the leering giant upon his way.

Putting a comforting hand upon his arm, Darcy spoke quietly to John, who recognised a friendly voice if not its owner and reached out for Darcy's hand. He strained to see who sat with him.

When Darcy said, "It is I," John immediately withdrew his proffered hand.

"Is his hate so strong that this boy will not allow comfort?" Darcy wondered to himself, but he saw it was not hatred but recompense that worried John, who was yet of the unlikely mind that Mr. Darcy had come all the way to France to seek vengeance upon a menacing groom.

For John said, "Aye guess yer can find no harsher due than this for me."

Retrieving John's hand, Darcy squeezed it in reassurance of no angry intent. It was apparent his wound was grave, but John did not betray the pain. Darcy warily lifted the bloody gauze and recoiled at the severity of the puncture.

"What was it?"

It was a reflex for Darcy to ask that. Immediately he realised it was unlikely John would have seen what hit him, but had no time to withdraw the query before John answered tersely, "Pistol lead."

"I see." Conversation dwindling, Darcy observed John's uniform. "A grenadier. Excellent."

Happy to have the honour of his service noted, he said, "Yer know yer soldierin' better'n yer sister."

However grievous his injuries, the volatility of subject that he had just broached was not lost upon John. If Mr. Darcy had not come to seek retribution, perchance he did not know he had fled Pemberley with Georgiana.

"Georgiana is here," Darcy told him.

"Hurt?" Alarmed, John tried to raise himself.

"No, no. As a nurse."

"Of course," John reassured himself. "Of course she is."

The only other news Darcy had was of Fitzwilliam, but he believed it would not be a consolation to John to know the good colonel in no better shape than was he. Stymied for a topic, Darcy sat in silence for a few moments. And John, perchance uneasy of his former employer at his bedside (or more likely uneasy because he had sold his former employer's horse and buggy for twenty pounds), attempted to make small talk himself.

"'ow're them 'orses?"

"They are quite well."

That was the final insult upon Darcy's intrinsic taciturnity. A mortally wounded boy was forced to make pleasantries with him. Under other circumstances, he might have been a little amused at the extent of his own congenital reserve, but not at that moment. Gently patting John's shoulder, he rose.

"I shall find Georgiana for you. Certainly she will be better company than I."

Horrified at John's injury, Georgiana hid her tears from him. That not a difficult deed, for he was growing increasingly weak, it being somewhat miraculous that he had lived as far as the steps of the hospital. She sat with John for some time, talking softly to him and listening to his ramblings. As he watched his sister sit and partake in easy conversation, Darcy found reproach in himself. Possibly, Elizabeth was right. If his shy sister could talk with such facility, perchance he should practise it more himself. For times like these, if nothing else.

But as he had not the time to practise, he turned his thoughts to a subject he knew well—that of detail. He saw now that they would have two wounded men for whom to care. It would not be a great problem, he reasoned; they would both fit in the back of the waggon. And Georgiana could probably be persuaded to stay at Roux's and not return to the hospital if she had two patients.

He refused to acknowledge either man's wounds were mortal. He would not have it. Out of the filthy hospital, they both might repair quite well. All this planning went for naught, however, for Georgiana came to her brother directly with a sorrowful report.

"John, I fear, will not last long. He gets weaker with each breath."

Darcy, who had compleatly forsaken (and already forgotten) his most recent employment, had been sitting as if in ecclesiastical vigilance over the entire ward. Thus, his solemnity was already in place as Georgiana related the gravity of John's condition. Had that not been daunting enough, there was further disquiet.

"John said a British officer shot him, but he is not entirely coherent. Perchance you can make better sense of it."

True, John rambled, and as Darcy sat next to him, he heard the telling of a battle that he did not want to envision. But, he heard quite clearly John say that his commanding officer shot him when John caught him in the act of stealing away under the colours of corporal.

Darcy said, rather than asked, for he thought the other not possible, "Pray, this was by way of a mistake?"

John answered the question only indirectly, "Aye thought 'im friendly enough," he said. "'e said 'e was from Derbyshire. 'e said Kympton was the living he should've 'ad. Aye should've known no officer befriends no corporal."

Stunned, Darcy silently shook his head in disbelief. Yet he knew that no other man could have uttered those words.

They had become Wickham's mantra, announced to anyone who would listen, "Kympton was the living I should have had."

It was not an unmitigated surprise for him to show a white tail-feather in the face of fire; Wickham's keenest instinct was, indeed, that of self-preservation. But Darcy could not believe that even Wickham would be so cowardly as to shoot a conscript who witnessed it. Thereupon, with uncivil clarity, it dawned upon him the magnitude of Wickham's treachery. Unknowingly, he had killed his own son to buy his silence. Worse was unimaginable. In time, Darcy would find gratitude that he had not had the opportunity to tell John of his true paternity. At least the lad would not have the additional misfortune to die knowing his own father was his murderer.

Increasingly, John's voice took upon a meandering turn, utterly unintelligible, until he drifted asleep altogether. As he watched John's chest struggle for breath, Darcy could think of nothing but the night he thought Elizabeth was dead, and it compleatly usurped his will. In defence of the possible mortification of actually weeping, he fled outside to gather himself.

Leaning against a wall, he gradually slid to a sitting position, his head betwixt his knees. He reached up to loosen his cravat, for he felt as if he was choking. His hand fell back, however, for his tie was not what constricted him. He had already surrendered it for use as a tourniquet. Ruthlessly, he tore at his top shirt button, determined to get more air. Although the button was not what strangled him, conquering so lowly a thing as that was a victory at that moment.

It took him a while to regain some sense of control, if not of circumstance, at least his own countenance. It was apparent to him that Georgiana did not know of John's earlier misapprehension about being his son. Darcy was exceedingly grateful he was spared the particular mortification of explaining the whys and wherefores of that situation to his sister. With renewed resolve, he returned inside and he and Georgiana both watched through the afternoon as John slowly and painfully died.

It was but one more Derbyshire youth vanquished, but John's death allowed Darcy to put a face on the multitudes that went before him.

Unable to bear the thought of his interment in the mass grave behind the hospital, Darcy decided to see to having John buried upon Roux's property. As he moved to make those arrangements, he saw another man, shot only in the leg, wearing a uniform and insignia identical to John's. He stopped and inquired if his officer was Major Wickham.

The man said, "Yea, but dead he is. Aye saw his body. He had a good horse—Aye donno what happened to him, but he were worth twenty of the major."

There was, no doubt, more than one British major of smaller value than his horse, but because Wickham always liked to be well-mounted, the sergeant's summation of his character seemed particularly keen to Darcy. He thanked the man mildly and walked on. So mildly did he respond, had anyone observed the exchange, the level of acquaintance betwixt Darcy and Major Wickham most certainly would not have been inferred. Those within the full ken of Wickham's dubious morals, however, would have understood Darcy's ambivalence.

Darcy did not investigate his own feelings upon the matter. He wondered only if the dead body the soldier witnessed was indeed Major Wickham or simply a corpse in his uniform jacket. It was obvious that query would lay unanswered, regardless how diligently he speculated. The single thing Darcy knew as true thereupon, was his own mind. For if he ever again saw Wickham alive, he intended to do everything within his ample power to render him not.

A messenger was hastened to Roux alerting him of need of a gravesite. Belatedly, Darcy realised Roux would ready a final resting-place befitting of Fitzwilliam's station, not that of a Pemberley groom. As he thought of that particular misunderstanding, it was with more amusement than he knew he should; but at the moment, black humour was the only kind to be had.

It was upon his re-entry to the building that he overheard an insistent conversation between several doctors and two guards. So urgent was their discourse, he slowed his steps long enough to overhear what was being discussed. He was staggered to hear someone speak of Putrid Fever and that quarantine was being instituted forthwith.

Putrid Fever, Gaol Fever, Louse Fever, Typhus. Many names, but they all meant the same: epidemic, plague. The wards had been tainted. Darcy was not surprised, for the filth that could not be overcome in so unclean a mass of injured men invited lice. The doctors intended to repair to another hospital site some ten miles away. The trail of wounded would be rerouted. Those who were in the hospital would stay, thus invoking a likely death sentence on them. Guards would assure no one came or left. Darcy begat a sedately frantic search for Georgiana.

Cornering her away from other patients, he explained that if they were to take leave they must immediately. Commandeering Mott, they each took an end of the stretcher, eased Fitzwilliam out the door, and carefully laid him in the waggon. The only benefit of the colonel's bandaged eyes was that he did not see them when they placed John's corpse next to him. It was wrapped in the fringed blanket originally meant to cover the man John had most admired. As Georgiana crawled into the bed of the waggon to steady Fitzwilliam, neither Darcy nor his sister spoke of the irony.

All loaded, Darcy turned to Mott and handed him a sovereign. "You did not see us take leave."

Mott plucked the coin from his hand and bit down upon it hard.

Gleefully, he said, "For a quid, Guv'nor, I'd strangle me own ma."

"No doubt," Darcy opined solemnly.

Not looking back, Darcy climbed upon the waggon and gave a decisive slap to the reins of the horses. The team strained against their harnesses and the waggon barely began to roll when they heard the last word Darcy wanted to have ringing in his ears.

"Halt!"

An officious guard had spied them and decided no one would take leave as of then and there. Word was not yet official, and was it, Darcy thought it most unlikely he would have complied with a demand to stay, regardless. The guard stepped into their path, one hand upon his gun, the flat of his other extended. So near to getting them all out of the hospital and in kinder hands, Darcy was not in a mood to debate.

"Stand aside," he commanded.

"I'm givin' the orders here. And Aye said halt," insisted the soldier unholstering his weapon.

Standing, Darcy put his hand to his blade, but did not yet draw it. All the man needed to know was that he would. Yet the man stood his ground. And as it is imprudent to issue a threat one does not intend to carry out, Darcy did not hesitate to draw his sword from its sheath and again demand the man to step aside. At the hubbub, another guard came over, long gun at the ready. Even though poised offensively, both men began to blink with rapidity under the cold stare of a man well prepared to face off with them both. A single blade was outmatched by one gun, not even considering two. Of this, Darcy cared little. The guards would step aside or he would have little decision but which of the men he would first run through.

Perchance the hue and cry initiated it, possibly not. But the first large drops of a summer storm began to fall upon Darcy's shoulders as he stood ready to do murder once again. The loud thock, thock, thock against his hat was overwhelmed by a thunder crack, and that detonating clap from the sky (however melodramatic) was a truer definition of his anger than any mere cannonade.

From behind him came the command, "Cease!"

It was accompanied by the cocking of a gun.

In unison, the guards' gazes forsook Darcy's angry face and rested just beyond his shoulder. There, they stared into the twin barrels of a military pistol. And if their faces bore a look of extended incredulity, Darcy's might have mirrored the same had he looked. But he needed not to turn around to know his sister stood behind him, owned the voice, and held the gun.

Prudently, the guards complied with Georgiana's demand, thus allowing Darcy to lower his sword and slap the reins against the team's back, with a sedate order to the horses to, "Walk on."

As they started forward with a jerk, the first guard saw a moment of vulnerability in Georgiana's unsteady footing. Not of a mind to lose his only recently obtained authority, he lowered his musket ominously at her and pulled back the breach. Darcy had only time to kick his boot upward at the gun, which, at this insult, discharged at the horizon and to the right of Darcy's head, almost dislodging him from the waggon. Recovering his seat and his anger in an instant, his sword found the man's gullet, its tip convincing the guard to stand back with no further commotion.

Thereupon, the small procession was allowed to start up the long road to healing.

80

When the address was located, Elizabeth was perplexed. It was not a building, shop, nor home. It appeared not to exist. There was only a park. She sat in the coach whilst trying to decide what to do, wondering if some person had played a hideous tease upon her. Her heart sank, and she scolded herself for not heeding Bingley's warnings.

Duly chastened, she decided since there were benches and it was the appointed hour, she would seat herself and see if anyone came about. Handed out of the coach, she disguised her pregnancy with a generous shawl, sat in an obvious spot beneath the shade of a large tree, and waited. Waiting an hour was no problem for this veteran of wait. She had just vowed she would sit there until twilight when she was approached.

It was not a man who came to her, but a woman. Elizabeth did not recognise her, but the woman sat next to her with no introduction of herself and simply asked, "Mrs. Darcy?" but it was not a true query; the woman obviously knew who she was.

Elizabeth acknowledged she was and queried anxiously, "Do you have word from Mr. Darcy?"

The woman took so murderously long a time in answering, Elizabeth thought it almost perverse. She endeavoured, however, to remain calm and wait what time this woman needed.

Finally, not answering her question, the woman instead asked as she fingered a locket, "Do you not remember me, Mrs. Darcy?"

Elizabeth's first response was a lack of recollection. She shook her head. Thereupon, she hesitated whilst eyeing her more carefully. The woman was quite toothsome and annoyingly familiar, but Elizabeth could not place her. She was very fair, with golden hair and slim waist. Upon a specific turn of her head, Elizabeth remembered the single time she had seen the woman. It was outside the elegant bagnio on Bond Street. The one that her husband said he had visited before they were married. This woman had stood poised to enter it.

She had a decided elegance in her address, but her accent was French, which answered at least one of Elizabeth's unasked questions. A subtle change upon Elizabeth's features was enough for a woman who had spent a lifetime in such matters to detect it.

She said, "I see you do."

Only momentarily detoured, Elizabeth quickly returned to her mission, "You have me at a disadvantage, forgive me, for you know my name, but I know not how you are called."

Beginning to wonder just what were this woman's wiles, Elizabeth decided to be forthright. She had no guile of her own, no time for chicanery. She desired only word of her husband, and if this woman would not cough it up forthwith, Elizabeth was truly sorry she had not brought her pistol.

The woman replied, "You may call me Juliette, for your husband does."

The reminder was not particularly relished, but Elizabeth said, "Then I will be Elizabeth to you. I assure you that I need only to know you have heard from Mr. Darcy and he is well."

When Elizabeth bade her to call her by her Christian name, Juliette appeared to be taken aback and sat looking at Elizabeth in a most direct fashion.

Finally, she said, "He was quite well one week ago."

At finally hearing first-hand that Darcy was yet alive, Elizabeth closed her eyes, and let out a deep breath of relief. Then she touched her fingers to her forehead, the release of tension leaving her feeling a little faint. Hastily recovering, she leaned forward in urgent enquiry.

"Can you tell me where he is, or his circumstance?"

She realised the mysteriousness of the letter had not been uncovered. For she could have learnt ten hours earlier by post that he was alive.

Juliette remained elusive, "I was in the company of your husband in France, near Lille."

Elizabeth remembered Darcy mentioned relations there before he left, and asked, "Is he there now? Was he well?" She did not query the circumstance or the connexion, only wanting to hear he was well.

"Where he is this day, I cannot say. But when I saw him, he was quite well. Quite well, indeed, but in need of comfort. As you might know, it is the comfort of such men as Darcy that I provide, no?"

What Juliette implied was hardly veiled and Elizabeth felt her cheeks begin to burn, hoping they were not in high enough colour to expose her ire. She had begun to question whether Darcy had actually bid the woman to bring her a message. That would be more than a little curious if he were truly in this woman's company in the manner she hinted. Under such perplexity, she was uncertain if she should discount all Juliette's information if part of it seemed false, or believe information selectively. It took her only a moment to decide to acknowledge the implication and speak the only way she knew how. Frankly.

Elizabeth said, "Let us have no misunderstanding. Though I doubt not my husband's love, I do not willingly share him. But if you saw him and gave him comfort when he needed it, you shall have my undying appreciation. I need only to know that he is well and not in danger."

Juliette had been paying rapt attention to Elizabeth's face, therefore, the moment her gaze lowered, Elizabeth by design looked down to see what had wrested her attention. They both sat for a moment looking at Elizabeth's unquestionably blossoming stomach. Thereupon, mortified, Elizabeth snatched up the end of her shawl that had dropped from her and repaired her concealment.

She not only was embarrassed by the exposure, she felt large and ungainly sitting next to the lovely, blonde woman. The lovely, blonde, lithe, French woman who said she was in her husband's company one week ago. And even though the last thing Elizabeth would have wanted from Juliette was sympathy, she saw Juliette's eyes, whose gaze had been quick and flinty, had softened.

It embarrassed her further that she had done the heedless and exposed her condition in public; she should have stayed in the coach like a lady. (Now that she knew Darcy was alive, it was easy to forget she was anxious beyond all caring only a few moments before.)

And of this Juliette spoke, but not in censure, "Forgive me, Elizabeth. It was unkind of me to demand you to come here and speak to a woman such as myself in public. I fear I misjudged you."

She looked off into the distance a moment and murmured, "I should have guessed that Darcy would not have married less."

As a woman whose life was one of disguise of every sort, Juliette had revealed much. Too much for Elizabeth not to understand the esteem that she must have felt for Darcy at one time. Thus, compassion allowed the flush of anger that had begun to creep up her neck to abate. Elizabeth realised she was undergoing some sort of test. To what gauge, she could not guess (and hoped the measure Juliette had underestimated of her was not her girth).

"I was in your husband's company at the home of his cousin. He knew I was to travel to London and inquired might I get word to you, for he knew of your fear for his safety. He thought it unlikely his other posts had reached you. There was a letter, but I destroyed it, for my party was accosted before we departed France and I could not have words in English upon my person. Had I thought to have him write it in French, I would have been happy to, how do you say...*oui*...translate."

Elizabeth almost offered that she could read French, thank you (which would have been a generous fabrication, but she so did not want to admit she was not conversant in French to this French woman who had seen her husband in France).

Prudently, she only inquired, "Did he say if he had yet found his sister?"

Juliette shook her head, and told her, "He did not tell me of his business. If that was his mission, I hope he finds her soon, for treachery rules France now. No one is safe."

That Darcy did not tell Juliette of his business was a reassurance of his fidelity, but learning of the continued peril in France compelled Elizabeth to prefer to fear for it than for his safety. She thought to change the subject, not truly wanting to hear the woman speak Darcy's name so intimately again.

Elizabeth asked, "Do you have family there?"

Juliette nodded.

"We both have reason to pray. I shall include yours in my own."

They both stood. Elizabeth re-engaged her shawl. That secured, she again thanked Juliette, who acknowledged it with a demure curtsy. Here, Elizabeth was torn by not wanting to not curtsy in return, lest Juliette take it as a cut, or attempt a curtsy and risk injury to her person (and mortification to her dignity). Hence, she gave more of a bow than curtsy, certain she looked awkward and unfeminine, then chastised herself for concern of something so shallow. As Elizabeth walked back to her coach, she felt drained but bathed in relief that Darcy was alive at least one week ago and able to get word to her.

Upon the long ride home it occurred to her that she had never once been in fear of anything but her husband's life whilst he had been gone. That she should fear for his faithfulness was no more likely to her, but it certainly now visited her thoughts.

For, howbeit Elizabeth had heard her husband addressed as "Darcy" by any number of friends and acquaintances, she had never felt quite the same twinge in her stomach as she did when Juliette said his name. Elizabeth could only imagine it as he must have heard it, Juliette's voice soft and fetching against his ear, her breath warm. In bed. Probably naked.

"Dar-cy," Elizabeth endeavoured to mimic Juliette's alluring accent.

"Dar-cy," she repeated.

She shook her head. It was useless. It was not possible for her to recreate Juliette's provocative lilt. That abandoned, she shook any picture from her mind of Darcy with Juliette, in the near or distant past. Her prayers for his safety had been answered. She chose to take the meeting with Juliette as it was: a way for him to get a message to her. As she thought about that, she was both amused and bewildered. It was an amusement to think of him having to request Juliette to contact her, and a bewilderment as to just why he did. Were circumstances that dire in France, or simply that serendipitous? She prayed for serendipity.

Her jealousy had been once piqued by Darcy's past and she had wished he had not known carnal embrace with any other women. Had he not had that connexion, she knew herself to have great need of information of him yet, and promised not to question what was behind them, for to-morrow seemed to carry a far greater burden.

Larger issues at rest, she fleetingly allowed herself to consider that it was Juliette who had schooled her husband so well in the art of love. For as beautiful as she was, Elizabeth believed she was older than was Darcy. Now she knew she was French as well. Elizabeth knew the French to be connoisseurs of pleasure. Some things were not difficult to surmise.

But there was one nagging query she thought she might ask Darcy when he returned. It was about the origin of particular acts of love. She was certain he had told her they were Latin.

Getting free of the hospital compound was only the first hurdle. The woods were alive with soldiers willingly hijacked from duty digging grave trenches to police the quarantine. Most had encamped adjacent to the hospital after bringing in the wounded and were happy to eschew their shovels for guns once again. Thus, they were enthusiastic to a fault whilst ensuring the integrity of their perimeter.

Belayed almost immediately by a ludicrous duo in arms (one long, lean, and hirsute, the other a short, stout pilgarlic), Darcy and Georgiana had only moments to concoct a story. The best they could do was throw the blanket across Fitzwilliam's face and innocently claim they were carrying off the dead for burial, supposing the just-relieved trench diggers would not deny someone else the job. It was the spare soldier who walked to the back of the waggon and lifted the edge of the blanket that covered John. With a distasteful sneer, he tossed the blanket back and told them to move along.

In any other circumstance, it would have been regrettable that Fitzwilliam had fallen unconscious from the pain of moving him. But as he did not stir whilst the man investigated the bodies, it was a necessary boon. But having their story believed once, it did not follow that it would be many times more. Thus, they left the conspicuity of the road. It was treacherous going, and several times they were well-nigh upended. Georgiana clung to the seat next to her brother, and the two reticent siblings shared barely a word. A look, a nod, a shrug spoke both question and answer.

Apart from the road, Darcy had only the most general knowledge of the whereabouts of Roux's guesthouse. Hence, he was grateful to see some of Roux's men near the villa in apparent watch for them. Two climbed into the back of the waggon, one giving direction from there. When the other moved to sit down next to John's body, the man accidentally kicked it as he fell to his seat when the waggon started away. He said, "*Pardon,*" before quite expeditiously understanding the affronted person was in no condition to find offence.

In levity or not, this was not witnessed by Georgiana and Darcy. Both looked earnestly ahead in anxious anticipation of refuge. Roux's hospitality was again bestowed. There were several servants at the guesthouse, they had it in order, and stood ready to serve tea. That most civilised of hospitalities had to await the removal of Fitzwilliam from the waggon and his being settled into the house. It was with that jostling that the consciousness that he had been fading in and out of during the trip was resurrected and along with it, the pain, and he moaned in agony. Whilst Georgiana tended Fitzwilliam, Darcy told a servant to tell her he had a task to which to attend. Thus, he was spared two miseries: the burden of Fitzwilliam's cries, and the heartbreak in Georgiana's eyes when he told her he had to take leave to bury John Christie's body.

That they had fled the hospital did not suppose them free of typhus. Fitzwilliam, because of his wounds, was most susceptible, but Georgiana, by reason of her nursing duties, was very vulnerable as well. Even his own health was at risk, certainly not to the same extent as theirs. Undoubtedly louse-ridden (not by reason of station but of army blankets), John's body had to be disposed of immediately.

It was less than a mile to the Roux family's cemetery, and Darcy was surprised at its size (the Roux branch of the family was apparently more prolific than the Darcy side). It sat next to a little chapel, picturesque but vacant. Forewarned of his coming, Darcy did not have to explain to the caretaker who he was or his reason for being there. He and another man stood with shovels in their hands, the grave already dug and ready for occupancy. They had a slat-board coffin before them, its lid resting against the side, in wait of its future inhabitant.

Lifting him by rigoured arms and legs, they quite unceremoniously plopped John's body into the coffin, and Darcy would have demanded caution had not the deed already been done. Immediate upon that affront, the caretaker reached out and rather roughly began to tug and yank at the rather fine blanket covering the corpse.

Darcy saw he meant to return it to him, and said, "*Non! Arrêtez vous!*" But he was too late, for before the man could stop, momentum drew the blanket from John's face. With all the death he had witnessed, Darcy did not understand why he could not bear to see John's dead countenance again. Nevertheless, it was revealed to him before the man could tuck the blanket back about him. The assault upon his sensibilities demanded Darcy take hasty leave. And he turned to do just that, when the caretaker called after him.

"*Pardon, monsieur. Comment il s'appelle?*"

Darcy stopped his retreat, turned and said firmly, "John. *Jean*, J-o-h-n." He turned to go again, and again he was stopped.

The man called, "John *quoi?*"

What was John's last name? A simple query. Few simpler. But some simple questions do not have simple answers. Darcy had no idea of John's surname. It was not "the groom," which was how he always had thought of him. Abigail's last name was lost to him as well. If he ever knew it. The one thing he did know, it was not Wickham, nor would it be so long as he had power over it.

Quite abruptly, he answered, "Darcy. John Darcy."

The man did no more than blink at this information, and he and his compatriot of spades put the lid upon the coffin. Darcy had taken himself quite unawares with his own unprecedented liberality with his heretofore-exalted family name. But it felt right. If it caused comment, he cared little. The consecration of name was compleated, yet he paused, reconsidering his leave taking. At the hospital, amid the moans and screams could be heard the constant drone of a priest who moved amongst the dying men anointing and exacting extreme unction. John had probably had some holy water splattered upon him, but Darcy did not think mass redemption enough. In lack of knowing John's religious persuasion for certain, Darcy chose to gift him his.

Hence, instead of hurrying away, Darcy stood and watched the men lower the coffin into the grave, and shovel the dirt over it. He endeavoured to retrieve some snatches of appropriate scriptures from his memory of his *Common Book of Prayer*, but with little success. Funeral words were not those he endeavoured to keep with him. But as the men finished their job and stood looking at him from their resting shovel handles, he spoke a prayer that did come to mind.

With the "amen" yet ringing, Darcy announced to the men who seemed startled at his directness. He told them to engrave the words *"Honneur, Courage, Bonté"* upon the headstone. He did not spell it in English, the translation was obvious. There were no mutes to hire, no watcher to guard the corpse, few refinements of passing were to be had. But Darcy did give the grave-diggers an extra coin to climb the church steeple and toll the bell. Thus, John was put to rest: with a first and last name, church bells, and at least one mourner.

The trip back to the guesthouse in the now empty waggon was grim for Darcy. He had thought that once he found Georgiana safe, he would be awash in joyous relief. But the burial of John in a land far from England made Darcy feel every mile of the distance betwixt France and home. And it was a lonely feeling.

This sense of desolation did not lift by the time he returned to the cottage. A melancholia settled over him that he would be unable to shake for some time. It was undoubtedly brought on by the horrific sights he had witnessed, John's death, Fitzwilliam's wounds, and being so far from Pemberley and Elizabeth. All were things that would have been hard enough to bear separately. Hence, glumness could be expected. And he probably would have had the strength to weather them had he not become aware that the percussion of the gun that had been fired at him, while sparing his head, had reinstated his deafness.

82

At first there was only a profound ringing sensation, tantamount to, if not surpassing, Darcy's previous impairment. This reverberation was a substantial annoyance, but he could nevertheless hear. However, just as MacFarqhuar had prophesied, it was an ominous knell. For in the intervening hours betwixt the gunshot and the burying of John Christie's body, what little Darcy heard became garbled. By the time he stood graveside, only the gravedigger's staccato delivery allowed him to understand a single word the man said. Upon the return to the cottage, the clattering of the waggon wheels was compleatly indiscernible.

Having ridden a nag, seconded a half-witted litter bearer, and well-nigh had his head blown off, another might have considered himself fortunate only to be in want of his auditory sense. Darcy, of course, was not another. His arrogance may have mitigated to a degree over the years; however, humility had most definitely not encroached upon his ego. To successfully eschew his disreputable mount and abdicate his labourer status (and Mott as well), only to be subjugated by such a ridiculous infirmity, was as infuriating to him as it was inescapable. Of course, that was the severest trial to Darcy—the very impotence of his will in the matter.

His pride, as always, demanded he mask any personal imperfection, thus he concealed his deafness with all the duplicity of a particularly artful card-sharp. In such close quarters with someone who knew him so well, this chicanery was unprofitable, for Georgiana found him out almost immediately. Quite aware (acutely, exceedingly, even excessively aware) of her brother's pride, she allowed him some time to think he had fooled her before telling him his charade was futile. Knowing their nature and relationship, not surprisingly she did not confront him directly with his deception.

Rather, she stood in front of him and inquired, "Did it happen from the gunshot at the hospital?"

He nodded. There was really nothing else to say.

There were far more pressing concerns. As Georgiana went about making a celandine poultice for Fitzwilliam's eyes and various herbal embrocations for his leg wounds, Darcy knew their most frightening predicament would be were any or all of them infected with typhus. That the case, Darcy dared not contaminate anyone else with the disease; he called together the servants Roux had assigned to them and frankly explained the danger of contagion if they stayed. Though refined in appearance, Roux's people were common folk, illiterate and superstitious. Hence, it was quite unexpected when not a single servant bolted for the door upon the announcement of possible plague. Their eyes widened and not a few took to clutching talismans, but none deserted Roux's cottage.

The matter of pestilence and death addressed, Darcy turned to a more daunting endeavour: that of speaking to his sister about her romantic entanglement.

For days he struggled with what to say to her, what to inquire of her, even whether to speak to her whilst she scurried about tending Fitzwilliam. The quarantine that confined them alleviated the possibility of Georgiana returning to aid at the hospital, and of that, Darcy was relieved. As the days passed, it appeared they would escape the epidemic, and he certainly did not want her to seek further risk. He could never compleatly shake his unease, but finally a little peace ensued.

Tranquillity, of course, being a relative thing. It seemed tranquil. It certainly sounded tranquil to Darcy (for the ringing had ceased and he heard little at all). The house was harmonious, placid, and calm. Then again, not at all. Georgiana busied herself in Fitzwilliam's sick-room, alternately reading to him when he was awake and embroidering when he was not. When her brother made a formal entry into the room each day to inquire of Fitzwilliam's condition, she was always (at whichever specific moment he chose to enter) toiling furiously amidst some inordinately intricate handwork and quite unable to extend their conversation beyond the perfunctory.

This dedication to her sewing was a subterfuge of limited effectiveness. Georgiana and Darcy both knew it was only a matter of time before he cornered her elsewhere in the cottage to confront her about the method and madness of her disappearance from Pemberley. Because the confrontation was inevitable, narrowing the field of contention to a manageable number of subjects would be his most trying difficulty. Georgiana's own most vexing perplexity was hardly a new one, that of being the sole officeholder of Sister to Fitzwilliam Darcy. For she knew that title demanded she give him an unabridged elucidation of the why, when, how, with whom, and wherefore of having absconded from Derbyshire.

Whilst they awaited for Fitzwilliam to heal enough to travel, idleness was not Darcy's weightiest vexation, merely the most central. Unimpaired by the constraint of time (and his deafness every excuse), he composed a detailed questionnaire about her disappearance for Georgiana to compleat, the ludicrousness of which was entirely lost upon his analytical sensibilities. Albeit they were quite similar in temperament, it is not argued that all wisdoms are necessarily distributed equally amongst siblings. Thus, Darcy would never understand, however logical the survey or industriously she endeavoured to account for the ambiguity of love, a document would never be able to uncover the vast shades of his sister's mind. Hence, the anticipated breviloquence of a written instrument of Georgiana's travels and travails was not to be. Any equivocation upon the matter was put to rest when she tore the unanswered instrument in half and handed it back to him. Of this, he was disproportionately unhappy.

Isolated and thwarted, not only by his own disability, but his sister's obstinacy as well, their sojourn at Lille became increasingly intolerable for Darcy. Georgiana went about her duties, humming with maddening congeniality. Diversions were few. His need to see Elizabeth manifested itself with an ache in his chest so palpable at times he actually feared it would literally burst his heart. Of this torment, of course, he spoke not a word, and endeavoured to soothe his soul by writing her endless letters.

Another excuse to be vexed that Georgiana had vandalised his set of inquiries was the scarcity of paper. (He did not reproach himself, however, for using precious paper to write them in the first place.) Thus, in addition to his usual small script, he resorted to the pauper's device of cross-writing a letter already filled front and back at ninety-degrees, thereby economically doubling the length of the letter. The added bother of this particular stratagem was that it was challenging to read (if not outright prohibitive), but Darcy knew well that circumstances made that not of great consideration.

Every day he compleated a letter, carefully folded and sealed it with red wax, thereupon, in his most elaborate script, directed it to Elizabeth. But these lengthy, heart-wrenching tomes to his wife journeyed not. Bundled in his lap, fertile with endearment but barren of destination, they sat as he awaited futilely upon the wide, bougainvillaea-shaded portico for some rider to happen by. Alas, most days the countryside was still as stone.

When Darcy did not sit, he paced. The only movement upon the road was the mysterious daily dispatch of Roux's waggon, empty but for a bevy of servants. Whatever the pilgrimage, it returned heavily laden, its contents shrouded by a tarp, his three men squeezed into the driver's seat. Day after day, without fail the waggon ventured. Aloof (some might even say supercilious), Darcy was not normally curious about a neighbour's business. However, unrelenting leisure might well drive the most indifferent of souls to scrutinise the most insignificant of endeavours.

Thus, when a goose intended for their supper took flight and had the misfortune to become entangled in the spokes of that waggon's passing wheels, Darcy took advantage of the ensuing chaos to stroll over to the arcane tumbrel, flip back the canvas and peer in.

Quite deliberately, and with the excuse of their possible typhus contamination, Darcy had refused Roux's many invitations to stay or even visit with him in his villa. It was quite obvious his cousin's manner of maintaining the lifestyle to which he was accustomed throughout some rather horrific social upheaval had been of dubious (if not outright dishonourable) means. As judgemental as he knew himself capable of being, Darcy did his best not to censure his cousin's life choices, not having had to live under the burden of extended revolution.

But his brief investigation of what was transported in Roux's waggon told him his cousin's avocation, which might have once been only considered unscrupulous, had now expanded into the undeniably felonious. For Roux's waggon had been filled with what could only be surmised as the spoils of war. Judging by the length of the daily trips this plunder came from his neighbours' vacant homes (having drunk the wine and admired the artwork, Roux knew just where any abandoned valuables would be found). Had he been confronted about his thievery, Roux might have justified it by pointing out that his own looting was hardly one step ahead of both armies. Marauders abounded. Napoleon's "scorched earth policy" was as much an excuse for pillaging as bringing the conquered to their knees by way of destitution, and hardly specific to the French.

Darcy knew Roux's merrymakers had abandoned his conviviality under the threat of a rather unpleasant pestilence, and one could only suppose that gentleman's trafficking in women thwarted, his boredom was eased by the thrill of larceny.

At least Darcy hoped it was monotony that drove his cousin's thievery, not an inborn criminality. Increasingly, the spectre of the Darcy family name besmirched by the inclusion of a libertine of Roux's magnitude was not a comfort.

Ennui the only thing accelerating with any rapidity in their little cottage, Darcy's substantial leisure allowed him to reflect upon the evening he had spent at Roux's. The disclosure that so close a friend and relative of his father's was an outright panderer was, indeed, a shocking revelation. But Darcy had initially concluded Roux must have descended of late into the occupation of buttock-peddler, else a man of his father's integrity would never have associated with him. Which was why contemplating upon just why Juliette Clisson was present at Roux's that eve was such an unsettling endeavour.

Initially, it seemed merely coincidental. Juliette was very much a demimondaine, that complementing Roux's inclinations quite fittingly. More than a few serendipitous turns of fate had altered Darcy's life (a chance encounter with Elizabeth led to their ultimate unity), therefore, he was not entirely disdainful of the part coincidence played in one's destiny. Nevertheless, just as Elizabeth's inability to dismiss him from her thoughts led her to visit Pemberley that day, thus allowing their re-acquaintance, he knew providence was almost always guided by connecting events. Darcy had not thought to query Juliette how she knew Roux, but he believed it quite probable theirs was not a new friendship.

As highly principled as he had known his father to be, Darcy had not once criticised that he had directed him to cool the youthful fever in his blood at a house of accommodation. Howbeit, he had chastised himself severely for accepting that advice with such enthusiasm. As to how, coincidentally, his father had directed him to the very house whence Juliette Clisson plied her trade, was a course of thought he believed it best not to pursue. Hence, he did not.

He pursued his sister. The time he did not spend searching the road for a surrogate post-boy, he stalked Georgiana. Possibly to deter her brother, she had no specific routine once leaving Fitzwilliam's sickroom. Thus, Darcy took to skulking about the hall, not unlike a particularly rapacious spider, awaiting his sister's inadvertent passing into his path. After a great deal of evasiveness (and no little ingenuity), Georgiana eventually bechanced upon him. Determined to discover unequivocally her romantic situation, he stepped in front of her, arms folded and a look upon his countenance that told her he had had quite enough of her intrigue. Knowing his quarry would slip away at any moment, he came directly to the point.

"Do you believe yourself in love with Fitzwilliam?"

At her brother's condescending implication that she truly did not know her own mind, she dropped her gaze to the floor and closed her eyes tightly in a vain endeavour to squelch her anger. Hence, when she did look to him, her eyes were defiant. With well-trained sufferance (and with compassion for his loss of hearing), she answered with a single nod.

"Does Fitzwilliam return your esteem?"

Although the question asked nothing more, neither nod nor shake of the head was offered. Georgiana merely shrugged. Thereupon, rather merrily, she encouraged her brother to let her pass with the back of her hand and flounced (yes, it was a flounce, he knew a flounce when he saw one) down the hall. This was an exasperating predicament. Captive of a house, hostage of his ears, now introduced to impudent flouncing from his own sister. It would not do.

As there was little alternative, his indignation was eventually exchanged for reluctant resignation. Fitzwilliam's recovery was slow, and Georgiana's devotion apparent. Acquiescing to Fitzwilliam's reluctance of being pitied, Darcy tried not to hover about him, often only coming to the door of the room to see how he was faring. From thence, he would, as often as not, observe Georgiana holding Fitzwilliam's hand as she bent over him, her ear turned to his lips. That luxury, of course, was denied to Darcy and there was little he would not have sacrificed just to hear the familiar cadence of Fitzwilliam's voice declaring himself better.

For Fitzwilliam truly did not look better. At least what you could see of him. For bandages yet covered his eyes and the side of his face. But his leg wound had stopped oozing, and he had ceased periods of delirium, both signs of improvement. The good tidings of these developments were, however, usurped for Darcy by a shock upon his sensibilities of unprecedented proportion.

For upon one of Darcy's trips to the door of Fitzwilliam's room, he accidently intruded upon the occasion of Fitzwilliam's daily sponge bath. The office of chief bather was held by Miss Georgiana Darcy.

"Georgiana!" Darcy said (or possibly shouted, for he spoke far more loudly than ever could be explained by his deafness).

Georgiana started at this and the bare arm she was slathering with soap slipped from her grip. Fitzwilliam, either used to Georgiana's ministrations or unaware it was she who was bathing him, had started as well. The provocation of Darcy's shouting out Georgiana's name in such an alarmed manner incited Fitzwilliam to believe they were somehow in harm's way and he flailed about in search of a weapon.

Georgiana endeavoured to calm him and said, "See what you have done?!" over her shoulder to Darcy.

Thereupon, with indignant impatience, she met her brother (who stood yet agape at the door) and led him firmly back to the drawing room, indicating there he was to stay.

He, however, was mid-sputter, "Georgiana, how can you behave in such an improper, incautious, indiscreet manner?! Have you gone mad?!" (Both brother and sister's remarks were more in exclamatory than query.)

She answered him slowly, mouthing her words in careful deference of his ears, "I am a nurse. How do you fancy the wounded to bathe?"

"You are not at the hospital now, and Fitzwilliam is not some anonymous patient. Have someone else to do it."

"Who do you propose? A maid. You?"

"I would sooner do it than have you."

Raising an eyebrow, she allowed them both to picture Darcy giving Fitzwilliam a bath. He might, perchance, oversee a bath, direct a manservant, she silently considered, but not bathe Fitzwilliam himself. Just as certain he would, as Georgiana thought not, Darcy stood his ground.

Georgiana heaved a sigh at her brother's lack of understanding. Truly, she had no way of explaining to him what she had seen and done since she left Pemberley. How altered she was. Forever altered. She opened her mouth to try to explain, then shook her head of the notion.

Instead, she said, simply and with finality, "I shall nurse him."

Darcy thought he saw what he considered an unhealthy degree of determination in his sister as she quitted the room. Perchance she was mad, he worried, for she certainly was not behaving in a rational manner. All the blood and death were enough to falter the hardiest of sensibilities. Yes, there was no question. His sister had gone daft. He had rescued her from the hospital, but he saw no way, save binding and trussing her as if a turkey, to save her from herself.

Fitzwilliam had been aware of Darcy's continued presence, but Georgiana had not told him of her brother's deafness. His outburst caused her to explain it. After the cursed bath, Darcy came again to the room and drew a chair next to the bed. Fitzwilliam reached out his hand and Darcy took it and held it, but not in feminine fashion by the fingers. This was a masculine gesture, designated as such by the grasping of the thumbs.

Just beginning to allow himself to believe Fitzwilliam would live, Darcy only then began to place himself in Fitzwilliam's proverbial boots. Survival was not always paramount. Life and living coexisted independently. Darcy thought of his own privilege and imagined living crippled and blind. It was unthinkable. For Fitzwilliam, it was worse yet. The younger brother of the Earl of Matlock would sit in bemedaled boredom in the sunroom at Whitemore and waste away.

Darcy cleared his throat several times before he could talk. Fitzwilliam acknowledged the emotion by a subtle pressure from his hand. All that he could muster to say was the observation of the ridiculous irony of their situation.

"What a sorry pair we are, Fitzwilliam. You cannot see, and I cannot hear. Together we make just one good man."

Fickleness of chance does betimes favour the infirm as it did at that moment. For had Darcy been able to hear, he most certainly would not have welcomed the reminder when Fitzwilliam laughed softly and made an assertion.

"At least I've got my ballocks, Darcy. At least I've got my ballocks."

A perturbation for Georgiana's brother, possibly. But a substantial consolation for Fitzwilliam.

Within a fortnight of Elizabeth's return from London, a portentous envoy hastened to Longbourn. This legate had the duty to inform Mrs. Lydia Bennet Wickham of her husband's valorous (if ultimately fatal) Napoleonic campaign.

Late of her father's house since Wickham's loudly lamented embarkation to Belgium, Lydia had been enjoying an extended holiday at the expense of her parents' nerves. Beyond the use of her husband's reluctant sallying forth into battle as a platform of self-promotion, she had not once considered he might actually be killed. Hence, upon learning of this serendipitous turn of events, she fell into a dreadful swoon. However her mother and father endeavoured, no vinaigrette-of-hartshorn could influence Lydia from the throes of bemoaning, bewailing bereavement.

In lieu of sending a cold post announcing their brother-in-law's demise, Mr. Bennet went to Derbyshire to tell Jane and Elizabeth himself. He undertook the journey solely to soothe the precipitousness of the message. This was an admirable intention, however, as a renowned poor traveller, his unannounced arrival was more ominous than any express.

The first to benefit from this harbinger of obituary was Jane. So roundly distraught was she, it was decided that she, Bingley, and Mr. Bennet should all go together to break the news of Wickham's death to Elizabeth. However, having spent precious little time in prayer for Wickham's uniformed hide, the arrival at Pemberley of the baleful trio well-nigh incited Elizabeth into a swoon herself. Fortuitously, her father foresaw she might think they brought ill-boding for her husband's life. Thus, he blurted out that it was not Darcy, but Wickham, who was heels foremost.

"Dead? Wickham?" she repeated incredulously.

"Gathered to God," assured Jane.

Hearing this revelation in the grand foyer, Elizabeth abruptly planted herself upon an ormolu ottoman and commenced to weep uncontrollably. Bingley, Jane, and Mr. Bennet took turns looking at each other quizzically at this unprecedented outburst, having it upon good authority that Elizabeth was not particularly fond of her brother-in-law. It was in the domain of this reflection that Mr. Bennet understood her true grief. That of newly exacerbated apprehension.

"There, there, Lizzy. Mr. Darcy is quite all right. It is only Wickham…" Mr. Bennet consoled.

"Papa!" Jane admonished.

"Yes, yes, Jane. She knows what I mean."

Yes, she did know what he meant, and having her father there to attempt to put his arms around her well-burgeoned stomach was more comfort than she thought possible to obtain. Mr. Bennet had ascertained from Bingley that Elizabeth had learnt Darcy was alive and at Roux's villa upon the eighteenth of June. He hastened to assure her that word had it that the fighting had ceased but for skirmishes upon the sixteenth. Hence, the worst was over and Darcy had survived.

Letting out a breath so deep it very nearly did make her faint, Elizabeth allowed herself to believe for the first time Darcy was finally out of harm's way. Thus, all put upon a sorrowful face and (in Jane's case, sincerely) set about mourning Lydia's husband.

It was decided over supper that this must be done in person and post-haste. But not so hastily lest Mr. Bennet not be able to rest adequately. Jane and Elizabeth had observed his puffy face and swollen ankles with trepidation.

"Just gout, my daughters, just gout. A rich man's affliction for certain, and what a mischievous game is played when such an ailment is visited upon such a lowly gentleman as myself!" he protested jovially.

Perchance it was merely the intensity of the summer air and not the spending of emotion of which Mr. Bennet was always so parsimonious that caused his heart to grieve him. In such a plight, rarely is it questioned whence it came. Elizabeth only knew one minute he was smiling over his meal, the next he was not. Slowly, he brought the palm of his hand to his chest and pressed it there. With that gesture came a grimace of pain.

"Papa!"

Elizabeth and Jane both leapt up, but Mr. Bennet's forehead had not brushed the table before Bingley reached him. A subdued bedlam ensued as servants were called to carry him upstairs and a rider dispatched for the physician. Once he was carried to a bedroom, he was presumptuously stripped to his small clothes, night-shirted, and sequestered into a sickbed, protesting cheerfully every step of the way. Both Elizabeth and Jane were affrighted to their shoes.

Thus, he assured them, "'Tis merely dyspepsia, my dears, I have not the neck for apoplexy."

Elizabeth almost smiled at that, but Mr. Bennet's face was contorted by another stab of pain. At that, even he gave up the pretence that nothing was wrong. His face took upon a cast of greyish-green and he lay back.

"What can I get you Papa? Calomel? Bitters?"

Dr. Upchurch (Carothers had been gathered to God the previous autumn) arrived directly to investigate the complaint and that done, he offered little encouragement, "I believe the gentleman is losing ground."

His daughters' distraught countenances announced the doctor's unfavourable diagnosis. Mr. Bennet reminded them that the doctor's vast medicinal bag of tricks had yet to be employed.

"He has come all this way in the dark. He shan't lose a patient so easily. Once dead, we are notoriously slow in paying his fee."

Although he was noticeably weaker, his good humour demanded a lack of pessimism. Moreover, Elizabeth reasoned, if he had suffered a stroke she knew there would have been some paralysis. Thus, she did her best not to think of the fear she had seen in her father's eyes, believing, somehow, that if he could live through the night, he would rally.

Jane and Elizabeth sat up with Dr. Upchurch as he periodically took Mr. Bennet's pulse. Each time he did, he raised an eyebrow and shook his head. But Mr. Bennet's breathing lost its pant and deepened before dawn. Elizabeth thought it a good sign.

"I did so want to outlive your mother, Lizzy. What will she do?" he queried. "What will she do?"

She could not believe that her father would be taken from her and allowed herself to join Jane in an uncomfortable upright nap. When the day did break, her father's face was turned to the light of the window. Seeing him, Elizabeth rose and placed the back of her fingers against his cool forehead. Softly, she called his name. He did not hear it.

Gently, she closed his eyes and then kissed his forehead. With stealth and determination, she recovered her seat next to Jane who was yet asleep, thus allowing her another hour of being a father's daughter.

Rather than returning to Hertfordshire to comfort Lydia, they brought renewed grief. Their small cortege followed Mr. Bennet's coffin slowly as it made its way upon a black caisson. The plumed feathers atop the funeral horses' heads bounced ludicrously. Yet Elizabeth could not keep herself from being entranced by their dance.

Ever fretful, Jane was concerned for Elizabeth, for the only tears her sister had shed were the very few that dropped from her eyes at his bedside. She feared her sister was slipping into the same melancholia from whence she very nearly did not recover after the death of her baby. Talking to her had not made head-way, for she responded appropriately, but with dispassion.

At Longbourn Mr. Bennet's coffin was set in the parlour, and as his body had been laid out at Pemberley, his family had nothing to do but keen.

In her childhood room, Elizabeth sat upon the side of the bed patiently awaiting for the others to retire. In time, when the house was quiet, she drew the shawl about her (indeed so well-worn it was getting a bit thread-bare) and padded barefoot down the stairs. Candles had been set at the base of the chairs that were fashioned into a makeshift bier supporting Mr. Bennet's coffin. They were the only lights in the room. Mary sat at her father's feet, a Bible clutched in her fingers, eyes shut tightly in prayer. When she heard Elizabeth, she silently rose and moved toward the stairs, her post replaced.

As she sat, Elizabeth placed her hand upon the smooth wood of the casket, then rested her cheek against its coolness. Time had suspended, thus she was unaware of how long she had been there when she heard her mother's voice, strangely softened.

"How shall we manage without him, Lizzy?"

Elizabeth did not raise her head, merely turned it by way of her forehead to rest upon her other cheek and looked toward where her mother had sat unobserved. Odd, Elizabeth had never known her mother to sit anywhere silently, as she did then.

"His last thoughts were of you, Mama," Elizabeth said, trying to contain any bitterness. Her mother said nothing.

"He said he was concerned for you, was he to die."

Her mother nodded, and yet sat silent. A substantial anomaly.

Elizabeth told her, "Do not fear, Mama. Jane and I shall take care of you, you will always have a home. I know of a house upon Pemberley you would like…"

"Thank you, Lizzy, but I cannot think of that now," her mother answered.

Elizabeth could see the rivulets of her tears gleaming in the candlelight. They sat in silence for some time before Elizabeth heard her mother sigh.

"No better man, my Lizzy. No better husband."

At this, Elizabeth returned to her alternate cheek, unable to look at her mother any further.

"How soon was it," she thought, "that the dead are brought to deity in the eyes of those who in life found them little regard."

She thought she had said it only to herself, but apparently did not, "That is not what you told Lydia."

"I told her what, Lizzy?"

Elizabeth did not want to quarrel with her mother. Particularly not over her father's yet uninterred corpse. But she could not remain silent just then in the dark. Had it been day and she were able to look at her mother's familiar countenance, she would remember whose daughter she yet was. In the pitch-gloom of the night, it was easy to forget she was a daughter still.

"That is not what you said to Lydia," she repeated, a little louder. "She said you told her Papa was faithless to you."

"Oh that Lydia. She told you that? That was not for your ears. She despaired so of Major Wickham. I thought she would not if she believed all men were as he…. It seemed right at the time Lizzy, for she was so very wretched. Was I amiss?"

Albeit it was the single time her mother had ever questioned the righteousness of her own actions, Elizabeth could not bring herself to tell her she was, indeed, quite wrong. The logic of disparaging her father to his daughter to ease the sins of her husband was lost upon Elizabeth, as was all her mother's reasoning.

But in the hours she sat at the foot of her father's coffin, in her father's house, she had the luxury of objectivity she had not held for some time. There she was Elizabeth alone, and not Darcy's wife. Having been so angry with her mother for so many years, the lucidity with which her own culpability came to her in the dark room was startling.

She had blamed her mother for Bingley's infidelity to Jane as much as Bingley himself. If she was honest, she knew she held her mother in reproach for the only serious rift betwixt herself and Darcy. The mere repeating of an accusation against her father had shaken her supposed august trust of her own husband. Had she no more fortitude than Lydia? She who found comfort in such a scurrilous story?

Elizabeth turned and looked at her mother again. Mrs. Bennet sat with her head resting against the back of the chair. She looked broken. Vulnerable. Again, Elizabeth closed her eyes, not in defence of the woeful sight, but of her own introspection.

The single good tiding (to which Elizabeth clung tenaciously) in this time of dreadful sadness was that with Napoleon's defeat, the fighting had ended and her husband had survived it. But however greatly it was anticipated, for weeks after hostilities had ceased, there was not another message from him.

Nor from anyone else of note. In this absence of enlightenment, Elizabeth could only conjecture that a lack of notification meant Fitzwilliam was not a casualty. Of this, she was exceedingly grateful, but Georgiana's circumstances were nevertheless an outright puzzle. Twice Bingley endeavoured to cross the Channel in search, but was denied by authorities. For word from the continent was grim: not only were marauding bands of plunderers keeping good folks inside, typhus had struck as well. The areas not in political upheaval were in quarantine. Everyone able to flee had fled. Both war and disease had commanded mass graves. Terrified and uncertain, Elizabeth had no notion what else to do but worry once more.

It was believed that in one of those graves rested Major George Wickham. For Lydia (who did not favour the appellation Widow Wickham, thinking it sounded too matronly), it was a trying time and one of great dilemma. Not of grief, but decorum, for it insisted the bereaved keep sober and mournful comportment, in neither of which she had any practise. In addition to the burden of countenance, she was demanded to wear black as well. She abhorred herself in black.

Was displeasure of her wardrobe not trial enough, there was another particularly ruthless turn. For the demise of her husband by way of battle required a steady stream of Whitehall garrisoned officers to make a pilgrimage of respect to his family. These were soldiers in name only, who chose not to soil their hands (or risk their comfortable lives) in battle, believing it duty enough to bask in the bravery of those who did (reflected glory better than no glory whatsoever). If there was any question of character of these failed sons of the peerage, it was not asked by Lydia.

The only interest she had was not one of integrity, but of uniform. Her greatest quandary was to decide whether Lancer, Dragoon, or Guard had a finer flourish to their uniform (eventually she decided in favour of the Hussars, for they wore rather fine beaver hats). Yes, handsome officer after handsome officer (all resplendent in cape and sword, which clearly defined handsome to Lydia) came to pay their devoirs, and propriety demanded she could not flirt and had to wear black.

Lydia loved her father, but he was dead and gone. (From the privilege of widowhood, she even believed she very nearly loved Wickham.) She had her whole life (or a goodly portion of it) in front of her and the confoundment of being denied opportunity to troll for a new husband from an uncommonly fertile pool vexed her to distraction. Had other been expected, her displeasure was not suffered in silence. She whined about it incessantly. Her chief occupations were whining when she was not in company and surreptitiously flirting when she was. For after some study before her mirror, Lydia perfected a wicked little smile that, if she could just get the right tilt of her fan, would promise any gentleman under her gaze that she was not all that sad.

There was ample audience to witness this devious coquetry, for bereavement required the Bingleys and Elizabeth stay at Longbourn for at least the month. Jane and Bingley were appropriately aghast (but not necessarily surprised) at Lydia's distaste of solemnity. Elizabeth cared little if Lydia was contemptuous of her husband's memory, but was determined she would not besmirch their father's. Thus, in exasperation at witnessing Lydia's repeated vamping from behind her fan, Elizabeth waited until the importuned officer had taken his leave, wrested Lydia's fan away, and rapped her soundly upon the top of her head with it.

"Lydia, I know you suffer cruelly at the loss of your father and husband both (it might have been presumed that this was mockery, but Elizabeth preferred to believe it not), but can you restrain your enthusiasm for widowhood at least until the passing bell ceases its reverberation?"

Hardly reprimanded, Lydia flounced over to a chair and sat in a disgusted heap, "Yes, I suffer cruelly!" she agreed, and thereupon glumly inquired, "Is there to be no diversion?"

"No. You are sad," Elizabeth assured her.

"Oh, Lizzy! 'Tis all so unfair!"

Thereupon, suddenly, a thought visited the unlikely neighbourhood of Lydia's limited intellect.

"Lizzy," she proclaimed, "it just occurred to me, that with Wickham and Papa dying almost simultaneously, I shall have to wear black for just one mourning period!"

"Happy thought indeed," Elizabeth feigned hearty agreement. "Concurrent death is much more pleasing than consecutive. What fortune!"

Lydia went in search of her mother to share her observation of luck. But Elizabeth knew that Mrs. Bennet would have no interest in Lydia's widowhood, for she was quite enmeshed in her own.

Although it was half-past four o'clock in the after-noon a full two weeks after Mr. Bennet's death, Mrs. Bennet had not yet been able to bring herself to rise and dress for the day. Her daughters took turns at her bedside, alternately patting her hand, bringing her tea, and exchanging tear-stained handkerchiefs for dry. (Lydia had abandoned tearful keening once officers began to call, for weeping made her eyes puffy.)

Inconsolable in the loss of her husband, Mrs. Bennet was additionally burdened by the no small matter of entailment of Longbourn to Charlotte Collins's unfortunate son. Again, Elizabeth patted her hand and assured her she would always have a home with her at Pemberley. This was sincerely offered, but Elizabeth could not help but cringe ever so slightly upon Darcy's behalf for when he learnt that he might well have Mrs. Bennet under (or even near) his roof permanently. The thought of that was a considerable trial, but most inadvertently, her mother cast aside that specific apprehension of Elizabeth's for far worse.

Mrs. Bennet's lack of amiability as a housemate would be a moot point if there were no house to plague.

"That is kind, Lizzy, but you may not have a home yourself! I fear Mr. Darcy is no more alive than Mr. Bennet or Wickham! You, my Lizzy, have no son! If this baby dies as the last or, heaven above help us, is a girl, Lady Catherine will have you out! Of that you can be sure!"

At the thought of her dear daughter's dilemma, Mrs. Bennet was nearly overcome with renewed sobs, "Lizzy, Lizzy! What are we to do? Bingley cannot take us all in!"

The spectre of Lady Catherine notwithstanding, more than anything Elizabeth wanted to be home at Pemberley and to wait for Darcy there. Betwixt Lydia's vulgar flirtations and her mother's relentless wailing, Elizabeth thought it quite possible she would run mad from the house. In lieu of the imprudence of that, she chose to take a walk outdoors instead.

She automatically picked up her shawl, and thereupon cast it impatiently aside. It was too warm for a shawl. Was she revealed great with child to someone whose sensibilities would be offended by the sight, they would just have to be sullied. The decision was made only in part due to the weather, the other fell to the sheer enormity of her person. It was simply difficult to disguise her girth.

It was a mystery to Elizabeth how Jane could conceal her pregnancies with such efficiency. For Elizabeth, no matter what manner of arrangement of shawl, her protuberance protruded. Kitty had blurted out that it was quite possibly the size of a small washtub and Elizabeth found no insult at the comparison. It was the size of a washtub. A lively washtub. The baby cast about her insides as if determined to find its own exit, and Elizabeth was certain she could see her skirt jump about as it did.

She fancied others could as well. For when they all sat about the parlour, all eyes rested upon her stomach. There would be short bursts of conversation; thereupon everyone would fall silent, their gazes studying her frock-skirt. It had transcended mere embarrassment and leapt into the world of outright mortification. With her first baby, Darcy had been at her side insisting upon the beauty of her form. It had been effortless then not to feel so very graceless. This time she felt like a particularly ungainly cow.

Beneath her dress and petticoats, she knew she looked like a particularly fecund bovine as well. But without her husband there to caress her bare belly, she alone was unsettled by knowing that this baby was undoubtedly larger than her last. That was the only benefit of Darcy's absence. He would be spared that worry. As she walked some ways down the lane, an unpropitious cramp nagged her.

Ponderously, she wended her way to the familiar oak and rested her unwieldy body against its trunk. She lay her cheek against its roughness and fingered the lines in the bark. It brought to mind how she had unceremoniously bitten Darcy's lip that day long past. She smiled at the recollection of her own discaution. Then, self-consciously, she looked about, for she realised she was embracing the tree. Given another moment she might have kissed it as well.

Wresting her affection from the tree Darcy had once leaned against, she rubbed the outline of the baby he had put in her. That was more rewarding, but only temporarily. Beleaguered by her own interminable worry for Darcy and Georgiana, Elizabeth began to harbour an irrational suspicion that Lady Catherine just might be able to put her out of Pemberley. Was Darcy not to return, was her baby not to survive, she considered it might well be a moot point. Even with so noble a motive as to spite Lady Catherine, she was not so very certain she could bear to stay there alone.

Resting her head back against the tree, she closed her eyes and sought the soothing vision of her husband. Time, grief, and worry were beginning to erode her memory of her husband's face, and for a brief panicky moment, she could not recall it. It was then that she was anointed with an undertaking of the utmost of importance. She vowed aloud she would repair that very day and return to Pemberley. There she would sit beneath Darcy's portrait in the gallery every day until their baby was born. Forgetting his face would be an impossibility.

Once the decision was made to repair to Derbyshire, Elizabeth altered her plans only as to the immediacy of the trip. As she hastened back to the house, she realised it was too late to take leave that very evening. Hence, she wiped her tears away with the hem of her skirt, walked back into the parlour, and announced to Jane and Bingley that she would take leave at first light. Jane was appalled.

She pleaded, "Lizzy, it was unsafe for you to have travelled here weeks ago. You must not journey again!"

"I intend to have my husband's baby in his home and be there when he returns. If I do not take leave immediately, it will be too late. I am quite adamant."

She spoke with such impressive finality that Jane opened her mouth to beseech her again, then stopped. Elizabeth's determined expression said it would not be wise to argue.

Bingley spoke instead, "If we cannot convince you not to travel, Jane and I shall go as well. You will not travel alone."

Such was Bingley's own resolve, Jane and Elizabeth both turned silently and looked at him, neither having heard him make an ultimatum before. Elizabeth thought of telling Bingley her travel decisions were quite her own, but decided not, by reason of…he was most probably right.

Hence, with her quest of hearth and home now a mission, Elizabeth entered the carriage that next morning with purposeful anticipation. The Bingleys sat upon either side of her just as resolutely, but with more trepidation than either of them wanted to keep to themselves. As they finished loading trunks into the boot, Mrs. Bennet (who had willed herself from her bed) came to wave a handkerchief in farewell and Jane endeavoured one last time to make Elizabeth listen to reason. Listen, if not to reason, at least to something.

"Lizzy, do reconsider. Do you feel well? Perchance you should rest more before you attempt this. Charles, hand Lizzy that pillow. Put it behind her back. Lizzy, do reconsider."

The coach drew away and Elizabeth said nothing in answer to Jane's solicitations, but simply patted her hand. Bingley patted Jane's other hand as well, for it was Jane who was the disordered party.

As they passed the Meryton churchyard, they looked across the stone fence at the grass that had begun to emerge atop their father's fresh grave. In the dawn's new light, it looked slightly bedraggled, yesterday's cut flowers having wilted in the summer air. Hating to see Mr. Bennet's final resting-place unkempt, Elizabeth almost called out for them to stop so she could replace the flowers with fresh ones, but she knew Kitty and Mary would do so by mid-morning. She hoped they would plant some sort of bulb that would not wane.

As the coach passed by the site, all those inside had turned their heads to gaze upon the grave. Once past, Jane and Bingley looked toward their destination. Only Elizabeth watched as the steeple of the church diminished into the distance.

By midday, it was suggested they stop near a grove of trees to stretch their limbs and partake of a bit of lunch. The same low pain that had plagued her earlier stole Elizabeth's appetite, but she spoke not of it, hoping the rest would aid her as well as the horses. They had barely laid out their repast before Elizabeth's ache announced its intensification in her back. With deliberate calm, she stood and stretched, well-aware Jane was watching her. Determined to keep her discomfort to herself, Elizabeth walked about a bit before proclaiming they had lost far too much time from the road.

When everyone sat and looked at her dumbly, she ordered, "Do not fart about!"

Alarmed at her dictatorial (and unprecedentedly coarse) directive, Jane and Bingley jumped up, not of a notion to deny her anything just then. Anxiously, Jane trailed about after Elizabeth, but Bingley looked more frightened by Elizabeth than for her. Elizabeth saw their confusion, but had neither the interest nor wherewithal to explain herself. By early afternoon, she had no need, for her pain had intensified long past hiding. Bingley ordered the coach to stop. Elizabeth insisted it not.

"I will not have this baby upon the road. I will have it at Pemberley. Move on!"

Bingley rapped the roof twice with his walking stick, but looked worriedly at his wife (Bingley's sensibilities were far too fragile to weather much female distress). Jane endeavoured reasoning again with her sister that they must stop at the first house they saw, but again Elizabeth refused.

"I will have this baby at Pemberley."

Finally, Jane motioned to Bingley to order the coach to stop regardless of her sister's admonitions. Elizabeth had lain back upon the seat opposite briefly but rose up at his interference, hanging onto the hand strap.

She said to Jane, whilst gifting Bingley a decidedly violent (Bingley would have described it maniacal) look, "Tell Charles Bingley that if he stops this carriage once more I shall…I shall…smite him!"

Bingley's notion that, in her condition, Elizabeth could not actually best him was not so strong as to stop him from urging the coach on again, this time shouting, "Make haste!" If they were to make this journey with Elizabeth labouring, they would do it, if not in comfort, then with speed.

The coach ride did not become truly horrific until the last few miles. Until then, Elizabeth's baby's imminent arrival had only been betrayed by her white-knuckled grip upon the hand strap and gritted teeth. Thus, when she put her feet upon the opposite seat, spread her knees and exhibited the unmistakable need to expel said infant, that the time for delivery was upon them was not misunderstood.

Hence, if her labouring traversed three counties, it culminated in Derbyshire.

A bombardment of docking vessels at the wharves down the Thames from London announced as shrilly as had the newspapers that Napoleon's threat had ended. The first to arrive were the proud Ships of the Line and frigates, laden with the heroes of Waterloo.

Each successive disembarkation featured the same performance to an ever-increasing crowd of cheering onlookers. Always first to come ashore were the officers, beplumed and besworded, taking each step down the gangplank as if it was the centre aisle at St. James. Upon the heels of that grandiloquent show was a substantially more rambunctious, but no less self-satisfied, mob of enlisted men, the two factions united within the complacency of enjoying their glory from the exceedingly fine vantage of good health.

It was only with the subsequent arrival of privateers did the true cost of victory unfold, and this tale was told as much from who did not put ashore as who did. For upon those creaking ships were thousands of the ambulatory amongst the wounded, their number only suggesting the men left in Belgium and France who were not. By then, there was neither music nor cheers to greet these less revered veterans, not that their wounds diminished their heroism, quite the contrary. It was simply a matter of aesthetics. Mangled men were not pretty. And as there was quite a troupe of returning soldiers who were, it was they who were called upon to personify triumph to the masses.

If the vast preponderance of citizens were satisfied by handsome pomp, there were many who were not. A largely tattered legion of wives and children stood yet upon the pier in vigilant hope of seeing a loved one, hobbling but alive, disgorged from the bowels of some straggling ship. With each passing day, then week, however, even these ignoble landings gradually dwindled. Those yet about who held out hope began to believe themselves forsaken. Amongst these forlorn few, Juliette Clisson stood quite apart.

It began as a simple act of kindness, but had since eclipsed pilgrimage and turned into an outright crusade.

As Juliette knew well, there was but one way from France to England and that was by way of the sea. By foregone assumption, it could be surmised that Mr. Darcy and party would return from the continent by way of London. Hence, rationalising that his wife's condition rendered such a vigil impossible for her, Juliette set about upon a daily campaign to the filthy, bustling dockside to await his arrival herself.

Having always quite diligently avoided any thought of whom Darcy had married, it had been a contradiction of emotions for Juliette when she finally met Elizabeth. Unable to ascertain from her long buried sentiments which she hoped for most—to find her unworthy or worthy—Juliette eventually made a conscious choice toward charity. To feel otherwise would be an abomination upon her own circumstance, and she refused to begrudge any woman such leverage. Hence, she would feel nothing but happiness for Darcy that his distinction was maintained in the woman with whom he had fallen in love. For even Juliette had to acknowledge it was quite remarkable for a woman of Elizabeth Darcy's station to meet with her in public. But for her to travel all the way from Pemberley to London in her exceedingly delicate condition…to do so was more than remarkable. It was quite astonishing.

With belated abashment, Juliette admitted to herself that she had quite maliciously put every obstacle in her way. Every humiliation. To no avail. Mrs. Darcy refused to be baited. A lady in the truest sense of that word.

Bloody hell.

No, Juliette reprimanded herself. It was as she had hoped. He deserved someone who loved him as had she. Someone honourable. Courageous. Kind. That this lady happened to be exceedingly pretty, was not, however, a particular comfort. A lady of station with such impressive probity could at least have the good graces to be plain. To have Darcy, integrity, and beauty was indefensible. The only deprivation incurred was the lack of children. Obviously, even that was remedied. The indignation at such incongruity of riches was enough to vex the hardiest of souls.

As Juliette was determined that no indefatigable fettles would eclipse her own, she set about to prove just that by naming herself watchkeeper over Elizabeth. And, as Juliette believed it highly likely that, however honourable, Mrs. Darcy would not fully appreciate patronage from her, these auspices were offered in silence. Each day Juliette came to the wharf to stand in Elizabeth's fecund stead, and every other week, she sent a discreet emissary to Derbyshire to learn if Mrs. Darcy had either delivered or had word from her husband. Upon the most recent reconnaissance, Juliette was informed that the family had gathered at Hertfordshire to grieve the death of Mr. Bennet.

Seldom was a death a boon, and unquestionably, Juliette did not wish Mr. Bennet ill-tidings. But his passing was out of her hands, thus she was free to see some good came of it, if only a small convenience to herself. For to give Darcy that message would be excuse enough to bring her to meet him at the pier.

She was much in want of justification. For after a week of coming to the wharves, it occurred to Juliette how odd it would appear to Darcy for her to be there to greet him (she thought he might not understand her self-proclaimed conservatorship of his family). Hence, every day as she alternately sat in her carriage and traversed the length of the wharf (with unladylike, long strides that betrayed her anxiety), she practised excuses for being there. All sounded quite flimsy until the recent news of his father-in-law's untimely death.

If she knew to conjure an excuse to present to Darcy for her presence, she did not bother to lie to herself. It was a silly folly. If she truly wanted to help, she could well afford to send a servant to stand upon the shore and watch for Darcy and his party. Truth was, she was so very anxious for his safety, she was drawn to the ships like a rat from Hameln. However honest Juliette was with herself, she did not investigate the contradiction of pursuit that was Darcy safe in England, he would be safe with his wife. After finding him well, there would be ample time for her to re-accustom herself to offering him no special regard. So, stand she did.

The furtive, hooded cloak she first wore was discarded, hot as it was. For she immediately saw there was no need for *incognita*. The dozen or so other women yet attending the dock were no more interested in her than she was in them. Upon occasion, in the monotony before the excitement of anticipating who would put ashore, Juliette would allow herself a little flight of fancy, imagining she was a wife or sweetheart not unlike the others who stood there with her. But she knew it was a frivolity to submit to such a capricious vagary. Her situation, of course, was not as the others.

It was a substantial vexation to her to know she would have to traverse the petard-strewn ground betwixt herself and disaffection for Darcy once again. Had she not had the poor timing to be at Roux's when Darcy passed through, she could have avoided a great deal of emotional bother. She believed, however, being able to see him once more was well worth the labourious duty of again purging him from her mind.

It had been nearly a half dozen years since she had last seen him upon the street in front of Harcourt. She remembered the day with unseemly clarity. It had been breezy; her skirt had whipped about. She was trying to contain it when she recognised him approaching, thus she had only a little time to pretend they were unacquainted before he passed. Even with his wife upon his arm, he had touched the brim of his hat in discreet acknowledgement to her. One would have thought that having a gentleman of his stature greet her in public as he had might have been a small victory. But it had not. He had made that gesture in the company of his wife.

It was at that moment Juliette knew that he had told her of their connexion.

It had been easier to accept no longer seeing him if she believed his absence was a matter of honour and at some personal sacrifice. She doubted quite seriously that he felt the need to unkennel his conscience of the indiscretion of his past. Thus, such a confidence shared with his wife revealed a marriage of more intimate regard than Juliette would have liked to have understood.

That day she renewed her resolve to forget him and had believed that endeavour successful. But when she saw him enter Roux's dining-room, she realised how very unprosperous her efforts had been. She had been flustered into a fit of nerves unlike any she recollected (save for that nasty guillotine incident). It was quite probable she visibly flushed and her only consolation was that he did not see her do it. For his reserve demanded that he acknowledge his introduction with no more than a cursory nod to his dinner companions.

Gathering all the aplomb her considerable experience granted her, she gave no further evidence of her disconcertion than her colour and continued to converse to her companion. However, when she thought herself unobserved she sneaked a few glances toward Darcy. It was the first time she had witnessed his behaviour amongst society.

As she would have guessed, he sat very straight and was quite solemn. It appeared time had altered him a very little, age thickening his lean body ever so slightly. Weariness, however, was etched upon his countenance and that incited a pang within Juliette that she would just as soon not have felt.

Continuing to ignore his presence, she listened as murmurings at her end of the table distinguished him, not only an aristocrat, but some sort of English diplomat as well. If, indeed, he was a government official, she thought that would be an odd turn of events for a man known for his taciturnity. But, she reasoned, one must never presume another's inclinations regardless how lengthy or intimate the connexion. For as aloof as she knew him to be, it was with outright astonishment that she had listened to the telling of that rage that had moved him to manslaughter.

That long past astoundment was well-nigh bested when he walked over to her in the drawing room that evening. Confoundment was something of which she had little experience. That night at Roux's was a series of disconcertions for Juliette, not the least of which occurred when Darcy bid her contact his wife.

It was apparent his reason for being in France was grave, and nonplussed as she was, for the first time her discretion failed her. She did not think to ask him if his business was governmental. That would have given her a source of small talk rather than remarking upon his company as she had. One might suggest with whom Darcy conversed, tarried, or slept was none of her business. By happy chance, he did not appear to understand that when a woman remarks upon a flirt, it is often because the *coquette* has trespassed (and Juliette had not spoken in defence of his wife).

Without hesitation she had agreed to pass on his letter, thereupon abandoning all pretence of disinterest, and watched him keenly the rest of the evening. Spirits being *de rigueur* in most bagnio assignations notwithstanding, in all the years she had known Darcy, she had never seen him have more than a single glass of sherry. She thought it unlikely that a man of his regulation would find drink a regular comfort, thus watched uneasily as he downed at least a carafe of wine before he retired.

It was that aberration that bade Juliette go to him that night in Lille, for something was clearly amiss. At the time, she was quite certain there was no cunning in her resolution. She had merely wanted to be able to talk to him more openly about what brought him there. Allow him to unburden himself. She knew unconditionally, however, that if he needed more than conversational consolation, she would happily supply it.

His door, however, opened so precipitously just as she stepped out of her own, it gave her a start. She very nearly fled back to her room, but held her ground by reason of what could only be described as prying. His arm was all she saw of him, but it told her a great deal. For it strongly encouraged a previous visitor to take leave. Thrust unceremoniously into the light of the corridor, the aforementioned visitor was revealed to be none other than Celeste Roux. A frightfully unhappy Celeste Roux, who announced this by stomping angrily away. Juliette duly noted that if Darcy chose feminine company, it was not in the manner of a virgin, however pretty and however anxious.

Feeling more than a little haughty that Darcy had rejected Mademoiselle Roux's company, Juliette almost took a step in the direction of his now soundly shut door. But she stopped. Thinking more rationally, she knew was he interested in her company, he would seek her. If not, she would find herself just as firmly in the corridor as Celeste. That rejection was not one she was inclined to incur.

She would leave it at that. And did. She closed her door that night in Lille, better prepared to miss an opportunity than obtain a disappointment. The next morning a servant brought a letter in his pen and directed to his wife. It did not bother her conscience to ponder opening it, nor salve it when she chose to not. However, she did decide to deliver it in person.

Regrettably, as those of her party walked up the gangplank to board their ship for England, women's purses were expropriated. (It was a considerable affront, one she would report to the captain, upon whose aegis she was allowed aboard.) Yet of the belief that Darcy was a British envoy, Juliette dared not have his letter confiscated. She discreetly removed it, tore it into tiny pieces and watched them float down to the water. She wished then she had read his letter to his wife, and wished it more when she talked to Elizabeth. At the very least she might have uncovered what had transpired in France with his sister. Perchance she should have told Elizabeth of the colossal misapprehension by others of Darcy's pursuits in France. No doubt, they both would have had a hearty laugh. The laconic Mr. Darcy, a diplomat, indeed.

As often as Darcy had not walked down the plank of any ship, Juliette's reverie was interrupted when he finally did. It took her a moment to realise it was actually him, and her knees buckled slightly with relief. She watched, her heart pounding in her ears, as he conversed with a uniformed man who thereupon scurried off to do some bidding. He stood there quite alone, but she chose not to go to him, enjoying her vantage of undetected observer. Apparently awaiting the man he sent off, he sat heavily upon a short barrel. For an infinitesimal moment, he looked haggard. Then, as if in rejuvenation, he rubbed his face with his hands and stood, composed.

The contemplation of his countenance was seductive, but Juliette knew he would not be alone long, thus she approached. He was facing away, observing the business upon the pier. She called his name. It was not proper for a lady to speak to a gentleman first; however, neither was it truly proper for a woman to be upon the wharf. When she called his name again louder and he did not yet turn about, it occurred to her that he had seen her and chose not to acknowledge her acquaintance in public.

"Foolish, foolish!" she admonished herself, both mortified and vexed at her own lack of circumspection.

At that moment, looking about the crowd, he did turn in her direction. Clearly, he was taken unawares at seeing her standing there. Without hesitation, he walked toward her, took her hand, and kissed it.

Such was her surprise, she apologised for what she had just been indignant, "Pray, forgive me for approaching you in such an unbefitting manner."

Flustered for the second time in so many meetings, she looked away.

"Care not," he assured her.

Thereupon, a look of enquiry overspread his face, and Juliette could see his mind questioning just why she was there. One chance meeting was a novelty, two, an intrigue.

"Were you able to get word to my wife? Do you know if she is well?"

Avoiding the exact wording of his query, for he did not ask her how she delivered his message, she said only, "Yes, she is well. I am here because, of course, she could not…"

He interrupted her, "Forgive me, I do not take your meaning. I understood you to say that she was well."

"She was well when last I heard…"

"You said she could not come here." His voice rising, he queried, "Why not, if she is well?"

Suddenly it dawned upon Juliette that Darcy was unaware of his wife's condition. Not daring to look into his eyes, she dropped hers from his gaze. For she had no notion if she should tell him, or what words to use to say it if she did. She searched for them upon the ground, not yet looking up.

Finally, she said to his boots, "Your wife is heavy with child."

Only then did she look at him. Darcy stood just as he had, his countenance unbetrayed by emotion. Juliette marvelled that even his reticent sensibilities could maintain an even keel upon hearing news of such substantial consequence. But he did. He stood there as if he had not heard, therefore, she repeated it for good measure, but this time looked at him full.

"Your wife is heavy with child."

"With child?" he repeated, apparently dumbfounded.

She nodded her head, and watched his face take a trip of emotions that would merit an atlas. For Juliette, it was an enjoyable revelation of his feelings, undisplayed as he had always kept them. But the last and most pronounced was of such decided apprehension, Juliette immediately recollected that his wife's only other laying-in had ended with a dead child. She did not know the circumstances, but his expression said this one was perilous as well.

He announced, "Forgive me, I must make haste," and distractedly turned to leave.

The man he had bid a few minutes before approached leading a carriage and a saddled horse tied to the back. Darcy spoke some instructions to him, pointed to the ship from which he had just disembarked, thereupon untied the horse from the coach. He grabbed the pommel as if to mount the horse, then stopped. He strode back to Juliette.

He said, "Pray, forgive me, for I did not thank you for coming here to tell me."

Looking at her curiously, as if to query, he then gave a slight shake of his head and said simply, "Thank you."

Abruptly, he drew her to his chest and kissed her upon the forehead. He mounted his horse and dug his heels quite soundly into its sides, encouraging it into a canter away. But Juliette could not see him do it for the tears in her eyes. She had walked half the distance to her own coach before she whirled and called after him. She had compleatly forgotten to tell him his wife was not at Pemberley, but at Longbourn.

"Darcy…Darcy!"

But he did not hear her.

The road was dry, hence dust curled behind the pounding hooves almost engulf-ing his horse and Darcy as he rode for Pemberley. Knowing it was reckless to travel with such haste upon an animal to whose stamina he could not attest, he strove on regardless. He knew the road home in his sleep, and thus, exactly where to stop to obtain another when this one inevitably faltered.

Each time he heeled to stop in a village, horse and rider both lathered and heaving, the event incited a small crowd to gather to see what manner of gentleman was in such a rush.

Dignity, however, was the least of his concerns, thus he paid little attention to the hubbub. The hauteur by which he had always presented himself to the world at large was outright abandoned by the time he reached the farthest reaches of Pemberley. For the summer heat not only caked dust upon his perspiring forehead, it demanded he discard his jacket entirely.

Once upon even more familiar ground, he cut off the main road to find a shorter route by the stables. It was there he saw his coach being unhitched from a team of horses that were lathered almost as generously as his own. He pulled to a stop but did not dismount, for he espied Edward Hardin as he stood before an opened door of the coach with a bucket of soapy water. The interior of the carriage was a bloody mess.

"Who travelled in this coach?" Darcy demanded.

His mouth slightly agape, Edward Hardin stood looking at the dirt-encrusted countenance of his long absent employer as if at an apparition. The man flinched when Darcy shouted the query at him a second time, but remained stunned yet. Too impatient to wait for information (and not certain he was sufficiently steeled to hear the answer), Darcy whirled his horse and kicked him toward the archway to the court and through it. At the doorsteps to Pemberley, he slung his leg over the neck of the horse and jumped down at a dead run.

Servants were by that time swarming and the door was thrown open for him, but only by the smallest margin, for he had taken the steps two at a time. Surprisingly, Bin-gley met him as he entered the vestibule.

Darcy offered no greeting, but demanded of him, "Is Elizabeth well?"

Bingley started to say something, stopped, looked down, then away. He held out one hand, palm up, and Darcy could not determine if this gesture was in supplication or in asking for help in explanation. That either was a possibility meant Bingley could not answer his question definitively with a "yes," and Darcy grabbed his lapel to encourage some response. One came not; hence, he shook him in the hope of rattling his vocal cords loose. Bingley's vest was so sticky with blood, it caught Darcy's atten-tion. He held up his stained hand before them, and both looked upon it with horror. A cold trepidation caused Darcy to abandon seeking a determination of Elizabeth's well-being from anyone other than Elizabeth, herself.

"Where is she? Where is Elizabeth?"

Bingley pointed upstairs and Darcy's boots assaulted them. At the top he took the corner by pivoting the newel post to speed himself, much as he did when a boy, and headed toward their rooms. Hannah had heard the commotion and opened the door in anticipation. He came to a skidding stop just inside.

He stood there, his chest heaving, less from exhaustion than emotion, for he could see Elizabeth there, the covers drawn up neatly beneath her chin. She lay still and white as death. No baby was in evidence.

Walking over to the edge of the bed, he kneeled and took her hand, softly calling her name.

"Lizzy," he said. "Lizzy."

Odd, the tricks one's mind plays. She would have sworn before God that it was her husband's voice she heard. But that was an impossibility.

Impossible or not, with great effort she turned upon her side and reached out, the allurement of his voice was irresistible. Grasping the side of the mattress, she tried to rise upon one arm, but she was too weak and collapsed upon it instead.

Again, she heard his voice calling her name and she opened her eyes, blinking wildly to clear the haze. The only thing within her focus was the floor, and upon it, a pair of boots. Tall boots. Large boots. Astoundingly large and decidedly dusty boots.

"Darcy."

Had she managed any tears, they would have been obliterated by the shower of kisses bestowed upon her face by her husband. She endeavoured to say more than just his name, but her voice was weak.

"Do not tire yourself, Lizzy."

There was little grander reason she could think of to exert herself, and she told him thus repeatedly. He, however, had whirled about demanding someone to tell him of her condition. Elizabeth tugged at his shirt, trying to get his attention once more, but failed. Jane, Hannah, Mrs. Reynolds, and Bingley too stood just beyond the world of her bed, peering upon them, smiling at the reunion. Darcy seemed reassured by such felicity, but confused.

"What?" he demanded. "What?!"

Elizabeth lifted her hand and pointed toward Hannah. Hannah was, indeed, holding a baby.

He looked again to Elizabeth and asked, incredulous, "Ours?"

Weakly, she smiled and nodded.

In another life, he might have rushed to look upon his child, but he did not. He took both of Elizabeth's hands and kissed the palms. Repeatedly. Thereupon he attended her lips, caressing her face as he did. It would have been expected that those in presence would have known to give their reunion some privacy but no one there was in a mind to take their leave. Hence, Darcy finally rose and walked over to look upon the countenance of his child. He did so not so much in curiosity, but as in believing that what was required. Having not had time to fully appreciate his father-hood, the magnitude of his altered situation was quite lost upon him.

The tiny bundle swaddled in Hannah's arms turned crimson as it began a squall of impressive decibel. Jane reached over and turned back the edge of the blanket revealing a dark-haired, red-faced, squirming infant. Darcy threw his head back with a hearty laugh of delight, now compleatly enlightened he was, indeed, a father.

Hannah laughed. Jane laughed as well. Bingley grabbed Mrs. Reynolds by the waist and swung her around, and the startled woman stopped laughing when he did. Bingley put her down a little meekly and walked over to stand behind Jane, his hands resting upon her shoulders.

It was only then that Darcy saw Jane also held a baby.

"My congratulations as well to you and Jane, Bingley," he said.

Everyone was looking at him so queerly, he was suddenly befuddled.

"Have I admired the wrong baby?"

He turned back to Elizabeth and bid, "Which is ours?"

She said, "Do you mean, sir, that we can keep but one?"

That he looked at her quite blankly revealed his deafness. Thus, she held out her arms, which he hastily reclaimed.

She held his face in her hands and said as clearly and plainly as she could, "They are both ours."

The rapture with which Darcy embraced not only his wife, but also his new-found fatherhood, transcended mere words. And eventually his reservoir of vigour was compleatly sapped by emotion and he fell fast asleep atop Elizabeth's covers. She had no way of knowing, of course, but concluded regardless, that it was the first peace he had secured for months. Hence, she was reassured, not affronted, by his relief.

The story of the birth of their babies could wait. That they and Elizabeth had survived the ordeal was all the information he wanted just at that particular moment. Elizabeth needed only to hear the murmured confirmation from him that Georgiana had returned to England unscathed to allow herself a serene rest as well. Hence, the blissful onlookers took their cue and retreated from the room, none realising that Darcy had not thought to inquire if either of his offspring was now heir to the vast fortune of Pemberley.

The babies favoured each other prodigiously, hence, their differing gender supplied the most efficient means of telling one from the other. This, as it happened, was of more immediate importance to their family than which would eventually inherit. And assured of lineage, Pemberley and the surrounding countryside feted the births with festivities unparalleled since the Darcys' wedding.

Whilst Derbyshire celebrated, Darcy embarked upon an individual interview of those present to learn eventually the full story of Elizabeth's pregnancy and the spectre of childbirth upon the road.

Most post hoc commentary had been jests by Elizabeth about the extent of her recent girth (now able to find more humour about it once her waistline was returned to an approximation of the past). Yet he uncovered that, though Jane actually delivered the babies, the dual birth explained Bingley's bloodied waistcoat. For his arms were commandeered as the most convenient repository for one of the squalling new-borns. Upon the new father's behalf, the fright and desperation during that event was ignored in favour of a telling that emphasised excitement and suspense. Much was the same for the tale of his ruptured hearing. The truth would be left to the ingenuity of each other's considerable imagination of what actually occurred.

It was within these conversations that Darcy learnt that, howbeit the family was blessed with two births, two deaths had occurred as well. When he heard from Bingley the sad news of Mr. Bennet's passing, he went directly to Elizabeth to console her. Possibly in want of not dwelling on that cheerless subject, she told her husband that Wickham had fallen in battle. She did so hesitantly, uncertain of just how that bit of information would sit upon him. He appeared to take it quite unremarkedly. Her father's death clearly was the more pertinent of the two.

The next day, understandably, Elizabeth was weak and bedridden yet. Even so, Jane had difficulty keeping her still, for she could not be happy but to have her husband and both babies in the bed with her. So roundly delighted to be home, Darcy was not inclined to leave her even for a moment, and was only coaxed from her side by the bell calling that Miss Georgiana had returned to Pemberley.

Fitzwilliam had fared poorly upon the trip home to England, but stoicism was part of his nature. Denial of pain was not a surprise, but he projected such cheerfulness about his circumstances, that Darcy knew that a farce as well. Fitzwilliam's vision and Darcy's hearing had repaired at about the same level. Fitzwilliam's sight was blurry and it left him dizzy. Darcy could hear, but mostly higher tones.

Of the two, fortune smiled most favourably on Darcy, for he could understand most of what Elizabeth said and could hear the babies when they had a notion to let out a wail. (Elizabeth assured him it was best his ears were disadvantaged at that particular time, for the noise the infants produced together was quite extraordinary.)

Still steadfastly at his side, Georgiana had accompanied Fitzwilliam to Whitemore, but the news of the babies' births bid her make haste to Pemberley. Seeing his sister standing safe within the walls of their home once again was a grand, but far too fleeting moment for Darcy. Quite precipitously, he was reminded that other ill-tidings were at hand and Elizabeth would have to be told.

As her recent company with her brother was both compact and extended, it could be understood if immediately after Georgiana gave her brother her congratulations in an unbridled embrace and kiss on the cheek, she relinquished his company to go to Elizabeth and have a look at her niece and nephew. Before she did so, Darcy told her of Mr. Bennet's recent death.

Then, rather mildly, he added, "I am told also that another loss has befallen the family. It is reported that George Wickham has evidently lost his life in valorous battle."

They stood looking at each other silently for a moment, for Georgiana knew of Wickham's treason.

Georgiana responded, "If Wickham shot John Christie in the stomach and left him to die, I hope he is burning in hell as we speak."

Darcy found no argument with that sentiment, but cautioned her, "With all that has bechanced, I have yet to tell Elizabeth that young John is dead, or that Fitzwilliam's wounds kept us in France. She thinks it was the quarantine alone."

Though it was not actually asked of her, Georgiana understood she had just inherited the unkind duty of delivering that information to Elizabeth, "I shall explain what has come to pass as best I can."

It was as Darcy had hoped, for he was not yet certain in his own mind "what had come to pass."

Perhaps filtered through Elizabeth he would understand it better himself.

Darcy did not inquire why Georgiana stayed with Elizabeth for an extended visit. In other circumstances, he would have interrupted such a lengthy stay, rousting the over-zealous confidant in defence of Elizabeth's rest. But he knew that it was probable Elizabeth would learn more of Georgiana's situation in those few hours than he had uncovered in all their time together in France, thus he kept himself downstairs and fretfully paced the room. Full curious, but still not disposed to expose it, he made a great show of a lack of interest in his sister's discourse, but wasted little time after Georgiana had left before returning to hear from Elizabeth what was unearthed.

Forthwith of other information, however, Elizabeth announced, "As soon as I am up and about there will be a wedding to plan. That is, of course, with your approval."

That Fitzwilliam and Georgiana had come to an understanding was not an unmitigated surprise, but Darcy was not yet certain what he thought of it. Fitzwilliam was quite unwell and it seemed premature to take so great a step as marriage. An engagement seemed too imprudent to him, even one done in the proper way.

"I think this should be postponed at least until Fitzwilliam can come to me and ask for her hand properly. If he is too unwell for that, he is surely too unwell to marry."

At that pronouncement, Darcy went over and peered at the baby resting in Elizabeth's arm, trying to determine its identity. Elizabeth called to the nurse to come take the babies, which surprised Darcy, for she had scarcely let them out of her sight. The babies gone, he sat down next to her plumping her pillows.

By all rights, Darcy should have taken notice of the solemnity of Elizabeth's countenance just then. But so all-consuming was his determination to be nothing but happy to be home, one must forgive him for looking to her in love rather than query. Thus, it was with reluctance that Elizabeth was compelled to readdress the issue of impending wedlock. It was only when she stopped his fussing with her comfort and took his hands in hers that he clearly looked at her countenance and all that it betrayed.

She said simply, "I fear 'tis impossible to wait until Fitzwilliam is fit. I understand that might take a year."

As Elizabeth spoke, she soothingly stroked his hands. This unmistakable gesture of solicitude was not misinterpreted, howbeit it did take a few moments for him to come to full realisation.

He asked regardless, "It is impossible to wait?"

"Yes."

With more than a little bitterness, he said, "I fancy this means Fitzwilliam is more fit than I imagined."

"But you see they must wed immediately?"

Elizabeth wanted to keep the conversation moving forward but, not unexpectedly, was unsuccessful.

Even more bitterly, he said, "I have spent the last months away from you in care of Fitzwilliam and I am repaid by this?"

"I truly do not believe this occurrence was staged for your injury, sir."

Elizabeth had a half-smile ready for the glare she knew she would receive. And the semi-smile did, if not eliminate, at least soften the truth of her words. He stood and did the inevitable of walking to the window and looking silently out across the grounds. Omnipotence had not lasted two days. He chuckled at the irony, thus alarming Elizabeth.

"Laughter was the last thing I would have thought to hear from you right now," she said.

He almost explained that he was laughing at himself, not the situation, but did not. Instead, he said as he turned around and faced her.

"Tell me, Mrs. Darcy, who shall I get to second Fitzwilliam?"

"Second him?"

"Yes, it must be someone hardy. Only a stout man can hold him up whilst I run him through. Perchance Bingley will do it."

Darcy said this with all due severity and Elizabeth was not entirely certain he was not serious. Not entirely certain he was not serious either, Darcy continued to speculate upon the duel this deflowerment demanded.

"Yes. It is my place to demand satisfaction upon this insult to the House of Pemberley. Is there a greater insult a gentleman can sustain than defilement of his sister?"

He had begun to pace with reclaimed anger.

She countered, "Possibly the insult to his character was he to draw the blood of a blind cripple?"

"That is my dilemma, is it not?"

"I think there is something else to consider."

She patted the bed next to her, inviting him to sit by her side again.

When he joined her, she said, "Georgiana has been frank with me, not in the particulars, but in general. I understand Fitzwilliam has been bedridden?"

"Yes. We left as soon as he could rise."

"Thereupon I think you will agree Georgiana was neither seduced nor over-powered."

In all the ill-humour of a humbling defeat, he stretched out upon the bed with her, and groused, "I shall never agree with that. I may not argue against it, but I most certainly will not agree."

It took Elizabeth some cajoling, some teasing, some encouragement, but eventually Darcy gave up the business of duelling Fitzwilliam. That misguided venture joined Elizabeth's scheming revenge of Charles Bingley's infidelity and was filed away under abandoned reprisals.

Perchance it was the rapidity of tumultuous events, or maybe Mrs. Reynolds' age simply told her it was time to rest, but sometime during that night her heart seized. Paralysed upon one side, she lay helpless in bed until the other servants became alarmed by her absence from duty at dawn. Mr. Darcy was called and the doctor fetched, but few held out hope of her recovery. Dr. Upchurch again came to impart ill-tidings, proclaiming her failing heart would cease directly.

Elizabeth insisted she be allowed downstairs to sit with the old woman, though Darcy argued against it. Knowing she was determined, he picked her up and carried her himself, though Cressida whined and circled his legs as he traversed the stairs, nearly causing additional catastrophe. (Troilus's absence declared his fate, thus Elizabeth was spared explaining to Darcy the exact circumstances of his demise.) Darcy could not bring himself to scold the dog and merely called for a servant to corral the widowed hound until he got Elizabeth safely to Mrs. Reynolds's bedside.

Both sat there for some time, until Darcy perceived Elizabeth's fatigue and insisted she return to her own bed. He, however, kept watch upon Mrs. Reynolds throughout the day, reporting her deteriorating condition to Elizabeth. It was late evening when the old woman truly began to fail. Again, he drew a chair to her bedside, this time reaching out to hold her knotted, spotted fingers as she endeavoured to speak.

"Take care, Mr. Darcy."

He assured her he would, and, expecting that was a good-bye, attempted to blink away the tears that stung his eyes. He thought it strange that in all that he had witnessed, death moved him not less, but more. All her qualms were not settled, however. She said a queer thing.

"But what of Wickham?"

Wickham? The last words upon her lips were of Wickham? That was an astonishment. Darcy could not fathom it, for Mrs. Reynolds despised Wickham nearly as dearly as did he. Endeavouring to reason such a blasphemy, he conjectured her wits had fled her waning body. She, however, looked so clearly in wait of an answer, he truly did not know what to say. Thus, he did not speak and merely waited for her possibly to reclaim her senses.

She spoke once more, but only the single word. "Wickham."

It took him a moment to realise she was gone, for her eyes, yet in enquiry, stared at him. Reaching out to close them, he called for the doctor to pronounce what he already knew was true. The room soon filled with weeping house servants, several covering their sobbing faces with their aprons. Reluctantly, Darcy left to tell Elizabeth of her passing. As he ascended the stairs his steps slowed, then came to a halt. A coldness descended upon him that was not reflected in the clamminess that claimed his armpits. He stood very still, as if frozen in place.

Wickham.

That despised name reverberated in his enfeebled ears. Again, he questioned himself as to why Mrs. Reynolds would inquire of Wickham upon her deathbed. For the first time since he had first heard and thereupon, in disgust, cast it away, he recollected what Roux had said about his father having a bastard child.

Wickham?

Not Wickham. Even if such abomination were true, he meant not Wickham...that simply could not be possible. Wickham was the son of old Mr. Wickham, Mr. Darcy's steward. He lived in the house with them after Mr. Wickham died because...his father was fond of him. Keenly fond of him, to have him live with his own son. In the upper floors of Pemberley.

Darcy took another few steps and stopped once again. Thereupon, he turned and went to his library. It was late in the day, but light had not quite quit for night. He looked out upon the long shadows across the grounds and thought. He thought of everything he could remember spoken of Wickham's circumstance at their home. Would not his father have told him had he a brother? He could not answer uneviquiv-ocally. For howbeit his father had always been keenly aware of and suffered not gladly the foibles of men, he had remained true to the unscrupulous George Wickham regardless. Was that from a sense of contrition?

It should not have been a surprise to Darcy that his thoughts turned to John Christie. He queried himself relentlessly as to what he would have done had he continued to believe that John was his own bastard son. If he were truly honest with himself in his inspection, he would have to acknowledge that, although he might unkennel that he had begat a chance-bairn to Elizabeth, it was unlikely that he would have had the courage to admit it to his sister and the world at large. There would have been small likelihood that he would have given him the name of Darcy, but he knew too that he would not simply dismiss him.

What would he have done? Taken him in to live in Pemberley? Seen to his education? Grant him a living? Most likely. Just as his father had done for Wickham.

Yes, that is exactly how he would have found compromise. Duty met, but the rules of station followed. Precisely as his father had done?

Briefly, he endeavoured to recollect a sketch of Mrs. Wickham's face. He could not. There was no face to attach to the memory of the mother of Wickham. The mistress of his father as well?

In the hours he sat in contemplation, he allowed the possibility of shared heritage to transmute into a reality. However, Darcy could not find time to inspect his heart for room to call Wickham his brother. But if it were true and Wickham (despicable Wickham) was his brother, thereupon John was not his son, but nevertheless, blood kin. Darcy's impetuous move to have him buried under the name of Darcy seemed suddenly serendipitous.

Filial pride was one of his keenest conceits. Among his dearest duties was never to disgrace his family or lose the influence of the Pemberley House. Elizabeth had once refused to be his wife by reason of his excessive pride of circumstance. However scrupulously he had endeavoured to prevent it, Elizabeth had suffered grievously from the necessity of producing Darcy progeny. He closed his eyes and almost snorted a laugh out loud. For Wickham may well be Darcy progeny. Wickham was issue. Was Wickham posterity? He prayed not.

After all the suffering he had witnessed and the reckoning he had dealt, once home at Pemberley with Elizabeth and their babies, he had once again fallen prey to the comforting indolence that compleat domination over one's circumstances provides. But it had been enjoyed for far too fleeting a time. Even Georgiana's considerable indiscretion seemed but a peccadillo upon a landscape that included Wickham as a bastard brother.

It would remain unknown if his opinion upon this matter would have been different had not Elizabeth just awarded him with an heir. As it was, he had no time to consider that, as confused as he was about every belief he had ever held dear. Darcy had always cherished his parents' marriage an inviolate ideal, and honoured his father above all men. Were things not as they seemed? Understanding that it all might take a lifetime, if forgiveness was demanded, he hoped he would one day be able to determine for whom it should be asked.

Not for a moment did Darcy consider Wickham to know of his connexion, for even he would not seduce his own sister. Too, had Wickham any knowledge or intimation that he was son to Mr. Darcy, he would have played his blackmail card long ago. No, Wickham did not know of this.

The single bit of mirth that Darcy could manage was in contemplation that cowardly, murderous Wickham had never learnt just how close he stood to the riches for which he had so eagerly yearned.

For Darcy knew that he would not deny Wickham. He would never trust him with any part of Pemberley, but would be honour-bound to give him another living, and when that was squandered, another after that. Thinking of having to readmit Wickham to the family was abhorrent and he reminded himself that Wickham was reported dead, not deserted. Yet Darcy felt that strange sick feeling of uncertainty, which stayed with him for some time.

90

It was only a day after Mrs. Reynolds was laid to rest that Darcy had an unusually long and private conversation with Lady Millhouse in his study. And, in time, Darcy did what Elizabeth thought was the unthinkable. He set up a trust for Wickham's children. He had not told Elizabeth; the information came from Lydia. Her sister's gratitude for this act of generosity was limited. For it was seen to that Lydia would have no access to these funds. It would not be released to her children until each reached their eighteenth birthday.

"Lizzy, can you not say something to Darcy? I have only Wickham's pension, my father's fifty pounds, and the money you and Jane send me. I am always a bit short and could so use more."

In answer, Elizabeth only closed her eyes, pursed her lips, and slowly shook her head.

Elizabeth did not query Darcy about this, nor inquire of him where he went upon a day-long pilgrimage soon after they had returned. As he had not offered, she did not inquire. But it came upon the heels of her compleat explanation of the circumstance of that unfortunate altercation with Lady Catherine.

Until then, Elizabeth had only remarked upon the encounter most jovially. She had implied that the entire matter fell to Lady Catherine's assertion that Darcy was dead. Knowing he would be decidedly displeased to learn that his aunt threatened to throw his wife out of his home was he not to return, she was taken unawares by his response.

"Why did you not tell her?"

"Pray, what? I told her emphatically to take her leave. What more could I have done sir, than, as I did, take aim upon the woman?"

"I would have taken great delight in knowing that you told her that she had only thought herself displeased in the past. For I thought you knew, Lizzy," he said.

When she looked at him in obvious ignorance of his reference, he told her, "I thought you knew. Had something bechanced me, regardless whether we had children, you would receive more than the Right of Dower. Beyond just one third of the income from Pemberley land, I had my solicitor see to it that you would be mistress of Pemberley House as long as you live. Lady Catherine has no rights over you."

"But..." she said.

"Lady Catherine has no rights over you," he repeated firmly.

The matter was dropped, and Elizabeth was slightly miffed that, howbeit he had smiled at her description (her compleat description) of Lady Catherine's hasty retreat from Pemberley, he did not show the indignation at that offence that she would have properly expected. As to where he went upon his excursion, had it not been for Georgiana, Elizabeth might never have learnt. Had it not been for a series of seriously amused servants, Georgiana might not have learnt it to tell her. For her brother had paid a visit to their aunt.

It was a surprise to Elizabeth, who had been sitting at her dressing table, when in ventured Georgiana. Her sister-in-law had never once come into her dressing room, hence, Elizabeth knew to belay her toilette. Georgiana did not call a greeting, but crossed the room and whispered directly into Elizabeth's ear.

She said, "'Tis only a rumour, of course, but I understand my brother visited Lady Catherine week last."

Elizabeth did not turn around but obtained Georgiana's gaze in the looking-glass. She continued, "'Tis said he told her if she should bother his wife again, he would see to it ('Make it his mission in life,' I believe were his exact words), that she would spend the rest of her days partaking of gruel, locked in a cell at the Lyme Institute for the Indigent Insane."

Georgiana said nothing more. Elizabeth could scarcely contain her smile until she left the room.

91

Hearing the distant cry of her babies, Elizabeth awakened early that day. Darcy lay asleep and was not awakened by her leaving, for it had become quite routine for her to go to them. Each day after the babies' break-fast, she had taken to bringing them by turn into the bed whilst he was yet asleep, and laying one upon his bare stomach. She waited for him to feel the tiny squirming body and awaken. She could not imagine a grander sight than to watch her husband open his eyes and look down upon the baby. For he would then draw it up until it was under his chin and kiss it upon the top of its head. He could always determine which baby it was upon beholding the crown of each head. Gerard Geoffrey's had a slight curl and grew in an orderly spiral. Jane Georgiana's had no rule to it at all.

"Just like her mother," he was wont to say.

That day she chose another course, for there was something to which she had to attend. The new mother intended to embark upon a seduction.

It was both a boon and a bother that Darcy's return had coincided with the culmination of her laying-in. Had she not been with child, their lengthy separation would have ended with their leaping into each other's outstretched, libidinous arms. That would have been an ecstatic moment, but its heat might not have allowed them the time they would need to adjust to the many alterations within their lives. With the babies literally betwixt them, their reunion was one that, by necessity, was not overcome by passionate longings.

But those longings simmered all the same. As trying as her still-birth had been, a timetable for re-establishing connubial congress post-delivery had not truly been affixed. Thus, the matter dangled about an absurdly long time (it did not truly dangle, for favours were dispensed and kindnesses abounded during periods of hockling about). Ultimately Elizabeth realised it fell upon her to ascertain, and thereupon announce to her husband, when her nether-regions were ready for unabridged, amorous embrace.

With this in mind, after tending the babies, she crept into her boudoir and dressed.

In time, Darcy lay half-awake, thus allowing his fragile ears to hear a skirl of a whistle. It was not a loud whistle. As it happened, it was of a puny wind, but it was a whistle. He rose and walked to door of the balcony, then over to the edge and looked down. There was Elizabeth, in a pair of his trousers, not side-saddle, but astride Boots. She was not looking at him, but at her fingers, in an effort to determine just what placement was needed for a louder whistle. She endeavoured once more with not much more luck.

Catching sight of his having spied her, she turned up her collar and called to him, "I dare you, Mr. Darcy, I dare you," and walked beneath the balcony towing Blackjack. She saw him laugh and shake his head and return inside. That perplexed her. She wondered if he would not come to a woman in men's pants, riding astride a horse and taunting him.

She had little time to spend on the query, for he reappeared doing a strange little hopping dance upon the balcony. Finally, he stopped hopping, put his boot against the top of the rail, and drew it hard onto his foot. Thereupon she saw he had put on his trousers and taken time only to tuck in part of his shirttail, and now booted, swung his leg over the rail as he waved her closer with Blackjack.

Climbing both feet over the wide stone rail, he sat upon the top briefly as if contemplating how to leap onto Blackjack without injury to his person. Gingerly, he dropped onto the saddle. This done, she handed him the reins.

"When you came for me, I came as I was."

"That is well enough for you, Elizabeth, but I shall not ride this horse without my breeches," he retorted.

At that, she suddenly kicked Boots and left Darcy and Blackjack standing. He responded immediately and she was but a half-dozen strides ahead of him, then she kicked Boots again to gain a few more.

He intended only to persuade her not to ride too aggressively so soon after giving birth. However, allowing another horse to outrun Blackjack was not in his nature, and any solicitous regard for Elizabeth's health was swamped by the spirit of competition. He spurred Blackjack forward, yet could not overtake Boots. It had been some time since he had enjoyed a race, but if he could not overtake a nursing mother astride a mare, he thought he would be most unhappy. The chance of which prodded him to urge Blackjack over a stone fence.

She made a hard left through the gate and, by virtue of his ignorance of their destination, he had to circle Blackjack to find her direction, thus losing what little he had gained. Frustrated that she was able to get out of sight so hastily, he wished he had brought his crop. As she had hers, he believed that was an unfair advantage.

They were far south-west of the house, upon the edge of a wood, when Darcy rounded the corner and saw Boots riderless and wheezing. He came to a skidding stop, called, "Lizzy, Lizzy," and dropped his own reins as he jumped down, turning frantically to locate her.

He could not imagine where she lay, for she was not within his sight. Then he heard that same feeble attempt at a whistle. He turned toward the sound. It came from the wood.

Seeing a figure disappearing quite fleetingly into the trees, he abandoned apprehension and reclaimed the chase. It took him little time to catch up to her once they were both on foot. Seeing he had heard her, Elizabeth ran with as much dispatch as she could in the languid grass able to find sun enough to grow betwixt the crowd of trees. He reached her just as her foot caught a sagging cuff and she fell.

Their momentum carried him down with her and they lay in laughing exhaustion a few moments, catching their breath. Thereupon Elizabeth sat up and leaned back against a tree. Darcy turned upon his side to look at her, resting his head against his hand. He lay still so long, just looking upon her, that Elizabeth became uneasy. She had successfully lured him to this spot, and wondered if she would have to be even more forward and say in words what she wanted of him.

Sooner than she expected, she found her answer. He reached out, grabbed her foot, and drew her to him. He rose upon his knees, yanked his shirt off over his head, and tossed it aside.

"You never cease to astound me, Lizzy."

"Pray, you have said you favour me coming to you."

"Indeed, I do. That is not of what I speak."

"Pray, what then?"

"Never once," he reached out and grasped both legs of her breeches, "have I attended to the removal of any trousers but my own."

"But husband," she smiled quite fetchingly, "these *are* yours."

In the next half year, the few letters Darcy had managed to hand to someone to carry from Belgium would betimes find way their to Pemberley, tattered, weathered, but intact. When the first one arrived, Elizabeth came upon it first, read it, and thereupon brought it to show him, thinking he would be amused he had found home first. When she realised it pained him to be reminded of that time, she notified the help to be certain if any more such posts arrived to bring them directly to her.

For she read and kept every one. It was through the letters that she eventually understood the peril and desperation that was endured. Darcy had forgotten that he had written to her when John died. He had forgotten that he had written of Wickham's treachery. Possibly, it was best he had, for Elizabeth surmised it unlikely to hear it from his lips (not in defence of Wickham's newly unsullied memory, but repugnance of speaking the name at all).

Hence, it was Elizabeth who addressed the subject, aghast at what she had read, and it gave Darcy momentum to tell her everything he had uncovered and believed. It was true. Wickham was a venal rogue who had murdered John to desert. The only uncertainty was whether he survived.

Elizabeth had thought him no worse than an ever-dissipating lecher, so she spent a few moments diligently excavating for some blame for herself that he was not unveiled for the venal rogue he truly was. So relentlessly did she propose herself somehow responsible for the train of events that had unfolded, that she was in danger of usurping Jane's firmly held office of martyr.

She sat there muttering these opinions to herself and was only distracted from her guilt of omission by Darcy drawing his chair next to hers. They had shared very serious moments of crisis, and she fully understood by his expression that what she had heard might be the worst, but would not be all. And that was alarming.

There was no way to say that Wickham was possibly his miscreant half-brother than just to speak the words. So he did. When he announced it, she almost laughed—but stopped herself—so astonishing was the revelation. Even fully explained, Elizabeth (not having the opportunity of discovery) would have been doubtful of the truth of it, had it not been verified by the independent information of Darcy's mother's good friend, Lady Millhouse.

The uncovering of the secret of Wickham's connexion with the family, of course, revealed the mystery behind the sadness she had sensed in Darcy's mother's portrait, but this was not an observation Elizabeth would have bestowed upon Darcy's already overworked sensibilities. Nor did she tell him of the conversation she had had with her mother over her own father's coffin. If she truly was to believe what she told her husband about accepting those they love for who they are, there was no point.

Lydia would spend a year happily glowing in widowhood, for Wickham was much improved as a dead war hero than a live philanderer. And Lydia would, eventually, give up claiming access to her sons' fortune and marry another major in the regulars. (There was an unfortunate incident when, a widow yet, Lydia produced a daughter of uncertain paternity. "That? Well, I couldn't help that," was her only explanation when she was scolded for the indiscretion.)

It was doubted her new husband fathered the child, but his new wife's easy virtue was overlooked by his own easy nature, hence, no true injury was inflicted. Lydia said that he was not quite so charming as Wickham, but he was quite dashing, and that met the only other standard Lydia set for a husband (that and a proposal). What he lost in beguiling wiles was made up for in great, if blind, devotion to his wife, which met the only standard her family hoped for him as well.

True love found Kitty by way of a vicar in Shropshire (nary a swoon came to pass during courtship, but bridesmaid Maria Lucas managed to be felled at the wedding breakfast). Mary was quite content to live a life of introspection under the unrelentingly disapproving gaze of her mother. Mrs. Bennet, however, would never tire of thanking Darcy for making arrangements with poor Charlotte and her unfortunate son for her to live out her life at Longbourn. (Her happiness at residing in Hertfordshire was exceeded only by his in that as well.)

Young Hinchcliffe was one of the Derbyshire soldiers who were left in a grave in France, forever removing from Darcy the opportunity to belittle. Young Henry Howgrave however, came home from war bemedaled and beribboned, was knighted, then elected to Parliament. It was in London that he met an exceedingly beautiful older woman and, thoroughly smitten, proposed marriage. There was talk at first that the lady of French birth was of dubious reputation, which only increased Howgrave's margin of victory when he was elected Prime Minister.

It was somewhat scandalous that his new wife took such an avid interest in her new husband's career and politicked for him relentlessly, awarding kisses to costermongers and butchers in exchange for their vote. When accused of relinquishing any claim to respectability by mingling with the coarse masses, Lady Juliette Howgrave merely tossed her curls. She was most happy in her elevated social status, but noted wryly to herself that, except for the currency, her situation had changed not a whit.

Never known to be the snitch to Lady Catherine, Cyril Smeads was given office as butler to Pemberley. But under the stern glare of Mr. Darcy, his guidance of the household became more outwardly circumspect. Goodwin and Hannah never actually found romance either with each other or another. Both remained quite content with continued furtive looks, rather than suffer the insult of sullied reality.

One of the lesser evils with which Darcy had to cope was an unexpected foaling by Boots. Darcy had always wanted to extend her bloodlines, but Elizabeth had not, always keeping her fastidiously in a stall when she was in season. In querying the grooms, it was understood the only horse that had been near her was Scimitar, the night before Fitzwilliam took him to France.

And, indeed, it was exactly ten months later (the precise date of Fitzwilliam's departure was etched in the Darcys' memory) when Boots presented without a complication. Elizabeth had insisted upon being called and, clad in coats over respective night-shirt and gown, she and Darcy went down to the stable to witness the birth. It was a beautiful young horse, all wobbly legs and stockinged feet. In want of hiding his pleasure at the sight, Darcy retook his position of opposition that the sire was Scimitar, not Blackjack. He groused about it unreasonably, and Elizabeth understood he did that in lieu of his sister's husband.

Once Darcy accepted the inevitable, he also admitted that the single man he could find no fault in as a husband to Georgiana was Colonel Fitzwilliam. No ambitions to entailment, after a lovely (but hurried) wedding at Pemberley, they were happy to reside at Whitemore and welcome their new daughter. Georgiana continued to write and reminded Fitzwilliam often how dashing he looked with a patch over one eye.

The colonel's leg wound did not entirely heal, but he insisted if his good leg was strong enough to lift him into a saddle, Scimitar's son's eyes would help him find his way.

So decidedly did he want to reach it, the crest of the knoll loomed before Wickham as precipitous as the cliffs of Dover. His horse's breathing was laboured, but he knew only that hill stood betwixt him and escape of Armageddon, hence he dug his heels into its flanks once more. The last few strides to the top of the hill seemed to take forever, but finally his mount conquered them. At the crown, Wickham stopped and giddily looked over his shoulder in reassurance that he was, indeed, free.

The cannons below were booming yet. He could see that his company's position was all but annihilated. A few scattered horses ran about, reins dangling precariously, skittishly trying to avoid the incoming fire. Grenades long expended, none of his men were standing, and only a few moving. Wickham stared at the sight dispassionately, turned, and kicked his horse into an easier lope down the reverse slope of the rise.

Yet in his pilfered corporal's uniform, he slowed to rid himself of the detestable jacket. The French were taking his flank and British forces ahead. Now that survival was likely, Wickham knew if he could get behind Anglo-Prussian lines without being stopped, there was a chance for compleat freedom. Not once in his life had he made an uncalculated move. It was a point of pride. But it had stayed only in the back of his mind, was he to fake his death, he could not sell his commission, Lydia would.

At the time, it had seemed unimportant. But as he wove his way through British lines toward Belgium, he thought again of what he had to sell or barter. It took him less than a mile of rumination before a scheme fell apparent. He spurred his horse past a plumed hat resting upon a sabre driven into the ground. Picking it up on the run, he pressed it upon his head then tapped it down. A small amusement crossed his mind and forced the corners of his mouth into an unseemly smile.

He rode on.

Have you been to Waterloo?
I have been to Waterloo.
'Tis no matter what you do,
If you've been to Waterloo.

acknowledgments

My eternal gratitude is extended to Deb Werksman, Sourcebooks Editor, who took up *The Bar Sinister* and had the vision to see what it could and should be. Deb told me that she would see to it that the essence of the book would not be compromised in the process of revision. She kept her word. Thank you, Deb. My thanks also go to Susie Benton, whose guidance through the sometimes treacherous editorial waters was both kind and patient.

Had it not been for my sister, Kathryn Baker (a brilliant writer in her own right), I would never have embarked on such an adventure. Her counsel and encouragement were invaluable.

Most of all I must thank my husband, Phil, for inspiring me to write and giving me the courage to follow through.

About the Author

Linda Berdoll is a self-described "Texas farm wife" whose interest in all things Austen was piqued by the BBC/A&E mini-series of *Pride and Prejudice*. Four years and much research later, her effort, *Mr. Darcy Takes a Wife* (originally titled *The Bar Sinister*) appeared, to the acclaim of readers and the horror of Jane Austen purists. This is Berdoll's first novel, but she has since published a humorous book of euphemisms. The sequel to the sequel, *Darcy & Elizabeth: Nights and Days at Pemberley*, is available now in stores everywhere. She and her husband live on a pecan farm in Del Valle, Texas. Although she admits that she eloped in a manner similar to Lydia Bennet's, to her great fortune it was with Darcy, not Wickham.

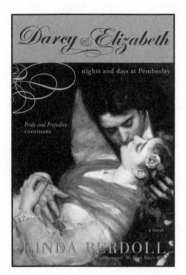